# STORMY WEATHER

## AND

# LUCKY YOU



**Carl Hiaasen** was born and raised in Florida. His other novels are *Tourist Season, Double Whammy, Skin Tight, Native Tongue* and *Strip Tease*, which together have been translated into twenty languages. Since 1979 he has worked at the *Miami Herald* as a magazine writer, investigative reporter and metropolitan columnist.

His latest novel is called *Sick Puppy* and is available in Pan paperback.

## ALSO BY CARL HIAASEN

Tourist Season
Double Whammy
Skin Tight
Native Tongue
Strip Tease
Sick Puppy

Carl Hiaasen Omnibus
(comprising: *Tourist Season, Double Whammy, Skin Tight*)

## AND WITH BILL MONTALBANO

Powder Burn
Trap Line
A Death in China

CARL HIAASEN

# STORMY WEATHER AND LUCKY YOU

PAN BOOKS

*Stormy Weather* first published 1995 by Alfred A. Knopf, Inc., New York,
first published in Great Britain 1995 by Macmillan,
first published in paperback 1996 by Pan Books
*Lucky You* first published 1997 by Alfred A. Knopf, Inc., New York,
first published in Great Britain 1997 by Macmillan,
first published in paperback 1998 by Pan Books

This omnibus edition published 2003 by Pan Books
an imprint of Pan Macmillan Ltd
Pan Macmillan, 20 New Wharf Road, London N1 9RR
Basingstoke and Oxford
Associated companies throughout the world
www.panmacmillan.com

ISBN 0 330 42098 4



1 3 5 7 9 8 6 4 2

A CIP catalogue record for this book is available from
the British Library.

Printed and bound in Great Britain by
Mackays of Chatham plc, Chatham, Kent

# STORMY WEATHER

*For Donna, Camille, Hugo and Andrew*

## Acknowledgements

For their expertise on the most esoteric subjects, I am deeply grateful to my good friends John Kipp (the finer points of skull collecting), Tim Chapman (the effects of canine shock collars on human volunteers) and Bob Branham (the care and handling of untamed South American coatimundis). I am also greatly indebted to my talented colleagues at the *Miami Herald*, whose superb journalism in the aftermath of Hurricane Andrew provided so much rich material for this novel.

**C.H.**

# ONE

**On August 23,** the day before the hurricane struck, Max and Bonnie Lamb awoke early, made love twice and rode the shuttle bus to Disney World. That evening they returned to the Peabody Hotel, showered separately, switched on the cable news and saw that the storm was heading directly for the southeastern tip of Florida. The TV weatherman warned that it was the fiercest in many years.

Max Lamb sat at the foot of the bed and gazed at the color radar image—a ragged flame-colored sphere, spinning counterclockwise toward the coast. He said, "Jesus, look at that."

A hurricane, Bonnie Lamb thought, on our honeymoon! As she slipped under the sheets, she heard the rain beating on the rental cars in the parking lot outside. "Is this part of it?" she asked. "All this weather?"

Her husband nodded. "We're on the edge of the edge."

Max Lamb seemed excited in a way that Bonnie found unsettling. She knew better than to suggest a sensible change of plans, such as hopping a plane back to La Guardia. Her new husband was no quitter; the reservations said five nights and six days, and by God that's how long they would stay. It was a special package rate; no refunds.

She said, "They'll probably close the park."

"Disney?" Max Lamb smiled. "Disney never closes. Not for plagues, famines, or even hurricanes." He rose to adjust the volume on the television. "Besides, the darn thing's three hundred miles away. The most we'll see up here is more rain."

Bonnie Lamb detected disappointment in her husband's tone. Hands on his hips, he stood nude in front of the TV screen; his pale shoulder blades and buttocks were streaked crimson from a day on the water flumes. Max was no athlete, but he'd done fine on the river slide. Bonnie wondered if it had gone to his head, for tonight he affected the square-shouldered posture of a college jock. She caught him glancing in the mirror, flexing his stringy biceps and sizing up his own nakedness. Maybe it was just a honeymoon thing.

The cable news was showing live video of elderly residents being evacuated from condominiums and apartment buildings on Miami Beach. Many of the old folks carried cats or poodles in their arms.

"So," said Bonnie Lamb, "we're still doing Epcot tomorrow?"

Her husband didn't answer.

"Honey?" she said. "Epcot?"

Max Lamb's attention was rooted to the hurricane news. "Oh sure," he said absently.

"You remembered the umbrellas?"

"Yes, Bonnie, in the car."

She asked him to turn off the television and come to bed. When he got beneath the covers, she moved closer, nipped his earlobes, played her fingers through the silky sprout of hair on his bony chest.

"Guess what I'm not wearing," she whispered.

"Ssshhh," said Max Lamb. "Listen to that rain."

Edie Marsh headed to Dade County from Palm Beach, where she'd spent six months trying to sleep with a Kennedy. She'd had the plan all worked out, how she'd seduce a young Kennedy and then threaten to run to the cops with a lurid tale of perversion, rape and torture. She'd hatched the scheme while watching the William Kennedy Smith trial on Court TV and noticing the breathless relief with which the famous clan had received the acquittal; all of them with those fantastic teeth, beaming at the cameras but wearing an expression that Edie Marsh had seen more than a few times in her twenty-nine action-packed years—the look of those who'd dodged a bullet. They'd have no stomach for another scandal, not right away. Next time there'd be a mad stampede for the Kennedy family checkbook, in order to make the problem go away. Edie had it all figured out.

She cleaned out her boyfriend's bank account and grabbed the Amtrak to West Palm, where she found a cheap duplex apartment. She spent her days sleeping, shoplifting cocktail dresses and painting her nails. Each night she'd cross the bridge to the rich island, where she assiduously loitered at Au Bar and the other trendy clubs. She overtipped bartenders and waitresses, with the understanding that they would instantly alert her when a Kennedy, *any* Kennedy, arrived. In this fashion she had quickly met two Shrivers and a distant Lawford, but to Edie they would have been borderline fucks. She was saving her charms for a direct heir, a pipeline to old Joe Kennedy's mother lode. One of the weekly tabloids had published a diagram of the family tree, which Edie Marsh had taped to the wall of the kitchen, next to a Far Side calendar. Right away Edie had ruled out screwing any Kennedys-by-marriage; the serious money followed the straightest lines of genealogy, as did the scandal hunters. Statistically it appeared her best target would be one of Ethel and Bobby's sons, since they'd had so many. Not that Edie wouldn't have crawled nude across broken glass for a whack at John Jr., but the odds of *him* strolling unescorted into a Palm Beach fern bar were laughable.

Besides, Edie Marsh was nothing if not a realist. John Kennedy Jr. had movie-star girlfriends, and Edie knew she was no movie star. Pretty, sure. Sexy in a low-cut Versace, you bet. But John-John probably wouldn't glance twice. Some of those cousins, though, Bobby's boys—Edie was sure she could do some damage there. Suck 'em cross-eyed, then phone the lawyers.

Unfortunately, six grueling months of barhopping produced only two encounters with *Kennedy* Kennedys. Neither tried to sleep with Edie; she couldn't believe it. One of the young men even took her on an actual date, but when they returned to her place he didn't so much as grope her boobs. Just pecked her good night and said thanks for a nice time. The perfect goddamn gentleman, she'd thought. Just my luck. Edie had tried valiantly to change his mind, practically pinned him to the hood of his car, kissed and rubbed and grabbed him. Nothing! Humiliating is what it was. After the young Kennedy departed, Edie Marsh had stalked to the bathroom and studied herself in the mirror. Maybe there was wax in her ears or spinach in her teeth, something gross to put the guy off. But no, she looked fine. Furiously she peeled off her stolen dress, appraised her figure and thought: Did the little snot think he's too good for *this*? What a joke, that Kennedy charm. The kid had all the charisma of oatmeal. He'd bored her to death long before the lobster entrée arrived. She'd felt like hopping on the tabletop and shrieking at the top of her lungs: Who gives a shit about illiteracy in South Boston? Tell me about Jackie and the Greek!

That dismal evening, it turned out, was Edie's last shot. The summer went dead in Palm Beach, and all the fuckable Kennedys traveled up to Hyannis. Edie was too broke to give chase.

The hurricane on the TV radar had given her a new idea. The storm was eight hundred miles away, churning up the Caribbean, when she phoned a man named Snapper, who was coming off a short hitch for manslaughter. Snapper got his nickname because of a crooked jaw, which had been made that way by a game warden and healed poorly. Edie Marsh arranged to meet him at a sports bar on the beach. Snapper listened to her plan and said it was the nuttiest fucking thing he'd ever heard because (a) the hurricane probably won't hit here and (b) somebody could get busted for heavy time.

Three days later, with the storm bearing down on Miami, Snapper called Edie Marsh and said what the hell, let's check it out. I got a guy, Snapper said, he knows about these things.

The guy's name was Avila, and formerly he had worked as a building inspector for Metropolitan Dade

County. Snapper and Edie met him at a convenience store on Dixie Highway in South Miami. The rain was deceptively light, given the proximity of the hurricane, but the clouds hung ominously low, an eerie yellow gauze.

They went in Avila's car, Snapper sitting next to Avila up front and Edie by herself in the back. They were going to a subdivision called Sugar Palm Hammocks: one hundred and sixty-four single-family homes platted sadistically on only forty acres of land. Without comment, Avila drove slowly through the streets. Many residents were outside, frantically nailing plywood to the windows of their homes.

"There's no yards," Snapper remarked.

Avila said, "Zero-lot lines is what we call it."

"How cozy," Edie Marsh said from the back seat. "What we need is a house that'll go to pieces in the storm."

Avila nodded confidently. "Take your pick. They're all coming down."

"No shit?"

"Yeah, honey, no shit."

Snapper turned to Edie Marsh and said, "Avila ought to know. He's the one inspected the damn things."

"Perfect," said Edie. She rolled down the window. "Then let's find something nice."

On instructions from the authorities, tourists by the thousands were bailing out of the Florida Keys. Traffic on northbound U.S. 1 was a wretched crawl, winking brake lights as far as the eye could see. Jack Fleming and Webo Drake had run out of beer at Big Pine. Now they were stuck behind a Greyhound bus halfway across the Seven Mile Bridge. The bus had stalled with transmission trouble. Jack Fleming and Webo Drake got out of the car—Jack's father's car—and started throwing empty Coors cans off the bridge. The two young men were still slightly trashed from a night at the Turtle Kraals in Key West, where the idea of getting stranded in a Force Four hurricane had sounded downright adventurous, a nifty yarn to tell the guys back at the Kappa Alpha house. The problem was, Jack and Webo had awakened to find themselves out of money as well as beer, with Jack's father expecting his almost-new Lexus to be returned . . . well, yesterday.

So here they were, stuck on one of the longest bridges in the world, with a monster tropical cyclone only a few hours away. The wind hummed across the Atlantic at a pitch that Jack Fleming and Webo Drake had never before heard; it rocked them on their heels when they got out of the car. Webo lobbed an empty Coors can toward the concrete rail, but the wind whipped it back hard, like a line drive. Naturally it then became a contest to see who had the best arm. In high school Jack Fleming had been a star pitcher, mainly sidearm, so his throws were not as disturbed by the gusts as those of Webo Drake, who had merely played backup quarterback for the junior varsity. Jack was leading, eight beer cans to six off the bridge, when a hand—an enormous brown hand—appeared with a wet slap on the rail.

Webo Drake glanced worriedly at his frat brother. Jack Fleming said, "Now what?"

A bearded man pulled himself up from a piling beneath the bridge. He was tall, with coarse silvery hair that hung in matted tangles to his shoulders. His bare chest was striped with thin pink abrasions. The man carried several coils of dirty rope under one arm. He wore camouflage trousers and old brown military boots with no laces. In his right hand was a crushed Coors can and a dead squirrel.

Jack Fleming said, "You a Cuban?"

Webo Drake was horrified.

Dropping his voice, Jack said: "No joke. I bet he's a rafter."

It made sense. This was where the refugees usually landed, in the Keys. Jack spoke loudly to the man with the rope: "*Usted Cubano?*"

The man brandished the beer can and said: "Usted un asshole?"

His voice was a rumble that fit his size. "Where do you dipshits get off," he said over the wind, "throwing your goddamn garbage in the water?" The man stepped forward and kicked out a rear passenger window of Jack's father's Lexus. He threw the empty beer can and the dead squirrel in the back seat. Then he grabbed Webo Drake by the belt of his jeans. "Your trousers dry?" the man asked.

Passengers in the Greyhound bus pressed their faces to the glass to see what was happening. Behind the Lexus, a family in a rented minivan could be observed locking the doors, a speedy drill they had obviously practiced before leaving the Miami airport.

Webo Drake said yes, his jeans were dry. The stranger said, "Then hold my eye." With an index finger he calmly removed a glass orb from his left socket and placed it carefully in one of Webo's pants pockets. "It loosed up on me," the stranger explained, "in all this spray."

Failing to perceive the gravity of the moment, Jack Fleming pointed at the shattered window of his father's luxury sedan. "Why the hell'd you do that?"

Webo, shaking: "Jack, it's all right."

The one-eyed man turned toward Jack Fleming. "I count thirteen fucking beer cans in the water and only one hole in your car. I'd say you got off easy."

"Forget about it," offered Webo Drake.

The stranger said, "I'm giving you boys a break because you're exceptionally young and stupid."

Ahead of them, the Greyhound bus wheezed, lurched and finally began to inch northward. The man with the rope opened the rear door of the Lexus and brushed the broken glass off the seat. "I need a lift up the road," he said.

Jack Fleming and Webo Drake said certainly, sir, that would be no trouble at all. It took forty-five minutes on the highway before they summoned the nerve to ask the one-eyed man what he was doing under the Seven Mile Bridge.

Waiting, the man replied.

For what? Webo asked.

Turn on the radio, the man said. If you don't mind.

News of the hurricane was on every station. The latest forecast put the storm heading due west across the Bahamas, toward a landfall somewhere between Key Largo and Miami Beach.

"Just as I thought," said the one-eyed man. "I was too far south. I could tell by the sky."

He had covered his head with a flowered shower cap; Jack Fleming noticed it in the rearview mirror, but withheld comment. The young man was more concerned about what to tell his father regarding the busted window, and also about the stubborn stain a dead squirrel might leave on fine leather upholstery.

Webo Drake asked the one-eyed man: "What's the rope for?"

"Good question," he said, but gave no explanation.

An hour later the road spread to four lanes and the traffic began to move at a better clip. Almost no cars were heading south. The highway split at North Key Largo, and the stranger instructed Jack Fleming to bear right on County Road 905.

"It says there's a toll," Jack said.

"Yeah?"

"Look, we're out of money."

A soggy ten-dollar bill landed on the front seat between Jack Fleming and Webo Drake. Again the earthquake voice: "Stop when we reach the bridge."

Twenty minutes later they approached the Card Sound Bridge, which crosses from North Key Largo to the mainland. Jack Fleming tapped the brakes and steered to the shoulder. "Not here," said the stranger. "All the way to the top."

"The top of the bridge?"

"Are you deaf, junior?"

Jack Fleming drove up the slope cautiously. The wind was ungodly, jostling the Lexus on its springs. At the crest of the span, Jack pulled over as far as he dared. The one-eyed man retrieved his glass eye from Webo Drake and got out of the car. He yanked the plastic cap off his head and jammed it into the waistband of his trousers.

"Come here," the stranger told the two young men. "Tie me." He popped the eye into its socket and cleaned it in a polishing motion with the corner of a bandanna.

Then he climbed over the rail and inserted his legs back under the gap, so he was kneeling on the precipice.

Other hurricane evacuees slowed their cars to observe the lunatic scene, but none dared to stop; the man being lashed to the bridge looked wild enough to deserve it. Jack Fleming and Webo Drake worked as swiftly as possible, given the force of the gusts and the rapidity with which their Key West hangovers were advancing. The stranger gave explicit instructions about how he was to be trussed, and the fraternity boys did what they were told. They knotted one end of the rope around the man's thick ankles and ran the other end over the concrete rail. After looping it four times around his chest, they cinched until he grunted. Then they threaded the rope under the rail and back to the ankles for the final knotting.

The product was a sturdy harness that allowed the stranger's arms to wave free. Webo Drake tested the knots and pronounced them tight. "Can we go now?" he asked the one-eyed man.

"By all means."

"What about the squirrel, sir?"

"It's all yours," the stranger said. "Enjoy."

Jack Fleming coasted the car downhill. At the foot of the bridge, he veered off the pavement to get clear of the traffic. Webo Drake found a rusty curtain rod in a pile of trash, and Jack used it to hoist the animal carcass out of his father's Lexus. Webo stood back, trying to light a cigaret.

Back on the bridge, under a murderous dark sky, the kneeling stranger raised both arms to the pulsing gray clouds. Bursts of hot wind made the man's hair stand up like a halo of silver sparks.

"Crazy fucker," Jack Fleming rasped. He stepped over the dead squirrel and threw the curtain rod into the mangroves. "You think he had a gun? Because that's what I'm telling my old man: Some nut with a gun kicked out the car window."

Webo Drake pointed with the cigaret and said, "Jack, you know what he's waiting for? That crazy idiot, he's waiting on the hurricane."

Although the young men stood two hundred yards away, they could see the one-eyed stranger grinning madly into the teeth of the rising wind. He wore a smile that blazed.

"Brother," Jack said to Webo, "let's get the hell out of here." The tollbooth was unmanned, so they blew through at fifty miles an hour, skidded into the parking lot of Alabama Jack's. There they used the one-eyed man's ten-dollar bill to purchase four cold cans of Cherry Coke, which they drank on the trip up Card Sound Road. When they were finished, they did not toss the empties from the car.

A noise awakened Bonnie Lamb. It was Max, snapping open a suitcase. She asked what in the world he was doing, fully dressed and packing his clothes at four in the morning. He said he wanted to surprise her.

"You're leaving me?" she asked. "After two nights."

Max Lamb smiled and came to the bed. "I'm packing for both of us."

He tried to stroke Bonnie's cheek, but she buried her face in the pillow, to block out the light. The rain was coming harder now, slapping horizontally against the windows of the high-rise hotel. She was glad her husband had come to his senses. They could do Epcot some other time.

She peered out of the pillow and said, "Honey, is the airport open?"

"I don't honestly know."

"Shouldn't you call first?"

"Why?" Max Lamb patted the blanket where it followed the curve of his wife's hips.

"We're flying home, aren't we?" Bonnie Lamb sat up. "That's why you're packing."

Her husband said no, we're not flying home. "We're going on an adventure."

"I see. Where, Max?"

"Miami."

"That's the surprise?"

"That's it." He tugged the covers away from her. "Come on, we've got a long drive—"

Bonnie Lamb didn't move. "You're serious."

"—and I want to teach you how to use the video camera."

She said, "I've got a better idea. Why don't we stay here and make love for the next three days. Dawn to dusk, OK? Tear the room to pieces. I mean, if it's adventure you want."

Max Lamb was up again, stuffing the suitcases. "You don't understand. This is a once-in-a-lifetime chance."

Right, Bonnie said, a chance to drown on our honeymoon. "I'd rather stay where it's warm and dry. I'll even watch *Emmanuelle VI* on the Spectravision, like you wanted last night." This she regarded as a significant concession.

"By the time we get to Miami," said Max, "the dangerous part will be over. In fact, it's probably over already."

"Then what's the point?"

"You'll see."

"Max, I don't want to do this. Please."

He gave her a stiff, fatherly hug. She knew he was about to speak to her as if she were six years old. "Bonnie," Max Lamb said to his new wife. "My beautiful little Bonnie, now listen. Disney World we can do anytime. Anytime we want. But how often does a hurricane hit? You heard the weatherman, honey. 'The Storm of the Century,' he called it. How often does a person get to see something like that!"

Bonnie Lamb couldn't stand her husband's lordly tone. She couldn't stand it so much that she'd have done anything to shut him up.

"All right, Max. Bring me my robe."

He kissed her noisily on the forehead. "Thatta girl."

# TWO

**Snapper and Edie Marsh** got two rooms at the Best Western in Pembroke Pines, thirty miles north of where the storm was predicted to come ashore. Snapper told the motel clerk that one room would be enough, but Edie said not on your damn life. The relationship had always been strictly business, Snapper being an occasional fence of women's wear and Edie being an occasional thief of same. Their new venture was to be another entrepreneurial partnership, more ambitious but not more intimate. Up front Edie alerted Snapper that she couldn't imagine a situation in which she'd have sex with him, even once. He did not seem poleaxed by the news.

She went to bed covering her ears, trying to shut out the hellish moan of the storm. It was more than she could bear alone. During the brief calm of the eye, she pounded on the door to Snapper's room and said she was scared half to death. Snapper said come on in, we're having ourselves a time.

Somewhere in the midst of a hurricane, he'd found a hooker. Edie was impressed. The woman clutched a half-empty bottle of Barbancourt between her breasts. Snapper had devoted himself to vodka; he wore a Marlins cap and red Jockey shorts, inside out. Candles gave the motel room a soft, religious lighting. The electricity had been out for two hours.

Edie Marsh introduced herself to the prostitute, whom Snapper had procured through a telephone escort service. Here was a dedicated employee! thought Edie.

The back side of the storm came up, a roar so unbearable that the three of them huddled like orphans on the floor. The candles flickered madly as the wind sucked at the windows. Edie could see the walls breathing—Christ, what a lousy idea this was! A large painting of a pelican fell, grazing one of the hooker's ankles. She cried out softly and gnawed at her artificial fingernails. Snapper kept to the vodka. Occasionally his free hand would turn up like a spider on Edie's thigh. She smashed it, but Snapper merely sighed.

By dawn the storm had crossed inland, and the high water was falling fast. Edie Marsh put on a conservative blue dress and dark nylons, and pinned her long brown hair in a bun. Snapper wore the only suit he owned, a slate pinstripe he'd purchased two years earlier for an ex-cellmate's funeral; the cuffed trousers stopped an inch shy of his shoetops. Edie chuckled and said that was perfect.

They dropped the prostitute at a Denny's restaurant and took the Turnpike south to see what the hurricane had done. Traffic was bumper-to-bumper lunacy, fire engines and cop cars and ambulances everywhere. The radio said Homestead had been blown off the map. The governor was sending the National Guard.

Snapper headed east on 152nd Street but immediately got disoriented. All traffic signals and street signs were down; Snapper couldn't find Sugar Palm Hammocks.

Edie Marsh became agitated. She kept repeating the address aloud: 14275 Noriega Parkway. One-four-two-seven-five. Tan house, brown shutters, swimming pool, two-car garage. Avila had guessed it was worth $185,000.

"If we don't hurry," Edie told Snapper, "if we don't get there soon—"

Snapper instructed her to shut the holy fuck up.

"Wasn't there a Dairy Queen?" Edie went on. "I remember him turning at a Dairy Queen or something."

Snapper said, "The Dairy Queen is gone. *Every* goddamn thing is gone, case you didn't notice. We're flying blind out here."

Edie had never seen such destruction; it looked like Castro had nuked the place. Houses without roofs, walls, windows. Trailers and cars crumpled like foil. Trees in the swimming pools. People weeping, Sweet Jesus, and everywhere the plonking of hammers and the growling of chain saws.

Snapper said they could do another house. "There's only about ten thousand to choose from."

"I suppose."

"What's so special about 1-4-2-7-5?"

"It had personality," Edie Marsh said.

Snapper drummed his knuckles on the steering wheel. "They all look the same. All these places, exactly the same."

His gun lay on the seat between them.

"Fine," said Edie, unsettled by the change of plans, the chaos, the grim dripping skies. "Fine, we'll find another one."

*

Max and Bonnie Lamb arrived in Dade County soon after daybreak. The roads were slick and gridlocked. The gray sky was growling with TV helicopters. The radio said two hundred thousand homes were seriously damaged or destroyed. Meanwhile the Red Cross was pleading for donations of food, water and clothing.

The Lambs exited the Turnpike at Quail Roost Drive. Bonnie was stunned by the devastation; Max himself was aglow. He held the Handycam on his lap as he steered. Every two or three blocks, he slowed to videotape spectacular rubble. A flattened hardware store. The remains of a Sizzler steak house. A school bus impaled by a forty-foot pine.

"Didn't I tell you?" Max Lamb was saying. "Isn't it amazing!"

Bonnie Lamb shuddered. She said they should stop at the nearest shelter and volunteer to help.

Max paid no attention. He parked in front of an exploded town house. The hurricane had thrown a motorboat into the living room. The family—a middle-aged Latin man, his wife, two little girls—stood in a daze on the sidewalk. They wore matching yellow rain slickers.

Max Lamb got out of the car. "Mind if I get some video?"

The man numbly consented. Max photographed the wrecked building from several dramatic angles. Then, stepping through the plaster and broken furniture and twisted toys, he casually entered the house. Bonnie couldn't believe it: He walked right through the gash that was once the front door!

She apologized to the family, but the man said he didn't mind; he'd need pictures anyway, for the insurance people. His daughters began to sob and tremble. Bonnie Lamb knelt to comfort them. Over her shoulder she caught sight of her husband with the camera at his eye, recording the scene through a broken window.

Later, in the rental car, she said: "That was the sickest thing I ever saw."

"Yes, it's very sad."

"I'm talking about you," Bonnie snapped.

"What?"

"Max, I want to go home."

"I bet we can sell some of this tape."

"Don't you dare."

Max said: "I bet we can sell it to C-SPAN. Pay for the whole honeymoon!"

Bonnie closed her eyes. What had she done? Was her mother right about this man? Latent asshole, her mother had whispered at the wedding. Was she right?

At dusk Edie Marsh swallowed two Darvons and reviewed the plan with Snapper, who was having second thoughts. He seemed troubled at the idea of waiting weeks for the payoff. Edie said there wasn't much choice, the way insurance worked. Snapper said he planned to keep his options open, just the same. Edie Marsh took it to mean he'd bug out on a moment's notice.

They had picked a house in a flattened development called Turtle Meadow, where the hurricane had peeled away all the roofs. Snapper said it was probably one of Avila's routes. He said Avila had bragged of inspecting eighty new homes a day without leaving the truck. "Rolling quotas," is what Avila called them. Snapper allowed that Avila wasn't much of a roof inspector, as he was deathly afraid of heights and therefore refused to take a ladder on his rounds. Consequently, Avila's roof certifications were done visually, from a vehicle, at speeds often exceeding thirty-five miles an hour. Snapper said Avila's swiftness and trusting attitude had made him a favorite among the local builders and contractors, especially at Christmastime.

Scanning the debris, Edie Marsh said Avila was damn lucky not to be in jail. That's why he quit when he did, Snapper explained. The bones told him it was time. That, and a grand jury.

Bones? said Edie.

You don't want to know, Snapper said. Honestly.

They were walking along the sidewalk, across the street from the house they had chosen on the drive-by that morning. Now the neighborhood was pitch black except for the erratic flicker of flashlights and the glow of a few small bonfires. Many families had abandoned the crumbled shells of their homes for nearby motels, but a few men had stayed to patrol against looters. The men wore pinched tense expressions and carried shotguns. Snapper was glad to be white and wearing a suit.

The house he and Edie Marsh had chosen wasn't empty, dark or quiet. A bare light bulb had been strung from the skeletal remains of the roof, and the gray-blue glow of a television set pulsed against the plaster. These luxuries were explained by the rumble of a portable generator. Edie and Snapper had seen a fat man gassing it up earlier in the day.

The street was either Turtle Meadow Lane or Calusa Drive, depending on which of the fallen street signs was accurate. The number "15600" was sprayed in red paint on an outside wall of the house, as was the name of the insurance company: "Midwest Casualty."

A big outfit, Edie noted. She'd seen the commercials on television; the company's symbol was a badger.

"A badger?" Snapper frowned. "The fuck does a badger have to do with insurance?"

"I dunno." Edie's mouth was dry. She felt sleepy. "What does a cougar have to do with cars? It's just advertising is all."

Snapper said, "The only thing I know about badgers is they're stubborn. And the last goddamn thing we need's a stubborn insurance company."

Edie said, "For heaven's sake—"

"Let's find another house."

"No!" Weaving slightly, she crossed the street toward 15600.

"You hear me?" Snapper called, then started after her.

Edie wheeled in the driveway. "Let's do it!" she said. "Right now, while it's quiet."

Snapper hesitated, working his jaw like a dazed boxer.

"Come on!" Edie tugged her hair out of the bun and mussed it into a nest in front of her face. Then she hitched her dress and raked her fingernails up both thighs, tearing tracks in her nylons.

Snapper checked to make sure none of the neighborhood vigilantes were watching. Edie picked a place on the driveway and stretched out, facedown. Using two broken roof trusses, Snapper did a superb job setting the scene. Edie was pinned.

From under the debris, she said, "Blood would help."

Snapper kicked a nail toward her left hand. "Take it easy."

Edie Marsh held her breath and scratched the point of the nail from her elbow to her wrist. It hurt like a bitch. She wiped her arm across one cheek to smear the blood for dramatic effect. On cue, Snapper began shouting for help. Edie was impressed; he sounded damn near sincere.

Max Lamb congratulated himself for stocking up on video supplies before they drove down from Orlando. Other tourists had not come so prepared for the hurricane and could be seen foraging through luggage in a manic search for spare tapes and batteries. Meanwhile, pausing only to reload, Max Lamb was compiling dramatic footage of a historic natural disaster. Even if C-SPAN wasn't interested, his friends in New York would be. Max was a junior account executive at a medium-sized advertising firm, and there were many persons whom he yearned to impress. Max was handy with the Sony, but it wouldn't hurt to seek professional assistance; he knew of a place on East Fiftieth Street that edited home videos and, for a small extra charge, added titles and credits. It would be perfect! Once Bonnie settled down, Max Lamb would ask her about throwing a cocktail party where they could screen the hurricane tapes for his clients and his colleagues at the agency.

Max trotted with predatory energy from one wrecked homestead to another, the video camera purring in his hand. He was so absorbed in recording the tragedy that he forgot about his wife, who had stopped following three blocks ago. Max had wanted to show Bonnie how to use the camera so he could pose amid hurricane debris; she'd told him she would rather swallow a gallon of lye.

For editing purposes, Max Lamb kept a mental inventory of his best shots. He had plenty of rubble scenes, and felt the need to temper the visual shock with moments of poignancy—vignettes that would capture the human toll, spiritual as well as physical.

A mangled bicycle grabbed Max's attention. The hurricane had wrapped it, as snug as a wedding band, around the trunk of a coconut palm. A boy no older than eight was trying to remove the bike. Max dropped to one knee and zoomed in on the youngster's face as he tugged grimly on the bent handlebars. The boy's expression was dull and cold, his lips pressed tight in concentration.

Max thought: He's in shock. Doesn't even know I'm here.

The youngster didn't seem to care that his bicycle was destroyed beyond repair. He simply wanted the tree to give it back. He pulled and pulled with all his might. The empty eyes showed no sign of frustration.

Amazing, Max Lamb thought as he peered through the viewfinder. *Amazing.*

Something jostled his right arm, and the boy's image in the viewfinder shook. A hand tugged at Max's sleeve. Cursing, he looked up from the Handycam.

It was a monkey.

Max Lamb pivoted on one heel and aimed the camera at the scrawny animal. Through the viewfinder he saw that the monkey had come through the storm in miserable shape. Its auburn fur was matted and crusty. A bruise as plump as a radish rose from the bridge of its broad velvet nose. The shoe-button eyes were squinty and ringed with milky ooze.

Swaying on its haunches, the monkey bared its gums in a woozy yawn. Listlessly it began to paw at its tail.

"See what we have here—a wild monkey!" Max narrated, for the benefit of future viewers. "Just look at this poor little fella. . . ."

From behind him, a flat voice: "Better watch it, mister." It was the boy with the broken bicycle.

Max, the Handycam still at his eye, said, "What's the matter, son?"

"Better watch out for that thing. My dad, he had to shoot one last night."

"Is that right?" Max smiled to himself. Why would anyone shoot a monkey?

"They're real sick. That's what my dad said."

"Well, I'll certainly be careful," said Max Lamb. He heard footsteps as the strange boy ran off.

Through the viewfinder, Max noticed the monkey's brow was twitching oddly. Suddenly it was airborne. Max lowered the camera just as the animal struck his face, knocking him backward. Miniature rubbery fingers dug at Max's nostrils and eyes. He cried out fearfully. The monkey's damp fur smelled awful.

Max Lamb began rolling in the dirt as if he were on fire. Screeching, the wiry little creature let go. Max sat up, scrubbing his face with the sleeves of his shirt. The stinging told him he'd been scratched. For starters he would require a tetanus booster, and then something more potent to counteract the monkey germs.

As he rose to his feet, Max heard chittering behind the palm tree. He was poised to run, until he spotted the monkey loping with an addled gait in the opposite direction. It was dragging something by a strap.

Max Lamb was enraged. The damn thing was stealing his Handycam! Idiotically he gave pursuit.

An hour later, when Bonnie Lamb went looking for her husband, he was gone.

Two uniformed Highway Patrol troopers stood in the rain at the top of the bridge. One was a tall, powerfully built black man. The other officer was a woman of milky smooth complexion and medium height, with a bun of reddish-brown hair. Together they leaned against the concrete rail and stared down a long length of broken rope, dangling in the breeze over the choppy brown water.

Five motorists had phoned on their cellulars to report that a crazy man was tied to the Card Sound Bridge. That was only hours before the hurricane, when every police officer within fifty miles had been busy evacuating the sane. Nobody had time for jumpers, so nobody checked the bridge.

The black trooper had been sent to Miami all the way from Liberty County, in northern Florida, to help clear traffic for the rescue convoys. At the command center he'd caught a glimpse of the incident notation in the dispatch log—"White male, 40–50 yrs old, 190–220 lbs, gray hair/beard, possible psych. case"—and decided to sneak down to North Key Largo for a look. Technically he was assigned to Homestead, but in the post-storm chaos it was easy to roam and not be missed. He had asked the other trooper to ride with him, and even though she was off duty she'd said yes.

Now motorists crossing the steep bridge braked in curiosity at the sight of the two troopers at the top. *What're they looking at, Mom? Is there a dead body in the water?*

Raindrops trickled from the brim of the black trooper's Stetson as he gazed across Biscayne Bay, leaden and frothy after the dreadful storm. He reached over the rail and hauled up the soggy rope. After examining the end of it, he showed the rope to the other trooper and said, with a weariness: "That's my boy."

The rope hadn't snapped in the hurricane. It had been cut with a knife.

# THREE

**Tony Torres sat in** what remained of his living room and sipped what remained of his Chivas. He found it amusing that his "Salesman of the Year" award had survived the hurricane; it was all that remained hanging on the rain-soaked walls. Tony Torres recalled the party two months earlier, when they'd given him the cheap laminated plaque. It was his reward for selling seventy-seven double-wide house trailers, eighteen more than any other salesman in the history of PreFab Luxury Homes, formerly Tropic Trailers, formerly A-Plus Affordable Homes, Ltd. In the cutthroat world of mobile-home sales, Tony Torres had become a star. His boss had presented the Chivas and a thousand-dollar bonus along with the plaque. They'd paid a waitress to dance topless on a table and sing "For He's a Jolly Good Fellow."

Oh well, Tony Torres thought. Life's a fucking roller coaster. He stroked the stock of the shotgun that lay across his globe-shaped lap, and remembered things he wished he didn't. For instance, that bullshit in the sales pitch about U.S. government safety regulations . . .

The Steens had questioned him thoroughly about hurricanes. So had the Ramirezes and the pain-in-the-ass Stichlers. So had Beatrice Jackson, the widow, and her no-neck son. Tony Torres always said what he'd been coached to say, that PreFab Luxury Homes built state-of-the-art homes guaranteed to withstand high winds. Uncle Sam set the specs. It's all there in the brochure!

So Tony's customers secured their mortgages and bought up the double-wides, and then the hurricane came and blew them away. All seventy-seven. The trailers imploded, exploded, popped off the tiedowns and took off like fucking aluminum ducks. Not one of the damn things made it through the storm. One minute they were pleasant-looking middle-class dwellings, with VCRs and convertible sofas and baby cribs . . . and the next minute they were shrapnel. Tony Torres had driven to the trailer park to see for himself. The place looked like a war zone. He was about to get out of the car when somebody recognized him—old man Stichler, who began spluttering insanely and hurling jagged debris at the salesman. Tony drove off at a high rate of speed. Later he learned that the widow Jackson was found dead in the wreckage of the trailer court.

Tony Torres was unfamiliar with remorse, but he did feel a stab of sorrow. The Chivas took care of that. How was I to know? he thought. I'm a salesman, not a goddamn engineer.

The more Tony drank, the less sympathy he retained for his customers. They goddamn well *knew*. Knew they were buying a tin can instead of a real house. Knew the risks, living in a hurricane zone. These were grown-ups, Tony Torres told himself. They made a choice.

Still, he anticipated trouble. The shotgun was a comfort. Unfortunately, anybody who wanted to track him down had only to look in the Dade County phone book. Being a salesman meant being available to all of humanity.

So let 'em come! Tony thought. Any moron customers got a problem, let 'em see what the storm did to *my* house. They get nasty, I turn the matter over to Señor Remington here.

Shouts rousted Tony Torres from the sticky embrace of his BarcaLounger. He took the gun and a flashlight to the front of the house. Standing in the driveway was a man with an unfortunate pin-striped suit and a face that appeared to have been modified with a crowbar.

"My sister!" the man exclaimed, pointing at a pile of busted lumber.

Tony Torres spotted the prone form of a woman under the trusses. Her eyes were half closed, and a fresh streak of blood colored her face. The woman groaned impressively. The man told Tony to call 911 rightaway.

"First tell me what happened," the salesman said.

"Just look—part of your damn roof fell down on her!"

"Hmmm," said Tony Torres.

"For Christ's sake, don't just stand there."

"Your sister, huh?" Tony walked up to the woman and shined the flashlight in her eyes. The woman squinted reflexively, raising both hands to block out the light.

Tony Torres said, "Guess you're not paralyzed, darling."

He tucked the flashlight under one arm and raised the shotgun toward the man. "Here's the deal, sport. The phones are blown, so we won't be calling 911 unless you got a cellular in your pants, and that looks more like a pistol to me. Second of all, even if we *could* call 911 we'll be waiting till Halloween. Every ambulance from here to Key West is busy because of the storm. Your 'sister' should've thought of that before her accident—"

"What the hell you—"

Tony Torres took the pistol from the man's waist. "Third of all," the salesman said, "my damn roof didn't fall on nobody. Those trusses came off the neighbor's house. That would be Mister Leonel Varga, next door. My own personal roof is lying in pieces somewhere out in the Everglades, is my guess."

From beneath the lumber, the woman said: "Shit, Snapper." The man shot her a glare, then looked away.

Tony Torres said: "I'm in the business of figuring people out quick. That's what a good salesman does. And if she's your sister, sport, then I'm twins with Mel Gibson."

The man with the crooked jaw shrugged.

"Point is," Tony said, "she ain't really hurt. You ain't really her brother. And whatever fucked-up plan you had for ripping me off is now officially terminated."

The man scowled bitterly. "Hey, it was *her* idea."

Tony ordered him to lift the wooden trusses off his partner. When the woman got up, the salesman noticed she was both attractive and intelligent-looking. He motioned with the shotgun.

"Both of you come inside. Hell, inside is pretty much outside, thanks to that goddamn storm. But come in, anyhow, 'cause I'd love to hear your story. I could use a laugh."

The woman smoothed the front of her dress. "We made a bad mistake. Just let us go, OK?"

Tony Torres smiled. "That's funny, darling." He swung the Remington toward the house and pulled the trigger. The blast tore a hole the size of a soccer ball in the garage door.

"Hush," said the drunken salesman, cupping a hand to one ear. "Hear that? Dead fucking silence. Shoot off a twelve-gauge and nobody cares. Nobody comes to see. Nobody comes to help. Know why? Because of the hurricane. The whole place is a madhouse!"

The man with the crooked jaw asked, more out of curiosity than concern: "What is it you want with us?"

"I haven't decided," said Tony Torres. "Let's have a drinky poo."

A week before the hurricane, Felix Mojack died of a viper bite to the ankle. Ownership of his failing wildlife-import business passed to a nephew, Augustine. On the rainy morning he learned of his uncle's death, Augustine was at home practicing his juggling. He had all the windows open, and the Black Crowes playing on the stereo. He was barefoot and wore only a pair of royal-blue gym shorts. He stood in the living room, juggling in time to the music. The objects that he juggled were human skulls; he was up to five at once. The faster Augustine juggled, the happier he was.

On the kitchen table was an envelope from Paine Webber. It contained a check for $21,344.55. Augustine had no need for or interest in the money. He was almost thirty-two years old, and his life was as simple and empty as one could be. Sometimes he deposited the Paine Webber dividends, and sometimes he mailed them off to charities, renegade political candidates or former girlfriends. Augustine sent not a penny to his father's defense lawyers; that was the old man's debt, and he could damn well settle it when he got out of prison.

Augustine's juggling was a private diversion. The skulls were artifacts and medical specimens he'd acquired from friends. When he had them up in the air—three, four, five skulls arcing fluidly from hand to hand—Augustine could feel the full rush of their faraway lives. It was inexplicably and perhaps unwholesomely exhilarating. Augustine didn't know their names, or how they'd lived or died, but from touching them he drew energy.

In his spare time Augustine read books and watched television and hiked what was left of the Florida wilderness. Even before he became wealthy—when he worked on his father's fishing boat, and later in law school—Augustine nursed an unspecific anger that he couldn't trace and wasn't sure he should. It manifested itself in the occasional urge to burn something down or blow something up—a high-rise, a new interstate highway, that sort of thing.

Now that Augustine had both the time and the money, he found himself without direction for these radical sentiments, and with no trustworthy knowledge of heavy explosives. Out of guilt, he donated large sums to respectable causes such as the Sierra Club and the Nature Conservancy. His ambition to noble violence remained a harmless fantasy. Meanwhile he bobbed through life's turbulence like driftwood.

The near-death experience that made Augustine so rich had given him zero insight into a grand purpose or cosmic destiny. Augustine barely remembered the damn Beechcraft going down. Certainly he saw no blinding white light at the end of a cool tunnel, heard no dead relatives calling to him from heaven. All he recalled of the coma that followed the accident was an agonizing and unquenchable thirst.

After recovering from his injuries, Augustine didn't return to the hamster-wheel routine of law school. The insurance settlement financed a comfortable aimlessness that many young men would have found appealing. Yet Augustine was deeply unhappy. One night, in a fit of depression, he violently purged his bookshelves of all genius talents who had died too young. This included his treasured Jack London.

Typically, Augustine was waiting for a woman to come along and fix him. So far, it hadn't happened.

One time a dancer whom Augustine was dating caught him juggling his skulls in the bedroom. She thought it was a stunt designed to provoke a reaction. She told him it wasn't funny, it was perverted. Then she moved to New York. A year or so later, for no particular reason, Augustine sent the woman one of his dividend checks from Paine Webber. She used the money to buy a Toyota Supra and sent Augustine a snapshot of herself, smiling and waving in the driver's seat. Augustine wondered who'd taken the picture and what he'd thought of the new car.

Augustine had no brothers and sisters, his mother was in Nevada and his father was in the slammer. The closest relative was his uncle Felix Mojack, the wildlife importer. As a boy, Augustine often visited his uncle's small cluttered farm out in the boondocks. It was more fun than going to the zoo, because Felix let Augustine help with the animals. In particular, Felix encouraged his nephew to familiarize himself with exotic snakes, as Felix himself was phobic (and, it turned out, fatally incompetent) when it came to handling reptiles.

After Augustine grew up, he saw less and less of his busy uncle. Progress conspired against Felix; development swept westward, and zoning regulations forced him to move his operation repeatedly. Nobody, it seemed, wished to build elementary schools or shopping malls within walking distance of caged jungle cats and wild cobras. The last time Felix Mojack was forced to relocate his animals, Augustine gave him ten thousand dollars for the move.

At the time of Felix's death, the farm inventory listed one male African lion, three cougars, a gelded Cape buffalo, two Kodiak bears, ninety-seven parrots and macaws, eight Nile crocodiles, forty-two turtles, seven hundred assorted lizards, ninety-three snakes (venomous and nonvenomous) and eighty-eight rhesus monkeys.

The animals were kept on a nine-acre spread off Krome Avenue, not far from the federal prison. The day after the funeral, Augustine drove out to the place alone. He had a feeling that his uncle ran a loose operation, and a tour of the facility corroborated his suspicion. The fencing was buckled and rusty, the cages needed new hinges, and the concrete reptile pits hadn't been drained and cleaned in months. In the tar-paper shed that Felix had used for an office, Augustine found paperwork confirming his uncle's low regard for U.S. Customs regulations.

It came as no surprise that Felix had been a smuggler; rather, Augustine was grateful that his uncle's choice of contraband had been exotic birds and snakes, and not something else. Wildlife, however, presented its own unique challenges. While bales of marijuana required no feeding, bears and cougars did. Lean and hungry was a mild description of the illegal menagerie; Augustine was appalled by the condition of some of the animals and presumed their deterioration was a result of his uncle's recent financial troubles. Fortunately, the two young Mexicans who worked for Felix Mojack graciously agreed to help out for a few days after his death. They stocked the freezers with raw meat for the large carnivores, bought boxloads of feed for the parrots and monkeys, and restocked on white mice and insects for the reptiles.

Meanwhile Augustine scrambled to locate a buyer for the animals, somebody qualified to take good care of them. Augustine was so preoccupied with the task that he didn't pay enough attention to news reports of a tropical storm intensifying in the Caribbean. Even when it bloomed into a hurricane, and Augustine saw the weather bulletin on television, he assumed it would do what most storms did in late summer—veer north, away from South Florida, on the prevailing Atlantic steering currents.

Once it became clear that the hurricane would strike southern Dade County with a direct hit, Augustine had little time to act. He was grimly aware what sustained one-hundred-mile-per-hour winds would do to his dead uncle's shabby farm. He spent the morning and afternoon on the telephone, trying to find a secure location for the animals. Interest invariably dropped off at the mention of a Cape buffalo. At dusk Augustine drove out to fasten tarps and tie-downs on the cages and pens. Sensing the advancing storm, the bears and big cats paced nervously, growling in agitation. The parrots were in a panic; the frenetic squawking attracted several large hawks to the nearby pines. Augustine stayed two hours and decided it was hopeless. He sent the Mexicans home and drove to a nearby Red Cross shelter to wait out the storm.

When he returned at dawn, the place was destroyed. The fencing was strewn like holiday tinsel across the property. The corrugated roofing had been peeled off the compound like a sardine tin. Except for a dozen befuddled turtles, all his uncle's wild animals had escaped into the scrub and marsh and, inevitably, the Miami suburbs. As soon as phone service was restored, Augustine notified the police what had happened. The dispatcher laconically estimated it would be five or six days before an officer could be spared, because everybody was working double shifts after the hurricane. When Augustine asked how far a Gaboon viper could travel in five or six days, the dispatcher said she'd try to send somebody out there sooner.

Augustine couldn't just sit and wait. The radio said a troop of storm-addled monkeys had invaded a residential subdivision off Quail Roost Drive, only miles from the farm. Augustine immediately loaded the truck with his uncle's dart rifle, two long-handled nooses, a loaded .38 Special, and a five-pound bag of soggy monkey chow.

He didn't know what else to do.

Canvassing the neighborhood in search of her husband, Bonnie Lamb encountered the dull-eyed boy with the broken bicycle. His description of the tourist jerk with the video camera fit Max too well.

"He ran after the monkey," the boy said.

Bonnie Lamb said, "What monkey?"

The boy explained. Bonnie assessed the information

calmly. "Which way did they go?" The boy pointed. Bonnie thanked him and offered to help pry his bicycle off the tree. The boy turned away, so she walked on.

Bonnie was puzzled by the monkey story, but most of the questions clouding her mind concerned Max Lamb's character. How could a man wander off and forget about his new wife? Why was he so fascinated with the hurricane ruins? How could he so cruelly intrude on the suffering of those who lived here?

During two years of courtship, Max had never seemed insensitive. At times he could be immature and self-centered, but Bonnie had never known a man who wasn't. In general, Max was a responsible and attentive person; more than just a hard worker, an achiever. Bonnie appreciated that, as her two previous boyfriends had taken a casual approach to the concept of full-time employment. Max impressed her with his seriousness and commitment, his buoyant determination to attain professional success and financial security. At thirty, Bonnie was at a point in life where she liked the prospect of security; she was tired of worrying about money, and about men who had none. Beyond that, she truly found Max Lamb attractive. He wasn't exceptionally handsome or romantic, but he was sincere—boyishly, completely, relentlessly sincere. His earnestness, even in bed, was endearing. This was a man Bonnie thought she could trust.

Until today, when he started acting like a creep.

The predawn expedition to Miami seemed, at first, a honeymoon lark—Max's way of showing his bride that he could be as wild and impulsive as her old boyfriends. Against her best instincts, Bonnie played along. She felt sure that seeing the hurricane's terrible destruction would end Max's documentary ambitions, that he'd put down the camera and join the volunteer relief workers, who were arriving by the busload.

But he didn't. He kept taping, becoming more and more excited, until Bonnie Lamb could no longer bear it. When he asked her to operate the camera while he posed on an overturned station wagon, Bonnie nearly slugged him. She quit tagging after Max because she didn't want to be seen with him. Her own husband.

In one gutted house she spotted an old woman, her mother's age, stepping through splintered bedroom furniture. The woman was calling the name of a pet kitten, which had disappeared in the storm. Bonnie Lamb offered to help search. The cat didn't turn up, but Bonnie did find the old woman's wedding album, beneath a shattered mirror. Bonnie cleared the broken glass and retrieved the album, damp but not ruined. Bonnie opened it to the date of inscription: December 11, 1949. When the old woman saw the album, she broke down in Bonnie's arms. With a twinge of shame, Bonnie glanced around to make sure that Max wasn't secretly filming them. Then she began to cry, too.

Later, resolved to confront her husband, Bonnie Lamb went to find him. If he refused to put away that stupid camera, she would demand the keys to the rental car. It promised to be the first hard test of the new marriage.

Two hours passed with no sign of Max, and Bonnie's anger dissolved into worry. The tale told by the boy with the broken bicycle ordinarily would have been comical, but Bonnie took it as further evidence of Max's reckless obsession. He was afraid of animals, even hamsters, a condition he blamed on an unspecified childhood trauma; to boldly pursue a wild monkey was definitely out of character. On the other hand, Max loved that damn Handycam. More than once he'd reminded Bonnie that it had cost seven hundred dollars, mail order from Hong Kong. She could easily envision him chasing a seven-hundred-dollar investment down the street. She could even envision him strangling the monkey for it, if necessary.

Another squall came, and Bonnie cursed mildly under her breath. There wasn't much left standing, in the way of shelter. She felt a shiver as the raindrops ran down her neck, and decided to return to the rental car and wait for Max there. Except she wasn't sure where the car was parked—without street signs or mailboxes, every block of the destroyed subdivision looked the same. Bonnie Lamb was lost.

She saw the helicopters wheeling overhead, heard the chorus of sirens in the distance, yet on the streets of the neighborhood there were no policemen, no soldiers, no proper authority to which a missing husband could be reported. Exhausted, Bonnie sat on a curb. To keep dry, she tried to balance a large square of plywood over her head. A gust of wind got under the board and pulled Bonnie over backward; as she went down, a corner of the board struck her sharply on the forehead.

She lay there stunned for several moments, staring at the muddy sky, blinking the raindrops from her eyes. A man appeared, standing over her. He wore a small rifle slung on one shoulder.

"Let me help," he said.

Bonnie Lamb allowed him to lift her from the wet grass. She noticed her blouse was soaked, and shyly folded her arms across her breasts. The man retrieved the plywood board and braced it at a generous angle against a concrete utility pole. There he and Bonnie Lamb took shelter from the slashing rain.

The man was in his early thirties, with good shoulders and tanned, strong-looking arms. He had short brown hair, a sharp chin and friendly blue eyes. He wore Rockport hiking shoes, which gave Bonnie a sense of relief. She couldn't imagine a psychopathic sex killer choosing Rockports.

"Do you live around here?" she asked.

The man shook his head. "Coral Gables."

"Is the gun loaded?"

"Sort of," the man said, without elaborating.

"My name is Bonnie."

"I'm Augustine."

"What are you doing out here?" she asked.

"Believe it or not," he said, "I'm looking for my monkeys."

Bonnie Lamb smiled. "What a coincidence."

Max Lamb woke up with a headache that was about to get worse. He found himself stripped to his underwear and bound to a pine tree. The tall man with the glass eye, the man who'd snatched him off the street as if he were a wayward toddler, was thrashing and flopping in a leafy clearing by the campfire. When the impressive seizure ended, the kidnapper gathered himself in a lotus position. Max Lamb noticed a thick black collar around the man's neck. In one hand he held a shiny cylinder that reminded Max of a remote control for a model car. The cylinder had a short rubber antenna and three colored buttons.

The one-eyed man was mumbling: "Too much juice, too much . . ." He wore a cheap plastic shower cap on his head. Max would have assumed he was a street person, except for the teeth; the kidnapper displayed outstanding orthodontics.

He seemed unaware that his captive was observing him. Deliberately the man extended both legs to brace himself, inhaled twice deeply, then pushed a red button on the remote-control cylinder. Instantly his body began to jerk like an enormous broken puppet. Max Lamb watched helplessly as the stranger writhed through the leaves toward the fire. His boots were in the flames when the fit finally ended. Then the man rose with a startling swiftness, stomping his huge feet until the soles cooled.

One hand went to his neck. "By God, that's better."

Max Lamb concluded it was a nightmare, and shut his eyes. When he opened them again, much later, he saw that the campfire was freshly stoked. The one-eyed kidnapper crouched nearby; now his neck was bare. He was feeding Oreo cookies to the larcenous monkey, which appeared to be regaining its health. Max was more certain than ever that what he'd witnessed earlier was a dream. He felt ready to assert himself.

"Where's my camera?" he demanded.

The kidnapper stood up, laughing through his wild beard. "Perfect," he said. "'Where's my camera?' That's just perfect."

In a hazardously patronizing tone, Max Lamb said: "Let me go, pardner. You don't *really* want to go to jail, do you?"

"Ha," the stranger said. He reached for the shiny black cylinder.

A bolt of fire passed through Max Lamb's neck. He

shuddered violently and gulped for breath. His tongue tasted of hot copper. Crimson spears of light punctured the night. Max warbled in fear.

"Shock collar," the kidnapper explained, unnecessarily. "The TriTronics 200. Three levels of stimulation. Range of one mile. Rechargeable nickel-cadmium batteries. Three-year warranty."

Max felt it now, stiff leather against the soft skin of his throat.

"State of the art," said the stranger. "You a bird hunter?"

Max mouthed the word "no."

"Well, trust me. Field trainers swear by these gizmos. Dogs get the message real quick, even Labs." The stranger twirled the remote control like a baton. "Me, I couldn't put one of these on an animal. Fact, I couldn't even try it on *you* without testing it myself. That's what a big old softy I am."

The kidnapper scratched the crown of the monkey's head. The monkey hopped back and bared its tiny teeth, which were flecked black with Oreo crumbs. The kidnapper laughed.

Max Lamb, quavering: "Keep it away from me!"

"Not an animal person, huh?"

"What is it you want?"

The stranger turned toward the fire.

Max said, "Is it money? Just take whatever I've got."

"Jesus, you're thick." The stranger pushed the red button, and Max Lamb thrashed briefly against his ropes. The monkey skittered away, out of the firelight.

Max looked up to see the psycho, taping him with the video camera! "Say cheese," the stranger said, aiming the Handycam with his good eye.

Max Lamb reddened. He felt spindly and pale in his underwear.

The man said, "I might send this up to Rodale and Burns. What d'you think—for the office Christmas bash? 'How I Spent My Florida Vacation,' starring Max Leo Lamb."

Max sagged. Rodale and Burns was the Madison Avenue advertising agency where he worked. The lunatic had been through his billfold.

"They call me Skink," the kidnapper said. He turned off the Handycam and carefully capped the lens. "But I prefer 'captain.'"

"Captain what?"

"Obviously you were impressed by the hurricane." The stranger packed the video camera in a canvas sleeve. "Myself, I was disappointed. I was hoping for something more . . . well, biblical."

Max Lamb said, as respectfully as possible: "It looked pretty bad to me."

"You hungry?" The kidnapper brought a burlap sack to the tree where his prisoner was tied.

"Oh God," said Max Lamb, staring inside the bag. "You can't be serious."

# FOUR

**Filling the BarcaLounger** like a stuffed tuna, Tony Torres encouraged Edie Marsh and Snapper to reveal the details of their aborted scam. Facing a loaded shotgun, they complied.

Snapper gestured sourly toward Edie, who said: "Simple. I fake a fall in your driveway. My 'brother' here threatens to sue. You freak out and offer us money."

"Because you guys know," Tony said, slapping a mosquito on his blubbery neck, "I'll be getting quite a wad of dough on account of the hurricane. Insurance dough."

"Exactly," Edie Marsh said. "Your place is wrecked, last thing you need is a lawsuit. So Snapper says here's an idea: Soon as your hurricane money comes in, cut us a piece and we call it even."

Tony Torres sucked his teeth in amusement. "How big a piece, darling?"

"Whatever we could take you for."

"Ah," said Tony.

"We figured you'd just factor us in the insurance claim. Jack up your losses by a few grand, who'd ever know?"

"Beautiful," Tony said.

"Oh yeah," said Snapper, "fucking genius. Look how good it worked."

He and Edie sat with their backs to the living-room wall; Snapper with his long legs drawn up, Edie's straight out, kneecaps pressed together. A picture of innocence, Tony Torres thought. The runs in her stockings were a nifty touch.

The carpet was sodden from the storm, but Edie Marsh didn't complain. Snapper felt the wetness creeping through the seat of his dress trousers—the annoyance was sufficient that he might kill Tony Torres, if the opportunity presented itself.

Deep in thought, the salesman slurped at a sweaty bottle of imported beer. He'd offered his captives a quart of warm Gatorade, which they'd refused without comment. A humid breeze blew through the fractures in the walls and rocked the bare sixty-watt bulb on its beam. Edie Marsh tilted her head and saw a spray of stars where Tony's ceiling had once been. The noise from the portable generator gave Snapper an oppressive headache.

Eventually, Tony Torres said: "You understand there's no law to speak of. The world's upside down, for the time being."

"You could kill us and get clean away with it. That's what you mean," Snapper said.

Edie looked at him. "You're a tremendous help."

Tony indicated that he preferred not to shoot them. "But here's my thinking," he said. "Tomorrow, maybe the day after, somebody from Midwest Casualty will come see about the house. I expect he'll say it's a total loss, unless he's blind as a bat. Anyway, the good news: I happen to own the place free and clear. Paid it off last

March." Tony paused to stifle a burp. "I was having a good run at the office, so what the hell. I paid the mortgage off."

Edie Marsh said: "Salesman of the Year." She had noticed the plaque.

"Mister," Snapper interjected, "you got somethin' I can put under my ass? The rug's all wet. A newspaper maybe?"

"Oh, I think you'll live," said the salesman. "Anyhow, since the bank don't own the house, all the insurance comes to me. As I say, there's the good news. The bad news is, half belongs to my wife. Her name's on the deed."

Snapper asked where she was. Tony Torres said she'd run off three months ago with a parapsychology professor from the university. He said they'd gotten into crystal healing and moved to Eugene, Oregon.

"In a VW van!" he scoffed. "But she'll be back for her cut. Of that there's no doubt. Neria will return. See where I'm headed?"

"Yeah," said Snapper. "You want us to kill your wife."

"Jesus, what a one-track mind you got. No, I don't want you to *kill* my wife." The salesman appealed to Edie Marsh. "You get it, don't you? Before they cut a check, the insurance company is gonna need both signatures. Me and the missus. And I also believe the adjuster might want to chat face-to-face. What'd you say your name was?"

"Edie."

"OK, Edie, you wanna be an actress here's your chance. When the man from Midwest Casualty shows up, you be Neria Torres. My loving wife." Tony smirked at the notion. "Well?"

Edie Marsh asked what was in it for her, and Tony Torres said ten grand. Edie said she'd have to think about it, which took about one one-hundredth of a second. She needed money.

"What about me?" Snapper asked.

Tony said, "I always wanted a bodyguard."

Snapper grunted skeptically. "How much?"

"Ten for you, too. It's more than fair."

Snapper admitted it was. "Why," he asked, with a trace of scorn, "do *you* need a bodyguard?"

"Some customers got really pissed off at me. It's a long boring story."

Edie Marsh said, "How pissed off?"

"I don't intend to find out," said Tony Torres. "Once I get the check, I'm gone."

"Where?"

"None a your damn business."

Middle America was what Tony had in mind. A handsome two-story house with a porch and a fireplace, on three-quarters of an acre outside Tulsa. What appealed to Tony about Middle America was the absence of hurricanes. There were tornadoes galore, but nobody expected any man-made structure (least of all, a trailer home) to withstand the terrible force of a tornado. Nobody would blame a person if the double-wides he sold blew to pieces, because that was the celestial nature of tornadoes. Tony Torres figured he would be safe from disgruntled customers in Tulsa.

Snapper said, "I'm gonna be a bodyguard, I'll need my gun."

Tony smiled. "No you won't. That face of yours is enough to scare the piss out of most mortal men. Which is perfect, because the people who're mad at me, they don't actually need to be shot. They just need to be scared. See where I'm headed?"

He took a length of bathroom pipe and smashed Snapper's pistol to pieces.

Edie Marsh said, "I've got a question, too."

"Well, bless your heart."

"What happens if your wife shows up?"

"We got probably six, seven days of breathing room," Tony Torres said. "However long it takes to drive that old van back from Oregon. See, Neria won't fly. She's terrified of planes."

Snapper remarked that money was known to make a person drive faster than usual, or overcome a fear of flying. Tony said he wasn't worried. "The radio said State Farm and Allstate are writing settlements already. Midwest won't be far behind—see, no company wants to look stingy in a national disaster."

Edie asked Tony Torres if he intended to hold them prisoner. He gave a great slobbering laugh and said hell, no, they could vamoose anytime they pleased. Edie stood and announced she was returning to the motel. Snapper rose warily, never taking his eyes off the shotgun.

He said to Tony: "Why are you doing this? Lettin' us walk out of here."

"Because you'll be back," the salesman said. "You most certainly will. I can see it in your eyes."

"Really?" Edie said, tartly.

"Really, darling. It's what I do for a living. Read people." The Naugahyde hissed as Tony Torres hoisted himself up from the BarcaLounger. "I need to take a leak," he declared. Then, with a hoot: "I'm sure you can find your way out!"

On the slow drive back to Pembroke Pines, Edie Marsh and Snapper mulled the options. Both of them were broke. Both recognized the post-hurricane turmoil as a golden opportunity. Both agreed that ten thousand dollars was a good week's work.

"Trouble is," Edie said, "I don't trust that asshole. What is it he sells?"

"Trailer homes."

"Good Lord."

"Then let's walk away," Snapper said, without conviction. "Try the slip-and-fall on somebody else."

Edie contemplated the ugly, self-inflicted scratch on her arm. Posing under a pile of lumber had been more uncomfortable than she'd anticipated. She wasn't eager to try it again.

"I'll coast with this jerkoff a day or two," she told Snapper. "You do what you want."

Snapper configured his crooked jaws into the semblance of a grin. "I know what you're thinkin'. I ain't no salesman, but I can read you just the same. You're thinkin' they's more than ten grand in this deal, you play it right. If *we* play it right."

"Why not." Edie Marsh pressed her cheek against the cool glass of the car's window. "It's about time my luck should change."

"*Our* luck," Snapper said, both hands tight on the wheel.

Augustine helped Bonnie Lamb search for her husband until nightfall. They failed to locate Max, but along the way they came upon an escaped male rhesus. It was up in a grapefruit tree, hurling unripened fruit at passing humans. Augustine shot the animal with a tranquilizer dart, and it toppled like a marionette. Augustine was dismayed to discover, stapled in one of its ears, a tag identifying it as property of the University of Miami.

He had captured somebody else's fugitive monkey.

"What now?" asked Bonnie Lamb, reasonably. She reached out to pet the stunned animal, then changed her mind. The rhesus studied her through dopey, half-closed eyes.

"You're a good shot," she said to Augustine.

He wasn't listening. "This isn't right," he muttered. He carried the limp monkey to the grapefruit tree and propped it gently in the crook of two boughs. Then he took Bonnie back to his truck. "It'll be dark soon," he said. "I forgot to bring a flashlight."

They drove through the subdivision for fifteen minutes until Bonnie Lamb spotted the rental car. Max wasn't there. Somebody had pried the trunk and stolen all the luggage, including Bonnie's purse.

Damn kids, Augustine said. Bonnie was too tired to cry. Max had the car keys, the credit cards, the money, the plane tickets. "I need to find a phone," she said. Her folks would wire some money.

Augustine drove to a police checkpoint, where Bonnie Lamb reported her husband missing. He was one of many, and not high on the list. Thousands who'd escaped their homes in the hurricane were being sought by worried relatives. For relief workers, reuniting local families was a priority; tracking wayward tourists was not.

A bank of six phones had been set up near the checkpoint, but the lines were long. Bonnie found the shortest one and settled in for a wait. She thanked Augustine for his help.

"What will you do tonight?" he asked.

"I'll be OK."

Bonnie was startled to hear him say: "No you won't."

He took her by the hand and led her to the pickup. It occurred to Bonnie that she ought to be afraid, but she felt illogically safe with this total stranger. It also occurred to her that panic would be a normal reaction to a husband's disappearance, but instead she felt an inappropriate calmness and lucidity. Probably just exhaustion, she thought.

Augustine drove back to the looted rental car. He scribbled a note and tucked it under one of the windshield wipers. "My phone number," he told Bonnie Lamb. "In case your husband shows up later tonight. This way he'll know where you are."

"We're going to your place?"

"Yes."

In the darkness, she couldn't see Augustine's expression. "It's madness out here," he said. "These idiots shoot at anything that moves."

Bonnie nodded. She'd been hearing distant gunfire from all directions. *Dade County is an armed camp.* That's what their travel agent had warned them. Death Wish Tours, he'd called it. *Only a fool would set foot south of Orlando.*

Crazy Max, thought Bonnie. What had possessed him?

"You know why my husband came down here?" she

said. "Know what he was doing when he got lost? Taking video of the wrecked houses. And the people, too."

"Why?" Augustine asked.

"Home movies. To show his pals back North."

"Jesus, that's—"

"Sick," Bonnie Lamb said. "'Sick' is the word for it."

Augustine said nothing more. Slowly he worked his way toward the Turnpike. The futility of the monkey hunt was evident; Augustine realized that most of his dead uncle's wild animals were irretrievable. The larger mammals would inevitably make their presence known—the Cape buffalo, the bears, the cougars—and the results were bound to be unfortunate. Meanwhile the snakes and crocodiles probably were celebrating freedom by copulating merrily in the Everglades, ensuring for their species a solid foothold in a new tropical habitat. Augustine felt it was morally wrong to interfere. An escaped cobra had as much natural right to a life in Florida as did all those retired garment workers from Queens. Natural selection would occur. The test applied to Max Lamb as well, but Augustine felt sorry for his wife. He would set aside his principles and help find her missing husband.

He drove using the high beams because there were no street lights, and the roads were a littered gauntlet of broken trees and utility poles, heaps of lumber and twisted metal, battered appliances and gutted sofas. They saw a Barbie dollhouse and a canopy bed and an antique china cabinet and a child's wheelchair and a typewriter and a tangle of golf clubs and a cedar hot tub, split in half like a coconut husk—Bonnie said it was as if a great supernatural fist had snatched up a hundred thousand lives and shaken the contents all over creation.

Augustine was thinking more in terms of a B-52 raid.

"Is this your first one?" Bonnie asked.

"Technically, no." He braked to swerve around a dead cow, bloated on the center line. "I was conceived during Donna—least that's what my mother said. A hurricane baby. That was 1960. Betsy I can barely remember because I was only five. We lost a few lime trees, but the house held up fine."

Bonnie said, "That's kind of romantic. Being conceived in the middle of a hurricane."

"My mother said it made perfect sense, considering how I turned out."

"And how *did* you turn out?" Bonnie asked.

"Reports differ."

Augustine edged the truck into a line of storm traffic crawling up the northbound ramp to the Turnpike. A rusty Ford with a crooked Georgia license plate cut them off. The car was packed with itinerant construction workers who'd been on the road for several days straight, apparently drinking the whole time. The driver, a shaggy blond with greenish teeth, leered and yelled an obscenity up at Bonnie Lamb. With one hand Augustine reached behind his seat and got the small rifle. Bracing it against the doorpost, he fired a tranquilizer dart cleanly into the belly of the redneck driver, who yipped and pitched sideways into the lap of one of his pals.

"Manners," said Augustine. He gunned the truck, nudging the stalled Ford off the pavement.

Bonnie Lamb thought: God, what am I doing?

*

They broke camp at midnight—Max Lamb, the rhesus monkey and the man who called himself Skink. Max was grateful that the man had allowed him to put on his shoes, because they walked for hours in pitch darkness through deep swamp and spiny thickets. Max's bare legs stung from the scratches and itched from the bug bites. He was terribly hungry but didn't complain, knowing the man had saved him the rump of the dead raccoon that was boiled for dinner. Max wanted no part of it.

They came to a canal. Skink untied Max's hands, unbuckled the shock collar and ordered him to swim. Max was halfway across when he saw the blue-black alligator slide out of the sawgrass. Skink told him to quit whimpering and kick; he himself swam with the rejuvenated monkey perched on his head. One huge hand held Max's precious Sony and the remote control for the dog collar high above the water.

After scrabbling ashore, Max said, "Captain, can we rest?"

"Ever seen a leech before? 'Cause there's a good one on your cheek."

After Max Lamb finished flaying himself, Skink retied his wrists and refastened the dog collar. Then he sprayed him down with insect repellent. Max croaked out a thank-you.

"Where are we?" he asked.

"The Everglades," Skink replied. "More or less."

"You promised I could call my wife."

"Soon."

They headed west, trudging through palmettos and pinelands shredded by the storm. The monkey scampered ahead, foraging wild berries and fruit buds.

Max said: "Are you going to kill me?"

Skink stopped walking. "Every time you ask that stupid question, you're going to get it." He set the remote on the weakest setting.

"Ready?"

Max Lamb clenched his lips. Skink stung him with a light jolt. The tourist twitched stoically. Soon they came to a Miccosukee village, which was not as badly damaged as Max Lamb would have imagined. Since the Indians were awake, cooking food, Max assumed it would soon be dawn. In open doorways the children gathered shyly to look at the two strange white men: Skink with his brambly hair, ill-fitting eye and mangy monkey, Max Lamb in his dirty underwear and dog collar.

Skink stopped at a wooden house and spoke quietly to a Miccosukee elder, who brought out a cellular phone. As he untied Max's hands, Skink warned: "One call is all you get. He says the battery's running low."

Max realized that he didn't know how to reach his wife. He had no idea where she was. So he called their apartment in New York and spoke to the answering machine: "Honey, I've been kidnapped—"

"Abducted!" Skink broke in. "Kidnapping implies ransom, Max. Don't fucking flatter yourself."

"OK, 'abducted.' Honey, I've been abducted. I can't say very much except I'm fine, all things considered. Please call my folks, and also call Pete up at Rodale about the Bronco billboard project. Tell him the race car should be red, not blue. The file's on my desk. . . . Bonnie, I'm not sure who's got me, or why, but I guess I'll find out soon enough. God, I hope you pick up this message—"

Skink snatched the phone. "I love you, Bonnie," he said. "Max forgot to tell you, so I will. Bye now."

They ate with the Miccosukees, who declined Skink's offer of boiled coon but generously shared helpings of fried panfish, yams, cornmeal muffins and citrus juice. Max Lamb ate heartily but, mindful of the electric dog collar, said little. After breakfast, Skink tied him to a cypress post and disappeared with several men of the tribe. When he returned, he declared it was time to leave.

Max said, "Where's my stuff?" He was worried about his billfold and clothes.

"Right here." Skink jerked a thumb toward his backpack.

"And my Sony?"

"Gave it to the old man. He's got seven grandchildren, so he'll have a ball."

"What about my tapes?"

Skink laughed. "He loved 'em. That monkey attack was something special. Max, lift your arms." He spritzed the prisoner with more bug juice.

Max Lamb, somberly: "That Handycam retails for about nine hundred bucks."

"It's not like I gave it away. I traded."

"For what?"

Skink chucked him on the shoulder. "I'll bet you've never been on an airboat."

"Oh no. Please."

"Hey, you wanted to see Florida."

It wasn't easy being a black Highway Patrol trooper in Florida. It was even harder if you were involved intimately with a white trooper, the way Jim Tile was involved with Brenda Rourke.

They'd met at a training seminar about the newest gadgets for clocking speeders. In the classroom they were seated next to each other. Jim Tile liked Brenda Rourke right away. She had a sane and healthy outlook on the job, and she made him laugh. They traded stories about freaky traffic stops, lousy pay and the impossible FHP bureaucracy. Because he was black, and few fellow officers were, Jim Tile rarely felt comfortable in a roomful of state troopers. But he felt fine next to Brenda Rourke, partly because she was a minority, too; the Highway Patrol employed even fewer women than blacks or Latins.

During one session, a buzz-cut redneck shot a rat-eyed look at Jim Tile to remind him that Trooper Rourke was a white girl, and that still counted for plenty in parts of Florida. Jim Tile didn't get up and move; he kept his seat beside Brenda. It took the cracker trooper only about two hours to quit glaring.

At the lunch break, Jim Tile and Brenda Rourke went to an Arby's. She was worried about her upcoming transfer to South Florida; Jim Tile couldn't say much to allay her fears. She said she was studying Spanish, in preparation for road duty in Miami. The first phrase she'd learned was: *Sale del carro con las manos arriba.* Out of the car with your hands up!

At the time, Jim Tile held no romantic intentions. Brenda Rourke was a nice person, that was all. He never even asked if she had a boyfriend. A few months later, when he was down in Dade County for a trial, he ran into her at FHP headquarters. Later they went to dinner and then to Brenda's apartment, where they were up until three in the morning, chatting, of all things—initially out of nervousness, and later out of an easy intimacy. The trial lasted six days, and every night Jim Tile found himself back at Brenda's place. Every morning they awakened exactly as they'd fallen asleep—her head in the crook of his right shoulder, his feet hanging off the short bed. He'd never felt so peaceful. After the trial ended and Jim Tile returned to North Florida, he and Brenda took turns commuting for long weekends.

He wasn't much of a talker, but Brenda could drag it out of him. She especially liked to hear about the time he was assigned to guard the governor of Florida—not just any governor, but the one who'd quit, disappeared and become a legendary recluse. Brenda had been in high school, but she remembered when it happened. The newspapers and TV had gone wild. "Mentally unstable," was what her twelfth-grade civics teacher had said of the runaway governor.

When Jim Tile had heard that, he threw back his head and laughed. Brenda would sit cross-legged on the carpet, her chin in her hands, engrossed by his stories of the one they now called Skink. Out of loyalty and prudence, Jim Tile didn't mention that he and the man had remained the closest of friends.

"I wish I'd met him," Brenda had said, in the past tense, as if Skink were dead. Because Jim Tile had, perhaps unconsciously, made it sound like he was.

Now, two years later, it seemed that Brenda's improbable wish might come true. The governor had surfaced in the hurricane zone.

On the ride back from Card Sound, she asked: "Why

would he tie himself to a bridge during a storm?" It was the logical question.

Jim Tile said, "He's been waiting for a big one."

"What for?"

"Brenda, I can't explain. It only makes sense if you know him."

She said nothing for a mile or two, then: "Why didn't you tell me that you two still talk?"

"Because we seldom do."

"Don't you trust me?"

"Of course." He pulled her close enough to steal a kiss.

She pulled away, a spark in her pale-blue eyes. "You're going to try to find him. Come on, Jim, be straight with me."

"I'm afraid he's got a loose wire. That's not good."

"This isn't the first time, is it?"

"No," said Jim Tile, "it's not the first time."

Brenda brought his hand to her lips and kissed his knuckles lightly. "It's OK, big guy. I understand about friends."

# FIVE

**When they got to** Augustine's house, Bonnie Lamb called her answering machine in New York. She listened twice to Max's message, then replayed it for Augustine.

"What do you think?" she asked.

"Not good. Is your husband worth a lot of money?"

"He does all right, but he's no millionaire."

"And his family?"

Bonnie said her husband's father was quite wealthy. "But I'm sure Max wasn't foolish enough to mention it to the kidnappers."

Augustine made no such assumption. He heated tomato soup for Bonnie and put clean linens on the bed in the guest room. Then he went to the den and called a friend with the FBI. By the time he got off the phone, Bonnie Lamb had fallen asleep on the living-room sofa. He carried her to the spare room and tucked her under the covers. Then he went to the kitchen and fixed two large rib-eye steaks and a baked potato, which he washed down with a cold bottle of Amstel.

Later he took a long hot shower and thought about how wonderful Mrs Lamb—warm and damp from the rain and sweat—had smelled in his arms. It felt good to have a woman in the house again, even for just a night. Augustine wrapped himself in a towel and stretched out on the hardwood floor in front of the television. He flipped back and forth between local news broadcasts, hoping not to see any of his dead uncle's wild animals running amok, or Mrs Lamb's husband being loaded into a coroner's wagon.

At midnight Augustine heard a cry from the guest room. He correctly surmised that Mrs Lamb had discovered his skull collection. He found her sitting up, the covers pulled to her chin. She was gazing at the wall.

"I thought it was a dream," she said.

"Please don't be afraid."

"Are they real?"

"Friends send them to me," Augustine said, "from abroad, mostly. One was a Christmas present from a fishing guide in Islamorada." He wasn't sure what Bonnie Lamb thought of his hobby, so he apologized for the fright. "Some people collect coins. I'm into forensic artifacts."

"Body parts?"

"Not fresh ones—artifacts. Believe it or not, a good skull is hard to come by."

That was the line that usually sent them bolting for the door. Bonnie didn't move.

"Can I look?"

Augustine took one from a shelf. She inspected it casually, as if it were a cantaloupe in a grocery store. Augustine smiled; he liked this lady.

"Male or female?" Bonnie turned the skull in her hands.

"Male, late twenties, early thirties. Guyanese, circa 1940. Came from a medical school in Texas."

Bonnie asked why the lower jaw was missing. Augustine explained that it fell off when the facial muscles decayed. Most old skulls were found without the mandible.

Lifting it by the eye sockets, Bonnie returned the spooky relic to its place on the wall. "How many have you got up there?"

"Nineteen."

She whistled. "And how many are women?"

"None," said Augustine. "They're all young males. So you've got nothing to worry your pretty head about."

She rolled her eyes at the joke, then asked: "Why all males?"

"To remind me of my own mortality."

Bonnie groaned. "You're one of *those*."

"Other times," Augustine said, "when I'm sure my life has gone to hell, I come in here and think about what happened to these poor bastards. It improves my outlook considerably."

She said, "Well, that makes about as much sense as everything else. Can I take a shower?"

Later, over coffee, he told her what the FBI man had said. "They'll treat your husband's disappearance as a kidnapping when there's a credible ransom demand. And he stressed the word 'credible.'"

"But what about the message on the machine? That other man's voice cutting in?"

"Of course they'll listen to it. But I've got to warn you, they're shorthanded right now. Lots of agents got hit hard by the storm, so they're out on personal leave."

Bonnie was exasperated by the lack of interest in Max's plight. Augustine explained that restless husbands often used natural disasters as a cover to flee their wives. Precious manpower and resources were wasted tracking them to the apartments, condominiums and houseboats of their respective mistresses. Consequently, post-hurricane reports of missing spouses were now received with chilly skepticism.

Bonnie Lamb said, "For God's sake, we just got married. Max wouldn't take off on a stunt like that."

Augustine shrugged. "People get cold feet."

She leaned across the kitchen table and took a swing at him. Augustine blocked the punch with a forearm. He told Mrs Lamb to settle down. Her cheeks were flushed and her eyes shone.

Augustine said, "I meant we can't rule out anything."

"But you heard that man on the answering machine!"

"Yeah, and I'm wondering why a serious kidnapper would be such a smartass. 'Don't flatter yourself, Max.' And then the guy gets on the line and says, 'I love you, Bonnie.' Just to needle your husband, see? Make him feel like shit." Augustine poured more coffee for both of them. He said, "There's something damn strange about it. That's all I'm saying."

Bonnie Lamb had to agree. "To leave his voice all over a telephone tape—"

"Exactly. The guy's either incredibly stupid, or he's got brass balls—"

"Or he just doesn't care," Bonnie said.

"You picked up on that, too."

"It's scary."

Augustine said, "I'm not so sure."

"Don't start again. Max is *not* faking this!"

"That stuff about having you call Pete at Rodale, the Bronco billboard—was he talking in code or what? Because some maniac kidnaps *me*, the last thing I'm worried about is keeping up with my ad accounts. What I'm worried about is saving my hide."

Bonnie looked away. "You don't know Max, what a workaholic he is."

Augustine pushed back from the table. Normally he wasn't wild about women who punched for no good reason.

"What do we do now?" She held the cup with both hands, shaking slightly. "You heard the man's tone."

"Yeah, I did."

"Let's agree he's not your average kidnapper. What is he?"

Augustine shook his head. "How would I know, Mrs Lamb?"

"It's Bonnie." She stood up, perfectly calm now, tightening the sash on the robe he'd loaned her. "Maybe together we can figure him out."

Augustine emptied his coffee in the sink. "I think we both need some sleep."

On the way back to Tony Torres's house, Edie Marsh asked Snapper if he had a stopwatch.

"Why?"

"Because I want to put a clock on this jerk," she said, "see how long it takes before he tries to screw me."

Snapper, who had daydreamed of doing the same thing, said: "I give him two days before he makes a move."

"I give him two hours," Edie said.

"So what'll you do? Ten grand's ten grand."

Edie said, "You better be joking. I'd shove hot daggers in my eyes before I'd let that pig touch me." It was a long bleak slide from dating a Kennedy to fucking a mobile-home salesman.

"What if he don't let up?" asked Snapper.

"Then I walk."

"Yeah, but—"

"Hey," Edie said, "you want the money so bad, *you* fuck him, OK? I think the two of you'd make a very cute couple."

Snapper didn't press the issue. He'd already hatched a backup plan, in case the Torres deal fell apart. Avila was in a happy mood when he'd called the motel. Apparently the *santería* saints had informed him he could become very rich by starting his own roofing business. The saints had pointed out that the hurricane left two hundred thousand people without shelter, and that many of these poor folks were so desperate to get their houses repaired that they wouldn't think of asking to see a valid contractor's license, which of course Avila did not possess.

"But you're afraid of heights," Snapper had reminded him.

"That's where you come in," Avila had said. "I'm the boss, you're the foreman. All we need is a crew."

"Meaning you won't be joining us up on the roof with the boiling tar in the hot sun."

"Jesus, Snap, somebody's got to handle the paperwork. Somebody's got to write up the contracts."

Snapper had inquired about the split. Avila said guys he knew were charging fifteen grand per roof, a third of it up front. He said some home owners were offering cash, to speed the job. Avila said there was enough work around to keep them busy for two years.

"Thanks to you," Snapper had said.

Avila failed to see irony in the fact that corruptly incompetent building inspections were a chief reason that so many roofs had blown off in the storm, and that so much new business was now available for incompetent roofers.

"You guys plan it this way?" Snapper had asked.

"Plan what?"

Snapper didn't trust Avila as far as he could spit, but the roofing option was something to consider if Torres went sour.

The trailer salesman also happened to be in sunny spirits when Snapper and Edie Marsh arrived. He was sprawled, shirtless, in a chaise on the front lawn. He wore Bermuda shorts and monogrammed socks pulled high on his hairy shins. The barrel of the shotgun poked out from a stack of newspapers on his lap. When Edie Marsh and Snapper got out of the car, Tony clapped his hands and exclaimed: "I knew you'd be back!"

"A regular Nostradamus," said Edie. "Is the electricity up yet? We picked up some stuff for the refrigerator."

Tony reported that the power remained off, and the portable generator had run out of gas overnight. He was storing food in two large Igloo coolers, packed with ice he'd purchased from gougers for twenty dollars a bag. The good news: Telephone service had been restored.

"And I got through immediately to Midwest Casualty," Tony said. "They're sending an adjuster today or tomorrow."

Edie thought: Too good to be true. "So we wait?"

"We wait," Tony said. "And remember, it's Neria. N-e-r-i-a. Middle initial, G as in Gómez. What'd you buy?"

"Tuna sandwiches," Snapper replied, "cheese, eggs, ice cream, Diet Sprite and stale fucking Lorna Doones.

There wasn't much to choose from." He iced the groceries, found a pool chair and took a position upwind of the sweaty Tony Torres. The sky had cleared and the summer sun blazed down, but it was pointless to look for shade. There wasn't any; all the trees in Turtle Meadow were leveled.

Tony complimented Edie Marsh for costuming herself as an authentic housewife—jeans, white Keds, a baggy blouse with the sleeves turned up. His only complaint was the sea-green scarf in her hair. He said, "Silk is a little much, considering the circumstances."

"Because it clashes with those gorgeous Bermudas of yours?" Edie glared at Tony Torres as if he were a maggot on a wedding cake. She was disinclined to remove the scarf, which was one of her favorites. She had boosted it from a Lord & Taylor's in Palm Beach.

"Suit yourself," said Tony. "Point is, details are damn important. It's the little things people notice."

"I'll try and keep that in mind."

Snapper said, "Hey, Mister Salesman of the Year, can we run the TV off that generator?"

Tony said sure, if they only had some gasoline.

Snapper tapped his wristwatch and said, "Sally Jessy comes on in twenty minutes. Men who seduce their daughter-in-law's mother-in-law."

"No shit? We could siphon your car." Tony pointed at the rubble of his garage. "There's a hose in there someplace."

Snapper went to find it. Edie Marsh said it was a lousy idea to siphon fuel from the car, since they might be needing speedy transportation. Snapper winked and told her not to worry. Off he went, ambling down the street, the garden hose coiled on his left shoulder.

Edie expropriated the pool chair. Tony Torres perked up. "Scoot closer, darling."

"Wonderful," she said, under her breath.

The salesman fanned himself with the Miami *Herald* sports pages. He said, "It just now hit me: Men who steal their daughter-in-law's mother-in-law. That's pretty funny! He don't look like a comedian, your partner, but that's a good one."

"Oh, he's full of surprises." Edie leaned back and closed her eyes. The sunshine felt good on her face.

The hurricane had transformed the trailer court into a sprawling aluminum junkyard. Ira Jackson found Lot 17 because of the bright yellow tape that police had roped around the remains of the double-wide mobile home where his mother, Beatrice, had died. After identifying her body at the morgue, Ira Jackson had driven directly to Suncoast Leisure Village, to see for himself.

Not one trailer had made it through the storm.

From the debris, Ira Jackson pulled his mother's Craftmatic adjustable bed. The mattress was curled up like a giant taco shell. Ira Jackson crawled inside and lay down.

He recalled, as if it were yesterday, the morning he and his mother met with the salesman to close the deal. The man's name was Tony. Tony Torres. He was fat, gassy and balding, yet extremely self-assured. Beatrice Jackson had been impressed with his pitch.

"*Mister Torres says it's built to go through a hurricane.*"

"*I find that hard to believe, Momma.*"

"*Oh yes, Mister Jackson, your mother's right. Our*

*prefabricated homes are made to withstand gusts up to one hundred twenty miles per hour. That's a U.S. government regulation. Otherwise we couldn't sell 'em!"*

Ira Jackson was in Chicago, beating up some scabs for a Teamsters local, when he'd heard about the hurricane headed for South Florida. He'd phoned his mother and urged her to move to a Red Cross shelter. She said it was out of the question.

"I can't leave Donald and Marla," she told her son.

Donald and Marla were Mrs Jackson's beloved miniature dachshunds. The hurricane shelter wouldn't allow pets.

So Ira's mother had stayed home out of loyalty to her dogs and a misplaced confidence that the mobile-home salesman had told the truth about how safe it was. Donald and Marla survived the hurricane by squeezing under an oak credenza and sharing a rawhide chew toy to pass the long night. A neighbor had rescued them the next morning and taken them to a vet.

Beatrice Jackson was not so lucky. Moments after the hurricane stripped the north wall off her double-wide, she was killed by a flying barbecue that belonged to one of her neighbors. The imprint of the grill remained visible on her face, peaceful as it was, lying in the Dade County morgue.

Beatrice's death had no effect whatsoever on the mood of her dachshunds, but her son was inconsolable. Ira Jackson raged at himself for letting his mother buy the trailer. It had been his idea for her to move to Florida—but that's what guys in his line of work did for their widowed mothers; got them out of the cold weather and into the sunshine.

God help me, Ira Jackson thought, tossing restively

on the mechanical mattress. I should've held off another year. Waited till I could afford to put her in a condo.

That cocksucker Torres. *A-hundred-twenty-mile-per-hour gusts*. What kind of scum would lie to a widow?

"Excuse me!"

Ira Jackson bolted upright to see a gray-haired man in a white undershirt and baggy pants. Skin and bones. Wire-rimmed eyeglasses that made him look like a heron. In one arm he carried a brown shopping bag.

"Have you seen an urn?" he asked.

"Jesus, what?"

"A blue urn. My wife's ashes. It's like a bottle."

Ira Jackson shook his head. "No, I haven't seen it." He rose to his feet. He noticed that the old man was shaking.

"I'm going to kill him," he said angrily.

Ira Jackson said, "Who?"

"That lying sonofabitch who sold me the double-wide. I saw him here after the hurricane, but he took off."

"Torres?"

"Yeah." The old man's cheeks colored. "I'd murder him, swear to God, if I could."

Ira Jackson said, "You'd get a medal for it." Humoring the guy, hoping he'd run out of steam and go away.

"Hell, you don't believe me."

"Sure I do." He was tempted to tell the old man to quit worrying, Señor Tony Torres would be taken care of. Most definitely. But Ira Jackson knew it would be foolish to draw attention to himself.

The old man said: "My name's Levon Stichler. I lived four lots over. Was it your mother that died here?"

Ira Jackson nodded.

Levon Stichler said, "I'm real sorry. I'm the one found her two dogs—they're at Dr Tyler's in Naranja."

"She'd appreciate that, my mother." Ira Jackson made a mental note to pick up the dachshunds before the vet's office closed.

The old man said, "My wife's ashes blew away in the hurricane."

"Yeah, well, if I come across a blue bottle—"

"What the hell could they do to me?" Levon Stichler wore a weird quavering smirk. "For killing him, what could they do? I'm seventy-one goddamn years old—what, life in prison? Big deal. I got nothing left anyhow."

Ira Jackson said, "I was you, I'd put it out of my mind. Scum like Torres, they usually get what they deserve."

"Not in my world," said Levon Stichler. But the widow Jackson's son had taken the wind out of his sails. "Hell, I don't know how to find the sonofabitch anyhow. Do you?"

"Wouldn't have a clue," Ira Jackson said.

Levon Stichler shrugged in resignation, and returned to the heap that once was his home. Ira Jackson watched him poking through the rubble, stooping every so often to examine a scrap. All around the trailer court, other neighbors of the late Beatrice Jackson could be seen hunched and scavenging, picking up pieces.

Her son opened his wallet, which contained: six hundred dollars cash, a picture of his mother taken in Atlantic City, three fake driver's licenses, a forged Social Security card, a stolen Delta Airlines frequent flyer card, and numerous scraps of paper with numerous phone numbers from the 718 area code. The wallet also held a few legitimate business cards, including one that said:

Antonio Torres
Senior Sales Associate
PreFab Luxury Homes
(305) 555-2200

The trailer salesman had jotted his home number on the back of the business card. Ira Jackson kicked through his mother's storm-soaked belongings until he found a Greater Miami telephone directory. The salesman's home number matched the one belonging to an A. R. Torres at 15600 Calusa Drive. Ira Jackson tore the page from the phone book. Carefully he folded it to fit inside his wallet, with the other important numbers.

Then he drove his fraudulently registered Coupe de Ville to a convenience store, where he purchased a Rand McNally road map of Dade County.

# SIX

**The vagabond monkey** chose to forgo the airboat experience. Max Lamb was given no choice. The one-eyed man strapped him to the passenger seat and off they went at fifty miles an hour, skimming the grass, cattails and lily pads. For a while they followed a canal that paralleled a two-lane highway; Max could make out the faces of motorists gaping at him in his underwear. It didn't occur to him to signal for help; the electrified dog collar had conditioned total passivity.

Riding high in the driver's perch, the man who called himself Skink sang at the top of his lungs. It sounded like "Desperado," an old Eagles tune. The familiar melody surfed above the ear-splitting roar of the airboat's engine; more than ever, Max Lamb believed he was in the grip of a madman.

Soon the airboat made a wide turn away from the road. It plowed a liquid trail through thickening marsh, the sawgrass hissing against the metal hull. The hurricane had bruised and gouged the swamp; smashed cypresses and pines littered the waters. Skink stopped singing and began to emit short honks and toots that Max Lamb assumed to be either wild bird calls or a fearsome attack of sinusitis. He was afraid to inquire.

At noon they stopped at a dry hammock, its once-lush branches now skeletal from the storm. Skink tied the airboat to a knuckled stand of roots. Evidence of previous campfires reassured Max Lamb that other humans had been there before. The kidnapper didn't bother to tie him; there was no place to run. With Skink's permission, Max put on his clothes to protect himself from the horseflies and mosquitoes. When he complained of being thirsty, Skink offered his own canteen. Max took a tentative swallow.

"Coconut milk?" he asked, hopefully.

"Something like that."

Max suggested that wearing the shock collar was no longer necessary. Skink whipped out the remote control, pushed the red button and said: "If you've got to ask, then it's still necessary."

Max jerked wordlessly on the damp ground until the pain stopped. Skink caught a mud turtle and made soup for lunch. Tending the fire, he said, "Max, I'll take three questions."

"Three?"

"For now. Let's see how it goes."

Max warily eyed the remote. Skink promised there would be no electronic penalty for dumb queries. "So fire away."

Max Lamb said, "All right. Who are you?"

"My name is Tyree. I served in the Vietnam conflict, and later as a governor of this fair state. I resigned because of disturbing moral and philosophical conflicts. The details would mean nothing to you."

Max Lamb failed to mask his disbelief. "You were governor? Come off it."

"Is that question number two?"

Impatiently, Max fingered the dog collar. "No, the second question is: Why me?"

"Because you made a splendid target of yourself. You with your video camera, desecrating the habitat."

Max Lamb got defensive. "I wasn't the only one taking pictures. I wasn't the only tourist out there."

"But you were the one I saw first." Skink poured hot soup into a tin cup and handed it to his sulking prisoner. "A hurricane is a holy thing," he said, "but you treated it as an amusement. Pissed me off, Max."

Skink lifted the pot off the hot coals and tipped it to his lips. Steam wisped from his mouth, fogging his glass eye. He put the pot down and wiped the turtle drippings from his chin. "I was tied up on a bridge," he said, "watching the storm roll out of the ocean. God, what a thing!"

He stepped toward Max Lamb and lifted him by the shirt, causing Max to drop the soup he had not touched.

Skink hoisted him to eye level and said: "Twenty years I waited for that storm. We were so close, so goddamn close. Two or three degrees to the north, and we're in business. . . ."

Max Lamb dangled in the stranger's iron clasp. Skink's good eye glistened with a furious, dreamy passion. "You're down to one question," he said, returning Max to his feet.

After settling himself, Max asked: "What happens now?"

Skink's stormy expression dissolved into a smile. "What happens now, Max, is that we travel together, sharing life's lessons."

"Oh." Max's eyes cut anxiously to the airboat.

The governor barked a laugh that scattered a flock of snowy egrets. He tousled his prisoner's hair and said, "We go with the tides!"

But a despairing Max Lamb couldn't face the prospect of true adventure. Now that it seemed he would not be murdered, he was burdened by another primal concern: *If I don't get back to New York, I'm going to lose my job.*

Edie Marsh was daydreaming about teak sailboats and handsome young Kennedys when she felt the moist hand of Tony Torres settle on her left breast. She cracked an eyelid and sighed.

"Quit squeezing. It's not a tomato."

"Can I see?" Tony asked.

"Absolutely not." But she heard the squeaky shift of weight as the salesman edged the chaise closer.

"Nobody's around," he said, fumbling with her buttons. Then an oily laugh: "I mean, you *are* my wife."

"Jesus." Edie felt the sun on her nipples and looked down. Well, there they were—the pig had undone her blouse. "Don't you understand English?"

Tony Torres contentedly appraised her breasts. "Yeah, darling, but who's got the shotgun."

"That's so romantic," Edie Marsh said. "Threaten to shoot me—there's no better way to put a girl in the mood. Fact, I'm all wet just thinking about it." She pushed his hand away and rebuttoned her blouse. "Where's my shades," she muttered.

Tony cradled the Remington across his belly. Sweat puddled at his navel. He said, "You *will* think about it. They all do."

"I think about cancer, too, but it doesn't make me horny." To Edie, the only attractive thing about Tony Torres was his gold Cartier wristwatch, which was probably engraved in such a gaudy way that it could not be prudently fenced.

He asked her: "Have you ever been with a bald man?"

"Nope. You ever seen venereal warts?"

The salesman snorted, turning away. "Somebody's in a pissy mood."

Edie Marsh dug the black Ray-Bans out of her purse and disappeared behind them. The shotgun made her nervous, but she resolved to stay cool. She tried to shut out the summer glare, the ceaseless drone of chain saws and dump trucks, and the rustle of Tony Torres reading the newspaper. The warmth of the sun made it easy for Edie Marsh to think of the duned shores at the Vineyard, or the private beaches of Manalapan.

Her reverie was interrupted by footsteps on the sidewalk across the street. She hoped it was Snapper, but it wasn't. It was a man walking two small dachshunds.

Edie felt Tony's hand on hers and heard him say, "Darling, would you squirt some Coppertone on my shoulders?"

Quickly she rose from the chair and crossed the road. The man was watching his dachshunds pee on the stem of a broken mailbox. He held both leashes in one hand, loosely. There was a melancholy slump to his shoulders that should have disappeared with the approach of a pretty woman, but did not.

Edie Marsh told him the dogs were adorable. When she stooped to pet them, the dachshunds simultaneously rolled over and began squirming like worms on a griddle.

"What're their names?"

"Donald and Marla," the man replied. He wasn't tall, but he was built like a furnace. He wore a peach knit shirt and khaki slacks. He said to Edie: "You live at that house?"

She saw Tony Torres eyeing them from the chaise. She asked the stranger if he was from the Midwest Casualty insurance company. He motioned sarcastically toward the dogs and said, "Sure. And my associates here are from Merrill Lynch."

The dachshunds were up, wagging their butts and licking at Edie's bare ankles. The man jerked his double chin toward Tony Torres and said, "You related to him? A wife or sister maybe."

"Please," Edie Marsh said, with an exaggerated shudder.

"OK, then I got some advice. Take a long fucking walk."

Edie's mind began to race. She looked in both directions down the street, but didn't see Snapper.

The man said, "The hell you waiting for?" He handed her the two leashes. "Go on, now."

Augustine awoke to the smell of coffee and the sounds of a married woman fixing breakfast in his kitchen. It seemed a suitable time to assess the situation.

His father was in prison, his mother was gone, and his dead uncle's wild animals had escaped among unsuspecting suburbanites. Augustine himself was free, too, in the truest and saddest sense. He had absolutely no personal responsibilities. How to explain such a condition to Bonnie Lamb?

My father was a fisherman. He ran drugs on the side, until he was arrested near the island of Andros.

My mother moved to Las Vegas and remarried. Her new husband plays tenor saxophone in Tony Bennett's orchestra.

My most recent ex-girlfriend was a leg model for a major hosiery concern. She saved her modeling money and bought a town house in Brentwood, California, where she fellates only circumcised movie agents, and the occasional director.

But what about you? Mrs Lamb will ask. What do you do for a living?

I read my bank statements.

And Mrs Lamb will react with polite curiosity, until I explain about the airplane accident.

It happened three years ago while flying back from Nassau after visiting my old man in Fox Hill Prison. I didn't realize the pilot was drunk until he T-boned the twin Beech into the fuselage of a Coast Guard helicopter, parked inside a hangar at the Opa-Locka airport.

Afterwards I slept for three months and seventeen days in the intensive care unit of Jackson Hospital. When I awoke, I was rich. The insurance carrier for the charter-air service had settled the case with an attorney whom I did not know and to this day have never met. A check for eight hundred thousand dollars appeared, and much to my surprise, I invested it wisely.

And Mrs Lamb, if I'm reading her right, will then say: So what is it you *do*?

Honestly, I'm not certain. . . .

The conversation, over bacon and French toast, didn't go precisely as Augustine had anticipated. At the end of his story, Bonnie Lamb looked over the rim of her coffee cup and asked: "Is that where you got the scar—from the plane crash?"

"Which scar?"

"The Y-shaped one on your lower back."

"No," said Augustine, guardedly. "That's something else." He made a mental note not to walk around without a shirt.

Later, clearing the kitchen table, Bonnie asked about his father.

"Extradited," Augustine reported, "but he much prefers Talladega to the Bahamas."

"Are you two close?"

"Sure," said Augustine. "Only seven hundred miles."

"How often do you go to see him?"

"Whenever I want to get angry and depressed."

Augustine often wished that the plane crash had wiped out his memory of that last visit at Fox Hill Prison, but it hadn't. They were supposed to talk about the extradition, about lining up a half-decent lawyer in the States, about maybe cutting a deal with prosecutors so that the old man might actually get out before the turn of the century.

But Augustine's father wanted to talk about something else when his son came to see him. He wanted a favor.

—Bollock, you remember Bollock? He owes me a piece of a shipment.

—The answer is no.

—Come on, A.G. I got lawyers to pay. Take Leaker and Ape along. They'll handle Bollock. Not the money, though. That I want in your hands only.

—Dad, I don't believe this. I just don't believe it. . . .

—Hey, go down to Nassau harbor. See what they

done to my boat! Ape says they stripped the radar and all the electric.

—So what. You didn't know how to use it anyway.

—Listen, wiseass, I was taking fire. It was the middle of the goddamn night.

—Still, it's not easy to park a sixty-foot long-liner in nine inches of water. How exactly did you manage that?

—Watch your tone, son!

—Grown man, hangin' out with guys called Leaker and Ape. Look where it got you.

—A.G., I'd love to keep strollin' down memory lane, but the guard says we're outta time. So will you do it? Go see Henry Bollock down on Big Pine. Get my slice and stick it in the Caymans. What's the harm?

—Pathetic.

—What?

—I said, you're pathetic.

—So I'll take that as a "no," you won't do this for me?

— Jesus Christ.

—You disappoint me, boy.

—And I'm proud of you, too, Dad. I bust my buttons every time your name comes up.

And Augustine recalled thinking, as he sat in the Beechcraft on the runway at Nassau: He's hopeless, my old man. He won't learn. He'll get out of prison and go right back to it.

A son looks a man square in the eye and calls him pathetic, *pathetic*, any other father would curse or cry or take a punch at the kid. Not mine. By God, not when there's drug money needs collecting. So how about it, A.G.?

Fuck him, thought Augustine. Not because of what

he'd done or what he'd been hauling, but because his stupid selfish greed had outlived the crime. Fuck him, Augustine thought, because it's hopeless. He was supposed to raise me, goddammit, I wasn't supposed to raise him.

And then the plane took off.

And then the plane went down.

And nothing was ever the same about the way Augustine saw the world, or his place in it. Sometimes he wasn't sure if it was the accident that had changed him, or the visit with his father at Fox Hill Prison.

At FBI headquarters, Bonnie Lamb spent an hour talking with maddeningly polite agents. One of them dialed her answering machine and dubbed Max's queer kidnap message. They urged her to notify the Bureau as soon as she received a credible ransom demand. Then, and only then, would a kidnap squad take over the case. The agents instructed Bonnie to check her machine often and be careful not to erase any tapes. They expressed no strong views about whether she ought to remain in Miami and search for her husband, or return to New York and wait.

The agents let Bonnie Lamb borrow a private office, where she tried with no luck to reach Max's parents, who were traveling in Europe. Next Bonnie phoned her own parents. Her mother sounded sincere in her alarm; her father, as usual, sounded helpless. He half-heartedly offered to fly to Florida, but Bonnie said it wasn't necessary. All she could do was wait for Max or the kidnapper to call again. Bonnie's mother promised to

FedEx some cash and an eight-by-ten photograph of Max, for the authorities.

Bonnie Lamb's last call was to Peter Archibald at the Rodale & Burns advertising agency in Manhattan. Max Lamb's colleague was shocked at Bonnie's news, but vowed to maintain the confidentiality requested by the FBI. When Bonnie passed along her husband's frantic instructions about the cigaret billboard, Peter Archibald said: "You married a real trouper, Bonnie."

"Thank you, Peter."

Augustine took her to a fish house for lunch. She ordered a gin-and-tonic, and said: "I want your honest opinion about the FBI guys."

"OK. I think they had problems with the tape."

"Max didn't sound scared enough."

"Possibly," Augustine said, "and, like I mentioned, he seemed a little too worried about the Marlboro account."

"It's Broncos," Bonnie corrected. From the way she winced at the gin, Augustine could tell she wasn't much of a drinker. "So they blew me off as a jilted wife."

"Not at all. They started a file. They're the best darn file-starters in the world. Then they'll send your tape to the audio lab. They'll probably even make a few phone calls. But you saw how deserted the place was—half their agents are home cleaning up storm damage."

She said, angrily, "The world doesn't stop for a hurricane."

"No," Augustine said, "but it wobbles like a sonofabitch. I'm having the shrimp, how about you?"

Mrs Lamb didn't speak again until they were in the

pickup truck, heading south to the hurricane zone. She asked Augustine to stop at the county morgue.

He thought: She couldn't have gotten this brainstorm *before* lunch.

Snapper had neither the ambition nor the energy to be a predator in the classic criminal mold. He saw himself strictly as a canny opportunist. He wouldn't endeavor to commit a first-degree felony unless the moment presented itself. He believed in serendipity, because it suited his style of minimal exertion.

He heard the kids coming long before he saw them. The souped-up Cherokee blasted Snoop Doggy Dogg through the neighborhood, rattling the few windows that the hurricane had not broken. The kids drove by once, circled the block, and cruised past again.

Snapper smiled to himself, thinking: It's the damn pinstripes. They think I'm carrying money.

He kept walking. When the Cherokee came around a third time, the rap music had been turned off. Stupid, Snapper thought. Why not take out a billboard: Watch us mug this guy!

As the Jeep rolled up behind him, Snapper stepped to the side and slowed his pace. He slipped Tony Torres's garden hose off his shoulder and carried it coiled in front of him. The Cherokee came alongside. One of the kids was hanging out the passenger window. He waved a chrome-plated pistol at Snapper.

"Hey, mud-fuckah," the kid said.

"Good mornin'," said Snapper. He deftly looped a coil of the garden hose around the kid's head and jerked him out of the truck. When the kid hit the pavement, he dropped the gun. Snapper picked it up. He stepped on the kid's chest and, with one hand, began twisting the hose tightly on the kid's throat.

The other muggers piled out of the Cherokee with the intention of rescuing their friend and killing the butt-ugly geek in the shiny suit, but the plan changed when they saw who had the pistol. Then they ran.

Snapper waited until the kid on the ground was almost unconscious before loosening the hose. "I need to borrow some gas," said Snapper, "to watch Sally Jessy."

The kid sat up slowly and rubbed his neck, which bled from the place where his three gold chains had cut into his flesh. He wore a tank top to show off the tattoos on his left biceps—a gang insignia and the nickname "Baby Raper."

Snapper said, "Baby, you got a gas can?"

"Fuck no." The kid answered in a raw whisper.

"Too bad. I'll have to take the whole truck."

"I don't care. Ain't mine."

"Yeah, that was my hunch."

The kid said, "Man, wus wrong wid yo face?"

"Excuse me?"

"I axed what's wrong wid yo mud-fuckin face."

Snapper went in the Cherokee and removed the Snoop Doggy Dogg compact disc from the stereo. He used the shiny side of the CD like a small mirror, pretending to admire himself in it.

"Looks fine to me," he said, after several moments.

The kid smirked. "Sheeeiiit."

Snapper put the pistol to the kid's temple and ordered him to get on his belly. Then he yanked the mugger's pants down to his ankles.

A Florida Power and Light cherry picker came steaming down the street. The kid shouted for help, but the driver kept going.

Twisting to look over his shoulder, Baby Raper saw Snapper hold the CD up to the sky, like a chrome communion wafer.

Snapper said: "Worst fuckin' excuse for music I ever heard."

"Man, whatcha gone do wid dat?"

"Guess."

Ira Jackson stood with his back to the sun. Tony Torres squinted, shielding his brow with one hand.

The salesman said: "Do I remember you? Course I remember you."

"My mother was Beatrice Jackson."

"I said I remember."

"She's dead."

"So I heard. I'm very sorry." Stretched in the chaise, Tony Torres felt vulnerable. He raised both knees to give himself a brace for the shotgun.

Ira Jackson asked Tony if he remembered anything else. "Such as what you promised my mother about the double-wide being as safe as a regular CBS house?"

"Whoa, sport, I said no such thing." Tony Torres was itching to get to his feet, but that was a major project. One wrong move, and the flimsy patio chair could collapse under his weight. "'Government approved,' is what I told you, Mister Jackson. Those were my exact words."

"My mother's dead. The double-wide went to pieces."

"Well, it was one hellacious hurricane. The Storm of the Century, they said on TV." Tony was beginning to wonder if this dumb ape didn't see the Remington aimed at his dick. "We're talking about a major natural disaster, sport. Look how it wrecked these houses. *My* house. Hell, it blew down the entire goddamn Homestead Air Force Base! There's no hiding from something like that. I'm sorry about your mother, Mister Jackson, but a trailer's a trailer."

"What happened to the tie-downs?"

Oh Christ, Tony thought. Who knew enough to look at the fucking tie-downs? He struggled to appear indignant. "I've got no idea what you're talking about."

Ira Jackson said, "I found two of 'em hanging off a piece of the double-wide. Straps were rotted. Augers cut off short. No anchor disks—this shit I saw for myself."

"I'm sure you're mistaken. They passed inspection, Mister Jackson. Every home we sold passed inspection." The confidence was gone from the salesman's tone. He was uneasy, arguing with a faceless silhouette.

"Admit it," Ira Jackson said. "Somebody cut the damn augers to save a few bucks on installation."

"Keep talkin' that way," warned Tony Torres, "and I'll sue your ass for slander."

Even before it was made a specified condition of his parole, Ira Jackson had never possessed a firearm. In his many years as a professional goon, it had been his experience that men who brandished guns invariably got shot with one. Ira Jackson favored the more personal touch afforded by crowbars, aluminum softball bats, nunchaku sticks, piano wire, cutlery, or gym socks filled with lead fishing sinkers. Any would have done the job nicely on Tony Torres, but Ira Jackson had brought nothing but his bare fists to the salesman's house.

"What is it you want?" Tony Torres demanded.

"An explanation."

"Which I just gave you." Tony's eyes watered from peering into the sun's glare, and he was growing worried. Edie the Ice Maiden had disappeared with Ira Jackson's dogs—what the hell was *that* all about? Were they in on something? And where was the freak in the bad suit, his so-called bodyguard?

Tony said to Ira Jackson: "I think it's time for you to go." He motioned with the shotgun toward the street.

"This is how you treat dissatisfied customers?"

A jittery laugh burst from the salesman. "Sport, you ain't here for no refund."

"You're right." Ira Jackson was pleased by the din of the neighborhood—hammers, drills, saws, electric generators. All the folks preoccupied with putting their homes back together. The noise would make it easier to cover the ruckus, if the mobile-home salesman tried to put up a struggle.

Tony Torres said, "You think I don't know to use this twelve-gauge, you're makin' a big mistake. Check out the hole in that garage door."

Ira Jackson whistled. "I'm impressed, Mister Torres. You shot a house."

Tony's expression hardened. "I'm counting to three."

"My mother was hit by a damn barbecue."

"*One!*" the salesman said. "Every second you look more like a looter, mister."

"You promised her the place was safe. All those poor people—how the hell do you sleep nights?"

"*Two!*"

"Relax, you fat fuck. I'm on my way." Ira Jackson turned and walked slowly toward the street.

Tony Torres took a deep breath; his tongue felt like sandpaper. He lowered the Remington until it rested on one of his kneecaps. He watched Beatrice Jackson's son pause in the driveway and kneel as if tying a shoe.

Craning to see, Tony shouted: "Move it, sport!"

The cinder block caught him by surprise—first, the sheer weight of it, thirty-odd pounds of solid concrete; second, the fact that Ira Jackson was able to throw such a hefty object, shot-putter style, with such distressing accuracy.

When it struck the salesman's chest, the cinder block knocked the shotgun from his hands, the beer from his bladder and the breath from his lungs. He made a sibilant exclamation, like a water bed rupturing.

So forceful was the cinder block's impact that it doubled Tony Torres at the waist, causing the chaise longue to spring on him like an oversized mousetrap. The moans he let out as Ira Jackson dragged him to the car were practically inaudible over the chorus of his neighbors' chain saws.

# SEVEN

**The Dade County** Medical Examiner's Office was quiet, neat and modern—nothing like Bonnie Lamb's notion of a big-city morgue. She admired the architect's thinking; the design of the building successfully avoided the theme of violent homicide. With its brisk and clerical-looking layout, it could have passed for the regional headquarters of an insurance company or a mortgage firm, except for the dead bodies in the north wing.

A friendly secretary brought coffee to Bonnie Lamb while Augustine spoke privately to an assistant medical examiner. The young doctor remembered Augustine from a week earlier, when he had come to claim his uncle's snakebitten remains. The medical examiner was intrigued to learn from Augustine that the tropical viper that had killed Felix Mojack now roamed free. He E-mailed a memorandum to Jackson Memorial, alerting the emergency room to requisition more antivenin, just in case. Then he took a Xeroxed copy of Bonnie Lamb's police report down the hall.

When he returned, the medical examiner said the morgue had two unidentified corpses that loosely matched the physical description of Max Lamb. Augustine relayed the news to Bonnie.

"You up for this?" he asked.

"If you go with me."

It was a long walk to the autopsy room, where the temperature seemed to drop fifteen degrees. Bonnie Lamb took Augustine's hand as they moved among the self-draining steel tables, where a half-dozen bodies were laid out in varying stages of dissection. The room gave off a cloying odor, the sickly-sweet commingling of chemicals and dead flesh. Augustine felt Bonnie's palm go cold. He asked her if she was going to faint.

"No," she said. "It's just . . . God, I thought they'd all be covered with sheets."

"Only in the movies."

The first John Doe had lank hair and sparse, uneven sideburns. He was the same race and age, but otherwise bore no resemblance to Max Lamb. The dead man's eyes were greenish blue; Max's were brown. Still, Bonnie stared.

"How did he die?"

Augustine asked: "Is it Max?"

She shook her head sharply. "But tell me how he died."

With a Bic pen, the young medical examiner pointed to a dime-sized hole beneath the dead man's left armpit. "Gunshot wound," he said.

Augustine and Bonnie Lamb followed the doctor to another table. Here the cause of death was no mystery. The second John Doe had been in a terrible accident. He was scalped and his face pulverized beyond recognition. A black track of autopsy stitches ran from his breast to his pelvis.

Bonnie stammered, "I don't know, I can't tell—"

"Look at his hands," the medical examiner said.

"No wedding ring," Augustine observed.

"Please. I want her to look," the medical examiner said. "We remove the jewelry for safekeeping."

Bonnie dazedly circled the table. The bluish pallor of the dead man's skin made it difficult to determine his natural complexion. He was built like Max—narrow shoulders, bony chest, with a veined roll of baby fat at the midsection. The arms and legs were lean and finely haired, like Max's. . . .

"Ma'am, what about the hands?"

Bonnie Lamb forced herself to look, and was glad she did. The hands were not her husband's; the fingernails were grubby and gnawed. Max believed religiously in manicures and buffing.

"No, it's not him." She spoke very softly, as if trying not to awaken the man with no face.

The doctor wanted to know if her husband had any birthmarks. Bonnie said she hadn't noticed, and felt guilty—as if she hadn't spent enough time examining the details of Max's trunk and extremities. Couldn't most lovers map their partner's most intimate blemishes?

"I remember a mole," she said in a helpful tone, "on one of his elbows."

"Which elbow?" asked the medical examiner.

"I don't recall."

"Like it matters," said Augustine, restlessly. "Check both his arms, OK?"

The doctor checked. The dead man's elbows had no moles. Bonnie turned away from the body and laid her head against Augustine's chest.

"He was driving a stolen motorcycle," the doctor explained, "with a stolen microwave strapped to the back."

Augustine sighed irritably. "A hurricane looter."

"Right. Smacked a lumber truck doing eighty."

"*Now* he tells us," said Bonnie Lamb.

The wash of relief didn't hit her until she was back in Augustine's pickup truck. *It wasn't Max at the morgue, because Max is still alive. This is good. This is cause to be thankful.* Then Bonnie began to tremble, imagining her husband gutted like a fish on a shiny steel tray.

When they returned to the neighborhood where Max Lamb had vanished, they found the rental car on its rims. The hood stood open and the radiator was gone. Augustine's note on the windshield wiper was untouched—a testament, he remarked, to the low literacy rate among car burglars. He offered to call a wrecker.

"Later," Bonnie said, tersely.

"That's what I meant. Later." He locked the truck and set the alarm.

They walked the streets for nearly two hours, Augustine with the .38 Special wedged in his belt. He thought Max Lamb's abductor might have holed up, so they checked every abandoned house in the subdivision. Walking from one block to the next, Bonnie struck up conversations with people who were patching their battered homes. She hoped one of them would remember seeing Max on the morning after the hurricane. Several residents offered colorful accounts of monkey sightings, but Bonnie spoke with no one who recalled the kidnapping of a tourist.

Augustine drove her to the Metro police checkpoint, where she contacted a towing service and the rental-car agency in Orlando. Then she made a call to the apartment in New York to get her messages. After listening for a minute, she pressed the pound button on the telephone and handed the receiver to Augustine.

"Unbelievable," she said.

It was Max Lamb's voice on the line. The static was so heavy he could have been calling from Tibet:

"Bonnie, darling, everything's OK. I don't believe my life's in danger, but I can't say when I'll be free. It's too hairy to explain over the phone—uh, hang on, he wants me to read something. Ready? Here goes:

"'I have nothing to do with the creaking machinery of humanity—I belong to the earth! I say that lying on my pillow and I can feel the horns sprouting from my temples.'"

After a scratchy pause: "Bonnie, honey, it sounds worse than it is. Please don't tell my folks a thing—I don't want Dad all worked up for no reason. And please call Pete and, uh, ask him to put me down for sick leave, just in case this situation drags out. And tell him to stall the sixth floor on the Bronco meeting next week. Don't forget, OK? Tell him under no circumstances should Bill Knapp be brought in. It's still my account. . . ."

Max Lamb's voice dissolved into fuzzy pops and echoes. Augustine hung up. He walked Bonnie back to the pickup.

She got in and said, "This is making me crazy."

"We'll call again from my house and get it on tape."

"Oh, I'm sure it'll jolt the FBI into action. Especially the poetry."

"Actually I think it's from a book."

"What does it mean?" she asked.

Augustine reached across her lap and placed the .38

Special in the glove compartment. "It means," he said, "your husband probably isn't as safe as he thinks."

By and large, the Highway Patrol troopers based in northern Florida were not overjoyed to learn of their temporary reassignment to southern Florida. Many would have preferred Beirut or Somalia. The exception was Jim Tile. A trip to Miami meant precious time with Brenda Rourke, although working double shifts in the hurricane zone left them scarcely enough energy to collapse in each other's arms.

Jim Tile hadn't counted on an intrusion by the governor, but it wasn't totally surprising. The man worshipped hurricanes. Ignoring his presence would have been selfish and irresponsible; the trooper didn't take the friendship that lightly, nor Skink's capacity for outstandingly rash behavior. Jim Tile had no choice but to try to stay close.

In the age of political correctness, a large black man in a crisply pressed police uniform could move at will through the corridors of white-cracker bureaucracy and never once be questioned. Jim Tile took full advantage in the days following the big storm. He mingled authoritatively with Dade County deputies, Homestead police, firefighters, Red Cross volunteers, National Guardsmen, the Army command and antsy emissaries of the Federal Emergency Management Agency. Between patrol shifts, Jim Tile helped himself to coffee and A-forms, 911 logs, computer printouts and handwritten incident reports—he scanned for nothing in particular; just a sign.

As it happened, though, madness flowed rampant in

the storm's wake. Jim Tile leafed through the paperwork, and thought: My Lord, people are cracking up all over town.

The machinery of rebuilding doubled as novel weapons for domestic violence. Thousands of hurricane victims had stampeded to purchase chain saws for clearing debris, and now the dangerous power tools were being employed to vent rage. A gentleman with a Black & Decker attempted to truncate a stubborn insurance adjuster in Homestead. An old woman in Florida City used a lightweight Sears to silence a neighbor's garrulous pet cockatoo. And in Sweetwater, two teenaged gang members successfully detached each other's arms (one left, one right) in a brief but spectacular duel of stolen Homelites.

If chain saws ruled the day, firearms ruled the night. Fearful of looters, vigilant home owners unloaded high-caliber semiautomatics at every rustle, scrape and scuff in the darkness. Preliminary casualties included seven cats, thirteen stray dogs, two opossums and a garbage truck, but no actual thieves. Residents of one rural neighborhood wildly fired dozens of rounds to repel what they described as a troop of marauding monkeys—an episode that Jim Tile dismissed as mass hallucination. He resolved to limit his investigative activities to daytime hours, whenever possible.

Nearly all the missing persons reported to authorities were locals who had fled the storm and lost contact with concerned relatives up North. Most turned up safe at shelters or in the homes of neighbors. But one case caught Jim Tile's attention: a man named Max Lamb.

According to the information filed by his wife, the Lambs drove to Miami on the morning after the hurricane struck. Mrs Lamb told police that her husband wanted to see the storm damage. The trooper wasn't surprised—the streets were clogged with out-of-towners who treated the hurricane zone as a tourist attraction.

Mr Max Lamb had left his rental car, in pursuit of video. It seemed improbable to Jim Tile that anybody from Manhattan could get lost on foot in the flat simple grid of a Florida subdivision. The trooper's suspicions were heightened by another incident, lost deep in the stack of files.

A seventy-four-year-old woman had called to say she had witnessed a possible assault. It was summarized in two short paragraphs, taken over the telephone by a dispatcher:

"Caller reports suspicious subject running along 10700 block of Quail Roost Drive, carrying another subject over his shoulder. Subject One is described as w/m, height and weight unknown. Subject Two is w/m, height and weight unknown.

"Caller reports Subject B appeared to be resisting, and was possibly nude. Subject A reported to be carrying a handgun with a flashing red light (??). Search of area by Units 2334 and 451I proved negative."

Jim Tile knew of no pistols with blinking red lights, but most hand-held video cameras had one. From a distance, a frightened elderly person might mistake a Sony for a Smith & Wesson.

Maybe the old woman had witnessed the abduction of Mr Max Lamb. Jim Tile hoped not. He hoped the Quail Roost sighting was just another weird Dade County roadside altercation and not the act of his volatile swamp-dwelling friend, who was known to hold ill-mannered tourists in low esteem.

The trooper made a copy of Mrs Lamb's report and slipped it in his briefcase along with several others. When he had some free time, he'd try to interview her.

There was only twenty minutes left for lunch with Brenda, before both of them had to start another shift. Being able to see her, even briefly, was well worth the ordeal of working the batty streets of South Florida.

Jim Tile was most displeased, therefore, to personally witness the hijacking of a Salvation Army truck while he was driving to the Red Lobster restaurant where Brenda waited. The trooper was obliged to give chase, and by the time it was over he'd missed his luncheon date.

As he disarmed and handcuffed the truck hijacker, Jim Tile wondered aloud why anybody with half a brain would use a MAC-10 to steal a truck full of secondhand clothes. The young man said his original intention was to spray-paint a gang insignia on the side of the Salvation Army truck, but before he could finish his tagging the driver took off. The young man explained that he'd had no choice, as a matter of self-respect, but to pull his submachine gun and, yo, steal the motherfucking truck.

As Trooper Jim Tile assisted the talkative hijacker into the cage of his patrol car, he silently vowed to redouble his efforts to persuade Brenda Rourke to transfer out of this hellhole called Miami, to a more civilized hellhole where they could work together.

Snapper was proud of how he'd acquired the Jeep Cherokee, but Edie Marsh showed no interest in his conquest.

"What's the story?" Snapper pointed at the dachshunds.

"Donald and Marla," Edie said, annoyed. The animals were pulling her back and forth across Tony Torres's front yard and peeing with wild abandon. Edie was amazed at the power in their stubby Vienna-sausage legs.

"By the way," she said, straining against the leashes, "it took that asshole all of three minutes before he grabbed my tits."

"Big deal, so you win the bet."

"Take these damn dogs!"

Snapper backed away. Numerous encounters with police German shepherds had left him with permanent scars, physical and mental. Over the years, Snapper had become a cat person.

"Just let 'em go," he said to Edie.

The moment she dropped the leashes, the two dachshunds curled up at her feet.

"Beautiful," Snapper said with a grunt. "Hey, look what I found." He flashed the chrome-plated pistol he'd taken from the gangsters. Palming the cheap gun, he noticed the chambers were empty. "Damn spades," he said, heaving it into the murky swimming pool.

Edie Marsh told Snapper about the tough guy with the New York accent who came for Tony Torres. "You picked a peachy time to disappear," she added.

"Shut the fuck up."

"Well, Tony's gone. Even his damn beach chair. Figure it out yourself."

"Shit."

"He won't be back," Edie said gravely. "Not in one piece, anyway."

A concrete block occupied the spot where Tony's chaise had been. Snapper cursed his rotten timing. The ten grand was history. Even in the unlikely event that the salesman returned, he'd never pay. Snapper had fucked up big-time; he wasn't cut out to be a bodyguard.

He said, "I don't guess you got a new plan."

A siren drowned Edie's reply, which she punctuated with a familiar hand gesture. An ambulance came speeding down Calusa Drive. Snapper figured it was carrying Baby Raper to the hospital, for some unusual surgery. Snapper wouldn't be surprised to read about it in a medical journal someday.

He spotted Tony Torres's Remington shotgun, broken into pieces on the driveway. Snapper thought: It's definitely time to abort the mission. Tomorrow he'd call Avila about the roofer's gig.

"I'll give you a lift," he said to Edie Marsh, "but not those damn dogs."

"Jesus, I can't just leave 'em here."

"Suit yourself." Snapper scooped three Heinekens from Tony's ice cooler, got in the souped-up Cherokee and drove off without so much as a wave.

Edie Marsh tethered Donald and Marla to a sprinkler in the backyard. Then she entered the ruined shell of the salesman's house, to check for items of value.

Skink ordered Max Lamb to disrobe and climb a tree. Max did as he was told. It was a leafless willow; Max sat carefully on a springy limb, his bare legs dangling. Beneath him Skink paced, fulminating. In one hand he displayed the remote-control unit for the electronic training collar.

"You people come down here—fucking yupsters with no knowledge, no appreciation, no *interest* in the natural history of the place, the ancient sweep of life. Disney World—Christ, Max, that's not Florida!" He pointed an incriminating finger at his captive. "I found the ticket stubs in your wallet, Tourist Boy."

Max was rattled; he'd assumed everybody liked Disney World. "Please," he said to Skink, "if you shock me now, I'll fall."

Skink pulled off his flowered cap and knelt by the dead embers of the campfire. Max Lamb was acutely worried. Coal-black mosquitoes swarmed his pale plump toes, but he didn't dare slap at them. He was afraid to move a muscle.

All day the kidnapper's spirits had seemed to improve. He'd even taken Max to a rest stop along the Tamiami Trail, so Max could call New York and leave Bonnie another message. While Max waited for the pay phone, Skink had dashed onto the highway to collect a fresh roadkill. His mood was loose, practically convivial. He sang during the entire airboat ride back to the cypress hammock; later he merely chided Max for not knowing that Neil Young had played guitar for Buffalo Springfield.

Max Lamb believed himself to be blessed with a winning personality, a delusion that led him to assume the kidnapper had grown fond of him. Max felt it was only a matter of time before he'd be able to shmooze his way to freedom. He put no stock in Skink's oral biography, and regarded the man as an unbalanced but moderately intelligent derelict; in short, a confused soul who could be won over with a thoughtful, low-key approach. And wasn't that an advertiser's forte—winning people over? Max believed he was making progress, too, with tepid conversation, pointless anecdotes and the occasional self-deprecatory joke. Skink certainly acted calmer, if not serene. Three hours had passed since he'd last triggered the canine shock collar; an encouraging lull, from Max's point of view.

Now, for reasons unknown, the one-eyed brute was seething again. To Max Lamb, he announced: "Pop quiz."

"On what?"

Skink rose slowly. He tucked the remote control in a back pocket. With both hands he gathered his wild hair and knotted it on one side of his head, above the ear—a misplaced mop of a ponytail. Then he removed his glass eye and polished it with spit and a crusty bandanna. Max became further alarmed.

"Who was here first," Skink asked, "the Seminoles or the Tequestas?"

"I, uh—I don't know." Max gripped the branch so hard that his knuckles turned pink.

Skink, replacing the artificial eyeball, retrieving the remote control from his pocket: "Who was Napoleon Bonaparte Broward?"

Max Lamb shook his head, helplessly. Skink shrugged. "How about Marjory Stoneman Douglas?"

"Yes, yes, wait a minute." The willow limb quivered under Max's nervous buttocks. "She wrote *The Yearling*!"

Moments later, regaining consciousness, he found himself in a fetal ball on a mossy patch of ground. Both knees were scraped from the fall. His throat and arms still burned from the dog collar's jolt. Opening his eyes, Max saw the toes of Skink's boots. He heard a voice as deep as thunder: "I should kill you."

"No, don't—"

"The arrogance of coming to a place like this and not knowing—"

"I'm sorry, captain."

"—not caring to learn—"

"I told you, I'm in advertising."

Skink slipped a hand under Max Lamb's chin. "What do you believe in?"

"For God's sake, it's my honeymoon." Max was on the slippery ledge of panic.

"What do you stand for? Tell me that, sir."

Max Lamb cringed. "I can't."

Skink chuckled bitterly. "For future reference, you got your Marjories mixed up. Rawlings wrote *The Yearling*; Douglas wrote *River of Grass*. I got a hunch you won't forget."

He cleaned the bloody scrapes on Max's legs and told him to put on his clothes. His confidence fractured, Max dressed in arthritic slow motion. "Are you ever going to let me go?"

Skink seemed not to have heard the question. "Know what I'd really like," he said, stoking a new fire. "I'd like to meet this bride of yours."

"That's impossible," Max said, hoarsely.

"Oh, nothing's impossible."

Among the stream of outlaws who raced south in the feverish hours following the hurricane was a man named Gil Peck. His plan was to pass himself off as an experienced mason, steal what he could in the way of advance deposits, then haul ass back to Alabama. The scam had worked flawlessly against victims of Hurricane

Hugo in South Carolina, and Gil Peck was confident it would work in Miami, too.

He arrived in a four-ton flatbed carrying a small but authentic-looking load of red bricks, which he'd ripped off from an unguarded construction site in Mobile—a new cancer wing for a pediatric hospital. Gil Peck had caught the festive groundbreaking on TV. That afternoon he'd backed up the flatbed, helped himself to the bricks and driven nonstop to South Florida.

So far, business was booming. Gil Peck had collected almost twenty-six hundred dollars in cash from half a dozen desperate home owners, all of whom expected him to return the following Saturday morning with his truckload of bricks. By then, of course, Gil Peck would be northbound and gone.

By day he worked the hustle, by night he scavenged hurricane debris. The big flatbed conveyed an air of authority, and no one questioned its presence. Even after curfew, the National Guardsmen waved him through the flashing barricades.

Many valuables had survived the storm's thrashing, and Gil Peck became an expert at mining rubble. An inventory of his two-day bounty included: a bagel toaster, a Stairmaster, a silver tea set, three offbrand assault rifles, a Panasonic cellular telephone, two pairs of men's golf spikes, a waterproof kilogram package of hashish, a brass chandelier, a scuba tank, a gold class ring from the University of Miami (1979), a set of police handcuffs, a collection of rare Finnish pornography, a Michael Jackson hand puppet, an unopened bottle of 100-milligram Darvocets, a boxed set of Willie Nelson albums, a Loomis fly rod, a birdcage and twenty-one pairs of women's bikini-style panties.

Exploring the demolished remains of a mobile-home park, Gil Peck was a happy fellow. There was a bounce to his step as he followed the yellow beam of the flashlight from one ruin to another. Thanks to the Guard, the Highway Patrol and the Dade County police, Gil Peck was completely alone and unmolested in the summer night; free to plunder.

And what he spied in the middle of a shuffleboard court made his greedy heart flutter with joy: a jumbo TV dish. The hurricane undoubtedly had uprooted it from some millionaire's estate and tossed it here, for Gil Peck to salvage. With the flashlight he traced the outer parabola and found one small dent. Otherwise the eight-foot satellite receiver was in top condition.

Gil Peck grinned and thought: Man, I must be living right. A dish that big was worth a couple-grand, easy. Gil Peck thought it might fit nicely in his own backyard, behind the chicken coops. He envisioned free HBO for the rest of his natural life.

He walked around to the other side to make sure there was no additional damage. He was shocked by what his flashlight revealed: Inside the TV dish was a dead man, splayed and mounted like a butterfly.

The dead man was impaled on the cone of the receiver pipe, but it wasn't the evil work of the hurricane. His hands and feet had been meticulously bound to the gridwork in a pose of crucifixion. The dead man himself was obese and balding, and bore no resemblance to the Jesus Christ of Gil Peck's strict Baptist upbringing. Nonetheless, the sight unnerved the bogus mason to the point of whimpering.

He switched off the flashlight and sat on the shuffleboard court to steady himself. Stealing the TV saucer obviously was out of the question; Gil Peck was working up the nerve to swipe the expensive watch he'd spotted on the crucified guy's left wrist.

Except for kissing his grandmother in her casket, Gil Peck had never touched a corpse before. Thank God, he thought, the guy's eyes are closed. Gingerly Gil Peck climbed into the satellite dish, which rocked under the added weight. Holding the flashlight in his mouth, he aimed the beam at the dead man's gold Cartier.

The clasp on the watchband was a bitch. Rigor mortis contributed to the difficulty of Gil Peck's task; the crucified guy refused to surrender the timepiece. The more Gil Peck struggled with the corpse, the more the TV saucer rolled back and forth on its axis, like a top. Gil Peck was getting dizzy and mad. Just as he managed to slip a penknife between the taut skin and the watchband, the dead man expelled an audible blast of postmortem flatulence. The detonation sent Gil Peck diving in terror from the satellite dish.

Edie Marsh paid a neighbor kid to siphon gas from Snapper's abandoned car and crank up Tony Torres's portable generator. Edie gave the kid a five-dollar bill that she'd found hidden with five others inside a toolbox in the salesman's garage. It was a pitiful excuse for a stash; Edie was sure there had to be more.

At dusk she gave up the search and planted herself in Tony's BarcaLounger, a crowbar at her side. She turned up the volume of the television as loudly as she could stand, to block out the rustles and whispers of the night. Without doors, windows or a roof, the Torres house was basically an open campsite. Outside was black and creepy; people wandered like spirits through the unlit streets. Edie Marsh had the jitters, being alone. She gladly would have fled in Tony's huge boat of a Chevrolet, if it hadn't been blocked in the driveway by Snapper's car, which Edie would have gladly swiped if only Snapper hadn't taken the damn keys with him. So she was stuck at the Torres house until daybreak, when it might be safe for a woman to travel on foot with two miniature dachshunds.

She planned to get out of Dade County before anything else went wrong. The expedition was a disaster, and Edie blamed no one but herself. Nothing in her modest criminal past had prepared her for the hazy and menacing vibe of the hurricane zone. Everyone was on edge; evil, violence and paranoia ripened in the shadows. Edie Marsh was out of her league here. Tomorrow she'd hitch a ride to West Palm and close up the apartment. Then she'd take the Amtrak home to Jacksonville, and try to make up with her boyfriend. She estimated that reconciliation would require at least a week's worth of blow jobs, considering how much she'd stolen from his checking account. But eventually he'd take her back. They always did.

Edie Marsh was suffering through a TV quiz show when she heard a man's voice calling from the front doorway. She thought: Tony! The pig is back.

She grabbed the crowbar and sprung from the chair. The man at the door raised his arms. "Easy," he said.

It wasn't Tony Torres. This person was a slender blond with round eyeglasses and a tan briefcase and matching Hush Puppy shoes. In one hand he carried a manila file folder.

"What do you want?" Edie held the crowbar casually, as if she carried it at all times.

"Didn't mean to scare you," the man said. "My name is Fred Dove. I'm with Midwest Casualty."

"Oh." Edie Marsh felt a pleasant tingle. Like the first time she'd met one of the young Kennedys.

With a glance at the file, Fred Dove said, "Maybe I've got the wrong street. This is 15600 Calusa?"

"That's correct."

"And you're Mrs Torres?"

Edie smiled. "Please," she said, "call me Neria."

# EIGHT

**Bonnie and Augustine** were cutting a pizza when Augustine's FBI friend stopped by to pick up the tape of Max Lamb's latest message. He listened to it several times on the cassette player in Augustine's living room. Bonnie studied the FBI man's expression, which remained intently neutral. She supposed it was something they worked on at the academy.

When he finished playing the tape, the FBI agent turned to Augustine and said, "I've read it somewhere. That 'creaking machinery of humanity.'"

"Me, too. I've been racking my brain."

"God, I can just see 'em up in Washington, giving it to a crack team of shrinks—"

"Or cryptographers," Augustine said.

The FBI man smiled. "Exactly." He accepted a hot slice of pepperoni for the road, and said good night.

Augustine asked Bonnie a question at which the agent had only hinted: Was it conceivable that Max Lamb could have written something like that himself?

"Never," she said. Her husband was into ditties and jingles, not metaphysics. "And he doesn't read much," she added. "The last book he finished was one of Trump's autobiographies."

It was enough to convince Augustine that Max Lamb

wasn't being coy on the phone; the mystery man was feeding him lines. Augustine didn't know why. The situation was exceedingly strange.

Bonnie took a shower. She came out wearing a baby-blue flannel nightshirt that Augustine recognized from a long-ago relationship. Bonnie had found it hanging in a closet.

"Is there a story to go with it?" she asked.

"A torrid one."

"Really?" Bonnie sat beside him on the sofa, at a purely friendly distance. "Let me guess: Flight attendant?"

Augustine said, "Letterman's a rerun."

"Cocktail waitress? Fashion model?"

"I'm beat." Augustine picked up a book, a biography of Lech Wałesa, and flipped it open to the middle.

"Aerobics instructor? Legal secretary?"

"Surgical intern," Augustine said. "She tried to cut out my kidneys one night in the shower."

"That's the scar on your back? The Y."

"At least she wasn't a urologist." He closed the book and picked up the channel changer for the television.

Bonnie said, "You cheated on her."

"Nope, but she thought I did. She also thought the bathtub was full of centipedes, Cuban spies were spiking her lemonade, and Richard Nixon was working the night shift at the Farm Store on Bird Road."

"Drug problem?"

"Evidently." Augustine found a Dodgers game on ESPN and tried to appear engrossed.

Bonnie Lamb asked to see the scar closely, but he declined. "The lady had poor technique," he said.

"She use a real scalpel?"

"No, a corkscrew."

"My God."

"What is it with women and scars?"

Bonnie said, "I knew it. You've been asked before."

Was she flirting? Augustine wasn't sure. He had no point of reference when it came to married women whose husbands recently had disappeared.

"How's this," he said. "You tell me all about your husband, and maybe I'll show you the damn scar."

"Deal," said Bonnie Lamb, tugging the nightshirt down to cover her knees.

Max Lamb met and fell in love with Bonnie Brooks when she was an assistant publicist for Crespo Mills Internationale, a leading producer of snack and breakfast foods. Rodale & Burns had won the lucrative Crespo advertising account, and assigned Max Lamb to develop the print and radio campaign for a new cereal called Plum Crunchies. Bonnie Brooks flew in from Crespo's Chicago headquarters to consult.

Basically, Plum Crunchies were ordinary sugar-coated cornflakes mixed with rock-hard fragments of dried plums—that is to say, prunes. The word "prune" was not to appear in any Plum Crunchies publicity or advertising, a corporate edict with which both Max Lamb and Bonnie Brooks wholeheartedly agreed. The target demographic was sweet-toothed youngsters aged fourteen and under, not constipated senior citizens.

On only their second date, at a Pakistani restaurant in Greenwich Village, Max sprung upon Bonnie his slogan for Crespo's new cereal: *You'll go plum loco for Plum Crunchies!*

"With p-l-u-m instead of p-l-u-m-b on the first reference," he was quick to explain.

Though she personally avoided the use of lame homonyms, Bonnie told Max the slogan had possibilities. She was trying not to dampen his enthusiasm; besides, he was the expert, the creative talent. All she did was bang out press releases.

On a napkin Max Lamb crudely sketched a jaunty, cockeyed mynah bird that was to be the cereal-box mascot for Plum Crunchies. Max said the bird would be colored purple ("like a plum!") and would be named Dinah the Mynah. Here Bonnie Brooks felt she should speak up, as a colleague, to remind Max Lamb of the many other cereals that already used bird logos (Froot Loops, Cocoa Puffs, Kellogg's Corn Flakes, and so on). In addition, she gently questioned the wisdom of naming the mynah bird after an aging, though much-beloved, TV singer.

Bonnie: "Is the bird supposed to be a woman?"

Max: "The bird has no particular gender."

Bonnie: "Well, do mynahs actually eat plums?"

Max: "You're adorable, you know that?"

He was falling for her, and she was falling (though a bit less precipitously) for him. As it turned out, Max's bosses at Rodale & Burns liked his slogan but hated the concept of Dinah the Mynah. The executives of Crespo Mills concurred. When the new cereal finally debuted, the box featured a likeness of basketball legend Patrick Ewing, slam-dunking a giddy cartoon plum. Surveys later revealed that many customers thought it was either an oversized grape or a prune. Plum Crunchies failed to capture a significant share of the fruited-branflake breakfast market and quietly disappeared forever from the shelves.

Bonnie and Max's long-distance romance endured. She found herself carried along by his energy, determination and self-confidence, misplaced as it often was. While Bonnie was bothered by Max's tendency to judge humankind strictly according to age, race, sex and median income, she attributed his cold eye to indoctrination by the advertising business. She herself had become cynical about the brain activity of the average consumer, given Crespo's worldwide success with such dubious food products as salted doughballs, whipped olive spread and shrimp-flavored popcorn.

In the early months of courtship, Max invented a game intended to impress Bonnie Brooks. He bet that he could guess precisely what model of automobile a person owned, based on his or her demeanor, wardrobe and physical appearance. The skill was intuitive, Max told Bonnie; a gift. He said it's what made him such a canny advertising pro. On dates, he'd sometimes follow strangers out of restaurants or movie theaters to see what they were driving. "Ha! A Lumina—what'd I tell ya? The guy had midsize written all over him!" Max would chirp when his guess was correct (which was, by Bonnie's generous reckoning, about five percent of the time). Before long, the car game grew tiresome and Bonnie Brooks asked Max Lamb to stop. He didn't take it personally; he was a hard man to insult. This, too, Bonnie attributed to the severe environment of Madison Avenue.

While Bonnie's father was amiably indifferent to Max, her mother was openly unfond of him. She felt he tried too hard, came on too strong; that he was trying to sell himself to Bonnie the same way he sold breakfast cereal and cigarets. It wasn't that Bonnie's mother thought Max Lamb was a phony; just the opposite. She believed he was exactly what he seemed to be—completely goal-driven, every waking moment. He was no different at home than he was at the office, no less consumed with attaining success. There was, said Bonnie's mother, a sneaky arrogance in Max Lamb's winning attitude. Bonnie thought it was an odd criticism, coming from a woman who had regarded Bonnie's previous boyfriends as timid, unmotivated losers. Still, her mother had never used the term "asshole" to describe Bonnie's other suitors. That she pinned it so quickly on Max Lamb nagged painfully at Bonnie until her wedding day.

Now, with Max apparently abducted by a raving madman, Bonnie fretted about something else her mother had often mentioned, a trait of Max's so obvious that even Bonnie had acknowledged it. Augustine knew what she was talking about.

"Your husband thinks he can outsmart anybody."

"Unfortunately," Bonnie said.

"I can tell from the phone tapes."

"Well," she said, fishing for encouragement, "he's managed to make it so far."

"Maybe he's learned when to keep his mouth shut." Augustine stood up and stretched his arms. "I'm tired. Can we do the scar thing some other time?"

Bonnie Lamb laughed and said sure. She waited until she heard the bedroom door shut before she phoned Pete Archibald at his home in Connecticut.

"Did I wake you?" she asked.

"Heck, no. Max said you might be calling."

Bonnie's words stuck in her throat. "You—Pete, you talked to him?"

"For about an hour."

"When?"

"Tonight. He's all frantic that Bill Knapp's gonna snake the Bronco cigaret account. I told him not to worry, Billy's tied up with the smokeless division on some stupid rodeo tour—"

"Pete, never mind all that. Where did Max call from?"

"I don't know, Bon. I assumed he'd spoken to you."

Bonnie strained to keep the hurt from her voice. "Did he tell you what happened?"

On the other end, Pete Archibald clucked and ummmed nervously. "Not all the gory details, Bonnie. Everybody—least all the couples I know—go through the occasional bedroom drama. Fights and whatnot. I don't blame you for not giving me the real story when you called before."

Bonnie Lamb's voice rose. "Peter, Max and I aren't fighting. And I *did* tell you the real story." She caught herself. "At least it was the story Max told me."

After an uncomfortable pause, Pete Archibald said, "Bon, you guys work it out, OK? I don't want to get in the middle."

"You're right, you're absolutely right." She noticed that her free hand was balled in a fist and she was rocking sideways in the chair. "Pete, I won't keep you. But maybe you could tell me what else Max said."

"Shop talk, Bonnie."

"For a whole hour?"

"Well, you know your husband. He gets rolling, you know what he's like."

Maybe I don't, Bonnie thought.

She said good-bye to Pete Archibald and hung up. Then she went to Augustine's room and knocked on the door. When he didn't answer, she slipped in and sat lightly on the corner of the bed. She thought he was asleep, until he rolled over and said: "Not a good night for the skull room, huh?"

Bonnie Lamb shook her head and began to cry.

Edie Marsh gave it her best shot. For a while, the plan went smoothly. The man from Midwest Casualty took meticulous notes as he followed her from room to room in the Torres house. Many of the couple's belongings had been pulverized beyond recognition, so Edie began embellishing losses to inflate the claim. She lovingly described the splintered remains of a china cabinet as a priceless antique that Tony inherited from a great-grandmother in San Juan. Pausing before a bare bedroom wall, she pointed to the nails upon which once hung two original (and very expensive) watercolors by the legendary Jean-Claude Jarou, a martyred Haitian artist whom Edie invented off the top of her head. A splintered bedroom bureau became the hand-hewn mahogany vault that had yielded eight cashmere sweaters to the merciless winds of the hurricane.

"Eight sweaters," said Fred Dove, glancing up from his clipboard. "In Miami?"

"The finest Scottish cashmeres—can you imagine? Ask your wife if it wouldn't break her heart."

Fred Dove took a small flashlight from his jacket and went outside to evaluate structural damage. Soon Edie heard barking from the backyard, followed by emphatic human profanities. By the time she got there, both dachshunds had gotten a piece of the insurance man. Edie led him inside, put him in the BarcaLounger, rolled up his cuffs and tended his bloody ankles with Evian and Ivory liquid, which she salvaged from the kitchen.

"I'm glad they're not rottweilers," said Fred Dove, soothed by Edie's ministrations with a soft towel.

Repeatedly she apologized for the attack. "For what it's worth, they've had all their shots," she said, with no supporting evidence whatsoever.

She instructed Fred Dove to stay in the recliner and keep his feet elevated, to slow the bleeding. Leaning back, he spotted Tony Torres's Salesman of the Year plaque on the wall. "Pretty impressive," Fred Dove said.

"Yes, it was quite a big day for us." Edie beamed, a game simulation of spousely pride.

"And where's Mister Torres tonight?"

Out of town, Edie replied, at a mobile-home convention in Dallas. For the second time, Fred Dove looked doubtful.

"Even with the hurricane? Must be a pretty important convention."

"It sure is," said Edie Marsh. "He's getting another award."

"Ah."

"So he *had* to go. I mean, it'd look bad if he didn't show up. Like he wasn't grateful or something."

Fred Dove said, "I suppose so. When will Mister Torres be returning to Miami?"

Edie sighed theatrically. "I just don't know. Soon, I hope."

The insurance man attempted to lower the recliner, but it kept springing to the sleep position. Finally Edie Marsh sat on the footrest, enabling Fred Dove to climb out. He said he wanted to reinspect the damage to the master bedroom. Edie said that was fine.

She was rinsing the bloody towel in a sink when the insurance man called. She hurried to the bedroom, where Fred Dove held up a framed photograph that he'd dug from the storm rubble. It was a picture of Tony Torres with a large dead fish. The fish had a mouth the size of a garbage pail.

"That's Tony on the left," Edie said with a dry, edgy laugh.

"Nice grouper. Where'd he catch it?"

"The ocean." Where else? thought Edie.

"And who's this?" The insurance man retrieved another frame off the floor. The glass was cracked, and the picture was puckered from storm water. It was a color nine-by-twelve, mounted inside gold filigree: Tony Torres with his arm around the waist of a petite but heavy-breasted Latin woman. Both of them wore loopy champagne smiles.

"His sister Maria," Edie blurted, sensing the game was about to end.

"She's in a wedding gown," Fred Dove remarked, with no trace of sarcasm. "And Mister Torres is wearing a black tuxedo and tails."

Edie said, "He was the best man."

"Really? His hand is on her bottom."

"They're very close," said Edie, "for a brother and sister." The words trailed off in defeat.

Fred Dove's shoulders stiffened, and his tone chilled. "Do you happen to have some identification? A driver's license would be good. Anything with a current photograph."

Edie Marsh said nothing. She feared compounding one felony with another.

"Let me guess," said the insurance man. "All your personal papers were lost in the hurricane."

Edie bowed her head, thinking: This can't be happening again. One of these days I've got to catch a break. She said, "Shit."

"Pardon?"

"I said 'shit.' Meaning, I give up." Edie couldn't believe it—a fucking *wedding* picture! Tony and the unfaithful witch he planned to rip off for half the hurricane money. Too bad Snapper bolted, she thought, because this was ten times better than Sally Jessy.

"Who are you?" Fred Dove was stern and official.

"Look, what happens now?"

"I'll tell you exactly what happens—"

At that moment, the electric generator ran out of gasoline, dying with a feeble series of burps. The lightbulb went dim and the television went black. The house at 15600 Calusa became suddenly as quiet as a chapel. The only sound was a faint jingle from the backyard, where the two dachshunds squirmed to pull free of their leashes.

In the darkness, Fred Dove reached for his flashlight. Edie Marsh intercepted his wrist and held on to it. She decided there was nothing to lose by trying.

"What are you doing?" the insurance man asked.

Edie brought his hand to her mouth. "What's it worth to you?"

Fred Dove stood as still as a statue.

"Come on," Edie said, her tongue brushing his knuckles, "what's it worth?"

The insurance man, in a shaky whisper: "What's *what* worth—not calling the police? Is that what you mean?"

Edie was smiling. Fred Dove could tell by the feel of her lips and teeth against his hand.

"What's this house insured for?" she asked.

"Why?"

"One twenty? One thirty?"

"One forty-one," said Fred Dove, thinking: Her breath is so *unbelievably* soft.

Edie switched to her sex-kitten voice, the one that had failed to galvanize the young Palm Beach Kennedy. "One forty-one? You sure, Mister Dove?"

"The structure, yes. Because of the swimming pool."

"Of course." She pressed closer, wishing she weren't wearing a bra but suspecting it didn't much matter. Poor Freddie's brakes were already smoking. She feathered her eyelashes against his neck and felt him bury his face in her hair.

The insurance man labored to speak. "What is it you want?"

"A partner," Edie Marsh replied, sealing the agreement with a long blind kiss.

Sergeant Cain Darby took his weekends with the National Guard as seriously as he took his regular job as a maximum-security-prison guard. Although he would have preferred to remain in Starke with the armed robbers and serial killers, duty called Cain Darby to South Florida on the day after the hurricane struck.

Commanding Darby's National Guard unit was the night manager of a Days Inn, who sternly instructed the troops not to fire their weapons unless fired upon themselves. From what Cain Darby knew of Miami, this scenario seemed not entirely improbable. Nonetheless, he understood that a Guardsman's chief mission was to maintain order in the streets, assist needy civilians and prevent looting.

The unit's first afternoon was spent erecting tents for the homeless and unloading heavy drums of fresh drinking water from the back of a Red Cross trailer. After supper, Cain Darby was posted to a curfew checkpoint on Quail Roost Drive, not far from the Florida Turnpike. Darby and another Guardsman, the foreman of a paper mill, took turns stopping the cars and trucks. Most drivers had good excuses for being on the road after curfew—some were searching for missing relatives, others were on their way to a hospital, and still others were simply lost in a place they no longer recognized. If questions arose about a driver's alibi, the paper-mill foreman deferred judgment to Sergeant Darby, due to his law-enforcement experience. Common violators were TV crews, sightseers, and teenagers who had come to steal. These cars Cain Darby interdicted and sent away, to the Turnpike ramp.

At midnight the paper-mill foreman returned to camp, leaving Sergeant Darby alone at the barricade. He dozed for what must have been two hours, until he was startled awake by loud snorting. Blearily he saw the shape of a large bear no more than thirty yards away, at the edge of a pine glade. Or maybe it was just a freak shadow, for it looked nothing like the chubby black bears that Cain Darby routinely poached from the Ocala National

Forest. The thing that he now *thought* he was seeing stood seven feet at the shoulders.

Cain Darby closed his eyes tightly to clear the sleep. Then he opened them again, very slowly. The huge shape was still there, a motionless phantasm. Common sense told him he was mistaken—they don't grow thousand-pound bears in Florida! But that's sure what it looked like. . . .

So he raised his rifle.

Then, from the corner of his eye, he spotted headlights barreling down Quail Roost Drive. He turned to see. Somebody was driving toward the roadblock like a bat out of hell. Judging by the rising chorus of sirens, half the Metro police force was on the chase.

When Cain Darby spun back toward the bear, or the shape that *looked* like a bear, it was gone. He lowered the gun and directed his attention to the maniac in the oncoming truck. Cain Darby struck an erect military pose in front of the candy-striped barricades—spine straight, legs apart, the rifle held at a ready angle across the chest.

A half mile behind the truck was a stream of flashing blue and red lights. The fugitive driver seemed undaunted. As the headlights drew closer, Sergeant Darby hurriedly weighed his options. The asshole wasn't going to stop, that much was clear. By now the man had (unless he was blind, drunk or both) seen the soldier standing in his path.

Yet the vehicle was not decelerating. If anything, it was gaining speed. Cain Darby cursed as he dashed out of the way. If there was one thing he found intolerable, it was disrespect for a uniform, whether it belonged to the Department of Corrections or the National Guard.

So he indignantly cranked off a few rounds as the idiot driver smashed through the barricade.

No one was more stunned than Cain Darby to see the speeding truck overshoot the Turnpike ramp and plunge full speed into a drainage canal; no one except the driver, Gil Peck. The sound of gunfire had destroyed his ragged reflexes, particularly his ability to locate the brake pedal. He couldn't believe some peckerwood Guardsman was shooting at him.

What did not surprise Gil Peck, considering his heavy cargo of stolen bricks, was how swiftly the flatbed sunk in the warm brown water. He squeezed through the window, swam to shore and began weeping at his own foul luck. All his hurricane booty was lost, except for the package of hash, which bobbed to the surface at the precise moment the first police car arrived.

Yet the drugs weren't the most serious of Gil Peck's legal concerns. As he was being handcuffed, he declared: "I didn't kill him!"

"Kill who?" the officer asked.

"The guy, you know. The guy at the trailer park." Gil Peck assumed that's why the cops were chasing him—they'd found the body of the crucified man.

But they hadn't. Gil Peck's nausea worsened. He should've kept his damn mouth shut. Now it was too late. Pink and blue bikini panties began to float up, like pale jellyfish, from the bed of the sunken truck.

The officer said: "What guy at what trailer park?"

Gil Peck told him about the dead man impaled in the TV dish. As other policemen arrived, Gil Peck repeated the story, and also his impassioned denials of guilt. One of the officers asked Gil Peck if he would take them to the body, and he agreed.

After the paramedics checked him for broken bones, the thief was toweled off and deposited in the back-seat cage of a Highway Patrol car. The trooper at the wheel was a large black man in a Stetson. On the way to the trailer court, Gil Peck delivered yet another excited monologue about his innocence.

"If you didn't do it," the trooper cut in, "why'd you run?"

"Scared, man." Gil Peck shivered. "You should see."

"Oh, I can't wait," the trooper said.

"You a Christian, sir?"

It was amazing, thought the trooper, how quickly the handcuffs induced spiritual devoutness. "Anyone read you your rights?" he asked the truck driver.

Gil Peck thrust his face to the mesh of the cage. "If you're a Christian, you gotta believe what I'm sayin'. It wasn't me that crucified the poor fucker."

But Jim Tile hoped with all his Christian heart that it was. Because the other prime suspect was someone he didn't want to arrest, unless there was no choice.

# NINE

**Skink eavesdropped leisurely** while Max Lamb made two calls. The phone booth was at a truck stop on Krome Avenue, the fringe of the Everglades. Longbeds overloaded with lumber, sheet glass and tar paper streamed south in ragged convoys to the hurricane zone. Nobody glanced twice at the unshaven man on the phone, despite the collar around his neck.

When Max Lamb hung up, Skink grabbed his arm and led him to the airboat, beached on the bank of a muddy canal. Skink ordered him to lie in the bow, and there he remained for two hours, his cheekbone vibrating against the hull. The howl of the aviation engine filled his ears. Skink was no longer singing harmony. Max Lamb wondered what he'd done to further annoy his abductor.

They stopped once. Skink left the airboat briefly and returned with a large cardboard box, which he set in the bow next to Max. They traveled until dusk. When Skink finally lifted him to his knees, Max was surprised to see the Indian village. They didn't stay long enough for Max to negotiate the return of his video camera. Skink borrowed a station wagon, put the box in the back, and buckled his prisoner on the passenger side. There was no sign of the monkey, and for that Max Lamb was grateful.

Skink put on the shower cap and started the car. Max needed to pee but was afraid to ask. He was no longer confident that he could talk his way out of the kidnapping.

"Is something wrong?" he asked.

Skink shot him a stony look. "I remember your wife from the hurricane video. Hugging two little Cuban girls."

"Yes, that was Bonnie."

"Beautiful woman. You zoomed in on her face."

"Can we stop the car," Max interrupted, squirming, "just for a minute?"

Skink kept his eyes on the road. "Your bride's got a good heart. That much is obvious from the video."

"A saint," Max agreed. He jammed both hands between his legs; he'd tie his dick in a Windsor before he'd wet himself in front of the governor.

"Why she's with you, I can't figure. It's a real puzzler," Skink said. He braked the car sharply. "Why didn't you try to phone her tonight? You call your buddy in New York. You call your folks in Milan-fucking-Italy. Why not Bonnie?"

"I don't know where she is. That damn answering machine—"

"And the crap about you and her having a fight—"

"I didn't want Peter to worry," Max said.

"Well, God forbid." Skink jammed the transmission into Park and flung himself out the door. He reappeared in the beam of the headlights, a hoary apparition crouched on the pavement. Max Lamb craned to see what he was doing.

Skink strolled back to the station wagon and tossed a dead opossum on the seat next to Max, who gasped and recoiled. A few miles later, Skink added a truck-flattened coachwhip snake to the evening's menu. Max forgot about his bladder until they made camp at an abandoned horse barn west of Krome.

The horses were gone, scattered by the storm; the owners had come by to retrieve the saddles and tack, and to scatter feed in case any of the animals returned. Max Lamb stood alone in the musky darkness and relieved himself torrentially. He considered running, but feared he wouldn't survive a single night alone in nature. In Max's mind, all Florida south of Orlando was an immense swamp, humidly teeming with feral beasts. Some had claws and poisonous fangs, some drove air-boats and feasted on roadkill. They were all the same to Max.

Skink appeared at his side to announce that dinner soon would be served. Max followed him into the stables. He asked if it was wise to make a campfire inside a barn. Skink replied that it was extremely dangerous, but cozy.

Max Lamb was impressed that the odor of horseshit could not be vanquished by a mere Force Four hurricane. On a positive note, the fragrance of dung completely neutralized the aroma of boiled opossum and pan-fried snake. After supper Skink stripped to his boxer shorts and did two hundred sit-ups in a cloud of ancient manure dust. Then he retrieved the large cardboard box from the car and brought it inside the barn. He asked Max if he wanted a cigaret.

"No, thanks," Max said. "I don't smoke."

"You're kidding."

"Never have," Max said.

"But you sell the stuff—"

"We do the advertising. That's it."

"Ah," Skink said. "Just the advertising." He picked his trousers off the floor and went through the pockets. Max Lamb thought he was looking for matches, but he wasn't. He was looking for the remote control to the shock collar.

When Max regained his senses, he lay in wet moldering hay. His eyeballs were jumping in their sockets, and his neck felt tingly and hot. He sat up and said, "What'd I do?"

"Surely you believe in the products you advertise."

"Look, I don't smoke."

"You could learn." With a pocketknife, Skink opened the cardboard box. The box was full of Bronco cigarets, probably four dozen cartons. Max Lamb failed to conceal his alarm.

The kidnapper asked how he could be sure of a product until he tested it himself. Grimly Max responded: "I also do the ads for raspberry-scented douche, but I don't use the stuff."

"Careful," said Skink, brightly, "or you'll give me another brainstorm." He opened a pack of Broncos. He tapped one out and inserted it between Max's lips. He struck a match on the wall of the barn and lit the cigaret.

"Well?"

Max spit out the cigaret. "This is ridiculous."

Skink retrieved the soggy Bronco and replaced it in Max's frowning mouth. "You got two choices," he said, fingering the remote control, "smoke or be smoked."

Reluctantly Max Lamb took a drag on the cigaret. Immediately he began to cough. It worsened as Skink tied him upright to a post. "You people are a riddle to me, Max. Why you come down here. Why you act the way you do. Why you live such lives."

"For God's sake—"

"Shut up now. Please."

Skink dug through the backpack and took out a Walkman. He chose a damp corner of the barn and put on the headphones. He lighted what appeared to be a joint, except it didn't smell like marijuana.

"What's that?" Max asked.

"Toad." Skink took a hit. After a few minutes, his good eye rolled back in his head and his neck went limp.

Max Lamb went through the Broncos like a machine. Whenever Skink opened an eye, he tapped a finger to his neck—a menacing reminder of the shock collar. Max smoked and smoked. He was finishing number twenty-three when Skink shook out of the stupor and rose.

"Damn good toad." He plucked the Bronco from Max's mouth.

"I feel sick, captain."

Skink untied him and told him to rest up. "Tomorrow you're going to leave a message for your wife. You're going to arrange a meeting."

"What for?"

"So I can observe the two of you together. The chemistry, the starry eyes, all that shit. OK?"

Skink went outside and crawled under the station wagon, where he curled up and began to snore. Max coughed himself to sleep in the barn.

Bonnie Lamb awoke in Augustine's arms. Her guilt was diluted by the observation that he was wearing jeans and a T-shirt. She didn't remember him dressing during the night, but obviously he had. She was reasonably sure that no sex had occurred; plenty of tears, yes, but no sex.

Bonnie wanted to pull away without waking him. Otherwise there might be an awkward moment, the two of them lying there embraced. Or maybe not. Maybe he'd know exactly what not to say. Clearly he was experienced with crying women, because he was exceptionally good at hugging and whispering. When she found herself thinking about how nice he smelled, Bonnie knew it was time to sneak out of bed.

As she'd hoped, Augustine had the good manners to pretend to stay asleep until she was safely in the kitchen, making coffee.

When he walked in, she felt herself blush. "I'm so sorry," she blurted, "for last night."

"Why? Did you take advantage of me?" He went to the refrigerator and took out a carton of eggs. "I'm a heavy sleeper," he said. "Easy prey for sex-crazed babes."

"Especially newlyweds."

"Oh, they're the worst," said Augustine. "Ravenous harlots. You want scrambled or fried?"

"Fried." She sat at the table. She tore open a packet of NutraSweet and managed to miss the coffee cup entirely. "Please believe me. I don't usually sleep with strange men."

"Sleeping is fine. It's the screwing you want to watch out for." He was peeling an orange at the sink. "Relax, OK? Nothing happened."

Bonnie smiled. "Can I at least say thanks, for being a friend."

"You're very welcome, Mrs Lamb." He glanced over his shoulder. "What's so funny?"

"The jeans."

"Don't tell me there's a hole."

"No. It's just—well, you got up in the middle of the night to put them on. It was a sweet gesture."

"Actually, it was more of a precaution." The eggs sizzled when Augustine dropped them into the hot pan. "I'm surprised you even noticed," he said, causing Bonnie to redden once more.

In the middle of breakfast, the phone rang. It was the Medical Examiner's Office—another John Doe was being hauled to the county morgue. The coroner on duty wanted Bonnie to stop by for a look. Augustine said she'd call him back. He put the phone down and told her.

"Can they make me go?"

"I don't think so."

"Because it's not Max," Bonnie said. "Max is too busy talking to Rodale and Burns."

"A white male is all they said. Apparent homicide."

The last word hung in the air like sulfur. Bonnie put down her fork. "It can't be him."

"Probably not," Augustine agreed. "We don't have to go."

She got up and went to the bathroom. Soon Augustine heard the shower running. He was washing the dishes when she came out. She was dressed. Her wet hair was brushed back, and she'd found the intern's rose lipstick in the medicine chest.

"I guess I need to be sure," she said.

Augustine nodded. "You'll feel better."

*

Snapper's real name was Lester Maddox Parsons. His mother named him after a Georgia politician best known for scaring off black restaurant customers with an ax handle. Snapper's mother believed Lester Maddox should be President of the United States and the whole white world; Snapper's father leaned toward James Earl Ray. When Snapper was barely seven years old, his parents took him to his first Ku Klux Klan rally; for the occasion, Mrs Parsons dressed her son in a costume sewn from white muslin pillowcases; she was especially proud of the pointy little hood. The other Klansmen and their wives fawned over Lester, remarking on the youngster's handsome Southern features—baffling praise, because all that was visible of young Lester were his beady brown eyes, peeping through the slits of his sheet. He thought: I could be a Negro, for all they know!

Still, the boy enjoyed Klan rallies because there was great barbecue and towering bonfires. He was disappointed when his family stopped attending, but he couldn't argue with his parents' reason for quitting. They referred to it as The Accident, and Lester would never forget the night. His father had gotten customarily shitfaced and, when the climactic moment came to light the cross, accidentally ignited the local Grand Kleagle instead. In the absence of a fire hose, the frantic Klansmen were forced to save their blazing comrade by spritzing him with well-shaken cans of Schlitz beer. Once the fire was extinguished, they placed the charred Kleagle in the bed of Lester's father's pickup and drove to the hospital. Although the man survived, his precious anonymity was lost forever. A local television crew happened to be outside the emergency room when the

Kleagle—hoodless, his sheet in scorched tatters—arrived. Once his involvement in the Klan was exposed on TV, the man resigned as district attorney and moved upstate to Macon. Lester's father blamed himself, a sentiment echoed in harsher terms by the other Klansmen. Morale in the local chapter further deteriorated when a newspaper revealed that the young doctor who had revived the dying Kleagle was a black man, possibly from Savannah.

The Parsonses decided to leave the Klan while it was still their choice to do so. Lester's father joined a segregated bowling league, while his mother mailed out flyers for J. B. Stoner, another famous racist who periodically ran for office. Politics bored young Lester, who turned his pubescent energies to crime. He dropped out of school on his fourteenth birthday, although his preoccupied parents didn't find out for nearly two years. By then the boy's income from stealing backhoes and bulldozers was twice his father's income from repairing them. The Parsonses strove not to know what their son was up to, even when it landed him in trouble. Lester's mother worried that the boy had a mean streak; his father said all boys do. Can't get by otherwise in this godforsaken world.

Lester Maddox Parsons was seventeen when he got his nickname. He was hot-wiring a farmer's tractor in a peanut field when a game warden snuck up behind him. Lester dove from the cab and took a punch at the man, who calmly reconfigured Lester's face with the butt of an Ithaca shotgun. He sat in the county jail for three days before a doctor came to examine his jaw, which was approximately thirty-six degrees out of alignment.

That it healed at all was a minor miracle; Snapper was spitting out snips of piano wire until he was twenty-two years old.

The Georgia prison system taught the young man an important lesson: It was best to keep one's opinions about race mingling to oneself. So when Avila introduced Snapper to the roofing crew, Snapper noted (but did not complain) that two of the four workers were as black as the tar they'd be mixing. The third roofer was a muscular young *Marielito* with the number "69" tattooed elegantly inside his lower lip. The fourth roofer was a white crackhead from Santa Rosa County who spoke a version of the English language that was utterly incomprehensible to Snapper and the others. Although each of the roofers owned long felony rap sheets, Snapper couldn't say that his feelings toward the crew approached anything close to kinship.

Avila sat the men down for a pep talk.

"Thanks to the hurricane, there's a hundred fifty thousand houses in Dade County need new roofs," he began. "Only a damn fool couldn't make money off these poor bastards."

The plan was to line up the maximum number of buyers and perform the minimum amount of actual roofing. By virtue of owning a suit and tie, Snapper was assigned the task of bullshitting potential customers through the fine print of the "contract," then collecting deposits.

"People are fucking desperate for new roofs," Avila said buoyantly. "They're getting rained on. Fried from the sun. Eat up by bugs. Faster they get a roof on their heads, the more they'll pay." He raised his palms to the sky. "Hey, do they really care about price? It's insurance money, for Christ's sake."

One of the roofers inquired how much manual labor would be involved. Avila said they should repair a small section on every house. "To put the people's minds at ease," he explained.

"What's a 'small' section?" the roofer demanded.

Another said, "It's fucking August out here, boss. I know guys that dropped dead of heatstroke."

Avila reassured the men they could get by with doing a square, maybe less, on each roof. "Then you can split. Time they figure out you won't be back, it's too late."

The crackhead mumbled something about contracting licenses. Avila turned to Snapper and said, "They ask about our license, you know what to do."

"Run?"

"*Exactamente!*"

Snapper wasn't pleased with his door-to-door role in the operation, particularly the odds of encountering large pet dogs. He said to Avila: "Sounds like too much talking to strangers. I hate that shit. Why don't you do the contracts?"

"Because I inspected some of these goddamn houses when I was with building-and-zoning."

"The owners don't know that."

Chango had warned Avila to be careful. Chango was Avila's personal *santería* deity. Avila had thanked him with a turtle and two rabbits.

"I'm keeping low," Avila told Snapper. "B-and-Z's got snitches all over the damn county. Somebody recognizes my face, we're screwed."

Snapper wasn't sure if Avila was paranoid or purely

lazy. "So where will you be exactly," he said, "when we're out on a job? Maybe some air-conditioned office." He heard the roofers snicker, a hopeful sign of solidarity.

But Avila was quick to assert his authority. "Job? This isn't no 'job,' it's an act. You boys aren't here 'cause you can mop tar. You're here 'cause you look like you can."

"What about me?" Snapper goaded. "How come *I* was hired?"

"Because we couldn't get Robert Redford." Avila stood up to signal the end of the meeting. "Snap, why the hell you *think* you got hired? So people would be sure to pay. *Comprende?* One look at that fucked-up face, and they know you mean business."

Maybe an ordinary criminal would've taken it as a compliment. Snapper did not.

All the mattresses in Tony Torres's house were soaked from the storm, so Edie Marsh had sex with the insurance man on the BarcaLounger. It was a noisy and precarious endeavor. Fred Dove was nervous, so Edie had to assist him each step of the way. Afterwards he said he must've slipped a disk. Edie was tempted to remark that he hadn't moved enough muscles to slip anything; instead she told him he was a stallion in technique and proportion. It was a strategy that seldom failed. Fred Dove contentedly fell asleep with his head on her shoulder and his legs snagged in the footrest, but not before promising to submit a boldly fraudulent damage claim for the Torres house and split the check with Edie Marsh.

An hour before dawn, Edie heard a terrible commotion in the backyard. She couldn't rise to investigate because she was pinned beneath the insurance man in the BarcaLounger. Judging from the tumult outside, Donald and Marla had gone rabid. The confrontation ended in a flurry of plaintive yips and a hair-raising roar. Edie Marsh didn't move until the sun came up. Then she stealthily roused Fred Dove, who panicked because he'd forgotten to phone his wife back in Omaha. Edie told him to hush up and put on his pants.

She led him to the backyard. The only signs of the two miniature dachshunds were limp leashes and empty collars. The Torres lawn was torn to shreds. Several large tracks were visible in the damp gray soil; deep raking tracks, with claws.

Fred Dove's left Hush Puppy fit easily one of the imprints. "Good Lord," he said, "and I wear a ten and a half."

Edie Marsh asked what kind of wild animal would make such a track. Fred Dove said it looked big enough to be a lion or a bear. "But I'm not a hunter," he added.

She said, "Can I come stay with you?"

"At the Ramada?"

"What—they don't allow women?"

"Edie, we shouldn't be seen together. Not if we're going through with this."

"You expect me to stay out here alone?"

"Look, I'm sorry about your dogs—"

"They weren't my goddamn dogs."

"Please, Edie."

With his round eyeglasses, Fred Dove reminded her of a serious young English teacher she'd known in high school. The man had worn Bass loafers with no socks and was obsessed with T. S. Eliot. Edie Marsh had screwed the guy twice in the faculty lounge, but he'd still given her a C on her final exam because (he claimed) she'd missed the whole point of "J. Alfred Prufrock." The experience had left Edie Marsh with a deep-seated mistrust of studious-looking men.

She said, "What do you mean, *if* we go through with this? We made a deal."

"Yes," Fred Dove said. "Yes, we did."

As he followed her into the house, she asked, "How soon can you get this done?"

"Well, I could file the claim this week—"

"Hundred percent loss?"

"That's right," replied the insurance man.

"A hundred and forty-one grand. Seventy-one for me, seventy for you."

"Right." For somebody about to score the windfall of a lifetime, Fred Dove was subdued. "My concern, again, is Mister Torres—"

"Like I told you last night, Tony's in some kind of serious jam. I doubt he'll be back."

"But didn't you say Mrs Torres, the real Mrs Torres, might be returning to Miami—"

"That's why you need to hurry," Edie Marsh said. "Tell the home office it's an emergency."

The insurance man pursed his lips. "Edie, every case is an emergency. There's been a hurricane, for God's sake."

Impassively, she watched him finish dressing. He spent five full minutes trying to smooth the wrinkles out of his sex-rumpled Dockers. When he asked to borrow an iron, Edie reminded him there was no electricity.

"How about taking me to breakfast," she said.

"I'm already late for an appointment in Cutler Ridge.

Some poor old man's got a Pontiac on top of his house."
Fred Dove kissed Edie on the forehead and followed up with the obligatory morning-after hug. "I'll be back tonight. Is nine all right?"

"Fine," she said. Tonight he'd undoubtedly bring condoms—one more comic speed bump on the highway to passion. She made a mental note to haul one of Tony's mattresses out in the sun to dry; another strenuous session in the BarcaLounger might put poor Freddie in traction.

"Bring the claim forms," she told him. "I want to see everything."

He jotted a reminder on his clipboard and slipped it into the briefcase.

"Oh yeah," Edie said. "I also need a couple gallons of gas from your car."

Fred Dove looked puzzled.

"For the generator," she explained. "A hot bath would be nice . . . since you won't let me share your tub at the Ramada."

"Oh, Edie—"

"And maybe a few bucks for groceries."

She softened up when the insurance man took out his wallet. "That's my boy." She kissed him on the neck and ended it with a little bite, just to prime the pump.

"I'm scared," he said.

"Don't be, sugar. It's a breeze." She took two twenties and sent him on his way.

# TEN

**On the drive** to the morgue, Augustine and Bonnie Lamb heard a news report about a fourteen-foot reticulated python that had turned up in the salad bar of a fast-food joint in Perrine.

"One of yours?" Bonnie asked.

"I'm wondering." It was impossible to know if the snake had belonged to Augustine's dead uncle; Felix Mojack's handwritten inventory was vague on details.

"He had a couple big ones," Augustine said, "but I never measured the damn things."

Bonnie said, "I hope they didn't kill it."

"Me, too." He was pleased that she was concerned for the welfare of a primeval reptile. Not all women would be.

"They could give it to a zoo," she said.

"Or turn it loose at the county commission."

"You're bad."

"I know," Augustine said. As legal custodian of the menagerie, he felt a twinge of responsibility for Bonnie Lamb's predicament. Without a monkey to chase, her husband probably wouldn't have been abducted. Maybe the culprit was one of Uncle Felix's rhesuses, maybe not.

Without reproach, Bonnie asked: "What'll you do if one of those critters kills a person?"

"Pray it was somebody who deserved it."

Bonnie was appalled. Augustine said, "I don't know what else to do, short of a safari. You know how big the Everglades are?"

They rode in silence for a while before Bonnie said: "You're right. They're free, and that's how it ought to be."

"I don't know how anything *ought* to be, but I know how it is. Hell, those cougars could be in Key Largo by now."

Bonnie Lamb smiled sadly. "I wish I was."

Before entering the chill of the Medical Examiner's Office, she put on a baggy ski sweater that Augustine had brought for the occasion. This time there were no preliminaries to the viewing. The same young coroner led them directly to the autopsy room, where the newly murdered John Doe was the center of attention. The corpse was surrounded by detectives, uniformed cops, and an unenthusiastic contingent of University of Miami medical students. They parted for Augustine and Bonnie Lamb.

A ruddy, gray-haired man in a lab coat stood at the head of the steel table. He nodded cordially and took a step back. Holding her breath, Bonnie lowered her eyes to the corpse. The man was potbellied and balding. His olive skin was covered from shoulder to toe with sprouts of shiny black hair. In the center of the chest was a gaping, raspberry-hued wound. His throat was a necklace of bruises that looked very much like purple fingerprints.

"It's not my husband," Bonnie Lamb said.

Augustine led her away. A tall black policeman followed.

"Mrs Lamb?"

Bonnie, on autopilot, kept moving.

"Mrs Lamb, I need to speak with you."

She turned. The policeman was broadly muscled and walked with a hitch in his right leg. He wore a state trooper's uniform and held a tan Stetson in his huge hands. He seemed as relieved to be out of the autopsy room as they were.

Augustine asked if there was a problem. The trooper suggested they go someplace to talk.

"About what?" Bonnie asked.

"Your husband's disappearance. I'm running down a few leads, that's all." The trooper's manner was uncharacteristically informal for a cop in uniform. He said, "Just a few questions, folks. I promise."

Augustine didn't understand why the Highway Patrol would take an interest in a missing-person case. He said, "She's already spoken to the FBI."

"This won't take long."

Bonnie said, "If you've got something new, anything, I'd like to hear about it."

"I know a great Italian place," the trooper said.

Augustine saw that Bonnie had made up her mind. "Is this official business?" he asked the trooper.

"Extremely unofficial." Jim Tile put on his hat. "Let's go eat," he said.

In the mid-1970s, a man named Clinton Tyree ran for governor of Florida. On paper he seemed an ideal candidate, a bold fresh voice in a cynical age. He was a rare native son, handsome, strapping; an ex-college football sensation and a decorated veteran of Vietnam.

On the campaign trail, he could talk smart in Palm Beach or play dumb in the Panhandle. The media were dazzled because he spoke in complete sentences, spontaneously and without index cards. Best of all, his private past was uncluttered by slimy business deals, the intricacies of which taxed the comprehension of journalists and readers alike.

Clinton Tyree's only political liability was a five-year stint as an English professor at the University of Florida, a job that historically would have marked a candidate as too thoughtful, educated and broad-minded for state office. But, in a stunning upset, voters forgave Clint Tyree's erudition and elected him governor.

Naively the Tallahassee establishment welcomed the new chief executive. The barkers, pimps and fast-change artists who controlled the legislature assumed that, like most of his predecessors, Clinton Tyree dutifully would slide into the program. He was, after all, a local boy. Surely he understood how things worked.

But behind the governor's movie-star smile was the incendiary fervor of a terrorist. He brought with him to the capital a passion so deep and untainted that it was utterly unrecognizable to other politicians; they quickly decided that Clinton Tyree was a crazy man. In his first post-election interview, he told *The New York Times* that Florida was being destroyed by unbridled growth, overdevelopment and pollution, and that the stinking root of those evils was greed. By way of illustration, he cited the Speaker of the Florida House for possessing "the ethics of an intestinal bacterium," merely because the man had accepted a free trip to Bangkok from a Miami Beach high-rise developer. Later Tyree went on radio urging visitors and would-be residents to stay out of the Sunshine State for a few years, "so we can gather our senses." He announced a goal of Negative Population Growth and proposed generous tax incentives for counties that significantly reduced human density. Tyree couldn't have caused more of an uproar had he been preaching satanism to preschoolers.

The view that the new governor was mentally unstable was reinforced by his refusal to accept bribes. More appallingly, he shared the details of these illicit offers with agents of the Federal Bureau of Investigation. In that manner, one of the state's richest and most politically connected land developers got shut down, indicted and convicted of corruption. Clearly Clinton Tyree was a menace.

No previous governor had dared to disrupt the business of paving Florida. For seventy glorious years, the state had shriveled safely in the grip of those most efficient at looting its resources. Suddenly this reckless young upstart was inciting folks like a damn communist. Save the rivers. Save the coasts. Save the Big Cypress. Where would it end? *Time* magazine put him on the cover. David Brinkley called him a New Populist. The National Audubon Society gave him a frigging medal. . . .

One night, in a curtained booth of a restaurant called the Silver Slipper, a pact was made to stop the madman. His heroics in Southeast Asia made him immune to customary smear tactics, so the only safe alternative was to neutralize him politically. It was a straightforward plan: No matter what the new governor wanted, the legislature and cabinet would do the opposite—a voting pattern to be ensured by magnanimous contributions from bankers, contractors, real estate brokers, hoteliers, farm conglomerates and other special-interest groups that were experiencing philosophical differences with Clinton Tyree.

The strategy succeeded. Even the governor's fellow Democrats felt sufficiently threatened by his reforms to abandon him without compunction. Once it became clear to Clint Tyree that the freeze was on, he slowly began to come apart. Each defeat in the legislature hit him like a sledge. His public appearances were marked by bilious oratory and dark mutterings. He lost weight and let his hair grow. During one cryptic press conference, he chose not to wear a shirt. He wrote acidulous letters on official stationery, and gave interviews in which he quoted at length from Carl Jung, Henry Thoreau and David Crosby. One night the state trooper assigned to guard the governor found him creeping through a graveyard; Clinton Tyree explained his intention was to dig up the remains of the late Napoleon Bonaparte Broward, the governor who had first schemed to drain the Everglades. Tyree's idea was to distribute Governor Broward's bones as souvenirs to visitors in the capitol rotunda.

Meanwhile the ravaging of Florida continued unabated, as did the incoming stampede. A thousand fortune-seekers took up residence in the state every day, and there was nothing Clint Tyree could do about it.

So he quit, fled Tallahassee on a melancholy morning in the back of a state limousine, and melted into the tangled wilderness. In the history of Florida, no governor had ever before resigned; in fact, no elected officeholder had made such an abrupt or eccentric exit from public life. Journalists and authors hunted the missing Clinton

Tyree but never caught up with him. He moved by night, fed off the road, and adopted the solitary existence of a swamp rattler. Those who encountered him knew him by the name of Skink, or simply "captain," a solemn hermitage interrupted by the occasional righteous arson, aggravated battery or highway sniping.

Only one man held the runaway governor's complete trust—the Highway Patrol trooper who had been assigned to guard him during the gubernatorial campaign and later had come to work at the governor's mansion; the same trooper who was driving the limousine on the day Clinton Tyree disappeared. It was he alone who knew the man's whereabouts, kept in touch and followed his movements; who was there to help when Clinton Tyree went around the bend, which he sometimes did. The trooper had been there soon after his friend lost an eye in a vicious beating; again after he shot up some rental cars in a roadside spree; again after he burned down an amusement park.

Some years were quieter than others.

"But he's been waiting for this hurricane," Jim Tile said, twirling a spoonful of spaghetti. "There's cause to be concerned."

Augustine said: "I've heard of this guy."

"Then you understand why I need to talk to Mrs Lamb."

"Mrs Lamb," Bonnie said, caustically, "can't believe what she's hearing. You think this lunatic's got Max?"

"An old lady in the neighborhood saw a man fitting the governor's description carrying a man fitting your husband's description. Over his shoulder. Buck naked." Jim Tile paused to allow Mrs Lamb to form a mental picture of the scene. He said, "I don't know about the lady's eyesight, but it's worth checking out. You mentioned a tape you made—the kidnapper's voice."

"It's back at the house," said Augustine.

"Would you mind if I listened to it?"

Bonnie said, "This is ludicrous, what you're saying—"

"Humor me," said Jim Tile.

Bonnie pushed away her plate of lasagna, half eaten. "What's your interest?"

"He's my friend. He's in trouble," the trooper said.

"All I care about is Max."

"They're both in danger."

Bonnie demanded to know about the fat man in the morgue. The trooper said he'd been strangled and impaled on a TV satellite dish. The motive didn't appear to be robbery.

"Did your 'friend' do that, too?"

"They're talking to some dumb goober from Alabama, but I don't know."

To Bonnie, it was all incredible. "You did say 'impaled'?"

"Yes, ma'am." The trooper didn't mention the mock crucifixion. Mrs Lamb was plenty upset already.

Through clenched teeth she said, "This place is insane."

Jim Tile was in full agreement. Tiredly he looked at Augustine. "I'm just tracking down a few leads."

"Come on back to the house. We'll play that tape for you."

Ira Jackson's intention had been to kill the mobile-home salesman and then drive home to New York and arrange his mother's funeral. To his dismay, the murder of Tony Torres left him restless and unfulfilled. Driving through the gutted hurricane zone, Ira Jackson realized what a pitifully insignificant little fuck Tony Torres had been. South Florida was crawling with guys who cheerfully sold death traps to widows. The evidence was plain: Ira Jackson knew shitty construction when he saw it, and he saw it everywhere. Homes in one subdivision came out of the storm with scarcely a shingle out of place; across the street, an equally high-priced development was obliterated, every house blown to pieces.

A goddamn disgrace, Ira Jackson thought. This was exactly the kind of thing that gave corruption a bad name. He recalled the cocky proclamation of Tony Torres: *Every home I've sold passed inspection.*

Undoubtedly it was true. Dade County's code inspectors were as culpable for the destruction as schmuck salesmen like Torres. To Ira Jackson's experienced eye, the substandard construction was too widespread to be explained by mere incompetence; a blind man would have red-tagged some of those cardboard subdivisions. Inspectors most certainly had been paid off with cash, booze, dope, broads, or all of the above. It happened in Brooklyn, too, but Brooklyn didn't get many hurricanes.

Ira Jackson angrily thought of the tie-downs that were supposed to anchor his late mother's double-wide trailer. Someone from the county should have noticed the rotted straps; someone should have examined the augers, to make sure they hadn't been sawed off. Ira Jackson wondered who that someone was, and how much he'd been bribed not to do his job.

He drove to the Metro building-and-zoning department to find out.

Snapper had sweated through his cheap suit. Mr Nathaniel Lewis was giving him a hard time about the deposit. Out in the truck, the phony roofers were drinking warm beer and arguing about sports.

"Four thousand down is totally out of line," Nathaniel Lewis was saying.

"All depends on how soon you want a roof. I figured you's in a hurry."

"Sure we're in a hurry. Just look at this place."

Snapper agreed that the house was in terrible shape; the Lewises had cut up plastic garbage bags and tacked them to the bare beams, to keep out the rain. "Look," said Snapper, "everybody's roof got blown away. Our phone's ringing off the hook. Four grand puts you top of the list. Priority One."

Nathaniel Lewis was sharper than Snapper preferred. "If your phone's ringin' off the hook, how is it you come knockin' on my door like some damn Jehovah. And how is it your crew's sittin' on their butts in the truck, if they's so much work to be done?"

"They're on a break," Snapper lied. "We're doing that duplex two blocks over. Save on gas money if we pick up a few more jobs in the neighborhood."

Lewis said, "Three down—and that's only if you start right away."

"We can handle that."

The crew ascended the skeleton of Lewis's roof. Snapper didn't have to tell the men to take their time;

that came naturally. Avila had said it was important to make lots of noise, like legitimate roofers, so the black guys staged a truss-hammering contest, with the Latin guy as referee. The white crackhead was left to cut plywood for the decking.

Snapper waited in the cab of the truck, which smelled like stale Coors and marijuana. Mercifully the sky darkened after about an hour, and a hard thunderstorm broke loose. While the roofers scrambled to load the truck, Snapper told Nathaniel Lewis they'd return first thing in the morning. Lewis handed him a cashier's check for three thousand dollars. The check was made out to Fortress Roofing, Avila's bogus company. Snapper thought it was a very amusing name.

He got in the stolen Jeep Cherokee and headed south. The crew followed in the truck. Avila had advised Snapper to move around, don't stay in one area. A smart strategy, Snapper agreed. They made it to Cutler Ridge ahead of the weather. Snapper found an expensive ranch-style house sitting on two acres of pinelands. Half the roof had been torn off by the hurricane. A Land Rover and a black Infiniti were parked in the tiled driveway.

Jackpot, Snapper thought.

The lady of the house let him in. Her name was Whitmark, and she was frantic for shelter. She'd been scouting the rain clouds on the horizon, and the possibility of more flooding in the living room had sent her dashing to the medicine chest. The "roofing foreman" listened to Mrs Whitmark's woeful story:

The pile carpet already was ruined, as was Mr Whitmark's state-of-the-art stereo system, and of course mildew had claimed all the drapery, the linens and half her winter evening wardrobe; the Italian leather sofa and the cherry buffet had been moved to the west wing, but—

"We can start this afternoon," Snapper cut in, "but we need a deposit."

Mrs Whitmark asked how much. Snapper pulled a figure out of his head: seven thousand dollars.

"You take cash, I assume."

"Sure," Snapper said, trying to sound matter-of-fact, like all his customers had seven grand lying around in cookie jars.

Mrs Whitmark left Snapper alone while she went for the money. He raised his eyes to the immense hole in the ceiling. At that moment, a sunbeam broke through the bruised clouds, flooding the house with golden light.

Snapper shielded his eyes. Was this a sign?

When Mrs Whitmark returned, she was flanked by two blackand-silver German shepherds.

Snapper went rigid. "Mother of Christ," he murmured.

"My babies," said Mrs Whitmark, fondly. "We don't have a problem with looters. Do we, sugars?" She stroked the larger dog under its chin. On command, both of them sat at her feet. They cocked their heads and gazed expectantly at Snapper, who felt a spasm in his colon.

His hands trembled so severely that he was barely able to write up the contract. Mrs Whitmark asked what had happened to his face. "Did you fall off a roof?"

"No," he said curtly. "Bungee accident."

Mrs Whitmark gave him the cash in a scented pink envelope. "How soon can you start?"

Snapper promised that the crew would return in half an hour. "We'll need to pick up some lumber. It's a big place you've got here."

Mrs Whitmark and her guard dogs accompanied Snapper to the front door. He kept both hands jammed in his pockets, in case one of the vicious bastards lunged for him. Of course, if they were trained like police K-9s, they wouldn't bother with his hands. They'd go straight for the balls.

"Hurry," Mrs Whitmark said, scanning the clouds with dilated pupils. "I don't like the looks of this sky."

Snapper walked to the truck and gave the crew the bad news. "She didn't go for it. Says her husband's already got a roofer lined up for the job. Some company from Palm Beach, she said."

"Thank God," said one of the black guys, yawning. "I'm beat, boss. How about we call it a day?"

"Fine by me," said Snapper.

Jim Tile rewound the tape and played it again.

"*Honey, I've been kidnapped—*"

"Abducted! *Kidnapping implies ransom, Max. Don't fucking flatter yourself. . . .*"

Bonnie Lamb said, "Well?"

"It's him," the trooper said.

"You're sure?"

"*I love you, Bonnie. Max forgot to tell you, so I will. Bye now. . . .*"

"Oh yeah," said Jim Tile. He popped the cassette out of the tape deck.

Bonnie asked Augustine to call his agent friend at the FBI. Augustine said it wasn't such a hot idea.

The trooper agreed. "They'll never find him. They don't know where to look, they don't know how."

"But you do?"

"What will probably happen," Jim Tile said, "is the governor will keep your husband until he gets bored with him."

"Then what?" Bonnie demanded. "He kills him?"

"Not unless your husband tries something stupid."

Augustine thought: We might have a problem.

The trooper told Bonnie Lamb not to panic; the governor wasn't irrational. There were ways to track him, make contact, engage in productive dialogue.

Bonnie excused herself and went to take some aspirin. Augustine walked outside with the trooper. "The FBI won't touch this," Jim Tile said, keeping his voice low. "There's no ransom demand, no interstate travel. It's hard for her to understand."

Augustine observed that Max Lamb wasn't helping matters, calling New York to check on his advertising accounts. "Not exactly your typical victim," he said.

Jim Tile got in the car and placed his Stetson on the seat. "I'll get back with you soon. Meanwhile go easy with the lady."

Augustine said, "You don't think he's crazy, do you?"

The trooper laughed. "Son, you heard the tape."

"Yeah. I don't think he's crazy, either."

"'Different' is the word. Seriously different." Jim Tile turned up the patrol car's radio to hear the latest hurricane dementia. The Highway Patrol dispatcher was directing troopers to the intersection of U.S. 1 and Kendall Drive, where a truck loaded with ice had overturned. A disturbance had erupted, and ambulances were on the way.

"Lord," Jim Tile said. "They're murdering each other over ice cubes." He sped off without saying good-bye.

Back in the house, Augustine was surprised to find Bonnie Lamb sitting next to the kitchen phone. At her elbow was a notepad upon which she had written several lines. He was struck by the elegance of her handwriting. Once, he'd dated a woman who dotted her *i*'s with perfect tiny circles; sometimes she drew happy faces inside the circles, sometimes she drew frowns. The woman had been a cheerleader for her college football team, and she couldn't get it out of her system.

Bonnie Lamb's handwriting bore no trace of retired cheerleader. "Directions," she replied, waving the paper.

"Where?"

"To see Max and this Skink person. They left directions on my machine."

She was excited. Augustine sat next to her. "What else did they say?"

"No police. No FBI. Max was very firm about it."

"And?"

"Four double-A batteries and a tape of *Exile on Main Street*. Dolby chrome oxide, whatever that means. And a bottle of pitted green olives, no pimientos."

"This would be the governor's shopping list?"

"Max hates green olives." Bonnie Lamb put her hand on Augustine's arm. "What do we do? You want to hear the message?"

"Let's go talk to them, if that's what they want."

"Bring your gun. I'm serious." Her eyes flashed. "We can kidnap Max from the kidnapper. Why not!"

"Settle down, please. When's the meeting?"

"Midnight tomorrow."

"Where?"

When she told him, he looked discouraged. "They'll never show. Not there."

"You're wrong," Bonnie Lamb said. "Where's that gun of yours?"

Augustine went to the living room and switched on the television. He channel-surfed until he found a Monty Python rerun; a classic, John Cleese buying a dead parrot. It never failed to make Augustine laugh.

Bonnie sat beside him on the sofa. When the Monty Python sketch ended, he turned to her and said, "You don't know a damn thing about guns."

# ELEVEN

**Max Lamb awoke** to these words: "You need a legacy."

He and Skink had bummed a ride in the back of a U-Haul truck. They were bucking down U.S. Highway One among two thousand cans of Campbell's broccoli cheese soup, which was being donated to hurricane victims by a Baptist church in Pascagoula, Mississippi. What the shipment lacked in variety it made up for in Christian goodwill.

"This," said the kidnapper, waving at the soup boxes, "is what people do for each other in times of catastrophe. They give help. You, on the other hand—"

"I said I was sorry."

"—you, Max, arrive with a video camera."

Max Lamb lit a cigaret. The governor had been in a rotten mood all day. First his favorite Stones tape broke, then the batteries crapped out in his Walkman.

Skink said, "The people who gave this soup, they went through Camille. Please assure me you know about Camille."

"Another hurricane?"

"A magnificent shitkicker of a hurricane. Max, I believe you're making progress."

The advertising man sucked apprehensively on the

Bronco. He said, "You were talking about getting a boat."

Skink said, "Everyone ought to have a legacy. Something to be remembered for. Let's hear some of your slogans."

"Not right now."

"I never see TV anymore, but some commercials I remember." The kidnapper pointed at the canyon of red-and-white soup cans. "'M'm, m'm good!' That was a classic, no?"

Unabashedly Max Lamb said, "You ever hear of Plum Crunchies? It was a breakfast cereal."

"A cereal," said Skink.

"'You'll go plum loco for Plum Crunchies!'"

The kidnapper frowned. From his camo trousers he produced a small felt box of the type used by jewelry stores. He opened it and removed a scorpion, which he placed on his bare brown wrist. The scorpion raised its fat claws, pinching the air in confusion. Max stared incredulously. The skin on his neck heated beneath the shock collar. He drew up his legs, preparing to spring from the truck if Skink tossed the awful creature at him.

"This little sucker," Skink said, "is from Southeast Asia. Recognized him right away." With a pinkie finger, he stroked the scorpion until it arched its venomous stinger.

Max Lamb asked how a Vietnamese scorpion got all the way to Florida. Skink said it was probably smuggled by importers. "Then, when the hurricane struck, Mortimer here made a dash for it. I found him in the horse barn. Remember Larks? 'Show us your Larks!'"

"Barely." Max was a kid when the Lark campaign hit TV.

Skink said: "That's what I mean by legacy. Does anyone remember who thought up Larks? But the Marlboro man, Christ, that's the most successful ad campaign in history."

It was a fact. Max Lamb wondered how Skink knew. He noticed that the scorpion had become tangled in the gray-blond hair on the captain's arm.

"What are you going to do with it?" Max asked.

No answer. He tried another strategy. "Bonnie is deathly afraid of insects."

Skink scooped the scorpion into the palm of one hand. "This ain't no insect, Max. It's an arachnid."

"Bugs is what I meant, captain. She's terrified of all bugs." Max was speaking for himself. Icy needles of anxiety pricked at his arms and legs. He struggled to connect the kidnapper's scorpion sympathies with his views of the Marlboro man. What was the psychopath trying to say?

"Can she swim, your Bonnie? Then she'll be fine." The governor popped the scorpion in his cheek and swallowed with an audible gulp.

"Oh Jesus," said Max.

After a suitable pause, Skink opened his mouth. The scorpion was curled placidly on his tongue, its pincers at rest.

Max Lamb stubbed out the Bronco and urgently lit another. He leaned his head against a crate of soup cans and said a silent prayer: Dear God, don't let Bonnie say anything to piss this guy off.

Avila's career as a county inspector was unremarkable except for the six months when he was the target of a police investigation. The cops had infiltrated the building department with an undercover man posing as a supervisor. The undercover man noticed, among a multitude of irregularities, that Avila was inspecting new roofs at a superhuman rate of about sixty a day, without benefit of a ladder. A surveillance team was put in place and observed that Avila never bothered to climb the roofs he was assigned to inspect. In fact, he seldom left his vehicle except for a regular two-hour buffet lunch at a nudie bar in Hialeah. It was noted that Avila drove past construction sites at such an impractical speed that contractors frequently had to jog after his truck in order to deliver their illicit gratuities. The transactions were captured with crystal clarity on videotape.

When the police investigation became public, a grand jury convened to ponder the filing of felony indictments. To give the appearance of concern, the building-and-zoning department reassigned Avila and several of his crooked colleagues to duties that were considered low-profile and menial, a status confirmed by the relatively puny size of the bribes. In Avila's case, he was relegated to inspecting mobile homes. It was a job for which he had no qualifications or enthusiasm. Trailers were trailers; to Avila, nothing but glorified sardine cans. The notion of "code enforcement" at a trailer park was oxymoronic; none of them, Avila knew, would survive the feeblest of hurricanes. Why go to the trouble of tying the damn things down?

But he made a show of logging inspections, taking what modest graft the mobile-home dealers would toss his way—fifty bucks here and there, a bottle of Old Grand-dad, porno tapes, an eight-ball of coke. Avila wasn't worried about police surveillance on his beat.

Authorities were concerned with protecting the upwardly mobile middle-class home buyer; nobody gave a shit what happened to people who bought trailers.

Except men like Ira Jackson, whose mother lived in one.

With the exception of the bus depot in downtown Guatemala City, the Dade County building department was the most disorganized and institutionally indifferent place that Ira Jackson had ever seen. It took ninety minutes to find a clerk who admitted to fluency in English, and another hour to get his hands on the documents for the Suncoast Leisure Village trailer park. Under the circumstances, Ira Jackson was mildly surprised that the file still existed. From what he saw, others were vanishing by the carload. Realizing the hurricane would bring scandal to the construction industry, developers, builders and compromised inspectors were taking bold steps to obscure their own roles in the crimes. As Ira Jackson elbowed his way to an empty chair, he recognized—amid the truly aggrieved—faces of the copiously guilty: brows damp, lips tight, eyes pinched and fretful. They were men who feared the prospect of public exposure, massive lawsuits or prison.

If only it were true, thought Ira Jackson. Experience had taught him otherwise. Bozos who rob liquor stores go to jail, not rich guys and bureaucrats and civil servants.

Ira Jackson thumbed through the trailer-court records until he found the name of the man who had botched the inspection of his mother's double-wide. He fought his way to the file counter and cornered a harried-looking clerk, who informed him that Mr Avila no longer was employed by Dade County.

Why not? Ira Jackson asked.

Because he quit, the clerk explained; started his own business. Since Ira Jackson was already agitated, the clerk saw no point in revealing that Avila's resignation was part of a plea-bargain agreement with the State Attorney's Office. That was a private matter that Mr Avila himself should share with Mr Jackson, if he so desired.

Ira Jackson said, "You got a current address, right?"

The clerk said it was beyond his authority to divulge that information. Ira Jackson reached across the counter and rested his hand, very lightly, on the young man's shoulder. "Listen to me, Paco," he said. "I'll come to your home. I'll harm your family. You understand? Even your pets."

The clerk nodded. "Be right back," he said.

Snapper was more annoyed than afraid when he saw the flashing blue lights in the rearview. He'd figured the Jeep Cherokee was already hot when he swiped it from the gangster rappers; he didn't figure the cops would be looking for it so soon. Not with all the hurricane emergencies.

Pulling to the side of the road, he wondered if Baby Raper had blabbed when he got to the hospital. No doubt the kid was ticked when Snapper retrofitted that compact disc up his ass, like a big shiny suppository.

But why would the cops care about *that*? Snapper thought: Maybe it's got nothing do with the gangster rapper or the stolen Jeep. Maybe it's just my driving.

The cop who stopped him was a female Highway Patrol trooper. She had pleasant features and pretty pale-blue eyes that reminded Snapper of a girl he'd tried to date back in Atlanta, some sort of turbocharged Catholic. The lady trooper's dark hair was pulled up under her hat, and she wore a gold wedding band that cried out for pawning. The holster appeared oversized and out of place on her hip. She shined a light in the Jeep and asked to see Snapper's driver's license.

"I left my wallet at home."

"No identification?"

"'Fraid not." For effect, he patted his pockets.

"What's your name?"

"Boris," said Snapper. He loved Boris and Natasha, from the old Rocky and Bullwinkle TV show.

"Boris what?" the trooper asked.

Snapper couldn't spell the cartoon Boris's last name, so he said, "Smith. Boris J. Smith."

The trooper's pale eyes seemed to darken, and the tone of her voice flattened. "Sir, I clocked you at seventy in a forty-five-mile-per-hour zone."

"No kidding." Snapper felt relieved. A stupid speeding ticket! Maybe she'd write him up without running the tag.

The trooper said: "It's against the law to operate a motor vehicle in Florida without a valid license. You're aware of that."

OK, Snapper thought, *two* tickets. Big fucking deal. But he noticed she wasn't calling him "Mister Smith."

"You're also aware that it's illegal to give false information to a law-enforcement officer?"

"Sure." Snapper cursed to himself The bitch wasn't buying it.

"Stay in your vehicle, please."

In the mirror, Snapper watched the flashlight bobbing

as the trooper walked back to her car. Undoubtedly she intended to call in the license plate on the Cherokee. Snapper felt his shoulders tighten. He had as much chance of explaining the stolen vehicle as he did explaining the seven thousand dollars in his suit.

He saw two choices. The first was to flee the scene, which was guaranteed to result in a chase, a messy crash and an arrest on numerous nonbondable felonies.

The second choice was to stop the lady trooper before she got on the radio. Which is what he did.

Some cons wouldn't hit a woman, but Snapper was neutral on the issue. A cop was a cop. The trooper spotted him coming but, encumbered by the steering wheel, had difficulty pulling that enormous Smith & Wesson out of its holster. She managed to get the snap undone, but by then it was good-night-nurse.

He took the flashlight, the gun and the wedding band, and left the trooper lying unconscious by the side of the road. Speeding away, he noticed a smudge of color on one of his knuckles.

Makeup, it looked like.

He didn't feel shame, regret or anything much at all.

Edie Marsh was beginning to appreciate the suffering of real hurricane victims. It rained three times during the day, leaving dirty puddles throughout the Torres house. The carpets squished underfoot, green frogs vaulted from wall to wall, and mosquitoes were hatching in one of the bathroom sinks. Even after the cloudbursts stopped, the exposed beams dripped for hours. Combined with the cacophony of neighborhood hammers and chain saws, the racket was driving Edie nuts. She walked outside and called halfheartedly for the missing dachshunds, an exercise that she abandoned swiftly after spying a fat brown snake. Edie's scream attracted a neighbor, who took a broom and scared the snake away. Then he inquired about Tony and Neria.

They're out of town, said Edie Marsh. They asked me to watch the place.

And you are . . . ?

A cousin, Edie replied, knowing she looked about as Latin as Goldie Hawn.

As soon as the neighbor left, Edie hurried into the house and stationed herself in Tony's recliner. She turned up the radio and laid the crowbar within arm's reach. When darkness came, the hammering and sawing stopped, and the noises of the neighborhood changed to bawling babies, scratchy radios and slamming doors. Edie began worrying about looters and rapists and the unknown predator that had slurped poor Donald and Marla like Tic Tacs. By the time Fred Dove showed up, she was a basket of nerves.

The insurance man brought a corsage of gardenias. Like he was picking her up for the prom!

Edie Marsh said, "You can't be serious."

"What's wrong? I couldn't find roses."

"Fred, I can't stay here anymore. Get me a room."

"Everything's going to be fine. Look, I brought wine."

"Fred?"

"And scented candles."

"Yo, Fred!"

"What?"

Edie steered him to a soggy sofa and sat him down. "Fred, this is business, not romance."

He looked hurt.

"Sweetie," she said, "we had sexual intercourse exactly one time. Don't worry, there's every chance in the world we'll do it again. But it isn't love and it isn't passion. It's a financial partnership."

The insurance man said, "You seduced me."

"Of course I did. And you were fantastic."

As Fred Dove's ego reinflated, his posture improved.

"But no more flowers," Edie scolded, "and no more wine. Just get me a room at the damn Ramada, OK?"

The insurance man solemnly agreed. "First thing tomorrow."

"Look at this place, honey. No roof. No glass in the windows. It's not a house, it's a damn cabana!"

"You're right, Edie, you can't stay here. I'll rejigger the expense account."

She rolled her eyes. "Fred, don't be so anal. We're about to rip off your employer for a hundred and forty-one thousand bucks, and you're pitching a hissy fit over a sixty-dollar motel room. Think about it."

"Please don't get angry."

"You've got the claim papers?"

"Right here."

After scanning the figures, Edie Marsh felt better. She plucked the gardenias from the corsage and arranged them in a coffeepot, which was full of lukewarm rain-water. She opened the bottle of Chablis, and they toasted to a successful venture. After four glasses, Edie felt comfortable enough to ask what the insurance man planned to do with his cut of the money.

"Buy a boat," Fred Dove said, "and sail to Bimini."

"What about wifey?"

"Who?" said Fred Dove. They laughed together. Then he asked Edie Marsh how she was going to spend her seventy-one grand.

"Hyannis Port," she said, without elaboration.

Later, when the Chablis was gone, Edie dragged a dry mattress into the living room, turned off the lightbulb and lit one of Fred Dove's candles, which smelled like malted milk. As Edie took off her clothes, she heard Fred groping inside his briefcase for a rubber. He tore the foil with his teeth and pressed the package into her hand.

Even when she was sober, condoms made Edie laugh. When drunk she found them downright hilarious, the silliest contraptions imaginable. For tonight Fred Dove had boldly chosen a red one, and Edie was no help whatsoever in putting it on. Neither, for that matter, was Fred. Edie's tittering had pretty well shattered the mood, undoing all the good work of the wine.

Flat on his back, the insurance man turned his head away. Edie Marsh slapped his legs apart and knelt between them. "Don't you quit on me," she scolded. "Pay attention, sweetie. Come on." Firmly she took hold of him.

"Could you just—?"

"No." It was always bad form to giggle in the middle of a blow job, and Fred Dove was the sort who'd never recover, emotionally. "Focus," she instructed him. "Remember how good it was last night."

Edie had gotten the condom partially deployed when she heard the electric generator cut off. Out of fuel, she figured. It could wait; Fred Jr was showing signs of life.

She heard a soft click, and suddenly the insurance man's festively crowned penis was illuminated in a circle of bright light. Edie Marsh let go and sat upright. Fred

Dove, his eyes shut tightly in concentration, said, "Don't stop now."

In the front doorway stood a man with a powerful flashlight.

"Candles," he said. "That's real fuckin' cozy."

Fred Dove's chest stopped moving, and one hand fumbled for his eyeglasses. Edie Marsh got up and folded her arms across her breasts. She said, "Thanks for knocking, asshole."

"I came back for my car." Snapper played the light up and down her body.

"It's in the driveway, right where you left it."

"What's the hurry," said Snapper, stepping into the house.

Bonnie Lamb went to Augustine's room at one-thirty in the morning. She climbed under the sheets without brushing against him even slightly. It wasn't easy, in a twin bed.

She whispered, "Are you sleeping?"

"Like a log."

"Sorry."

He rolled over to face her. "You need a pillow?"

"I need a hug."

"Bad idea."

"Why?"

"I'm slightly on the naked side. I wasn't expecting company."

"Apology number two," she said.

"Close your eyes, Mrs Lamb." He got up and pulled on a pair of loose khakis. No shirt, she observed, unalarmed. He slipped under the covers and held her.

His skin was warm and smooth against her cheek, and when he moved she felt a taut, shifting wedge of muscle. Max's physical topography was entirely different, but Bonnie pushed the thought from her mind. It wasn't fair to compare hugging prowess. Not now.

She asked Augustine if he'd ever been married. He said no.

"Engaged?"

"Three times."

Bonnie raised her head. "You're kidding."

"Unfortunately not." In the artificial twilight, Augustine saw she was smiling. "This amuses you?"

"Intrigues me," she said. "Three times?"

"They all came to their senses."

"We're talking about three different women. No repeats?"

"Correct," said Augustine.

"I've got to ask what happened. You don't have to answer, but I've got to ask."

"Well, the first one married a successful personal-injury lawyer—he's doing class-action breast-implant litigation; the second one started an architecture firm and is currently a mistress to a Venezuelan cabinet minister; and the third one is starring on a popular Cuban soap opera—she plays Miriam, the jealous schizophrenic. So I would say," Augustine concluded, "that each of them made a wise decision by ending our relationship."

Bonnie Lamb said, "I bet you let them keep the engagement rings."

"Hey, it's only money."

"And you still watch the soap opera, don't you?"

"She's quite good in it. Very convincing."

Bonnie said, "What an unusual guy."

"You feeling better? My personal problems always seem to cheer people up."

She put her head down. "I'm worried about tomorrow, about seeing Max again."

Augustine told her it was normal to be nervous. "I'm a little antsy myself."

"Will you bring the gun?"

"Let's play it by ear." He seriously doubted if the governor would appear, much less deliver Bonnie's husband.

"Are you scared?" When she spoke, he could feel her soft breath on his chest.

"Restless," he said, "not scared."

"Hey."

"Hey what?"

"You getting excited?"

Augustine shifted in embarrassment. What did she expect? He said, "My turn to apologize."

But she didn't move. So he took a slow quiet breath and tried to focus on something else . . . say, Uncle Felix's fugitive monkeys. How far had they scattered? How were they coping with freedom?

Augustine's self-imposed pondering was interrupted when Bonnie Lamb said: "What if Max is different now? Maybe something's happened to him."

Augustine thought: Something's happened, all right. You can damn sure bet on it.

But what he told Bonnie was: "Your husband's hanging in there. You wait and see."

# TWELVE

**Skink said,** "Care for some toad?"

The shock collar had done its job; Max Lamb was unconditionally conditioned. If the captain wanted him to smoke toad, he would smoke toad.

"It's an offer, not a command," Skink said, by way of clarification.

"Then no, thanks."

Max Lamb squinted into the warm salty night. Somewhere out there, Bonnie was searching. Max was neither as anxious nor as hopeful as he should have been, and he wondered why; his reaction to practically every circumstance was muted, as if key brain synapses had been cauterized by the ordeal of the kidnapping. For instance, he had failed to raise even a meek objection at the Key Biscayne golf course, where they'd stopped to free the Asian scorpion. Skink had tenderly deposited the venomous bug in the cup on the eighteenth green. "The mayor's favorite course," he'd explained. "Call me an optimist." Max had stood by wordlessly.

Now they were on a wooden stilt house in the middle of the bay. Skink dangled his long legs off the end of a dock, which was twisted and buckled like a Chinese parade dragon. The hurricane had sucked the wooden pilings from their holes. Most of the other stilt houses were shorn at the stems, but this one had outlasted the storm, though barely. It lurched and creaked in the thickish breeze; Max Lamb suspected it was sinking with the tide. Skink said the house belonged to a man who'd retired on disability from the State Attorney's Office. The man recently had married a beautiful twelve-string guitarist and moved to the island of Exuma.

Under a swinging lantern, Skink lighted another exotic-smelling joint; marijuana and French onion soup, thought Max Lamb. Something strong and cheesy.

"The toad itself is toxic," Skink explained. "*Bufo marinus*. A South American import—overran the local species. Sound familiar?" He took a long sibilant drag. "The glands of Señor Bufo perspire a milky sap that can kill a full-grown Doberman in six minutes flat."

To Max, it didn't sound like a substance that one should be inhaling.

"There's a special process," Skink said, "of extraction." He took another huge hit.

"What does it do, this toad sap?"

"Nothing. Everything. What all good drugs do, I suppose. Psychoneurotic roulette." Skink's chin dropped to his chest. His good eye fluttered and closed. His breathing rose to a startling volume; the exhalations sounded like the brakes of a subway train. For fifteen minutes Max Lamb didn't make a move; the notion to escape never occurred to him, such was the Pavlovian influence of the collar.

In the interval of enforced suspension, Max's thoughts drifted to Bill Knapp up at Rodale. The scheming viper undoubtedly had his sights on Max's corner office, with its partially obstructed but nonetheless energizing view of Madison Avenue. Each day lost to the ambivalent kidnapper was a potential day of advancement for Billy the Backstabber; Max Lamb was burning to return to the agency and crush the devious little fucker's ambitions. Brutal humiliation was called for, and Max hoped he was up to the task. Darkly he imagined Billy Knapp a jobless, wifeless, homeless, toothless wretch, hunched over a can of Sterno in a wintry alley, sucking on a moist spliff laced with poisonous toad sweat . . .

When Skink snapped awake, he coughed hard and flipped the butt of the dead joint into the storm-silted water. Not far from the house, the broken mast of a submerged sailboat protruded from the waves. Skink pointed at the ghostly wreck but said nothing. His leathery finger stayed in the air for an exceptionally long time.

"Tell me," he said to Max Lamb, "the most breathtaking place you've ever seen."

"Yellowstone Park. We took a bus tour."

"Good God."

"So what?"

"Outside Yellowstone they've got a grizzly-bear theme park. Did you go? I mean, some truly sad cases—no claws, no testicles. They're about as wild as goddamn hamsters, but tourists line up to see 'em. Deballed grizzly bears!"

Rapidly Skink shook his head back and forth, as if trying to roust a bumblebee from his ear. Max Lamb wasn't sure how the conversation had gone so far astray. He did not share the madman's compassion for the altered grizzly bears; removing the claws seemed an entirely sensible procedure, liability-wise, for a public amusement park. But Max knew there was no percentage in arguing. He remained quiet as Skink withdrew into a heap on the planks of the spavined deck. The kidnapper trembled and heaved and cried out names that Max Lamb didn't recognize. A half hour later he was up, scouting the starlit horizons.

"You all right?" Max asked.

Skink nodded soberly. "The down side of toad. I do apologize."

"Are you sure Bonnie can find us out here?"

"Why in the name of God would you marry a woman who can't follow simple directions?"

"But it's so dark—"

The trip to Stiltsville had frightened Max Lamb beyond exclamation—full throttle, no running lights, a wet nasty chop in an open skiff. Infinitely more harrowing than the airboat. The hurricane had turned the bay into a spectral gauntlet of sunken yachts, trawlers, cabin cruisers and runabouts. On the way out, Skink had removed his glass eye and pressed it, for safekeeping, into the palm of Max's right hand. Max had clenched it as if it were the Hope diamond.

"Your wife," Skink was saying, "will surely hook up with somebody who knows the way."

"I could use a cigaret. Please, captain."

Skink groped in his coat until he came up with a fresh pack. He tossed it, along with a lighter, to his captive.

Max Lamb was embarrassed that he'd so quickly become hooked on the infamously harsh Broncos. Around the agency they were jokingly known as Bronchials, such was their killer reputation with anti-smoking zealots. Max attributed his hazardous new habit to severe stress, not a weakness of character. In the advertising business it was essential to remain immune from the base appetites that tyrannized the average consumer.

Skink said: "What else have you to show for yourself?"

"I'm not sure what you mean."

"Slogans, tiger. Besides the Plum Crispies."

"Crunchies," said Max, tightly.

The dock shimmied as Skink rose to his feet. Max braced himself against a half-rotted beam. There was nowhere to go; the old man who ferried them across the bay had snatched Skink's fifty dollars and hastily aimed the skiff back toward the mainland.

Skink swung the lantern around and around his head. Caught in the erratic strobe, Max said, "All right, captain, here's one: 'That fresh good-morning feeling, all day long.'"

"Product name?"

"Intimate Mist."

"No!" The lantern hissed as Skink put it down.

Max tried not to sound defensive. "It's a feminine hygiene item. Very popular."

"The raspberry rinse! Sweet Jesus, I thought you were joking. This is the sum of your life achievements—*douche* jingles?"

"No," Max snapped. "Soft drinks, gasoline additives, laser copiers—I've worked on plenty of accounts." He wondered what had impelled him to mention the Intimate Mist campaign. Was it an unconscious act of masochism, or carelessness caused by fatigue?

Skink sat heavily on the porch, which was canted at an alarming angle toward the bay. "I do hear a boat," he said.

Max stared curiously across the water. He heard nothing but the slap of waves and the scattered piping of seagulls. He asked, "What happens now?"

There was no reply. Max Lamb saw, in the yellow flicker of the lantern, a smile cross the crazy man's face.

"You seriously don't want any ransom?"

"I didn't say that. *Money* is what I don't want."

"Then what?" Max flicked his cigaret into the water. "Tell me what the hell it's all about. I'm sick of this game, I really am!"

Skink was amused by the display of anger. Maybe there was hope for the precious little bastard. "What I want," he said to Max Lamb, "is to spend some time with your wife. She intrigues me."

"In what way?"

"Clinically. Anthropologically. What in the world does she see in you? How do you two fit?" Skink gave a mischievous wink. "I like mysteries."

"If you touch her—"

"What a brave young stud!"

Max Lamb took two steps toward the madman, but froze when Skink raised a hand to his own throat. *The collar!* Max felt a hot sizzle shoot from his scalp down the length of his spine. Instantly he foresaw himself hopping like a puppet. Had he known that the battery in the Tri-Tronics remote control had been dead for the past six hours, it wouldn't have softened his reaction. He was a slave to his subconscious. He had come to understand that the anticipation of pain was more immobilizing than the pain itself—though the knowledge didn't help him.

When Max settled down, Skink assured him he had no carnal interest in his wife. "Christ, I'm not trying to get laid; I'm trying to figure out man's place in the food chain." His long arms swept an arc across the stars. "A riddle of the times, Tourist Boy. Five thousand years ago we're doodling on the walls of caves. Today we're writing odes to fruit-flavored douche."

"It's a job," Max Lamb replied petulantly. "Get over it."

Skink yawned like a gorged hyena. "That's a damn big engine coming. I hope your Bonnie wasn't foolish enough to call the police."

"I warned her not to."

Skink went on: "My opinion about your wife will be shaped by how she handles this situation. Whom she brings. Her attitude. Her composure."

Max Lamb asked Skink if he had a gun. Skink clicked his tongue against his front teeth. "See the running lights?"

"No."

"Toward Key Biscayne. Over there."

"Oh, yeah."

"Two engines, it sounds like. I'm guessing twin Mercs."

Somebody aboard the boat had a powerful spotlight. It swept back and forth across the flats of Stiltsville. As the craft drew nearer, the white light settled on the porch of the stilt house. Skink seemed unconcerned.

He began to remove toads from his pockets; gray, jowly, scowling, lump-covered toads, some as large as Idaho potatoes. Max Lamb counted eleven. Skink lined them up side by side at his feet. Max had nothing to add to the scenario, perhaps it was all a dream, beginning with the mangy hurricane monkey, and soon he'd awaken in bed with Bonnie. . . .

The pudgy Bufo toads began to squirm and huff and pee. Skink rebuked them with a murmur. When the beam of the speedboat's spotlight hit them, the toads blinked their moist globular eyes and jumped toward it. One by one they leaped off the dock and plopped into the water. Skink hooted mirthfully. "South, boys! To Havana, San Juan, wherever the hell you came from!"

Max watched the toads disappear; some kicked for the depths, others bobbed on the foamy crests of waves. Max didn't know what would happen to them, nor did he care. They were just ugly toads, and barracudas could devour them, as far as he was concerned. His only interest was in drawing a lesson from the episode, one that might be employed to handle the cyclopean kidnapper.

But Skink already seemed to have forgotten about the Bufos. Once more he was rhapsodizing about the hurricane. "Look at Cape Florida, every last tree flattened—forest to moonscape in thirty blessed minutes!"

"The boat—"

"You ponder that."

"It's flashing a light at us—"

"The gorgeous fury inside that storm. And you with your video camera." Skink sighed disappointedly. "'Sin is a thing that writes itself across a man's face.' Oscar Wilde. I don't expect you've read him."

Max's silence affirmed it.

"Well, I've been waiting," said Skink, "to see it written across your face. Sin."

"What I did was harmless, OK? Maybe a bit insensitive, but harmless. You've made your point, captain. Let me go now."

The speedboat was close enough to see it was metallic

blue with a white jagged stripe, like a lightning bolt, along the hull. Two figures were visible at the console.

"There she is," said Max.

"And no cops." Skink waved the boat in.

One of the figures moved to the bow and tossed a rope. Skink caught it and tied off. As soon as the rope came tight, the twin outboards went quiet. The current nudged the stern of the boat against the pilings, into the lantern's penumbra.

Max Lamb saw that it was Bonnie on the bow. When he called her name, she stepped to the dock and hugged him in a nurselike fashion, consoling him as if he were a toddler with a skinned knee. Max received the attention with manly reserve; he was conscious of being watched not only by his captor but by Bonnie's male escort.

Skink smiled at the reunion scene, and slipped back into the shadows of the stilt house. The driver of the boat made no move to get out. He was young and broad-shouldered, and comfortable on the open water. He wore a pale-blue pullover, cutoffs and no shoes. He seemed unaffected by navigating a pitch-black bay mined with overturned hulls and floating timbers.

From the darkness, Skink asked the young man for his name.

"Augustine," he answered.

"You have the ransom?"

"Sure do."

Bonnie Lamb said: "Don't worry, he's not the police."

"I can see that," came Skink's voice.

The boat driver stepped to the gunwale. He handed Bonnie a shopping bag, which she gave to her husband, who handed it to the kidnapper in the shadows.

Max Lamb said: "Bonnie, honey, the captain wants to talk to you. Then he'll let me go."

"I'm considering it," Skink said.

"Talk to me about what?"

The driver of the boat reached inside the console and came out with a can of beer. He took a swallow and leaned one hip against the steering wheel.

Bonnie Lamb asked her husband: "What's that on your neck?" It looked like some appalling implement of bondage; she'd seen similar items in the display windows of leather shops in Greenwich Village.

Skink came into the light. "It's a training device. Lie down, Max."

Bonnie Lamb studied the tall, disheveled stranger. He was all the state trooper had promised, and more. In size he appeared capable of anything, yet Bonnie felt in no way threatened.

"Max, now!" the kidnapper said to her husband.

Obediently Max Lamb lay prone on the wooden dock. When Skink told him to roll over, like a dog, he did.

Bonnie was embarrassed for her husband. The kidnapper noticed, and apologized. He instructed Max to get up.

The shopping bag contained everything Skink had demanded. Within moments the new batteries were inserted in the Walkman, and "Tumbling Dice" was spilling out of his earphones. He opened the jar of green olives and poured them into his gleaming bucket of a mouth.

Bonnie Lamb asked Max what in God's name was going on.

"Later," he whispered.

"Tell me now!"

"She deserves to know," the kidnapper interjected, spraying olive juice. "She's risking her life, being out here with a nutcase like me."

Bonnie Lamb had dressed for a boat ride—blue slicker, jeans and deck shoes. Good stuff but practical, Skink noticed, none of that catalog nonsense from California. He pulled off the earphones and complimented Bonnie for her common sense. Then he instructed her husband to remove the shock collar and toss it in the sea.

Max's hands quavered at his neck. Skink told him to go ahead, dammit, off with it! Max's lips tightened in determination, but he couldn't make himself touch it. Finally it was his wife who stepped forward, unhooked the clasp and removed the Tri-Tronics dog trainer. She examined it in the light of the lantern.

"Sick," she said to Skink, and set the collar on the dock.

From his jacket he took a videotape cassette. He tossed it to Bonnie Lamb, who caught it with both hands. "Your hubbie's home movies from the hurricane. Talk about sick."

Bonnie wheeled and threw the cassette into the bay.

The girl had fire! Skink liked her already. Nervously Max lighted a cigaret.

His wife wouldn't have been more repulsed had he jabbed a hypodermic full of heroin in his arm. She said, "Since when do you smoke?"

"If you put the collar back on him," Skink volunteered helpfully, "I can teach him to quit."

Max Lamb told Skink to get on with it. "You said you wanted to talk to her, so talk."

"No, I said I wanted to spend time with her."

Bonnie turned toward the barefoot young man at the helm of the striped speedboat. He apparently had nothing to say. His demeanor was casual, almost bored.

"Where," Bonnie asked the kidnapper, "did you want to spend time? And doing what?"

"Not what you think," Max Lamb cut in.

Skink put on his plastic shower cap. "The hurricane has set me on a new rhythm. I feel it ticking."

He put his hands on Bonnie's shoulders, gently moving her to Max's side. From the governor's shadow she felt his stare. He was studying them, her and Max, like they were lab rats. Then she heard him mutter: "I still don't see how."

Tersely Bonnie said, "Just tell us what you want."

"Watch it," Max advised. "He's been smoking dope."

Skink looked away, toward the ocean. "No offense, Mrs Lamb, but your husband has put me sorely off the human race. A feminine counterpoint would be nice."

Bonnie was surprised by a pleasurable shiver, goose-flesh rising on her neck. The stranger's voice was soothing and hypnotic, a wild broad river; she could have listened to him all night. Mad is what he was, demonstrably mad. But his story fascinated her. Once a governor, the trooper had said. Bonnie longed to know more.

Yet here was her husband, exhausted, sunburned, emotionally sapped. She ought to tend to him. Poor Max had been through hell.

"I only want to talk," the kidnapper said.

"All right," Bonnie told him, "but just for a little while."

He cupped a hand to his mouth. "You, Augustine! Take Mister Lamb to safety. He needs a shower and a shave and possibly a stool softener. Return at dawn for his wife."

Skink grabbed Max under the arms and lowered him to the speedboat. He cut the line with a pocketknife, pushing the bow away from the sagging stilt house. He flung one arm around Bonnie and with the other began to wave. As the boat drifted out of the lantern's glow, Skink saw a third figure rise in the stern of the boat—where had *he* been hiding? Then the young man at the wheel brought a rifle to his shoulder.

"Damn," said Skink, pushing Bonnie Lamb from the line of fire.

Something stung him fiercely, spinning him clockwise and down. He was still spinning when he hit the warm water, and wondering why his arms and legs weren't working, wondering why he hadn't heard a shot or seen a muzzle flash, wondering if perhaps he was already dead.

# THIRTEEN

**Late on the night** of August 27, with a warm breeze at his back and nine cold Budweisers in his belly, Keith Higstrom decided to go hunting. His friends declined to accompany him, as Keith was as clumsy and unreliable a shooter as he was a drunk.

Truthfully there wasn't much to hunt in South Florida, the wild game having long ago fled or died. However, the hurricane had dispersed throughout the suburbs an exotic new quarry: livestock. Mile upon mile of ranch posts in rural Dade County had been uprooted, freeing herds of cattle and horses to explore vistas beyond their mucky flooded pastures. Motivated more by dull hunger than by native inquisitiveness, the animals began appearing in places where they were not customarily encountered. One such place was Keith Higstrom's neighborhood, a subdivision of indistinguishable clam-colored houses, stacked twenty deep and twenty-five across and bordered on every side by bankrupt strip shopping malls.

It was here Keith Higstrom had spent his childhood. His father's family had moved to Miami from northern Minnesota in the early 1940s bringing an affinity for long guns and an appetite for the great outdoors. An impressionable boy, Keith had listened to hunting yarns his entire life—timber wolves and trophy black bears in the north woods, white-tailed deer and wild turkeys in the Florida scrub. The head of an eight-point buck, stoic but marble-eyed, hung over the Higstrom dinner table; the tawny pelt of a prized panther was tacked spread-eagle on the west wall of the den. At age five, Keith began collecting in leatherbound volumes each edition of *Outdoor Life, Field & Stream* and *Sports Afield*. His most treasured possession was an autographed photo of the famous Joe Foss, standing over a dead grizzly. At age six, young Keith got a Daisy popgun, a BB pistol at age nine, a pellet rifle at age eleven, and his first .22 at thirteen.

Yet . . . even plinking beer cans at the local rock pit, the boy displayed an unfailing lack of proficiency with firearms. His father was more than slightly disappointed. Young Keith was a pure menace with a gun. Practice brought no improvement, nor did experimenting with different styles of weapons. Scopes didn't help. Tripods didn't help. Recoil cushions didn't help. Even goddamn breathing exercises didn't help.

Often these father–son target practices disintegrated into sulking and tears until the elder Higstrom relented, allowing young Keith to fire a few rounds with a twelve-gauge Mossberg, just so he could have the experience of hitting *something*. Clearly the family lineage of crack dead-eye shots had come to a sorry end. Keith's father returned from these outings looking pale and shaken, although he said nothing to Keith's mother about what he'd witnessed at the rock pit.

Fortunately, by the time Keith was old enough to go out hunting, there was practically nothing left to shoot in Miami except for rats and low-flying seagulls. Every autumn, Keith badgered his father into taking him to the Big Cypress Swamp or private hunting camps in the Everglades, where the deer were chased into high water by airboats and shot at point-blank range. The elder Higstrom dreaded these excursions and found no sport in the killing, but his son couldn't have been happier had he been lobbing grenades at crippled fawns.

It was on one such miserable morning that Keith Higstrom's father swore off hunting forever. They were riding a tank-sized swamp buggy in hot pursuit of a scraggly, half-senile bobcat. Suddenly Keith began firing wildly at an object high in the sky—a bald eagle, it turned out, a federally protected species. The attempted felony was not consummated, due to the young man's shaky aim, but in the fever of the moment he managed to blow off his father's left ear.

Deafened, blood-drenched, writhing facedown in Everglades marl, the elder Higstrom experienced a peculiar catharsis, an unexpected soothing of the soul, as if a cool white sheet were slowly being drawn over his head. Yes, his injury was terrible, and the deafness would (if he came clean about it) cost him his job as an air traffic controller. On the other hand, he could never again be forced to go hunting with his excitable son!

Keith Higstrom couldn't duck responsibility for the accident, nor the guilt that went with it. His father recovered from the gunshot wound, and was kind enough not to bring it up more than once or twice a day. Before long, Keith's remorse gave way to an unspoken resentment, for he perceived that his father was using the missing ear as an excuse to avoid their weekend expeditions. A plastic surgeon had attached a durable polyurethane facsimile to the left side of the elder

Higstrom's head, while a high-tech hearing aid had restored the old man's auditory capacity to eighty-one percent of what it was before the Everglades mishap. Yet he stubbornly refused to pick up a gun. Doctor's orders, he squawked.

For Keith, outdoor companionship was increasingly hard to come by. His friends always seemed to have prior commitments whenever Keith invited them to go hunting. Frustrated and restless, he spent long sullen weekends cleaning his guns and watching videotapes of his favorite *American Sportsman* episodes. Whenever his trigger finger got itchy, he'd drive out the Tamiami Trail and park by the canal. As soon as darkness fell, Keith would load a double-barrel shotgun, strap on a head-lamp and stalk along the shoreline. His usual targets were turtles and opossums; anything faster or smarter generally eluded him.

Shortly after the hurricane, Keith Higstrom noticed four dairy cows and a palomino mare grazing on his neighbor's front lawn. Everyone on the block was gathered on the sidewalk, laughing and taking pictures; a light moment of relief in the otherwise somber aftermath of the storm. That night, drinking with his buddies at an Irish bar on Kendall Drive, Keith asked: "How much does a cow weigh?"

One of Keith's friends said, "I give up, Higstrom. How much does a cow weigh?"

"It's not a joke. More than an elk? Because I got cows loose on my street."

One of his friends said, "From the hurricane."

"Yeah, but how big do you figure? More than a mulie?" Keith Higstrom drained his Budweiser and stood up. "Let's go hunting, boys."

"Sit down, Higstrom."

"You pussies coming or not?"

"Have another beer, Keith."

With a burp, he charged out the door. He drove home, slipped into the den, and removed his grandfather's old .30-06 from the maple gun cabinet. He dropped a box of bullets, and giggled drunkenly when nobody woke up. He pulled on his boots and his mail-order camo jumpsuit, strapped on the headlamp, and went looking for a cow to shoot.

They were no longer grazing in his neighbor's front yard. Dropping into an exaggerated half crouch, Keith Higstrom weaved down the block. He felt light as a feather, lethal as a snake. The rifle was slick and magnificent in his hands. His plan was to tie the dead cow on the front fender of his Honda Civic and drive all the way back to Kendall, back to the Irish bar where his chickenshit pals were drinking. Keith Higstrom chuckled in advance at the spectacle.

For cover he used mounds of hurricane debris, shuffling noisily from one to another. The street was empty and black and shadowless; the homes on the north side still had no electricity. Passing the Ullmans' house, Keith Higstrom heard something in the backyard—deep raspy snorting. He thought it might be the runaway palomino. As he snuck around the corner of the garage, the beam of Keith Higstrom's headlamp illuminated a pair of glistening indigo eyes, as large as ashtrays.

"God damn," he exclaimed.

An enormous animal stood next to the Ullmans' half-drained swimming pool. The light from Keith's headlamp played up and down its blue-black flanks. This was no ordinary cow. For starters, it was as big as a tractor.

Its sharp horns were lavishly curved and downslung, upside down from those of domestic American stock.

Keith Higstrom knew exactly what he was looking at. Hadn't he watched Jimmy Dean and Curt Gowdy shoot one of the very same majestic bastards on *The American Sportsman*? But that was in Africa, for Christ's sake. Not Miami, Florida.

It occurred to Keith that he might be suffering the effects of too much alcohol, that the gigantic oval-eyed ungulate glaring at him was merely a Budweiser-enhanced Angus.

Then it snorted again, expelling twin strings of dewy snot. The animal lowered its head and, with hooves the size of laundry irons, decisively pawed a trench in the Ullmans' newly replanted Bermuda sod.

"Shit on a biscuit," Keith Higstrom said, raising his grandfather's rifle. "That's a Cape buffalo!"

He fired and, naturally, missed. Twice.

The gunshots awakened Mr Ullman, a banker by trade and a recent arrival from Copenhagen, who looked out the bedroom window just in time to see a tremendous bull galloping across his yard with a thrashing young American impaled on its rack. Mr Ullman quickly telephoned the police and informed them, as urgently as his newly acquired English would allow, that an "unlucky cowboy is being perforated seriously." Eventually the police figured out what Mr Ullman was trying to say.

Two hours later, a police dispatcher phoned Augustine's house with a message: His dead uncle's missing Cape buffalo, identified by an ear tag, had turned up in the produce aisle of a storm-gutted supermarket. Unfortunately, there was trouble. The dispatcher requested that Augustine call Animal Control as soon as possible.

Augustine didn't check his answering machine for several hours, because he was out on Biscayne Bay with Bonnie Lamb.

They had borrowed the speedboat from one of Augustine's friends, an airline pilot. The pilot owed Augustine a favor from a long-ago divorce, when Augustine had let him bury $45,000 worth of gold Krugerrands behind Augustine's garage, to conceal them from his future ex-wife's private investigator. After the divorce litigation ended, the airline pilot was left with nothing but the hidden stash of coins. He immediately depleted them on a ninety-one-pound fashion model, who later abandoned him at a five-star hotel in Morocco. Although years had passed, the pilot never forgot Augustine's act of friendship in a time of personal crisis.

The speedboat was on a trailer at a marina in North Miami Beach, untouched by the hurricane. Augustine and Bonnie Lamb met Jim Tile there. His eyes were red and his voice was raw. He told them that a close friend, a female trooper, had been savagely beaten by a car thief, and that he would have preferred to be out on road patrol, hunting for the gutless low-life sonofabitch.

As distracted as he was, Jim Tile also seemed visibly anxious about the boat trip. Even in the dark, the bay looked rough and tricky. Oddly, Bonnie Lamb wasn't worried. Maybe it was the way Augustine handled himself behind the wheel; steering casually with two fingers as he aimed, with his free hand, the spotlight.

Smoothly he weaved around massive tree limbs and wind-split lumber and ghostly capsized hulls. The scary ride temporarily took Jim Tile's mind off the image of Brenda on an ambulance stretcher. . . .

Bonnie was anticipating her first sight of the man called Skink. She kept thinking about the bloodied corpse in the morgue—impaled on a TV dish, the trooper had said. Was Skink the killer? To hear the trooper tell it, the ex-governor was not a nut of the certifiable, Mansonesque strain. Rather, he was launched on a mission: a reckless doomed mission, boisterously outside the law. Bonnie was intrigued by bold eccentrics. She wasn't afraid of Skink, not with the trooper and Augustine at her side. In an odd way, although she'd never admit it, she looked forward to confronting the kidnapper almost as much as to reuniting with her husband. . . .

Now Jim Tile and Augustine were struggling to drag the unconscious man over the gunwale of the speedboat. His clothes were soaked, adding to his considerable bulk. Bonnie Lamb tried to help. Augustine got a silvery handful of the man's hair, the trooper had him by the belt loops, Bonnie dug her fingers in the tongues of his boots—and finally the kidnapper was on the deck, vomiting seawater.

From the bow came a whine of disgust: Max Lamb, arms folded, face pinched, sucking a Bronco cigaret. Bonnie turned back to the tranquilized stranger. The trooper knelt beside him. With a handkerchief he cleaned the foul splatter off Skink's face; the glass eye needed special attention.

Augustine said, "He's breathing."

A volcanic cough, and then: "I saw lobsters big as Sonny Liston." Skink raised his head.

Jim Tile said, "Be still now."

"My Walkman!"

"We'll get you a new one. Now lie still."

Skink lowered his head with a sharp clunk. Humming, he shut both eyes.

Bonnie Lamb asked, "What do we do with him?"

Max laughed acidly. "He's going to jail, what'd you think?"

Bonnie looked at Augustine, who said, "It's up to Jim. He's the law."

The trooper had a thermos open, trying to get some hot coffee into his groggy friend. Bonnie put her hands under the kidnapper's head to help him drink. Augustine went to the console and started the boat. Over the noise of the engines, Bonnie asked Jim Tile if she should sit with the man during the ride back, in case he got ill again. The trooper leaned close and in a low voice said: "He's all right now. Go check on your husband."

"OK," Bonnie said. She was glad for the darkness, so the trooper couldn't see her blush. Neither could Max.

The conversation between Gar Whitmark and his wife was not a loving one. That she had handed seven thousand cash to a band of crooked roofers was infuriating enough; that she had failed to ask the name of the one taking the money was unforgivably stupid. The only clue in tracking the thieves was the piece of yellow paper that had been given by the phony roofing foreman to Mrs Whitmark, the yellow paper intended to double as a receipt and an estimate, the yellow paper that Mrs Whitmark had instantly misplaced.

Gar Whitmark's anger had another facet. He was by

trade a builder of residential subdivisions, and was therefore personally familiar with every honest, competent roofer in Dade County. The list was not voluminous, but from it Gar Whitmark had intended to select the crew that would rebuild the roof of his gutted home. He'd left messages with a half-dozen companies, and had explained (repeatedly) to his wife that it would take time to line up the job. The hurricane had launched a drooling Klondike stampede among roofers—the best ones were swamped with emergency work and likely would be engaged for months to come. Meanwhile out-of-towners were pouring into Miami by the truckload; some were capable and experienced, some were hapless and inept, and many were gypsy impostors. All arrived to find boundless opportunity.

The typical hurricane victim, frantic for shelter, was forced to trust his instincts when choosing a roof builder. Unfortunately, the instincts of the typical hurricane victim in such matters were not acute. Gar Whitmark, however, had the twin advantages of knowing the cast of characters and possessing the clout to divert the best of them to his own pressing needs. With little trouble he located a top-notch roofer who agreed to put all other contracts aside to tackle Gar Whitmark's roof (Whitmark being one of the most prolific home builders—and employers of roofing contractors—in all South Florida). However, the craftsman whom Whitmark selected first had to replace two other roofs: his own, and that of his wife's mother.

Gar Whitmark gave the man seven days to patch up the family roofs. The delay proved unbearable for Mrs Whitmark, whose roaring anxiety at the chance of more rain-stained Chippendales was no match for her customary palliative dosages of sedatives, muscle relaxants, sleep aids and mood elevators. To Mrs Whitmark, the unexpected appearance of willing roofers at the door had been a godsend. She thought her husband would be grateful for her initiative—it would be one less problem for him to worry about, what with all the nasty threats of negligence suits from customers whose Whitmark Signature homes had disintegrated like soggy cardboard in the hurricane.

Standing in the living room, the rain beating a tattoo on his blue-veined forehead, Gar Whitmark instructed his wife to immediately locate the goddamn receipt or estimate or whatever the goddamn so-called foreman had called it. After an hour's search, the crucial yellow paper turned up neatly folded in Mrs Whitmark's high-school yearbook; Gar Whitmark couldn't imagine why his wife had put it there, or how she found it. Nor could she explain it herself—her brain was too jumbled by the hurricane.

The receipt bore the name of "Fortress Roofing," which brought a bitter cackle from Gar Whitmark. At least the scammers had a sense of irony! Gar Whitmark dialed the number and got an answering machine. He hung up and called the director of the county building-and-zoning department, who owed his job to seven of the county commissioners, who owed their jobs to Gar Whitmark's generous campaign contributions. As Gar Whitmark anticipated, the building director expressed shock and alarm that a fraud was perpetrated on Gar Whitmark's wife, and promised a thorough criminal investigation.

No, he hadn't ever heard of Fortress Roofing—but he'd damn sure find out who was behind it.

Sooner the better, said Gar Whitmark, toweling the

rainwater from his stinging scalp, which bristled with fifty pink-stemmed, freshly implanted hair plugs.

Fifteen minutes later, the building director phoned back to report, mournfully, that Fortress Roofing had never obtained a valid Dade County contractor's license and was therefore an unknown outlaw entity.

In a fury, Gar Whitmark began contacting roofers he knew—some honest, some not. The name Fortress struck a note with one or two, who said they'd recently lost crew to the new company. The sonofabitch owner, they said, was an ex-inspector named Avila. Dirty as they come, the roofers warned.

Gar Whitmark knew Avila quite well, having successfully bribed him for many years. All those times Gar Whitmark's subcontractors had slipped booty to the greedy bastard! Cash, booze, porn—Avila had a taste for the hard stuff; girl-on-girl, if Gar Whitmark remembered correctly.

He called his secretary, whose fingers swiftly punched up a highly confidential computer file of corrupt and/or corruptible officials in Dade, Broward, Palm Beach, Lee and Monroe Counties. It was a lengthy roster, alphabetized for convenience. Avila's name and unlisted home phone number winked fatefully at the bottom of the first screen.

Gar Whitmark waited until three in the morning before phoning.

"This is your old friend Gar Whitmark," he said. "Your crew of gypsy fakers hit my wife for seven grand. My wife is not well, Avila. If I don't see my money by tomorrow morning, you'll be in the county jail by tomorrow night. And I will arrange for you to share a cell with Paul Pick-Percy."

The threat brutally jarred Avila wide awake. Paul Pick-Percy was a notorious cannibal. Currently he awaited trial on charges of killing and eating his landlord, who had neglected to repair a leaky ball cock in Paul Pick-Percy's toilet tank. Recently Paul Pick-Percy had also been found guilty of killing and eating a tardy cable-TV repairman and a rude tollbooth attendant.

Avila said: "Seven thousand? Mister Whitmark, I swear to God I don't know nothing about this."

"Suit yourself—"

"Wait, now hold on. . . ." Avila sat upright in bed. "Tell me supposedly what happened, OK?"

"There is no fucking 'supposedly.'" Gar Whitmark related his wife's pitiable tale.

"And the truck was ours, you're sure?"

"I'm holding the receipt, dipshit. 'Fortress Roofing' is what it says."

Avila grimaced. "Who signed it?"

Gar Whitmark said the signature was illegible. "My wife said the guy had a fucked-up jaw made him look like a moray eel. Plus he wore a bad suit."

"Shit," Avila said. Exactly what he'd feared.

"Is this ringing a bell?" Gar Whitmark's sarcasm was heavy and ominous.

Avila sagged against the headboard of his bed. "Sir, you'll get your money back first thing."

"Damn straight. And a new roof as well."

"What?"

"You heard me, noodle dick. The seven grand your people stole, plus you're picking up the bill when my new roof gets done. By real roofers."

Avila's stomach pitched. Gar Whitmark probably lived in a goddamn ranch house way down south, with all the other millionaires. Avila figured he'd be looking at twenty thousand, easy, for a new roof job. He said, "That ain't really fair."

"You'd rather do dinner with Chef Pick-Percy?"

"Aw, Christ, Mister Whitmark."

"I didn't think so."

Avila got out of bed and went to the backyard to round up two roosters, which he took to the garage for beheading. He hoped the sacrifice would be favorably received. After a short scuffle, the deed was done. Avila dripped the warm blood into a plastic pail filled with pennies, bleached cat bones and turtle shells. The pail was placed at the feet of a ceramic statue of Chango, the saint of lightning and fire. The child-sized statue wore a robe, colored beads and a gold-plated crown. Kneeling in beseechment, Avila raised his blood-flecked arms toward the heavens and asked Chango to please strike Snapper dead as a fucking doornail for screwing up the roofer scam.

Avila wasn't sure the ceremony would work. He was relatively new to the study of *santería* and, characteristically, hadn't bothered to research it thoroughly. Avila had begun dabbling in the blood practices when he first learned the authorities were investigating him for bribery; several cocaine dealers of his acquaintance swore that *santería* worship had kept them out of jail, so Avila figured there was nothing to lose by trying. In Hialeah he conferred with a genuine *santero* priest, who offered to teach him the secrets of the religion, rooted in ancient Afro-Cuban customs. The history was infinitely too deep and mystical for Avila, and soon he grew impatient with the lessons.

All he really wanted, he explained to the *santero*, was the ability to put curses on his enemies. Lethal curses.

The priest wailed and told him to get lost. But Avila went home convinced that, from the mumbo jumbo he'd seen, he could teach himself the basics of hexing. For his deity Avila picked the saint Chango, because he liked the macho name. For his first target he chose the county prosecutor leading the investigation against corrupt building inspectors.

Pennies were easy to come by, as were old animal bones; Avila's grandmother lived four blocks from a pet cemetery in Medley. Obtaining blood was the biggest obstacle for Avila, who had no zeal for performing live sacrifices. The first few times, he tried pleasing Chango by sprinkling the coins and bones with steak juices and homemade bouillon. Nothing happened. Evidently the *santería* saints preferred the fresh stuff.

One rainy Sunday afternoon, Avila bought himself a live chicken. His wife was cooking a big dinner for the cousins, so she banished Avila from the kitchen. He put a Ginsu knife in his back pocket and smuggled the victim to the garage. As soon as Avila began spreading newspapers on the floor, the chicken sensed trouble. Avila was astounded that a puny five-pound bird could make such a racket or put up such spirited resistance. The crudely staged sacrifice eventually was completed, but Avila emerged scratched, pecked and smeared with bloody feathers. So was his wife's cream-colored Buick Electra. Her ear-splitting tirade caused the cousins to forgo dessert and head home early.

Two days later, the magic happened. The prosecutor targeted by Avila's chicken curse fell and dislocated a shoulder in the shower. At the time, he was in the company of an athletic prostitute named Kandi, who was thoughtful enough not only to call 911 but to make herself available for numerous press interviews. Given the media uproar, the State Attorney suggested that the fallen prosecutor take an indefinite leave of absence.

The corruption investigation wasn't derailed, merely reassigned. Nevertheless, Avila was convinced that the *santería* spell was a success. Later attempts to replicate the results proved fruitless (and messy), but Avila blamed his own inexperience, plus a lack of suitable facilities. Perhaps, during the sacrifices, he was chanting the wrong phrases, or chanting the right phrases in the wrong order. Perhaps he was performing the ceremonies at a bad time of day for the mercurial Chango. Or perhaps Avila was simply using inferior poultry.

While he ended up plea-bargaining with the replacement prosecutor, Avila's faith in the witchcraft of bones and blood remained unshaken. He decided Snapper's transgression was heinous enough to merit the offering of two chickens instead of one. If that didn't work, he'd invest in a billy goat.

The roosters did not succumb quietly, the clamor awakening Avila's wife, aunt and mother. The women burst into the garage to find Avila singing Spanish gibberish to his cherished ceramic statue. Avila's wife instantly spied red droplets and a waxen fragment of chicken beak on the left front fender of her Electra, and savagely took to striking her husband with a garden rake.

On the other side of Dade County, Snapper dozed

peacefully in a dead man's Naugahyde recliner. He felt no pain from the supernatural hand of Chango, nor did he feel the hateful glare of Edie Marsh, who was stretched out on the mildewed carpet and trussed to a naked insurance man.

# FOURTEEN

**As the candles** melted to lumps, Snapper's shadow flickered and shrunk on the pale bare walls. His profile reminded Edie Marsh of a miniature tyrannosaurus.

For laughs, he refused to let Fred Dove remove the red condom.

"That's mean," Edie said.

"Well, I'm one mean motherfucker," Snapper proclaimed. "You don't believe me, there's a lady cop in the hospital you should see."

When he yawned, the misaligned mandible waggled horizontally, then appeared to disengage altogether from his face. He looked like a snake trying to swallow an egg.

Edie said, "What is it you want?"

"You know damn well." Snapper held the flashlight on Fred Dove's retreating cock. "Where'd you find a red rubber?" he asked. "Mail order, I bet. Looks like a Santy Claus hat."

From the floor, the insurance man gave a disconsolate whimper. Edie leaned her head against the small of his back. Snapper had positioned them butt-to-butt, binding their hands with a curtain sash. In Fred Dove's briefcase Snapper found the business cards and policy folders from Midwest Casualty. From that it was easy to figure out—Edie on her knees, and so on. Snapper marveled at the exquisite timing of his entrance.

He said, "Fair is fair. A three-way split."

"But you took off!" Edie objected. "You left me here with that asshole Tony."

Snapper shrugged. "I changed my mind. I'm allowed. So how much money we talkin' about?"

"Fuck you," said Edie Marsh.

Without leaving the recliner, Snapper cocked one leg and kicked her in the side of the head. The sound of the blow was sickening. Edie moaned but didn't cry.

"For God's sake." Fred Dove's voice cracked, as if he were the one who'd been clobbered.

Snapper said, "Then tell me how much."

"Don't you dare." Edie was woozy, but sharply she dug both elbows into Fred Dove's ribs.

"I'm waiting," said Snapper.

Edie felt the insurance man stiffen against the ropes. Then she heard him say: "A hundred forty-one thousand dollars."

"Moron!" Edie hissed.

"But you won't get a dime," Fred Dove warned Snapper, "without me and Edie."

"That a fact?"

"Yes, sir."

"Not a goddamn cent," Edie agreed, "because guess who's getting the settlement check. *Missus* Neria Torres. Me."

Snapper aimed the flashlight on Edie's face, which bore a puffy salmon imprint of his shoe. "Sweetie," he said, "it's hard to sign a check if you're in a body cast. Understand?"

She turned away from the harsh light and silently cursed her lousy taste in convicts.

Fred Dove said to Snapper: "You ought to untie us."

"Well, listen to Santy Claus!"

Edie's pulse jackhammered in her temples. "You know what it is, Fred? Snapper's jealous. See, it's not about the insurance money. It's that I was going to make love to you—"

"Haw!" Snapper exclaimed.

"—and he knows," Edie went on, "he knows I wouldn't do it with him for all the money in Fort Knox!"

Snapper laughed. Nudging Fred Dove with a toe, he said, "Don't kid yourself, bubba. She'd fuck a syphilitic porky-pine, she thought there was a dollar in it."

"Nice talk," Edie said. God Almighty, her head hurt.

The insurance man fought to steady his nerves. He was flabbergasted to find himself in the middle of something so ugly, complicated and dangerous. Only hours ago the arrangement seemed foolproof and exciting: a modestly fraudulent claim, a beautiful and uninhibited co-conspirator, a wild fling in an abandoned hurricane house.

A bright-red condom seemed appropriate.

Then out of nowhere appeared this Snapper person, a hard-looking sort and an authentic criminal, judging by what Fred Dove had seen and heard. The insurance man didn't want such a violent character for a third partner. On the other hand, he didn't want to die or be harmed seriously enough to require hospitalization. Blue Cross would demand facts, as would Fred Dove's wife.

So he offered Snapper forty-seven thousand dollars. "That's how it splits three ways."

Snapper swung the flashlight to Fred Dove's face. He said, "You figured that up in your head? No pencil and paper, that's pretty good."

Yeah, thought Edie Marsh. Thank you, Dr Einstein.

Fred Dove said to Snapper: "Do we have a deal?"

"Fair is fair." He rose from the BarcaLounger and made his way to the garage. Within moments the portable generator belched to life. Snapper returned to the living room and turned on the solitary lightbulb. Then, kneeling beside Fred Dove and Edie Marsh, he cut the curtain sash off their wrists.

"Let's go eat," he said. "I'm fuckin' starved."

Fred Dove rose shakily. He modestly locked his hands in front of his crotch. "I'm taking this thing off," he declared.

"The rubber?" Snapper gave him a thumbs-up. "You do that." He glanced at Edie, who made no effort to cover her breasts or anything else. She eyed Snapper in a dark poisonous way.

He said, "That's how you goin' to Denny's? Fine by me. Maybe we'll get a free pie."

Wordlessly Edie walked behind the Naugahyde recliner, picked up the crowbar she'd left there, took two steps toward Snapper, and swung at him with all her strength. He went down squalling.

Weapon in hand, Edie Marsh straddled him. Her damp and tangled hair had fallen to cover the bruised half of her face. To Fred Dove, she looked untamed and dazzling and alarmingly capable of homicide. He feared he was about to witness his first.

Edie inserted the sharp end of the crowbar between Snapper's deviated jawbones, pinning his bloodless tongue to his teeth.

"Kick me again," she said, "and I'll have your balls in a blender."

Fred Dove snatched his pants and his briefcase, and ran.

They returned the borrowed speedboat to the marina and went back to Coral Gables. With great effort they carried the man known as Skink into Augustine's house.

Max Lamb was unnerved by the wall of grinning skulls, but said nothing as he made his way down the hall to the shower. Augustine got on the telephone to sort out what had happened with his dead uncle's Cape buffalo. Bonnie fixed a pot of coffee and took it to the guest room, where the governor was recovering from the animal dart. He and Jim Tile were talking when Bonnie walked in. She wanted to stay and listen to this improbable stranger, but she felt she was intruding. The men's conversation was serious, held in low tones. She heard Skink say:

"Brenda's a strong one. She'll make it."

Then, Jim Tile: "I've tried every prayer I know."

As Bonnie slipped out the door, she encountered Max, sucking on a cigaret as he emerged from the bathroom. She resolved to be forbearing about her husband's odious new habit, which he blamed on the battlefield stress of the abduction.

She followed him to the living room and sat beside him on the sofa. There, in sensational detail, he described the torture he'd received at the hands of the one-eyed misfit.

"The dog collar," Bonnie Lamb said.

"That's right. Look at my neck." Max opened the top

buttons of his shirt, which he'd borrowed from Augustine. "See the burns? See?"

Bonnie didn't notice any marks, but nodded sympathetically. "So you definitely want to prosecute."

"Absolutely!" Max Lamb detected doubt in his wife's voice. "Christ, Bonnie, he could've murdered me."

She squeezed his hand. "I still don't understand why—why he did it in the first place."

"With a fruitcake like that, who knows." Max Lamb purposely didn't mention Skink's disgust with the hurricane videos; he remembered that Bonnie felt the same way.

She said, "I think he needs professional help."

"No, sweetheart, he needs a professional jail." Max lifted his chin and blew smoke at the ceiling.

"Honey, let's think about this—"

But he pulled away from her, bolting for the phone, which Augustine had just hung up. "I'd better call Pete Archibald," Max Lamb said over his shoulder, "let everyone at Rodale know I'm OK."

Bonnie Lamb got up and went to the guest room. The governor was sitting upright in bed, but his eyes were half shut. His ragged beard was finely crusted with ocean salt. Jim Tile, his Stetson tucked under one arm, stood near the window.

Bonnie poured each of them another cup of coffee. "How's he feeling?" she whispered.

Skink's good eye blinked open. "Better," he said, thickly.

She set the coffeepot on the bedstand. "It was monkey tranquilizer," she explained.

"Never to be combined with psychoactive drugs," said Skink, "particularly toad sweat."

Bonnie looked at Jim Tile, who said, "I asked him."

"Asked me what?" Skink rasped.

"About the dead guy in the TV dish," the trooper said. Then, to Bonnie: "He didn't do it."

"Though I do admire the style," said Skink.

Bonnie Lamb did a poor job of masking her doubt. Skink peered sternly. "I didn't kill that fellow, Mrs Lamb. But I damn sure wouldn't tell you if I had."

"I believe you. I do."

The governor finished the coffee and asked for another cup. He told Bonnie it was the best he'd ever tasted. "And I like your boy," he said, gesturing toward the wall of skulls. "I like what he's done with the place."

Bonnie said: "He's not my boy. Just a friend."

Skink nodded. "We all need one of those." With difficulty he rolled out of bed and began stripping off his wet clothes. Jim Tile led him to the shower and started the water. When the trooper returned, carrying the governor's plastic cap, he asked Bonnie Lamb what her husband intended to do.

"He wants to prosecute." She sat on the edge of the bed, listening to the shower run.

Augustine came into the room and said, "Well?"

"I can arrest him tonight," Jim Tile told Bonnie, "if your husband comes to the substation and files charges. What happens then is up to the State Attorney."

"You'd do that—arrest your own friend?"

"Better me than a stranger," the trooper said. "Don't feel bad about this, Mrs Lamb. Your husband's got every right."

"Yes, I know." Prosecuting the governor was the right thing—a person couldn't be allowed to run around kidnapping tourists, no matter how offensively they behaved. Yet Bonnie was saddened by the idea of Skink's going to jail. It was naive, she knew, but that's how she felt.

Jim Tile was questioning Augustine about the skulls on the wall. "Cuban voodoo?"

"No, nothing like that."

"Nineteen is what I count," the trooper said. "I won't ask where you got 'em. They're too clean for homicides."

Bonnie Lamb said, "They're medical specimens."

"Whatever you say." After twenty years of attending head-on collisions, Jim Tile had a well-earned aversion to human body parts. "Specimens it is," he said.

Augustine removed five of the skulls from the shelves and lined them up on the hardwood floor, at his feet. Then he picked up three and began to juggle.

The trooper said, "I'll be damned."

As he juggled, Augustine thought about the drunken young fool who tried to shoot his uncle's Cape buffalo. What a sad, dumb way to die. Fluidly he snatched a fourth skull off the floor and put it in rotation; then the fifth.

Bonnie Lamb found herself smiling at the performance in spite of its creepiness. The governor emerged from the shower in a cloud of steam, naked except for a sky-blue towel around his neck. His thick silver hair sent snaky tails of water down his chest. He used a corner of the towel to dab the condensation off his glass eye. He beamed when he saw Augustine's juggling.

Jim Tile felt dizzy, watching the skulls fly. Max Lamb appeared in the doorway. His expression instantly changed from curiosity to revulsion, as if a switch had been flipped inside his head. Bonnie knew what he was going to say before the words left his lips: "You think *this* is funny?"

Augustine continued juggling. It was unclear whether he, or the governor's nudity, was the object of Max Lamb's disapproval.

The trooper said, "It's been a long night, man."

"Bonnie, we're leaving." Max's tone was patronizing and snarky. "Did you hear me? Playtime is over."

She was infuriated that her husband would speak to her that way in front of strangers. She stormed from the room.

"Oh, Max?" Skink, wearing a sly smile, touched a finger to his own throat. Max Lamb's neck tingled the old Tri-Tronics tingle. He jumped reflexively, banging against the door.

From the backpack Skink retrieved Max's billfold and the keys to the rental car. He dropped them in Max's hand. Max mumbled a thank-you and went after Bonnie.

Augustine stopped juggling, catching the skulls one by one. Carefully he returned them to their place on the wall.

The governor tugged the towel from his neck and began drying his arms and legs. "I like that girl," he said to Augustine. "How about you?"

"What's not to like."

"You've got a big decision to make."

"That's very funny. She's married."

"Love is just a kiss away. So the song says." Playfully Skink seized Jim Tile by the elbows. "Tell me, Officer. Am I arrested or not?"

"That's up to Mister Max Lamb."

"I need to know."

"They're talking it over," Jim Tile said.

"Because if I'm not bound for jail, I'd dearly love to go find the bastard who beat up your Brenda."

For a moment the trooper seemed to sag under the weight of his grief. His eyes welled up, but he kept himself from breaking down.

Skink said, "Jim, please. I live for opportunities like this."

"You've had enough excitement. We all have."

"You, son!" the governor barked at Augustine. "You had enough excitement?"

"Well, they just shot my water buffalo at a supermarket—"

"Ho!" Skink exclaimed.

"—but I'd be honored to help." The skull juggling had left Augustine energetic and primed. He was in the mood for a new project, now that Bonnie's husband was safe.

"You think about what I said," Skink told Jim Tile. "In the meantime, I'm damn near hungry enough to eat processed food. How about you guys?"

He charged toward the door, but the trooper blocked his path. "Put on your pants, captain. Please."

The corpse of Tony Torres lay unclaimed and unidentified in the morgue. Each morning Ira Jackson checked the *Herald*, but in the reams of hurricane news there was no mention of a crucified mobile-home salesman. Ira Jackson took this as affirmation of Tony Torres's worthlessness and insignificance; his death didn't rate one lousy paragraph in the newspaper.

Ira Jackson turned his vengeful attentions toward

Avila, the inspector who had corruptly rubber-stamped the permits for the late Beatrice Jackson's trailer home. Ira Jackson believed Avila was as culpable as Tony Torres for the tragedy that had claimed the life of his trusting mother.

Early on the morning of August 28, Ira Jackson drove to the address he'd pried from the reluctant clerk at the Metro building department. A woman with a heavy accent answered the front door. Ira Jackson asked to speak to Señor Avila.

"He bissy eng de grotch."

"Please tell him it's important."

"Hokay, but he berry bissy."

"I'll wait," said Ira Jackson.

Avila was scrubbing rooster blood off the whitewalls of his wife's Buick when his mother announced he had a visitor. Avila swore and kicked at the bucket of soap. It had to be Gar Whitmark, harassing him for the seven grand. What did he expect Avila to do—rob a fucking bank!

But it wasn't Whitmark at the door. It was a stocky middle-aged stranger with a chopped haircut, a gold chain around his neck and a smudge of white powder on his upper lip. Avila recognized the powder as doughnut dust. He wondered if the guy was a cop.

"My name is Rick," said Ira Jackson, extending a pudgy scarred hand. "Rick Reynolds." When the man smiled, a smear of grape jelly was visible on his bottom row of teeth.

Avila said, "I'm kinda busy right now."

"I was driving by and saw the truck." Ira Jackson pointed. "Fortress Roofing—that's you, right?"

Avila didn't answer yes or no. His eyes flicked to his

truck at the curb, and the Cadillac parked behind it. The man wasn't a cop, not with a flashy car like that.

"The storm tore off my roof. I need a new one ASAP."

Avila said, "We're booked solid. I'm really sorry."

He hated to turn down a willing sucker, but it would be suicidal to run a scam on someone who knew where he lived. Especially someone with forearms the size of fence posts.

Avila made a mental note to move the roofing truck off the street, to a place where passersby couldn't see it.

Ira Jackson licked the doughnut sugar from his lip. "I'll make it worth your while," he said.

"Wish I could help."

"How's ten thousand sound? On top of your regular price."

Try as he might, Avila couldn't conceal his interest. The guy had a New York accent; they did things in a big way up there.

"That's ten thousand cash," Ira Jackson added. "See, it's my grandmother, she lives with us. Ninety years old and suddenly it's raining buckets on her head. The roof's flat-out gone."

Avila feigned compassion. "Ninety years old? Bless her heart." He stepped outside and closed the door behind him. "Problem is, I've got a dozen other jobs waiting."

"Fifteen thousand," Ira Jackson said, "if you move me to the top of the list."

Avila rubbed his stubbled chin and eyed the visitor. How often, he thought, does fifteen grand come knocking at the door? A rip-off was out of the question, but another option loomed. Radical, to be sure, but do-able:

Avila could build the man a legitimate, complete roof. Use the cash to settle up with Gar Whitmark. Naturally the crew would piss and moan, spoiled bastards. Properly installing a roof was a hard, hot, exhausting job. Perhaps desperate times called for honest work.

"I see," remarked Ira Jackson, "your place came through the hurricane pretty good."

"We were a long way from the eye, thank God."

"Thank God is right."

"Where exactly do you live, Mister Reynolds? Maybe I can squeeze you on the schedule."

"Fantastic."

"I'll send a man out for an estimate," Avila said. Then he remembered there was no man to send; the thieving Snapper had skipped.

Ira Jackson said, "I'd prefer it was you personally."

"Sure, Mister Reynolds. How about tomorrow first thing?"

"How about right now? We can ride in my car."

Avila couldn't think of a single reason not to go, and fifteen thousand reasons why he should.

When Max Lamb put down the phone, his face was gray and his mouth was slack. He looked as if he'd been diagnosed with a terminal illness. The reality was no less grave, as far as the Rodale & Burns agency was concerned. On the other end of the line, easygoing Pete Archibald had sounded funereal and defeated. The news from New York was bad indeed.

The National Institutes of Health had scheduled a press conference to further enumerate the health hazards of cigaret smoking. Ordinarily the advertising world would scarcely take notice, so routine and predictable were these dire outcries. No matter how harrowing the medical revelations, the impact on retail cigaret sales seldom lasted more than a few weeks. This time, though, the government had used sophisticated technology to test specific brands for concentrations of tars, nicotine and other assorted carcinogens. Broncos rated first; Bronco Menthols rated second, Lady Broncos third. Epidemiologically, they were the most lethal products in the history of tobacco cultivation. Smoking a Bronco, in the lamentably quotable words of one wiseass NIH scientist, was "only slightly safer than sucking on the tailpipe of a Chevrolet Suburban."

Details of the NIH bombshell had quickly leaked to Durham Gas Meat & Tobacco, manufacturer of Broncos and other fine products. The company's knee-jerk response was a heated threat to cancel its advertising in all newspapers and magazines that intended to report the government's findings. That bombastically idiotic maneuver, Max Lamb knew, would itself become front-page headlines if sane heads didn't prevail. Max had to get back to New York as soon as possible.

When he told his wife, she said: "Right now?"

As if she didn't understand the gravity of the crisis.

"In my business," Max explained impatiently, "this is a flaming 747 full of orphans, plowing into a mountainside."

"Is it true about Broncos?"

"Probably. That's not the problem. They can't start yanking their ads; there's serious money at stake. Double-digit millions."

"Max."

"What?"

"Please put out that damn cigaret."

"Jesus, Bonnie, listen to yourself."

They were sitting in wicker chairs on Augustine's patio. It was three or four in the morning. Inside the house, Neil Young played on the stereo. Through the French doors Bonnie Lamb saw Augustine in the kitchen. He noticed she was watching, and shot her a quick shy smile. The black trooper and the one-eyed governor were standing over the stove; it smelled like they were frying bacon and ham.

Max Lamb said, "We'll catch the first plane." He stubbed out his Bronco and flipped the butt into a birdbath.

"What about *him*?" Bonnie cut her eyes toward the kitchen window, where Skink could be seen breaking eggs at the sink. She said to Max, "You wanted to file charges, didn't you? Put him in jail where he belongs."

"Honey, there's no time. After the NIH mess blows over, we'll fly back and take care of that maniac. Don't worry."

Bonnie Lamb said, "If they let him go now . . ." She finished the sentence in her head.

If they let him go now, they'll never find him again. He'll vanish like a ghost in the swamp. And wouldn't that be a darn shame.

Bonnie bewildered herself with such sentiment. What's wrong with me? The man abducted and abused my husband. Why don't I want to see him punished?

"You're right," she said to Max. "You should go back to New York as soon as you can."

With a frown, he reached over and lightly smacked a mosquito on her arm. "What does that mean—you're not coming?"

"Max, I'm not up for a plane trip this morning. My stomach's in knots."

"Take some Mylanta."

"I did," Bonnie lied. "Maybe it was the boat ride."

"You'll feel better later."

"I'm sure I will."

He said he'd get her a room near the airport. "Take a long nap," he suggested, "and catch an evening flight."

"Sounds good."

Poor Max, she thought. He hasn't got a clue.

# FIFTEEN

**Bonnie Brooks's father** worked in the circulation department of the Chicago *Tribune*, and her mother was a buyer for Sears. They had an apartment in the city and a summer cabin on the boundary waters in Minnesota. Bonnie, an only child, had mixed memories of family vacations. Her father was an unadventurous fellow for whom the northern wilderness held no allure. Because he couldn't swim and was allergic to deerflies, he avoided the lakes. Instead he stayed in the cabin and assembled model airplanes; classic German Fokkers were his passion. The tedious hobby was made more so by her father's chronic ham-fistedness, which turned the simplest glue job into high drama. Bonnie and her mother stayed out of the way, to avoid being blamed for disturbing his concentration.

While her father toiled over the model planes, Bonnie's mother paddled her across the wooded lakes in an old birch canoe. Bonnie remembered those happy mornings—trailing her fingertips in the chilly water, feeling the sunlight warm the back of her neck. Her mother was not the stealthiest of paddlers, but they saw their share of wildlife—deer, squirrels, beavers, the occasional moose. Bonnie recalled asking, more than once, why her folks had bought the cabin if her father was so averse to the outdoors. Her mother always explained: "It was either here or Wisconsin."

Bonnie Brooks attended Northwestern University and, to her father's puzzlement, majored in journalism. Soon she embarked on her first serious romance, with a divorced adjunct professor who claimed to have won prizes for his reportage of the Vietnam War. The absence of plaques in the professor's office Bonnie naively attributed to modesty. For Christmas she decided to surprise him with a framed, laminated copy of his front-page scoop about the mining of Haiphong harbor. Yet when Bonnie searched the college's microfilm of the San Francisco *Chronicle*, for whom her lover had supposedly worked, she found not a single bylined story bearing his name. Demonstrating the blood instincts of a seasoned reporter, she contacted the newspaper's personnel department and (using harmless subterfuge) was able to determine that the closest her heroic seducer had ever come to Southeast Asia was the copy desk of the *Chronicle*'s Seattle bureau.

Bonnie Brooks acted decisively. First she dumped the jerk, then she got him fired from the university. Subsequent boyfriends were more loyal and forthcoming, but what they lacked in dishonesty they made up for with indolence. Bonnie's mother grew tired of cooking them meals and deflecting their halfhearted offers to help dry the dishes. She couldn't wait for her daughter to graduate from school and find herself a grown-up man.

Good or bad, jobs in journalism were hard to come by. Like many of her classmates, Bonnie Brooks wound up writing publicity blurbs and press releases. She went to work first for the City of Chicago Parks Department and then for a baby-food company that was eventually purchased by Crespo Mills Internationale. There Bonnie was promoted to the job of assistant corporate publicist. The title was attached to a salary that ten tough years in most city newsrooms wouldn't have earned. As for the writing, it was as elementary as it was unsatisfying. In addition to pabulums and breakfast cereals, Crespo Mills manufactured whipped condiment spreads, peanut butter, granola bars, cookies, crackers, trail mix, flavored popcorn, bread sticks and three styles of croutons. In no time, Bonnie Brooks ran out of appetizing adjectives. Attempts at lyrical originality were discouraged by her Crespo supervisors; during one especially dreary streak, she was required to use the word "tasty" in fourteen consecutive press releases. When Max Lamb asked her to marry him and move to New York, Bonnie didn't hesitate to quit her job.

Max could take only a few days off from work, so they decided to take their honeymoon at Disney World—a corny choice, but Bonnie figured anything was better than Niagara Falls. She knew that a waterfall, no matter how grandiose, wouldn't hold Max's interest. Neither, it turned out, did Mickey Mouse. Two days at the Magic Kingdom and Max was as antsy as a cat burglar.

Then the hurricane blew in, and he just *had* to go see. . . .

Bonnie had wanted to stay in Orlando, stay cuddled under the scratchy motel sheets and make love while the rain drummed on the windows. Why wasn't that enough for him?

She'd almost asked that very question as they sat in the dark on Augustine's patio after the adventure in Stiltsville. And later, on the way to the airport. And again, standing at the Delta gate, when he'd hugged her in a loose and distracted way, his hair and shirt reeking of cigarets.

But Bonnie hadn't asked. The moment wasn't right; he was a man with a purpose. A grown-up man, just like her mother wanted her to find. Except her mother thought Max was an asshole. Her father, well, he thought Max Lamb was a fine young fella. He thought all Bonnie's boyfriends had been fine young fellas.

She wondered what her father would think of her now, on the way to a hospital, scrunched in the front seat of a pickup truck between a one-eyed, toad-smoking kidnapper and a plane-crash survivor who juggled skulls.

Brenda Rourke's head was fractured in three places, and one of her cheeks needed reconstruction. She was bleeding under the right temporal bone, but doctors had managed to stanch it. A plastic surgeon had repaired a U-shaped gash on her forehead, stitching the loose flap above the hairline.

Bonnie Lamb had never seen such terrible wounds. Even the governor seemed shaken. Augustine fastened his eyes on his shoetops—the sounds and smells of the hospital were too familiar. He felt parched.

Jim Tile held both of Brenda's hands in one of his own. Her eyes were open but unfocused; she had no sense of anyone besides Jim at her bedside. She was trying to talk through the drugs and the pain; he leaned closer to listen.

After a while he straightened, announcing in a low, angry voice, "The bastard stole her ring. Her mother's wedding ring."

Skink slipped from the room so quietly that Bonnie and Augustine didn't notice immediately. There was no trace of him outside the door, but a rush of blue and white uniforms attracted them to the end of the hall. The governor was in the nursery, strolling among the newborns. He carried an infant in the crook of each arm. The babies slept soundly, and he studied them with profound sadness. To Bonnie Lamb he appeared harmless, despite the rebellious beard and the grubby combat pants and the army boots. A trio of husky orderlies conferred at a water fountain; apparently a negotiation had already been attempted, with poor results. Calmly Jim Tile entered the nursery and returned the infants to their glass cribs.

Nobody intervened when the trooper led Skink out of the hospital, because it looked like a routine arrest; another loony street case hauled to the stockade: Jim Tile, his arm around the madman, walking him briskly down the maze of pale-green corridors; the two of them talking intently; Bonnie and Augustine dodging wheelchairs and gurneys and trying to keep up.

When they reached the parking lot, Jim Tile said he had to go to work. "The President's coming, and guess who gets to clear traffic."

He folded a piece of paper into Skink's hand and got into the patrol car. Wordlessly Skink settled in the bed of Augustine's pickup and lay down. His good eye was fixed on the clouds, and his arms were folded across his chest.

Augustine asked Jim Tile: "What do we do with him?"

"That's entirely up to you." The trooper sounded exhausted.

Bonnie Lamb asked about Brenda Rourke. Jim Tile said the doctors expected her to pull through.

"What about the guy who did it?"

"They haven't caught him," the trooper replied, "and they won't." He strapped on the seat belt, locked the door, adjusted his sunglasses. "Place used to be something special," he said absently. "Long, long time ago."

A feral cry rose from the bed of the pickup truck. Jim Tile blinked over the rims of his shades. "It was nice meeting you, Mrs Lamb. You and your husband do what's right. The captain, he'll understand."

Then the trooper drove off.

On the way to the airport hotel, where Max Lamb had reserved a day room for her, Bonnie slid across the front seat and rested her cheek on Augustine's shoulder. He was dreading this part, saying good-bye. It was always easier as a bitter cleaving, when suitcases snapped shut, doors slammed, taxis screeched out of the driveway. He checked the dashboard clock—less than three hours until her flight.

Through the back window of the truck, Bonnie saw that Skink had pulled the flowered cap over his face and drawn himself into a loose-jointed variation of a fetal curl.

She said, "I wonder what's on that piece of paper."

"My guess," said Augustine, "it's either a name or an address."

"Of what?"

"It's just a guess," he said, but he told her anyway.

That night he didn't have to say good-bye, because Bonnie Lamb didn't go home to New York. She canceled her flight and returned to Augustine's house. Her phone messages for Max were not returned until after midnight, when she was already asleep in the skull room.

Shortly after noon on August 28, the telephone in Tony Torres's kitchen started ringing.

Snapper told Edie Marsh to get it.

"*You* get it," she said.

"Real funny."

Snapper couldn't walk; the blow from the crowbar had messed up his right leg. He was laid out in the BarcaLounger with his knee packed in three bags of ice, which Edie had purchased for fifty dollars on Quail Roost Drive from some traveling bandit in a fish truck. The fifty bucks came out of Snapper's big score against the Whitmarks. He didn't tell Edie Marsh how much money remained in his pocket. He also didn't mention the trooper's gun in the Cherokee, in the event she blew her top again.

The phone continued ringing. "Answer it," Snapper said. "Maybe it's your Santy Claus boyfriend."

Edie picked up the phone. On the other end, a woman's voice said: "Hullo?"

Edie hung up. "It wasn't Fred," she said.

"The fuck was it?"

"I didn't ask, Snapper. We're not supposed to be here, remember?" She said it sounded like long distance.

"What if it's the insurance company? Maybe the check's ready."

Edie said, "No. Fred would tell me."

Snapper hacked out a laugh. "Fred's gone, you dumb twat. You scared him off!"

"How much you wanna bet."

"Right, he can't stay away, you're such a fantastic piece a ass."

"You can't even imagine," Edie said, showing some tongue. Maybe she wasn't hot enough for a young Kennedy, but she was the best thing young Mr Dove had ever seen. Besides, he couldn't back out of the deal now. He'd already put in for the phony claim.

Again the phone rang. Edie Marsh said, "Shit."

"For Christ's sake, gimme a hand." Snapper writhed irritably on the BarcaLounger. "Come on!"

Bracing a forearm on Edie's shoulder, he hobbled to the kitchen. She plucked the receiver off the hook and handed it to him.

"Yo," Snapper said.

"Hullo?" A woman. "Tony, is that you?"

"Hmmphrr," answered Snapper, cautiously.

"It's me. Neria."

Who? Frigid drops from the ice pack dripped down Snapper's injured leg. The purple kneecap felt as if it were about to burst, like a rotten mango. Edie pressed close, trying to hear what the caller was saying.

"Tony, I been tryin' to get through for days. What's with the house?"

Then Snapper remembered: The wife! Tony Torres had said her name was Miriam or Neria, some Cuban thing. He'd also said she'd be coming back for her cut of the insurance.

"Bad connection," Snapper mumbled into the receiver.

"What's going on? I call next door and Mister Varga, he said the hurricane totaled our house and now there's strangers living there. Some woman, Tony. You hear me? And Mister Varga said you shot a hole in the garage. What the hell's going on down there?"

Snapper held the receiver at arm's length, like it was a stick of dynamite. His bottom jaw shoveled in and out; the joints of his face made a popping sound that gave Edie the creeps.

"Tony?" squeaked the voice on the telephone.

Edie took it from Snapper's hand and said, "I'm very sorry. You've got the wrong number." Then she hung up.

At first all Snapper could say was, "Goddamn."

"The wife?"

"Yeah. Goddamn."

Edie Marsh helped him pogo to the chair. The ice crunched as he sat down. "Where's your Santy Claus boyfriend live?"

"Some Ramada."

"Goddamn. We don't got much time."

Edie said, "Where's Mrs Torres? Is she here in Miami?"

"Hell if I know. Get me to the car."

"I've got some more bad news. The dogs came back this morning."

"The wiener dogs?"

"We can't just leave them here. They need to be fed."

With both hands Snapper choked his throbbing leg and said, "Never again. I swear to Christ."

"Oh yeah," Edie Marsh said, "like this is some fun picnic for me. Here, give me your arm."

Avila's new customer took the Turnpike south. Before long the Cadillac was pinned in traffic—construction trucks, eighteen-wheelers, Army convoys, ambulances, sightseers, National Guardsmen, and hundreds of queasy insurance adjusters, all heading into the hurricane zone. Ground Zero.

"Looks like a bombing range," said the man calling himself Rick Reynolds.

"Sure does. Where's your house?"

"We got a ways yet." As the car inched along, the man turned up the radio: Rush Limbaugh, making wisecracks about the wife of some candidate. Avila didn't think the jokes were all that funny, but the man chuckled loyally. After the program ended, a news report announced that the President of the United States was flying to Miami to see the storm damage firsthand.

"Great," said Avila. "You think traffic sucks now, just wait."

The man said, "Yeah, one time I got stuck behind Reagan's motorcade in the Holland Tunnel. Talk about a fuck story—two hours we're breathing fumes."

Avila inquired how long the man had been in Dade County. Couple months, he answered. Moved down from New York.

"And I never saw nuthin' like this."

Avila said, "Me, neither."

"I don't get it. Some houses go down like dominoes, some don't lose a shingle. How's that happen?"

Avila checked his wristwatch. He wondered if the guy had the fifteen grand on him, or maybe in the trunk of the car. He glanced in the back seat: a crumpled road map and two empty Mister Donut boxes.

The man said, "My guess is somebody got paid off. There's no other way to make sense of it."

Avila kept his eyes ahead. "This ain't New York," he said. Finally the traffic started to move.

The customer said a trailer park not far from his neighborhood got blown to smithereens. "Old lady was killed," he said.

"Man, that's rough."

"Wonderful old lady. But every single trailer got destroyed, every damn one."

Avila said, "Storm of the century."

"No, but here's the thing. The tie-downs on those mobile homes was rotted out. The augers was sawed off. Anchor disks missing. Now you tell me some inspector didn't get greased."

Avila shifted uncomfortably. "Straps rot fast in this heat. How much farther?"

"Not long."

The customer picked up Krome Avenue to 168th Street. There he turned back east and drove for a mile to a subdivision called Fox Hollow, which had eroded to more or less bare foundations in the hurricane. The man parked in front of the skeletal remains of a small tract home.

Avila got out of the Cadillac and said, "God, you weren't kidding."

The roof of the house was totally blown away; gables, beams, trusses, everything. Avila was stunned that Mr Reynolds was allowing his family to remain in such an unprotected structure. Avila followed him inside, stepping over the wind-flattened doors. The place looked abandoned except for the kitchen, where a pack of stray dogs fought over rancid hamburger in the overturned refrigerator. Avila's customer grabbed an aluminum baseball bat and chased the mongrels off.

Peeking into the flooded bedrooms, Avila saw no sign of the customer's family. Immediately he felt the whole day go sour. Just to be sure, he said, "So where's your ninety-year-old grandmother?"

"Dead and buried," Ira Jackson replied, slapping the bat in the palm of one hand, "on beautiful Staten Island."

As the man from New York prepared to nail him to a pine tree, Avila concluded that Snapper was responsible for hiring the attacker.

Clearly the plan was to murder Avila and take control of his crooked roofers. Where was the mighty fist of Chango? Avila wondered grimly. Had the double-chicken sacrifice misfired?

Then the man from New York explained himself—who he was, what had happened to his mother, and why Avila must die a horrible drawn-out death. At first Avila pleaded innocence, feigning outrage at the fate of Beatrice Jackson. Soon he realized that the survival skills so essential to a county bureaucrat—the ability on a moment's notice to shift blame, dodge responsibility and misplace crucial paperwork—were of no use to him now.

Avila reasoned it was better to tell the truth than to have it tortured out of him. So, out of sheer bladder-shriveling fear, he confessed to Ira Jackson.

Yes, it was he who'd been assigned to approve the mobile homes at Suncoast Leisure Village. And yes, he'd failed to perform thorough and timely inspections. And—yes, yes! God forgive me!—he'd taken bribes to overlook code violations.

"Didn't you see those goddamn rotten straps?" demanded Ira Jackson, who was making a crucifix with fallen roof beams.

"No," Avila admitted.

"The augers?"

"No, I swear."

"Never even checked?" Ira Jackson pounded ferociously with a hammer.

"I didn't see them," Avila said morosely, "because I never drove out there."

Ira Jackson's hammer halted in midair. Avila, who was lashed to a broken commode in a bathroom, lowered his eyes in a pantomime of shame. That's when he saw that the toilet bowl was alive with bright-green frogs and mottled brown snakes, splashing beneath him in fetid water.

With a shiver he said, "I never went to the trailer park. The guy sent me the money—"

"How much?"

"Fifty bucks a unit. He sent it to the office, so I figured what the hell, why waste gas? Instead of driving all the way down there, I . . ." Here Avila caught himself. It seemed unnecessary to reveal that he'd played golf on the afternoon he was supposed to inspect Suncoast Leisure Village.

". . . I didn't go."

"You're shittin' me."

"No. I'm very, very sorry."

The expression on Ira Jackson's face caused Avila to reevaluate his decision to be candid. Evidently the doughnut man intended to torture him, no matter what. Ira Jackson bent over the crucifix and went back to work.

Raising his voice over the racket, Avila said, "Christ, if I knew what he was doing with those trailers, he never woulda got permits. You gotta believe me, there's no amount of money would make me take a pass on cut augers. No way!"

"Shut up." Ira Jackson carried the cross to the backyard and began nailing it to the trunk of a pine. It had been a tall lush tree until the hurricane sheared off the top thirty feet; now it was merely a bark-covered pole.

With each plonk of the hammer, Avila's spirits sank. He said a prayer to Chango, then tried a "Hail Mary" in the wan hope that traditional Catholic entreaty would be more potent in staving off a crucifixion.

As the man from New York dragged him to the tree, Avila cried, "Please, I'll do anything you want!"

"OK," said Ira Jackson, "I want you to die."

He positioned Avila upright against the cross and wrapped duct tape around his ankles and wrists to minimize the squirming. Avila shut his eyes when he saw the doughnut man snatch up the hammer. The moment the cold point of the nail punctured his palm, Avila emitted a puppy yelp and fainted.

When he awoke, he saw that Chango had answered his prayers with a fury.

# SIXTEEN

**At nine sharp** on the morning of August 31, an attractive brunette woman carrying two miniature dachshunds walked into a Hialeah branch of the Barnett Bank and opened an account under the name of "Neria G. Torres."

For identification, the woman provided an expired automobile registration and a handful of soggy mail. The bank officer politely requested a driver's license or passport, any document bearing a photograph. The woman said her most personal papers, including driver's license, were washed away by the hurricane. As the bank officer questioned her more closely, the woman became distraught. Soon her little dogs began to bark plangently; one of them squirted from her arms and dashed in circles around the lobby, nipping at other customers. To quiet the scene, the banker agreed to accept the woman's auto registration as identification. His own aunt had lost all her immigration papers in the storm, so Mrs Torres's excuse seemed plausible. To open the account she gave him one hundred dollars cash, and said she'd be back in a few days to deposit a large insurance check.

"You're lucky they settled so fast," the banker remarked. "My aunt's having a terrible time with her company."

The woman said her homeowner policy was with Midwest Casualty. "I've got a *great* insurance man," she added.

Later, when Edie Marsh told the story to Fred Dove, he reacted with the weakest twitch of an ironic smile. Under the woeful circumstances, it was as good as a cartwheel.

Edie, Snapper and the two noisy wiener dogs had moved into his room at the Ramada. No other accommodations were available for a radius of sixty miles, because the hotels were jammed full of displaced families, relief volunteers, journalists, construction workers and insurance adjusters. Fred Dove felt trapped. His fear of getting arrested for fraud was now compounded by a fear that his wife would call the motel room, then Edie Marsh or Snapper would answer the phone and the wiener dogs would start howling, leaving Fred Dove to invent an explanation that no sensible woman in Omaha, Nebraska, would ever accept.

"Cheer up," Edie told him. "We're all set at the bank."

"Good," he said in a brittle tone.

The long tense weekend had abraded the insurance man's nerves—Snapper, gimping irritably around the small motel room, slugging down vodka, threatening to blast the yappy dachshunds with a massive black handgun he claimed to have stolen from a police officer.

No wonder I'm edgy, thought Fred Dove.

To deepen the gloom, sharing the cramped room with Snapper and the dogs left the insurance man no opportunity for intimacy with Edie Marsh. Not that he could have availed himself of a sexual invitation; the withering effect of Snapper's previous coital interruption endured, as Snapper continued to tease Fred Dove about the red condom.

Also looming large was the question of Edie's aptitude for violence—a disconcerting vision of the crowbar episode was scorched into Fred Dove's memory. He worried that she or Snapper might endeavor to murder each other at any moment.

Edie stretched out next to him on the bed. "You're miserable," she observed.

"Yes indeed," said the insurance man.

With his bum leg elevated, Snapper was stationed in an armchair three and one half feet from the television screen. Every so often he would take a futile swipe at Donald or Marla, and tell them to shut the holy fuck up.

"Sally Jessy," Edie whispered. Fred Dove sighed.

On the TV, a woman in a dreadful yellow wig was accusing her gap-toothed white-trash husband of screwing her younger sister. Instead of denying it, the husband said damn right, and it was the best nooky I ever had. Instantly the sister, also wearing a dreadful wig and lacking in teeth, piped up to say she couldn't get enough. Sally Jessy exhaled in weary dismay, the studio audience hooted, and Snapper let out a war whoop that set off the dogs once again.

"If the phone rings," Fred Dove said, "please don't answer."

Edie Marsh didn't need to ask why.

"You got any kids?" she asked.

The insurance man said he had two, a boy and a girl. He thought Edie might follow up and ask about their ages, what grades they were in, and so on. But she showed no interest.

She said, "Cheer up, OK? Think about your cruise to Bimini."

"Look, I was wondering—"

Snapper, growling over one shoulder: "You two mind? I'm tryin' to watch the fuckin' show."

Edie signaled for Fred Dove to follow her to the bathroom. He perked up, anticipating a discreet blow job or something along those lines.

But Edie only wanted a quiet place to chat. They perched their butts on the edge of the bathtub. She stroked his hand and said, "Tell me, sugar. What's on your mind?"

"OK, the company sends me the check—"

"Right."

"I give it to you," said Fred Dove, "and you deposit it in the bank."

"Right."

"And then?"

Edie Marsh answered with exaggerated clarity, like a schoolteacher coaxing an exceptionally dull-witted pupil. "*Then*, Fred, I go back to the bank in a couple days and cut *three* separate cashier's checks for forty-seven thousand *each*. Just like we agreed."

Undeterred by the condescension, he said: "Don't forget the hundred dollars I gave you to open the account."

Edie let go of his hand and brushed it, like a cockroach, off her lap. Lord, what an anal dweeb! "Yes, Freddie, I'll make absolutely sure your check says forty-seven thousand *one hundred*. OK? Feel better?"

The insurance man grunted unhappily. "I won't feel better till it's over."

Edie Marsh didn't inform Fred Dove about the phone call from the real Neria Torres. She didn't want to spook him out of the scam.

"The best part about this deal," she said, "is that nobody's in a position to screw anyone else. You've got shit on me, I've got shit on you, and we've both got plenty of shit on Snapper. That's why it's going down so clean."

Fred Dove said, "That gun of his scares me to death."

"Not much we can do. The asshole digs guns."

Outside, Donald and Marla began scratching at the bathroom door in the frenetic manner of deranged badgers.

"Let's get out there," Edie Marsh said, "before Snapper loses it."

"This is nuts!"

Edie mechanically guided Fred Dove's head to her bosom. "Don't you worry," she said, and he was momentarily transported to a warm, fragrant valley, where no harm could ever come.

Then, on the other side of the door, a gun went off, the dachshunds bayed and Snapper bellowed profanely.

"Jesus!" Edie exclaimed.

The insurance man burrowed in her cleavage. "What're we going to do?" he asked, desolately.

Avila thought: I'm either dead or dreaming.

Because it should hurt worse than this, being nailed to a cross. Even if it's only one hand, it should hurt like a mother. I ought to be screaming at the top of my lungs, instead of just hanging here with a dull ache. Hanging like a wet flag and staring at . . .

It *must* be a dream.

Because they don't have lions in Florida. And that's what that monster is, a full-grown African lion. King of the motherfucking jungle. So real you can see the red-brown stains on its mouth. So real you can smell its piss. So real you can hear the dead man's spine dear God Almighty being crunched in its fangs.

The lion was eating the doughnut man.

Avila was frozen in the pose of a scarecrow. He was afraid to blink. Between bites, the big cat would glance up, yawn, lick its paws, shake the gnats off its mane. Avila noticed a blue tag fastened to one of its ears, but that wasn't important.

The important thing was: He definitely wasn't dreaming. The lion was real. Clearly it was sent to save his life.

And not by the Catholic God—Catholics had no expertise in the summoning of demonic jungle beasts. No, it was a funkier, more mystical deity who had answered Avila's plea from the cross.

*Gracias*, Chango! *Muchas gracias*.

When I get home, Avila promised his *santería* guardian, I shall make an offering worthy of royalty. Chickens, rabbits. Perhaps I'll even spring for a goat.

In the meantime, Avila implored, please make the lion go away so I can get this fucking nail out of my hand!

The big cat dined leisurely, no more than fifteen yards from the pine tree. Ira Jackson's hammer lay where he'd dropped it, at Avila's feet. From marks on the ground, it appeared that the doughnut man had been jumped from behind, swiftly done in, and dragged to the dry weedy patch where the lion now sat, possessively attending the disemboweled, disarticulated corpse. Ira Jackson's gold chain dangled like spaghetti from the cat's whiskered maw. It disappeared with a flick of the tongue.

Avila's knowledge of lion eating habits was sketchy, but he couldn't believe the animal could still be hungry after devouring the substantial Mr Jackson. Despite the worsening pain in his hand, Avila remained rock steady against the cross until the lion quit munching and nodded off.

Slowly Avila turned his head to examine the nasty puncture. His palm was striped with congealed blood. The nail had penetrated the tough fleshy web between the second and third fingers, which wiggled feebly at Avila's silent bidding. A moral victory, of sorts—Ira Jackson had failed to break any major bones.

Keeping a close watch on the snoozing lion, and moving with glacial deliberation, Avila tugged his good hand free of the duct tape. Slowly he reached across and began to work the nail loose from the punctured palm. The undertaking caused less agony than he'd anticipated; perhaps Chango had anesthetized him as well.

Luckily, the wood of the makeshift crucifix was soft. In less than a minute the nail pulled out, and Avila's hand fell free, with only a modest geyser of blood. He inserted the hand forcefully between his shaking knees, and bit his lower lip to stifle a cry. The lion did not stir. The exhaust of its snore fluttered the bright remains of Ira Jackson's sports shirt, which clung like a lobster bib to the big cat's throat.

While the beast slept, Avila unwrapped the sticky tape from his ankles. As he furtively inched clear of the pine tree, his eyes fell on a partially masticated chunk of bone—a wee remnant of the doughnut man, but a potent talisman for future *santería* rites.

Avila pocketed the moist prize and stole away.

Skink chose to spend the night in the back of the pickup truck. Shortly after ten, Augustine emerged from the house with a hot Cuban sandwich and two bottles of beer. Skink winked appreciatively and sat up. He finished the sandwich in four huge bites, guzzled the beer and said: "So she stayed."

"I don't know why."

"Because she's never seen the likes of you."

"Or you," said Augustine.

"And because her husband behaved poorly."

Augustine slouched against the fender. "She's here, and I'm glad about it. Which makes me quite the model of rectitude—a woman on her honeymoon, for Christ's sake."

Skink arched a tangled eyebrow. "A new low?"

"Oh yes."

"Her decision, son. Don't beat yourself up."

Anxiety, not guilt, gnawed at Augustine. On his present course, he would very soon fall in love with Mrs Max Lamb. How much fragrant late-night snuggling could a man endure? And Bonnie was an ardent snuggler, even in platonic mode. Augustine was racked with worry. He had no chance whatsoever, not with her hair smelling like bougainvilleas, not with that velvet slope of neck, not with those denim-blue eyes. He couldn't recall being with a woman who felt so *right*, nestled in his embrace. Even her slumbering snorts and sniffles soothed him—that's how hard he was falling.

It's just a kiss away. Like Mick and Keith said.

A newly married woman. Brilliant.

Unconsciously Augustine found himself gazing at the window of the guest room. Soon Bonnie's shadow crossed behind the drapes. Then the lights went off.

Skink poked him sharply. "Settle down. Nothing'll happen unless she wants it to." He stood in the bed of the pickup for a series of twisting calisthenics, accompanied by preternaturally asthmatic grunts. That went on for twenty full minutes under the stars. Augustine watched without interrupting. Afterwards Skink sat down heavily, rocking the truck.

Pointing at the remaining beer, he said: "You gonna drink that?"

"Help yourself."

"You're a patient young man."

"I've got nothing but time," Augustine said. Why rush the guy?

Skink threw back his head and tilted the beer bottle until it was empty. Pensively he said: "You never know how these things'll play out."

"Doesn't matter, captain. I'm in."

"OK. Here." He handed Augustine the scrap of paper that Jim Tile had given him at the hospital. On the paper, the trooper had written:

black Jp. Cherokee
BZQ-42F

Augustine was impressed that Brenda Rourke remembered the license tag, or anything else, after the hideous beating.

Skink said, "The plate's stolen. No surprise there."

"The driver?"

"White non-Latin male, late thirties. Deformed jaw, according to Trooper Rourke. Plus he wore a pinstriped suit."

Skink returned to a sprawled position. He folded his arms under his head.

Augustine peered over the side of the truck. "Where do we start?" The man could be all the way to Atlanta by now.

"I've got some ideas," said the governor.

Augustine was doubtful. "The cops'll find him first."

"They're all on hurricane duty, double shifts. Even the detectives are directing traffic." Skink chuckled quietly. "It's not a bad time to be a fugitive."

Augustine felt something brush his leg—a neighbor's orange tabby. When he reached to pet it, the cat scooted beneath the pickup.

The governor said, "I'm doing this for Jim. It's not often he asks."

"But there's other reasons."

Skink nodded. "True. I'm not fond of shitheads who beat up women. And the storm has left me, well, unfulfilled. . . ."

It hadn't been the cataclysmic purgative he had hoped for and prophesied. Ideally a hurricane should drive people out, not bring people in. The high number of new arrivals to South Florida was merely depressing; the moral caliber of the fortune-seekers was appalling—low-life hustlers, slick-talking scammers and cold-blooded opportunists, not to mention pure gangsters and thugs. Precisely the kind of creeps who would cave in a lady's face.

"Do not," Skink said, "expect me to control my temper."

"Wouldn't dream of it," said Augustine.

The light in the guest bedroom went on. Augustine found Bonnie Lamb sitting up in bed. For a nightgown she wore a long white T-shirt that she'd found in a drawer: Tom Petty and the Heartbreakers. Augustine had purchased it at a concert at the Miami Arena. The woman whom he'd taken to the show, the psychotic doctor who later tried to filet him in the shower, had bought a black shirt to match her biker boots. At the time, Augustine had found the ensemble fetching, in a faux-trashy way.

"Max call yet?" Bonnie asked.

Augustine checked the answering machine. No messages. He returned to the bedroom and told her.

She said, "I've been married one week and a day. What's the matter with me?" She drew her knees to her chest. "I should be home."

Exactly! thought Augustine. Absolutely right!

"You think my husband's a jerk?"

"Not at all," Augustine lied, decorously.

"Then why hasn't he called." It was not a question. Bonnie Lamb said, "Come here."

She made room under the covers, but Augustine positioned himself chastely on the edge of the bed.

"You must think I'm crazy," said Bonnie.

"No."

"My heart is upside down. That's the only way to describe it."

Augustine said, "Stay as long as you want."

"I want to go along with you and . . . him. The kidnapper."

"Why?"

"Oh, I don't know. Probably goes back to Max, or my dad and his model airplanes, or my wretched childhood, even though my memories are quite wonderful. It's got to be something. Happy normal little girls don't grow up to dump their husbands, do they?" Bonnie Lamb switched off the lamp. "You want to lie down?"

"Better not," said Augustine.

In the dark, her hand found his cheek. She said, "Here's my idea: I think we should sleep together."

"But we *have* slept together, Mrs Lamb." That without missing a beat. Augustine commended himself—a little humor to cut the tension.

Bonnie said, "Come on. You know what I mean."

"Make love?"

"Oh, you're a quick one." She grabbed his shoulders and pulled him down. His head came to rest on a pillow. Before he could get up she was on top, pinning his arms. Impishly she planted her chin on his breastbone. In the light slanting through the window, Augustine was able to see her smile, the liveliness of her eyes and—behind her—the wall of gaping skulls.

Bonnie Lamb said, "Making love with you might clear my thinking."

"So would electroshock therapy."

"I'm very serious."

"And very married," said Augustine.

"Yes, but you're still getting hard."

"Thanks for the bulletin."

She let go of his arms, took his face in both hands. Her smile disappeared, and sadness entered her voice.

"Don't be such a smartass," she whispered. "Can't you understand—I don't know what else to do. I tried crying; it doesn't work."

"I'm sorry—"

"I feel closer to you than I've ever felt to Max. That's not a good sign."

"No, it isn't."

"Especially after a week of marriage. My own husband—and already I feel old and invisible when we're together." She took his shirt in her fists. "God, you know what? Forget everything I said."

"Yeah, right."

"Then you've thought about it, too."

"Constantly," said Augustine. Then, in a burst of foolish virtue: "But it would sure be wrong."

Her breasts were lined up just below his rib cage. They rose ever so slightly when she took a breath. Friendship, he reminded himself, could be excruciating.

Bonnie asked, "What happens now?"

"Oh, my erection will eventually go away. Then we can both get some sleep."

She lowered her eyes. Blushing? In the shadows it was hard to tell. She said, "No, I meant with the governor. What're you two guys up to?"

"Hair-raising thrills and high-speed adventure."

Bonnie nestled closer and settled in for the night. Augustine was severely tempted to stroke her hair, or kiss the top of her head, or trace a finger along that famous velvet slope of her neckline. But, with idiotic decency, he held back.

Mrs Max Lamb fell asleep long before he did. Shortly after midnight, the telephone began to ring in the kitchen. Augustine didn't get out of bed to answer it, because he didn't want to wake his new friend. He probably could have moved her gently to one side of the bed, but he didn't even try.

She was sleeping so soundly, and he felt so good.

# SEVENTEEN

**Bonnie Lamb rolled over** at three in the morning, freeing Augustine to rise and answer the phone, which had been ringing intermittently for hours.

Naturally it was Bonnie's husband in New York. Augustine anticipated a lively exchange.

"What's going on!" Max Lamb demanded.

"Bonnie's fine. She's asleep."

"Answer me!"

"She left you several messages. She wasn't up to the airplane trip—"

"Wake her, please. Tell her it's important."

As he waited, Max Lamb reflected over the unalloyed rottenness of his long thankless day. The NIH press conference declaiming the hazards of Bronco cigarets made CNN, MTV and all the networks, followed of course by prominent barbs in the Leno and Letterman monologues. The wiseass MTV coverage was particularly aggravating because it struck directly at young female smokers, a key market component of Bronco's booming sales growth. Front-page stories were expected the following morning in the *Times*, the *Wall Street Journal* and the Washington *Post*. The word "disaster" was insufficient to describe the crisis, as the splenetic chairman of Durham Gas Meat & Tobacco adamantly insisted on a total advertising embargo against all publications reporting the NIH findings—which was to say, all newspapers and magazines in the United States. The atmosphere at Rodale & Burns was sepulchral, due to the many millions of dollars that the agency stood to lose if Bronco's print ads were yanked. Max Lamb had spent the better part of the afternoon attempting to contact DGM&T's chairman in Guadalajara, where he was receiving thrice-daily injections of homogenized sheep semen to arrest the malignant tumors in his lungs. Workers at the clinic said the chairman was taking no calls, and refused to patch Max Lamb through to the old geezer's room.

And if that wasn't enough, Max now had to deal with a flighty, recalcitrant wife in Florida.

Bonnie's voice was husky from sleep. "Honey?" she said.

Max gripped the receiver as if it were the neck of a squirming rattlesnake. "Exactly what's going on down there!"

"I'm sorry. I need a few more days."

"Why aren't you at the motel?"

"I fell asleep here."

"With the skulls? Jesus Christ, Bonnie."

When Max Lamb got highly agitated, he acquired a frenetic rasp that his coworkers likened to that of an asthmatic on amphetamines. Bonnie didn't blame her husband for getting upset that she was with Augustine. Trying to explain was pointless, because she didn't yet comprehend it herself. Her attempted seduction—*that* she understood too well. But the urge to go road-tripping with the governor, the lack of interest in returning home to begin her new marriage . . . confusing emotions, indeed.

"I still don't feel very well, Max. Maybe it's exhaustion."

"You can sleep on the plane. Or in a damn motel."

"All right, honey, I'll get a room."

"Has he tried anything?"

"No!" Bonnie said sharply. "He's been a perfect gentleman." Thinking: *I'm* the one you've got to worry about, buddy boy.

"I don't trust him." Max Lamb's normal vibrant voice had returned, indicating a beneficial drop in blood pressure.

Bonnie decided it was safe to point out that if it weren't for Augustine, Max would still be kidnapped.

That provoked a grinding silence on the other end. Then: "There's something not right about him."

"Oh, and you're perfectly normal, Max. Driving hundreds of miles to take movies of wrecked houses and crying babies."

A movement by Augustine caught Bonnie Lamb's attention. With a mischievous grin, he produced three plump grapefruits and began to juggle, dancing barefoot around the kitchen. Bonnie covered her mouth to keep from giggling into the phone.

She heard Max say, "I'm flying to Mexico tomorrow. When I get back, I expect you to be here."

Bonnie's eyes followed the flying citrus.

"Of course I'll be there." The promise sounded so anemic that her husband couldn't possibly have believed it. Bonnie felt a wave of sadness. Max wasn't stupid; surely he knew something was wrong. She took a slow deep breath. Augustine slipped out of the kitchen and left her alone.

"Bonnie?"

"Yes, honey."

"Don't you want to know why I'm going to Mexico?"

"Mexico," she said, pensively. Thinking: He's going to *Mexico*.

Asking: "Will you be gone long, Max?"

And wondering: Who's this strange, reckless woman who has climbed inside my skin!

Avila didn't tell his wife about his harrowing brush with crucifixion, for she would've massaged it into a divine parable and shared it with all the neighbors. Once, Avila's wife had seen the face of the Virgin Mary in a boysenberry pancake, and phoned every TV station in Miami. No telling how far she'd run with a lion story.

Locking himself in the bathroom, Avila bandaged his throbbing hand and waited for his wife to depart for the grocery store. When the coast was clear, he grabbed a shovel from the garage, crept to the backyard and excavated a Tupperware box full of cash that was buried under a mango tree. The money was his wife's brother's share of a small-time marijuana venture. Avila's wife's brother resided in state prison for numerous felony convictions unrelated to the pot, so Avila and his wife had promised to baby-sit the cash until his parole, sometime around the turn of the century. Avila didn't approve of pilfering a relative's life savings, but it was an emergency. If Gar Whitmark didn't get his seven grand immediately he would call the authorities and have Avila thrown in a cell with a voracious pervert. That's how powerful Whitmark was, or so Avila believed.

He dug energetically for the Tupperware, ignoring the

pain of the nail wound. He was spurred by the putrid-sweet stench of rotting mangos, and a fear that one of his many in-laws would arrive unannounced—Avila wanted nobody to know he'd been ripped off by one of his own crooked roofers. He unearthed the container without difficulty, and eagerly pried off the lid. He removed seventy damp one-hundred-dollar bills and wadded them into a pocket. But something wasn't right: Money appeared to be missing from his wife's brother's stash. Avila's suspicion was confirmed by a hasty count; the Tupperware box was short by an additional four grand.

Dumb bitches! Avila steamed. They've been losing at Indian bingo again. His wife and her mother were practically addicted.

To confront the women would have given Avila great pleasure, but it also would've exposed his own clandestine filching. Ruefully he reburied the Tupperware, and concealed the disturbed topsoil with a mat of leaves and lawn cuttings. Then he drove to the Gar Whitmark Building, where he was made to wait in the lobby for ninety minutes, like a common peon.

When a secretary finally led him into Gar Whitmark's private office, Avila spoiled any chance for a civil exchange by asking the corporate titan what the hell was wrong with his scalp, was that a fungus or what? Avila, who had never before seen hair plugs, hadn't meant to be rude, but Gar Whitmark reacted explosively. He shoved Avila to the floor, snatched the seven grand from his hand, knelt heavily on his chest and spewed verbal abuse. Whitmark wasn't a large man, but he was fit from many afternoons of country-club tennis. Avila chose not to resist; he was thinking lawsuit. Whitmark's eyes bulged in rage, and he cursed himself breathless, but he did not punch Avila even once. Instead he got up, smoothed the breast of his Italian suit, straightened his necktie and presented the disheveled con man with an itemized estimate from Killebrew Roofing Co. for the staggering sum of $23,250.

Avila was crestfallen, though not totally surprised: Whitmark had selected the best, and most expensive, roofers in all South Florida. Also, the most honest. From his days as a crooked inspector, Avila sourly recalled the few times he'd tried to shake down Killebrew crews for payoffs, only to be chased like a skunk from the construction sites. Killebrew, like Gar Whitmark, had some heavy juice downtown.

Avila pretended to study the estimate while he thought up a diplomatic response.

Whitmark said: "They start work next week. Adjust your finances accordingly."

"Jesus, I don't have twenty-three grand." There—he'd said it.

"You're making me weep." Gar Whitmark clicked his teeth.

With a bandaged hand Avila waved the Killebrew paper in tepid indignation. "I could do this same job for half as much!"

Whitmark snorted. "I wouldn't let you put the roof on a fucking doghouse." He handed Avila a Xeroxed clipping from the newspaper. "You either come up with the money or go to jail. *Comprende*, Señor Dipshit?"

The newspaper article said the Dade State Attorney was appointing a special squad of prosecutors to crack down on dishonest contractors preying on hurricane victims.

"One phone call," said Whitmark, "and you're on your way to the buttfuck motel."

Avila bowed his head. The sight of his blackened fingernails reminded him of the buried Tupperware box. Hell, there was only twelve, maybe thirteen grand left in it. He was screwed.

"My wife's still a wreck from what your people did. You wouldn't believe the goddamn pharmacy bill." Whitmark pointed at the door and told Avila good-bye. "We'll talk," he said, ominously.

On the way home, Avila dejectedly mulled his options. How often could he turn to Chango without offending Him, or appearing selfish? Yet the *santero* priest who trained Avila had mentioned no numerical limit on supernatural requests. Tonight, Avila decided, I'll do a goat—no, *two* goats!

And tomorrow I will hunt that bastard Snapper.

The Church of High Pentecostal Rumination, headquartered in Chicoryville, Florida, attended all natural disasters in the western hemisphere. Earthquake, flood and hurricane zones proved fertile territories for conversion and recruitment of sinners. Less than thirty-six hours after the killer storm smashed Dade County, an experienced team of seven Ruminator missionaries was dispatched in a leased Dodge minivan. Hotel beds were scarce, so they shared a room at a Ramada Inn off the Turnpike. There was no complaining.

Every morning, the missionaries preached, consoled and distributed pamphlets. Then they stood in line for free army lunches at the tent city, and returned to the motel for two hours of quiet contemplation and gin rummy. The Ramada offered free cable TV, which allowed the Ruminators to view a half-dozen different religious broadcasts at any time of day. One afternoon, in the absence of a pure Pentecostal preacher, they settled on Pat Robertson and the *700 Club*. The Ruminators didn't share Robertson's paranoid worldview, but they admired his life-or-death style of fund-raising and hoped to pick up some pointers.

Toward the end of the program, Reverend Robertson closed his eyes and prayed. The Ruminators joined hands—no easy task, since four of them were on one bed and three were on the other. The prayer was not one they recognized from the Scriptures; evidently Reverend Robertson had composed it personally, since it contained several references to his post office box in Virginia. Nonetheless, it was a pretty good prayer, fervently rendered, and the Ruminator missionaries were enjoying it.

No sooner had Reverend Robertson exhaled the word "Amen" when the motel room was rocked by a muffled detonation, and the television set exploded before the missionaries' startled eyes. Reverend Robertson's squinting visage vaporized in a gout of acrid blue smoke, and his whiny beseechment faded in a sprinkle of falling glass. The Ruminators scrambled off the beds, dropped to their knees and burst into a hymn, "Nearer My God to Thee." That's how the manager of the Ramada found them, fifteen minutes later, when he came to apologize.

"Some asshole downstairs shot off a .357," he announced.

All singing ceased. The motel manager pushed the

broken television away from the wall and pointed to a ragged hole in the carpet. "From the bullet," he explained. "Don't worry. I kicked 'em out."

"A gun?" cried a Ruminator elder, springing to his feet.

"That ain't the worst of it," the motel manager said. "They had dogs in the room! You believe that? Chewin' up the bedspreads and God knows *what*." He promised to bring the Ruminators another TV set, but warned them to keep their hymn singing at a low volume, so as not to disturb other guests.

"Everybody's on edge," the manager added, unnecessarily.

After he left, the missionaries locked the door and held a solemn meeting. They agreed they'd done all they could for the good people of South Florida, and quickly packed their bags.

"Well, that was brilliant."

Snapper told Edie Marsh to shut up and quit beating it to death. What's done is done.

"No, really," she said, "getting us thrown out of the only hotel room between here and Daytona Beach. Absolute genius."

With a gaseous hiss, Snapper sagged into the Barca-Lounger. She had some nerve giving him shit, after the way she'd fucked up his leg with that crowbar. Who wouldn't be in a lousy mood, their goddamn knee all swollen up like a Georgia ham.

He said, "It's your fault, you and them dogs. Hey, get me a Coors."

On the drive back to the Torres house, they had

stopped at a 7-Eleven for gas, ice and supplies. Fred Dove had purchased Tylenol and peppermint Tic Tacs before lugubriously departing for a busy afternoon of storm-damage estimates. He drove off with the hollow stare of a man whose life had abruptly gone to ruin.

Edie Marsh pulled a beer from the cooler and tossed it underhanded at Snapper. "We're lucky we're not in jail," she said for the fifth time.

"Dogs wouldn't shut up."

"So you shot a hole in the ceiling."

"Damn straight." Snapper arranged his lower jaw to accommodate the stream of Coors. He reminded Edie of Popeye in the old Saturday cartoons.

"I'm gonna do them fuckin' mutts," he said. "Tonight when you're sleeping. That'll leave me three bullets, too, so don't get no ideas."

"Wow, a math whiz," said Edie, "on top of all your other talents."

"You don't believe me?"

"The dogs are tied outside. They're not bothering anybody."

When Snapper finished the beer, he crumpled the can and tossed it on the carpet. Then he took out the pistol and started spinning the cylinder, something he'd obviously picked up from a movie. Edie Marsh ignored him. She went to the garage to put more gasoline in the generator—they needed electricity to run the TV, without which Snapper would become unmanageable.

Sure enough, by the time she returned to the living room, he was contentedly camped out in front of *Oprah*.

"Hookers," he reported, riveted to the screen.

"Your lucky day."

Edie Marsh felt gummy with perspiration. The hurricane had eviscerated the elaborate ductwork of Tony Torres's air-conditioning system. Even if the unit had worked, there were no doors, windows or roof to keep cooled air in the house. Edie went to the bedroom and changed from her banking dress to a pair of Mrs Torres's expensive white linen shorts and a beige short-sleeved pullover. She would have been inconsolable if the borrowed clothes had fit her, but thank God they didn't; Mrs Torres was easily three sizes larger. The bagginess provided welcomed ventilation in the tropical humidity, and was not entirely unattractive.

Edie Marsh was appraising her new look in the mirror when the phone started ringing. Snapper hollered for her to pick up, goddammit!

Not given to premonitions, Edie experienced a powerful one that proved true. When she answered the telephone, a long-distance operator asked if she would accept collect charges from a "Neria in Memphis."

*Memphis*! The witch was heading south!

"I don't know anybody named Neria," Edie said, straining to stay calm.

"Is this 305-443-1676?"

"I'm not sure. See, I don't live here—I was walking past the house when I noticed the phone."

"Ma'am, please—"

"Operator, in case you haven't heard, we had a terrible hurricane down here!"

Neria's voice: "I want to speak to my husband. Ask her if Antonio Torres is around."

Edie Marsh said, "Look, the house is empty. I was walking past and I thought it might be somebody's relative calling. An emergency maybe. The man who stayed here, he's gone. Loaded his stuff in a Ryder truck and moved out Friday. Up to New York, is what he said."

"Thank you," said the operator.

"What! What's your name, lady?" Neria asked excitedly.

"Thank you," the operator repeated, trying to cut the conversation short.

But Edie was rolling. "Him and some young lady had a rental truck. Maybe his wife. She looked twenty-three, twenty-four. Long blond hair."

Neria, exploding: "No, *I'm* the wife! That's my house!"

Sure, thought Edie, now that insurance money is in the air. Dump the granola-head professor and come running back to blimpy old Tony.

"Brooklyn," Edie embellished. "I think he said Brooklyn."

"Sonofabitch," Neria moaned.

Curtly the operator asked Mrs Torres if she wished to try another telephone number. No reply. She'd hung up. Edie Marsh did, too.

Her heart drummed against her ribs. Unconsciously she rubbed her damp palms on the rump of Mrs Torres's lovely linen shorts. Then she hurried to the garage and located a pair of small green-handled wire cutters.

From the living room, Snapper called: "Who the hell was that? The wife again?" When he heard the garage door, he yelled, "Hey, I'm talkin' to you!"

Edie Marsh didn't hear him. She was sneaking next door to clip the telephone lines, so that Neria Torres could not call Mr Varga to check out the wild story about Tony and the young blonde and the Ryder truck.

The license tag on the black Cherokee was stolen from a Camaro on the morning after the hurricane, in a subdivision called Turtle Meadow. That's where Augustine was headed when Skink directed him to stop at a makeshift tent city, which the National Guard had erected for those made homeless by the hurricane.

Skink bounded from the truck and stalked through rows of open tents. Bonnie and Augustine kept a few steps behind, taking in the sobering scene. Dazed eyes followed them. Men and women sprawled listlessly on army cots, dull-eyed teenagers waded barefoot through milky puddles, children clung fiercely to new dolls handed out by the Red Cross.

"All these souls!" Skink cried, simian arms waving in agitation.

The soldiers assumed he was shell-shocked from the storm. They let him alone.

At the front of a ragged line, Guardsmen gave out plastic bottles of Evian. Skink kept marching. A small boy in a muddy diaper scurried across his path. With one hand he scooped the child to eye level.

Bonnie Lamb nudged Augustine. "What do we do?"

When they reached Skink's side, they heard him singing in a voice that was startlingly high and tender:

*It's just a box of rain,*
*I don't know who put it here.*
*Believe it if you need it,*
*Or leave it if you dare.*

The little boy—scarcely two years old, Bonnie guessed—had chubby cheeks, curly brown hair and a scrape healing on his brow. He wore a sleeveless cotton shirt with a Batman logo. He smiled at the song and tugged curiously on a silver sprout of the stranger's beard. A light mist fell from scuffed clouds.

Augustine reached for Skink's shoulder. "Captain?"

Skink, to the boy: "What's your name?"

The reply was a bashful giggle. Skink peered at the child. "You won't ever forget, will you? Hurricanes are an eviction notice from God. Go tell your people."

He resumed singing, in a nasal pitch imposed by tiny fingers pinching his nostrils.

*And it's just a box of rain,*
*Or a ribbon in your hair.*
*Such a long, long time to be gone*
*And a short time to be there.*

The child clapped. Skink kissed him lightly on the forehead. He said, "You're good company, sonny. How's your spirit of adventure?"

"No!" Bonnie Lamb stepped forward. "We're not taking him. Don't even think about it."

"He'd enjoy himself, would he not?"

"Captain, please." Augustine lifted the boy and handed him to Bonnie, who hurried to find the parents before the wild man changed his mind.

The pewter sky filled with a loud thwocking drone. People in the Evian line pointed to a covey of drab military helicopters, flying low. The choppers began to circle, causing the tents to flutter and snap. Quickly a procession of police cars, government sedans, black Chevy Blazers and TV trucks entered the compound.

Skink said, "Ha! Our Commander in Chief."

Five Secret Service types piled out of one of the Blazers, followed by the President. He wore, over a shirt and necktie, a navy-blue rain slicker with an emblem on the breast. He waved toward the television cameras, then compulsively began to shake the hands of every National Guardsman and Army soldier he saw. This peculiar behavior might have continued until dusk had not one of the President's many aides (also in a blue slicker) whispered in his ear. At that point a family of authentic hurricane refugees, carefully screened and selected from the sweltering masses, was brought to meet and be photographed with the President. Included in the family was the obligatory darling infant, over whom the leader of the free world labored to coo and fuss. The photo opportunity lasted less than three minutes, after which the President resumed his obsessive fraternizing with anyone wearing a uniform. These unnatural affections were extended to a snowy-haired officer of the local Salvation Army, around whom the Commander in Chief flung a ropy arm. "So," he chirped at the befuddled old-timer, "what outfit you with?"

A short distance away, Augustine stood with his arms folded. "Pathetic," he said.

Skink agreed. "Check the glaze in his eyes. There's nothing worse than a Republican on Halcion."

As soon as Bonnie Lamb returned, they left for Turtle Meadow.

# EIGHTEEN

**Skink had gotten** the address from the police report, courtesy of Jim Tile. The mailboxes and street signs were down, so it took some searching to find the house. Because of his respectable and clean-cut appearance, Augustine was chosen to make the inquiry. Skink waited in the back of the pickup truck, singing the chorus from "Ventilator Blues." Bonnie Lamb wasn't familiar with the song, but she enjoyed Skink's bluesy bass voice. She stood by the truck, keeping an eye on him.

Augustine was met at the door by a tired-looking woman in a pink housedress. She said, "The trooper mentioned you'd be by." Her tone was as lifeless as her stare; she'd been whipped by the hurricane.

"It's been, like, three days since I called the cops."

"We're stretched pretty thin," Augustine said.

The woman's entire family—husband, four children, two cats—was bivouacked in the master bedroom, beneath the only swatch of roof that the hurricane hadn't blown away. The husband wore a lime mesh tank top, baggy shorts, sandals and a Cleveland Indians cap. He had a stubble of gray-flecked beard. He tended a small Sterno stove on the dresser; six cans of pork and beans were lined up, the lids removed. The kids were preoccupied with battery-operated Game Boys, beeping like miniature radars.

"We still got no electric," the woman said to Augustine. She told her husband it was the man the Highway Patrol sent about the stolen license plate. The husband asked Augustine why he wasn't wearing a police uniform.

"Because I'm a detective," Augustine said. "Plainclothes."

"Oh."

"Tell me what happened."

"These four kids pulled up and took the tag off my Camaro. I was out'n the yard, burying the fish—see, when the power went off it took care of the aquarium, so we had dead guppies—"

"Sailfin mollies!" interjected one of the kids.

"Anyway, I had to bury the damn things before they stunk up the place. That's when this Jeep comes up, four colored guys, stereo cranked full blast. They take a screwdriver and set to work on the Camaro. Me standin' right there!"

The woman said, "I knew something was wrong. I brought the children inside the bedroom."

Her husband dumped two cans of pork and beans into a small pot, which he held over the royal-blue flame of the Sterno. "So I run over with a shovel and say what do you think you're up to, and one of the brothers flashes a gun and tells me to you-know-what. I didn't argue, I backed right off. Getting shot over a damn license plate was *not* on my agenda, you understand."

Augustine said, "Then what happened?"

"They slapped the tag on the Jeep and hauled ass.

You could hear that so-called music for about five miles."

The wife added, "David's got a pistol and he knows how to use it. But—"

"Not over a thirty-dollar license plate," said her husband.

Augustine commended David for being so level-headed. "Let me double-check the tag number." He took out the folded piece of paper and read it aloud: "BZQ-42F."

"Right," said David, "but it's not on that Jeep no more."

"How do you know?"

"I saw it the other day, goin' down Calusa."

"The same one?"

"Black Cherokee. Mags, tinted windows. I'd bet the farm it's the same truck. I could tell by the mud flaps."

The woman frowned. "Tell him about *those*."

"Mud flaps like what you see on them eighteen-wheelers. You know, fancy, with naked ladies."

"In chrome," the woman said. "That's how we knew it was the same one—"

Augustine said, "Where's Calusa?"

"—only some white guy was driving it."

"What'd he look like?"

"Not friendly," said the husband.

The wife said, "Watch the beans, David. And tell him about the music."

"That's the other thing," David said, stirring the pot. "He had that damn stereo all the way loud, same as the colored kids. Only it wasn't rap music, it was Travis Tritt. I thought it was weird, this guy in a business suit and a niggered-up Jeep, listenin' to Travis Tritt."

"David!" The woman reddened with genuine offense. Augustine liked her. He surmised that she was the strength of the outfit.

Her husband, halfway apologizing for the slur: "Aw, you know what I mean. All that chrome and tint, the guy didn't fit."

Augustine recalled Brenda Rourke's description of the attacker. "You're sure about the suit?"

"Clear as day."

The woman said, "We figured maybe he's the boss. Maybe the kids who stole our license plate work for him."

"It's possible," said Augustine. He sort of enjoyed playing a cop, ferreting fresh trails.

"You say he looked unfriendly. What do you mean?"

David spooned the pork and beans into matching ceramic bowls. "His face," he said. "You wouldn't forget it."

The wife said, "We were on our way to the Circle K for ice. At first I thought he had on a Halloween mask, the man in the Jeep. That's how odd he was—wait, Jeremy, that's too hot!" She intercepted her youngest son, lunging for the beans.

Augustine thanked them, on behalf of the Metropolitan Dade County Police, for their cooperation. He promised to do his best to retrieve the stolen license plate. "I've only got one more question."

"Where's Calusa?" said David, smiling.

"Exactly."

"Margo can do you a map. Use one them napkins."

*

Avila's wife found him writhing on the floor of the garage, near the Buick. He was bleeding from a large puncture in the groin. One of the sacrificial billy goats, anticipating its fate, had gored him.

"Where are they?" demanded Avila's wife, in Spanish.

Through clenched teeth, Avila confessed that both goats had escaped.

"I tole you! I tole you!" his wife cried, switching to English. She rolled Avila on his back and opened his trousers to examine the injury. "Chew need a tennis shot," she said.

"Take me to the doctor."

"Not in *my* car! I done wanno blood on de 'polstery."

"Then help me to the goddamn truck."

"Chew a mess."

"You want me to die right here on the floor? Is that what you want?"

Avila had purchased the billy goats from the nephew of a *santero* priest in Sweetwater. The nephew owned a farm on which he raised fighting cocks and livestock for religious oblations. The two goats had cost Avila a total of three hundred dollars, and they didn't get along. They'd butted heads and kicked at each other continually on the return trip to Avila's house. Somehow he had managed to wrestle both animals into the open garage, but before he could attach the tethers and shut the door, a liquid wildness had come into their huge amber eyes. Avila wondered if they'd sensed Chango's supernatural presence, or merely smelled the blood and entrails from past *santería* offerings. In any event, the goats went absolutely berserk and destroyed a perfectly good riding mower, among other items. The larger of the two billies gouged Avila cleanly with a horn before clacking off into the neighborhood.

Avila's wife scolded him zealously on the drive to the hospital. "Three hunnert bucks! Chew fucking crazy!" When swearing she customarily dropped her Spanish for English, due to the richer, more emphatic variety of profanities.

Avila snarled back: "Don't talk to me about money. You and *mamí* been losin' your fat asses at the Miccosukee bingo, no? So don't talk to me about crazy."

He checked the wound in his groin; it was the size of a fifty-cent piece. The bleeding had stopped, but the pain was fiery. He felt clammy and light-headed.

Oh, Chango, Avila thought. What have I done to anger you?

In the emergency room, a businesslike nurse eased him onto a gurney and connected him to a glorious bag of I.V. Demerol. Avila told the doctor that he'd fallen on a rusty lawn sprinkler. The doctor said he was lucky it didn't sever an artery. He asked about the dirty bandage on Avila's left hand, and Avila said it was a nasty golfing blister. Nothing to worry about.

As the pain receded, his mind drifted into a fuzzy free fall. Snapper's lopsided face appeared in a cloud.

*I will find you, coño!* Avila vowed.

But how?

Dreamily he recalled the night they'd first met. It was in a supper club on LeJeune Road. Snapper was at the bar with two women from an escort service. The women wore caked mascara and towering hair. Avila made friends. He had cash in his pocket, having moments earlier collected a bribe from a fellow who retailed fiberglass roof shingles of questionable durability. The hookers told Avila the name of the escort service was Gentlemen's Choice, and it was open seven days a week. They said Snapper was a regular customer, one of their best. They said he was taking them out on the town to celebrate, on account he was going off to prison for three to five years and wouldn't be getting much pussy, professional or otherwise. Snapper told Avila he'd killed some shithead dope dealer that nobody cared about. Prosecutors had let him cop to a manslaughter-one, and with any luck he'd get out of the joint in twenty months. Avila didn't believe a word the guy was saying, but he thought the manslaughter routine was a pretty good line to use on the babes. He bought several rounds of drinks for Snapper and the prostitutes, in hopes that Snapper might start feeling generous. And that's exactly what happened. When Avila returned from the men's room, the one he liked—a gregarious platinum blonde, Morganna was her name—whispered in his ear that Snapper said it was OK, as long as Avila paid his share. So they'd all gone to a fleabag motel on West Flagler and had quite a time. Morganna proved full of energy and imagination, well worth the shingle money.

Narcotic memories took Avila's mind off the vigorous suturing that was being done on a freshly shaved triangle five inches due southwest of his navel. Then, giddily, it came to him from out of the clouds—one obvious way for Avila to track that cocksucker Snapper and recover the seven grand.

A lead, is what cops would call it.

Not exactly a red-hot lead, but better than nothing.

*

Another curious neighbor dropped by, asking about Tony. Edie Marsh used the same ludicrous story about being a distant Torres cousin who was watching the place as a favor. She made no effort to explain Snapper, snoring in the recliner, a gun on his lap.

Fred Dove drove up a few minutes later, while Edie was walking Donald and Marla in the front yard. The insurance man looked more cheerless and pallid than ever. From the way he snatched the briefcase off the seat of the car, Edie sensed an urgency to his gloom.

"My supervisor," he announced, "wants to see the house."

"Is he suspicious?"

"No. Routine claims review."

"Then what's the problem, Fred? Show him the house."

He gave a bitter laugh and spun away. Edie tied up the dogs and followed him inside.

"The problem is," Fred Dove said, "Mister Reedy will want to chat with 'Mister and Mrs Torres.'" Loudly he dropped his briefcase on the kitchen counter, rousing Snapper.

Edie said, "Don't panic. We can handle it."

"Don't panic? The company wants to know why I got kicked out of the motel. My wife wants to know where I'm staying, and with whom. Dennis Reedy will be here tomorrow to interview two claimants that I cannot produce. Personally, I think it's an excellent time to panic."

"Hey, Santy Claus!" It was Snapper, hollering from the living room. "You got the insurance check?"

Edie Marsh went to the doorway and said, "Not yet."

"Then shut him up."

Fred Dove dropped his voice. "I can't stay here with that maniac. It's impossible."

"His leg hurts," said Edie. She had given Snapper the last of her Darvons, which evidently were beginning to wear off. "Look, I'm not thrilled about the setup, either. But it's this or go camp in the woods."

The insurance man removed his glasses and pressed his thumbs against his temples. A mosquito landed on one of his eyelids. He shook his head like a spaniel until it floated away. "We can't go through with this," he said, dolorously.

"Yes we can, sweetie. I'll be Mrs Torres. Snapper is Tony."

Fred Dove sagged. "You don't exactly look Cuban. Neither of you, for God's sake." He punched a cabinet door and cried out, "What was I *thinking*!"

Snapper declared that Fred Dove was on the brink of dismemberment unless he immediately shut the fuck up. Edie Marsh led the distraught insurance man into Neria's bedroom closet. She shut the door and kissed him with expert tenderness. Simultaneously she unzipped his pants. Fred jumped at her touch, warm but unexpected. Edie squeezed gently, until he was calm and quite helpless.

"This Dennis Reedy," she whispered, "what's he like?"

Fred Dove squirmed pleasurably.

"Tough guy? Tightass? What's his deal?"

"He seems all right," the insurance man said. He'd dealt with Reedy only once, in a flooded subdivision outside Dallas. Reedy was gruff but fair. He had approved most of Fred Dove's damage estimates, with only minor adjustments.

Edie's free hand pulled down Fred's pants. She said, "We'll go over the claim papers tonight, in case he makes it a quiz."

"What about Snapper?"

"Let me handle that. We'll have a rehearsal."

"What are you doing?" The insurance man nearly lost his balance.

"What does it look like, Fred. Will Mister Reedy have our check?"

In stuporous bliss, Fred Dove gazed at the top of Edie's head. Fingers explored her silken hair; his own fingers, judging by the familiar gold wedding band and the University of Nebraska class ring. Fred Dove struggled for clarity. It was no time for an out-of-body experience; for this long-awaited moment, he wanted sensual acuity and superior muscle control.

The insurance man struggled to purge his mind of worry and guilt, to make way for oncoming ecstasy. He inhaled deeply. The closet smelled of old gardenias and mildew: Neria Torres's pre-professor wardrobe, damp and musty from the storm. Fred Dove felt stifled, though a vital part of him was not.

Without using her hands, Edie Marsh leaned him against the wall for leverage. He released her hair and rapturously locked a monkey grip on the wooden dowel. His upturned face was obstructed by the silken armpit of somebody's wedding gown.

Suddenly he had a humiliating flashback to what had happened the last time, when Snapper interrupted them on the floor of the living room. To prevent a recurrence, Fred groped for the doorknob and held it shut.

From below, Edie Marsh paused to inquire again: "Will Reedy have the settlement check?"

"N-no. The check always comes from Omaha."

"Shit."

Fred Dove wasn't sure whether he heard her say it, or felt her say it. The important thing was, she didn't stop.

When Augustine came out to the truck, Bonnie Lamb and the governor were gone. He found them a few blocks away, behind a deserted hurricane house. Skink was kneeling next to a swimming pool, scooping chubby brown toads out of the rancid water and slipping them into his pockets. Bonnie was busy fending off the mosquitoes that hovered in an inky cloud around her face.

Augustine related what he'd learned about the black Jeep Cherokee. Skink said, "Where's Calusa Drive?"

"They drew me a map."

"Are we going now?" Bonnie asked.

"Tomorrow," Skink said. "We'll need daylight."

He and Augustine decided to spend the night nearby. They found an empty field and built a campfire from storm debris. Nearby another small fire glowed, flickering from the mouth of a fifty-five-gallon drum—itinerant laborers from Ohio. Two of them wandered over in search of crack. Augustine spooked them off with a casual display of the .38. Skink disappeared with the toads into a scrubby palmetto thicket.

Bonnie said, "What's DMT?"

"A Wall Street drug," Augustine replied. "Before our time."

"He said he dries the toad poison and smokes it. He said it's a chemical strain of DMT."

"I believe I'll stick to beer." Augustine got two

sleeping bags from the cab of the truck. He shook them out and spread them near the fire.

She said, "I'm sorry about last night."

"Quit saying that." Like it would have been the worst mistake of her entire life.

"I don't know what's wrong with me," she said.

Augustine arranged some dead branches on the fire. "Nothing's wrong with you, Bonnie. You're so normal it's scary." He sat cross-legged on one of the sleeping bags.

"Come here," he said. When he put his arms around her, she felt completely relaxed and secure. Then he said: "I can take you to the airport."

"No!"

"Because after tonight, you'll be in the thick of it."

Bonnie Lamb said, "That's what I want. Max got his adventure, I want mine."

A reedy howl rose from the palmettos, diffusing into a creepy rumble of laughter.

Bufo madness, thought Augustine. Bonnie stiffened in his embrace. Firmly she said, "I'm not leaving now. No way."

He lifted her chin. "This is not a well person. This is a man who put a shock collar on your husband, a man who gets high off frog slime. He's done things you don't want to know about, probably even killed people."

"At least he believes in *some*thing."

"Good Lord, Bonnie."

"Then why are *you* here? If he's so dangerous, if he's so crazy—"

"Who said he was crazy."

"Answer the question, Señor Herrera."

Augustine blinked at the firelight. "I'm not so tightly wrapped myself. That should be obvious."

Bonnie Lamb pressed closer. She wondered why she so enjoyed the fact that both of these new men were unpredictable and impulsive—opposites of the man she'd married. Max was exceptionally reliable, but he was neither deep nor enigmatic. Five minutes with Max and you had the whole menu.

She said, "I suppose I'm rebelling. Against what, I don't know. It's a first for me."

Augustine rebuked himself for showing off with the skulls; what woman could resist such charm? Bonnie laughed softly.

"Seriously," he said, "there's a big difference between your situation and mine. You've got a husband and a life. I've got nothing else to do, and nothing to lose by not doing it."

"Your uncle's animals?"

"Long gone," he said. "Anyway, there's worse places than Miami to be for a monkey. They'll make out fine." After a rueful pause: "I do feel lousy about the water buffalo."

Bonnie said there was no point trying to analyze motivation. Both of them were rational, mature, intelligent adults. Certainly they knew what they were doing, even if they didn't know why.

From the thicket, another penetrating wail.

Bonnie stared toward the palmettos. "I get the feeling he could take us or leave us."

"Exactly." Augustine came right out and asked her if she truly loved her husband.

She answered unhesitantly: "I don't know. So there."

Without warning, the governor crashed shirtless out of the trees. He was feverish, drenched in sweat. His good eye was as bright as a radish; the glass one was turned askew, showing yellowed bone in the socket. Bonnie hurried to his side.

"Damn," he wheezed, "was that some bad toad!"

Augustine doubted Skink's technique for removing the toxin and processing it for inhalation. Based on the man's present state, it seemed likely that he'd bungled the pharmacology.

"Sit here by the fire," Bonnie told him.

He held out his hands, which were filled with leathery, lightly freckled eggs. Augustine counted twelve in all. Skink palmed them like golf balls.

"Supper!" he exulted.

"What are they?"

"Eggs, my boy!"

"Of what?"

"I don't have a clue." The governor stalked toward the laborers' camp, returning five minutes later with a fry pan and a squeeze bottle of ketchup.

Regardless of species, the eggs tasted dandy scrambled. Augustine was impressed, watching Bonnie dig in.

When they finished eating, Skink said it was time to hit the rack. "Big day ahead. You take the sleeping bags, I'll be in the scrub." And he was gone.

Augustine returned the fry pan to the Ohio contingent, which was amiably drunk and nonthreatening. He and Bonnie stayed up watching the flames die, sitting close but saying little. At the first onslaught of mosquitoes, they dove into one of the sleeping bags and zipped it over their heads. Like two turtles, Bonnie said, sharing the same shell.

They hugged each other in the blackness, laughing uncontrollably. After Bonnie caught her breath, she said, "God, it's hot in here."

"August in Florida."

"Well, I'm taking off my clothes."

"You aren't."

"Oh yes. And you're going to help."

"Bonnie, we should get some sleep. Big day tomorrow."

"I need a big night to take my mind off it." She got tangled while wriggling out of her top. "Give me a hand, kind sir."

Augustine did as he was told. They were, after all, rational, mature, intelligent adults.

# NINETEEN

**The death of** Tony Torres did not go unnoticed by homicide detectives, crucifixions being rare even in Miami. However, most murder investigations were stuck on hold in the frenetic days following the hurricane. With the roadways in disorder, the police department was precariously shorthanded; every available officer of every rank was put to work directing traffic, chasing looters or escorting relief convoys. In the case of Juan Doe #92–312 (the whimsical caption on Tony Torres's homicide file), the lack of urgency to investigate was reinforced by the fact that no friends or relatives appeared to identify the corpse, which indicated to police that nobody was searching for him, which further suggested that nobody much cared he was dead.

Two days after the body was found, a fingerprint technician faxed the morgue to say that a proper name now could be attached to the crucified man: Antonio Rodrigo Guevara-Torres, age forty-five. The prints of the late Mr Torres were on file because he had, during one rocky stretch of his adult life, written thirty-seven consecutive bum checks. Had one of those checks not been made out to the Police Benevolent Association, Tony Torres likely would have escaped prosecution. To avoid jail, he pleaded guilty and swore to make full restitution, a pledge quickly forgotten amid the pressure of his demanding new job as a junior sales associate at a trailer-home franchise called A-Plus Affordable Homes.

Because the arrest report was old, the home address and telephone number listed for Tony Torres were no good. The current yellow pages showed no listing for A-Plus Affordable. Three fruitless inquiries sufficiently discouraged the young detective to whom the case of the crucified check-kiter had been assigned. He was relieved when his lieutenant ordered him to put the homicide file aside and drive down to Cutler Ridge, where he parked squarely in the center of the intersection of Eureka Drive and 117th Avenue, in order to block traffic for the presidential motorcade.

The young detective didn't think again of the murdered check-bouncing mobile-home salesman until two days later, when the police department got a call from an agitated woman claiming to be the victim's wife.

Avila phoned the Gentlemen's Choice escort service and asked for Morganna. She got on the line and said, "I haven't used that name in six months. It's Jasmine now."

"OK. Jasmine."

"Do I know you, honey?"

Avila reminded her of their torrid drunken night at the motel on West Flagler Street.

"Gee," she said, "that narrows it down to about ninety guys."

"You had a friend. Daphne, Diane, something like that. Redhead with a tattoo on her left tit."

Jasmine said, "What kinda tattoo?"

"I think it was a balloon or something."

"Don't ring a bell."

Avila said, "The guy you were with, you'd definitely remember. Scary dude with a seriously fucked-up face."

"Little Pepe that got burned?"

"No, it wasn't Pepe with the burns. Man's name was Snapper. His jaws stuck out all gross and crooked. You remember. It was a party before he went upstate."

"Nope, still no bell," said Jasmine. "What're you doing tonight, sweetheart? You need a date?"

What a cold shitty world, thought Avila. There was no such thing as a friendly favor anymore; everybody had their greedy paws out.

"Meet me at Cisco's," he told her tersely. "Nine o'clock at the bar."

"That's my boy."

"You still a blonde?"

"If you want."

Avila arrived twenty minutes late; he had taken a long hot shower following another furtive raid on the buried Tupperware stash. The stitches in his groin still stung from the soaking.

Jasmine sat at the bar, sipping Perrier from the bottle. She wore a subtle scarlet miniskirt and an alarming Carol Channing-style wig. Her perfume smelled like a fruit stand. Avila sat down carefully and ordered a beer. He folded a hundred-dollar bill into Jasmine's empty hand.

She smiled. "I *do* remember you now."

"What about Snapper?"

"You're a squeaker."

"*Cómo?*"

"You squeak when you fuck. Like a happy little hamster."

Avila flushed, and lunged for his beer.

"Don't be embarrassed," Jasmine said. She took his left wrist and examined the beads of his *santería* bracelet. "I remember this, too. Some sorta voodoo."

Avila pulled away. "Has Daphne heard from Snapper lately?"

"It's not Daphne anymore. It's Bridget." Jasmine dug a pack of Marlboros out of her purse. "Matter of fact, she spent the hurricane with him. Drunk as a skunk at some motel up in Broward."

Avila made no move to light her cigaret. He said, "When's the last time she saw him?"

"Just yesterday."

"Yesterday!"

It was too good to be true! Thank you, mighty Chango! Avila was awestruck and humbled.

Jasmine said, "That Snapper calls all the time, ever since he got out of Sumter. She's put her meathooks in that boy. By the way, her tattoo—it's not a balloon, it's a lollipop." Jasmine laughed. "But you were on the money about which tit."

"So where's Snapper?"

"Sugar, how should I know? He's Daphne's trick."

"You mean Bridget."

Jasmine bowed. "Touché," she said, good-naturedly.

Avila produced another hundred-dollar bill. He put it flat on the bar, beneath the Perrier bottle. "Is he at a motel?" he asked.

"A house, I think."

"Where?"

"I gotta ask her," Jasmine said.

"You need a quarter for the phone?"

"She's working tonight. Give me your number."

Avila wrote it in the margin of the damp C-note. Jasmine put it in her purse.

"I'm hungry," she said.

"I'm not."

"What's the matter?" She gave his knee a squeeze. "Oh, I know. I know why you're pissed."

"You don't know a damn thing."

"Yes I do. You're mad 'cause of what I said about the way you are in bed."

Avila shot to his feet and called for the check. Jasmine tugged him back to the barstool. Pressing her chest against his arm, she whispered, "Hey, it's all right. I thought it was cute."

"I don't *squeak*," Avila said coldly.

"You're right," said Jasmine. "You're absolutely right. Come on, honey, couldn't you go for a steak?"

Edie Marsh and Snapper had gotten into a nasty argument over the call girl. Edie had said it was no time for screwing—they needed to practice their husband-and-wife routine for when Fred Dove's boss showed up. Snapper had told her to lighten up or shut her trap. Watching the panel of saucy prostitutes on *Oprah* had made him think about licking the former Daphne's lollipop.

She was delighted to hear from him, the escort service business being slow as molasses after the hurricane. She caught a taxi to the Torres house, but got there late because the driver got lost in the pitch darkness and traffic confusion.

There was no door on which to knock, so Bridget

strolled in unannounced. Edie Marsh and Snapper were glaring at each other by candlelight in the living room.

"Hello again," Bridget said to Edie, who nodded testily.

Bridget scampered to the BarcaLounger and sprawled across Snapper's lap. She scissored her chubby legs in the air and smooched his neck (the disaligned jaws made mouth-kissing problematic).

Snapper said, "You're sittin' on my gun."

Bridget wriggled girlishly as he extricated the pistol. She said, "Baby, what happened to your leg?"

"Ask Little Miss Psychobitch."

Bridget stared at Edie Marsh. "He hit me," Edie said, remorselessly, "so I hit him back."

"With a fucking crowbar."

"Ouch," said the hooker.

Snapper told Edie to go walk the damn dogs for a couple hours.

Bridget said, "You got dogs? Where?" She sat up excitedly. "I love dogs."

"Just take off your clothes," Snapper said. "Where's the Stoli?"

"All the liquor stores were boarded up."

"Mother of Christ!"

Edie Marsh said, "Look, Bridget, nothing personal against you. But we've got a very important meeting tomorrow morning—"

"Wait, now," Snapper cut in. "You're sayin' there's no vodka? Did I hear right?"

"Baby, the storm, remember? Everything's shut down."

"Bullshit. You didn't even try."

"Chill out," said Bridget. "We don't need booze for a party."

Edie Marsh tried once more: "All I'm asking is that you're gone in the morning, OK? There's a man coming to the house, he won't understand."

"No problem, hon."

"Nothing personal."

Bridget laughed. "It's not like I had my heart set on staying over in *this* dump."

Edie said, "You should see the bathrooms. There's mosquitoes *this* big hatching in the toilets!"

Bridget made a face and pressed her knees together. Snapper said: "Edie, I'm countin' to ten. Get your lazy ass in gear."

Donald and Marla began yipping in the backyard.

"Are those your puppies?" Bridget sprang from Snapper's lap and hurried to what once had been French doors. "They sound adorable—what kind?" She peered expectantly into the night.

Snapper gimped to her side. "Fertilizer hounds," he said.

"Fertilizer hounds?"

"When I get done with 'em, yeah. That's the only goddamn thing they'll be good for." He raised the pistol and fired twice at the infernal yowling. Bridget let out a cry and covered her ears. Edie Marsh came up from behind and kicked Snapper in the crook of his bum right leg. He went down with a surprised grunt.

Outside, the volume of doggy racket increased by many decibels. Donald and Marla were hysterical with fear. Edie Marsh hurried outside to untangle the leashes before they garroted each other. Bridget knelt at Snapper's side and scolded him for being such a meanie.

The way Levon Stichler figured it, he had nothing to lose. The hurricane had taken everything, including the urn containing the ashes of his recently departed wife. The life in which he had invested most of his military pension had been reduced to broken glass and razor tinsel. Hours of painstaking salvage had yielded not enough dry belongings to fill a tackle box. Levon Stichler's neighbors at the trailer court were in the same abject fix. Within twenty-four hours, his shock and despair had distilled into high-octane anger. Someone must pay! Levon Stichler thundered. And logically that someone should be the smirking sonofabitch who'd sold them those mobile homes, the glib fat thief who'd promised them that the structures were government certified and hurricane-proof.

Levon Stichler had spotted Tony Torres at the trailer court on the morning after the hurricane, but the mangy prick had fled like a coyote. Levon Stichler had fumed for a few days, gathering what valuables he could find among the trailer's debris until county workers showed up to bulldoze the remains. The old man considered returning to Saint Paul, where his only daughter lived, but the thought of long frigid winters—and sharing space with six hyperactive grandchildren—was more than he could face.

There would be no northward migration. Levon Stichler considered his life to be officially ruined, and considered one man to be morally responsible for the tragedy. He would know no peace until Tony Torres was dead. Killing the salesman might even make Levon Stichler a hero, at least in the eyes of his trailer-court neighbors—that's what the old man convinced himself. He envisioned public sympathy and national headlines, possibly a visit from Connie Chung. And prison wouldn't be such an awful place; a damn sight safer than a double-wide trailer. Haw! Levon Stichler told no one of his mission. The hurricane hadn't actually driven him insane, but that's what he intended to plead at the trial. The Alzheimer's defense was another promising option. But first he had to devise a convincingly eccentric murder.

As soon as he settled on a plan, Levon Stichler called PreFab Luxury Homes. The phone rang over and over, causing the old man to wonder if the storm had put the trailer-home company out of business. In fact, PreFab Luxury was enjoying a banner week, thanks to a massive requisition from the Federal Emergency Management Agency. Uncle Sam, it seemed, was generously providing trailers to homeless storm victims. Many of the miserably displaced souls who'd been living in PreFab Luxury trailers when the hurricane wiped them out would be living in a PreFab Luxury product once again. Neither the company nor the federal government thought it necessary to inform tenants of the irony.

Eventually a receptionist answered the telephone, and made a point of mentioning how busy they all were. Levon Stichler asked to speak to Mr Torres. The woman said that Tony apparently was taking some personal leave after the storm and that nobody knew when he'd return to the office. Levon Stichler gathered that he wasn't the first dissatisfied customer to make inquiries.

The receptionist politely declined to divulge the salesman's home number.

From his sodden telephone directory, Levon Stichler carefully removed the page listing the names and addresses of all the Antonio Torreses in Greater Miami. Then he got in the car, filled up the tank and began the hunt.

On the first day, Levon Stichler eliminated from the list three auto mechanics, a scuba instructor, a thoracic surgeon, a palmist, two lawyers and a university professor. All were named Antonio Torres, but none was the scoundrel whom Levon Stichler sought. He was exhausted, but resolute.

On the second day, Levon Stichler continued to winnow the roster of candidates: a stockbroker, a nurseryman, a shrimper, a police officer, two electricians, an optometrist and a greenskeeper. Another Tony Torres, unkempt and clearly impaired, tried to sell him a bag of bootleg Dilaudids; still another threatened to decapitate him with a hoe.

The third day of the manhunt brought Levon Stichler to the Turtle Meadow subdivision and 15600 Calusa Drive. By then he'd seen enough hurricane destruction to be utterly unmoved by the sight of another gutted, roofless home. At least it still had walls, which was more than Levon Stichler could say for his own.

A pretty Anglo woman met him at the open front doorway. She wore baggy jeans and a long lavender T-shirt. Levon Stichler noticed she was barefoot and (unless his seventy-one-year-old eyeballs were mistaken) she was not wearing a bra. Her toenails were the shade of red hibiscus.

He said, "Is this the Torres residence?"

The woman said yes.

"Antonio Torres? The salesman?"

"That's right." The woman held out a hand. "I'm Mrs Torres. Come on in, we've been expecting you."

Levon Stichler jerked and said, "What?"

He followed the barefoot braless woman into the house. She led him to the kitchen, which was a shambles.

"Where's your husband?"

"In the bedroom. Is Mister Dove on the way?"

"I don't know," answered Levon Stichler, thinking: Who the hell is Mr Dove?

"Listen, Mrs Torres—"

"Please. It's Neria." The woman excused herself to tend the generator, which was in the garage. When she returned to the kitchen, she turned on the electric coffeemaker and made three cups.

Levon Stichler thanked her, stiffly, and took a sip. The wife would be a problem; he needed to have Tony Torres alone.

The barefoot woman stirred two spoonfuls of sugar into her coffee. "Is this your first stop of the day?"

"Sure is," said Levon Stichler, hopelessly puzzled. Having never before murdered anybody, he was full of the jitters. He glanced at his wristwatch so often that the woman couldn't help but notice.

She said, "Tony's in the shower. He'll be out very soon."

"That's OK."

"Is the coffee all right? Sorry there's no cream."

Levon Stichler said, "It's fine."

She seemed like a nice enough person. What was she doing with a crooked slob like Torres?

He heard muffled noises from another room, two

voices: a man's guttural laughter and a woman's high-pitched giggle. Levon Stichler reached slowly into the right pocket of his windbreaker. His hand tightened on the cool shaft of the weapon.

"Honey?" the barefoot woman called. "Mister Reedy's waiting."

*Reedy?* Levon Stichler's bold determination began to dissolve in a muddle. Something was awry with this particular Tony Torres. Yet Levon had spied the Salesman of the Year plaque on the wall, *PreFab Luxury Homes*, in raised gold lettering. Had to be the same creep.

Levon Stichler knew he must act swiftly, or lose forever the opportunity to avenge. He removed the concealed weapon from his jacket and raised it, ominously, for the wife to see.

"You better leave," he advised.

Calmly she set her coffee cup on the counter. Her brow furrowed, but not in fear; more as if she were stymied on a crossword puzzle. "What *is* that?" Pointing at the thing in Levon Stichler's hand.

"What's it look like?"

"A giant screw?"

"It's an auger spike, Mrs Torres. It was supposed to anchor my trailer in the storm."

Levon Stichler had choreographed the crime a hundred times in his mind, most recently while sharpening the point of the auger on a whetstone wheel. The fat face of Tony Torres would make an easy target. Either of those cavernous hairy nostrils could be forcibly modified to accept the steel bit, which would (according to Levon's calculation) extrude well beyond the nasal cavity and into the brainpan.

The barefoot woman said, "Excuse me, but are you fucking nuts?"

Before Levon Stichler could respond, the tall shape of a man materialized in the kitchen doorway. Levon Stichler aimed the spike like a lance, and charged. The woman shouted a sharp warning, and the man threw himself backward onto the wet tile floor. The auger impaled itself in the wooden shelf of a cabinet; with both hands Levon Stichler could not pull it free. Frantically he looked down at his intended victim.

"Oh shit," he said. "You're not the one." He released his grip on the spike. "You're not the one who sold me the double-wide!"

Another woman—wild-looking and half dressed—burst from the bedroom. Together she and the barefoot one helped Snapper rise to his feet.

In an accusatory tone, Levon Stichler said, "You are *not* Tony Torres."

"Like hell," Snapper said.

Edie Marsh moved between the two men. "Honey," she said, facing Snapper, "Mister Reedy here appears to be nuts."

"Worse than nuts," Bridget asserted.

"My name's not Reedy."

Edie wheeled on the old man. "Wait a second—you aren't from Midwest Casualty?"

Levon Stichler, who by now had gotten a close-up look at Snapper's feral eyes and disfigured mug, felt his brittle old bones turn to powder. "Where's Mister Torres?" he asked, with noticeably less spunk.

Edie sighed in annoyance. "Incredible," she said to Snapper. "He's not Reedy. Can you believe this shit?"

Snapper wanted to be sure for himself. He leaned forward until he was two inches from the old man's nose. "You're not from the insurance company? You're not Dove's boss?"

Misjudging the situation, Levon Stichler emphatically shook his head no. Edie Marsh stepped out of the way so Snapper could punch him into unconsciousness.

They sat on the rolled-up sleeping bags and waited for the governor to wake up in the palmettos.

Augustine assumed, as men sometimes do when they've had a particularly glorious time, that he should apologize.

Bonnie Lamb said, "For what? It was my idea."

"No, no, no. You're supposed to say it was all a terrible mistake. You got carried away. You don't know what got into you. Now you feel rotten and cheap and used, and you want to rush home to your husband."

"Actually I feel pretty terrific."

"Me, too." Augustine kissed her. "Forgive me, but I was raised Catholic. I can't be sure I've had fun unless I feel guilty afterwards."

"Oh, it's guilt you're talking about? Sure I feel guilty. So should you, allowing yourself to be seduced by a newlywed." She stood up and stretched her arms. "However, Señor Herrera, there's a big difference between guilt and remorse. I don't feel any remorse."

Augustine said, "Me, neither. And I feel guilty that I don't."

Bonnie whooped and climbed on his back. They rolled to the ground in an amorous tangle.

Skink came out of the thicket and smiled. "Animals!" he bellowed, evangelically. "No better than animals, rutting in public!"

Bonnie and Augustine got up and brushed themselves off. The governor was a sight. Twigs and wet leaves stuck to his knotted hair. Gossamer strands of a broken spider's web glistened from his chin.

He tromped melodramatically toward the campfire, shouting: "Fornicators! Fellaters! You ought to be ashamed!"

Augustine winked at Bonnie Lamb. "That's one I hadn't thought of: shame."

"Yeah, that's a killer."

The governor announced he had a tasty surprise for breakfast. "Your carnal frolics awoke me last night," he said, "so I went walking the roads."

From his fatigues he produced two small, freshly skinned carcasses. "Who wants rabbit," he asked, "and who wants the squirrel?"

Later they doused the fire and loaded the truck. Using the hand-drawn map that Augustine had been given by the helpful Margo and David, they located Calusa Drive with no difficulty. The black Jeep Cherokee was parked halfway down the street, in front of a badly damaged house; the bawdy mud flaps were impossible to miss. Skink told Augustine to keep driving. They left the pickup half a mile away and backtracked on foot.

Bonnie Lamb noticed, uneasily, that Augustine wasn't carrying either the pistol or the dart rifle. "Scouting mission," he explained.

They stayed off Calusa and approached on a parallel street, one block north. When they got close, they cut through a yard and slipped into an abandoned house directly across from 15600. From the broken window of a front bedroom, they had a clear view of the front door, the garage, the black Cherokee and two other cars in the driveway.

Margo and David were right. Their stolen license plate had been removed from the Jeep. Skink said: "Here's what happened. After the guy beat up Brenda, he pulled the tag from the Cherokee and tossed it. What's on there now probably came off that Chevy."

The car parked nearest to the garage was a late-model Caprice. The license plate was missing. The second car was a rusty barge of an Oldsmobile with a lacerated vinyl top and no hubcaps. Augustine said it would be useful to know how many people were inside the house. Skink grunted in assent.

Bonnie tried to guess what the next move would be. Notifying the police, she surmised, was not in the governor's plans. Looking around, she felt a stab of melancholy. The room had belonged to a baby. Gaily colored plastic toys were strewn on the floor; a sodden stuffed teddy bear lay facedown in a dank puddle of rainwater. Mounted on the facing wall were wooden cutouts of popular Disney characters—Mickey Mouse, Donald Duck, Snow White. Oddly, they made Bonnie Lamb think of her honeymoon and Max. The first thing he'd bought at the Magic Kingdom was a Mickey golf cap.

I should've known then and there, she thought. Bless his heart, he probably couldn't help it.

She got up to see the baby's crib. A mobile of tropical butterflies, fastened to the rail, had been snapped at the stem. The mattress was splotched with dark greenish mildew. Shiny red ants trooped across the fuzzy pink blanket. Bonnie wondered what had happened to the infant and her parents. Surely they escaped before the roof blew off.

Augustine waved her back to the broken window. Heart skipping, she knelt between the two men. *What am I doing? Where is this heading?*

Another car drives up to 15600 Calusa. A white compact.

Man gets out. Bony and clerical-looking. Gray hair. Brown windbreaker, loose dark trousers. Reminds Bonnie of her landlord back in Chicago. What was his name? Wife taught piano. What the heck was his name?

Standing by his car, the old man puts on a pair of reading glasses. Looks at a piece of paper, then up at the numerals painted on the house. Nods. Takes off the glasses. Tucks them in the left pocket of his windbreaker. Pats the right pocket, as if checking for something.

Awfully hot for a jacket, Bonnie's thinking. Summertime in Miami, how can a person be chilly?

"Where does *he* fit?" said Augustine.

"Contractor. Utility worker. Something like that," Skink speculated.

Bonnie Lamb watches the old man straighten himself, stride purposefully to the doorway. Into the house he goes.

Augustine said, "I thought I saw a woman."

"Yes." Skink scratched thoughtfully at his beard.

Creedlow! Bonnie thinks. That's the ex-landlord's name. James Creedlow. His wife, the piano teacher, her name was Regina. Chicago wasn't so long ago—Bonnie feels ditzy for not remembering. James and Regina Creedlow, of course.

Augustine said, "What now, captain?"

Skink settled his bristly chin on the windowsill. "We wait."

Two hours later, the old man still hasn't come out of the house at 15600 Calusa Drive. Bonnie's worried.

Then another car pulls up.

# TWENTY

**Neria Torres had** no desire to drive all the way to Brooklyn in search of a thieving husband.

"Then fly," suggested Celeste, the graduate student who shared the Volkswagen van with Neria and Neria's lover, the professor.

The professor's name was Charles Gabler. His field of interest was parapsychology. "Neria won't fly," he said. "She's afraid to death of airplanes."

"Wow," said Celeste, cooking on a portable stove in the back of the van. She was in charge of the macrobiotic menu.

Neria said, "It's not just the flying, it's Brooklyn. How would I find Tony in a place like that?"

"I know how," Celeste piped. "Hire a psychic."

"Great idea. We'll call Kreskin."

The professor said, "Neria, there's no need to be snide."

"Oh yes, there is."

She and Dr Gabler had been sorely low of funds when he'd proposed that young Celeste join them a week earlier as they prepared to depart Eugene, Oregon, for Miami. Young Celeste had been blessed with a comfortable trust fund, a generous heart and handsome gravity-defying breasts. Neria was under no illusions about the professor's motives, but she tried to put aside her concerns. They needed gas money, and young Celeste kept a world of credit cards in her purse. Somewhere near Salina, Kansas, Neria felt the need to inform Dr Gabler that he was paying too much attention to their travel companion, that his behavior was not only rude but disrespectful, and that the Great Plains in the heat of summer was no place to relearn the basics of hitchhiking. The professor seemed to take the warning to heart.

In truth, Neria was growing bored with Dr Gabler and his absurd blue and red crystals. Mystic healing, my ass—a box of Milk Duds starts to look pretty mystical, you smoke enough dope. Which was how the professor spent most of his waking hours, sluggishly bequeathing the driving duties to Neria and Celeste.

"I'd rather go to Miami anyway," Celeste said, measuring out two cups of brown rice. "I'd like to work in one of those tent cities. Cook for the homeless, if they need me."

The professor regarded Neria Torres through bloodshot hound-dog eyes. "Darling, it's entirely up to you. We'll go wherever you wish."

"Wow," said Neria. The mockery was lost on Celeste, who was immersed in a complex recipe. Neria declared she was going for a walk, and exited the van.

They had parked at a public campground off Interstate 20, outside Atlanta, to discuss which way to go—New York or Miami, north or south. Neria Torres replayed in her mind the upsetting conversation with the stranger who'd answered Tony's telephone. The more Neria thought about it, the more doubts she had. Not that her piggy husband wasn't capable of falling for a twenty-four-year-old blonde; rather, it was highly implausible that one would fall for him. And Brooklyn? Hardly a boomtown for the mobile-home trade. The stranger's story didn't add up.

Neria Torres had tried to confirm the lurid details with Varga, the nosy next-door neighbor, but his telephone was out of order. Neria was certain about two things: She was entitled to half the hurricane money for the house in Miami. And her estranged husband was dodging her.

New York was an astronomic long shot. At least in Florida there'd be a trail. Neria decided they should head for Miami, as originally planned.

She thought of a way to widen the net: Why not let the cops search for Tony, too? They were the pros, after all. Neria backtracked through the campground to a phone booth, where she used her husband's PIN number to call the Metro-Dade police and make a missing-person report.

After a desk officer took the information, he put Neria Torres on hold. She waited several minutes, growing increasingly impatient. The sky began to drizzle. Neria fumed. She thought of Dr Gabler and young Celeste, together in the back of the Volkswagen van. She wondered if the professor was demonstrating his "human Ouija board" exercise, the one he'd worked so charmingly on Neria herself.

Around Neria's neck hung a polished stalk of rose quartz, which Dr Gabler had given her to help channel untapped torrents of "unconditional love." Dickhead! thought Neria. At that very moment he was probably tuning young Celeste's inner chakras. Until she'd met the professor, Neria Torres hadn't known what a chakra was. Celeste undoubtedly did. She and Dr Gabler seemed to operate on the same wavelength.

The drizzle turned to a hard rain. Under Neria's feet, the red Georgia clay turned to slop. A man with a newspaper over his head came up behind her and stood uncomfortably close. He employed noisy, urgent breathing to emphasize his need for the telephone. Neria cursed aloud and slammed down the receiver.

On the other end, at Metro police headquarters in Miami, the desk officer had been diligently cross-checking the missing husband against a list of unclaimed bodies in the morgue. He was surprised to get a possible hit: One dead man had the same name, same date of birth, same extravagant brand of wristwatch.

The officer immediately had transferred Mrs Torres's phone call to the Homicide division. By the time a detective picked up, nobody was on the line.

Max Lamb flew from New York to San Diego to Guadalajara, where he slept for eleven hours. He woke up and called the airport hotel in Miami. Bonnie hadn't checked in. Max lit a Bronco cigaret and fell back on the pillow.

He chewed over a scenario in which his new wife might be cheating on him with one of two certifiable lunatics, or both. He couldn't conceive of it. The Bonnie Brooks he knew wasn't a free spirit—that was one of the things he loved about her. Steady and predictable, that was Bonnie. To Max's knowledge, the most impulsive thing she'd ever done was to hurl a stale pizza, Frisbee style, out the apartment window in Manhattan. When it came to sex, she was practically old-fashioned. She hadn't slept with *him* until their seventh date.

So it took only minutes for Max Lamb to dismiss his worries about Bonnie's fidelity. The ability to delude oneself on such matters was a benefit of owning a grossly inflated ego. Bottom line: Max couldn't imagine that Bonnie would desire another man. Especially *those* types of men: outlaws and psychos. Impossible! He snickered, blowing smoke at the notion. She was punishing him, that was all; obviously she was still ticked off about the hurricane excursion.

Scrubbing in the shower, Max Lamb refocused on the task at hand: the obstreperous Clyde Nottage Jr, ailing chairman of Durham Gas Meat & Tobacco. Max's orders were to talk some sense into the old fart, make him understand the grievous consequences of withdrawing all those expensive advertisements from print. Before Max Lamb had left New York, four Rodale & Burns executive vice presidents had individually briefed him on the importance of the Guadalajara mission. Success, Max knew, would guarantee a long and lucrative career at the agency. A home run, is how one of the honchos had put it. Turning the old man around would be a grand-slam homer in the bottom of the ninth. Clyde Nottage was one crusty old prick.

A cab took Max Lamb to the Aragon Clinic, a two-story stucco building, freshly painted and lushly landscaped, in a residential sub-division of the city. The lobby of the clinic showed evidence of recent remodeling, which unfortunately had not included central air. Max loosened his necktie and took a seat. On a glass table was a stack of informational pamphlets printed in Spanish. Curious, Max picked one up. On the first page was a drawing of a male sheep with an arrow pointing between its hind legs.

Max returned the pamphlet to the table. He wanted a smoke, but a sign on the wall said "No Fumar." A drop of sweat rolled down his jawline. Max dabbed it away with a handkerchief.

A man wearing a white medical coat came out; a pale-eyed American in his mid-sixties. He introduced himself as Dr Caulk, Mr Nottage's physician.

"When may I see him?" Max Lamb asked.

"In a few minutes. He's finishing his treatment."

"How's he doing?"

"Better, by and large," said Dr Caulk, enigmatically.

The chat turned to the clinic, and cancer. The doctor asked Max Lamb if he was a smoker.

"Just started."

"Started?" The doctor looked incredulous.

"Long story," Max said.

"Mister Nottage smokes four packs a day."

"I'd heard six."

"Oh, we've got him down to four," said the doctor. He gave the impression it was a contest of wills.

Max Lamb inquired about the unusual nature of the tumor treatments. Dr Caulk took full credit.

"We're really onto something," he told Max. "So far, the results have been quite astounding."

"What made you think to try . . . you know—"

"Sheep semen?" Dr Caulk gave a wise smile. "Actually it's quite an interesting story."

As Max Lamb listened, he wondered if the deepening consternation showed on his face. The Caulk therapy was based entirely upon the casual observation that male sheep have a low incidence of lung cancer.

"Compared to . . . ?"

The doctor slyly wagged a finger at Max. "Now you sound just like the FDA." He folded his hands and leaned forward. "I suppose you're curious about how we collect the semen."

"Not in the slightest," said Max, forcefully.

A mountainous nurse appeared at the doctor's shoulder. She said Mr Nottage's afternoon treatment was completed. Dr Caulk took Max to the old man's room.

Outside the door, the doctor dropped his voice. "I'll leave you two alone. Lately he's been a bit cranky with me."

Max Lamb had met Clyde Nottage Jr only once before, on a golf course in Raleigh. The robust, fiery, blue-eyed curmudgeon that he remembered bore no resemblance to the gaunt, gray-skinned invalid in the hospital bed.

Until Clyde Nottage opened his mouth: "The hell you staring at, boy?"

Max pulled a chair to the side of the bed. He sat down and positioned the briefcase on his lap.

"Gimme cigaret," Nottage muttered.

As Max inserted a Bronco in the old man's bloodless lips, he said, "Sir, did the doctor tell you I was coming? How are you feeling?"

Nottage ignored him. He plucked the cigaret from his mouth and eyed it ruefully. "What they say is true, all true. About these goddamn things causing cancer. I know it's a fact. So do you. So does the goddamn guv'ment."

Max Lamb was uneasy. "It's a choice people make," he said.

Nottage laughed, a tubercular snuffle. With a shaky hand he returned the cigaret to his mouth. Max lit it for him.

The old man said, "They got you trained good. Look at me, boy—you heard about the sheep jizz?"

"Yes, sir."

"I got a tumor the size of a Cuban mango in my chest, and I'm down to sheep jizz. My last earthly hope."

"The doctor said—"

"Oh, fuck him." Nottage paused to suck defiantly on the Bronco. "You're here about the ads, right? Rodale sent you to change my mind."

"Sir, the NIH report was news—bad news, to be sure. But they were only doing their jobs, the newspapers and magazines. They *had* to print the story; it was all over television—"

Clyde Nottage laughed until his nose ran. He wiped it with a hairless withered forearm. "Christ, you missed the point. They all did."

The old man's jocular tone gave Max a false burst of hope.

"I yanked those damn ads," Nottage went on, "because I was pissed. That much is true. But I wasn't mad they published the cancer report."

"Then why?"

An inch of dead ash fell from the old man's cigaret onto the sheets. He tried to blow it away, but the exertion of laughing had sapped him; his lungs moaned under the strain. After regaining his breath, he said: "The real reason I was pissed, they're fuckin' hypocrites. They tell the whole world we peddle poison, put it on the front page. Yet they're delighted to take our money and advertise that very same poison. Greedy cocksucking hypocrites, and you may quote me to the boys in New York."

Max Lamb realized the conversation had taken a perilous turn. He said, "It's just business, sir."

"Well, it's a business I'm gettin' out of. Right now. Before I leave this sorry world."

Max waited for a punch line that didn't come. He felt a quaking in his bowels.

Clyde Nottage deposited the smoldering Bronco butt in a plastic cup of orange juice. "As of this morning, Durham Gas Meat & Tobacco is Durham Gas Meat."

"Please," Max Lamb blurted. "Wait on this, please. You're not feeling well enough to make such an important decision."

"I'm dying, you fucking idiot. Three times a day some nurse looks like Pancho Villa shoots sheep cum into my belly. Damn right I don't feel well. Gimme Kleenex."

Max handed him a box of tissues from the bed tray. Nottage snatched one and hacked fiercely into it.

"Mister Nottage, I urge you not to do anything right now."

"Hell, it's already done. Made the call this morning." Nottage spit again. He opened the tissue and examined the contents with a clinical eye. "Last time I checked, I still had fifty-one percent of the company stock. You wasted a perfectly good airplane ticket, boy. The decision's made."

Max Lamb, queasy with despair, began to protest. Nottage hunched forward, cupped his palms to his face and broke into a volcanic spasm of coughing.

Max jumped away from the bed. "Shall I get Dr Caulk?"

The old man gazed into his hands and said, "Oh shit."

Max edged closer. "Are you all right?"

"Considering I'm holding a piece of my own goddamn lung."

"God!" Max turned away.

"Who knows," the old man mused, "it might be worth something someday. Put it in the Smithsonian, like Dillinger's dick."

He drew back his frail right arm and lobbed the rancid chunk of tissue at the wall, where it hung like a gob of salsa.

Max Lamb bolted from the room. Moments later, Clyde Nottage Jr put his head on the pillow and died with a merry wheeze. The expression on his face was purely triumphant.

Dennis Reedy possessed an inner radar for potential trouble. His legendary instincts had saved Midwest Casualty many millions of dollars over the years, so his services as a claims supervisor were prized at the home office in Omaha. Reedy was an obvious choice to lead the Hurricane Crisis Team: South Florida was the insurance-scam capital of the nation, and Reedy knew the territory inside and out.

His radar went on full alert at 15600 Calusa Drive. The injury to the man's jaw was old, and healed. But there was another prospective problem.

"Mister Torres," Reedy said, "how'd you hurt that leg?"

Annoyed, the man looked up from the BarcaLounger. "It was the storm," he said.

Reedy turned stiffly to Fred Dove. "You didn't mention this."

"They're not filing a claim on the injury."

Reedy suppressed the urge to guffaw in young Fred Dove's face. Antonio Torres was a textbook profile of a nuisance claimant. He was disfigured, morose and unsociable—precisely the sort of malcontent who'd have no qualms about defrauding an insurance company. The notion might not have occurred to Torres yet, but it would.

Dennis Reedy asked him how the accident had happened. Mr Torres shot a look at Mrs Torres, standing next to Fred Dove. Reedy detected nervous animosity in the husband's expression.

Mr Torres began to speak, but his wife cut in to answer: "Tony got hit by a roof beam."

"Oh?"

"While he was walking the dogs. Down the end of the street."

Fred Dove smiled inwardly with relief. Boy, she was good. And quick!

Reedy said, "So the accident didn't happen here on the property?"

"No," replied Edie Marsh, "but I wish it did. Then we'd know who to sue."

They all chuckled, except Snapper. He stared contemptuously at the emblem of a growling badger, stitched to the breast of Dennis Reedy's corporate blazer.

"I hope you don't mind my asking about the accident," said Reedy, "but it's important for us to know all the circumstances—so there's not a misunderstanding later down the road."

Edie Marsh nodded cooperatively. "Well, like I

explained to Mister Dove, I told Tony don't you walk those dogs in the storm. It won't kill us if they pee on the carpet or wherever. But would he listen? They're like his little babies—Donald and Marla is what he named them. Spoiled rotten, too. We don't have children, you understand."

She gave Snapper a sad wifely smile. The look he sent back was murderous. She said, "Tony waited till the eye passed over and the wind died before he went outside. 'Fore long it started blowing hard all over again, and before Tony could make it back with the dogs, he got hit by a beam off somebody's roof. Tore up his knee pretty bad."

Reedy nodded neutrally. "Mister Torres, where did this accident occur?"

"Down the end of the street. Like she said." Snapper spoke in a dull monotone. He hated answering questions from pencil dicks like Reedy.

"Do you recall the address, Mister Torres?"

"No, man, the rain was a mess."

"Have you seen a doctor?"

"I'll be OK."

"I think you should go to a doctor."

Fred Dove said, "I suggested the same thing."

"Oh, Tony's stubborn as a mule." Edie Marsh took Dennis Reedy's arm. "Let me show you the rest of the house."

Reedy spent an hour combing through the place. Fred Dove was a jumble of nerves, but Edie stayed cool. Flirting with Reedy was out of the question; she could tell he was an old pro. She steered him away from the hall closet where the crazy geezer with the auger spike was propped, bound and gagged.

Snapper remained sourly camped in front of the television. Edie reminded him that the portable generator was low on gas, but he paid no attention. Donahue was doing a panel on interracial lesbian marriages, and Snapper was riveted in disgust. White chicks eating black chicks! That's what they seemed to be getting at—and there's old Phil, acting like everything's perfectly normal, like he's interviewing the fucking Osmonds!

After inspecting the property, Dennis Reedy settled in the kitchen to work up the final numbers. His fingers were a blur on the calculator keypad. Fred Dove and Edie Marsh traded anticipatory glances. Reedy scratched some figures on a long sheet of paper and slid it across the counter. Edie scanned it. It was a detailed claims form she hadn't seen before.

Reedy said, "Mister Dove estimated the loss of contents at sixty-five. That's a little high, so I'm recommending sixty." He pointed with the eraser end of his pencil. "That brings the total to two hundred and one thousand. See?"

Edie Marsh was baffled. "Contents?" Then, catching on: "Oh yes, of course." She felt like a total fool. She'd assumed the estimate for the house included the Torreses' personal belongings. Fred Dove gave her a sneaky wink.

"One-forty-one for the dwelling," explained Dennis Reedy, "plus sixty for the contents."

Edie said, "Well, I guess that'll have to do." She did a fine job of acting disappointed.

"And we'd like your husband to sign a release confirming that he will not file a medical claim related to his knee injury. Otherwise the settlement process could become quite complicated. Under the circumstances, you probably don't want any delays in receiving your payment."

"Tony'll sign," said Edie. "Let me have it."

She went to the living room and knelt by the Barca-Lounger. "We're in great shape," she whispered, and placed both documents—the liability waiver and the claims agreement—on the armrest. "Remember," she said, "it's Torres with an *s*."

Snapper barely took his eyes off the television while he forged Tony's signature. "You believe these perverts?" he said, pointing at Phil's panel. "Bring me a damn beer."

Back in the kitchen, Edie Marsh thanked Dennis Reedy for his time. "How long before we get the money?"

"A couple days. You're at the top of the list."

"That's wonderful, Mister Reedy!"

Fred Dove said, "You've seen our commercials, Mrs Torres. We're the fastest in the business."

Christ, Edie thought, Fred's really overdoing it. But, with the exception of the chatty cartoon badger, she did recall being impressed by Midwest Casualty's TV spots. One in particular showed an intrepid company representative delivering claims checks, by rowboat, to Mississippi flood victims.

"I've got a laptop at the hotel," Dennis Reedy was saying. "We file by modem direct to Omaha, every night."

Edie said, "That's incredible." A couple days! But what about that extra sixty grand?

As soon as Reedy went outside, Fred Dove took her in his arms. When he tried to kiss her, she pushed him away and said, "You *knew*."

"It was supposed to be a surprise."

"Oh, right."

"I swear! Sixty thousand extra, for you and me."

"Freddie, don't screw around."

"How could I steal it, Edie? The check will be made out to 'Mister and Mrs Torres.' That's you guys. Think about it."

Irritably she paced the kitchen. "I'm so stupid," she muttered. "Jesus."

Of course the furnishings would be separate, along with the clothes and appliances and every stupid little doodad inside the place. Fred Dove said, "You never filed a big claim before. You wouldn't know."

"Dwelling *and* contents."

"Exactly."

She stopped pacing and lowered her voice. "Snapper didn't look at the new numbers."

Fred Dove gave her a thumbs-up. "That was my next question."

"I kept my hand over the papers so he wouldn't see."

"Good girl."

"Can we get two checks instead of one?"

"I think so, Edie. Sure."

"One for the dwelling, one for the contents."

"That's the idea," the insurance man said. "An extra sixty for you and me. But don't say a word about this."

"No shit, Sherlock. He's still got three bullets left, remember?" She pecked Fred Dove on the lips and aimed him out the back door.

# TWENTY-ONE

**Skink and Bonnie Lamb** kept watch over the house on Calusa while Augustine returned to the pickup truck for the guns. He wasn't in the mood to shoot at anybody, even with monkey tranquilizer. Making love to Bonnie had left him recklessly serene and sleepy-headed. He resolved to shake himself out of it.

First he attempted to depress himself with misgivings and high-minded reproach. The woman was married, newly married! She was confused, lonely, vulnerable—Augustine piled it on, struggling to feel like a worthless low-life piece of shit. But he was too happy. Bonnie dazzled him with her nerve. Augustine hadn't ever been with a woman who would stoically snack on roadkill, or fail to complain about mosquitoes. Moreover, she seemed to understand the psychotherapeutic benefits of skull juggling. "Touching death," she'd said, "or maybe teasing it."

In the aftermath of passion, zipped naked into a sleeping bag, a lover's groggiest murmurs can be mistaken for piercing insight. Augustine had cautioned himself against drawing too much from those tender exhausted moments with Bonnie Lamb. Yet here he was with a soaring heart and the hint of a goddamn spring in his step. Would he ever learn?

As much as he craved her company, Augustine was apprehensive about Bonnie's joining Skink's expedition. He feared that he'd worry about her to distraction, and he needed his brain to be clear, uncluttered. As long as the governor ran the show, trouble was positively guaranteed. Augustine was counting on it; he couldn't wait. Finally he was on the verge of recapturing, at least temporarily, direction and purpose.

Bonnie was a complication. A week ago Augustine had nothing to lose, and now he had something. Everything. Love's lousy timing, he thought.

Secret moves would be easier with only the two of them, he and Skink. But Bonnie demanded to be in the middle, playing Etta to their Butch and Sundance. The governor didn't seem to care; of course, he lived in a different universe. "'Happiness is never grand,'" he'd whispered to Augustine. "Aldous Huxley. 'Being contented has none of the glamour of a good fight against misfortune.' You think about that."

When Augustine got to the truck, he broke down the dart rifle and concealed the pieces in a gym bag. The .38 pistol he tucked in the gut of his jeans, beneath his shirt. He slung the gym bag over his shoulder and began hiking back toward Calusa, wondering if Huxley was right.

As soon as Dennis Reedy and Fred Dove drove away, Edie Marsh hauled Levon Stichler out of the closet. Snapper wasn't much help. He claimed to be saving his energy.

Edie poked the old man with a bare toe. "So what are we going to do with him?" It was a question of paramount interest to Levon Stichler as well. His eyes widened in anticipation of Snapper's answer, which was:

"Dump him."

"Where?" asked Edie.

"Far away," Snapper said. "Fucker meant to kill me."

"It was a pitiful try, you've got to admit."

"So? It's the thought that counts."

Edie said, "Look at him, Snapper. He's not worth the bullet."

Levon Stichler wasn't the slightest bit insulted. Edie pulled the gag from his mouth, prompting the old man to spit repeatedly on the floor. The gag was a dust cloth that tasted pungently of furniture wax.

"Thank you," he panted.

"Shut up, asshole," said Snapper.

Edie Marsh said: "What's your name, Grampy?"

Levon Stichler told her. He explained why he'd come to assassinate the mobile-home salesman.

"Well, somebody beat you to it." Edie described the visit by the burly fellow with the two dachshunds. "He took your scumbag Tony away. I'm certain he won't be back."

"Oh," said Levon Stichler. "Who are you?"

Snapper gave Edie a cranky look. "See? I told you we gotta kill the fucker."

The old man immediately apologized for being so nosy. Snapper said it didn't matter, they were going to dump him anyway.

Levon said, "That's really not necessary." When he began to plead his case, Snapper decided to gag him again. The old man coughed out the dust rag, crying, "Please—I've got a heart condition!"

"Good." Snapper ordered Edie Marsh to go fetch the

auger spike. Levon Stichler got the message. He stopped talking and allowed his mouth to be muffled.

"Cover his eyes, too," said Snapper.

Edie used a black chiffon scarf that she'd found in Neria Torres's underwear drawer. It made for quite a classy blindfold.

"That too tight?" she asked.

Levon Stichler grunted meekly in the negative.

"Now what?" she said to Snapper.

He shrugged unhappily. "You got any more them Darvons? My fucking leg's on fire."

"Honey, I sure don't—"

"Shit!" With his good leg he kicked Levon Stichler in the ribs, for no reason except that the old man was a convenient target. Edie pulled Snapper aside and told him to get a grip, for Christ's sake.

Under her breath: "It's all working out, OK? Reedy signed off on the settlement. All that's left is to wait for the money. Kill this geezer, you'll screw up everything."

Snapper worked his jaw like a steam shovel. His eyes were shot with pain and hangover. "Well, I can't think of nothin' else to do."

Edie said: "Listen. We put old Levon in the car and haul him out to the boonies. We tell him to take his sweet time walking back, otherwise we'll track down each of his grandchildren and . . . oh, I don't know—"

"Skin 'em like pigs?"

"Fine. Whatever. The point is to scare the hell out of him, and he'll forget about everything. All he wants to do is live."

Snapper said, "My goddamn leg's near to bust open."

"Go watch TV. I'll look for some pills."

Edie searched the medicine cabinets to see if any

useful pharmaceuticals had survived the hurricane. The best she could do was an unopened bottle of Midols. She told Snapper it was generic codeine, and pressed five tablets into his hand. He washed them down with a slug of warm Budweiser.

Edie said, "Is there gas in the Jeep?"

"Yeah. After Sally Jessy we'll go."

"And what is today's topic?"

"Boob jobs gone bad."

"How cheery," said Edie. She went outside to walk Donald and Marla.

After days in a morphine fog, Trooper Brenda Rourke finally felt better. The plastic surgeon promised to get her on the operating-room schedule by the end of the week.

Through the bandages she told Jim Tile: "You look whipped, big guy."

"We're still on double shifts. It's like Daytona out there."

Brenda asked if he'd heard what happened. "Some pawnshop off Kendall—the creep tried to hock my mom's ring."

"Same guy?"

"Sounds like it. The clerk was impressed by the face."

Jim Tile said, "Well, it's a start."

But the news worried him. He had unleashed the governor to deal with Brenda's attacker on the assumption that the governor would move faster than police. However, the pawnshop incident freshened the trail. Now it was possible that Skink's pursuit of the man in the black Cherokee would put him on a collision course with detectives. It was not a happy scenario to contemplate.

"I must look like hell," Brenda said, "because I've never seen you so gloomy."

Of course he'd let it get to him—Brenda lying pale and shattered in the hospital. In his work Jim Tile had seen plenty of blood, pain and heartache, yet he'd never felt such blinding anger as he had that first day at Brenda's bedside. Trusting the justice system to deal with her attacker had struck the trooper as laughably naive, certainly futile. This was a special monster. It was evident by what he'd done to her. The guy hated either women, cops or both. In any case, he was a menace. He needed to be cut from the herd.

Now, upon reflection, Jim Tile wished he'd let his inner rage subside before he'd made the move. When Brenda remembered the tag number off the Cherokee, he should've sent it up the chain of command; played it by the book. Turning the governor loose was a rash, foolhardy impulse; vigilante madness. Brenda would recover from the beating, but now Jim Tile had put his dear old friend at dire risk. It would be damn near impossible to call him off.

"I need to ask you something," Brenda said.

"Sure."

"A detective from Metro Robbery came by today. Also a woman from the State Attorney. They didn't know about the black Jeep."

"Hmmm."

"About the license plate—I figured you'd given them the numbers."

"I made a mistake, Bren."

"You forgot?"

"No, I didn't forget. I made a mistake."

Jim Tile sat on the edge of the bed and told her what he'd done. Afterwards she remained quiet, except to make small talk when a nurse came to dress her wounds.

Later, when she and Jim Tile were alone again, Brenda said, "So you found your crazy friend. How?"

"Doesn't matter."

"And he was right here, in this room, and you didn't introduce me?"

Jim Tile chuckled. "You were zonked, darling."

Brenda stroked his hand. He could tell she was still thinking about it. Finally she said, "Boy, you must really love me, to do something like this."

"I screwed up bad. I'm sorry."

"Enough already. I've got one question."

"OK."

"What are the odds," Brenda said, "that your friend will catch up with the asshole who got my mother's ring?"

"The odds are pretty good."

Brenda Rourke nodded and closed her eyes. Jim Tile waited until her breathing was strong and regular; waited until he was certain it was a deep healthy sleep, and not something else. Before leaving, he kissed her cheek, in a gap between bandages, and was comforted by the warmth of her skin. He felt pretty sure he saw the trace of a smile on her lips.

Skink's forehead was propped on the windowsill. He hadn't made a sound in an hour, hadn't stirred when Augustine left to get the guns. Bonnie Lamb didn't know if he was dozing or ignoring her.

"This was the baby's room. Did you notice?" she said.

Nothing.

"Are you awake?"

Still no response.

A yellowjacket flew through the broken-out window and took an instant liking to Skink's pungent mane. Bonnie shooed it away. From across the street, at 15600 Calusa, came the sound of dogs barking.

Eventually the governor spoke. "Oh, they'll be back." He didn't raise his head from the sill.

"Who?"

"Folks who own the baby."

"How can you be sure?"

Silence.

"Maybe the hurricane was all they could take."

"Optimist," Skink grumbled.

Glancing again at the drowned teddy bear, Bonnie thought that no family deserved to have their life shattered in such a harrowing way. The governor seemed to be reading her mind.

He said, "I'm sorry it happened to them. I'm sorry they were here in the first place."

"And you'll be even sorrier if they come back."

Skink looked up, blinking like a sleepy porch lizard. "It's a hurricane zone," he said simply.

Bonnie thought he ought to hear an outsider's point of view. "People come here because they think it's better than where they were. They believe the postcards, and you know what? For lots of them, it *is* better than where they came from, whether it's Long Island or Des Moines or Havana. Life is brighter, so it's worth the risks. Maybe even hurricanes."

The governor used his functional eye to scan the baby's room. He said, "Fuck with Mother Nature and she'll fuck back."

"People have dreams, that's all. Like the settlers of the old West."

"Oh, child."

"What?" Bonnie said, indignantly.

"Tell me what's left to settle." Skink lowered his head again.

She tugged on the sleeve of his camo shirt. "I want you to show me what you showed Max. The wildest part."

Skink clucked. "Why? Your husband certainly wasn't impressed."

"I'm not like Max."

"Let us fervently hope not."

"Please. Will you show me?"

Once more, no reply. Bonnie wished Augustine would hurry back. She returned her attention to the house where the black Cherokee was parked, and thought about what they'd witnessed during the long hot morning.

A half hour after the old man had arrived, a taxi pulled up. Out the doorway of 15600 Calusa had scurried a redheaded woman in a tight shiny cocktail dress and formidable high heels. Augustine and Bonnie agreed she looked like a prostitute. As the woman had wriggled herself into the back of the cab, Skink remarked that her bold stockings would make a superb mullet seine.

A short time later, a teal-blue Taurus had stopped in the driveway. The governor said it had to be a rental, because only rental companies bought teal-blue cars.

Two men had gotten out of the Taurus; neither had a disfigured jaw. The younger one was a trim-looking blond who wore eyeglasses and carried a tan briefcase. The older, heavier one had cropped dark hair and carried a clipboard; his bearing was one of authority—probably ex-military, Skink guessed, a sergeant in his youth. The two men had stayed in the house for a long time. Finally the older one had come out alone. He'd sat in the driver's side of the car, with the door open, and jotted notes. Soon the man with the briefcase had appeared around the corner of the house, from the backyard, and together they'd departed.

While the visitors didn't appear to be violent desperadoes, Skink said that one could never be certain in Miami. Augustine got the hint, and went to fetch the guns from the pickup truck.

Now the governor had his forehead on the sill, and he'd begun to hum. Bonnie asked the name of the song.

"'Number Nine Dream,'" he said.

"I don't know that one."

She wanted so much to hear about his life. She wanted him to open up and tell the most thrilling and shocking of true stories.

"Sing it for me," she said.

"Some other time." Skink pointed across the street. A man and a woman were leaving the house.

Bonnie Lamb stared. "What in the world are they doing?"

The governor rose quickly. "Come, child," he said.

After the Sally Jessy show ended, Snapper made a couple of phone calls to set something up. Exactly what, Edie

Marsh wasn't sure. Evidently he'd gotten a brainstorm about what to do with the old man, short of murder.

"Gimme hand," he said to Edie, and began tearing the living-room drapes off the rods. The drapes were whorehouse pink, heavy and dank from rain. They spread the fabric in a crude square on the floor. Then they put Levon Stichler in the middle and rolled him up inside.

To Edie, it resembled an enormous strawberry pastry. She said, "I hope he can breathe."

Snapper punched the pink bundle. "Hey, asshole. You got air?"

The gagged old man responded with an expressive groan. Snapper said, "He's OK. Let's haul his ass out to the Jeep."

Levon Stichler wasn't easy to carry. Snapper took the heavy end, but each step was agony to his shattered knee. They dropped the old man several times before they made it to the driveway. Each time it happened, Snapper swore vehemently and danced a tortured one-legged jig around the pink bundle. Edie Marsh opened the rear hatch of the Cherokee, and somehow they managed to fold Levon Stichler into the cargo well.

Snapper was leaning against the bumper, waiting for the searing pain in his leg to ebb, when he spotted the tall stranger coming toward them from the abandoned house across the street. The man was dressed in army greens. His long wild hair looked like frosted hemp. At first Snapper thought he was a street person, maybe a Vietnam vet or one of those cracked-out losers who lived under the interstate. Except he was walking too fast and purposefully to be a bum. He was moving like he had food in his stomach, good hard muscles, and something serious on his mind. Ten yards behind, hurrying to catch up, was a respectable-looking young woman.

Edie Marsh said, "Oh shit," and slammed the hatch of the Jeep. She told Snapper not to say a damn word; she'd do the talking.

As the stranger approached, Snapper straightened on both legs. The pain in his injured knee caused him to grind his mismatched molars. He slipped a hand inside his suit jacket.

"Excuse us," said the stranger. The woman, looking nervous, stood behind him.

Edie Marsh said, helpfully, "Are you lost?"

The stranger beamed—a striking smile, full of bright movie-star teeth. Snapper tensed; this was no interstate bum.

"What a fine question!" the man said to Edie. Then he turned to Snapper. "Sir, you and I have something in common."

Snapper scowled. "The fuck you talkin' about?"

"See here." The stranger calmly pried out one of his eyeballs and held it up, like a polished gemstone, for Snapper to examine. Snapper felt himself keeling, and steadied himself against the truck. The sight of the shrunken socket was more sickening than that of the glistening prosthesis.

"It's glass," the man said. "A minor disability, just like your jaw. But we both struggle with the mirror, do we not?"

"I got no problems in that department," Snapper said, though he could not look the stranger in the face. "Are you some fuckin' preacher or what?"

Edie Marsh cut in: "Mister, I don't mean to be rude, but we've got to be on our way. We've got an appointment downtown."

The stranger had a darkly elusive charm, a dangerous and disorganized intelligence that put Edie on edge. He appeared content at the prospect of physical confrontation. The pretty young woman, tame and fine-featured, seemed an unlikely partner; Edie wondered if she was a captive.

The tall stranger cocked back his head and deftly reinserted the glass eye. Then, blinking for focus, he said, "OK, kids. Let's have a peek in that snazzy Jeep."

Snapper whipped out the .357 and pointed it at a button in the center of the man's broad chest. "Get in," he snarled.

Again the stranger grinned. "We thought you'd never ask!" The young woman clutched one of his arms and tried to suppress her trembling.

Augustine noticed a young towheaded boy, rigid in a shredded patio chair outside a battered house. Most of the roof was gone, so a skin of cheap blue plastic had been stapled to the beams for shade and shelter. It puckered and flapped in the breeze.

The towheaded boy looked only ten or eleven years old. He held a stainless-steel Ruger Mini-14, which he raised from his lap as Augustine passed on the sidewalk. In a thin high pitch, the boy yelled: "Looters will be shot!"

The warning matched a message spray-painted in two-foot letters on the front wall: LOOTERS BEWAIR!!

Augustine turned to face the child. "I'm not a looter. Where's your father?"

"Out for lumber. He told me watch the place."

"You're doing a good job." Augustine stared at the powerful rifle. A bank robber had used the same model to shoot down five FBI agents in Suniland, a few years back.

The boy explained: "We had looters, night after the hurry-cane. We were stayin' with Uncle Rick, he lives somewheres called Dania. They came through while we's gone."

Augustine slowly stepped forward for a closer look. The clip was fitted flush in the Ruger; all systems Go. The boy wore a severe expression, squinting at Augustine as if he stood a hundred yards away. The boy fidgeted in the flimsy chair. One side of his mouth wormed into a creepy lopsided frown. Augustine half expected to hear banjo music.

The boy went on: "They got our TVs and CD player. My dad's toolbox, too. I'm 'posed to shoot the bastards they come back."

"Did you ever fire that gun before?"

"All the time." The child's hard gray-blue eyes flickered with the lie. The Mini-14 was heavy. His little arms were tired from holding it. "You better go on now," he advised.

Augustine nodded, backing away. "Just be careful, all right? You don't want to hurt the wrong person."

"My dad said he's gone booby-trap everything so's next time they'll be damn sorry. He went to the hardware store. My mom and Debbie are still up at Uncle Rick's. Debbie's my half-sister, she's seven."

"Promise you'll be careful with the gun."

"She stepped on a rusty nail and got infected."

"Promise me you'll take it easy."

"OK," said the boy. A droplet of sweat rolled down a pink, sunburned cheek. It surely tickled, but the boy never took a hand off the rifle.

Augustine waved good-bye and went on up the road. When he arrived at the house where he'd left Bonnie Lamb and the governor, he found it empty. Across the street, at 15600 Calusa, the black Jeep Cherokee was gone from the driveway.

# TWENTY-TWO

**Augustine sprinted across** the street. He pulled the pistol when he reached the doorway. There was no answer when he called Bonnie's name. Cautiously he went through the house. It was empty of life. The air was stale; mildew and sweat, except for one of the bedrooms—strong perfume and sex. A hall closet was open, revealing nothing unusual. A plaque on the living-room wall indicated the house belonged to a salesman, Antonio Torres. The hurricane had done quite a number on the place. In the backyard Augustine saw two miniature dachshunds tied to a sprinkler. They barked excitedly when they spotted him.

He sat down in a Naugahyde recliner and tried to reconstruct what could have happened in the twenty minutes he'd been gone. Obviously something had inspired the governor to make his move. Surely he'd ordered Bonnie to wait across the street, but she'd probably followed him just the same. Augustine had to assume they were now in the Jeep with the bad guy, headed for an unknown destination.

Augustine tore through the house once more, searching for clues. In the rubble of the funky-smelling bedroom was an album of water-stained photographs: the salesman, his spouse, and a multitude of well-fed relatives. Brenda Rourke had not recalled her attacker as an overweight Hispanic male, and the pictures of Antonio Torres showed no obvious facial deformity. Augustine decided it couldn't be the same man. He moved to the kitchen.

Hidden in a large saucepan, in a cupboard over the double sink, was a woman's leather purse. Inside was a wallet containing a Florida driver's license for one Edith Deborah Marsh, white female. Date of birth: 5–7–63. The address was an apartment in West Palm Beach. The picture on the license was unusually revealing: a pretty young lady with smoky, predatory eyes. The photo tech at the driver's bureau had outdone himself. Folded neatly in the woman's purse were pink carbons of two insurance settlements from Midwest Casualty, one for $60,000 and one for $141,000. The claims were for hurricane damage to the house at 15600 Calusa, and bore signatures of Antonio and Neria Torres. Interestingly, the insurance papers were dated that very day. Augustine was intrigued that Ms Edith Marsh would have these documents in her possession, and took the liberty of transferring them to his own pocket.

It was an interesting twist, but Augustine doubted it would help him locate Bonnie and the governor. The key to the mystery was the creep with the crooked jaw. He'd be the one carrying Brenda Rourke's service revolver. He'd be the one at the wheel of the Cherokee. Yet the house yielded no traceable signs.

With every passing moment, the creep was getting farther away. Augustine experienced a flutter of panic, thinking of what might happen. It was inconceivable that the governor would be cooperative during an abduction. Resistance was in the man's blood. A .357 aimed at his forehead would only enhance the challenge. And if he screwed up, Bonnie Lamb would be lost.

Augustine ached with dread. His impulse was to get in the truck and start driving; desperate widening grids and circles, in a wild hope of spotting the Jeep. The creep had only a short head start, but also the considerable advantage of knowing which direction he was going.

Then Augustine thought of Jim Tile, the state trooper. One shout on the police radio and every cop in South Florida would know to keep an eye open for the Cherokee. Augustine had made a point of memorizing the new tag: PPZ–350. Save the Manatee.

He picked up the kitchen phone to get the number for the Highway Patrol. That's when he noticed his old friend, the redial button.

He'd learned the trick while keeping house with the demented surgical intern, the one who ultimately knifed him in the shower. Whenever he found her gone, Augustine would touch the redial button to determine if she'd been phoning around town to score more Dilaudid, or pawn items stolen from his house. Before long he was able to recognize the voices of her various dope dealers and fences, before hanging up. In that way, the redial button had been a valuable tool for predicting his girlfriend's moods and tracing missing property.

So he punched it now, to find out the last number dialed from 15600 Calusa before Skink and Bonnie disappeared. After three rings, a friendly female voice answered:

"Paradise Palms. Can I help you?"

Augustine hesitated. He knew of only one Paradise

Palms, a seaside motel down in Islamorada. He gave it a shot. "My brother just called a little while ago. From Miami."

"Oh yes. Mister Horn's friend."

"Pardon me?"

"The owner. Mister Horn. Your brother's name is Lester?"

"Right," said Augustine, flying blind.

"He's the only Miami booking we've had today. Did he want to cancel?"

"Oh no," Augustine said. "No, I just want to make sure the reservation is all set. See, we're supposed to surprise him down there—it's his birthday tomorrow. We're going to take him deep-sea fishing."

The woman at the motel said the dolphin were hitting offshore, and advised him to try the docks at Bud 'n' Mary's to arrange a charter. "Would you like me to call over there?"

"No, that's all right."

"Does Mister Horn know?"

"Know what?" said Augustine.

"That it's Lester's birthday. He'll be so sorry he missed it—he's in Tampa on business."

"Oh, that's too bad," Augustine said. "I meant to ask—what time's my brother getting in? So we can make sure everything's arranged. You know, for the surprise party."

"Of course. He told us to expect him late this afternoon."

"That's perfect."

"And don't you worry. I won't say a word to spoil it."

Augustine said, “Ma’am, I cannot thank you enough.”

After a day of inept drinking and arduous self-pity, Max Lamb took a flight from Guadalajara to Miami. There he intended to quit smoking, reclaim his brainwashed spouse and reconstruct his life. Another honeymoon was essential—but, this time, someplace far from Florida.

Hawaii, Max thought. Maybe even Australia.

His head was a cinder block. The tequila hangover fueled vivid, horrific dreams on the plane. Once he awakened clawing at an invisible shock collar, his neck on fire. In the nightmare it was Bonnie and not the kidnapper wielding the Tri-Tronics remote control, diabolically pushing the buttons. An hour later came another dream; again his wife. This time they were making love on the deck of an airboat, skimming across the Everglades under a blue porcelain sky. Bonnie was on top of him with her eyes half open, the sawgrass whipping her cheeks. Clinging to her bare shoulder was a monkey—the same psoriatic pest that Max had videotaped after the hurricane! In the dream, Max couldn’t see the face of the airboat driver, but believed it was the quiet young man who juggled skulls. As Bonnie bucked her hips, the vile monkey hung on like a tiny wrangler. Suddenly it rose on its hind legs to display a miniature pink erection. That’s when Max screamed and woke up. He was wide-eyed but calmer by the time the plane landed.

Then, at the Miami airport, his tequila phantasms were reignited by a newspaper headline:

Remains in Fox Hollow Identified as Mob Figure; Believed Mauled, Devoured by Escaped Cat

Max bought the paper and read the story in horror. A gangster named Ira Jackson had been gobbled by a wild lion that broke out of a wildlife farm during the storm. The gruesome details heightened the urgency of Max's mission.

He arrived at Augustine's home with a prepared speech and, if necessary, a legal threat. The lights were off. Nobody answered the door. In the absence of confrontation, Max was emboldened to slip around to the backyard.

The sliding glass door on the porch was unlocked. Inside the house, it was stuffy and warm. Max started the air conditioner and turned on every lamp he could find. He wanted to advertise his presence; he didn't want to be found creeping through the halls in darkness, like a common burglar.

Thrilled by his own daring, Max combed the place for signs of his wife. Hanging in a closet was the outfit she'd worn on the day he was kidnapped. Since the rental car had been looted of their belongings, Max reasoned that Bonnie must now be wearing somebody else's clothes, or her folks had wired some cash—or perhaps Augustine had bought her an expensive new wardrobe. Wasn't that what wife-stealers did?

Max Lamb forced himself to enter the guest room. He purposely avoided the wall of skulls, but shuddered anyway under the dissipated stares. He was pleased to find the bed linens rumpled exclusively on the left side—Bonnie's favorite. A depression in the lone pillow seemed, upon inspection, to match the shape of a young woman's head. The bed showed no manifest evidence of male visitation.

An oak dresser yielded an assortment of female clothing, from bras to blue jeans, in an intriguing range of sizes. Relics of Augustine's ex-girlfriends, Max assumed. One of them must have stood six feet two, judging by the Amazonian cut of her black exercise leggings. Max located several petite items that would have fit his wife, including a pair of powder-blue sweat socks in a tidy mound on the hardwood floor. His outlook improved; at least she was wearing borrowed clothes.

He steeled himself for the next survey: Augustine's room.

The man's bed looked like a grenade had been set off under the sheets. Max Lamb thought: He's either having fantastic sex or horrible nightmares. The disarray made it impossible to determine if two persons had shared the mattress; the cast of *A Chorus Line* could have slept there, for all Max could tell.

Uncertainty nibbled at his ego. He got an idea—distasteful but effective. He bent over Augustine's bed and put his nose to the linens, whiffing for a trace of Bonnie's perfume. Uncharacteristically, Max Lamb couldn't recall the brand name of the fragrance, but he'd never forget its orchard scent.

He sniffed in imaginary grids, starting at the headboard and working his way down the mattress. An explosive sneeze announced his findings: Paco Rabanne for men. Max recognized the scent because he wore it himself (in spite of a near-incapacitating allergy) every Monday, for the sixth-floor meetings at Rodale.

Paco and laundry bleach, that's all Max detected on Augustine's sheets.

One more place to check: the wastebasket in the bathroom. Grimly Max pawed through the litter: no used condoms, thank God.

Later, stretched out on Augustine's sofa, Max realized that Bonnie's faithfulness, or possible lack thereof, wasn't the most pressing issue. It was her sanity. Somehow they'd snowed her, those madmen. Like some weird cult—one eats road pizza, the other fondles human skulls.

How could such a bright girl let herself be brainwashed by such freaks!

Max Lamb decided on a bold move. He composed a script for himself and rehearsed it for an hour before picking up the phone. Then he dialed the apartment in New York and left the message for his wandering wife. The ultimatum.

Afterwards Max called back to hear how it sounded on the answering machine. His voice was so steely that he scarcely recognized himself.

Excellent, he thought. Just what Bonnie needs to hear.

If only she calls.

Avila's wife snidely announced that his expensive *santería* goats were in the custody of Animal Control. One had been captured grazing along the shoulder of the Don Shula Expressway, while the other had turned up at a car wash, butting its horns through the grillwork of a leased Jaguar sedan. Avila's wife said it made the Channel 7 news.

"So? What do you want *me* to do?" Avila demanded.

"Oh, forget about! Three hundred dollars, chew jess forget about!"

"You want me to steal the goats back? OK, tonight I'll drive to the animal shelter and break down the fence and kidnap the damn things. That make you happy? While I'm there I'll grab you some kittens and puppies, too. Maybe a big fat guinea pig for your mother, no?"

"I hate chew! I hate chew!"

Avila shook his head. "Here we go again."

"Chew and Chango, your faggot *orícha*!"

"Louder," Avila said. "Maybe you can wake some of your dead relatives in Havana."

The phone rang. He picked it up and turned his back on his wife, who hurled a can of black beans and stormed from the kitchen in a gust of English expletives.

It was Jasmine on the line. She asked, "What's all that noise?"

"Marriage," Avila said.

"Well, love, I'm sitting here with Bridget, and guess where we're going tonight."

"To blow somebody?"

"God, look who's in a piss-poor mood."

"Sorry," Avila said. "It's been a shitty day."

"We're driving to the Keys."

"Yeah?"

"To meet your friend," said Jasmine.

"No shit? Where?"

"Some motel on the ocean. Can you believe he's payin' the both of us to baby-sit some old-timer."

"Who?" Avila couldn't imagine what new scam Snapper was running.

Jasmine said, "Just some yutz, I don't know. We're

supposed to keep him busy for a couple days, take some dirty pictures. Five hundred each is what your friend's giving us."

"Geez, that sucks."

"Business is slow, sweetie. The hurricane turned all our regulars into decent, faithful, God-fearing family men."

Avila heard Bridget's giggle in the background. Jasmine said, "So five hundred looks pretty sweet right about now."

"You can double it if you give up the name of the motel."

"Why do you think we called? Aren't you proud of me?"

Avila said, "You're the best."

"But listen, honey, we need to know—"

"Let me talk to Bridget."

"Nope, we want to know what you got in mind. Because both of us are on probation, as usual—"

"Don't worry," Avila said.

"—and we don't need no more trouble, legally speaking."

"Relax, I said."

"You ain't gonna kill this guy?"

"Which guy—Snapper? Hell, no, he owes me money is all. What time are you meeting him?"

Jasmine said, "Around eight."

Avila checked his wristwatch. "You girls ain't gonna make Key West by eight o'clock unless you got a rocket car."

"Not Key West, honey. Islamorada."

It was seventy-five miles closer, but Avila still wasn't

certain he could get there in time. First he had to make an offering; such a momentous trip was unthinkable without an offering.

He said, "Jasmine, what's the name of the motel?"

"Not till you promise me and Bridget won't get in trouble."

"Jesus, I already told you."

She said, "Here's the deal, so listen. You gotta wait till we get our money from your friend Snapper. Then you gotta promise not to shoot anybody in front of us, OK?"

Avila said, "On my wife's future grave."

"Also, you gotta promise to pay us what you said—five hundred each."

"Yep."

"Plus two stone crab dinners. That's Bridget's idea."

"No problem," Avila said. Informing the prostitutes that stone crabs were out of season would only have muddled the negotiation.

"The name," Avila pressed.

"Paradise Palms. I've never been there before. Bridget, neither, but Snapper promised it's really nice."

"Compared to prison, I'm sure it's the fucking Ritz. What's the room number?"

Jasmine asked Bridget. Bridget didn't know.

"Doesn't matter," Avila said. "I'll track you down."

"Remember what you promised!"

"Yeah, I'll try. It's already been at least seven seconds."

"Well, sweetheart, we better cruise."

Avila was about to set the receiver on the cradle when he remembered something. "Hey! Jasmine, wait!"

"Yeah, what."

"Did you tell her about me?"

"Bridget? I didn't tell her nuthin'." Jasmine sounded puzzled. "What's to tell?"

"Nuthin'."

"Oh . . . you mean about—"

"Don't say it!"

Jasmine said, "Honey, I would *never*. That was between you and me. Honest to God."

"'Cause the other night you said I was better." How valiantly Avila had labored to stifle his vocalizing during the lovemaking! What few sounds he'd made were not, by any stretch of the imagination, squeaks.

"The other night you were just great," said Jasmine. "Fantastic, even. Better than I remembered."

Avila said, "Same goes for you, too."

Later, driving to Sweetwater for the chickens, he couldn't stop thinking about the call girl's sultry compliment. Whether she meant a word of it or not wasn't worth speculating on; the concept of sincerity was so foreign to Avila's own life that he felt unqualified to pass judgment on Jasmine. He was just glad she'd quit calling herself Morganna—what a clunker of a name to remember in the heat of passion!

The combined effect of marijuana and methaqualone on Dr Charles Gabler's judgment was not salutary. Never was it more evident than late on the night of September 1, at a roadside motel off Interstate 10 near Bonifay, Florida. Overtaken with desire, the professor slipped out of the twin bed he shared with the sleeping Neria Torres, and slipped into the twin bed occupied by the wakeful young graduate student, Celeste. As he ardently attached himself to one of Celeste's creamy breasts, Dr Gabler was becalmed by a warm, harmonious confluence of physical and metaphysical currents. His timing couldn't have been worse.

Neria Torres had been reevaluating the parameters of her relationship with the professor ever since they'd pulled off a highway outside Jackson, Mississippi, so he could take a leak. Sitting in the driver's seat, watching Dr Gabler try to tinkle in some azaleas, Neria had thought: I don't find this cute anymore.

As the professor had tottered back toward the van, the beams of the headlights dramatically illuminated the ruby-colored crystals dangling from the lanyard around his neck.

"Oh wow," young Celeste had exclaimed, suffused with mystic awe and Humboldt County's finest.

That was the moment when Neria Torres had looked into her future and decided that the professor should share no large part of it; specifically, the insurance settlement from the hurricane. Neria envisioned a scenario in which Dr Gabler might endeavor to sweet-talk her out of a portion of the money—he would probably call it a friendly loan—and then flee in the dead of night with his nubile protégée. After all, that's pretty much what he'd done to his previous lover, a vendor of fine macramés, when Neria Torres entered his life.

Even if the professor harbored no selfish designs on the hurricane booty, Neria had a pragmatic reason to dump him: His appearance in Miami would complicate the duel with her estranged husband over the insurance settlement. Considering the tainted circumstance of her departure from the household, Neria doubted that Tony would be in a mood to forgive and forget. Her inability to make contact in the days following the storm was foreboding—the vindictive bastard obviously intended to pocket her half of the windfall. If the battle went to court, Dr Gabler's bleary presence during the proceedings would not, Neria Torres knew, work in her favor.

These were the thoughts she carried into sleep at the motel in Bonifay. Had it been a deeper sleep, or had the room's Eisenhower-vintage cooling unit been a few decibels louder, Neria Torres might not have been awakened by the muffled suckling and amorous hmmm-hmmms from the nearby bed. But awakened she was.

Except for cracking her eyelids, Neria didn't move a muscle at first. Instead she lay listening in disgusted fascination, struggling to arrange her emotions. On the one hand, she was vastly relieved to have found a solid excuse for jettisoning the professor. On the other hand, she was furious that the sneaky little shit would be so crude and thoughtless. Over the years, Tony Torres undoubtedly had cheated on her now and again—but never while she was sleeping in the same room!

Eventually, it was the immodest giggling of young Celeste that galvanized Neria Torres. She sprang from the bed, turned on all the lights, snatched up the velvet satchel containing Dr Gabler's special healing crystals and began whaling deliriously on the writhing mound of bedsheets. The satchel was heavy and the stones were sharp, taking a toll on the professor's unfirm flesh. With an effeminate cry, he scuttled to the bathroom and chained the door. Meanwhile the graduate student cowered nude and tearful on the mattress. The stubble on Dr Gabler's chin had left a telltale path of abraded, roseate blotches from her neck to her quivering belly. Neria Torres noticed, with fierce satisfaction, a faint comma of a scar beneath each of young Celeste's perfect breasts; an Earth Mother with implants!

Repeatedly she gasped, "I'm sorry, Neria, please don't kill me! Please don't . . ."

Neria threw the satchel of crystals to the floor. "Celeste, you know what I hope for you? I hope that asshole hiding in the john is the highlight of your entire goddamn life. Now where's the keys to the van?"

Hours later, at a busy truck stop in Gainesville, Neria tried another call to Mr Varga, her former neighbor in Miami. This time his phone was working; Varga answered on the third ring. He insisted he knew nothing about Neria's husband and a young blond hussy loading up a rental truck.

"Fact, I haven't seen Tony since maybe two days after the hurricane."

"Are there still strangers at the house?" Neria asked.

"All the time, people come and go. But no blondes."

"Who are they, Leon?"

"I don't know. Friends and cousins of Tony, I heard. They got two dogs bark half the night. I figured Tony's letting 'em watch the place."

Varga shared his theory: Neria's husband was lying low, due to adverse publicity about the mobile-home industry. "Every damn one blew to smithereens in the storm," Varga related. "The papers and TV are making a big stink. Supposedly there's going to be an investigation. The FBI is what they say."

"Oh, come off it."

"That's the rumor," Varga said. "Your Tony, he's no fool. I think he's making himself invisible till all this cools down, these people come to their senses. I mean, it's not *his* fault those trailers fell apart. God's will is what it was. He's testing us, same as He did with Noah."

"Except Noah wasn't insured," said Neria Torres.

Mr Varga was right about one thing: Tony wouldn't stick around if there was heat. His style was to take a nice hotel room and ride things out. In the meantime, he'd have some of his deadbeat relatives or white-trash salesmen pals stay with their bimbos in the house on Calusa. Tony wouldn't be far away; never would he skip town without getting his paws on the Midwest Casualty money.

Neria was buoyed. The story about the young blonde and Brooklyn obviously was bullshit, a ruse cooked up by her husband. Wishful thinking, too, Neria mused. Talking to Mr Varga validated her decision to return to Miami.

"Are you really heading home?" he asked. "You and the mister give it one more try?"

"Stranger things have happened," said Neria Torres. She made Mr Varga swear on a stack of Holy Bibles not to breathe a word. She said it would ruin everything if Tony found out she was coming.

# TWENTY-THREE

**Snapper instructed Edie Marsh** to take the Turnpike, and watch the damn speedometer. He was pressed against the passenger-side door, keeping the stolen .357 pointed at the freak in the army greens. The young woman was no immediate threat.

The stranger blinked like a craggy tortoise. He said: "How much you get for her ring?"

Snapper frowned. The fucker *knew*—but how?

Edie Marsh didn't take her eyes off the road. "What's he talking about? Whose ring?"

Snapper spied, in the lower margin of his vision, the wandering prow of his jawbone. He said, "Everybody shut the fuck up!"

Leaning forward, the longhair said to Edie: "Your rough-tough boyfriend beat up a policewoman. Ripped off her gun and her mother's wedding band—he didn't tell you?"

Edie shivered. Maybe it was his breath on the nape of her neck, or the slow rumble of his voice, or what he was saying. Meanwhile Snapper waved the police pistol and hollered for the whole world to shut up or fucking die!

He jammed a CD into the dashboard stereo: ninety-five decibels of country heartache. Within minutes his fury passed, soothed by Reba's crooning or possibly the five white pills Edie had given him back at the house.

OK, boy, now *think*.

The original plan was to waylay the nutty old man with the hookers. No problem there. A guy Snapper knew from his Lauderdale days, Johnny Horn, had a small motel down in the Keys. Ideal spot for Levon Stichler to take a short vacation. Snapper's idea was to get one a them cheap disposable cameras, so the hookers could take some pictures, the kind a respectable man wouldn't want his grandkiddies to see. Two or three days tied naked to a motel bed, the old fart wouldn't care to recall he'd ever set foot at 15600 Calusa Drive. If he promised to behave, then possibly the disposable camera would get disposed of. The old man could make his way back to Miami with nothing but a bed rash and a sore cock to show for the experience.

Best of all, Snapper wouldn't have to pay for the motel room in the Keys, because Johnny Horn owed him a favor. Two years back, Snapper had more or less repossessed a Corvette convertible from the freeloading boyfriend of one of Johnny Horn's ex-wives. Snapper had driven the Corvette straight to the Port of Miami and, in broad daylight, parked it on a container ship bound for Cartagena. It was a high-risk deal, and Johnny said for Snapper to call the Paradise Palms anytime he needed a place to crash or hide out or take some girl.

Snapper had dreamed up the plan for old man Stichler all by himself, without Edie's input. He surely didn't want to throw all that cleverness out the window, but he couldn't conceive of how to fit the new intruders into his scheme, and he was too fogged from the pills to improvise. It seemed easier to kill the one-eyed freak and his woman companion—and as long as Snapper was being so bold, why not do loony old Levon as well? That way, Snapper reasoned, he wouldn't have to pay the two whores anything, except for gas money and possibly a seafood dinner.

On the downside: How to get rid of three dead bodies? The logistics were daunting. Snapper suspected that his droopy brain wasn't up to the challenge. Killing took energy, and Snapper all of a sudden felt like sleeping for three weeks solid.

He worked up a pep talk for himself, recalling what a wise guy once told him in prison: *Dumping bodies is like buying real estate—location, location, location.* Snapper thought: Look around, boy. You got your mangrove islands, your Everglades, your Atlantic-mother-fucking-Ocean. What more you want? A fast shot to the head, then let the sharks or the gators or the crabs finish the job. What's so damn difficult about that?

But Jesus, the stakes were high; one measly fuckup and it's back to Raiford for the rest of my life. Probably locked in a ten-by-ten with some humongous horny black faggot weight lifter. Clean and jerk my skinny ass till I walk like Julia Roberts.

And shooting people *is* awful noisy. Edie Marsh wouldn't go for it, Snapper knew for a fact. She'd make quite a stink. And killing Edie with the others was impractical because (a) he didn't have enough bullets and (b) he couldn't cash the insurance checks without her. *Damn.*

"What is it?" Edie shouted over Reba.

Snapper made a sarcastic zipper motion across his lips. He thought: I'm so goddamn tired. If only I could have a nap, it would come to me. A new plan.

The one-eyed stranger began to sing along with the stereo. Snapper scrutinized him coldly. How'd he know about the lady trooper? Snapper's hands had a slight tremor. His lips were as dry as ash. What if the bitch had gone and died? What if first she'd gotten a good look at him, or maybe the Jeep? What if it was already on TV, and every cop in Florida was in the hunt?

Snapper told himself to knock it off, think positive. For the first time in days, his busted-up knee didn't hurt so much. That was something to be glad about.

The young woman in the back seat joined her flaky companion in song. She was winging it with the lyrics, but that was all right with Snapper; her voice was pretty.

Edie Marsh tapped the rim of the steering wheel and acted peeved at the amateur chorus. After about three minutes she reached out and poked the Off button on the CD player. Reba fell silent, and so did the chorus.

Snapper announced that the next selection was Travis Tritt.

"Spare us," Edie said.

"Hell's your problem?"

The woman in the back seat spoke up: "My name's Bonnie. This is the governor. He prefers to be called 'captain.'"

"Skink will be fine," said the one-eyed man. "And I would kill for some Allman Brothers."

Snapper demanded to know what they wanted, why they'd been snooping at the Torres house. The man who called himself Skink said: "We were looking for you."

"How come?"

"As a favor to a friend. You wouldn't know him."

Edie Marsh said, "You're not making a damn bit of sense."

Something shifted in the bed of the Jeep. The sound was followed by a faint quavering moan.

From the woman, Bonnie: "What are your names?"

Edie Marsh rolled her eyes. Bonnie caught it in the rearview.

Snapper said, "Fuckin' idiots, the both of 'em."

"All I meant," said Bonnie Lamb, "is what should we call you?"

"I'm Farrah Fawcett," Edie said. Nodding at Snapper: "He's Ryan O'Neal."

In discouragement, Bonnie turned toward the window. "Just forget it."

A warm hand settled on Edie's shoulder. "Whoever you are," Skink said intimately, "you make a truly lovely couple."

"Fuck you."

Snapper lunged across the seat and stuck the barrel of the .357 in a crease of the stranger's cheek. "You think I don't got the balls to shoot?"

Skink nonchalantly pushed the gun away. He eased back in the seat and folded his arms. His fearless attitude distracted Edie Marsh. Snapper commanded her to pull off at the next exit. He needed to find a bathroom.

Having never been abducted at gunpoint, Bonnie Lamb wasn't as scared as she thought she ought to be. She attributed the unexpected composure to her resolve for adventure and to the governor's implausibly confident air. Based on nothing but blind faith, Bonnie was sure that Skink wouldn't allow them to be harmed by a deformed auto thief. The guy's erratic gun handling was nerve-racking, but somehow not so menacing with another woman in the Jeep. Bonnie Lamb could tell that she wasn't some dull-eyed trailer-park tramp; she was a sharp cookie, and not especially afraid of the dolt with the pistol. Bonnie had a feeling there wouldn't be any killing inside the truck.

She wondered what Max Lamb would think if he could see her now. Probably best that he couldn't. She felt terrible about hurting her husband, but did she miss him? It didn't feel like it. Perhaps she was doing Max the biggest favor of his life. Having waited all of one week to commit adultery with a near-total stranger, Bonnie surmised that she had, in the parlance of pop psychotherapy, "unresolved issues" to confront. Poor eager Max was a victim of misleading packaging. He thought he was getting one sort of woman when he was getting another. For that Bonnie felt guilty.

She vowed not to depress herself by overanalyzing her instant attraction to Augustine. She wished he were there, and wondered how he would ever find them on the road. Bonnie herself had no clue which way they were headed.

"South," the governor reported. "And south is good."

The man with the pistol snarled: "Quiet, asshole."

Suddenly Bonnie got an eerie hologrammic vision of the gunman's naked skull on the wall of Augustine's guest room. The broken mandible caused the bony orb to rest with a sinister tilt on the shelf; a pirate's crooked grin. Then Bonnie had a flash of Augustine, juggling the gunman's skull with the others.

From a pocket Skink withdrew a squirming Bufo toad, which immediately peed on him. The man with the .357 sneered.

The woman who was driving glanced over her shoulder. "What now?" she grumbled.

"Smoke the sweat," Skink said, cupping the toad and its amber piddle in his palm, "and then you see mastodons."

"Get that stinking thing outta here," said the gunman.

"Did you know mastodons once roamed Florida? Eons before your ancestors began their ruinous copulations. Mastodons as big as cement trucks!" Skink put the toad out the window. Then he wiped the toad pee on the sleeve of the gunman's pinstriped suit.

"You fuck!" Snapper took aim at Skink's good eye.

The woman at the wheel told him to cool it—other drivers were staring. She turned off at the next exit and pulled into an abandoned service station. The hurricane had blown down the gas pumps like dominoes. Looters had cleaned out the garage. On the roof lay the remains of a Mazda Miata, squashed upside down like a bright lady-bug.

While the gunman left the Jeep to relieve himself behind the building, the woman reluctantly took charge of the .357. She looked so uncomfortable that Bonnie Lamb felt a little sorry for her; the poor girl could barely hoist the darn thing. Surely, Bonnie thought, now was the moment for Skink to make his move.

But he didn't. Instead he smiled at the woman in the driver's seat and said, "You're truly pretty. And aware of it, of course. The guiding force for most of your life, I imagine—your good looks."

The woman blushed, then toughened.

"Where'd you spend the storm?" Skink asked.

"In a motel. With Mel Gibson there," the woman said, nodding toward Snapper, "and a hooker."

"I was tied to a bridge. You should try it sometime."

"Right."

Bonnie Lamb said, "He isn't kidding."

The woman shifted the .357 to her other hand. "What on earth are you people doing? Who sent you to the house—Tony's wife?" She turned around on her knees, bracing her gun arm on the front seat. "Bonnie, dear," she said sharply. "I'd really appreciate some answers."

"Would you believe I'm on my honeymoon."

"You're joking." The woman glanced doubtfully at Skink.

Bonnie said, "Oh, not *him*. My husband's in Mexico."

"Boy, are you ever lost," said the woman.

Bonnie shook her head. "Not really."

The storm had knocked down the traffic signal at Florida City, or what was left of Florida City. A tired policeman in a yellow rainsuit directed traffic at the intersection. Edie Marsh tensed behind the wheel of the Jeep. She told Snapper to make sure the gun was out of sight. As they passed the officer, Bonnie Lamb figured it would be a fine time to poke her head out the window and shout for help, but Skink offered no encouraging signal. His chin had drooped back to his chest.

Most of the street signs remained down from the hurricane, but Bonnie saw one indicating they were about to enter the Fabulous Florida Keys. Snapper was apprehensive about possible checkpoints along Highway One, so he instructed Edie Marsh to use Card Sound Road instead.

"There's a toll," she noted.

"So?"

"I left my purse at the house."

Snapper said, "Jesus, I got money."

"I bet you do." Edie Marsh couldn't stop thinking about what the one-eyed stranger had said: Snapper assaulting a woman cop and swiping her mother's ring.

"How much *did* you get for it?" she asked.

"For what?"

"The ring." Edie stared ahead at the flat strip of road, which stretched eastward as far as she could see.

Snapper muttered obscenely. He fished in his coat and came out with a plain gold wedding band. He held it three inches from Edie's face.

"Happy?" he said.

The sight of the stolen ring affected Edie in an unexpected way: She felt repulsed, then dejected. She tried to picture the policewoman, wondered if she was married or had children, wondered what dreadful things Snapper had done to her.

Lord, Edie thought. What a small, disappointing life I've made for myself. She wanted to believe it would've been different if only she'd talked that shy young Kennedy into the sack. But she was no longer sure.

"I couldn't pawn it," Snapper was saying. "Damn thing's engraved, nobody'll touch it."

"What does it say?" Edie asked quietly. "On the ring."

"Who cares."

"Come on. What does it say?"

The woman in the back seat sat forward, also curious, as Snapper read the inscription aloud: "'For My Cynthia. Always.'" He gave a scornful laugh and hung his bony arm out the window, preparing to toss the ring from the truck.

"Don't do that," Edie said, backing off the accelerator.

"The fuck not? If I can't hock the goddamn thing, I'm gone dump it. Case we get pulled over."

Edie Marsh said, "Just don't, OK?"

"Oops. Too late." He cocked his arm and threw the ring as far as he could. It plopped into a roadside canal, breaking the surface with concentric circles.

Edie saw everything from the corner of her eye. "You lousy prick." Her voice was as hard as marble. The woman in the back seat felt the Jeep gain speed.

Defiantly Snapper waved the heavy black pistol. "Maybe you never heard of somethin' called 'possession of stolen property'—it's a motherfuckin' felony, case you didn't know. Here's another beauty: Vi-o-lay-shun o' pro-bay-shun! Translated: My skinny white ass goes straight to Starke, I get caught. Do not pass Go, do not collect any hurricane money. So fuck the cop's jewelry, unnerstand?"

Edie Marsh said nothing. She willed herself to concentrate on the slick two-lane blacktop, which intermittently was strewn with pine boughs, palmetto fronds and loose sheets of plywood. A regular obstacle course. Edie checked the speedometer: ninety-two miles per hour. Not bad for a city girl.

Snapper, ordering her to slow down, couldn't keep the raw nervousness out of his voice. Edie acted as if she didn't hear a word.

The one who called himself Skink didn't stir from his nap, trance, coma, whatever it was. Meanwhile the young newlywed (Edie noticed in the rearview) carefully removed her own wedding band from her finger.

The tollbooth was empty and the gate was up. Edie didn't bother to slow down. Bonnie Lamb held her breath.

When they blew through the narrow lane, Snapper exclaimed, "Jesus!"

As the Jeep climbed the steep bridge, Skink raised his head. "This is the place."

"Where you spent the storm?" Bonnie asked.

He nodded. "Glorious."

Beneath them, broken sunlight painted Biscayne Bay in shifting stripes of copper and slate. Ahead, a bloom of lavender clouds dumped chutes of rain on the green mangrove shorelines of North Key Largo. As the truck crested the bridge, Skink pointed out a pod of bottle-nosed dolphins rolling along the edge of a choppy boat channel. From such a height the arched flanks of the creatures resembled glinting slivers of jet ceramic, covered and then uncovered by foamy waves.

"Just look," said Bonnie Lamb. The governor was right—it was purely spectacular up here.

Even Edie Marsh was impressed. She curbed the Jeep on the downhill slope and turned off the key. She strained to keep the rollicking dolphins in view.

Snapper fumed impatiently. "What *is* this shit?" He jabbed Edie in the arm with the .357. "Hey you, drive."

"Take it easy."

"I said fucking *drive*."

"And I said take it fucking easy."

Edie was livid. The last time Snapper had seen that hateful glare was moments before she'd bludgeoned his leg with the crowbar iron. He cocked the revolver. "Don't be a cunt."

"Excuse me?" One eyebrow arched. "What'd you say?"

Bonnie Lamb feared that Edie was going to lose her mind and go for Snapper's throat, at which point she certainly would be shot dead. Snapper jammed the gun flush against her right breast.

The governor was unaware. He had everted the upper half of his torso out the window to watch the dolphins make their way north, and also to enjoy a fresh sprinkle that had begun to fall. Bonnie tried to grab his hand, but it was too large. She settled for squeezing two of his fingers. Gradually Skink drew himself back into the Jeep and appraised the tense drama unfolding in the front seat.

"You heard me," Snapper was saying.

"So that *was* you," Edie said, "calling me a cunt."

Violently Snapper twisted the gun barrel, bunching the fabric of Edie's blouse and wringing the soft flesh beneath it. God, Bonnie thought, that's got to hurt.

Edie Marsh didn't let it show.

"Drive!" Snapper told her again.

"When I'm through watching Flipper."

"Fuck Flipper." Snapper raised the .357 and fired once through the top of the Jeep.

Bonnie Lamb cried out and covered her ears. Edie Marsh clutched the steering wheel to steady herself. The pain in her right breast made her wonder briefly if she was shot. She wasn't.

Snapper cheerlessly eyed the hole in the roof of the truck; the acrid whiff of cordite made him sneeze. "God bless me," he said, with a dark chuckle.

A door opened. Skink got out of the Jeep to stretch. "Don't you love this place!" He unfolded his long arms toward the clouds. "Don't it bring out the beast in your soul!"

Glorious, Bonnie agreed silently. That's the word for it.

"Get back in the car," Snapper barked.

Skink obliged, shaking the raindrops from his hair like a sheep dog. Without a word, Edie Marsh started the engine and drove on.

# TWENTY-FOUR

**"What do you mean,** no roosters?"

The owner of the *botánica* apologized. It had been a busy week for fowl. He offered Avila a sacrificial billy goat instead.

Avila said, "No way, José." The sutures from his goring itched constantly. "I never heard anyone running outta roosters. What else you got?"

"Turtles."

"I don't got time to do turtles," Avila said. Removing the shells was a messy chore. "You got any pigeons?"

"Sorry, meng."

"Lambs?"

"Tomorrow morning."

"How about cats?"

"No, meng, hiss no legal."

"Yeah, like you give a shit." Avila checked his wristwatch; he had to hurry, do this thing then get on the road to the Keys. "OK, señor, what *do* you got?"

The shop owner led him to a small storage room and pointed at a wooden crate. Inside, Avila could make out a furry brown animal the size of a beagle. It had shoe-button eyes, an anteater nose, and a long slender tail circled with black rings.

Avila said, "What, some kinda raccoon?"

"Coatimundi. From South America."

The animal chittered inquisitively and poked its velvety nostrils through the slats of the crate. It was one of the oddest creatures Avila had ever seen.

"Big medicine," promised the shop owner.

"I need something for Chango."

"Oh, Chango would love heem." The shop owner had astutely pegged Avila for a rank amateur who knew next to nothing about *santería*. The shop owner said, "*Sí, es muy bueno por Chango.*"

Avila said, "Will it bite?"

"No, my freng. See?" The *botánica* man tickled the coati's moist nose. "Like a puppy dog."

"OK, how much?"

"Seventy-five."

"Here's sixty, *chico*. Help me carry it to the car."

As he drove up to the house, Avila saw the Buick backing out of the driveway; his wife and her mother, undoubtedly off to Indian bingo. He waved. They waved.

Avila gloated. Perfect timing. For once I'll have the place to myself. Quickly he dragged the wooden crate into the garage and lowered the electric door. The coati huffed in objection. From a cane-wicker chest Avila hastily removed the implements of sacrifice—tarnished pennies, coconut husks, the bleached ribs of a cat, polished turtle shells, and an old pewter goblet. From a galvanized lockbox Avila took his newest, and potentially most powerful, artifact—the gnawed chip of bone belonging to the evil man who had tried to crucify him. Reverently, and with high hopes, Avila placed the bone in the pewter goblet, soon to be filled with animal blood.

For sustenance Chango was known to favor dry wine and candies; the best Avila could do, on short notice, was a pitcher of sangria and a roll of stale wintergreen Life Savers. He lighted three tall candles and arranged them triangularly on the cement floor of the garage. Inside the triangle, he began to set up the altar. The coatimundi had gone silent; Avila felt its stare from between the slats. Could it know? He whisked the thought from his mind.

The final item to be removed from the wicker chest was the most important: a ten-inch hunting knife, with a handle carved from genuine elk antler. The knife was an antique, made in Wyoming. Avila had received it as a bribe when he worked as a county building inspector—a Christmas offering from an unlicensed roofer hoping that Avila might overlook a seriously defective scissor truss. Somehow Avila had found it in his heart to do just that.

Vigorously he sharpened the hunting knife on a whetstone. The coati began to pace and snort. Avila discreetly concealed the gleaming blade from the doomed animal. Then he stepped inside the triangle of candles and improvised a short prayer to Chango, who (Avila trusted) would understand that he was pressed for time.

Afterwards he took a pry bar and started peeling the wooden slats off the crate. The sacramental coati became highly agitated. Avila attempted to soothe it with soft words, but the beast wasn't fooled. It shot from the crate and tore crazed circles throughout the garage, scattering cat bones and tipping two of the *santería* candles. Avila tried to subdue the coati by stunning it with the pry bar, but it was too swift and agile. Like a monkey, it vertically scampered up a wall of metal shelves and bounded onto the ceiling track of the electric door-opener. There it perched, using its remarkable tail for balance, squealing and baring sharp yellow teeth. Meanwhile one of the *santería* candles rolled beneath Avila's lawn mower, igniting the gas tank. Cursing bitterly, Avila ran to the kitchen for the fire extinguisher. When he returned to the garage, he was confronted with fresh disaster.

The electric door was open. In the driveway was his wife's Buick, idling. Why she had come back, Avila didn't know. Perhaps she'd decided to pilfer the buried Tupperware for extra bingo money. It truly didn't matter.

Apparently her mother had emerged from the car first. The scene that greeted Avila was so stupefying that he temporarily forgot about the flaming lawn mower. For reasons beyond human comprehension, the overwrought coatimundi had jumped from its roost in the garage, dashed outdoors and scaled Avila's mother-in-law. Now the creature was nesting in the woman's coiffure, a brittle edifice of chromium orange. Avila had always believed that his wife's mother wore wigs, but here was persuasive evidence that her fantastic mop was genuine. She shrieked and spun about the front yard, flailing spastically at the demon on her scalp. The jabbering coati dug in with all four claws. No hairpiece, Avila decided, could withstand such a test.

His wife bilingually shouted that he should do something, for God's sake, don't just stand there! The pry bar was out of the question; one misplaced blow and that would be the end of his mother-in-law. So Avila tried the fire extinguisher. He unloaded at point-blank range, soaping the stubborn animal with sodium bicarbonate.

The coati snarled and snapped but, incredibly, refused to vacate the old woman's hair. In the turmoil it was inevitable that some of the cold mist from the fire extinguisher would hit Avila's mother-in-law, who mashed her knuckles to her eyes and began a blind run. Avila gave chase for three-quarters of a block, periodically firing short bursts, but the old woman showed surprising speed.

Avila gave up and trotted home to extinguish the fire in the garage. Afterwards he rolled the charred lawn mower to the backyard and hosed it down. His distraught wife remained sprawled across the hood of the Buick, crying: "*Mamí, mamí*, luke what chew did to my *mamí*!"

Above her keening rose the unmistakable whine of sirens—someone on the block had probably called the fire department. Avila thought: Why can't people mind their own goddamn business! He was steaming as he hurried to his car.

At the very moment he fit the key in the ignition, the passenger window exploded. Avila nearly wet himself in shock. There stood his wife, beet-faced and seething, holding the iron pry bar.

"Chew fucking bastard!" she cried.

Avila jammed his heel to the accelerator and sped away.

"O Chango, Chango," he whispered, brushing chunks of glass from his lap. "I know I fucked up again, but don't abandon me now. Not tonight."

A peculiar trait of this hurricane, Jim Tile marveled on the drive along North Key Largo, was the dramatic definition of its swath. The eye had come ashore like a bullet, devastating a thin corridor but leaving virtually untouched the coastline to the immediate north and south. August hurricanes are seldom so courteous. Its bands had battered the vacation estates of ritzy Ocean Reef and stripped a long stretch of mangrove. Yet two miles down the shore, the mangroves flourished, leafy and lush, offering no clue that a killer storm had passed nearby. A ramshackle trailer park stood undamaged; not a window was broken, not a tree was uprooted.

Phenomenal, thought Jim Tile.

He goosed the Crown Victoria to an invigorating ninety-five; blue lights, no siren. At high speeds the big Ford whistled like a bottle rocket.

Paradise Palms was a lead but not a lock. Augustine had done his best in a tough situation, the trick with the redial button was slick. Maybe the guy who'd beaten up Brenda was in the black Jeep Cherokee. Augustine didn't know for sure. Maybe they were headed to the Keys, maybe not. Maybe they'd stay with the Jeep, or maybe they'd ditch it for another car.

The only certainty was that they were transporting Skink and the tourist woman, Augustine's girlfriend. The circumstances of the abduction, and its purpose, remained a mystery. Augustine had promised to lie back and wait at Paradise Palms, and the trooper told him that was an excellent idea. One-man rescues only worked in the movies.

The old road from Ocean Reef rejoined Highway One below Jewfish Creek, where it split into four lanes. The traffic thickened, so Jim Tile slowed to seventy miles per hour, weaving deftly between the Winnebagos and rental cars. It was the time of late summer when the setting sun could torment inexperienced drivers, but there was no glare from the west tonight. A bruised wall of advancing weather shaded the horizon and cast sooty twilight over the islands and the water. Lightning strobed high in distant clouds over Florida Bay. Its exquisite sparking was wasted on Jim Tile, who dourly contemplated the prospect of hard rain. A chase was tricky enough when the roads were bone dry.

On Plantation Key the highway narrowed again, and as the traffic merged to two lanes, Jim Tile thought he spotted the black Cherokee not far ahead. Quickly he turned off the blue lights. It had to be the same Jeep; the shiny mud flaps were as preposterous as Augustine had described them.

Four vehicles separated Jim Tile from the Jeep—three passenger cars, and a station wagon towing a fishing boat on a wobbly trailer. The boat was tall and beamy enough to make it hard for those in the Jeep to see the marked police car in the stacked traffic behind them. Already the rain was falling, fat drops popping sporadically on the hood of the Ford. The thickening sky promised a deluge.

The station wagon in front of Jim Tile began an untimely, though predictable, deceleration. Bad omens abounded: Michigan license plates suggested unfamiliarity with local landmarks; the driver and a female passenger were gesticulating heatedly, indicating a marital-type disagreement. Most distressing, from Jim Tile's point of view: A third passenger clearly could be seen unfolding a road map as large as a tablecloth.

They're lost, the trooper thought. Lost in the Florida Keys. Where there was only one way in and out. Amazing.

Now the map was being passed to the front seat, where the driver and his wife pawed at it competitively. The station wagon began snaking back and forth, followed somewhat indecisively by the boat trailer. Two McDonald's bags flew from one of the car's windows, exploding unwanted French fries and ketchup packets on the shoulder of the highway.

"Pigs," Jim Tile said aloud. He scowled at the speedometer: thirty-two damn miles per hour. If he tried to pass, the guy in the Jeep might see him coming. The trooper boiled. As the rain fell harder, he went to his windshield wipers and headlights.

The sluggish station wagon stayed ahead of him for the entire length of Plantation Key, until its sole operative brake light began to flicker. The rig meandered to a dead stop.

Dispiritedly, Jim Tile put the patrol car in Park, thinking: This ain't my day.

Ahead rose the Snake Creek drawbridge. The black Jeep and the three cars behind it easily crossed before the warning gates came down. The moron in the station wagon would have beaten it, too, had he ventured to touch the accelerator.

Now the trooper was stuck. The Jeep was on the other side of the waterway, out of sight. Jim Tile stepped from his car and slammed the door. With raindrops trickling off the brim of his Stetson, he approached the witless driver of the station wagon and asked for a license, registration and proof of insurance. In the eight minutes that passed before the Snake Creek bridge came down, the trooper managed to weigh the bewildered tourist with seven separate traffic citations, at least three of which would inconveniently require a personal appearance in court.

On the way to the Torres house, Fred Dove stopped to buy flowers and white wine. He wanted Edie Marsh to know he was proud of her performance as Neria, devoted wife of Tony.

When the insurance man pulled up to 15600 Calusa, he saw that the Jeep wasn't in the driveway. His heart quickened at the possibility that Snapper was gone, leaving him alone with Edie. Not that she was fussy about privacy, but Fred Dove was. He couldn't perform at full throttle, sexually, as long as a homicidal maniac was watching TV in an adjoining room. Snapper's loud and truculent presence was deflating in all respects.

Nobody answered when the insurance man rapped on the wooden doorjamb. He stepped into the Torres house and called Edie's name. The only reply came from the two miniature dachshunds, barking in the backyard; they sounded tired and hoarse.

The ugly Naugahyde recliner in the living room was unoccupied, and the television was off. Fred Dove was encouraged—no Snapper. Inside the house, the light was fading. When the insurance man flipped a lamp switch, nothing happened. The generator wasn't running; out of gas, probably. He found Snapper's flashlight and peeked in the rooms, hoping to spy Edie napping languorously on a mattress. She wasn't.

Fred Dove saw her purse on the kitchen counter. Her wallet lay open on top. Inside he found twenty-two dollars and a Visa card. Fred Dove was relieved; at least the house hadn't been robbed. He held Edie's driver's license under the flashlight; her expression in the photograph spooked him. It was not a portrait of pure trustworthiness and devotion.

Oh well, he thought, lots of girls look like Lizzie Borden on their driver's license.

The insurance man returned to the living room, lit a candle and sat in the recliner. He wondered where Edie had gone and why she'd left her purse when she knew the streets were crawling with looters. It seemed like she'd departed in a hurry, probably in the Jeep with Snapper.

Fred Dove settled in for a wait. The candle smelled of vanilla. The cozy way it lighted the walls reminded him of the night they nearly made love on the floor, the night Snapper barged in. The humiliation of that moment still stung; it had invested Snapper with indomitable power over the insurance man. That, plus the loaded gun. Fred Dove could hardly wait until the psycho thug was paid off. Then he and Edie would be free of him.

Every so often the insurance man switched on the flashlight and reexamined Edie's picture on the driver's license. The vulturine eyes did not soften. Fred Dove wondered if it was her deviousness that he found so arousing. The notion disturbed him, so he retreated to innocuous diversions. He hadn't known, for example, that her middle name was Deborah. It was a name he liked: plucky, Midwestern and reliable-sounding. He was willing to bet that if you went through every women's prison in America, you wouldn't find a half-dozen Deborahs. Perhaps the name had been taken from one of Edie's grandmothers, or that of a special aunt. In any event, he regarded it as a positive sign.

He wondered, too, about the apartment listed as her address in West Palm: what kind of art Edie had hung on the walls, what color towels were folded in the bathroom, what sort of homey magnets were stuck on her refrigerator door. Linus and Snoopy? Garfield the Cat? If *only*, Fred Dove thought. He thought about Edie's bed, too. He hoped it was king-sized, brass or a big wooden four-poster—anything but a water bed, which negatively affected his thrusting techniques. Fred Dove hoped the sheets on Edie's bed were imported silk, and that one day she would invite him to lie down on them.

The insurance man stayed in the recliner for more than two hours, long after the neighborhood chain saws and hammers had fallen silent. He finally arose to take a position near a windowpane, in glum preparation to witness the vandalism of his rental car by a group of swaggering, loud-talking teenagers. Mercifully they ignored Fred Dove's drab sedan, but minutes after they passed the house he heard a pop-pop that could have been the backfire of an automobile, or gunshots. In the backyard Donald and Marla dissolved in frenzy, striking up an irksome chorus with half a dozen other vigilant dogs on the block. Fred Dove's nerves were fraying fast. He returned Edie's driver's license to the purse. Hurriedly he arranged the flowers in a vase and placed it next to the unopened wine on the dining-room table. Then he blew out the candle and went outside to check on the dachshunds.

Tangled impressively in their leashes, the animals whimpered out of hunger, loneliness and general anxiety. Their low-density memories still twitched from the near-fatal encounter with the prowling bear. The moment Fred Dove set them free, the dachshunds clambered up his lap and licked his chin shamelessly. He was suckered into giving them a short walk.

Admiring the unfettered mirth with which Donald and Marla pranced and peed, the insurance man was bothered by the idea that they might spend the whole night outdoors and unattended. He wrote Edie a note and folded it on top of her purse. Then he led the two wiener dogs to his rented sedan, drove back to the motel and smuggled them in a laundry bag up to his room. It was marginally better than all-night movies on cable.

The motels in the Upper Keys were filling with out-of-town insurance adjusters. The clerk at the Paradise Palms said she felt uncomfortable, profiting off the hurricane.

"But a customer's a customer. Can I have your name?"

Augustine introduced himself as Lester's brother. "I phoned earlier. What's his room number?"

"He's not here yet." The clerk leaned across the counter and whispered: "But your sisters checked in about twenty minutes ago. Room 255. I mean, I'm assuming sisters, on account of they're Parsons, too."

"Parsons indeed." Augustine nodded and acted pleased. Sisters? He couldn't imagine.

He paid for his room with cash. The clerk said, "Those girls know how to dress for a party, I'll sure say that."

"Oh boy," said Augustine. "What have they done now?"

"Don't you go fussing—let 'em have their fun, all right?" She handed him his key. "You're in 240. I tried to put you in the unit next door, but some wise guy from Prudential, he didn't want to switch."

"That's quite all right."

Once inside his room, Augustine put the loaded .38 on the bureau, near the door. He took the parts of the dart rifle from the gym bag and laid them on the bedspread. The muscles of his neck were in knots. He wished he'd brought a few skulls, for relaxation.

Augustine turned up the TV while he assembled the tranquilizer gun. He was surprised that he'd beaten the black Jeep to Islamorada, hadn't even passed it on the eighteen-mile stretch south of Florida City. He wondered if they'd turned on Card Sound Road, or stopped someplace else—and why. His worst fear, the thing he kept pushing out of his mind, was that the creep with the crooked jaw had already killed Skink and Bonnie, and dumped them. There were only about a hundred ideal locations between Homestead and Key Largo; years might pass before the bodies were found.

Well, he'd know soon enough. If the asshole showed up without them, then Augustine would know.

If the asshole showed up at all. Augustine still wasn't sure if "Lester Parsons" was the man with the crooked jaw.

He stood the dart rifle in a closet and put the pistol in his waistband, under the tail of his shirt. Rain whipped his face as soon as he stepped out the door. He shielded his eyes and hurried along the walkway to Room 255. He knocked seven times in a neighborly cadence—shave-and-a-haircut, two bits—to give the false impression that he was expected.

The door was flung open by a fragrant redheaded woman in high heels and a luminous green bikini. Augustine recognized her as the hooker in fishnets from 15600 Calusa.

An orange sucker was tattooed on the freckled slope of her left breast. In her left hand was a frosty Rum Runner.

She said, "Shit, I thought you were Snapper."

"Wrong room," said Augustine. "I'm sorry."

"Don't be."

Another woman came out of the bathroom, saying, "Goddamn this rain. I wanted to go in the pool." She wore a silver one-piece suit, an explosive white-blonde wig and gold hoop earrings. When she saw Augustine in the doorway, she said, "Who're you?"

"I thought this was my sister's room, but I guess I'm at the wrong motel."

The redhead introduced herself as Bridget. "You wanna come in and dry off?"

"Not if it gets Snapper mad." Augustine was thinking: Snapper—now what the hell kind of name is *that*?

The redhead laughed. "Yeah, he's quite the jealous maniac. Come on in."

The blonde said, "Jesus, Bridget, they're gonna be here any second—"

But Augustine was already inside the room, scouting unobtrusively: an overnight bag, two cosmetic cases, a cocktail dress on a hanger. Nothing out of the ordinary. Bridget tossed him a towel. She said her friend's name was Jasmine. They were from Miami.

"My name's George," said Augustine, "from California." Inanely he shook hands with the hookers.

Bridget held on, examining his ring finger. "Not married?"

"Afraid not." Augustine gently tugged free.

Jasmine told Bridget to forget it, they didn't have enough time. Bridget said they wouldn't need much.

"George looks like a fast starter." She winked somewhat mechanically at Augustine. "You want some fun until the rain stops?"

"Thanks, but I really can't stay."

"Hundred bucks," Bridget suggested. "Double date."

Jasmine pulled a long white T-shirt over her swimsuit. She griped: "Hey, do I get a vote in this? A hundred for what?"

Bridget slipped a milky arm around Augustine's waist and pulled him close. The obvious implant in her left breast felt like a sack of nickels against his rib cage. "Seventy-five," she said, dropping her eyes to the bright tattoo, "and I'll give you a taste of my Tootsie Pop."

"Can't," Augustine said. "Diabetic."

Jasmine gave a biting laugh. "You're both pitiful. Bridget, let 'George from California' go find his sisters." She sat cross-legged on the bed and applied pungent glue to a broken artificial fingernail. "Boy, this weather's suck-o," she muttered, to no one.

Bridget's motivational hug went slack, and slowly she recoiled from Augustine's side. "Our man George has a gun." She announced it with a mix of alarm and regret. "I felt it."

Jasmine, blowing on her glue job, looked up. "Goddamn, Bridget, I knew it! You happy now? We're busted."

"No you're not." Augustine took out the pistol and

displayed it in a loose and casual way, hoping to quell their concerns. "I'm not a cop, I promise."

Jasmine's eyes narrowed. "Shit, *now* I know. The squeaker sent you."

"Who?"

"Avila."

"Never heard of him."

Bridget backpedaled to the bed and sat next to her friend. Nervously she crossed her arms over her breasts. "Then who the hell are you, *George*? What is it you're after?"

"Information."

"Yeah, right."

"Really. I just want you to tell me about this 'Snapper,'" said Augustine, "and I also want to know if you two ladies can keep a secret."

# TWENTY-FIVE

**The professor's VW van** ran out of gas two miles shy of the Fort Drum service plaza. Neria Torres stood by the Turnpike and flagged down a truck. It was an old Chevy pickup; three men in the cab, four others sprawled in the bed. They were from Tennessee. Neria wasn't crazy about the odds.

"Looking for work," explained the driver, a wiry, unshaven fellow with biblical tattoos on both arms. He said his first name was Matthew and his middle name was Luke.

Neria was nervous nonetheless. The men stared ravenously. "What do you guys do?" she asked.

"Construction. We're here for the hurricane." Matthew had a spare gas can. He poured four gallons into the van. Neria thanked him.

She said, "All I can give you is three bucks."

"That's fine."

"What kind of construction?"

Matthew said: "Any damn thing we can find." The other men laughed. "We do trees, also. I got chain saw experience," Matthew added.

Neria Torres didn't ask if the crew was licensed to do business in Florida. She knew the answer. The men climbed out of the truck to stretch their legs and urinate.

One of them was actually mannered enough to turn his back while unzipping.

Neria decided it was a good time to go. Matthew stood between her and the van. "I dint ketch your name."

"Neria."

"That's Cuban, right?"

"Yes."

"You don't talk with no accent."

She thought: Well, thank you, Gomer. "I was born in Miami," she said.

Matthew seemed pleased. "So you're on the way home—hey, how'd you make out in the big blow?"

Neria said, "I won't know till I get there."

"We do residential."

"Do you really."

"Wood or masonry, it don't matter. Also roofs. We got a helluva tar man." Matthew pointed. "That bald guy doin' his bidness in the bushes—he worked on that new Wal-Mart in Chat'nooga. My wife's cousin Chip."

Neria Torres said, "From what I understand, you won't have a bit of trouble finding jobs when you get to Dade County."

"Hey, what about your place?"

"I don't know. I haven't seen it yet."

"So it could be totaled," Matthew said, hopefully.

Slowly Neria opened the door of the van. Only when it stubbed his shoulder blades did Matthew move out of the way.

Neria got behind the wheel and revved the engine. "Tell you what. When I get home and see how the roof looks, then I'll give you a call. Where you staying?"

The other workers laughed again. "Sterno Hilton," said Matthew. "See, we're campin' out." He said they couldn't afford a motel, no way.

Neria fumbled in the console until she found a gnawed stub of pencil and one of the professor's matchbooks, which reeked of weed. She wrote down a bogus telephone number and gave it to Matthew. "OK, then, you call *me*."

He didn't even glance at the number. "I got a better idea. Since none of us ever been to Miami before . . ."

Oh no! she thought. Please no.

". . . we'll just follow you down. That way, we're sure not to get lost. And if your place needs work, we can git on it rightaways."

Matthew's plan was well received by his crew. Neria said, uselessly: "I don't think that's a good idea."

"We got references."

She was eyeing the pickup truck, wondering if there was a chance in hell that the professor's van could outrun it.

"We kicked some ass over Charleston," Matthew was saying, "after Hurricane Hugo."

Neria said, "It's getting pretty late."

"We'll be right behind you."

And they were, all the way down the Turnpike.

The truck's solitary headlight, stuck on high beam, illuminated the interior of the VW van like a TV studio. Neria stiffened in the harsh brightness, knowing that seven pairs of inbred male eyes were fixed on the back of her head. She drove ludicrously slow, hoping the rednecks would grow impatient and decide to pass. They didn't.

All she could do was make the best of it. Even if the Neanderthals didn't know a thing about construction, they might be helpful in tracking a thieving husband.

Max Lamb cracked the door to poke his head out. He'd never met an FBI man before. This one didn't look like Efrem Zimbalist Jr. He wore a green Polo shirt, tan Dockers and cordovan Bass Weejuns. He also toted a bag from Ace Hardware.

When it came to name brands, Max was nothing if not observant. He believed it was part of his job, knowing who in America was buying what.

The agent said, "Is Augustine home?"

"No, he isn't."

"Who are you?"

"Could I see some ID?" Max asked.

The agent showed him a badge in a billfold. Max told him to come in. They sat in the living room. Max asked what was in the bag, and the agent said it was drill bits. "Storm sucked the cabinets right out of my kitchen," he explained.

"Black and Decker?"

"Makita."

"That's a first-rate tool," said Max.

The agent was exceedingly patient. "You're a friend of Augustine's?"

"Sort of. My name is Max Lamb."

"Really? I'm glad to see you're all right."

Max's eyebrows hopped.

"From the kidnapping," the agent said. "You're the one who was kidnapped, right?"

"Yes!" Max's spirits skied, realizing that Bonnie had

been so concerned that she'd called the FBI. It was proof of her devotion.

The agent said, "She played the tape for me, the message you left on the answering machine."

"Then you heard his voice—the guy who snatched me." Max got a Michelob from the refrigerator. The FBI man accepted a Sprite.

"Where's your wife?" he asked.

"I don't know."

Excitedly Max Lamb related the whole story, from his kidnapping on Calusa Drive to the midnight rescue in Stiltsville, up to Bonnie's disappearance with Augustine and the deranged one-eyed governor. The FBI man listened with what seemed to be genuine interest, but took no notes. Max wondered if they were specially trained to remember everything they heard.

"These are dangerous men," he told the agent, portentously.

"Was your wife taken against her will?"

"No, sir. That's why they're so dangerous."

"You say he put a collar on your neck."

"A shock collar," Max said gravely, "the kind used to train hunting dogs."

The FBI man asked if the kidnapper had done the same thing to Bonnie. Max said he didn't think so. "She's very trusting and impressionable. They took advantage of that."

"What's Augustine's role in all this?"

"I believe," said Max, "the kidnapper has brainwashed him, too." He got another beer and tore into a bag of pretzels.

The agent said, "Prosecution won't be easy. It's your word against his."

"But you believe me, don't you?"

"Mister Lamb, it doesn't matter what I believe. Put yourself in the jury box. This is a very weird story you'll be asking them to swallow. . . ."

Max shot to his feet. His cheeks were stuffed with pretzel fragments. "Jeshush Chritht, mahh wife's misshing!"

"I understand. I'd be upset, too." The FBI man was maddeningly agreeable and polite. "And I'm not trying to tell you what to do. But you need to know what you're up against."

Max sat down, glowering.

The agent explained that the Bureau seldom got involved unless a ransom demand was issued. "There was none in your case. There's been none for your wife."

"Well, *I* think her life's in danger," Max said, "and I think you people are in deep trouble if something happens to her."

"Believe me, Mister Lamb, I understand your frustration."

No you don't, Max fumed silently, or you wouldn't talk to me like I was ten years old.

The agent said, "Have you spoken to the police?"

Max told him about the black state trooper who was acquainted with the kidnapper. "He said I was entitled to press charges. He said he'd take me down to the station."

The FBI man nodded. "That's the best way to go, if you've got your mind made up."

Max told the agent there was something he definitely ought to see. He led him to Augustine's guest room and showed him the wall of skulls. "Tell me honestly," he said to the FBI man, "wouldn't you be worried? He *juggles* those damn things."

"Augustine? Yeah."

"You know?"

"He won't hurt your wife, Mister Lamb."

"Gee, I feel so much better."

The agent seemed impervious to sarcasm. "You'll hear from Mrs Lamb sooner or later. That's my guess. If you don't, call me. Or call me even if you do." He handed his card to Max, who affected hard-bitten skepticism as he studied it. Then he walked toward the kitchen, the agent following.

"I was wondering," the FBI man said, "did Augustine give you a key?"

Max turned.

"To the house," the agent said.

"No, sir. The sliding door was open."

"So you just walked in. He doesn't know you're here?"

"Well . . ." It hadn't occurred to Max Lamb that he was breaking the law. For one infuriating moment, he thought the FBI man was preparing to arrest him.

But the agent said: "That's a swell way to get your head shot off—being in somebody's house without them knowing. Especially here in Miami."

Max, grinding his teeth, realized the impossibly upside-down nature of the situation. He was wasting his breath. A state trooper is friends with the kidnapper, an FBI man is friends with the skull collector.

"You know what I really want?" Max drained his beer with a flourish, set the bottle down hard on the counter. "All I want is to find my wife, put her on a plane and go home to New York. Forget about this fucked-up place, forget about this hurricane."

The agent said, "That's a damn good plan, Mister Lamb."

# TWENTY-SIX

**Snapper made Edie Marsh** pull over at a liquor store in Islamorada.

"Not now," she said.

"I *got* to."

"We're almost there."

A rumble from the back seat: "Let the man have a drink."

She parked behind the store, away from the road. Jim Tile didn't see the black Cherokee as he sped past. Neither did Avila, ten minutes later.

Snapper wouldn't be talked out of his craving, and Edie was worried. She knew firsthand the folly of mixing booze with Midols. Double dosed, Snapper might hibernate for a month.

The woman named Bonnie asked for a cold Coke. "I'm burning up."

"Welcome to Florida," said Edie.

Snapper tossed three ten-dollar bills on her lap. "Johnnie Red," he said.

"Bad idea when you're full of codeines."

"Shit, I've handled ten times worse. Besides, it don't feel like codeine you gave me."

Edie said, "Your knee quit hurting, right? The bottle said 'codeine.'"

Snapper switched the .357 to his left hand. With his right hand he twisted Edie's hair, as if he were uprooting a clump of weeds. When she cried out, he said: "I don't give a fuck if the medicine bottle said turpentine. Go get my Johnnie Walker."

Edie pulled free and jumped out of the Jeep. She flipped him the finger as she went through the door of the liquor store. Snapper said, "Stubborn bitch."

"Feisty," Skink agreed.

Bonnie Lamb felt like her skin was sizzling. She thought it would be glorious to bury herself in fresh snow. "Honest to God, it's so hot. I feel like taking off my clothes."

She couldn't believe she'd said it aloud.

Snapper was startled, and too confused for lust. "Jesus Christ, what's a matter with you people."

Bonnie said, "I'm smothering."

His eyes wandered to the young woman's chest. Nothing like a pair of tits to fuck up the balance of power. He knew that if she flashed those babies, his position instantly would be weakened, his authority diminished. It was a lost advantage that even the .357 could not restore.

"Keep your goddamn shirt on," he told her.

"Don't worry." Bonnie fanned herself in nervous embarrassment. In the back of the Jeep, Levon Stichler mewled inquiringly, trussed in his cocoon of moldy carpet. Skink figured the old man must have been listening, wondering if he was missing something.

Edie Marsh returned from the store. Her hair sparkled with tiny raindrops. She handed Bonnie a can of Dr Pepper. "The Cokes weren't cold. Here, asshole."

She shoved a brown paper bag at Snapper. He took out the Johnnie Walker bottle and opened it with one hand. He threw back his head and chugged, as if from a canteen.

"Take it easy," Edie admonished.

Contemptuously he smacked his lips. "I bet you'd look good completely bald," he said to her. "That guy on the new *Star Trek*, Gene Luke—you and him could pass for twins."

Edie said, "Touch my hair again. Just try."

He swung the .357 until the barrel came to rest on the tip of Edie's nose. He cocked the hammer and said: "Come on. Somebody talk me out of it."

Bonnie thought: Oh God, please don't. She shivered in sweat.

Snapper took another sloppy swig of whiskey. The one-eyed man reminded him of the ammunition shortage. "Shoot her, that'd leave only one bullet for the rest of us."

"There's other ways besides the gun."

Skink let loose an avalanche of laughter. "Son, I'm fairly immune to blunt objects and sharp instruments."

Edie's pitch was more blunt. "Pull the trigger," she said to Snapper, "and kiss your hurricane money goodbye. Forty-seven grand goes out the window with my brains."

Snapper's bad mandible began to creak; a sign, Skink hoped, of possible cogitation. The moron was deciding between the long-term rewards from the money and the short-term satisfaction from shooting her. Apparently it wasn't an easy choice.

Skink said, "Consider it an IQ test, chief."

Impulsively Bonnie Lamb opened the cold Dr Pepper and poured it under her blouse; a fizzing caramel torrent from the cleft of her neck to her tummy.

"Stop!" Snapper yelled. "You stop that crazy shit!"

"I'm suffocating in here—"

"I don't care! I don't fucking care."

Bonnie was so light-headed from the heat that Snapper's fury didn't register. "I'm sorry," she said, "I'm really sorry, but it's a hundred degrees in this stupid truck."

The soda pop soaked through her top, so that Snapper could see the lacy outline of a bra and a pale damp oval of bare belly. Skink asked Edie Marsh to put on the air conditioner.

"I tried. It's broken." Edie's voice was empty.

"Don't even think about getting naked," Snapper warned Bonnie, "or I'll kill you." His head jangled with loud voices, some his own. In exasperation he shouted: "You don't think I'd shoot all you crazy shits? You don't believe me? Check the fuckin' hole in the roof a this Jeep!"

Yeah, Edie thought. Matches the one between your ears.

"Can we get on with this?" she said sourly. "It *is* awfully damn humid."

As Bonnie's skin cooled off, she heard herself apologizing repeatedly. Yet it was absurd to be ashamed. Why should she care what two common criminals thought of her?

But she did care. She couldn't help herself. It was the way she'd been raised: A proper young woman did not douse herself with soda pop in front of total strangers, even felons.

"It's all right," Skink said. "You're scared, that's all."

"I guess I am."

Snapper heard her. With a vulgar chuckle, he said, "Good. Scared is damn well what you ought to be." He was halfway to shitfaced.

Edie drove slowly, fretfully. The man was a keeling wreck. *How could they possibly pull this off?* She devised a fantasy scenario: If Snapper passed out drunk, she'd push him from the Jeep. Then she'd tell the eccentric couple in the back seat that she was very, very sorry—it was all a terrible misunderstanding. She'd promise them Snapper's share of the Midwest Casualty settlement if they'd forget the whole dreadful evening. She would drive them back to Miami without delay and (to prove she was basically a decent person) offer to replace the gold ring stolen from the lady trooper. The unconscious Snapper would be run over on the highway by a passing shrimp truck and no longer pose a menace to society, or to Edie's future.

Unfortunately, Snapper wasn't nodding off. The Johnnie Walker bottle lay capped on the dashboard. Now he was playing with the gun, spinning the cylinder and humming mischievously.

Edie Marsh said, "Could you please not do that?"

Snapper gurgled crapulously, his jaw jutting like a window box. "You're so hot and sweaty, Edie, you oughta do what she almost done. Take off your clothes."

"You'd like that, wouldn't you."

"I would *love* it. Wouldn't y'all?" He waggled the .357 at Skink and Bonnie Lamb. "Come on, wouldn't ya like to see Edie's tits? They're cuties."

Bonnie felt crummy that she'd given Snapper the idea.

Skink said, "Speaking for myself, yes, I'm sure they're delightful. But some other time."

Edie Marsh felt herself blush. Nobody spoke. Snapper began to hum again, accompanied by the metered squeak of the windshield wipers. Ahead, on the ocean side of the highway, Edie saw the electric-blue sign for the Paradise Palms Resort Motel.

Skink shook Levon Stichler out of the carpet, dumping him like a sack of flour on the terrazzo. Somebody yanked off the gag and the blindfold.

The old man's eyes watered at the sudden brightness.

A woman's voice: "You again."

Levon blinked until a face came into focus—the redhead from the hurricane house at Turtle Meadow. The chiffon scarf, Levon's blinder, dangled from her festively painted fingernails. Standing next to the redhead was a wild-looking blonde. She said, "What's your name, sweetheart?"

The redhead wore a diaphanous black bustier, fishnet stockings and stiletto heels. The blonde wore a silver lamé teddy that made her shimmer like the hood ornament on a Silver Shadow. The air was sugary with perfume; pure heaven, after three hours of gagging on mildew and carpet fuzz. When Levon Stichler sat up, he found himself in the center of an attentive circle: the two prostitutes, the thug in the pinstriped suit, the pretty long-haired brunette, another young woman, with creamy skin and delicate features, and a large bearded man wearing a flowered shower cap. The bearded man was polishing a glass eye on the sleeve of his jacket. They were gathered in a small motel room.

Levon Stichler said: "What's this all about?"

The prostitutes introduced themselves. Bridget and Jasmine.

Snapper dropped to a crouch. Roughly he pinched the back of the old man's neck. "You tried to kill me, 'member?"

"It was a mistake. I told you."

"Here's the deal: You're gone stay down here two, maybe three days with the girls. They're gone fuck ya and blow ya till you can't walk. Plus they gone take some pitchers."

Levon was skeptical. The man reeked of liquor and spoke as if he had a mouthful of marbles.

"Just shoot me and get it over with."

"We're not shooting anybody." It was the pretty brunette. "Honest," she said, "long as you behave."

Snapper said, "Maybe you're too old to get it up or maybe you like guys—I don't fuckin' care. Point is, you stay here with these girls till I call and say it's OK to leave. Then what you do, you take your sweet time gettin' back to Miami. By that I mean, stand on the highway with your thumb out. Unnerstand?"

Levon stammered and blinked. Snapper swatted him twice across the face.

Edie Marsh said: "I don't think Mister Stichler realizes the alternative. The alternative is we go to the cops and tell how you tried to murder Snapper and rape me with that trailer spike. Your family'll think you've gone senile. The photographs won't help—Grandpa doing pony rides with two call girls."

Levon glanced up at Bridget and Jasmine. They were large and scary. He could tell they'd worked together before.

"Think of it as a vacation," said Edie. "Hey, you're allowed to have fun."

"I wish I could."

"Uh-oh." Bridget knelt beside him. "Prostate?"

The old man nodded somberly. "It was removed last year."

Jasmine told him to cheer up. "We'll think of something."

Skink, fitting his glass eye into its socket, advised Levon Stichler to do what he was told. "It's still better than getting shot."

Bridget said, "Gee, thanks."

Snapper paid the prostitutes from a wad of the stolen roofing money, which they counted, divided and put away. They turned their backs so he wouldn't peek inside their pocketbooks, which bulged with the other cash given to them ten minutes earlier by Avila, and ten minutes before that by the good-looking young man with the .38 Special.

"Is there ice in the bucket?" Bonnie Lamb asked. The hooker named Jasmine told her to help herself. Bonnie scooped two handfuls of cubes and pressed them to her cheeks.

The one-eyed man helped the prostitutes lift Levon Stichler to his feet. Snapper poked the old man's Adam's apple with the barrel of the gun. "Don't try nuthin' stupid," he said. "These young girls can crack coconuts in their legs. Killing a skinny old fart like you is no problem whassoever."

Levon Stichler didn't doubt it for a moment. "Don't worry, mister. I'm no hero."

The redhead pinched his butt playfully. "We'll see about that."

Augustine was hiding behind a Dumpster when the black Cherokee with the cheesy mud flaps arrived at the Paradise Palms. His spirits leaped when he saw Bonnie Lamb get out, followed by the governor. The driver was a brown-haired woman in a lavender top; probably the one from the driver's license photo, Edith Deborah Marsh, age twenty-nine. She was the next to get out of the Jeep. From the passenger side: a lanky sallow man in a rumpled suit, no necktie. He carried a gun and a bottle, and seemed unsteady. His crooked jaw was made conspicuous by a street light. Augustine had no doubt. It was him; the one who'd attacked Brenda Rourke, the one the prostitutes had told him about. Snapper in real life, "Lester Parsons" on the motel register.

The man opened the hatch of the Cherokee and barked something at Skink, who removed a long lumpy bundle and hoisted it across his back. Once the procession disappeared into the motel, Augustine ran to the Jeep, climbed in the cargo well and quietly closed the hatch. He flattened himself below the rear window, placing the .38 at his right side. With both hands he held the dart rifle across his chest.

This, he thought, would be something to tell the old man. Make those fat wormy veins in his temples pop up.

Dad wouldn't dream of risking his neck unless vast sums of money were at stake. Love, loyalty and honor weren't part of the dope smuggler's creed. Augustine could hear the incredulity: *A.G., why the hell would you do such a crazy thing?*

Because the man deserved it. He beat up a lady cop and stole her mother's wedding ring. He was scum.

*Don't be an idiot. You could've been killed.*

He kidnapped the woman I love.

*I raised an idiot!*

No you didn't. You didn't raise anybody.

Whenever Augustine wrote his father, he made a point of mentioning how much money he'd given away to ex-girlfriends, obscure charities and ultraliberal political causes. He imagined his father's face turning gray with dismay.

*You disappoint me, A.G.*

This from a dumb shit who ran aground at full throttle with thirty-three kilos in the bilge and the entire Bahamian National Defense Force in pursuit.

"You disappoint me."

Right. Augustine listened to the rain thrumming against the roof of the truck. It made him drowsy.

He hadn't expected to see his father waiting when he awoke from the coma, so he wasn't disappointed. Predominantly he was thrilled to be alive. The person at his bedside was a middle-aged Haitian nurse named Lucy. She told him about the plane crash, the months of slumber. Augustine hugged her tearfully. Lucy showed him a letter from his father, sent from the prison in Talladega; she'd read the letter aloud to Augustine when he was unconscious. She volunteered to read it again.

*Son, I hope you are alive to read these words. I'm sorry the way things turned out.* Dad should've signed off right there, but grace and decency were never his strong suits.

*Everything I did was for you*, he wrote. *Every move I made, right or wrong.*

Which was crap, an unnecessary lie. It mildly saddened Augustine but didn't embitter him. He was beyond all that. The airplane accident had pruned his emotions down to the roots. Nothing affected him the way it had before, which was fine. He decided everyone could benefit from a short coma. Wipe the slate clean.

So what if it took him years to come up with a new agenda? Here it was. Here *she* was.

Dad would not approve. Fortunately, Dad was not a factor.

Augustine heard the closing of a door, footsteps slapping in the puddles, voices advancing across the motel parking lot. He took three deep breaths. Checked the safety on the dart rifle.

He was glad for the weather, which misted the Jeep's windows and made him invisible from the outside. The voices grew sharper—two men arguing. Augustine didn't recognize them. Perhaps Snapper and somebody else, but who?

Loud words broke through the whisper of the rain. Augustine decided not to give himself away unless Bonnie Lamb was in trouble. The argument moved closer. Then came a deep huff, the sounds of a clumsy struggle; a bottle shattering on the pavement.

One of the men blurted: "Hold the damn gun while I strangle this fucker."

*

Snapper's consternation about the two remaining bullets in the .357 was well founded. A crack marksman he was not.

A police report dated July 7, 1989, showed that one Lester Maddox Parsons was arrested for shooting Theodore "Sunny" Shea outside the Satellite Grille in Dania, Florida. The victim was not just a garden-variety crack dealer, as Snapper claimed after the incident. In truth, Sunny Shea was his longtime business partner. The scope of their enterprises extended beyond drugs to stolen guns, jewelry, clothing, patio furniture, stereos, even a shipment of baby food on one occasion. Eventually Sunny Shea came to suspect Snapper of cheating him on the proceeds, and confronted him with the accusation one humid summer night in the doorway of the Satellite Grille, before sixteen eyewitnesses.

Snapper's indignant response was to display a 9mm Glock (swiped from the glove box of an unmarked Coral Springs police car) and attempt to empty said weapon into Sunny Shea. In all, Snapper fired eleven times from a distance of eight feet. Only six rounds struck Sunny Shea, and not one nicked a vital organ—quite a feat, considering that Sunny Shea weighed only one hundred thirty pounds and hadn't an ounce of fat on his body. The hapless shooting exhibition was even more remarkable because Snapper was stone sober at the time.

Sunny Shea never lost consciousness, and was extremely cooperative when police inquired about the identity of his assailant. The two detectives who hauled Lester Maddox Parsons to the Broward County Jail ridiculed him mercilessly about his lousy aim.

The next morning, when they came to his cell to inform him that the charge of attempted first-degree murder had been upgraded, Snapper glowed with vindication. Then he learned it wasn't one of his shots that had killed his scrawny, obnoxious partner—some bonehead in the emergency room had injected Theodore "Sunny" Shea with an antibiotic to which he was virulently, and fatally, allergic.

Snapper pleaded out to a chickenshit manslaughter and got easy time, but his confidence in the efficacy of handguns was ruined forever. Two bullets in a .357 was scarcely better than no bullets at all.

Which was why he didn't want to waste them on Avila, the whiny spic. He was the last guy on earth that Snapper expected to see at Paradise Palms. He'd materialized like a drowned ghost out of the rainstorm, bitching about the roofing deposit that Snapper had ripped off from Mrs Whitmark.

"You know who she is? You know who she's married to?" Avila was screeching. Skink and the two women retreated to a dry vantage, under the eaves of the motel, while Avila chased Snapper around the parking lot like a terrier. Their conversation was difficult to follow, but Edie Marsh got the substance of it: Snapper had made a seven-thousand-dollar score.

Funny how he'd forgotten to tell her about it. Same as the wedding ring.

The pistol in Snapper's possession worried Avila but didn't deter him. For eighty miles he'd been praying for Chango's protection, and felt moderately imbued. Snapper appeared frazzled and shaky, possibly visited by black spirits.

Avila said, "Gimme the money."

"Eat shit," Snapper growled.

When he turned away, Avila hopped on his back.

Snapper shook him off. Avila pounced again, ripping Snapper's suit and knocking the Johnnie Walker from his hand. The two men locked together, spinning in the mist. Ultimately Snapper backed into a sabal palm tree, slamming Avila against the trunk. He made a true squeak as he slid to the ground.

Snapper, panting, weaved toward Edie: "Hold the damn gun while I strangle this fucker."

Halfheartedly she took the pistol and held it on Bonnie and Skink. Snapper fell upon Avila and breathlessly beat him. Avila was surprised by the clarity of the pain. When his nose exploded under Snapper's fist, he realized he'd been foolhardy to count on beatific intervention. Evidently Chango hadn't forgiven him for the aborted coati sacrifice.

As Snapper's grimy fingernails closed upon his throat, Avila inventoried the multiple sources of his agony: the fractured nose, the sliver of broken whiskey bottle in his right thigh, the unhealed crucifixion hole in his left hand, the goat-related goring in his groin and, soon, a crushed larynx.

He thought: Forget the seven grand. Screw Gar Whitmark. It's time to run.

Avila brought his right knee hard to Snapper's crotch. Snapper's eyelids fluttered but he didn't release his grip on Avila's neck. Avila kneed him twice more, ultimately producing the desired result. Snapper moaned and rolled away. Avila struggled to his feet. He took three steps and slipped. When he got up again, he heard Snapper rising behind him. Frantically Avila bolted for the road.

*

The rain made it hard to discern the details of the two men running along Highway One. Neither was large enough to be the governor, or physically fit enough to be Augustine. From where his Highway Patrol car was parked, a hundred yards away, Jim Tile was unable to see if the tall man had a crooked jaw. He might have been any old Keys drunk in a soggy pinstriped suit.

The black Jeep was still parked at the Paradise Palms. The trooper decided to sit still and wait.

Avila made it half a mile before he ran out of strength. He stopped on the Tea-Table Bridge and doubled over, sucking air. He tried to flag passing motorists, but none found room in their icy hearts for a bedraggled, saliva-flecked, blood-spattered hitchhiker. Avila was further dejected to see, framed in the window of a speeding Airstream, a freckle-faced teenaged girl, snapping his photograph.

What a sick world, he thought, when an injured human being becomes a roadside amusement.

Meanwhile, out of the veil of rain came Snapper. He was shambling like a zombie across the bridge. For a weapon he'd selected a rusty axle from an abandoned Jet Ski trailer.

Avila raised both arms in supplication. "Let's forget the whole thing, OK?"

"Don't move." Snapper gripped the axle at one end and brought it high over his head, like a sledgehammer.

With a morose peep, Avila hurled himself sideways off the bridge. The drop was only fourteen feet, but given his dread of heights, it might as well have been fourteen stories. Avila was mildly amazed to survive the impact.

The water was warm and the tide was strong. He let it carry him out the channel toward the ocean, because he wasn't strong enough to swim against it. When the sodden weight of his clothing began to drag him under, he kicked off his shoes and pants, and stripped out of his shirt. Soon the lights from the Overseas Highway were absorbed by darkness and bad weather. Avila could see nothing but the occasional high-altitude flash of heat lightning. When a heavy object thumped him in the small of the back, he was sure it was the snout of a great white shark and that death was imminent.

But it was only a piece of plywood. Avila clung to it like a crippled frog. He thought of a sublime irony—what if the life-saving lumber had blown off one of the roofs that he'd been bribed not to inspect? Perhaps it was Chango's idea of a practical joke.

All night long, adrift in the chop, Avila cursed the hurricane for bringing him such misery: the sadistic doughnut man, Whitmark and, of course, Snapper. The rainfall stopped at dawn but the sun never broke free of the clouds. It was midafternoon before Avila heard an engine. As he shouted for help, a tall white fishing boat idled within hailing distance. Avila waved. The skipper and his tropically garbed clients waved back.

"Hang in there, *amigo*," the skipper yelled, and trolled away.

Twenty minutes later, a Coast Guard boat arrived and took Avila aboard. The crew gave him dry clothes, hot coffee and homemade chili. He ate in appreciative silence. Afterwards he was led belowdeck to a small briefing room, where he was greeted by a man from the Immigration and Naturalization Service.

In halting Spanish, the immigration man asked Avila

for the name of the Cuban port he had fled. Avila laughed and explained that he was from Miami.

"Then what're you doing out here in your underwear?"

Avila said a robber was chasing him down the road, so he jumped off a bridge in Islamorada.

"Tell the truth," the immigration man said sternly. "Obviously you're a rafter. Now where did you come from—Havana? Mariel?"

Avila was about to argue when it dawned on him that there was no faster way to shed his burdens. What could he look forward to in his current life but an unforgiving wife, a traumatized mother-in-law, personal bankruptcy, the wrath of Gar Whitmark and a possible criminal indictment?

He asked the immigration man: "What will happen to me if I confess?"

"Nothing. You'll be processed at Krome and most likely released."

"If I am a political refugee."

"That's the usual procedure."

"*Sí*," Avila said. "*Yo soy balsero.*" I am a rafter.

The immigration man seemed so relieved that Avila was left to conclude (as a former civil servant himself) that he'd saved the man mountains of paperwork.

"*Su nombre, por favor?*"

"Juan," Avila replied. "Juan Gómez. From Havana."

"And your occupation in Cuba?"

"I was a building inspector."

# TWENTY-SEVEN

**They waited in** the Jeep—Edie Marsh up front, holding the revolver; Bonnie Lamb pressed against the governor in the back seat.

It was Bonnie who said: "What if he doesn't come back?"

Edie was thinking the same thing. Hoping it. The problem was, Snapper had the damn car keys. She asked the man in the shower cap: "You know how to hot-wire one of these?"

"That would be illegal."

The cinematic smile startled her. She said, "Why aren't you afraid?"

"Of what?"

"The gun. Dying. Anything."

Bonnie said she was frightened enough for all of them. The rain slackened; still no sign of Snapper, or Avila. Edie had difficulty keeping her eyes off the man called Skink.

"What is it," he said. "My hat?"

She lifted the .357. "You could take this away from me anytime you wanted. You know it."

"Maybe I don't want to."

That's what scared her. What was the point of holding a gun on a person like this?

He said, "I won't hurt you." Again with the smile.

Edie Marsh was a sucker for laugh lines around the eyes. She said to Bonnie: "I think I know what you see in this guy."

"We're just friends."

"Really? Then maybe you can tell me," Edie said, "what's he got planned?"

"I honestly don't know. I wish I did."

Edie was all clammy shakes, roiled emotions. In the motel room, depositing Mr Stichler with the two hookers, she'd caught something on the TV that got her daydreaming—a news clip of the President of the United States touring the hurricane damage. At his side was a tall, boyishly attractive man in his thirties, whom the TV newscasters identified as the President's son. When they said he lived in Miami, Edie Marsh got a whimsical flash. So what if he wasn't a Kennedy? And maybe he was too much of a good young Republican to pick up some hot girl in a bar and get raunchy. Or just maybe he'd been waiting his whole repressed life to do exactly that. And he *was* the President's son. It was something to consider, Edie mused, for the future. Particularly if the hurricane scam continued to unravel at its current pace.

She put Snapper's gun on the seat. "Get out of here," she told Skink and Bonnie. "Go on. I'll tell him you pushed me down and got away."

Bonnie looked over at the governor, who said: "Now's your chance, girl."

"What about you?"

He shook his head. "I made a promise to Jim."

"Who the hell's Jim?" asked Edie Marsh.

Bonnie said: "Then I guess we're staying."

Skink encouraged her to make a dash for it. "Go call Augustine. Let him know you're OK."

"Nope," Bonnie said.

"And your husband, too."

"No! Not until it's over."

Edie was exasperated, her nerves worn ragged. Snapper was right; they *are* nuts. "Fine," she said, "you two fruitballs stay if you want, but I'm outta here."

Skink said: "Excellent decision."

"Tell him I went to use the bathroom."

"No problem," said Bonnie.

"I got my period or something."

"Right."

Skink leaned forward. "Could you hand me the gun?"

"Why not," Edie said. Perhaps the smiler would shoot Snapper dead. There were about forty-seven thousand reasons that Edie wasn't upset at the idea, not including the barrel-shaped bruise on her right breast.

She was passing the .357 to Skink when he waved her off, saying: "On second thought—"

Edie turned and let out a gasp. It was Snapper's face, dripping wet, pressed to the window of the Jeep. The bent nose and misshapen mouth made him look like a gargoyle.

"Miss me, bay-beeee?" he crooned, pallid lips wriggling like flatworms against the glass.

Jim Tile was tempted to call for backup, though it would spell the end of the governor's elaborate reclusion.

Long ago they'd made a pact: no cavalry, unless innocent lives were in peril. The trooper was thinking of the tourist woman as more or less innocent. She and Skink might be dead already.

Glumly Jim Tile watched the rain drench the passing cars on Highway One. Again he castigated himself for letting his emotions get the better of his brain. Brenda was alive. He should've thanked God, then let it go.

But he didn't. And the governor had had little trouble talking him out of the license-tag number.

"Pest control" was what Skink had called it, as they were leaving the hospital.

"Whoever did that to Mrs Rourke is not a viable member of the species. Not a welcome donor to the gene pool. Wouldn't Darwin himself agree?"

And the trooper had merely said: "Be careful."

"Jim, we're infested with these mutant shitheads. Look what they've done to the place."

The trooper, locked in some cold distant zone: "The tag's probably stolen off another car. It may lead you nowhere."

The governor, momentarily shaking loose of his friend's firm grip: "They're turning it into a sump hole. Some with guns, some with briefcases—it's all the same goddamn crime."

"Pest control."

"We do what we can."

"Be careful, captain."

Then he'd flashed those movie-star pearlies, the ones that had gotten him elected. And Jim Tile stood back and let him go. Let him stalk the man in the black Jeep Cherokee.

Which was now parked in a windy drizzle outside the Paradise Palms. The trooper counted three figures inside the truck; two of them, he hoped, were Skink and Bonnie Lamb.

A dark shape near the road caught his attention.

The tall man in the suit was hurrying along the gravel shoulder of Highway One. There was a tippiness to his gait; he seemed well challenged to keep a straight course, clear of the speeding cars. He flinched when the high beams of a gasoline tanker caught him in the face.

This time Jim Tile got a good look at the misaligned jaws.

He watched the man pass beneath the bright electric sign in front of the motel. He saw him walk up to the Jeep, lean close to a window. Then the man ran around to the driver's side, opened the door and got in. Smoke puffed from the truck's exhaust pipe. The brake lights flickered.

Jim Tile said, "Hello," and started his engine.

Suddenly, all around, the night was diced into blues and whites.

Snapper was backing the Jeep out, chortling about what had happened to Avila: "Dumb fuck went straight off the bridge, you shoulda seen— Hey! Hey, what the hell . . ."

Bright lights started strobing everywhere. In the reflection of the puddles. On the coral-colored walls of the motel. In the fronds of the sabal palms.

Snapper shoved the Jeep into Neutral. "Fucking cops!"

"No way," Edie said. But she knew he was right.

A figure in gray was approaching the Cherokee. Snapper rolled down the window. It was a state trooper;

big black sonofabitch, too. He'd parked his patrol car at an angle, to block the exit.

Snapper's mind raced, half drunk, half wired: Christ Almighty, would Momma and Pappy pitch a fit they ever heard I got taken down by a nigger cop. Momma especially.

In a flash Snapper figured out what must've happened: The lady trooper either was alive, or had survived long enough after the beating to give a description of the Jeep, and maybe even of Snapper himself.

So this was the big black posse.

Snapper knew he should've ditched the Cherokee after it happened. Sure, park the fucker in the nearest canal and call it a deal. But, oh Jesus, how he loved that stereo system! Reba, Garth, Hank Jr., they'd never sounded so sweet. His whole life Snapper had wanted a car with decent speakers. So he'd stayed with the stolen Jeep because of its awesome stereo—and here was the price to be paid.

A big black motherfucker of a cop, coming across the parking lot, drawing his gun.

The one-eyed man tapped him on the shoulder. "Haul ass, chief."

"Huh?"

"That's what I'd do."

"No," murmured Edie Marsh. "We've had it."

Snapper told her to shut up. He snatched the .357 off the seat, pointed it out the window and somehow managed to shoot the trooper in the center of the chest. The man fell backward, landing with a splash.

"Good night, nigger," Snapper said.

Skink went rigid. Bonnie and Edie screamed. Snapper slammed the Jeep into gear and peeled rubber.

"You see thaa-aatt?" he whinnied. "One shot, one nigger cop! Whooheee! One shot!"

In the cargo well of the Cherokee, Augustine popped up on one knee. The stubby dart rifle was at his shoulder, the sights trained on the ragged hairline of Snapper's neck. He was surprised when Skink turned and shoved him back to the floor.

That's when the rear window of the Jeep vaporized.

The explosion caught Snapper furrowed in concentration, as he labored to steer around the parked Highway Patrol car, lit up like a Mardi Gras float.

Snapper ducked, peering up at the rearview. He saw the black trooper lying in a puddle, his arm waving but not aiming the smoking gun. Then the trooper went limp, and Snapper cackled.

The Cherokee fishtailed on the rain-slicked asphalt as it entered the highway. Edie Marsh hunched like an aged nun, sobbing into her hands. Skink had pulled Bonnie Lamb into his lap, out of the gunfire's path. Huddled in the cargo hatch, Augustine silently plucked nuggets of safety glass from his clothes.

Snapper was loopy on Midols, Johnnie Walker and pure criminal adrenaline. "You see that big nigger go down?" he yammered at the top of his lungs. "You see him go down!"

Christophe Michel spent the night of the hurricane in the safe and convivial atmosphere of Key West. At noon the next morning he put on the television and recognized, with cramps of dread, the bombed-out remains of a luxury housing development called Gables-on-the-Bay. The subdivision had been built by a company called

Zenith Custom Homes, which not only employed Christophe Michel as a senior structural engineer but advertised his ecumenical credentials in its sales brochures. Michel had been recruited from one of France's oldest engineering firms, which had not energetically protested his departure. Among the fields in which Michel sorely lacked experience was that of girding single-family structures to withstand the force of tropical cyclones. His new employer assured him there was nothing to it, and FedExed him a copy of the South Florida Building Code, which weighed several pounds. Christophe Michel skimmed it on the flight from Orly to Miami.

He got along fine at Zenith, once he understood that cost containment was higher on the list of corporate priorities than ensuring structural integrity. To justify its preposterously inflated prices, the company had hyped Gables-on-the-Bay as "South Florida's first hurricane-proof community." Much in the same way, Michel later reflected, that the *Titanic* was promoted as unsinkable.

All week the news from Dade County worsened. The newspaper hired its own construction engineers to inspect the storm rubble, uncovering so many design flaws that an unabridged listing was possible only in the tiniest of agate type. One of the engineers sarcastically remarked that Gables-on-the-Bay should have been called Gables-*in*-the-Bay—a quote so colorful that it merited enlargement, in boldface, on the front page.

With home owners picketing Zenith headquarters and demanding a grand jury, Christophe Michel prudently planned his departure from the United States. He closed his bank accounts, shuttered the condo in Key West, packed the Seville and set out for the mainland.

The rain did nothing for his fragile confidence in

American traffic. Every bend and rise in the overseas highway was a trial of reflexes and composure. Michel finished his last cigaret while crossing the Bahia Honda Bridge, and by Islamorada had gnawed his forty-dollar manicure to slaw. At the first break in the weather, he stopped at a Circle K for a carton of Broncos, an American brand to which he unaccountably had become devoted.

When he returned to the Seville, four strangers emerged from the shadows. One of them put a gun to his belly.

"Give us your goddamn car," the man said.

"Certainly."

"Don't stare at me like that!"

"Sorry." The engineer's trained eye calculated the skew of the man's jawbone at thirty-five degrees off center.

"I got one bullet left!"

"I believe you," said Christophe Michel.

The disfigured gunman told him to go back in the store and count backward from one hundred, slowly.

Michel asked, "May I keep my suitcase?"

"Fuck, no!"

"I understand."

He was counting aloud as he walked for the second time into the Circle K. The clerk at the register asked if something was wrong. Michel, fumbling to light a Bronco, nodded explicitly.

"My life savings just drove away," he said. "May I borrow the telephone?"

*

Bonnie Lamb expected Skink to erupt in homicidal fury upon seeing his best friend shot down. He didn't. Bonnie worried about the listless sag to his shoulders, the near feebleness of his movements. He wore the numb, unfocused glaze of the heavily sedated. Bonnie was sorry to see the governor's high spirits extinguished.

Meanwhile Snapper ranted and swore because the Seville had no CD player, only a tape deck, and here he'd gone to all the goddamn trouble of removing his compact discs from the Jeep before they'd ditched it behind the convenience store.

Bonnie squeezed Skink's arm and asked if he was all right. He shifted his feet, and something rattled metallically on the floorboard. He picked it up and asked, "What's this?"

It was a red pronged instrument, with a black plastic grip and a chrome key lock.

Snapper looked over his shoulder and sniggered. "The Club!"

"The what?"

Bonnie Lamb said, "You know. That thing they advertise all the time on TV."

"I watch no television," Skink said.

Snapper hooted. "The Club, for Chrissakes. The Club! See, you lock it across't here"—he patted the steering wheel—"so your car don't get stolen."

"Really?"

"Yeah. Lotta good it did that dickhead back at the Circle K." Snapper's laughter had a ring of triumph.

Edie Marsh was struggling to collect herself after the shooting. Even in the darkness, Bonnie could see fresh tears shining in her eyelashes.

"I had this boyfriend," Edie sniffled, "he put one of those on his new Firebird. They got it anyway. Right out of the driveway, broad daylight. What they did, they iced the lock and cracked it with a hammer."

Snapper said, "No shit? Froze it?"

"Yeah." Edie couldn't come to terms with what had happened at the Paradise Palms, the wrongness and maddening stupidity of it. They'd never get away now. Never. Killing a cop! How had a harmless insurance scam come so unhinged?

Skink was impressed with the ingenious simplicity of The Club. He took special interest in the notched slide mechanism, which allowed the pronged ends to be fitted snugly into almost any large aperture.

"See, that way you can't turn the wheel," Snapper was explaining, still enjoying the irony, "so nobody can drive off with your fancy new Cadillac Seville. 'Less they put a fuckin' gun in your ribs. Ha! Accept no imitations!"

Skink set the device down.

"Accept no imitations!" Snapper crowed again, waving the .357.

The governor's gaze turned out the window, drifting again. Teasingly, Bonnie said: "I can't believe you've never seen one of those."

This time the smile was sad. "I lead a sheltered life."

Edie Marsh wondered if Snapper could have picked a dumber location to shoot a cop—a county of slender, connected islands, with only one way out. She kept checking for blue police lights behind them.

Snapper told her to knock it off, she was making everyone a nervous wreck. "Another half hour we're home free," he said, "back on the mainland. Then we find another car."

"One with a CD player, I bet."

"Damn right."

The Seville got boxed in behind a slow beer truck. They wound up stopped at the traffic light in Key Largo. Again Edie snuck a peek behind them. Snapper heard a gasp.

"What!" He spun his head. "Is it cops?"

"No. The Jeep!"

"You're crazy, that ain't possible—"

"Right behind us," Edie said.

Bonnie Lamb began to turn around, but Skink held her shoulder. The light turned green. Snapper floored the Seville, zipped smartly between the beer truck and a meandering Toyota. He said: "You crazy twat, there's only about a million goddamn black Jeeps on the road."

"Yeah?" Edie said. "With bullet holes in the roof?" She could see a bud of mushroomed steel above the passenger side.

"Jesus." Snapper used the barrel of the .357 to adjust the rearview mirror. "Jesus, you sure?"

The Cherokee was still on their bumper. Bonnie noticed the governor wore a faint smile. Edie picked up on it, too. She said, "What's going on? Who's that behind us?"

Skink shrugged. Snapper said: "How 'bout this? I don't care who's back there, because he's already one dead cocksucker. That's 'zackly how many shots I got left."

In what seemed to Bonnie as a single fluid motion, the governor reached across the seat, wrenched the .357

from Snapper's hand and fired it point-blank into the Cadillac's dashboard.

Then he dropped it on Snapper's lap and said: "Now you've got jackshit."

Snapper labored not to pile the car into a utility pole. Edie Marsh's ears rang from the gun blast, although she wasn't surprised by what had happened. It had only been a matter of time. The smiler had been humoring them.

One thought reverberated in Bonnie Lamb's head: What now? What in the world will he do next?

Snapper, straining not to appear frightened, hollering at Skink over his shoulder: "Try anything, *anything*, I fuckin' swear we're all going off a bridge. You unnerstand? We'll all be dead."

"Eyes on the road, chief."

"Don't touch me, goddammit!"

Skink placed his chin next to the headrest, inches from Snapper's right ear. He said, "That cop you shot, he was a friend of mine."

Edie Marsh's chin dropped. "Tell me it wasn't 'Jim.'"

"It was."

"Naturally." She sighed disconsolately.

"So what?" Snapper said. His shoulders bunched. "Like I'm supposed to know. Fucking cop's a cop."

To Bonnie, the social dynamics inside the carjacked Seville were surreal. Logically the abduction should have ended once Snapper's gun was out of bullets. Yet here they were, riding along as if nothing had changed. They might as well be on a double date. Stop for pizza and milk shakes.

She said: "Can I ask something: Where are we going? Is somebody in charge now?"

Snapper said, "*I* am, goddammit. Long as I'm drivin'—"

He felt Edie jab him in the side. "The Jeep," she said, pointing. "Check it out."

The black truck was in the left lane, keeping speed with the Cadillac. Snapper pressed the accelerator, but the Jeep stayed even.

"Well, shit," he grumbled. Edie was right. It was the same truck they'd abandoned ten minutes earlier. Snapper was totally baffled. Who could it be?

They watched the Cherokee's front passenger window roll down. The ghost driver steered with his left hand. His eyes were locked on the highway. In the oncoming headlights Snapper caught sight of the man's face, which he didn't recognize. He did, however, note that the stranger definitely wasn't wearing a Highway Patrol uniform. The observation gave Snapper an utterly misplaced sense of relief.

Bonnie Lamb recognized the other driver immediately. She gave a clandestine wave. So did the governor.

"What's going on!" Edie Marsh was on her knees, pointing and shouting. "What's going on! Who is *that* sonofabitch!"

She was more dejected than startled when the Jeep's driver one-handedly raised a rifle. By the time Snapper saw it, he'd already heard the shot.

*Pffttt*. Like a kid's airgun.

Then a painful sting under one ear; liquid heat flooding down through his arms, his chest, his legs. He went slack and listed starboard, mumbling, "What the fuh, what the fuh—"

Skink said it was a superb time for Edie to assist at the wheel. "Take it steady," he added. "We're coasting."

Reaching across Snapper's body, she anxiously guided the Seville to the gravel shoulder of the highway. The black Jeep smoothly swung in ahead of them.

Edie bit her lip. "I can't believe this. I just can't."

"Me, neither," said Bonnie Lamb. She was out the door, running toward Augustine, before the car stopped rolling.

# TWENTY-EIGHT

**Jim Tile once** played tight end for the University of Florida. In his junior year, during the final home game of the season, a scrawny Alabama cornerback speared his crimson helmet full tilt into Jim Tile's sternum. Jim Tile held on to the football but completely forgot how to breathe.

That's how he felt now, lying in clammy rainwater, staring up at the worried face of a platinum-haired hooker. The impact of the shot had deflated Jim Tile's lungs, which were screaming silently for air. The emergency lights of the patrol car blinked blue-white-blue in the reflection in the prostitute's eyes.

Jim Tile understood that he couldn't be dying—it only felt that way. The asshole's bullet wasn't lodged in vital bronchial tissue; it was stuck in a layer of blessedly impenetrable Du Pont Kevlar. Like most police officers, Jim Tile detested the vest, particularly in the summer—it was hot, bulky, itchy. But he wore it because he'd promised his mother, his nieces, his uncle and of course Brenda, who wore one of her own. Working for the Highway Patrol was statistically the most dangerous job in law enforcement. Naturally it also paid the worst. Only after numerous officers had been gunned down were bulletproof vests requisitioned for the state patrol, whose budget was so threadbare that the purchase was made possible only by soliciting outside donations.

Long before that, Jim Tile's loved ones had decided he shouldn't wait for the state legislature to demonstrate its heartfelt concern for police officers. The Kevlar vest was a family Christmas present. Jim Tile didn't always wear it while patrolling rural parts of the Panhandle, but in Miami he wouldn't go to church without it. He was glad he had strapped it on today.

If only he could remember how to breathe.

"Take it easy, baby," the hooker kept saying. "Take it easy. We called 911."

As Jim Tile sat upright, he emitted a sucking sound that reminded the prostitute of a broken garbage disposal. When she smacked him between the shoulders, a mashed chunk of lead fell from a dime-sized hole in Jim Tile's shirt and plopped into the puddle. He picked it up: the slug from a .357.

Jim Tile asked, "Where'd they go?" His voice was a frail rattle. With difficulty he holstered his service revolver.

"Don't you move," said the woman.

"Did I hit him?"

"Sit still."

"Ma'am, help me up. Please."

He was shuffling for his car when the fire truck arrived. The paramedics made him lie down while they stripped off his shirt and the vest. They told him he was going to have an extremely nasty bruise. They told him he was a very lucky man.

By the time the paramedics were done, the parking lot of the Paradise Palms was clogged with curious locals, wandering tourists and motel guests, a fleet of

Monroe County deputies, two TV news vans and three gleaming, undented Highway Patrol cruisers belonging to Jim Tile's supervisors. They gathered under black umbrellas to fill out their reports.

Meanwhile the shooter was speeding up Highway One with the governor and the newlywed.

A lieutenant told Jim Tile not to worry, they'd never make it out of the Keys.

"Sir, I'd like to be part of the pursuit. I feel fine."

"You're not going anywhere." The lieutenant softened the command with a fraternal chuckle. "Hell, Jimbo, we're just gettin' started."

He handed the trooper a stack of forms and a pen.

The body of Tony Torres inevitably became a subject of interest to a newspaper reporter working on hurricane-related casualties. The autopsy report did not use the term "crucifixion," but the silhouette diagram of puncture wounds told the whole grisly story. To avert embarrassing publicity, the police made a hasty effort to reignite the investigation, dormant since the aborted phone call from a woman claiming to be the dead man's widow. Within a day, a veteran homicide detective named Brickhouse was able to turn up a recent address for the murdered Tony Torres. This was done by tracing the victim's Cartier wristwatch to a Bal Harbour jeweler, who remembered Tony as an overbearing jerk, and kept detailed receipts of the transaction in anticipation of future disputes. The jeweler was not crestfallen at the news of Señor Torres's demise, and graciously gave the detective the address he sought. While the police department's Public Information division stalled the newspaper reporter, Brickhouse drove down to the address in Turtle Meadow.

There he found an abandoned hurricane house with a late-model Chevrolet and a clunker Oldsmobile parked in front. The Chevy's license plate had been removed, but the VIN number came back to Antonio Rodrigo Guevara-Torres, the victim. The tag on the rusty Olds was registered to one Lester Maddox Parsons. Brickhouse radioed for a criminal history, which might or might not be ready when he got back to the office in the morning; the hurricane had unleashed electronic gremlins inside the computers.

The detective's natural impulse was to enter the house, which would have been fairly easy in the absence of doors. The problem wasn't so much that Brickhouse didn't have a warrant; it was the old man next door, watching curiously from the timber shell of his front porch. He would be the defense lawyer's first witness at a suppression hearing, if an unlawful search of the victim's residence turned up evidence.

So Brickhouse stayed in the yard, peeking through broken windows and busted doorways. He noted a gas-powered generator in the garage, wine and flowers in the dining room, a woman's purse, half-melted candles, an Igloo cooler positioned next to a BarcaLounger—definitive signs of post-hurricane habitation. Everything else was standard storm debris. Brickhouse saw no obvious bloodstains, which fit his original theory that the mobile-home salesman had been taken elsewhere to be crucified.

The detective strolled over to chat with the snoopy neighbor, who gave his name as Leonel Varga. He told a jumbled but colorful yarn about sinister-looking visitors, mysterious leggy women and insufferable barking dogs. Brickhouse took notes courteously. Varga said Mr and Mrs Torres were separated, although she'd recently phoned to say she was coming home.

"But it's a secret," he added.

"You bet," Brickhouse said. Before knocking off for the evening, he tacked his card to the doorjamb at 15600 Calusa.

That's where Neria Torres found it at dawn.

Matthew's pickup truck had followed her all the way from Fort Drum to the house at Turtle Meadow. The seven Tennesseeans swarmed the battered building in orgiastic wonderment at the employment opportunity that God had wrought. Matthew dramatically announced they should commence repairs immediately.

Neria said, "Not just yet. You help me find my husband, then I'll let you do some work on the house."

"I guess, sure. Where's he at?"

"First I've got to make some calls."

"Sure," Matthew said. "Meantime we should get a jump on things." He asked Neria's permission to borrow some tools from the garage.

"Just hold on," she told him.

But they were already ascending the roof and rafters, like a troop of hairless chimpanzees. Neria let it go. The sight of the place disturbed her more than she had anticipated. She'd seen the hurricane destruction on CNN, but standing ankle-deep in it was different; overwhelming, if the debris once was your home. The sight of her mildewed wedding pictures in the wreckage brought a sentimental pang, but it was quickly deadened by the discovery of flowers and a bottle of wine in the dining room. Neria Torres assumed Tony had bought them for a bimbo.

She fingered the detective's card. She hoped it meant that the cops had tossed her asshole husband in jail, leaving her a clear path toward reclaiming half the marital property. Or possibly more.

She heard a mechanical roar from the garage; the resourceful Tennesseeans had found fuel for the generator. A bare lightbulb flickered on and off in the living room.

Leonel Varga, still in his bathrobe, came over to say hello. He assured her that the police detective was a nice man.

"What did he want? Is it about Tony?"

"I think so. He didn't say." Mr Varga stared up at the busy figures of the men on the roof beams, backlit by the molten sunrise. "You found some roofers?"

Neria Torres said, "Oh, I seriously doubt it."

She dialed the private number that Detective Brickhouse had penciled on the back of the business card. He answered the phone like a man accustomed to being awakened by strangers. He said, "I'm glad you called."

"Is it about Tony?"

"Yeah, I'm afraid it is."

"Don't tell me he's in jail," said Neria, hoping dearly that Brickhouse would tell her precisely that.

"No," the detective said. "Mrs Torres, your husband's dead."

"Oh God. Oh God. Oh God." Neria's mind was skipping like a flat rock on a river.

"I'm sorry—"

"You sure?" she asked. "Are you sure it's Antonio?"

"We should take a ride up to the morgue. You're home now?"

"Yes. Yes, I'm back."

Brickhouse said, "I've got to be in court this morning. How about if I swing by around noon? We'll go together. Give us some time to chat."

"About what?"

"It looks like Antonio was murdered."

"How? Murdered?"

"We'll talk later, Mrs Torres. Get some rest now."

Neria didn't know what she felt, or what she ought to feel. The corpse in the morgue was the man she'd married. A corpulent creep, to be sure, but still the husband she had once believed she loved. Shock was natural. Curiosity. A selfish stab of fear. Maybe even sorrow. Tony had his piggish side, but even so . . .

Her gaze settled for the first time on the purse. A woman's purse, opened, on the kitchen counter. On top was a note printed in block letters and signed with the initials "F.D." The note said the author was keeping the dogs at the motel. The note began with "My Sexy Darling" and ended with "Love Always."

Dogs? Neria Torres thought.

She wondered if Tony was the same man as "F.D." and, if so, what insipid nickname the initials stood for. Fat Dipshit?

Curiously she went through the contents of the purse. A driver's license identified the owner as Edith Deborah Marsh. Neria noted the date of birth, working the arithmetic in her head. Twenty-nine years old, this one.

*Tony, you dirty old perv.*

Neria appraised the face in the photograph. A ball-buster; Tony must've had his fat hands full. Neria took unaccountable satisfaction from the fact that young Edith was a dagger-eyed brunette, not some dippy blonde.

From behind her came the sound of roupy breathing. Neria wheeled, to find Matthew looming at her shoulder.

"Christ!"

"I dint mean to scare ya."

"What is it? What do you want?"

"It's started up to rain."

"I noticed."

"Seemed like a good spot for a break. We was headed to a hardware store for some roof paper, nails, wood—stuff like that."

"Lumber," Neria Torres said archly. "In the construction business, it's called 'lumber.' Not wood."

"Sure." He was scratching at his Old Testament tattoos.

She said, "So go already."

"Yeah, well, we need some money. For the lumber."

"Matthew, there's something I've got to tell you."

"Sure."

"My husband's been murdered. A police detective is coming out here soon."

Matthew took a step back and said, "Sweet Jesus, I'm so sorry." He began to improvise a prayer, but Neria cut him off.

"You and your crew," she said, "you *are* licensed in Dade County, aren't you? I mean, there won't be any problem if the detective wants to ask some questions . . . ?"

The Tennesseeans were packed and gone within fifteen minutes. Neria found the solitude relaxing: a light whisper of rain, the occasional whine of a mosquito. She thought of Tony, wondered whom he'd pissed off to get himself killed—maybe tough young Edith! Neria thought of the professor, too, wondered how he and his Earth Mother blow-job artist were getting along with no wheels.

She also thought of the many things she didn't want to do, such as move back into the gutted husk at 15600 Calusa. Or be interviewed by a homicide detective. Or go to the morgue to view her estranged husband's body.

Money was the immediate problem. Neria wondered if careless Tony had left her name on any of the bank accounts, and what (if anything) remained in them. The most valuable item at the house was his car, untouched by the hurricane. Neria located the spare key in the garage, but the engine wouldn't turn over.

"Need some help?"

It was a clean-shaven young man in a Federal Express uniform. He had an envelope for Neria Torres. She signed for it, laid it on the front seat of Tony's Chevy.

The kid said, "I got jumpers in the truck."

"Would you mind?"

They had the car started in no time. Neria idled the engine and waited for the battery to recharge. The FedEx kid said it sounded good. Halfway to the truck, he stopped and turned.

"Hey, somebody swiped your license plate."

"Shit." Neria got out to see for herself. The FedEx driver said it was probably a looter.

"Everybody around here's getting ripped off," he explained.

"I didn't even notice. Thanks."

As soon as he left, Neria opened the FedEx envelope. Her delirious shriek drew nosy Mr Varga to his front porch. He was shirtless, a toothbrush in one cheek. In fascination he watched his neighbor practically bound up the sidewalk into her house.

The envelope contained two checks made out to Antonio and Neria Torres. The checks were issued by the Midwest Life and Casualty Company of Omaha, Nebraska. They totaled $201,000. The stubs said: "Hurricane losses."

Shortly after noon, when Detective Brickhouse arrived at 15600 Calusa, he found the house empty again. The Chevrolet was gone, as was the widow of Antonio Torres. A torn Federal Express envelope lay on the driveway, near the rusty Oldsmobile. Mr Varga, the neighbor, informed the detective that Neria Torres sped off without even waving good-bye.

Brickhouse was backing out of the driveway when a rental car pulled up. A thin blond man wearing round eyeglasses got out. Brickhouse noticed the man had tan Hush Puppies and was carrying a box of Whitman chocolates. High-pitched barking could be heard from the back seat of the visitor's car.

The detective called the man over. "Are you looking for Mrs Torres?"

The man hesitated. Brickhouse identified himself. The man blinked repeatedly, as if his glasses were smudged.

He said, "I don't know anybody named Torres. Guess I've got the wrong address." Speedily he returned to his car.

Brickhouse leaned out the window. "Hey, who's the candy for?"

"My mother!" Fred Dove replied, over the barking.

The detective watched the confused young man drive away, and wondered why he'd lied. Even crackheads know how to find their own mother's house. Brickhouse briefly considered tailing the guy, but decided it would be a waste of time. Whoever crucified Tony Torres wasn't wearing Hush Puppies. Brickhouse would have bet his pension on it.

Augustine parked at a phone booth behind a gas station. The governor had them wait while he made a call. He came back humming a Beatles tune.

"Jim's alive," he said.

Edie Marsh leaned forward. "Your friend! How do you know?"

"There's a number where we leave messages for each other."

Bonnie asked if he was hurt badly.

"Nope. He took it in the vest."

Augustine shook a fist in elation. Everybody's mood perked up, even Edie's. Skink told Bonnie she could call her mother, but make it fast. It went like this:

"Mom, something's happened."

"I guessed as much."

"Between Max and me."

"Oh no." Bonnie's mother, laboring to sound properly dismayed, when Bonnie knew how she truly felt.

"What'd he do, sweetie?"

"Nothing, Mom. It's all me."

"Did you have a fight?" her mother asked.

"Listen, I've met two unusual men. I believe I've fallen in love with one of them."

"On your honeymoon, Bonnie?"

"I'm afraid so."

"What does he do?"

"He's not certain," Bonnie said.

"These men, are they dangerous?"

"Not to me. Mom, they're totally different from anyone I've ever known. It's a very . . . primitive charisma."

"Let's not mention that last part to your father."

Next Bonnie phoned the apartment in New York. When she got back to the Seville, she told Skink to go on without her.

"Max left a message on the machine." She didn't look at Augustine when she said it. Couldn't look at him.

Bonnie repeated her husband's message. "He says it's over if I don't meet with him."

"It's over regardless," Skink said.

"Please."

"Call back and leave your own message." The governor gave her the details—the place, the time, who would be there.

After Bonnie finished with the phone, Skink made another call himself. When they got back in the car, Augustine punched the accelerator and peeled rubber. Bonnie put her hand on his arm. He gave a tight, rueful smile.

They made the 905 turnoff in the nick of time. Already the northbound traffic was stacked past Lake Surprise; Skink surmised that the police had raised the Jewfish Creek drawbridge for their roadblock. He predicted they'd set up another one at Card Sound, as soon as more patrol cars arrived from the mainland.

Edie Marsh said, "So where are we going?"

"Patience."

The two of them sat together in the back seat. On the

governor's lap was a Bill Blass suitcase, removed from the Cadillac's trunk to make space for the blacked-out Snapper.

Skink said, "Driver, dome light! *Por favor.*"

Augustine began pushing dashboard buttons until the ceiling lights came on. Skink broke the locks off the suitcase and opened it.

"What have we here!" he said.

The troopers waited all night at Jewfish Creek. As Jim Tile predicted the black Jeep Cherokee never appeared, nor did the silver Cadillac stolen from a customer at a Key Largo convenience store. The French victim had dryly described the armed carjacker as "a poster boy for TMJ."

At daybreak the cops gave up the roadblock and fanned through the Upper Keys. It would take three days to locate the Seville, abandoned on a disused smugglers' trail off County Road 905, only a few miles from the exclusive Ocean Reef Club. The police would wait another forty-eight hours before announcing the discovery of the vehicle. They omitted mention of the bullet hole in its dashboard, as they didn't wish to unduly alarm Ocean Reef's residents and guests, which included some of the most socially prominent, politically influential and chronically impatient taxpayers in the eastern United States. Many were already in a cranky mood, due to the inconvenient damaging of their vacation homes by the hurricane. News that a murderous criminal might be lurking in the mangroves would touch off heated high-level communiqués with Tallahassee and

Washington, D.C. The Ocean Reef crowd didn't mess around.

As it turned out, there was no danger whatsoever.

Most newly married men, faced with unexpected desertion, would have been manic with grief, jealousy and anger. Max Lamb, however, was blessed by a hearty, blinding preoccupation with his career.

A nettlesome thought kept scrolling across his mind, and it had nothing to do with his runaway wife. It was something the nutty kidnapper had told him: *You need a legacy*.

They'd been riding in the back of a U-Haul truck, discussing unforgettable advertising slogans. Max hadn't anything zippy to brag about except the short-lived Plum Crunchies ditty. Since the failure of the cereal campaign, the sixth floor had deployed him more often for billboard concepts and print graphics, and not as much on the verbally creative side.

Which stung, because Max considered himself a genuinely glib and talented wordsmith. He believed it was well within his reach to write an advertising catchphrase that would embed itself in the national lexicon—one of those classics the kidnapper had mentioned. A legacy, if you will.

Now that Bronco cigarets were history, Max was left to review the potential of his other accounts. The hypercarbonated soda served on the plane to Miami put him in mind of Old Faithful Root Beer. Old Faithful's popularity had peaked in the summer of 1962, and since then its share of the global soft-drink market had fizzled to a microscopic sliver. Rodale's mission was to revive

Old Faithful in the consciousness of the consumer, and to that end the eccentric Mormon family that owned the company was willing to spend a respectable seven-figure sum.

Around Rodale & Burns, the Old Faithful Root Beer account was regarded as a lucrative but hopeless loser. Nobody liked the stuff because one sixteen-ounce bottle induced thunderous belching that often lasted for days. At a party, Pete Archibald drunkenly offered a joke slogan: "The root beer you'll never forget—because it won't let you!"

Lying there alone in Augustine's house, Max Lamb savored the prospect of single-handedly resuscitating Old Faithful. It was the sort of coup that could make him a legend on Madison Avenue. For inspiration he turned on the Home Shopping Network. Into the wee hours he tinkered determinedly with beverage-related alliterations, allusions, puns, verses and metaphors. Bonnie didn't cross his mind.

Eventually Max struck on a winner, something that sounded like good silly fun to kids, and at the same time titillating to teens and young adults:

"Old Faithful Root Beer—Makes You Tingle in Places You Didn't Know You Had Places!"

Max Lamb was so excited he couldn't sleep. Once more he tried calling the apartment in New York. No Bonnie, but the answering machine emitted a telltale beep. He punched the three-digit code and waited.

Bonnie had gotten his message—and left him a reply that caused him to forget temporarily about the Old Faithful account. The flesh under Max's shirt collar prickled and perspired, and stayed feverish until dawn.

He wasn't surprised by the symptoms. The downside of seeing his wife would be seeing the deranged kidnapper again. Only an idiot wouldn't be scared shitless.

# TWENTY-NINE

**Snapper regained consciousness** with the dreamy impression of being someplace he hadn't been in twenty-two years—a dentist's chair. He sensed the dentist hovering, and felt large deft hands working inside his mouth. The last time Snapper had a cavity filled, he'd reflexively chomped off the top joint of the dentist's right thumb. This time he was becalmed by the ejaculate of the dart rifle.

"Lester Maddox Parsons!" The dentist, attempting to wake him.

Snapper opened his eyes in a fog bank. Looming out of the psychedelic mist was a silvery-bearded grin. A dentist in a plastic shower cap? Snapper squirmed.

"Whhaannffrr?" he inquired.

"Relax, chief."

The dentist's basso chuckle rolled like a freight train through Snapper's cranium. His jaws were wedged wide, as if awaiting the drill. Come on, he thought, get it over with.

He heard buzzing. Good!

But the buzzing wasn't in his mouth; it was in his ears. Bugs. Fucking bugs flying in his ears!

"Hrrrnnnff!" Snapper shook his head violently. It hurt. All of a sudden he was drenched by a wave of salty water. What he didn't cough up settled as a lukewarm puddle in his protruded mandible, which functioned as a natural cistern.

Now he was completely awake. Now he remembered. The fog cleared from his mind. He saw a campfire. Edie, sweaty and barefoot. And the young broad, Bonnie, with her arms around the asshole punk who'd shot him.

"Yo, Lester." It was the giant one-eyed fruitcake, holding an empty bucket. There was no dentist.

But Snapper definitely felt a cold steel object bracing his jaws open, digging into the roof of his mouth, pinching the tender web of flesh beneath his tongue; something so heavy that it caused his head to nod forward, something that extended diagonally upward from his chin to beyond his forehead.

A heavy bar of some type. Snapper crossed his eyes to put it in focus. The bar was red.

Oh fuck.

He wailed, trying to rise. His legs tangled. With rubbery arms he flailed uselessly at the thing locked in his mouth.

Skink held up a small chrome key and said, "Accept no imitations."

"Nnnnngggggoooo!!"

"You shot my friend. You called him a nigger." Skink shrugged in resignation. "You beat up a lady, stole her momma's wedding ring, dumped her on the roadside. What choice have you left me?"

He took Snapper by the hair and dragged him, blubbering, to the shore of a broad milky-green creek.

"What choice?" Skink repeated, softly.

"Unngh! Unnngggghhhh!"

"Sure. *Now* you're sorry."

Edie, Bonnie and Augustine appeared on the bank. Skink crouched in the mud next to Snapper.

"Here's the deal. Most any other species, you'd have been dead long ago. Ever heard of Charles Darwin?"

Mosquitoes tickled Snapper's eyelids as he nodded his head.

"Good," Skink said. "Then you might understand what's about to happen." He turned to the others. "Somebody tell Mister Lester Maddox Parsons where we are."

Augustine said: "Crocodile Lakes."

"Yes indeedy." Skink rose. Once more he displayed the chrome key, the only thing that could unlock The Club from Snapper's achingly prolongated jowls.

Skink threw it in the water. He said, "Crocodile Lakes Wildlife Refuge. Guess how it got its name."

Mournfully Snapper stared at the circle of ripples where the key had plopped into the creek.

They'd stopped once along County Road 905, so Skink could snatch a dead diamondback off the blacktop.

"Don't tell me," said Edie. "It tastes just like chicken."

The governor, coiling the limp rattlesnake at his feet, pretended to be insulted. He told Edie she was much too pretty to be such a cynic. He snapped off the snake's rattle and presented it to her for a souvenir.

"Just what I always wanted." She dropped it in the ashtray.

After ditching the car, Skink made a torch from a gummy stump of pine. For nearly two hours he led them through a shadowed canopy of buttonwoods, poisonwoods, figs, pigeon plums and mahogany. He'd slung Snapper over his shoulder like a sack of oats. In his right hand he held the torch; in his other was the Bill Blass suitcase. Edie Marsh followed along a path hardly wide enough for a rabbit. Bonnie went next, with Augustine close behind, carrying (at Skink's instruction) the tranquilizer rifle and The Club. The .38 Special was in his belt.

Eventually they entered a small clearing. In the center was a ring of sooty stones; a campfire site. A few yards away sat a junked truck with freckles of rust and a faded orange stripe. Bolted to the roof was a bar of cracked red lights. Bonnie and Augustine stepped closer—it was an old Monroe County ambulance, propped on cinder blocks. Augustine opened the tailgate and whistled appreciatively. The ambulance was full of books.

The governor deposited Snapper on the ground, propped against a scabby tree trunk. He went to a spot on the other side of the clearing and kicked at the leaves and loose twigs, exposing an olive-drab tarpaulin. Rummaging beneath it, he came out with a tin of bread crumbs, a jar of vegetable oil, a five-gallon jug of fresh water and a waxy stick of army insect repellent, which he passed around.

While he collected dry wood for the fire, Edie Marsh came up beside him. "Where are we?"

"Middle of nowhere."

"Why?"

"Because there's no better place to be."

They gathered to watch him skin the rattler. Edie was impressed by his enormous hands, sure and swift and completely at ease with the knife.

As the fire sparked up, Augustine pulled Bonnie closer and buried his face in the silkiness of her hair. He was soothed by the soft crackle of tinder; the owl piping on a distant wire; raccoons trilling and fussing in the shadows; the whoosh of nighthawks scooping insects above the firelit treetops. The sole discordant note was the stuporous snore of Lester Maddox Parsons.

The air tasted fresh; the rain was done for a while. Augustine wouldn't have traded places with another soul. Crocodile Lakes on a warm September night was fine. He kissed Bonnie lightly, having no special plans beyond the moment. He willed himself not to worry about Max Lamb, who would be coming tomorrow on a mission to retrieve his bride.

Skink began spooning out chunks of pan-fried snake. Edie Marsh facetiously said it was impolite not to save some for Snapper. Skink declared that he wouldn't so dishonor the memory of a dead reptile.

That's when he'd asked Augustine for The Club.

He turned his back to the others while he fitted it under Snapper's papery gray lips. Bonnie believed the procedure would have been physically impossible, were it not for the preexisting crookedness of those saurian jawbones. Afterwards nobody said a word, until Snapper made a groggy inquisitive murmur.

Skink bent over him. "Lester?"

"Mmmmmfrrrtthh."

"Lester Maddox Parsons!"

Snapper's eyelids fluttered. The governor asked Augustine to take a bucket down to the creek and get some water to wake up the sorry sonofabitch.

*

The pink-orange parfait of dawn failed to elevate Edie's spirits. She was sticky, scratched, hot, parched, filthy, as wretched as she'd ever been. She wanted to cry and pull at her hair and scream. She wanted to make a scene. Most of all she wanted to escape, but that was impossible. She was trapped on all sides by humming crackling wilderness; it might as well have been a twelve-foot wall of barbed wire. Her hands and feet weren't shackled. The governor held no gun to her head. Nothing whatsoever prevented her from running, except the grim certainty that she'd never find her way out, that she'd become blindly lost in the woods and starve, and that her emaciated body would be torn apart and devoured by crocodiles, rattlers and ravenous tropical ants. The prospect of an anonymous death in the swamps offended Edie's dignity. She didn't want her sun-bleached bones to be found by hunters, fishermen or bird-watchers; pieced together by wisecracking medical students and coroners; identified by X-rays from her childhood orthodontist.

She approached the governor. "I want to talk."

He was mumbling to himself, feeling around in his shirt. "Damn," he said. "Out of toad." He glanced at Edie: "You're a woman of the world. Ever smoke Bufo?"

"We need to talk," she said. "Alone."

"If it's about the suitcase, forget it."

"It's not that."

"All right, then. Soon as I finish chatting with Lester."

"No, now!"

Skink cupped her chin in one of his huge, rough palms. Edie Marsh sensed that he could break her neck as effortlessly as twisting the cap off a beer. He said, "You've got shitty manners. Go sit with the others."

Bonnie and Augustine were kneeling in the back of the junked ambulance, poring through Skink's library. Edie couldn't understand how they could seem so unconcerned.

She said, "We've got to do something." It came out like a command.

Augustine was showing Bonnie a first edition of *Absalom, Absalom*. He glanced up at Edie and said, "It's a ride. When it's over, it's over."

"But who *is* he?" She pointed toward Skink. Then, facing Bonnie: "Aren't you afraid? God, am I the only one with brains enough to be scared?"

"Last night I was," Bonnie said. "Not now."

Augustine told Edie to quiet down. "It'll be over when he says so. In the meantime, please do your best not to piss him off."

Edie was jarred by the harshness of Augustine's tone. He jerked a thumb toward Snapper, agape by the campfire. "What're you doing with that shitbird, anyway?"

Bonnie cut in: "Let's drop the whole thing."

"No, it's all right. I want to explain," said Edie. "It was just business. We were working a deal together."

"A scam."

"Insurance money," she admitted, "from the hurricane." She caught Bonnie staring. "Welcome to the real world, princess."

"So when's the big payoff?" Augustine asked.

Edie laughed ruefully. "The adjuster said any day. Said it was coming Federal Express. And here I am, lost in the middle of the fucking Everglades."

"It's not the Everglades," said Augustine. "In fact, this is Saint-Tropez compared to the Everglades. But I can see why you're upset, watching two hundred grand fly away."

Edie Marsh was dumbfounded. Bonnie said, "You're joking. Two hundred thousand dollars?"

"Two hundred and one." Augustine chided Edie with a wink.

She asked, almost inaudibly: "How'd you know?"

"You left something in the house on Calusa."

"Oh shit."

He unfolded the pink carbons of the Midwest Casualty claim—Edie recognized the cartoon badger at the top of the page. Augustine ripped the carbons into pieces. He said, "I were you, I'd come up with a clever excuse why your pocketbook might be in that particular kitchen. The police'll be mighty curious."

"Shit."

"What I'm saying is, don't be in such a rush to get back to civilization." He turned back to the governor's books.

Edie bit her lower lip. Lord, sometimes it was tough to stay cool. She felt like breaking down again. "What's this all about—some kind of game?"

"I don't think so," Bonnie said.

"Jesus Christ."

"Ride it out. Hang on till it's over."

Not me, thought Edie. No fucking way.

The Club exaggerated Snapper's pre-exaggerated features. It pushed the top half of his mug into pudgy creases, like a shar-pei puppy; the eyes were moist slits, the nose pugged nearly to his brow. The rest was all maw.

"An authentic mouth-breather," Skink said, studying him as if he were a museum piece.

"Fhhhrrrggaaah," Snapper retorted. His elbows stung from scrapes received when the lunatic had dragged him to the creek.

Now the lunatic was saying: "God, I hate the word 'nigger.' Back at the motel I considered killing you when you said it. Blowing your three pitiful teaspoons of brain matter all over the Jeep. Even if you hadn't shot my friend, the thought would've crossed my mind."

Snapper stopped moaning. Worked at controlling his slobber. Watched gnats and mosquitoes float in and out of his mouth.

"Nothing to be done about that." Skink flicked at the insects. He'd already spread a generous sheen of repellent on his captive's neck and arms. "'Not to be taken internally.' Says so right on the package."

Snapper nodded submissively.

"Lester Maddox Parsons is the name on your license. Wild guess says you're named after that clay-brained Georgia bigot. Am I right?"

A weaker nod.

"So you started out two strikes against you. That's a shame, Lester, but I expect even if your folks had called you Gandhi, you still would've grown up to be a world-class dickhead. Here, let me show you something."

The governor yanked the Bill Blass suitcase from under his butt. He positioned it in front of Snapper and opened it with a gay flourish. "Drool away," he said.

Snapper rose to his haunches. The suitcase was packed with money: bank-wrapped bundles of twenties.

"Ninety-four thousand dollars," Skink reported.

"Plus assorted shirts, socks and casual wear. Two packs of French condoms, a set of gold cuff links, a tube of generic lubricant—what else? Oh yes, personal papers."

He probed in the luggage. "Bank statements, newspaper clippings about the hurricane. And this . . ."

It was a glossy color sales brochure for a real estate project called Gables-on-the-Bay. Skink sat next to Snapper and opened the brochure.

"There's our boy. Christophe Michel. 'Internationally renowned construction engineer.' See, here's his picture."

Snapper recognized him as the dork at the Circle K.

"What would you do," Skink mused, "if you designed all these absurdly expensive homes—and they fell down in the first big blow. I believe a smart person would grab the money and split, before subpoenas started flying. I believe that was Monsieur Michel's plan."

Snapper didn't give two shits about the Frenchman. He was transfixed by the sight of so much money. He would have gaped rapturously even if his jaws weren't bolted open. He remembered a Sally Jessy, or maybe it was a Donahue, with some hotel maid from Miami Beach who'd found like forty-two grand under a bed. The maid, for some reason, instead of grabbing the dough she'd turned it in to the manager! That's how come she'd got on Sally Jessy; the theme that day was "honest people." Snapper remembered shouting at the TV screen: What a dumb cunt! They'd showed a picture of the cash, and he'd almost come in his pants.

And here he was staring at twice as much. In person.

"Whhrrrrooognnn? Whhhaaakkkfff?"

"Good question, Lester."

Without warning, the one-eyed freak stood up, unbuttoned his army trousers, whipped out his unit and—to Snapper's mortification—urinated prodigiously upon the hurricane money.

Woefully Snapper rocked on his heels. He felt sick. Skink tucked himself in and went for the monkey rifle. He opened the chamber, peered inside. Then he strolled over to Snapper, flipped him on his belly and shot a tranquilizer dart into his ass. Right away the fog rolled in and Snapper got drowsy. The last thing he heard came from Skink.

"Who wants to go for a swim?"

Bonnie and Augustine stayed to look at the books while the governor took Edie to the creek. She wanted to talk; Skink wanted to get wet. He stripped, starting with the shower cap.

As he stepped into the water, she said: "What about the crocodiles?"

"They won't bother us. There aren't enough of them left to bother anybody. I wish there were."

Serenely he sank beneath the surface, then burst into the air, shaking bubbles and spray from his beard. He was as brown as a manatee, and so large he seemed to bridge the creek. Edie was unprepared for the sight of his body: the lodgepole arms and broad chest, his bare neck as thick as a cypress trunk. The baggy army fatigues had given none of it away.

"Coming in?"

"Only if we can talk," she said.

"What else *would* we do?"

Edie thought: There's that damn smile again. She asked him to turn around while she took off her clothes.

He heard her slip into the creek. Then he felt her slender arms and legs; she was clinging to his back. As he moved into deeper water, she wrapped herself around his thighs.

"I'm a little scared," she said.

"Haw! You and I are the scariest beasts in the jungle."

Edie's mouth was at his ear. "I want to go back to Miami."

"So go."

"But I don't know the way out."

The governor was treading against the push of a strong tidal current. It cleaved around their bobbing heads as if they were dead stumps in the creek.

Edie's breath quickened from the thrill of being in fast water. She said, "From the minute you and Pollyanna showed up at the house, I knew it was over. Snapper's gun—it meant nothing. We didn't kidnap you; you kidnapped us!"

"Nature imposes hierarchy. Always," Skink said.

Edie, in a taut whisper: "Please. Show me the way out of here."

"And I was so sure you'd be angling for that suitcase."

"No way," she said, although it fleetingly had crossed her mind. Instead she'd decided to concentrate on getting out of the Keys alive.

A small silver fish jumped nearby. Playfully Skink swiped at it. He said, "Edie, your opinion of men—it's not good. That much we share. Christ, imagine what Florida would look like today if women had been in charge of the program! Imagine a beach or two with no ugly high-rises. Imagine a lake without golf courses." He clapped his hands, making a merry splash.

Edie said, "You're wrong."

"Darling, I can dream." He felt her lips feather against his neck. Then a tongue, followed by the unsubtle suggestion of a nibble. He said, "And what was that?"

"What do you think."

When she kissed him again, they went down. The saltiness burned her eyes, but she opened them anyway. He was smiling at her, blowing bubbles. They surfaced together and laughed. Carefully she repositioned herself, climbing around him as if he were a tree—hanging from his rock-hard forearms and shoulders, bracing her knees against his hipbones as she swung to the front. All the time she felt him easing toward a shallower spot in the creek, so he could stand while holding her.

Now they were eye-to-eye, green water foaming up between them. Edie said, "Well?"

"Weren't you the one worried about crocodiles?"

"He'd have to eat both of us, wouldn't he?"

"At the moment, yes."

"That means he'd have to be awfully big and hungry."

Skink said, "We should be quiet, just in case. Certain noises do attract them." He sounded serious.

"How quiet?" Lightly she brushed her nipples along the lines of his ribs.

"Very quiet. Not a sound."

"That's impossible." She felt his hands on the curve of her bottom. He was lifting her, keeping her in a gentle suspension. Then he was inside her. Just like that.

"Hush," he said.

"I can't."

"Yes you can, Edie."

They made love so slowly that often it seemed they weren't moving a muscle. All sense of touch and motion came from the warm summer tide that rushed past and around and between them. In the mangroves an outraged heron squawked. More silver mullets jumped toward the shallows. A long black snake drifted by, indifferently riding the slick of the current as if it were floating on jade-colored silk.

Edie Marsh was good. She hardly made a sound. For quite a while she even forgot the purpose of the seduction.

Afterwards she wanted to dry off and take a nap together, but Skink said there was no time. They dressed quickly. Without a word he led her through the tangled woods. Edie saw no particular trail; at times it seemed they were hiking in circles. Once they reached a paved road, he took her arm. They walked another mile to an intersection with a flashing traffic light. A sign said that one road went to Miami, the other toward Key West.

Skink told her to wait there.

"For what?"

"Somebody's taking you to the mainland. He'll be coming soon."

Edie was caught by surprise. "Who?"

"Relax."

"But I wanted *you* to take me."

"Sorry," said Skink. "This is as far as I go."

"It's going to rain again."

"Yep."

"I heard lightning!" Edie said.

"So don't fly any kites."

"When did you plan this? Dropping me out here . . ." She was angry now. She realized he'd always meant to let her go—which meant the sex-in-the-creek had been unnecessary.

Not that she hadn't enjoyed it, or wouldn't love to try it again, but still she felt tricked.

"Why didn't you tell me last night?"

Skink flashed her the politician's smile. "Slipped my mind."

"Asshole." She picked a leaf out of her wet hair and peevishly flicked it into the wind. Swatted a horsefly off her ankle. Folded her arms and glared.

He leaned down and kissed her forehead. "Look on the bright side, girl. You got over your fear of crocodiles."

# THIRTY

**At half past noon,** a police cruiser stopped at the intersection of Card Sound Road and County Road 905. A broad-shouldered black man in casual street clothes honked twice at Edie Marsh. As he motioned her to the car, she recognized him as the cop whom Snapper had shot outside Paradise Palms.

"You might not believe this," she said, "but I'm really glad you're OK."

"Thanks for your concern." His tone was so neutral that she almost didn't catch the sarcasm. He wore reflector sunglasses and had a toothpick in the corner of his mouth. When he reached across to open the door, Edie glimpsed a white mat of bandage between the middle buttons of his shirt.

"You're Jim, right? I'm Edie."

"I figured."

He took the road toward Miami. Edie assumed she was being arrested. She said, "For what it's worth, I didn't think he would shoot."

"Funny thing about morons with guns."

"Look, I know where he is. I can show you where he is."

Jim Tile said, "I already know."

Then she understood. The trooper had no intention of trying to find Snapper. It was over for Snapper.

"What about me?" she asked, inwardly speculating on the multitude of felonies for which she could be prosecuted. Attempted murder. Fleeing the scene. Aiding and abetting. Auto theft. Not to mention insurance fraud, which the trooper might or might not know about, depending on what the governor had told him.

"So what happens to me?" she asked again.

"Last night I got a message saying a lady needed a ride to the mainland."

"And you had nothing better to do."

From miles behind the sunglasses: "It was an old friend who called."

Edie Marsh kept trying to play tough. It wasn't easy. No other cars were in sight. The guy could rape me, kill me, dump my body in the swamp. Who'd ever know? Plus he was a cop.

She said, "You didn't answer my question."

The toothpick bobbed. "The answer is: Nothing. Nothing's going to happen to you. The friend who left a message put in a good word."

"Yeah?"

"'Jail will not make an impression on this woman. Don't waste your time.' That's a quote."

Edie reddened. "Some good word."

"So you get a free ride to Florida City. Period."

After crossing the Card Sound Bridge, the trooper stopped at Alabama Jack's. He asked Edie if she wanted a fish sandwich or a burger.

"I'm barefoot," she said.

Finally he broke a smile. "I don't believe there's a dress code."

Over lunch, Edie Marsh tried again. "I got sick when

Snapper pulled the trigger," she said, "back at the motel, I swear. It's the last thing I wanted."

Jim Tile said it didn't matter one way or the other. To appear friendly, Edie asked how long he'd been assigned to Miami.

"Ten days."

"You came for the hurricane?"

"Just like you," he said, letting her know he had her pegged.

On their way out of the restaurant, he bought her an extra order of fries and a Coke for the road. In the car, Edie tried to keep the conversation moving. She felt more secure when he was talking, instead of staring ahead like a sphinx, working that damn toothpick.

She asked if she could see the bulletproof vest. He said he'd had to turn it in at headquarters, for evidence. She asked if the bullet made a hole and he said no, more of a dimple.

"Bet you didn't think hurricane duty would be so hairy."

Jim Tile fiddled with the squelch on the radio.

Edie said, "What's the craziest thing you've seen so far?"

"Besides your geek partner shooting at me?"

"Yeah, besides that."

"The President of the United States," he said, "trying to hammer a nail into a piece of plywood. Took him at least nine tries."

Edie straightened. "You saw the President!"

"Yeah. We had motorcade duty."

Thoughtfully she munched on a French fry. "Did you see his son, too?"

"They were riding in the same limo."

"I didn't know he lived in Miami, the President's son."

"Lucky him," the trooper said.

Edie Marsh, sipping her Coke, trying not to be too obvious: "I wonder where his house is, somebody like that. Key Biscayne probably, or maybe the Gables. Sometimes I wonder about famous people. Where they eat out. Where they get their cars waxed. Who's their dentist. I mean, think about it: The President's kid, he still has to get his teeth cleaned. Don't you ever wonder about stuff like that?"

"Never." Fat raindrops slapped on the windshield. Still the trooper stayed camped behind the sunglasses.

Edie didn't give up. "You got a girlfriend?" she asked.

"Yes."

Finally, Edie thought. Something to run with. "Where is she?"

"In the hospital," Jim Tile said. "Your buddy beat her to a pulp."

"Oh God, no. . . ."

He saw that she'd spilled the Coke, and that she didn't even know it.

"God, I'm so sorry," she was saying. "I swear, I didn't—will she be all right?"

Jim Tile offered a handful of paper napkins. Edie tried to sop the soda off her lap. Her hands were shaky.

"I didn't know," she said, more than once. She recalled the engraving on the mother's wedding band, the one that Snapper had stolen. "Cynthia" was the name on the ring, the mother of the trooper's girlfriend.

Now Edie felt close to the crime. Now she felt truly sick.

Jim Tile said, "The doctors think she'll be OK."

All Edie could do was nod; she was tapped out. The trooper turned up the volume of the police radio. When they reached the mainland, he stopped at a boarded-up McDonald's. The hurricane had blown out the doors and windows.

A teal-blue compact was parked under a naked palm tree. A man in a green Day-Glo rain poncho was sitting on the hood; from the sharp creases, it appeared that his poncho was brand-new. The man hopped down when he saw the Highway Patrol car.

"Who's that?" Edie asked.

"Watch out for broken glass," Jim Tile said.

"You're leaving me here?"

"Yes, ma'am."

When Edie Marsh got out, the man got in. The trooper told him to shut the door and fasten his seat belt. Edie didn't back away from the car; she just stood there, crossing her arms in a halfhearted sulk. The effect was impaired by the slashing rain, which caused her to blink and squint, and by the stormy wind, which made her hair thrash like a pom-pom.

Through the weather she shouted at Jim Tile: "What am I supposed to do now?"

"Count your blessings," he said. Then he made a U-turn and headed back toward Key Largo.

Bonnie gave Augustine a nervous kiss before she left camp with Skink. Her husband was on his way. They were to meet at the road.

Alone, Augustine tried to read, huddled in the old ambulance to keep the pages dry. But he couldn't concentrate. His imagination was inventing dialogue for

Bonnie and Max's reunion. In his head there were two versions of the script; one for a sad good-bye, one for I'm-sorry-let's-try-again.

Part of him expected not to see Bonnie again, expected her to change her mind and fly back to New York. Augustine had accustomed himself to such letdowns.

On the other hand, none of his three ex-fiancées would have lasted so long in the deep woods without a tantrum or a scene. Bonnie Lamb was very different from the others. Augustine hoped she was different enough not to run away.

Despite his emotional distress, Augustine kept a watch on Snapper, still zonked from the monkey tranquilizer. It wouldn't be long before the dumb cracker woke up blathering. Except for the cheap pinstripe suit, he reminded Augustine of the empty-eyed types his father used to hire as boat crew.

Another thing that got him thinking about his old man was the lousy weather. Augustine recalled a gray September afternoon when his father had dumped sixty bales overboard in the mistaken belief that an oncoming vessel was a Coast Guard patrol, when in fact it was a Hatteras full of hard-drinking surgeons on their way to Cat Cay. The marijuana bobbed on seven-foot swells in the Gulf Stream while Augustine's father frantically recruited friends, neighbors, cousins, dock rats and Augustine himself for the salvage. Using boat hooks and fish gaffs, they retrieved all but four bales, which were snatched up by the agile crew of a passing Greek tanker. Later that night, when the load was safe and drying in a warehouse, Augustine's father threw a party for his helpers. Everybody got stoned except Augustine, who was only twelve years old at the time. Already he knew he wasn't cut out for his old man's fishing business.

Augustine climbed out of the ambulance and stretched. A redtailed hawk hunted in tight circles above the campsite. Augustine walked over to the place where Snapper slept. The governor had left the hurricane money lying in the suitcase, reeking of urine. Augustine nudged Snapper with his shoe. Nothing. He grasped The Club and turned the man's head back and forth. He was as limp as a rag doll. The motion caused a slight stir and a sleepy gargle, but the eyelids remained closed. Augustine lifted one of Snapper's hands and pinched a thumbnail, very hard. The guy didn't flinch.

Dreamland, thought Augustine. No need to tie him up.

He found the sight and sound of Lester Maddox Parsons particularly depressing when married to the fear that Bonnie Lamb wasn't coming back. Sharing camp with a shitbird criminal had no appeal. The smell of fast-moving rain, the high coasting of the hawk, the cool green embrace of the hardwoods—all spoiled by Snapper's sour presence.

Augustine couldn't wait there anymore. It was worse than being alone.

Jim Tile said, "Where's the young man?"

"Library," said Skink.

They were in the trooper's car, near the trail upon which Skink had led Bonnie to the road. She and her husband were sitting side by side on one of the metal rails that ran the perimeter of Crocodile Lakes. The police car was parked seventy-five yards away; it was the best that Jim Tile and Skink could offer for privacy. Even from that distance, in the rain, Max Lamb was highly visible in the neon poncho.

"His old man's in prison." Skink was still talking about Augustine. "You'll love this: She says he was conceived in a hurricane."

"Which one?"

"Donna."

Jim Tile smiled. "That's something."

"Thirty-two years later: another storm, another beginning. The boy's star-crossed, don't you think?"

The trooper chuckled. "I think you're full of it." There was affection in the remark. "What's the story with the father?"

"Smuggler," Skink said, "and not a talented one."

Jim Tile considered that for a moment. "Well, I like the young man. He's all right."

"Yes, he is."

The trooper put on the windshield wipers. They could see—by the movement of the poncho—that Bonnie's husband was up and pacing.

"*Him* I don't envy," Jim Tile said.

Skink shrugged. He hadn't completely forgiven Max Lamb for bringing his Handycam to Miami. He said, "Lemme see where you got shot."

The trooper unbuttoned his shirt and peeled away the bandage. Even with the vest to stop it, the slug had raised a plum-colored bruise on Jim Tile's sternum. The governor whistled and said, "You and Brenda need a vacation."

"They say maybe ten days she'll be out of the hospital."

"Take her to the islands," Skink suggested.

"She's never been to the West. She loves horses."

"The mountains, then. Wyoming."

The trooper said, "She'd go for that."

"Anywhere, Jim. Away from this place is the main thing."

"Yeah." He turned off the wipers. The heavy rain gathered like syrup on the windshield. They did not speak of Snapper.

"Which one is it?" Max Lamb asked.

He hoped it was the kidnapper, the wilder one. That would bolster his theory that his wife had lost her mind; a weather-related version of the Stockholm Syndrome. That would make it easier to accept, easier to explain to his friends and parents. Bonnie had been mesmerized by a drug-crazed hermit. Manson minus the Family.

Bonnie said, "Max, the problem is *me*."

When she knew it wasn't, not entirely. She'd watched him, after stepping from the police car, jump at the sight of a puny marsh rabbit as if it were a hundred-pound timber wolf.

Now he was saying, "Bonnie, you've been brainwashed."

"Nobody—"

"Did you sleep with him?"

"Who?"

"Either of them."

"No!" To cover the lie, Bonnie aimed for a tone of indignation.

"But you wanted to."

Max Lamb rose, raindrops beading on the plastic

poncho. "You're telling me that this"—with a mordant sweep of an arm—"you prefer *this* to the city!"

She sighed. "I wouldn't mind seeing a baby crocodile. That's all I said." She was aware of how outrageous it must have sounded to someone like Max.

"He's got you smoking that shit, doesn't he?"

"Oh please."

Back and forth he paced. "I can't believe this is happening."

"Me, neither," she said. "I'm sorry, Max."

He squared his shoulders and spun away, toward the lakes. He was too mad to weep, too insulted to beg. Also, it had dawned on him that Bonnie might be right, that perhaps he didn't know her very well. Even if she changed her mind and returned with him to New York, he constantly would be worrying that she might flip out again. What happened out here had sprained their relationship, probably permanently.

Turning to face her, his voice leaden with disappointment, Max said, "I thought you were more . . . centered."

"Me, too." To argue would only drag things out. Bonnie was determined to be agreeable and apologetic, no matter what he said. She had to leave him with *something*—if not his pride, then his swollen sense of male superiority. She figured it was a small price, to help get him through the hurt.

"Last chance," Max Lamb said. He groped under the bright poncho and pulled out a pair of airline tickets.

"I'm sorry," said Bonnie, shaking her head.

"Do you love me or not?"

"Max, I don't know."

He tucked the tickets away. "This is unbelievable."

She got up and kissed him good-bye. Her eyes were rimmed with tears, though Max probably didn't notice, with all the raindrops on her face.

"Call me," he said bitterly, "when you figure yourself out."

Alone, he walked back to the patrol car. The kidnapper held the door for him.

Max was quiet on the drive back to the mainland; an accusatory silence. The state trooper was friends with the maniac who'd kidnapped Max and brainwashed his wife. The trooper had a moral and legal duty to stop the seduction, or at least try. That was Max's personal opinion.

When they got to the boarded-up McDonald's, Max told him: "You make sure that nutty one-eyed bastard takes care of her."

It was meant to carry the weight of a warning, and ordinarily Jim Tile would have been amused at Max's hubris. But he pitied him for the bad news he was about to deliver.

"She'll never see the governor again," the trooper said, "after today."

"Then—"

"I think you're confused," said the trooper. "The young fella with the skulls, that's who she fell for."

"Jesus." Max Lamb looked disgusted.

As Jim Tile drove away, he could see him in the rearview—stomping around the parking lot in the rain, kicking at puddles, flapping like a giant Day-Glo bat.

*

They were a mile from the road when Augustine appeared on the trail. Bonnie ran to him. They were still holding each other when Skink announced he was heading back to camp.

Augustine took Bonnie to the creek. He cleared a dry patch of bank and they sat down. She saw that he'd brought a paperback book from the ambulance.

"Oh, you're going to read me sonnets!" She clasped both hands to her breasts, pretending to swoon.

"Don't be a smartass," Augustine said, mussing her hair. "Remember the first time your husband called after the kidnapping—the message he left on the answering machine?"

Bonnie no longer regarded it as that—a kidnapping—but she supposed it was. Technically.

Augustine said, "The governor had him read something over the phone. Well, I found it." He pointed to the title on the spine of the book. *Tropic of Cancer*, by Henry Miller.

"Listen," said Augustine:

"'Once I thought that to be human was the highest aim a man could have, but I see now that it was meant to destroy me. Today I am proud to say that I am *inhuman*, that I belong not to men and governments, that I have nothing to do with creeds and principles. I have nothing to do with the creaking machinery of humanity—I belong to the earth! I say that lying on my pillow and I can feel the horns sprouting from my temples.'"

He handed the novel to Bonnie. She saw that Skink had underlined the passage in red ink.

"It's him, all right."

"Or me," said Augustine. "On a given day."

The sky was turning purple and contused. Overhead a string of turkey buzzards coasted on the freshening breeze. In the distance there was a broken tumble of thunder. Augustine asked Bonnie what happened with Max.

"He's going back alone," she said. "You know, it's crossed my mind that I'm cracking up." She took out her wedding ring. Augustine figured she was going to either slip it on her finger or toss it in the creek.

"Don't," he said, covering both possibilities.

"I'll send it back to him. I don't know how else to handle it." Her voice was thin and sad. Hurriedly she put the ring away.

Augustine asked, "What do you want to do?"

"Be with you for a while. Is that OK?"

"Perfect."

Brightening, Bonnie said, "What about you, Mister Live-for-Today?"

"You'll be pleased to know I've got a plan."

"That's hard to believe."

"Really," he said. "I'm going to sell Uncle Felix's farm, or what's left of it. And my house, too. Then I intend to find someplace just like this and start again. Someplace on the far edge of things. Still interested?"

"I don't know. Will there be cable?"

"No way."

"Rattlesnakes?"

"Possibly."

"Boy. The edge of the edge." Bonnie pretended to be mulling.

He said, "Ever heard of the Ten Thousand Islands?"

"Somebody counted them all?"

"No, dear. That would take a lifetime."

"Is that your plan?" she asked.

Augustine was familiar with the partner-choosing dilemma. She was deciding whether she wanted an anchor or a sail. He said, "There's a town called Chokoloskee. You might hate it."

"Baloney. Stay right here." Bonnie hopped to her feet.

"Now where are you going?"

"Back to camp for some poetry."

"Sit down. I'm not finished."

She spanked his arm away. "You read to me. Now I'm going to read to you."

What Bonnie had in mind, dashing up the trail, was Whitman. Somewhere in the rusted ambulance was a hardbound volume of "Song of Myself," a poem she'd loved since high school. One line in particular—"In vain the mastodon retreats from its own powder'd bones"—reminded her of Skink.

As she entered the campsite, she spotted him motionless on the ground. Snapper craned over him, making throaty snarls. He was coming down from a sulfurous rage. In one hand was a piece of burnt wood that Bonnie recognized as the governor's hiking torch.

She stood rigid, her fists balled at her sides. Snapper wore a contorted expression made no less malignant by the red-and-chrome bar clamped to his face. He was unaware of Bonnie watching from the tree line. He dropped the torch, snatched up the suitcase and began to run.

Insanely she went after him.

# THIRTY-ONE

**Snapper had been** awakened by a cool drizzle. The campsite was still. The one-eyed lunatic was asleep, stretched out in his grubby army duds beneath a tree. There was no sign of Edie Marsh, or the sharpshooter, or the weird broad who'd doused herself with soda pop in the Jeep.

Slowly Snapper sat up. His eyes were crusty and his mouth was ash dry. A clot of black dirt stuck to one eyebrow: For the umpteenth time he tried unsuccessfully to wrench The Club out of his gums. The pain was hideous, as if the bones of his face were spring-loaded to blow apart. He was grateful he couldn't see himself; he must've looked like a fucking circus freak. Bucket-Mouth Man. Dorks lining up to toss softballs down his gullet.

Jesus H. Christ, he thought, I gotta clear the cobwebs.

There on the ground was the suitcase full of cash, yawning, where Skink had left it. The smell pungently reminded Snapper that it hadn't been a nightmare: The asshole had actually pissed on ninety-four thousand perfectly good U.S. dollars.

Snapper tested his legs; left, right, together. Next he clenched his hands, flexed his arms. So far, so good. The second tranquilizer dart finally had worn off.

He rose to his feet. Tenuously he took one step toward the cash. Then another. The iron bar on his jaws was so cumbersome that he almost lost his balance and toppled forward. He tried to hold his breath while he latched the suitcase, but the aroma was unavoidable. Snapper found the water jug and emptied it into his throat. His spluttering failed to disturb the dozing lunatic.

Snapper spied a handy weapon—a length of gummy wood, one end charred.

The big dork must've heard him coming, because he tried to roll away when Snapper swung. The blow caught the man in a shoulder instead of the head, but Snapper heard bones crack. He knew it hurt.

"Ahhheeegggnnn!" he brayed, swinging again and again until the fucker quit rolling and just lay there making a faint hiss, like a tire going flat.

Bonnie had always been scrappy for her size. In junior high she had chased down a boy who'd lifted her skirt in the school cafeteria. The boy's name was Eric Schultz. He was almost six feet tall, foul-mouthed and cocky, a star of the basketball team. He outweighed Bonnie by eighty pounds. When he tried to run away, she tackled him, held him down and punched him in the testicles. Eric Schultz missed the first and second rounds of the basketball playoffs. Bonnie Brooks was suspended from class for three days. Her father said it was worth it; he was proud. Bonnie's mother said she overreacted, because the boy Eric had been held back twice for eighth grade. Bonnie's mother said he'd probably done what he had to Bonnie because he didn't know any better. *He does now*, Bonnie had said. She agreed with her father: Stupidity was an overworked excuse.

With his bum knee, Snapper was easy to catch. His speed was further hindered by the unwieldy facial contraption, which snagged in the vines and branches. He went down in the same basic configuration as had Eric Schultz—limbs splayed, nose down. It took only a moment for Snapper to realize it was a woman hanging off his shoulders, and not a large one. The casual manner in which he shook free suggested to Bonnie that her rabbit punches were ineffective. Unlike young Eric Schultz, Lester Maddox Parsons had been to prison, where he'd learned much about dirty fighting. He wasn't about to let a one-hundred-pound girl get a clear shot at his jewels.

With both arms he swung the Frenchman's suitcase, knocking Bonnie sideways against the gnarled trunk of an old buttonwood. She landed flat on her back, punching frenetically. The red steel bar across Snapper's cheeks blocked her best jabs. He quickly pinned her wrists, but she stopped kicking only when he dug a knee into her pubic bone.

Beneath the dull deadening weight of his torso, she gradually lost sight of the buzzards and the gathering clouds. Her next view was a glistening, pink, fistulous cave—his mouth, stretched in the shape of a permanent scream. He panted from exertion; hot, necrotic gusts. Bonnie wanted to gag. Something wet and wormy settled on the cleft of her chin.

A lip.

She took it in her teeth and bit hard. Snapper yowled and pulled away. A half second later, Bonnie was stunned by a sharp blow to her temple. The Club. The bastard was trying to beat her with it, using frenzied, snorting sweeps of his head. She had no way to protect herself. Snapper wouldn't release her arms because he didn't need his own for the attack; his gourd was doing all the work. Bonnie was dazed by another white burst of pain. She shut her eyes so she wouldn't have to see his goggling wet hole of a face. She made herself go limp, thinking that unconsciousness would be fine and dandy.

Snapper imagined himself a wild bull in the ring; goring at will. The bitch was helpless beneath him, hardly twitching. He paused to catch his breath, spit blood, and congratulate himself for so cleverly converting a handicap to a martial asset. The cop on the TV commercial was right; The Club was indestructible! Despite the stinging of his lip and the burning in his knee and the electric throbbing in the joints of his jaw, Snapper didn't feel so bad. His pride outweighed the pain. Certainly he'd earned the rights to the Frenchman's hurricane money.

That's when a hand moved between his legs; lightly, like a sparrow on a branch.

"Nnnngggguuuhhh!!"

The bitch grabbed him. Snapper bellowed. He thrashed his head, trying to pummel her with the heavy end of The Club. Then he realized it couldn't be the girl squeezing his balls, because both her wrists remained pinned in the dirt. She wasn't moving a muscle. It had to be somebody else.

Then, from a distance, he heard: "No! Don't do that."

He tried to hold still. Tried to breathe without

whimpering. Tried to turn ever so slightly, to see who the fuck had at least one (and possibly both) of his nuts in their fingers.

Again the voice, this time closer: “Don’t do it! Don’t!”

The one-eyed freak, calling out.

Who’s he talking to? Snapper wondered. Don’t do *what*?

Then the gun went off at his head, and he knew.

Max Lamb was surprised to find a woman sleeping in the front seat of his rental car. He recognized her as the one whom the state trooper had dropped off in the parking lot earlier that afternoon.

She sat up, brushing her long brown hair from her eyes. “It was raining. I had no place to go.” Not the least bit bashful.

“That’s OK,” Max said. He wormed out of the Day-Glo poncho and tossed it in the back seat.

“My name is Edie.” She reached out to shake his hand.

He took it, stiffly. She had a strong grip.

“I’m Max,” he said. Then he heard himself saying: “You need a lift back to Miami?”

Edie Marsh nodded gratefully. That’s what she’d been counting on. One way or another, all rental cars ultimately returned to Miami.

She said, “I would’ve tried hitching a ride, but there was lightning.”

“Yeah, I heard.”

Somehow Max missed the ramp to the Turnpike; it

wasn't easy, but he did. Edie didn't complain. A lift was a lift. All the roads went the same direction anyway.

"Where are you from, Max?" He looked perfectly harmless, but still she wanted to get him talking. Silent brooding made her edgy.

"New York. I'm in advertising."

"No kidding."

And off he went. During the next hour, Edie learned a great deal about Madison Avenue. Max was absolutely elated to discover that she'd been a glutton for Plum Crunchies cereal. And she remembered his slogan, word for word!

"What others have you done?" she asked brightly.

Max was tempted to tell her about Intimate Mist but thought better of it. Not everyone felt comfortable on the subject of douches.

"Bronco cigarets," he said.

"Really!"

"Speaking of which, would you mind if I smoked?"

"Not at all," said Edie Marsh.

He offered her a menthol. She declined politely. As smoke filled the car, she rolled down the window and tried not to cough herself blue. "When are you going back to New York?"

"Tomorrow," Max said. He grew quiet again.

Edie said: "If you tell me, I'll tell you."

Max looked perplexed.

She said, "You know—what we were doing with that cop. Me coming, you going."

"Oh." After a pause: "I'm not in any kind of trouble, if that's what you mean."

Dryly she said, "I had a hunch you're no Ted Bundy."

What eyes! Max thought. What an interesting woman! He had reason to believe she was aware of her impact.

He said, "How about this: If you don't tell me, I won't tell you. What's over is over."

"I like that approach."

"Let's just agree we've had a bad day."

"And how."

In South Dade they hit heavy traffic where the storm had blown ashore, taking down everything. Edie Marsh had seen the destruction the day after the hurricane, but it seemed much worse to her now. She was surprised to find herself fighting back tears.

Out of nowhere Max said: "Hey, I bet I can guess what kind of car you drive." Apparently trying to take their minds off what they saw: two unshaven men, on a street corner, fighting over a five-gallon jug of fresh water. Their wives and children watching anxiously from the sidewalk.

"Seriously," Max was saying. "It's a knack I've got. Matching people to their cars."

"Based on . . . ?"

"Intuition, I guess you'd say."

Edie said, "OK, give it a try."

Max, eyeing her up and down, like he was guessing her weight: "Nissan 300?"

"Nope."

"A 280Z?"

"Try an Acclaim."

He winced. "I had you figured for a sports import."

"Well, I'm flattered," Edie said, with a soft laugh.

There was a brutal truth at the heart of Max's silly game. Eligible young Kennedys and even sons of sitting presidents did not customarily flag down women in 1987 Plymouths.

Later, after Max had found the Turnpike extension and made his way downtown, he said: "Where can I drop you?"

"Let me think about that," said Edie Marsh.

"Captain, have you got a mirror?"

"No."

"Good," Bonnie said.

She felt a raw knot rising on her forehead, another on a cheekbone. Augustine assured her that she didn't look as bad as she thought. "But you could use some ice."

"Later." She was watching Skink. "I know somebody who ought to be in a hospital."

"No," said the governor.

"Augustine says your collarbone is broken."

"I believe he's right."

"And several ribs."

"I shall call you Nurse Nightingale."

"Why are you so stubborn?"

"I know a doctor in Tavernier."

"And how do you plan to get there?"

"Walking upright," Skink replied. "One of the few commendable traits of our species."

Bonnie told him to quit being ridiculous. "You're in terrible pain, I can tell."

"The whole world's in pain, girl."

She looked imploringly to Augustine. "Talk to him, please."

"He's a grown man, Bonnie. Now hold still."

He was cleaning her face with his shirt, which he'd

wadded up and soaked in the creek. Skink perched on a nearby log, his arms crossed tightly. Moments earlier they'd watched him gobble a dozen Anacins from a plastic bottle he located under the camp tarpaulin. Bonnie boldly swallowed three.

No aspirins were offered to Snapper, who was bound with a corroded tow-truck chain to the buttonwood tree. He was caked with soggy leaves, mulch and dried blood. His cheap suit was filthy and torn. During the struggle, Augustine had made him dig a short trench with his mandible, so his maw was full of stones and loose soil, like a planter. In addition, he was missing an earlobe, which Augustine had shot off at point-blank range. It was inconceivable to Snapper that such a chickenshit wound could be so excruciating.

Skink said to Augustine: "I thought sure you were going to kill him."

"It was tempting."

"My way's better."

"After what he did to Jim's girlfriend?"

"Yes. Even after that." The governor bowed his head. He was hurting.

Augustine was drained. The adrenaline had emptied out in a clammy torrent. He no longer entertained the idea of murdering Snapper, and doubted if he was even capable of it. An hour ago, yes. Not now. It was probably a good time to leave.

Bonnie studied his expression as he tended her cheeks and brow. "You OK?" she said.

"I don't know. The way he hurt you—"

"Hey, I asked for it."

"But you wouldn't be out here if it weren't for me."

Playfully she jabbed a finger in his side. "What makes you so sure? Maybe I'm here because of *him*."

Skink grinned but didn't look up. Augustine had to laugh, too. That's why we're both here, he thought. Because of him.

"Would it be bad manners," Bonnie said to Skink, "if I asked what you plan to do with the money."

His chin came off his chest. "Oh. That." Grimacing, he rose from the log. "Lester, you awake? Yo, Lester!"

"Ghhhnungggh."

The governor used his feet to push the Frenchman's suitcase across the clearing to the buttonwood tree, where he kicked the latches open. Snapper regarded the bundled cash with a mixture of undisguised longing and suspicion. He wondered what sick stunt the fucker was cooking up now.

Only the bills on top were wet. Skink swept them aside with his hands. Bonnie and Augustine walked over to see.

The governor said, "You guys want any of this?" They shook their heads.

"Me, neither," he muttered. "Just more shit to lug around." He addressed Snapper: "Chief, I'm sure there was a time in your sorry-ass life when ninety-four grand would've come in handy. Believe me when I tell you those days are over."

Skink took a matchbook from his pocket. He asked Bonnie and Augustine to do the honors. Snapper spewed dirt and thrashed inconsolably against the chains.

The money gave off a rich, sweet scent as it burned.

*

Later he unlocked the truck chain holding Snapper to the tree. Plaintively Snapper pointed at the red brace fastened in his mouth. Skink shook his head.

"Here's the deal, Lester. Don't be here when I get back. Do not fuck with my camp, do not fuck with my books. It's about to rain like hell, so lie back and drink as much as you can. You'll need it."

Snapper didn't respond. Augustine stepped up. He took out the .38 Special and said, "Try to follow us out, I'll blow your head off."

Bonnie shuddered. The governor removed a few items from beneath the tarpaulin and placed them in a backpack. Then he lighted the torch and led the others into the trees.

Snapper had no desire to follow; he was glad the crazy fuckers were gone. A gust churned the cinders at his feet, blew a flurry into his lap. He ran his fingers through the ashes, brought a handful to his nose. It didn't even smell like money anymore.

Later he awoke to the hard rustle of leaves. The rain came driving down. Snapper took the man's advice. He filled up on it.

At daybreak he would start his march.

They broke a fresh trail through the hardwoods. Bonnie was worried that Snapper would be able to use it to find his way out. "Not across a lake," Skink said.

She hooked her fingers in Augustine's belt as they swam. The governor hoisted the torch, his boots and the backpack over his head, to keep them dry. Augustine was astounded that the man could swim so well with a fractured collarbone. The crossing took less than fifteen minutes, though it seemed an eternity to Bonnie. She was unable to convince herself that crocodiles shunned firelight.

Afterwards they rested on shore. Skink, struggling into his laceless boots: "If he gets out of here, he deserves to be free."

Augustine said, "But he won't."

"No, he'll go the wrong way. That's his nature."

Then Skink was moving again, an orange flame weaving through the trees ahead of them. Bonnie, hurrying to keep up: "So something'll get him. Panthers or something."

Augustine said, "Nothing so exotic, Mrs Lamb."

"Then what?"

"Time. Time will get him."

"Exactly!" the governor boomed. "It's the arc of all life. For Lester we merely hasten the sad promenade. Tonight we are Darwin's elves."

Bonnie quickened her pace. She felt happy to be with them, out in the middle of nowhere. Ahead on the trail, Skink was singing to himself. Feeling the horns sprouting from his temples, she supposed.

Two hours later they emerged from the woods. A rip of wind braced them.

"Oh brother," Augustine said, "any second now."

With a grimace, Skink removed the backpack. "This is for your hike."

"It's not that far."

"Take it, just in case."

Bonnie said, "God, your eye."

A stalk of holly berries garnished the empty withered

socket. The governor groped at himself. "Damn. I guess it fell out."

Bonnie could hardly look at him.

"It's all right," he said. "I got a whole box of extras somewhere."

She said, "Don't be foolish. Go to the mainland with us."

"No!"

A mud-gray wall of rain came hissing down the road. Bonnie shivered as it hit them. Skink leaned close to Augustine: "Give it a couple three months, at least."

"You bet."

"For what?" Bonnie asked.

"Before I try to find that place again," Augustine said.

"Why go back?"

"Science," said Augustine.

"Nostalgia," said the governor.

The squall doused the torch, which he lobbed into a stand of red mangroves. He tucked his hair under the plastic shower cap and said good-bye. Bonnie kissed him on the chin and told him to be careful. Augustine gave an affable salute.

For a while they could make out his tall shape, stalking south, under violet flashbursts of high lightning. Then he was gone. The weather covered him like a shroud.

They turned and went the other way. Augustine walked fast on the blacktop, the backpack jouncing on his bare shoulders.

"Hey, the scar is looking good," Bonnie said.

"You still like it?"

"Beauty." She could see it vividly whenever the sky

lit up. "A corkscrew in the shower—you weren't kidding?"

"God, I wish," said Augustine.

They heard a car behind them. As it approached, the headlights elongated their shadows on the pavement. Augustine asked Bonnie if she wanted to hitch a ride. She said no. They stepped off the road to let the car go by.

Soon they reached the tall bridge at Card Sound. Augustine said it was time to rest. He unzipped the backpack to see what the governor had packed: a coil of rope, two knives, four bandannas, a tube of antiseptic, a waterproof box of matches, a bottle of fresh water, chlorine tablets, some oranges, a stick of bug repellent, four cans of lentil soup and a tin of unidentifiable dried meat.

Augustine and Bonnie shared the water, then started up the bridge.

Needles of rain stung Bonnie's bruises as she climbed the long slope. She tasted brine on the wind, and wasn't embarrassed to clutch Augustine's right arm—the gusts were so strong they nearly lifted her off the ground.

"Maybe it's another hurricane!"

"Not hardly," he said.

They stopped at the top. Augustine threw the pistol as far as he could. Bonnie peered over the concrete rail to watch the splash, a silent punctuation. Augustine placed his hands firmly on her waist, holding her steady. She liked the way it felt, the trust involved.

Far below, the bay was frothed and corrugated; a treacherously different place from the first time Bonnie saw it. Not a night for dolphins.

She drew Augustine closer and kissed him for a long time. Then she spun him around and groped in the backpack.

"What're you doing?" he shouted over the slap of the rain.

"Hush."

When he turned back, her eyes were shining. In her hands was the coil of rope.

"Tie me to the bridge," she said.

# EPILOGUE

The marriage of **Bonnie Brooks** and **Max Lamb** was discreetly annulled by a judge who happened to be a skiing companion of Max Lamb's father. Max returned to Rodale & Burns, pouring his energies into a new advertising campaign for Old Faithful Root Beer. Spurred by Max's simpleminded jingle, the company soon reported a 24 percent jump in domestic sales. Max was promoted to the sixth floor and put in charge of an $18 million account for a low-fat malt liquor called Steed.

By the end of the year, Max and **Edie Marsh** were engaged. They got an apartment on the Upper West Side of Manhattan, where Edie became active in charity circles. Two years after the hurricane, while attending a Kenny G concert to benefit victims of a Colombian mud slide, Edie met the same young Kennedy she'd long ago tried so avidly to debauch. She was mildly amazed when, while greeting her, he slipped a tongue in her ear. Max said it surely was her imagination.

**Brenda Rourke** recovered fully from her injuries and returned to the Highway Patrol. She requested and received a transfer to northern Florida, where she and **Jim Tile** built a small house on the Ochlockonee River.

For Christmas he gave her an engraved gold replica of her mother's wedding ring, and two full-grown rottweilers from Stuttgart.

After being rescued in the ocean off Islamorada, **Avila** was taken to Miami's Krome Detention Center and processed as "Juan Gómez Duran," a rafter fleeing political oppression in Havana. He was held at Krome for nine days, until a Spanish-language radio station sponsored his release. In return, brave "Sẽnor Gómez" agreed to share the details of high-seas escape with radio listeners, who were moved by his heart-wrenching story but puzzled by his wildly inaccurate references to Cuban geography. Afterwards Avila packed up and moved to Fort Myers, on the west coast of Florida, where he was immediately hired as a code-enforcement officer for the local building-and-zoning department. During his first four weeks on the job, Avila approved 212 new homes—a record for a single inspector that stands to this day. Nineteen months after the hurricane, while preparing a sacrifice to Chango on the patio of his luxurious new waterfront town house, Avila was severely bitten on the thigh by a hydrophobic rabbit. Too embarrassed to seek medical attention, he died twenty-two days later in his hot tub. In honor of his short but productive tenure as a code inspector, the Lee County Home Builders Association established the Juan Gómez Duran Scholarship Fund.

One day after the state trooper was shot in the parking lot, paramedics again were summoned to the Paradise Palms Motel in the Florida Keys. This time a guest named **Levon Stichler** had suffered a mild myocardial infarction. On the ride to the emergency room, the old man deliriously insisted he'd been held captive at the motel by two bossy prostitutes. Doctors at Mariners Hospital notified Levon Stichler's daughter in Saint Paul, who was understandably alarmed to learn of her father's hallucinations. After hanging up the phone, she informed her children that Grandpa would be coming to stay for a while.

The gnawed remains of **Ira Jackson**, identified by X-rays, were cremated and interred at a private ceremony on Staten Island. Several Teamster bosses sent flowers, as did the retired comptroller of the Central States Pension Fund. Three weeks after the hurricane, the African lion that attacked Ira Jackson was captured while foraging in a Dumpster behind a Pizza Hut in Perrine. The tranquilized animal was dipped, vaccinated, wormed and nicknamed "Pepperoni." It is now on display at a wildlife park in West Palm Beach.

The murder of **Tony Torres** remains unsolved, although police suspect his wife of arranging the crime so that she could hoard the hurricane money from Midwest Casualty. Detectives seeking to question **Neria Torres** learned that she'd moved to Belize, leased an oceanfront villa and taken up with an expatriate American fishing guide. A court-ordered inspection of her late husband's bank records revealed that before leaving the United States, Mrs Torres moved $201,000 through a single checking account. The house at 15600 Calusa was never repaired and remained abandoned for twenty-two months, until it was finally condemned and destroyed.

Five weeks after the hurricane, **Fred Dove** went home to Omaha and presented his wife with two miniature dachshunds orphaned by the storm. He, **Dennis Reedy** and eight other Midwest Casualty adjusters were honored for their heroic work on the Florida crisis-response team. To publicize its swift and compassionate processing of hurricane claims, the company featured the men in a national television commercial that aired during the Bob Hope Christmas Special. Fred Dove was hopeful that **Edie Marsh** would contact him after the commercial was broadcast, but he never heard from her again.

Faced with a class-action lawsuit by 186 customers whose homes had more or less collapsed in the hurricane, builder **Gar Whitmark** declared bankruptcy and revived his construction companies under different names. He was killed thirteen months later in a freak accident on a job site, when high winds from a tropical storm knocked a bucket of hot tar off a roof and through the windshield of his Infiniti Q45. His troubled widow gave up prescription medicine and joined the Church of Scientology, to which she donated her late husband's entire estate.

The body of **Clyde Nottage Jr.** was flown from Guadalajara to Durham, North Carolina, where—at his family's request—an autopsy was performed at the Duke University Medical Center. Four days later, Mexican authorities arrested **Dr. Alan Caulk**, seized his laboratory and deported him to the Bahamas. Oddly, no sheep were ever found at the Aragon Clinic.

Despite contradictory affidavits from two preeminent psychiatrists, attorneys for **Durham Gas Meat & Tobacco** persuaded a judge in Raleigh to declare Clyde Nottage Jr mentally unfit. The posthumous certification was based on disturbing medical evidence supplied by Mexican officials, and sealed forever by the North Carolina courts. Sixty days after Nottage's death, DGM&T resumed production of Bronco cigarets. The advertising contract with Rodale & Burns was not renewed.

Eleven months after the hurricane, a biologist for the US Fish and Wildlife Service made a gruesome find in a remote upland area of the Crocodile Lakes Wildlife Refuge in North Key Largo: a deformed human jaw. Locked to the bone was an adjustable iron bar popularly used to deter auto theft. Dental X-rays identified the owner of the mandible as **Lester Maddox Parsons,** a career felon and convicted killer wanted for violent assaults on two Florida Highway Patrol officers. According to the Monroe County Medical Examiner, evidence at the scene indicated that Parsons likely starved to death. A search of the hammocks turned up the remaining pieces of his skeleton, except for the skull.

**Augustine Herrera** sold his late uncle's wildlife farm and moved with **Bonnie Brooks** to Chokoloskee, a fishing village on the edge of Florida's Ten Thousand Islands. There he bought a crab boat and built a pineboard house with space for a large library, including a wall for his collection of skulls, now numbering twenty.

**Bonnie Brooks** took up watercolors, cycling and outdoor photography. Her remarkable picture of a pair of bald eagles nesting in the boughs of a cypress made the cover of *Audubon* magazine.

Most of the wild animals that escaped from **Felix Mojack's** farm during the hurricane were recaptured or, unfortunately, killed by armed home owners. The exceptions include one female cougar, forty-four rare birds, more than three hundred exotic lizards, thirty-eight snakes (venomous and nonvenomous) and twenty-nine adult rhesus monkeys, which have organized into several wily troops that roam Dade County to this day.

# LUCKY YOU

*For Laureen,*
*one in a million*

# ONE

**On the afternoon** of November 25, a woman named JoLayne Lucks drove to the Grab N'Go minimart in Grange, Florida, and purchased spearmint Certs, unwaxed dental floss and one ticket for the state Lotto.

JoLayne Lucks played the same numbers she'd played every Saturday for five years: 17–19–22–24–27–30.

The significance of her Lotto numbers was this: each represented an age at which she had jettisoned a burdensome man. At 17 it was Rick the Pontiac mechanic. At 19 it was Rick's brother, Robert. At 22 it was a stockbroker named Colavito, twice JoLayne's age, who'd delivered on none of his promises. At 24 it was a policeman, another Robert, who got in trouble for fixing traffic tickets in exchange for sex. At 27 it was Neal the chiropractor, a well-meaning but unbearable codependent.

And at 30 JoLayne dumped Lawrence, a lawyer, her one and only husband. Lawrence had been notified of his disbarment exactly one week after he and JoLayne were married, but she stuck with him for almost a year. JoLayne was fond of Lawrence and wanted to believe his earnest denials regarding the multiple fraud convictions that precipitated his trouble with the Florida Bar. While appealing his case, Lawrence took a job as a toll taker on the Beeline Expressway, a plucky career realignment that nearly won JoLayne's heart. Then one night he was caught making off with a thirty-pound sack of loose change, mostly quarters and dimes. Before he could post bail, JoLayne packed up most of his belongings, including his expensive Hermès neckties, and gave them to the Salvation Army. Then she filed for divorce.

Five years later she was still single and unattached when, to her vast amusement, she won the Florida Lotto. She happened to be sitting with a plate of turkey leftovers in front of the television at 11 p.m., when the winning numbers were announced.

JoLayne Lucks didn't faint, shriek or dance wildly around the house. She smiled, though, thinking of the six discarded men from her past life; thinking how, in spite of themselves, they'd finally amounted to something.

Twenty-eight million dollars, to be precise.

One hour earlier and almost three hundred miles away, a candy-red Dodge Ram pulled into a convenience store in Florida City. Two men got out of the truck: Bodean Gazzer, known locally as Bode, and his companion Chub, who claimed to have no last name. Although they parked in a handicapped-only zone, neither man was physically disabled in any way.

Bode Gazzer was five feet six and had never forgiven his parents for it. He wore three-inch snakeskin shit-kickers and walked with a swagger that suggested not brawn so much as hemorrhoidal tribulation. Chub was a beer-gutted six two, moist-eyed, ponytailed and unshaven. He carried a loaded gun at all times and was Bode Gazzer's best and only friend.

They had known each other two months. Bode

Gazzer had gone to Chub to buy a counterfeit handicapped sticker that would get him the choicest parking spot at Probation & Parole, or any of the other state offices where his attendance was occasionally required.

Like its mangy tenant, Chub's house trailer emitted a damp fungal reek. Chub had just printed a new batch of the fake emblems, which he laconically fanned like a poker deck on the kitchen counter. The workmanship (in sharp contrast to the surroundings) was impeccable – the universal wheelchair symbol set crisply against a navy-blue background. No traffic cop in the world would question it.

Chub had asked Bode Gazzer what type he wanted – a bumper insignia, a tag for the rearview or a dashboard placard. Bode said a simple window tag would be fine.

"Two hunnert bucks," said Chub, scratching his scalp with a salad fork.

"I'm a little short on cash. You like lobster?"

"Who don't?"

So they'd worked out a trade – the bogus disabled-parking permit in exchange for ten pounds of fresh Florida lobster, which Bode Gazzer had stolen from a trapline off Key Largo. It was inevitable that the poacher and the counterfeiter would bond, sharing as they did a blanket contempt for government, taxes, homosexuals, immigrants, minorities, gun laws, assertive women and honest work.

Chub never thought of himself as having a political agenda until he met Bode Gazzer, who helped organize Chub's multitude of hatreds into a single venomous philosophy. Chub believed Bode Gazzer was the smartest person he'd ever met, and was flattered when his new pal suggested they form a militia.

"You mean like what blowed up that courthouse in Nebraska?"

"Oklahoma," Bode Gazzer said sharply, "and that was the government did it, to frame those two white boys. No, I'm talking 'bout a *militia*. Armed, disciplined and well-regulated. Like it says in the Second Amendment."

Chub scratched a chigger bite on his neck. "Reg'lated by who, if I might ast?"

"By you, me, Smith and Wesson."

"And that's allowed?"

"Says right in the motherfuckin' Constitution."

"OK then," said Chub.

Bode Gazzer had gone on to explain how the United States of America was about to be taken over by a New World Tribunal, armed by foreign-speaking NATO troops who were massing across the Mexican border and also at secret locations in the Bahamas.

Chub glanced warily toward the horizon. "The Bahamas?" He and Bode were in Bode's cousin's nineteen-foot outboard, robbing traps off Rodriguez Key.

Bode Gazzer said: "There's seven hundred islands in the Bahamas, my friend, and most are uninhabited."

Chub got the message. "Jesus Willy Christ," he said, and began pulling the lobster pots with heightened urgency.

To run a proper militia would be expensive, and neither Chub nor Bode Gazzer had any money; Bode's net worth was tied up in the new Dodge truck, Chub's in his illegal printshop and arsenal. So they began playing the state lottery, which Bode asserted was the only decent generous thing the government of Florida had ever done for its people.

Every Saturday night, wherever they happened to be, the two men would pull into the nearest convenience store, park brazenly in the blue handicapped zone, march inside and purchase five Lotto tickets. They played no special numbers; often they were drinking, so it was easier to use the Quick Pick, letting the computer do the brainwork.

On the night of November 25, Bode Gazzer and Chub bought their five lottery tickets and three six-packs of beer at the Florida City 7-Eleven. They were nowhere near a television an hour later, when the winning numbers were announced.

Instead they were parked along a dirt road on a tree farm, a few miles from the Turkey Point nuclear reactor. Bode Gazzer was sitting on the hood of the Dodge pickup, aiming one of Chub's Ruger assault rifles at a U.S. government mailbox they'd stolen from a street corner in Homestead. An act of revolutionary protest, Bode had said, like the Boston Tea Party.

The mailbox was centered in the headlight beams of the truck. Bode and Chub took turns with the Ruger until they were out of ammo and Budweisers. Then they sorted through the mail, hoping for loose cash or personal checks, but all they found was junk. Afterwards they fell asleep in the flatbed. Shortly after dawn they were rousted by two large Hispanics, undoubtedly the foremen of the tree farm, who swiped the Ruger and chased them off the property.

It was some time later, after returning to Chub's trailer, that they learned of their extraordinary good fortune. Bode Gazzer was on the toilet, Chub was stretched on the convertible sofa in front of the TV. A pretty blond newscaster gave out the previous night's winning Lotto numbers, which Chub scribbled on the back of his latest eviction notice.

Moments later, when Bode heard the shouting, he came lurching from the bathroom with his jeans and boxer shorts bunched at his knees. Chub was waving the ticket, hopping and whooping like he was on fire.

Bodean Gazzer said: "You're shittin' me."

"We won it, man! We won!"

Bode lunged for the ticket, but Chub held it out of reach.

"Give it here!" Bode demanded, swiping at air, his genitals flopping ludicrously.

Chub laughed. "Pull up your pants, for Christ's sake." He handed the ticket to Bode, who recited the numbers out loud.

"You're sure?" he kept asking.

"I wrote 'em down, Bode. Yeah, I'm sure."

"My God. *My God*. Twenty-eight million dollars."

"But here's what else: They's two winning tickets is what the news said."

Bode Gazzer's eyes puckered into a hard squint. "The hell you say!"

"Two tickets won. Which is still, what, fourteen million 'tween us. You believe it?"

Bode's tongue, lumpy and blotched as a toad, probed at the corners of his mouth. He looked to be working up a spit. "Who's got the other one? The other goddamn ticket."

"TV didn't say."

"How can we find out?"

Chub said, "Christ, who gives a shit? Long as we get fourteen million, I don't care if Jesse Fucking Jackson's got the other ticket."

Now Bode Gazzer's stubbled cheeks began to twitch. He fingered the Lotto coupon and said: "There must be a way to find out. Don't you think? Find out who's this shitweasel with the other ticket. There's gotta be a way."

"Why?" Chub asked, but it was awhile before he got an answer.

Sunday morning, Tom Krome refused to go to church. The woman who'd slept with him the night before – Katie was her name; strawberry blond, freckles on her shoulders – said they should go and seek forgiveness for what they had done.

"Which part?" asked Tom Krome.

"You know darn well."

Krome covered his face with a pillow. Katie kept talking, putting on her pantyhose.

She said, "I'm sorry, Tommy, it's the way I'm made. It's time you should know."

"You think it's wrong?"

"What?"

He peeped out from beneath the pillow. "You think we did something wrong?"

"No. But God might not agree."

"So it's precautionary, this church visit."

Now Katie was at the mirror, fixing her hair in a bun. "Are you coming or not? How do I look?"

"Chaste," said Tom Krome.

The phone rang.

"Chased? No, sweetheart, that was last night. Get the telephone, please."

Katie put on her high heels, balancing storklike on

elegant slender legs. "You honestly won't go? To church, Tom, I can't believe it."

"Yeah, I'm one heathen bastard." Krome picked up the phone.

She waited, arms folded, at the bedroom door.

Krome covered the receiver and said, "Sinclair."

"On a Sunday morning?"

"I'm afraid so." Krome tried to sound disappointed but he was thinking: There *is* a God.

Sinclair's title at *The Register* was Assistant Deputy Managing Editor of Features and Style. He relied on the fact that nobody outside the newspaper business understood the insignificance of his position. At smaller papers it was one of the least nerve-racking and lowest-profile jobs. Sinclair couldn't have been happier. Most of his reporters and editors were young and unabashedly grateful to be employed, and they did whatever Sinclair told them.

His biggest problem was Tom Krome, who also happened to be his best writer. Krome's background was hard news, which had made him impossibly cynical and suspicious of all authority. Sinclair was scared of Krome; he'd heard stories. Also, at thirty-five Krome was older by two years, so he held the advantage of age as well as experience. Sinclair realized there was no possibility, none whatsoever, that Krome would ever respect him.

His fear – in fact, Sinclair's most serious concern as the ADME of Features and Style – was that Krome might someday humiliate him in front of the staff. Figuratively cut off his nuts in front of Marie or Jacquelyn, or one of the clerks. Sinclair felt he could not psychologically endure such an episode, so he had resolved to keep Krome away from the newspaper office as much as possible. To that end, Sinclair committed ninety-five percent of his meager travel budget to assignments that kept Krome safely out of town. It worked out fine: Tom seemed content to be gone, and Sinclair was able to relax at the office.

The most challenging of Sinclair's responsibilities was handing out lame story assignments. Calling Tom Krome at home was particularly trying; usually Sinclair had to shout to make himself heard above the loud rock music or women's voices in the background. He could only imagine how Krome lived.

Sinclair had never before phoned on a Sunday. He apologized numerous times.

Tom Krome said: "Don't worry about it."

Sinclair was encouraged. He said, "I didn't think this one could wait."

Krome had no trouble containing his excitement. Whatever Sinclair was calling about, it wasn't breaking news. Breaking fluff, maybe, but not news. He blew a kiss to Katie and waved her off to church.

"I got a tip," Sinclair said.

"*You* got a tip."

"My brother-in-law phoned this morning. He lives over in Grange."

Krome thought: Uh-oh. Crafts show. I will murder this fucker if he makes me cover another crafts show.

But Sinclair said: "You play the lottery, Tom?"

"Only when it's up to forty million bucks or so. Anything less is chump change."

No reaction from Sinclair, who was deep into his pitch: "There were two winners last night. One in Dade

County, the other in Grange. My brother-in-law knows the woman. Her name is – are you ready for this? – Lucks."

Inwardly Tom Krome groaned. It was the quintessential Sinclair headline: LADY LUCKS WINS THE LOTTO!

You had your irony. You had your alliteration.

And you had your frothy, utterly forgettable feature story. Sinclair called them Feel Goods. He believed it was the mission of his department to make readers forget all the nastiness they were getting in other sections of the newspaper. He wanted them to feel good about their lives, their religion, their families, their neighbors, their world.

Once he'd posted a memo setting forth his philosophy of feature writing. Somebody – Sinclair suspected Tom Krome – had nailed a dead rat to it.

"How much she win?" Krome asked.

"The pot was twenty-eight million, so she'll get half. What do you think, Tom?"

"Depends."

"She works for a veterinarian. Loves animals, Roddy says."

"That's nice."

"Plus she's black."

"Ah," said Krome. The white editors who ran the newspaper loved positive stories about minorities; Sinclair obviously smelled a year-end bonus.

"Roddy says she's a trip."

Krome said, "Roddy would be your brother-in-law?" The tipster.

"Right. He says she's a character, this JoLayne Lucks." The headline dancing in Sinclair's brain actually was: LUCKS BE A LADY!

Tom Krome said: "This Roddy person is married to your sister?"

"Joan. Yes, that's right," Sinclair answered, edgily.

"What the hell's your sister doing in Grange?"

Grange was a truck-stop town known mainly for its miracles, stigmata, visitations and weeping Madonnas. It was a must-see on the Christian tourist circuit.

Sinclair said, "Joan's a teacher. Roddy works for the state." Sinclair wanted to make clear they weren't nut-cases but were responsible citizens. He noticed his palms had gotten damp from talking to Tom Krome for too long.

"This Lady Lucks," Krome said, in a tone designed to cast scorn on the inevitable headline, "is she a Jesus freak? Because I'm in no mood to be preached at."

"Tom, I really wouldn't know."

"She says Jesus gave her those lucky numbers, end of story. I'm coming home. You understand?"

Sinclair said, "Roddy didn't mention anything like that."

Solemnly Krome played his ace. "Think of the letters we'll get."

"What do you mean?" Sinclair hated letters almost as much as he hated telephone calls. The best stories were those that produced no reaction, one way or another, from readers. "What kind of mail?" he asked.

"Tons," Krome replied, "if we do a piece saying Jesus is a gambling tout. Can you imagine? Hell, you'll probably hear from Ralph Reed himself. Next they'll be boycotting our advertisers."

Firmly Sinclair said: "So let's stay away from that angle. By all means." After a pause: "Maybe this isn't such a hot idea."

On the other end, Tom Krome smiled. "I'll drive up to Grange this afternoon. Check it out and let you know."

"OK," Sinclair said. "Go check it out. You want my sister's phone number?"

"That's not necessary," said Krome.

Sinclair experienced a small shudder of relief.

Demencio was refilling the fiberglass Madonna when his wife, Trish, hurried outside to say that somebody in town won the lottery.

"I don't suppose it's us," said Demencio.

"Rumor is JoLayne Lucks."

"Figures."

Demencio removed the top of the Madonna's head and reached inside the statue to retrieve a plastic bottle that had once held the wiper fluid in a 1989 Civic hatchback. These days the jug held tap water, lightly scented with perfume.

Trish said, "You're almost out of Charlie."

Demencio nodded irritably. That would be a problem. It was important to use a fragrance the righteous faithful wouldn't recognize; otherwise suspicions would be stirred. Once he'd experimented with Lady Stetson and there was nearly an uprising. The third pilgrim in line, a buzzardly bank teller from Huntsville, had sniffed it out instantly: "Hey, Mother Mary's crying Coty tears!"

The woman was discreetly whisked away from the shrine before trouble started. Demencio had vowed to be more careful. Scenting the Madonna's tears was a fine touch, he thought. The devout souls who waited so long in the hot Florida sun deserved more than a drop of salty water on their fingertips – this was supposed to be Jesus' mother, for heaven's sake. Her tears *ought* to smell special.

Trish held the plastic bottle while Demencio poured the last of the Charlie perfume. Again she marveled at how small and childlike his brown hands were. And steady. He would've made a wonderful surgeon, her husband, if only he'd had the chance. If only he'd been born in, say, Boston, Massachusetts, instead of Hialeah, Florida.

Demencio replaced the plastic bottle inside the Madonna. Clear thin tubes ran upward from the bottle's cap to the inside of the statue's eyelids, where the clever Demencio had drilled pinprick-sized holes. A thicker black tube ran internally down the length of the statue and emerged from another hole in her right heel. The black air tube connected to a small rubber bulb, which could be operated by hand or foot. Squeezing the bulb forced the phony tears out of the bottle, up the twin tubes and into the Madonna's eyes.

There was an art to it, and Demencio fancied himself one of the best in the business. He kept the tears small, subtle and paced at intervals. The longer the crowd was made to linger, the more soft drinks, angel food cake, T-shirts, Bibles, holy candles and sunblock they purchased.

From Demencio, of course.

Most everybody in Grange knew what he was up to, but they didn't say much. Some were too busy running their own scams. Besides, tourists were tourists and there wasn't much difference, when you got down to the core morality of it, between Mickey Mouse and a fiberglass Madonna.

Trish liked to say: "All we're really selling is hope."

Demencio liked to say: "I'd rather peddle religion than a phony goddamn rodent."

He made decent money, though he wasn't rich and probably never would be. Not like Miss JoLayne Lucks, whose astounding and undeserved windfall he now contemplated.

"How much she win?" he asked his wife.

"Fourteen million, if it's true."

"She's not sure?"

"She not sayin'."

Demencio snorted. Anybody else, they'd be hooting and hollering all over town. *Fourteen million bucks*!

Trish said, "All they announced is there's two winning tickets. One was bought down around Homestead, the other was in Grange."

"The Grab N'Go?"

"Yep. The way they figured out who, the store only sold twenty-two Lotto tickets all last week. Twenty-one is accounted for. JoLayne's is the only one left."

Demencio fitted the fiberglass Madonna back together. "So what's she up to?"

Trish reported that, according to neighbors, JoLayne Lucks had not come out of her house all morning and was not answering the telephone.

"Maybe she ain't home," Demencio said. He carried the Madonna into the house. Trish followed. He set the statue in a corner, next to his golf bag.

"Let's go see her," he said.

"Why?" Trish wondered what Demencio was planning. They barely knew the Lucks woman to say hello.

"Bring her some angel food cake," Demencio proposed. "It's a neighborly thing on a Sunday morning. I mean, why the hell not?"

# TWO

**JoLayne Lucks didn't** expect to see Trish and Demencio on her front porch, and Demencio didn't expect to see so much of JoLayne's legs. She appeared in a peach-colored jogging bra and sky-blue panties.

"I wasn't ready for company," she said in a sleepy voice.

Trish: "We'll drop by another time."

"Whatcha got there?"

Demencio said, "Cake."

He was transfixed by JoLayne's perfectly muscled calves. How'd they get like that? He never saw her running.

"Come on in," she said, and Demencio – shaking free of his wife's grip – went on.

They stood, each holding one side of the cake plate, while JoLayne Lucks went to put on a pair of jeans. The small tidy house showed no signs of a post-lottery celebration. Trish remarked on the handsome piano in the living room; Demencio eyed an aquarium full of baby turtles – there must have been fifty of them, paddling full tilt and goggled-eyed against the glass.

To Trish he said, "I wonder what *that's* all about."

"You hush. They're pets is all."

JoLayne returned with her hair under a baseball cap,

which Demencio found intriguing and sexy – the attitude as much as the style. JoLayne told Trish the cake looked delicious.

"Angel food," Demencio's wife said. "My grandma's recipe. On my mother's side."

"Sit down, please." JoLayne carried the plate to the kitchen counter. Trish and Demencio sat stiffly on an antique cherrywood love seat.

He said, "Those your turtles?"

JoLayne Lucks gave a bright smile. "Would you like one?"

Demencio shook his head. Trish, by way of explanation: "We've got a jealous old tomcat."

JoLayne peeled the plastic wrapping from the cake and broke off a chunk with her fingers. Serenely she popped it in her mouth. "What brings you folks by?"

Trish glanced at Demencio, who shifted in the love seat. "Well," he said, "here's the thing – we heard about your good fortune. You know . . ."

JoLayne gave him no help. She was savoring the angel food.

Demencio said, "About the Lotto, I mean."

One of her fine brown eyebrows arched. She kept chewing. Demencio fumbled with a strategy. The woman seemed slightly spacey.

Trish came to the rescue. "We stopped over to say congratulations. Nothing like this ever happens in Grange."

"No?" With a lizard flick of her tongue, JoLayne Lucks removed a crumb from one of her sparkling cobalt fingernails. "I thought miracles happen all the time around here. Most every Sunday, right?"

Demencio reddened, perceiving a dig at his Madonna

concession. Trish, courageously: "What I meant, JoLayne, was nobody's ever won anything. Nobody I can recall."

"Well, you might be right."

"It's just a shame you've got to split the jackpot with somebody else." Trish spoke with true sympathy. "Not that fourteen million bucks is anything to sneeze at, but it'd be nice if you were the only winner. Nice for Grange, too."

Demencio shot a glare at his wife. "It's still nice for Grange," he said. "It'll put us on the map, for damn sure."

JoLayne Lucks said, "Ya'll want some coffee?"

"So what's next, girl?" Trish asked.

"I thought I'd feed the turtles."

Trish chuckled uneasily. "You know what I mean. Maybe a new car? A place at the beach?"

JoLayne Lucks cocked her head. "You're losing me now."

Demencio had had enough. He stood up, hitching at his trousers. "I won't lie. We came to ask a favor."

JoLayne beamed. "That's more like it." She noticed how Trish's hands had balled with tension.

Demencio forced a cough, to clear his throat. "Pretty soon you'll be all famous, in the newspapers and TV. My idea was maybe when they ask where your Lotto luck came from, you could put in a good word."

"For you?"

"For the Madonna, yes."

"But I've never even been to the shrine."

"I know, I know." Demencio held up his hands. "It's just an idea. I can't promise hardly anything in return. I mean, you're a millionaire now."

Although he sorely hoped JoLayne wouldn't ask for a commission on his take, he was prepared to part with ten percent.

Trish, quietly: "It'd just be a favor, like he said. Pure and simple. A favor for a neighbor."

"Christmas is coming," Demencio added. "Any little thing would help. Anything you could do."

JoLayne Lucks walked them, one on each arm, to the door. She said, "Well, it's surely something to think about. And, Trish, that's glorious cake."

"You're so kind."

"Sure you don't fancy a turtle?"

In tandem, Demencio and his wife edged off the porch. "Thanks just the same," they said, and walked home in silence. Trish pondered the possibility she'd gotten some bad information, as JoLayne Lucks didn't behave like a woman who'd won a free toaster, much less a Lotto jackpot. Demencio, meanwhile, had concluded JoLayne Lucks was either a borderline psycho or a brilliant faker, and that further investigation was necessary.

Bodean James Gazzer had spent thirty-one years perfecting the art of assigning blame. His personal credo – *Everything bad that happens is someone else's fault* – could, with imagination, be stretched to fit any circumstance. Bode stretched it.

The intestinal unrest that occasionally afflicted him surely was the result of drinking milk taken from secretly irradiated cows. The roaches in his apartment were planted by his filthy immigrant next-door neighbors. His dire financial plight was caused by runaway bank computers and conniving Wall Street Zionists; his bad luck in the South Florida job market, prejudice against English-speaking applicants. Even the lousy weather had a culprit: air pollution from Canada, diluting the ozone and derailing the jet stream.

Bode Gazzer's accusatory talents were honed at an early age. The youngest of three sons, he veered astray to develop a precocious fondness for truancy, vandalism and shoplifting. His parents, both teachers, earnestly tried to redirect the boy, only to hear themselves lashingly blamed for his troubles. Bode took the position that he was persecuted because he was short, and that his shortness was attributable to his mother's careless dietary practices (and his father's gluttonous complicity) during pregnancy. That both Jean and Randall Gazzer were genetically slight of stature was immaterial to young Bode – from television he'd gathered that humans as a species were getting taller with evolution, and he therefore expected to surpass his parents, if only by an inch or two. Yet Bode stopped growing in eighth grade, a fact lugubriously chronicled in the family's bimonthly measuring ceremonies, conducted at the kitchen doorjamb. A multicolored sequence of pencil slashes confirmed Bode's worst fears: His two older brothers were still ascending positively, while he himself was finished, capped off at the ripe old age of fourteen.

The bitter realization hardened Bode Gazzer against his MSG-gobbling parents, and society at large. He became "the bad element" in the neighborhood, the cocky ringleader of misdemeanors and minor felonies. He worked diligently at being a hood, taking up unfiltered cigarets, public spitting and gratuitous profanity. Every so often he purposely provoked his brothers into beating him up, so he could tell friends he'd been in a savage gang fight.

Bode's schoolteacher parents didn't believe in whippings and (except for one occasion) never laid a glove on him. Jean and Randall Gazzer preferred "talking out" problems with their children, and spent many hours around the supper table "interacting" earnestly with the insolent Bodean. He was more than a match. Not only had he acquired the rhetorical skills of his mother and father, he was boundlessly creative. No matter what happened, Bode always produced an elaborate excuse from which he would not budge, even in the face of overwhelming evidence.

By the time he turned eighteen, his juvenile arrest record filled three pages, and his weary parents had put themselves in the hands of a Zen counselor. Bode had come to relish his role as the family outlaw, the bad seed, the misunderstood one. He could explain everything and would, at the drop of a hat. By the time he turned twenty-two, he was living on beer, bold talk and a multitude of convenient resentments. "I'm on God's shit list," he'd announce in barrooms, "so keep your damn distance."

A series of unhealthy friendships eventually drew Bode Gazzer into the culture of hate and hardcore bigotry. Previously, when dishing out fault for his plight, Bode had targeted generic authority figures – parents, brothers, cops, judges – without considering factors such as race, religion or ethnicity. He'd swung broadly, and without much impact. But xenophobia and racism infused his griping with new vitriol. Now it wasn't just some storm-trooper cop who busted Bode with stolen VCRs, it was the *Cuban* storm-trooper cop who obviously had a hard-on for Anglos; it wasn't just the double-talking defense lawyer who sold Bode down the river, it was the double-talking *Jew* defense lawyer who clearly held a vendetta against Christians; and it wasn't just the cokehead bondsman who refused to put up Bode's bail, it was the cokehead *Negro* bondsman who wanted him to stay in jail and get cornholed to death.

Bode Gazzer's political awakening coincided with an overdue revision of his illicit habits. He'd made up his mind to forsake burglaries, car thefts and other property offenses in favor of forgeries, check kiting and other so-called paper crimes, for which judges seldom dispensed state prison time.

As it happened, the hate movement in which Bode had taken an interest strongly espoused fraud as a form of civil disobedience. Militia pamphlets proclaimed that ripping off banks, utilities and credit-card companies was a just repudiation of the United States government and all the liberals, Jews, faggots, lesbians, Negroes, environmentalists and communists who infested it. Bode Gazzer admired the logic. However, he proved only slightly more skillful at passing bad checks than he was at hot-wiring Oldsmobiles.

Between always-brief jail stints, he'd decorated the inside of his apartment with antigovernment posters purchased at various gun shows: David Koresh, Randy Weaver and Gordon Kahl were featured heroically.

Whenever Chub visited the place, he raised a long-necked Budweiser in salute to the martyrs honored on Bode's wall. Through television he'd acquired a vague awareness of Koresh and Weaver, but he knew little about Kahl except that he'd been a Dakota farmer and tax protester, and that the feds had shot the shit out of him.

"Goddamn storm troopers," Chub snarled now, parroting a term he'd picked up at a small but lively militia meeting on Big Pine Key. He carried his beer to a futon sofa, where he plopped down splay-legged and relaxed. Quickly his thoughts drifted from the fallen patriots to his own sunny fortunes.

Bode Gazzer hunched at the dinette, a newspaper spread under his nose. He'd been in a spiteful mood since learning from a state lottery pamphlet that he and Chub wouldn't be receiving the $14 million all at once – it was to be dispensed in equal payments over twenty years.

Worse: The payments would be taxed!

Chub, who wasn't bad with numbers, attempted to cheer Bode Gazzer with the fact that $700,000 a year, even before taxes, was still a very large piece of change.

"Not large enough to outfit a patriot force," Bode snapped.

Chub said, "Rules is rules. The hell can you do?" He got up to turn on the TV. Nothing happened. "This busted or what?"

Bode smoothed the wrinkles from the newspaper and said: "Christ, don't you get it? This is everything we've been talkin' about, everything worth fightin' for – life, liberty, pursuit and happiness all rolled up in one."

Chub thwacked the broken television with the flat of his hand. He wasn't in the mood for one of Bode's speeches yet it now seemed inescapable.

Bode Gazzer continued: "Finally we hit it big and what happens? The state of motherfucking Florida is gonna pay us in drips and draps. Then, whatever we get is snatched by the Infernal Revenue!"

Listening to his friend, Chub's high feelings about their good luck began to ebb. He'd always viewed the lottery as a potential way to get tons of free money without doing jackshit. But the way Bode explained it, the Lotto was just another sinister example of government intrusion, tax abuse and liberal deceit.

"You think it's a accident we gotta share this money with somebody else?"

With the mouth of the beer bottle, Chub massaged the furry nape of his neck. He wondered what his friend was getting at.

Bode rapped his knuckles on the dinette. "Here's my prediction: The shitweasel holding the other Lotto ticket, he's either a Negro, Jew or Cuban type."

"Go on!"

"That's how they do it, Chub. To fuck over decent Americans such as you and me. You think they're gonna let two white boys take the whole jackpot? Not these days, no way!" Bode's nose angled back toward the newspaper. "Where's Grange? Over near Tampa?"

Chub was stunned at his friend's theory. He didn't understand how the lottery could be rigged. If it was, how had he and Bode managed to win even half?

During the brief span of their friendship, Bodean Gazzer had invoked conspiracies to explain numerous puzzling occurrences – for instance, how come there was usually a big airplane crash at Christmastime.

Bode knew the answer, and naturally it involved the U.S. government. The Federal Aviation Administration was in perpetual danger of having its budget slashed, the crucial vote customarily coming in December before Congress adjourned for the holidays. Consequently (Bode revealed to Chub) the FAA always sabotaged an airliner around Christmas, knowing politicians wouldn't have the nerve to cut the funding for air safety while the world watched mangled bodies being pulled out of a charred fuselage.

"Think about it," Bode Gazzer had said – and Chub did. A government plot seemed more plausible than grim coincidence, all those plane crashes.

Corrupting the state Lotto, however, was something else. Chub didn't think even the liberals could pull it off.

"It don't add up," he said sullenly. Plenty of regular white folks had won, too; he'd seen their faces on TV. Speaking of which, he wished the goddamn thing wasn't busted so he could watch football and not have to think about what Bode Gazzer was saying.

"You'll see," Bode told him. "You'll see I'm right. Now, where the hell's Grange, Florida?"

Chub muttered, "Upstate."

"Big help you are. Everything's upstate from here."

From his studded belt Chub took a Colt Python .357 and shot several holes in David Koresh's cheeks.

Bode Gazzer leaned back from the dinette. "What's *your* damn problem?"

"I don't like the way I feel." Chub tucked the gun in the waist of his trousers, the barrel hot against his thigh. Without flinching he said: "Man wins fourteen million bucks, he oughta feel good. And I don't."

"Exactly!" Bode Gazzer charged across the room and seized Chub in a clammy tremble of an embrace. "Now you see" – Bode's voice dropping to a whisper – "what this country of ours has come to. You see what the battle is all about!"

Chub nodded solemnly, withholding his concern that a battle sounded like damn hard work, and hard work sounded like the last damn thing a brand-new millionaire ought to be doing.

The downsizing trend that swept newspapers in the early nineties was aimed at sustaining the bloated profit margins in which the industry had wallowed for most of the century. A new soulless breed of corporate managers, unburdened by a passion for serious journalism, found an easy way to reduce the cost of publishing a daily newspaper. The first casualty was depth.

Cutting the amount of space devoted to news instantly justified cutting the staff. At many papers, downsizing was the favored excuse for eliminating such luxuries as police desks, suburban editions, foreign bureaus, medical writers, environmental specialists and, of course, investigative teams (which were always antagonizing civic titans and important advertisers). As newspapers grew thinner and shallower, the men who published them worked harder to assure Wall Street that readers neither noticed nor cared.

It was Tom Krome's misfortune to have found a comfortable niche with a respectable but doomed newspaper, and to have been laid off at a time when the business was glutted with hungry experienced writers. It was his further misfortune to have been peaking in his career as an investigative reporter at a time when most newspapers no longer wished to pay for those particular skills.

*The Register*, for example, was in the market for a

divorce columnist. Sinclair had made the pitch at Krome's job interview.

"We're looking for something funny," Sinclair had said. "Upbeat."

"Upbeat?"

"There's a growing readership out there," Sinclair had said. "You ever been through a divorce?"

"No," Krome had lied.

"Perfect. No baggage, no bitterness, no bile."

Sinclair's fetish for alliteration – it was Krome's first exposure.

"But your ad in *E&P* said 'feature writer.' "

"This would be a feature, Tom. Five hundred words. Twice a week."

Krome had thought: I know what I'll do – I'll move to Alaska! Gut salmon on the slime line. In winters, work on a novel.

"Sorry I wasted your time." He'd stood up, shaken Sinclair's hand (which had, actually, a limp, slick, dead-salmon quality), and flown home to New York.

A week later, the editor had called and offered Krome a feature-writing position at $38,000 a year. No divorce column, thank God – *The Register*'s managing editor, it turned out, had seen nothing upbeat in the topic. "Four-time loser," Sinclair had explained in a whisper.

Tom Krome took the feature-writing job because he needed the money. He was saving for a cabin on Kodiak Island or possibly up near Fairbanks, where he'd live by himself. He intended to buy a snowmobile and photograph wild wolves, caribou and eventually a grizzly bear. He intended to write a novel about a fictional actress named Mary Andrea Finley, based on a true person named Mary Andrea Finley, who in real life had spent the last four years successfully preventing Tom Krome from divorcing her.

He was packing for the Lotto story when Katie returned from church.

"Where to?" Her purse hit the kitchen table like a cinder block.

"A place called Grange," Tom Krome said.

"I've been there," Katie said testily. *A place called Grange*. Like she didn't even know it was a town. "That's where they have the sightings," she said.

"Right." Krome wondered if Katie was one of the religious pilgrims. Anything was possible; he'd known her only two weeks.

She said, "They've got a Mother Mary that cries." She went to the refrigerator. Poured herself a glass of grapefruit juice; Krome, waiting for more about Grange. "And on the highway," she said, between sips, "in the middle of the highway, the face of Jesus Christ."

Tom Krome said, "I heard about that."

"A stain," Katie elaborated. "Dark violet. Like blood."

Or possibly transmission fluid, Krome thought.

"I've only been there once," Katie said. "We stopped for gas on the way to Clearwater."

Krome was relieved to hear she wasn't a Grange regular. He tossed a stack of clean Jockey shorts into the suitcase. "What was your impression of the place?"

"Weird." Katie finished the fruit juice, washed the glass. She slipped out of her shoes and took a seat at the table, where she had a good view of Tom packing. "I didn't see the crying Madonna, just the Road-Stain Jesus. But the whole town struck me as weird."

Krome suppressed a smile. He was counting on weird.

Katie asked, "When will you be back?"

"Day or two."

"You gonna call me?"

Krome looked up. "Sure, Katie."

"When you get to Grange, I mean."

"Oh . . . sure."

"You thought I meant for you to call when you get back. Didn't you?"

Krome marveled at how, with no effort, he'd gotten himself into a downward-spiraling conversation before noon on a Sunday morning. He was simply trying to pack, for God's sake, yet he'd apparently managed to hurt Katie's feelings.

His theory: It was the pause between the "oh" and the "sure" that had tripped her alarm.

Surrender was the only option: Yes, yes, sweet Katherine, forgive me. You're right, I'm a total shit, insensitive and self-absorbed. What was I thinking! *Of course* I'll call as soon as I get to Grange.

"Katie," he said, "I'll call as soon as I get to Grange."

"It's OK. I know you'll be busy."

Krome closed the suitcase, snapped the latches. "I want to call, all right?"

"OK, but not too late."

"Yes, I remember."

"Art gets home – "

"At six-thirty. I remember."

Art being Katie's husband. Circuit Judge Arthur Battenkill Jr.

Krome felt bad about betraying Art, even though he didn't know the man, and even though Art was cheating on Katie with both his secretaries. This was widely known, Katie had assured him, unbuckling his pants on their second "date." An eye for an eye, she'd said; that's straight from the Bible.

Still, Tom Krome felt guilty. It was nothing new; possibly it was even necessary. Beginning in his teenage years, guilt had played a defining role in every romance Tom Krome ever had. These days it was a steady if oppressive companion in his divorce.

Katie Battenkill had poleaxed him with her fine alert features and lusty wholesomeness. She'd chased after him, literally, one day while he was jogging downtown. He'd gotten tangled in a charity street march – he couldn't recall whether it was for a disease or a disorder – and clumsily slapped some money in her hand. Next thing he knew: footsteps running behind him. She caught up, too. They had lunch at a pizza joint, where the first thing out of Katie's mouth was: "I'm married and I've never done this before. God, I'm starved." Tom Krome liked her tremendously, but he realized that Art was very much part of the equation. Katie was working things out in her own way, and Krome understood his role. It suited him fine, for now.

Barefoot in her nylons, Katie followed him out to the car. He got in and, perhaps too hastily, fit the key in the ignition. She leaned over and kissed him goodbye; quite a long kiss. Afterwards she lingered at the car door. He noticed she was holding a disposable camera.

"For your trip," she said, handing it to him. "There's five shots left. Maybe six."

Krome thanked her but explained it was unnecessary. Sinclair would be sending a staff photographer if the lottery story panned out.

"That's for the newspaper," Katie said. "This is for me. Could you take a picture of the weeping Madonna?"

For a moment Krome thought she was kidding. She wasn't.

"Please, Tom?"

He put the cardboard camera in his jacket. "What if she's not crying? The Virgin Mary. You still want a picture?"

Katie didn't catch the sarcasm that leaked into his voice. "Oh yes," she said ardently. "Even without the tears."

# THREE

**The mayor of** Grange, Jerry Wicks, complimented JoLayne Lucks on her cooters.

"My babies," she said fondly. Her blue fingernails sparkled as she shredded a head of iceberg lettuce into the aquarium. The turtles commenced a mute scramble for supper.

Jerry Wicks said, "How many you got there?"

"Forty-six, I believe."

"My, my."

"There's red-bellies, Suwanees and two young peninsulars, which I am told will grow up to be something special. And see how they all get along!"

"Yes, ma'am." Jerry Wicks couldn't tell one from another. He was impressed, however, by the volume of noise made by the feeding reptiles. He was quite certain the crunching would drive him insane if he lingered too long.

"JoLayne, the reason I came by – there's talk you won the Lotto!"

JoLayne Lucks dried her hands on a towel. She offered the mayor a glass of limeade, which he declined.

"It's your own private business," he went on, "and there's no need to tell me yes or no. But if it's true, nobody deserves it more than you . . ."

"And why's that?"

Jerry Wicks was stumped for a reply. Ordinarily he wasn't nervous around pretty women, but this afternoon JoLayne Lucks possessed an uncommonly powerful aura; a fragrant dazzle, a mischievous twinkling that made him feel both silly and careless. He wanted to run away before she had him down on the floor, howling like a coon hound.

"The reason I'm here, JoLayne, I'm thinking about the town. It'd be great for Grange if it was true. About you winning."

"Publicitywise," she said.

"Exactly," he exclaimed with relief. "It would be such a welcome change from the usual . . ."

"Freak shit?"

The mayor winced. "Well, I wouldn't . . ."

"Like the road stain or the weepy Virgin," JoLayne said, "or Mister Amador's phony stigmata."

Dominick Amador was a local builder who'd lost his contracting license after the walls of the Saint Arthur catechism school collapsed for no good reason during a summer squall. Dominick Amador's buddies advised him to relocate to Dade County, where it was safe for incompetent contractors, but Dominick wanted to stay in Grange with his wife and girlfriends. So one night he got hammered on Black Jack and Xanax, and (using a three-eighth-inch wood bit) drilled a perfect hole in each of his palms. Now Amador was one of the stars of Grange's Christian pilgrim tour, touting himself as a carpenter ("just like Jesus!") and assiduously picking at the circular wounds in his hands to keep them authentically unscabbed and bloody. There were rumors he was planning to drill his feet soon.

The mayor said to JoLayne Lucks: "See here, I'm not one to pass judgment on others."

"But you're a religious man," she said. "Do *you* believe?"

Jerry Wicks wondered how the conversation had drifted so far off course. He said, "What I personally believe isn't important. Others do – I've seen it in their eyes."

JoLayne popped a Certs. She was sorry about putting the mayor on the spot. Jerry wasn't a bad fellow, just soft. Thin blond hair going gray at the sides. Pink slack cheeks, a picket line of tiny perfect teeth, and sparse guileless eyebrows. Jerry ran an insurance business he'd inherited from his mother; homeowners and auto, mostly. He was harmless and chubby. JoLayne kept all her coverage with him; most everyone in town did.

Jerry said, "I guess the point to be made, it'd be good for Grange to get a different slant of publicity."

"Let the world know," JoLayne agreed, "there's normal folks who live here, too."

"Right," said the mayor.

"Not just Jesus freaks and scammers."

The blunt words caused in Jerry Wicks a pain similar to an abdominal cramp. "JoLayne, *please*."

"Oh, I'm sorry to be such a cynical young lady. Don't ask how I got this way."

By now the mayor realized JoLayne Lucks had no intention of telling him whether or not she'd won the Lotto. The rhythmic munch of her hungry cooters had become almost unbearable.

"You want one?" she asked. "For Jerry junior?"

Jerry Wicks said no thanks. He eyed the teeming aquarium and thought: Look who's talking about freaks.

JoLayne reached across the kitchen table and tweaked him in the ribs. "Hey, cheer up."

The mayor turned to gooseflesh at her touch; he smiled bashfully and looked away. He beheld a fleeting impure fantasy: JoLayne's blue fingernails raking slowly across his pallid, acne-scarred shoulder blades.

Teasingly she said, "You came here to tell me something, Jerry. So let's hear it already, 'fore we both die of old age."

"Yes, all right. There's a newspaper reporter coming into town. From *The Register.* He's got a reservation at the bed-and-breakfast – Mrs. Hendricks told me."

"For tonight?"

"That's what she said. Anyhow, he's looking for the lottery winner. To do a feature story, is my guess."

"Oh," said JoLayne Lucks.

"Nothing to worry about." As mayor, Jerry Wicks had experience dealing with the press. He said, "They love to write about ordinary people who make it big."

"Really." JoLayne pursed her lips.

"Human interest, they call it." The mayor wanted to reassure her there was nothing to fear from giving interviews. He hoped she would be cooperative and friendly, since the image of Grange was at stake.

JoLayne said, "Do I have to talk to him?"

"No." Jerry Wicks' heart sank.

"Because I'm fond of my privacy."

"The man doesn't have to come to the house. Fact, it'd be better if he didn't." The mayor was worried about JoLayne's turtle hobby, and what cruel fun a snotty city reporter might have with that. "Maybe you could meet him at the restaurant in the Holiday Inn."

"Yum," said JoLayne.

The phone on the kitchen wall rang. She stood up. "I've got some errands. Thanks for stopping over."

Jerry Wicks said, "I just thought you should know what's ahead. Winning the Lotto is very big news."

"Must be," JoLayne Lucks said.

The mayor told her goodbye and let himself out. As he walked from the porch to the driveway, he could hear JoLayne's telephone ringing and ringing and ringing.

Chub said they should drive directly to Tallahassee and claim their half of the $28 million jackpot as soon as humanly possible. Bodean Gazzer said nope, not just yet.

"We got one hundred and eighty days to pick it up. That's six whole months." He loaded a cold twelve-pack into the truck. "Right now we gotta find that other ticket before whoever's got it cashes in."

"Maybe they already done it. Maybe it's too late."

"Don't think so negative."

"*Life* is fucking negative," Chub noted.

Bode spread a striped beach towel on the passenger half of the front seat, to shield the new upholstery from the gun grease and sweat that was Chub's natural marinade. Chub took mild offense at the precaution but said nothing.

A few minutes later, speeding along the turnpike, Bode Gazzer summarized his plan: "Break in, rip off the ticket, then split."

"Happens we can't find it?" Chub asked. "What supposed they hid it too good?"

"There you go again."

"I ain't interested in felony time."

"Relax, goddammit."

"I mean, my God, we's millionaires," Chub went on. "Millionaires, they don't do b-and-e's!"

"No, but they steal just the same. We use crowbars, they use Jews and briefcases."

As usual, Bode had a point. Chub hunkered down with a Budweiser to think on it.

Bode said, "Hey, I don't wanna go to jail, either. Say we go up on charges, who'd take over the White Rebels?"

The White Rebel Brotherhood is what Bodean Gazzer had decided to call his new militia. Chub didn't fuss about the name; it wasn't as if they'd be printing up business cards.

Bode said, "Hey, d'you finish that book I gave you? On how to be a survivalist?"

"No, I did not." Chub had gotten as far as the business on eating bugs, and that was it. "How to Tell Toxic Insects from Edible Insects." Jesus Willy Christ.

"I didn't see no chapter on prime rib," he grumbled.

To ease the tension, Bode asked Chub if he'd like to make a bet on who was holding the other winning Lotto numbers. "I got ten bucks says it's a Negro. You want to take Jews, or Cubans?"

Chub had never met a white supremacist who said "Negro" instead of "nigger." "Is they a difference?" he inquired sarcastically.

"No, sir," said Bode.

"Then why don't you call 'em what they is?"

Bode clenched the steering wheel. "I could call 'em coconuts and what's the damn difference? One word's no better than another."

Chub chuckled. "Coconuts."

"How about you make yourself useful. Find a radio station plays some white music, if that's possible."

"S'matter? You ain't fond a these *Negro* rappers?"

"Eat me," Bode Gazzer said.

He was ashamed to admit the truth, that he couldn't speak the word "nigger." He'd done so only once in his life, at age twelve, and his father had promptly hauled him outside and whipped his hairless bare ass with a razor strop. Then his mother had dragged him into the kitchen and washed his mouth out with Comet cleanser and vinegar. It was the worst (and only) corporal punishment of Bode Gazzer's childhood, and he'd never forgiven his parents. He'd also never forgotten the ghastly caustic taste of Comet, the scorch of which still revisited his tender throat at the mere whisper of "nigger." Uttering it aloud was out of the question.

Which was a major handicap for a self-proclaimed racist and militiaman. Bode Gazzer worked around it.

Changing the subject, he said to Chub: "You need some camos, buddy."

"I don't think so."

"What size pants you wear?"

Chub slumped in the seat and pretended he was trying to sleep. He didn't want to ride all the way to Grange. He didn't want to break into a stranger's house and steal a Lotto ticket.

And he sure as hell didn't want to wear camouflage clothes. Bode Gazzer's entire wardrobe was camo, which he'd ordered from the Cabela's fall catalog on a stolen MasterCard number. Bode believed camo garb would be essential for survival when the NATO troops invaded from the Bahamas and the White Rebel Brotherhood took to the woods. Until Bode opened his closet, Chub had had no idea that camo came in so many shrub-and-twig styles. There was your basic Trebark (Bode's parka);

your Realtree (Bode's rainsuit); your Mossy Oak, Timber Ghost and Treestand (Bode's collection of jumpsuits, shirts and trousers), your Konifer (Bode's snake-proof chaps) and your Tru-Leaf (Bode's all-weather mountain boots).

Chub didn't dispute Bode's pronouncement that such a selection of camos, properly matched, would make a man invisible among the oaks and pines. Having grown up in the mountains of north Georgia, Chub didn't want to be invisible in the woods. He wanted to be seen and heard. He especially wanted not to be mistaken for a tree by a rambunctious bear or a randy bobcat.

He said to Bode Gazzer: "You dress up your way, I'll dress up mine."

Bode peevishly scooped a fresh beer off the floorboard and popped the tab. "Remember what the Constitution says? 'Well-*regulated* militia.' Regulated means discipline, OK? And discipline starts with uniforms."

Bode took a slug and wedged the beer can in the crotch of his Mossy Oak trousers, to free both hands for steering. Chub leaned against the door, his ponytail leaving an oily smear on the window. He said, "I ain't wearin' no camo."

"Why not, goddammit!"

" 'Cause it makes you look like a fuckin' compost heap."

Bode Gazzer jerked the truck onto the shoulder of the highway. Angrily he stomped the brake.

"You listen – " he began.

"No, *you* listen!" Chub said, and was upon him in a second.

Bode felt the barrel of the Colt poking the soft part of his throat, right about where his tongue was attached on the inside. He felt Chub's hot beery breath on his forehead.

"Let's not fight," Bode pleaded, hoarsely.

"Won't be a fight. Be a killin'."

"Hey, brother, we're partners."

Chub said, "Then where's *our* ticket, dickface?"

"The lottery ticket?"

"No, the fucking laundry ticket." Chub cocked the pistol. "Where's it at?"

"Don't do this."

"I'm countin' to five."

"In my wallet. Inside a rubber."

Chub grinned crookedly. "Lemme see."

"A Trojan. One a them ribbed jobbers, nonlubricated." Bode removed it from his wallet and showed Chub what he'd done the night before – opening the plastic foil with a razor and folding the Lotto ticket inside the rolled-up condom.

Chub returned the gun to his pants and slid back to the passenger side. "That's pretty slick, I gotta admit. Nobody steals another man's rubbers. Steals every other damn thing, but not that."

"Exactly," Bode said. As soon as his heart stopped skipping, he put the truck in gear and eased back on the turnpike.

Chub watched him in a neutral but not entirely innocuous way. He said: "You understand what coulda happened? That we wouldn't be partners no more if I blowed your brains all over this truck and took the Lotto stub for m'self."

Bode nodded tightly. Until now it hadn't occurred that Chub might rip him off. Obviously it was something to think about. He said, "It's gonna work out fine. You'll see."

"OK," said Chub. He opened a beer: warm and fizzy. He closed his eyes and sucked down half the can. He wanted to trust Bode Gazzer but it wasn't always easy. *Negro*, for God's sake. Why'd he keep on with that word? It troubled Chub, made him wonder if Bode wasn't all he claimed to be.

Then he had another thought. "They a whorehouse in Grange?"

"Who knows," Bode said, "and who cares."

"Just don't forget where you hid our ticket."

"Gimme a break, Chub."

"Be helluva way to lose out on fourteen million bucks, winds up in the sheets of some whorehouse."

Bode Gazzer stared straight ahead at the highway. He said, "Man, you got a wild imagination."

The brains of a goddamn squirrel, but a wild imagination.

Tom Krome didn't wait to unpack; tossed his carry bag on the bed and dashed out. The owner of the bed-and-breakfast was pleased to give directions to the home of Miss JoLayne Lucks, at the corner of Cocoa and Hubbard across from the park. Krome's plan was to drop in with sincere apologies, invite Miss Lucks to a proper dinner, then ease into the interview gradually.

His experience as a visiting journalist in small towns was that some folks would tell you their life story at the drop of a hat, and others wouldn't say boo if your hair was on fire. Waiting on the woman's porch, Krome didn't know what to expect. He had knocked: No reply. He knocked again. Lights shone in the living room, and Krome heard music from a radio.

He walked around to the backyard and rose on his toes, to peer in the kitchen window. There were signs of a finished meal on the table: a setting for one. Coffee cup, salad bowl, a bare plate with a half-nibbled biscuit.

When Krome returned to the porch, the door stood open. The radio was off, the house was still.

"Hello!" he called.

He took a half step inside. The first thing he noticed was the aquarium. The second thing was water on the hardwood floor; a trail of drips.

From down the hall, a woman's voice: "Shut the door, please. Are you the reporter?"

"Yes, that's right." Tom Krome wondered how she knew. "Are you JoLayne?"

"What is it you want? I'm really not up for this."

Krome said, "You all right?"

"Come see for yourself."

She was sitting in the bathtub, with soap bubbles up to her breasts. She had a towel on her hair and a shotgun in her hands. Krome raised his arms and said, "I'm not going to hurt you."

"No shit," said JoLayne Lucks. "I've got a twelve-gauge and all you've got is a tape recorder."

Krome nodded. The Pearlcorder he used for interviews was cupped in his right hand.

"Sure is tiny," JoLayne remarked. "Sit down." She motioned with the gun toward the commode. "What's your name?"

"Tom Krome. I'm with *The Register*." He sat where she told him to sit.

She said, "I've had more company today than I can stand. Is this what it's like to be rich?"

Krome smiled inwardly. She was going to be one helluva story.

"Take out the cassette," JoLayne Lucks told him, "and drop it in the tub."

Krome played along. "Anything else?"

"Yeah. Quit staring."

"I'm sorry."

"Don't tell me you never saw a woman take a bath. Oh my, is it the bubbles? They sure don't last long."

Krome locked his eyes on the ceiling. "I can come back tomorrow."

JoLayne said, "Would you kindly stand up. Good. Now turn around. Get the robe off that hook and hand it to me – without peeking, please."

He heard the slosh of her climbing out of the tub. Then the lights in the bathroom went out.

"That was me," she said. "Don't try anything."

It was so dark that Krome couldn't see his own nose. He felt something sharp at his back.

"Gun," JoLayne explained.

"Gotcha."

"I want you to take off your clothes."

"For Christ's sake."

"And get in the bathtub."

"No!" he said.

"You want your interview, Mr. Krome?"

Until that moment, everything that had happened in the house of JoLayne Lucks was splendid material for Krome's feature story. But not this part, the disrobing-at-gunpoint of the reporter. Sinclair would never be told.

Once Krome was in the water, JoLayne Lucks turned

on the lights. She stood the shotgun against the toilet, and knelt next to the tub. "How you feeling?" she asked.

"Ridiculous."

"Well, you shouldn't. You're a good-enough-looking man." She peeled the towel off her head and shook her hair.

Tom Krome roiled the water to churn up more soap bubbles, in a futile effort to conceal his shriveled cock. JoLayne thought that was absolutely adorable. Krome fidgeted self-consciously. He reflected on the difficult and occasionally dangerous situations in which he'd found himself as a reporter – urban riots, drug busts, hurricanes, police shootouts, even a foreign coup. Yet he'd never felt so stymied and helpless. The woman had thought it out very carefully.

"Why are you doing this?" he asked.

"Because I was scared of you."

"There's nothing to be scared of."

"Oh, I can see that."

He laughed then. Couldn't help it. JoLayne Lucks laughed, too. "You gotta admit it breaks the ice."

Krome said, "You left the front door open."

"I sure did."

"And that's what you do when you're scared? Leave the door open and wait buck naked in the bath?"

"With a Remington," JoLayne reminded him, "full of nickel turkey load. Gift from Daddy." She ran some hot water into the tub. "You gettin' chilly?"

Krome kept his hands folded across his groin. There was no sense trying to act casual, but he did. JoLayne put her chin on the edge of the tub. "What do you want to know, Mr. Krome?"

"Did you win the lottery?"

"Yes, I won the lottery."

"Why aren't you happy about it?"

"Who says I'm not?"

"Will you keep your job at Dr. Crawford's?" The lady at the bed-and-breakfast had told him JoLayne Lucks worked at the veterinary clinic.

She said, "Hey, your fingers are pruning up."

Krome was determined to overcome the distraction of his own nakedness. "Can I ask a favor? There's a notebook and a ballpoint pen in the pocket of my pants."

"Oh, no you don't."

"But you promised."

"I beg your pardon?" She picked up the gun again; gonged the barrel loudly against the tub's iron faucet, which protruded from the wall between Krome's feet.

OK, he thought. We'll do it her way.

"JoLayne, have you ever won anything before?"

"Bikini contest at Daytona. I was eighteen, for heaven's sake, but I know what you're thinking." She rolled her eyes.

Krome said, "What was the prize?"

"Two hundred bucks." She paused. Puffed her cheeks. Propped the shotgun against the sink. "Look, I can't lie. It was a wet T-shirt contest. I tell people it was bikinis because it doesn't sound so slutty."

"Heck, you were just a kid."

"But you'd put it in the newspaper anyway. It's too juicy *not* to."

She was right: It was an irresistible anecdote – yet one that could be retold tastefully, even poignantly, as JoLayne Lucks would appreciate when she finally saw Tom Krome's feature article. In the meantime he could do little but gaze at the glassy bubbles that clung to the wet hair on his chest. He felt disarmed and preposterous.

"What are you afraid of?" he asked JoLayne.

"I've got just an awful feeling."

"Like a vision?" Krome was fishing to see if she was one of the local paranormals. He hoped not, even though it would've made for a more colorful story.

"Not a vision, just a feeling," she said. "The way you can sometimes feel a storm coming, even when there's not a cloud in the sky."

It was agony, hearing one good quote after another slip away untranscribed. Again he begged for his notebook.

JoLayne shook her head. "This isn't the interview, Mr. Krome. This is the *pre*-interview."

"But Miss Lucks – "

"Fourteen million dollars is a mountain of money. I believe it will attract a bad element." She reached into the water – deftly insinuating her hand under Tom Krome's butt – and yanked the drain plug out of the bathtub.

"Dry off and get dressed," she told him. "How do you like your coffee?"

# FOUR

**Demencio was carrying** out the garbage when the red pickup rolled to a stop under the streetlight. Two men got out and stretched. The shorter one wore pointed cowboy boots and olive-drab camouflage, like a deer hunter. The taller one had a scraggy ponytail and sunken drugged-out eyes.

Demencio said: "Visitation's over."

"Visitation of what?" asked the hunter.

"The Madonna."

"She die?" The ponytailed one spun toward his friend. "Goddamn, you hear that?"

Demencio dropped the garbage bag on the curb. "I'm talking about Madonna, the Virgin Mary. Jesus' mother."

"Not the singer?"

"Nope, not the singer."

The hunter said, "What's a 'visitation'?"

"People travel from all over to pray at the Madonna's statue. Sometimes she cries real tears."

"No shit?"

"No shit," said Demencio. "Come back tomorrow and see for yourself."

The ponytailed man said, "How much you charge?"

"Whatever you can spare, sir. We take donations

only." Demencio was trying to be polite, but the two men made him edgy. Hicks he could handle; hardcore rednecks scared him.

The strangers whispered back and forth, then the camouflaged one spoke up again: "Hey, Julio, we in Grange?"

Demencio, feeling his neck go tight: "Yeah, that's right."

"Is there a 7-Eleven somewheres nearby?"

"All we got is the Grab N'Go." Demencio pointed down the street. "About half a mile."

"Thank you kindly," said the hunter.

"Double for me," said the ponytailed man.

Before the pickup drove away, Demencio noticed a red-white-and-blue sticker on the rear bumper: MARK FUHRMAN FOR PRESIDENT.

Definitely not pilgrims, Demencio thought.

Chub was intrigued by what the Cuban had said. A statue that cries? About what?

"You'd cry, too," said Bodean Gazzer, "if you was stuck in a shithole town like this."

"So you don't believe him."

"No, I do not."

Chub said, "I seen weepin' Virgin Marys on TV before."

"I've seen Bugs Bunny on TV, too. That make him real? Maybe you think there's a real rabbit that sings and dances dressed up in a fucking tuxedo – "

"Ain't the same thing." Chub was insulted by Bode's acid sarcasm. Sometimes his friend seemed to forget who had the gun.

"Here we are!" Bode declared, waving at a flashing sign that spelled out GRAB N'GO. He parked in the handicapped space by the front door and flipped on the dome light inside the truck. From a pocket he took out the folded clipping from *The Miami Herald*. The story said the second winning lottery ticket had been purchased "in the rural community of Grange." The winner, it reported, hadn't yet come forward to claim his or her share of the prize.

Bode read this aloud to Chub, who said: "Can't be many Lotto joints in a town this size."

"Let's ask," said Bode.

They went into the Grab N'Go and picked up two twelve-packs of beer, a cellophane bag of beefalo jerky, a carton of Camels and a walnut coffee cake. While the clerk rang them up, Bode inquired about Lotto tickets.

"How many you want? We're the only game in town," the clerk said.

"Is that a fact." Bode Gazzer gave a smug wink at Chub.

The clerk was eighteen, maybe nineteen. He was heavyset and freshly sunburned. He had a burr cut and a steep pimpled nose. A plastic tag identified him as SHINER.

He said, "Maybe you guys heard – this store had the winning ticket yesterday."

"Go on!"

"God's truth. I sold it to the woman myself."

Bode Gazzer lit a cigaret. "Right here? No way."

Chub said, "Sounds like a line a shit to me."

"No, I swear." With a finger the clerk crossed his heart. "Girl name of JoLayne Lucks."

"Yeah? How much she win?" Chub asked.

"Well, first it was twenty-eight million, but come to find out she's gotta split it. Someone else had the same numbers, is what the news said. Somebody down around Miami."

"Is that a fact?" Bode paid for the beer and groceries. Then he tossed a five-dollar bill on the counter. "Tell you what, Mister Shiner. Give me five Quick Picks, assuming you still got the magic touch."

The clerk smiled. "You come to the right place. Town's famous for miracles." He pulled the tickets from the Lotto machine and handed them to Bodean Gazzer.

Chub said, "She a local gal, this Joleen?"

"Lives acrost from the park. And it's *JoLayne*."

Chub, scratching his neck: "I wonder if she's lookin' for a husband."

The clerk grinned and lowered his voice. "No offense, sir, but she's a little too tan for you."

They all had a laugh. Bode and Chub said goodbye and walked out to the truck. For a while the two men sat in the cab, drinking beer, gnawing on jerky, not speaking a word.

Finally Chub said, "So it's just like you said."

"Yup. Just like I said."

"Goddamn. A *Negro*." With both hands Chub tore into the coffee cake.

"Eat quick," Bode told him. "We got work to do."

Tom Krome spent three hours with JoLayne Lucks. To call it an interview was a stretch. He'd never met anyone, politicians and convicts included, who could so adroitly steer conversation in a wrong direction. JoLayne Lucks held the added advantages of soft eyes and charm, to which Krome easily succumbed. By the end of the evening, she knew everything important there was to know about him, while he knew next to nothing about her. Even the turtles remained an enigma.

"Where'd you get them?" he asked.

"Creeks. Hey, I like your wristwatch."

"Thanks. It was a gift."

"From a lady friend, I'll bet!"

"My wife, a long time ago."

"How long you been married?"

"We're divorcing . . ." And away he'd go.

At half past ten JoLayne's father called from Atlanta. She apologized for not picking up when he'd phoned earlier. She said she'd had company.

When Tom Krome rose to leave, JoLayne told her father to hang on. She led Krome to the door and said it had been a pleasure to make his acquaintance.

"May I come back tomorrow," he asked, "and take some notes?"

"Nope."

She gave him a gentle nudge. The screen door slapped shut between them.

"I've decided," she said, "not to be in your newspaper."

"Please."

"Sorry."

Tom Krome said, "You don't understand."

"Not everybody wants to be famous."

He felt her slipping away. "Please. One hour with the tape recorder. It'll be fine, you'll see."

That was the lie, of course. No matter what Krome wrote about JoLayne Lucks winning the lottery, it wouldn't be fine. Nothing positive could come from telling the whole world you're a millionaire, and JoLayne was smart enough to know it.

She said, "I'm sorry for your trouble, but I prefer to keep my privacy."

"You really don't have a choice." That was the part she didn't understand.

JoLayne stepped closer to the screen. "What do you mean?"

Krome shrugged apologetically. "There's going to be a story in the papers, one way or another. This is news. This is the way it works."

She turned and disappeared into the house.

Krome stood on the porch, contemplating the hum and bubble of the aquarium pump. He felt like a shitheel, but that was nothing new. He took out one of his business cards and wrote on the back of it: "Please call if you change your mind."

He inserted the card in the doorjamb and returned to the bed-and-breakfast. In his room he saw a note on the dresser: Katie had phoned. So had Dick Turnquist.

Krome sat heavily on the edge of the bed, pondering the slim likelihood that his New York divorce lawyer had tracked him down in Grange, Florida, on a Sunday night to deliver good tidings. He waited twenty minutes before making the call.

JoLayne Lucks worked as an assistant to Dr. Cecil Crawford, the town veterinarian. JoLayne had been trained as a registered nurse, and easily could have earned twice as much money at the county hospital if she hadn't preferred animal patients over human ones. And she excelled at her job. Everyone in Grange who owned a pet knew JoLayne Lucks. Where Doc Crawford could be cranky and terse, JoLayne was all tenderness and concern. That she was rumored to be eccentric in her private life was intriguing but immaterial; she had a special way with the animals. Just about everybody was fond of her, including a number of lifelong bigots who confided that she was the only black person they'd ever trusted. JoLayne found it interesting that so many of the local racists owned small, neurotic, ill-tempered breeds of dogs. The women favored toy poodles; the men, grossly overfed Chihuahuas. In Dade County, where JoLayne grew up, it was German shepherds and pit bulls.

The job at Dr. Crawford's clinic was only JoLayne's second since leaving nursing school. Her first job was at the infamously exotic emergency room of Jackson Memorial Hospital, in downtown Miami. That's where JoLayne had met three of the six serious men in her life:

Dan Colavito, the stockbroker, who on a daily basis would promise to give up cigars, cocaine and over-the counter biotechs. He'd arrived on a Saturday night at Jackson with four broken toes, the consequence of dashing into the middle of Ocean Drive and kicking (for no apparent reason) what turned out to be Julio Iglesias' personal limousine;

Robert Nossario, the policeman, who would spend his road shifts stopping attractive young female drivers, few of whom had committed an actual traffic offense. Officer Nossario had been brought to the emergency room complaining of a severely bruised testicle, the result (or so he said) of falling on his nightstick while trying to subdue a burglary suspect;

Dr. Neal Grossberger, the young chiropractor, who would phone JoLayne at least twice an hour when she was home, and who would weep like a drunk when she'd refuse to wear the portable pager he'd bought her (baby blue, to match her hospital scrubs), and who couldn't get dressed in the morning without calling to ask what socks he should wear. Neal had come breathlessly to the hospital after consuming a suspect gooseneck clam, and had waited seven hours in the emergency room for what he'd predicted would be a virulent onset of salmonella, which never arrived.

JoLayne Lucks finally quit the hospital after meeting and marrying Lawrence Dwyer, the lawyer. Like JoLayne's other lovers, Lawrence had good qualities that were instantly obvious and bad qualities that took a bit longer to surface. It was Lawrence who'd suggested to JoLayne that they move upstate to Grange, where he could concentrate on fighting his disbarment, absent from big-city distractions such as vengeful ex-clients. Such was JoLayne's affection for Lawrence (and her determination to make the marriage work) that she'd declined to read the four loose-leaf volumes of trial transcripts from his Miami fraud conviction. She'd chosen instead to believe her husband's claim of complete innocence, which relied on a complicated theory of prosecutorial entrapment, judicial conspiracy and a careless bookkeeper whose "zeroes looked exactly like sixes!"

In Grange it had been JoLayne who'd found the old house on Cocoa and Hubbard, and JoLayne who'd put up the down payment. She had been touched and secretly proud when Lawrence took the job as a toll taker on the Beeline Expressway – until he got arrested for stealing the jumbo-sized bag of change. That evening, after boxing all her husband's clothes, jewelry and toiletries for the Salvation Army, JoLayne made a backyard bonfire of his law books, files, depositions and correspondence with the Florida Bar. After the divorce she asked Dr. Crawford if she could cut back to three days a week at the animal clinic; she said she needed time to herself.

That's when she started exploring Simmons Wood, a rolling splash of oak, pine and palmetto scrub on the outskirts of town. Once or twice a week, JoLayne would park on the main highway, hop the short wire fence and disappear into the tree line. Every green thicket was an adventure, every clearing was a sanctuary. She kept a spiral notebook of the wildlife she saw: snakes, opossums, raccoons, foxes, a bobcat, a half dozen species of tiny warblers. The baby turtles came from a creek – JoLayne didn't know the name. The creek water was the color of apricot tea, and it ran through a stand of mossy oaks down to a sandy, undercut bluff. That was where JoLayne usually stopped to rest and eat lunch. One afternoon she counted eleven little cooters perched on flat rocks and logs. She loved the way they craned their painted necks and poked out their scaly legs to catch the sunlight. When a small alligator swam by, JoLayne tossed it part of her ham sandwich, to keep its mind off the turtles.

She never thought of taking the little fellows out of the creek, until that day she'd parked on the edge of Simmons Wood and noticed a freshly painted FOR SALE sign facing the highway: 44 acres, zoned commercial. At first JoLayne thought it was a mistake. Forty-four acres couldn't be right – it sounded too small. The Wood seemed to go on forever when JoLayne was walking there. She'd driven straight back to town and stopped at the Grange courthouse to check the plat book. On paper

Simmons Wood was shaped like a kidney, which surprised JoLayne. On her hikes she'd tried not to think of the place as having boundaries, but there they were. The FOR SALE sign had been correct on the acreage, too. JoLayne had hurried home and phoned the real estate company named on the sign. The agent, a friend of JoLayne's, told her the property was grandfathered for development into a retail shopping mall. The next morning, JoLayne started taking the baby turtles from the creek. She couldn't bear the thought of them being buried alive by bulldozers. She would have tried to save the other animals, too, but almost everything else was too fast to catch, or too hard to handle. So she'd concentrated on the cooters, and from a pet-supply catalog at Dr. Crawford's she'd ordered the largest aquarium she could afford.

And when JoLayne Lucks learned she'd won the Florida lottery, she knew immediately what to do with the money: She would buy Simmons Wood and save it.

She was sitting at the kitchen table, working up the numbers on a pocket calculator, when she heard a sharp knock from the porch. She figured it must be Tom, the newspaperman, giving it one more shot. Who else would be so brash as to drop by at midnight?

The screen door opened before JoLayne got there. A stranger stepped into her living room. He was dressed like a hunter.

Krome asked, "Did you find her?"

"Yes," said Dick Turnquist.

"Where?"

"I hesitate to tell you."

"Then don't," said Krome. He lay on the sheets with his fingers interlocked behind his head. To keep the receiver at his ear he'd propped it in the fleshy pocket above his collarbone. Years of talking to editors from motel rooms had led him to perfect a supine, hands-free technique for using the telephone.

Turnquist said, "She's checked herself into rehab, Tom. Says she's hooked on antidepressants."

"That's ridiculous."

"Says she's eating Prozacs like Pez."

"I want her served."

"Tried," Turnquist said. "The judge says leave her alone. Wants a hearing to find out if she is of 'diminished mental capacity.' "

Krome cackled bitterly. Turnquist was sympathetic.

Mary Andrea Finley Krome had been resisting divorce for almost four years. She could not be assuaged with offers of excessive alimony or a cash buyout. *I don't want money, I want Tom.* No one was more baffled than Tom himself, who was acutely aware of his deficiencies as a domestic companion. The dispute had been brutally elongated because the case was filed in Brooklyn, which was, with the possible exception of Vatican City, the worst place in the world to expedite a divorce. Further complicating the procedure was the fact that the estranged Mrs. Krome was an accomplished stage actress who was capable, as she demonstrated time and again, of convincing the most hard-bitten judge of her fragile mental condition. She also had a habit of disappearing for months at a time with obscure road shows – most recently it was a musical adaptation of *The Silence of the Lambs* – which made it difficult to serve her with court summonses.

Tom Krome said, "Dick, I can't take much more."

"The competency hearing is set two weeks from tomorrow."

"How long can she drag this out?"

"You mean, what's the record?"

Krome sat up in bed. He caught the phone before it hit his lap. He put the receiver flush to his lips and said loudly: "*Does she even have a goddamn lawyer yet*?"

"I doubt it," said Dick Turnquist. "Get some rest, Tom."

"Where is she?"

"Mary Andrea?"

"Where's this rehab center?" Krome asked.

"You don't want to know."

"Oh, let me guess. Switzerland?"

"Maui."

"Fuck."

Dick Turnquist said things could be worse. Tom Krome said he didn't think so. He gave the lawyer permission to round up a couple of expert witnesses on Prozac for the upcoming hearing.

"Shouldn't be hard," Krome added. "Who wouldn't love a free trip to Hawaii?"

Two hours later, he was startled awake by the light graze of fingernails on his cheek.

*Katie*. Krome realized he'd fallen asleep without locking his door. Moron! He sprung upright.

The room was black. He smelled perfumed soap.

"Katherine?" Christ, she must've run out on her husband!

"No, it's me. Please don't turn on the light."

He felt the mattress shift as JoLayne Lucks sat beside him. In the darkness she found one of his hands and brought it to her face.

"Oh no," said Krome.

"There were two of them." Her voice was thick.

"Let me see."

"Keep it dark. Please, Tom."

He traced along her forehead, down her cheeks. One of her eyes was swollen shut – a raw knot, hot to the touch. Her top lip was split open, bloody and crusting.

"Jesus," Krome sighed. He made her lie down. "I'm calling a doctor."

"No," JoLayne said.

"And the cops."

"Don't!"

Krome felt like his chest would explode. Gently JoLayne pulled him down, so they were lying side by side.

"They got the ticket," she whispered.

It took a moment for him to understand: the lottery ticket, of course.

"They made me give it to them," she said.

"Who?"

"I never saw them before. There were two of them."

Krome heard her swallow, fighting the tears. His head was thundering – he had to do something. Get the woman to a hospital. Notify the police. Interview the neighbors in case somebody saw something, heard something . . .

But Tom Krome couldn't move. JoLayne Lucks hung on to his arm as if she were drowning. He turned on his side and carefully embraced her.

She shivered and said, "They *made* me give it to them."

"It's OK."

"No – "

"You're going to be all right. That's the important thing."

"No," she cried, "you don't understand."

A few minutes later, after her breathing settled, Krome reached over to the bedstand and turned on the lamp. JoLayne closed her eyes while he studied the cuts and bruises.

"What else did they do?" he asked.

"Punched me in the stomach. And other places."

JoLayne saw his eyes flash, his jaw tighten. He told her: "It's time to get up. We've got to do something about this."

"Damn right," she said. "That's why I came to you."

# FIVE

**They took turns** examining themselves in the rearview mirror, Chub swearing extravagantly: "Goddamn nigger bitch, goddamn we shoulda kilt her."

"Yeah, yeah," said Bodean Gazzer.

They both hurt like hell and looked worse. Chub had deep scratches down his cheeks, and his left eyelid was sliced in half – one ragged flap blinked, the other didn't. He was soiled with blood, mostly his own.

He said, "I never seen such fuckin' fingernails. You?"

Bode muttered in assent. His face and throat bore numerous purple-welted bite marks. The crazy cunt had also chewed off a substantial segment of one eyebrow, and Bode was having a time plugging the hole.

In a worn voice, he said: "Important thing is we got the ticket."

"Which I'll hang on to," Chub said, "just to be safe." And to make things even, he thought. No way was he about to let Bode Gazzer hold *both* Lotto tickets.

"Fine with me," Bode said, though it wasn't. He was in too much pain to argue. He'd never seen a woman fight so ferociously. Christ, she'd left them looking like gator puke!

Chub said, "They's animals. Total goddamn animals."

Bode agreed. "White girl'd never fuss like that. Not even for fourteen million bucks."

"I'm serious, we shoulda kilt her."

"Right. Wasn't you the one had no interest in jail time?"

"Bode, go fuck yourself."

Chub pressed a sodden bandanna to his tattered eyelid. He remembered how relieved he'd been to learn that the woman who'd hit the lottery numbers was black. What a weight off his shoulders! If she'd been white – especially a white Christian woman, elderly, like his granny – Chub knew he wouldn't have had the guts to go through with the robbery. Much less slug her in the face and the privates, as was necessary with that wild JoLayne bitch.

And a white girl, you shove a pistol in her lips and she'll do whatever she's told. Not this one.

*Where's the ticket?*

Not a word.

*Where's the goddamn ticket?*

And Bode Gazzer saying, "Hey, genius, she can't talk with a gun in her mouth."

And Chub removing it, only to have the woman spit all over the barrel. Then she'd spit on him, too.

Leaving Chub and Bode to conclude there wasn't a damn thing they could do to this person, in the way of rape or torture, to make her give up that ticket.

It had been Bode's idea to shoot one of the turtles.

Give him credit, Chub thought, for figuring out the woman's weakness.

Grabbing a baby turtle from the tank, setting it at JoLayne's feet, chuckling in anticipation as it started marching toward her bare toes.

And Chub, firing a round into the center of the turtle's shell, sending it skidding like a tiny green hockey puck across the floor, bouncing off walls and corners.

That's when the woman broke down and told them where she'd hidden the Lotto stub. Inside the piano, of all places! What a racket they'd made, getting it out of there.

But they'd done it. Now here they were, parked in the amber glow of a streetlight; taking turns with the rearview, checking how badly the nigger girl had messed them up.

Chub's multiple lacerations gave a striped effect to his long sunken face. The softest breeze stung like hot acid. He said, "I reckon I need stitches."

Bode Gazzer, shaking his head: "No doctors till we git home." Then he got a good look at Chub's seeping cuts and, recognizing a threat to his new truck's gorgeous upholstery, announced, "Band-Aids. That's what we'll get."

He made a U-turn on the highway and drove back to town at high speed. His destination was the Grab N'Go, where they would purchase first-aid supplies and also settle a piece of militia business.

Shiner's teenage years had been tolerable until his mother had gotten religion. Before then, she'd allowed him to play football without a helmet, shoot his .22 inside the city limits, go bass fishing with cherry bombs, smoke cigarets, bother the girls and skip school at least twice a week.

One night Shiner had returned home late from a Whitesnake concert in Tampa to find his mother waiting in the kitchen. She was wearing plastic thong sandals, a shortie nightgown and her ex-husband's mustard blazer, left over from his days at Century 21 – for Shiner, a jarring apparition. Wordlessly his mother had taken his hand and led him out the front door. In the moonlight they'd traipsed half a mile to the intersection where Sebring Street meets the highway. There Shiner's mother had dropped to her knees and begun to pray. Not polite praying, either; moans and wails that fractured the peacefulness of the night.

Shiner had been further dumbfounded and embarrassed to watch his mother crawl into the road and nuzzle her cheek to the grimy pavement.

"Ma," he'd said. "Cut it out."

"Don't you see Him?"

"See who? You're gonna get runned over."

"Shiner, don't you see Him?" She'd bounced to her feet. "Son, it's Jesus. Look there! Our Lord and Savior! Don't you see His face in the road?"

Shiner had walked to the spot and peered intently. "It's just an oil stain, Ma. Or maybe brake fluid."

"No! It's the face of Jesus Christ."

"OK, I'm outta here."

"Shiner!"

He'd figured the Jesus thing would blow over once she'd sobered up, but he was wrong. His mother had spent the whole next day praying at the edge of the road, and the day after as well. Some vacationing Christians gave her an ice-blue parasol and a Styrofoam cooler full of soda pop. The following Saturday, a reporter from a TV station in Orlando came to town with a camera crew. Soon the Road-Stain Jesus was regionally famous, as was

Shiner's mother. Nothing much went right for him after that.

One day he came home to find her burning his collection of heavy metal CDs, which she had taken to calling "devil wafers." She forbade him to drink beer or smoke cigarets, and threatened to withhold his five-dollar weekly allowance if he didn't stay home Friday nights and sing hymns. To get out of the house (and far away from the pilgrims who came regularly to snap his mother's picture) Shiner joined the army. In less than a month he washed out of basic training, and returned to Grange twenty pounds lighter but infinitely more sullen than when he'd left. To a depressed job market Shiner brought neither an adequate education nor practical work skills, so he wound up working the graveyard shift at the Grab N'Go, doubles on Saturday. Not much happened except for the stickups, which occurred every second or third weekend. Some nights barely a half dozen customers came through the door, leaving Shiner loads of free time to paw through the latest *Hustler* or *Swank*. He was always careful to sneak the nudie magazines back to the frozen-food aisle, the only place in the store that was blocked from the fish-eye gaze of the security camera. Shiner would dissect the magazines and arrange his favorite snatch shots across the Plexiglas lid of the ice-cream freezer – it was colder than a frog's balls back there, but he couldn't risk getting caught at the front of the store. His mother would be ruined if her only son got fired for whacking off on the job, especially on videotape. Even though Shiner was mad at his Ma, he didn't want to hurt her feelings.

At 2 a.m. on the morning of November 27, he was hunched feverishly over a *Best of Jugs* when he heard the jingle of the cat bell that was fastened to the store's front door. He tucked himself in and hurried up toward the register. It took him a moment to recognize the two customers as the same men who'd stopped by earlier in the evening for jerky and Quick Picks. Clearly they'd been in an awesome bar fight.

"The hell happened to you boys?" Shiner asked.

The short one, dressed in camo, asked for Band-Aids. The one with the ponytail requested malt liquor. Shiner obliged – finally, some excitement! He helped the men clean and bind their multiple wounds. The camouflaged one introduced himself as Bodean Gazzer, Bode for short. He said his friend was called Chub.

"Pleased to meetcha," said Shiner.

"Son, we need your help."

"OK."

Bode said, "You believe in God and family?"

Shiner hesitated. Not this again – more pilgrims!

But then Chub said, "You believe in guns?"

"The right to bear arms," Bode Gazzer clarified. "It's in the Constitution."

"Sure," said Shiner.

"You got a gun?"

"Course," Shiner answered.

"Excellent. And the white man – you believe in the white man?"

"Goddamn right!"

"Good," Bode Gazzer said.

He told Shiner to take a hard look at himself. Look at where he'd ended up, behind the counter of a miserable motherfucking convenience store, waiting on Cubans and Negroes and Jews and probably even a few Indians.

Chub said, "How old are you, boy?"

"Nineteen."

"And this is your grand plan for life?" Chub sneered as he waved a hand around the store. "This is your, whatchamacallit, your birthright?"

"Hell, no." Shiner found it difficult to meet Chub's gaze; the split eyelid was distracting and creepy. The closed portion hung pale and unblinking, a torn drape behind which the yolky bloodshot eyeball would intermittently disappear.

"I bet you didn't know," Bode Gazzer said, "your hard-earned tax dollars are payin' for a crack NATO army to invade the U.S.A."

Shiner had no clue what the camouflaged man was talking about, though he didn't let on. He'd never heard of NATO and in his entire life hadn't paid enough in income taxes to finance a box of bullets, much less a whole invasion.

Headlights in the parking lot caught his attention: a Dodge Caravan full of tourists, pulling up to the gas pumps.

Chub frowned. "Tell 'em you're closed."

"What?"

"Now!" Bode barked.

The clerk did as he was told. When he came back in the store, he found the men whispering to each other.

The one called Chub said, "We's just sayin' you'd make a fine recruit."

"For what?" Shiner asked.

Bode lowered his voice. "You got any interest in saving America from certain doom?"

"I guess. Sure." Then, after thinking about it: "Would I have to quit my job?"

Bode Gazzer nodded portentously. "Soon," he said.

Shiner listened as the men explained where America had gone wrong, allowing Washington to fall into the hands of communists, lesbians, queers and race mixers. Shiner was annoyed to learn he probably would have *owned* the Grab N'Go by now if it weren't for something called "affirmative action" – a law evidently dreamed up by the commies to help blacks take over the nation.

Pretty soon Shiner's universe began to make more sense. He was pleased to learn it wasn't all his doing, this sorry-ass excuse for a life. No, it was the result of a complicated and diabolical plot, a vast conspiracy against the ordinary working white man. All this time there'd been a heavy boot on Shiner's neck, and he hadn't even known! Out of ignorance he'd always assumed it was his own damn fault – first quitting high school, then crapping out of the army. He'd been unaware of the larger, darker forces at work, "oppressing" him and "subordinating" him. *Enslaving* him, Chub added.

Thinking about it made Shiner angry, but also oddly elated. Bode Gazzer and Chub were doing wonders for his self-esteem. They gave him a sense of worth. They gave him pride. Best of all, they gave him an excuse for his failures; someone else to blame! Shiner was invigorated with relief.

"How come you guys know so much?"

"We learned the hard way," Bode said.

Chub cut in: "You say you got a gun?"

"Yep," Shiner said. "Marlin .22."

Chub snorted. "No, boy, I said *a gun.*"

In more detail Bode Gazzer explained about the impending invasion of NATO troops from the Bahamas and their mission of imposing a totalitarian world regime on the United States. Shiner's eyes grew wide at the mention of the White Rebel Brotherhood.

"I've heard of 'em!" the young man exclaimed.

"You have?" Chub shot a beady look at Bode, who shrugged.

Shiner said, "Yeah. It's a band, right?"

"No, dickbrain, it's not a band. It's a militia," Chub said.

"A well-regulated militia," Bode added, "like they talk about in the Second Amendment."

"Oh," said Shiner. He hadn't read the first one yet.

In a low confiding tone, Bode Gazzer said the White Rebel Brotherhood was preparing for prolonged armed resistance – *heavily* armed resistance – to any forces, foreign or domestic, that posed a threat to something called the "sovereignty" of private American citizens.

Bode laid a hand on the back of Shiner's neck. With a friendly squeeze: "So what do you say?"

"Sounds like a plan."

"You want into the WRB?"

"You're kiddin'!"

Chub said, "Answer the man. Yes or no."

"Sure," Shiner chirped. "What do I gotta do?"

"A favor," Chub said. "It's easy."

"More like a assignment," said Bode Gazzer. "Think of it like a test."

Shiner's expression clouded. He hated tests, especially multiple choice. That's how he'd blown the SATs.

Chub sensed the boy's consternation. "Forget 'test,' " he told him. "It's a favor, that's all. A favor for your new white brothers."

Instantly Shiner brightened.

*

When Tom Krome saw JoLayne's living room, he told her (for the fourth time) to call the police. The house was a mother lode of evidence: fingerprints, footprints, plenty of blood to be typed. JoLayne Lucks said absolutely not, no way, and started cleaning up. Reluctantly Krome helped. There wasn't much to be done about the gutted piano, or the bullet hole in the wood floor. The blood mopped up with ammonia and water.

Afterwards, while JoLayne took a shower, Krome buried the dead turtle under a lime tree in the backyard. When he came back inside, she was standing there, bundled in her robe.

Dripping water. Shredding lettuce into the aquarium.

"Well, the others seem fine," she said quietly.

Krome led her away from the turtles. "What've you got against calling the cops?"

JoLayne pulled free, snatched up a broom. "They wouldn't believe me."

"How could they not? Look in the mirror."

"I'm not talking about the beating. I'm talking about the Lotto ticket."

"What about it?" Krome said.

"I've got no proof I ever had it. Which makes it damn hard to claim it was stolen."

She had a point. Florida's lottery computer kept track of how many winning tickets were bought and where, but there was no way of identifying the owners. That's because Lotto numbers were sold over the counter with the beer and cigarets; trying to keep track of customers' names – hundreds of thousands – would have been impossible. Consequently the lottery bureau had one intractable criterion for claiming the jackpot: possession of the winning ticket. If you didn't have it, you didn't get the money – no matter what your excuse. Over the years, once-in-a-lifetime fortunes had been lost to hungry puppies and teething infants and washing machines and toilets and house fires.

And now robbers.

Tom Krome was torn between his sympathy for JoLayne Lucks and the realization that he'd stumbled into a pretty good news story. He must have done a poor job of masking his anticipation, because JoLayne said: "I'm begging you not to write about this."

"But it'll flush the bastards out."

"And I'll never, ever get the money. Don't you see? They'd burn the damn ticket before they'd go to jail. Burn it or bury it."

Krome lifted his feet to make way for JoLayne's fierce, metronomic sweeping.

"If these guys get spooked," she went on, "that fourteen-million-dollar stub of paper is garbage. They see a newspaper headline about what they did . . . well, it's all over. Same if I go to the police."

She probably was right, Krome thought. But wouldn't the robbers assume JoLayne would report the theft? That's what most people would do.

He no longer heard the manic whisk of her sweeping. She was in the kitchen, leaning on the broom in front of the open refrigerator, letting the cool air soothe the cuts and bruises on her face.

Tom Krome said, "I'll put some ice in a bag."

JoLayne shook her head. The house was silent except for the drone of the aquarium pump and the turtles' steady munching of lettuce.

After a few moments, she said: "All right, here it is. They said they'd come back and kill me if I told anyone about the lottery ticket. They said they'd come back and shoot my babies, one at a time. Then me."

A chill went down Krome's arms.

JoLayne Lucks went on: "They told me to say my boyfriend beat me up. That's what I'm supposed to tell the doctor! 'What boyfriend?' I say. 'I don't have a boyfriend.' And the short one goes, 'You do now,' and he punches me in the tits."

Suddenly Krome couldn't breathe. He stumbled out the back door. JoLayne found him on his knees in the tomato patch. She stroked his hair and told him to take it easy. Before long, the crashing in his ears faded away. She brought him a glass of cold juice, and they sat together on an iron bench facing a birdbath.

In a raw voice, Krome said: "You can identify these guys?"

"Of course."

"They belong in jail."

"Tom – "

"Here's what you do: Go to the cops and the lottery bureau, and tell them everything that happened. About the robbery and the death threats. Give a statement, file a report. And then let the authorities wait for these bastards – "

"No."

"Listen. These guys will surface soon. They've only got six months to claim that jackpot."

"Tom, that's what I'm trying to tell you. *I* don't have six months. I need the money now."

Krome looked at her. "What in the world for?"

"I just do."

"Forget the money – "

"I can't."

"But these guys are monsters. They're going to hurt someone else the way they hurt you. Maybe worse."

"Not necessarily," JoLayne said. "Not if we stop them first."

The incredible part was, she meant it. Krome would have laughed except he didn't want to hurt her feelings.

JoLayne, pinching his right knee: "We could do it. You and me, we could find them."

"To borrow an old expression: No fucking way."

"They're driving a bright-red pickup."

"I don't care if they're in the starship *Enterprise*."

"Tom, please."

He held her hands. "In my business, fear is a sane and very healthy emotion. That's because death and disaster aren't abstractions. They're as goddamn real as real can be."

"Suppose I told you why I need the money. Would it make a difference?"

"JoLayne, I don't think so." It tore him up to look at her, at what they'd done.

She pulled away and walked to the aquarium. Krome could hear her talking – to herself, to the turtles, or maybe to the men who'd beaten her so badly.

"I'm truly sorry," he said.

When JoLayne turned around, she didn't appear upset. "Just think," she said mischievously, "if I get that lottery ticket back. Think of the fantastic story you'll be missing."

Tom Krome smiled. "You're ruthless, you know that?"

"I'm also right. Please help me find them."

He said, "I've got a better idea. May I borrow the phone?"

Shiner awoke to the sight of his mother hovering over him. She was dressed in the white bridal gown that she always wore on Mondays to the Road-Stain Jesus. The outfit was a smash with the Christian tourists – it wasn't uncommon for Shiner's Ma to come home with two hundred dollars in cash from donations. Monday was her best day of the week, pilgrimwise.

Now she told Shiner to get his fat ass downstairs. There was company waiting in the Florida room.

"And I'm already an hour late," she said, cuffing him so hard that he retreated under the blanket.

He listened to the rustle of the wedding dress as she hurried downstairs. Then came the slam of the front door.

Shiner pulled on some jeans and went to see who was waiting. The woman he recognized, with apprehension, as JoLayne Lucks. The man he didn't know.

JoLayne said, "Sorry to wake you, but it's sort of an emergency."

She introduced her friend as Tom, who shook Shiner's hand and said, "The day guy at the store gave me your address. Said you wouldn't mind."

Shiner nodded absently. He wasn't a young man who had an easy time putting two and two together, but he quickly made the connection between JoLayne's battered face and those of his new white rebel brothers, Chub and Bodean. Out of simple courtesy Shiner probably should've asked JoLayne who popped her in the kisser, but he didn't trust himself with the question; didn't trust himself to keep a straight face.

The man named Tom sat next to Shiner on the divan. He wasn't dressed like a cop, but Shiner resolved to be careful anyway.

JoLayne said, "I've got a big problem. You remember the Lotto ticket I bought Saturday afternoon at the store? Well, I've lost it. Don't ask me how, Lord, it's a long story. The point is, you're the only one besides me who knows I bought it. You're my only witness."

Shiner was a mumbler when he got nervous. "Saturday?"

He didn't look at JoLayne Lucks but instead kept his eyes on the folds of his belly, which still bore wrinkle marks from the bedsheets.

Finally he said: "I don't remember seein' you Saturday."

JoLayne couldn't hear the words, Shiner was speaking so low. "What?" she said.

"I don't remember seein' you in the store Saturday. Sure it wasn't last week?" Shiner began fiddling with the curly black hairs around his navel.

JoLayne came over and lifted his chin. "Look at me."

He flinched at the prospect of her blue fingernails in his throat.

She said, "Every Saturday I play the same numbers. Every Saturday I come to the Grab N'Go and buy my ticket. You know what happened this time, don't you? You know I won."

Shiner pushed her hand away. "Maybe you come in Saturday, maybe you didn't. Anyhow, I don't look at the numbers."

JoLayne Lucks stepped back. She seemed quite angry.

The man named Tom spoke up: "Son, surely you know that one of the two winning Lotto tickets came from your store."

"Yeah, I do. Tallahassee phoned up about it."

"Well, if Miss Lucks didn't have the numbers, who did?"

Shiner licked his lips and thought: Damn. This high-stakes lying was harder than he figured it would be. But a blood oath was a blood oath.

He said, "There was a fella came in late off the highway. Got a Quick Pick and a six-pack of Bud Lights."

"Wait, wait – you're telling me," JoLayne protested, her voice rising, "you're telling me some . . . *stranger* bought the winning ticket."

"Ma'am, I don't honestly know who's got what. I just run the machine, I don't pay no 'tention to the damn numbers."

"Shiner, you know it was my ticket. Why are you lying? Why?"

"I ain't." It came out as mush.

The man named Tom asked: "This mystery man who came in late and bought the Quick Pick – who was he?"

Shiner slid his hands under his butt, to conceal the tremor. He said, "I never seen him before. Just some tall skinny guy with a ponytail."

"Oh no." JoLayne turned to her friend. "What do you say now, Mister No Fucking Way?" Then she ran out of the house.

The man named Tom didn't leave right away, which made Shiner jittery. Later he watched from the window as the man put an arm around JoLayne Lucks when they walked off, down Sebring Street.

Shiner sucked on a cigaret and recalled what Bode and Chub had told him: *Your word against hers, son.*

So it was done. And no fuckups!

Presto, Shiner thought. I'm in the brotherhood.

But for the rest of the morning he couldn't stop thinking about what JoLayne's friend had told him before walking out.

*We'll be talking again, you and I.*

Like hell, Shiner thought. He'll have to find me first.

# SIX

**Mary Andrea Finley** Krome wasn't addicted to Prozac or anything else. Nor was she chronically depressed, psychologically unstable, schizoid or suicidal.

She was, however, stubborn. And it was her very strong desire to not be a divorced woman.

Her marriage to Tom Krome wasn't ideal; in fact, it had become more or less an empty sketch. Yet that was a tradition among Finley women, hooking up with handsome, self-absorbed men who quickly lost interest in them.

They'd met in Manhattan, in a coffee shop near Radio City. Mary Andrea had initiated contact after noticing that the intent, good-looking man at the end of the counter was reading a biography of Ibsen. What Mary Andrea hadn't known was that the book had been forced upon Tom Krome by a young woman he was dating (a drama major at NYU), and that he would've much rather been delving into the complete life story of Moose Skowron. Nonetheless, Krome was pleased when the auburn-haired stranger moved three stools closer and said she'd once read for a small part in *A Doll's House*.

The attraction was instant, though more physical than either of them cared to admit. At the time, Tom Krome was working on a newspaper investigation of Medicaid bills. He was on the trail of a crooked radiologist who spent his Tuesday mornings playing squash at the Downtown Athletic Club instead of reading myelograms, as he'd claimed, while billing the government thousands of dollars. Mary Andrea Finley was auditioning for the role of the restless farm wife in a Sam Shepard play.

She and Tom dated for five weeks and then got married at a Catholic church in Park Slope. After that they didn't see each other much, which meant it took longer to discover they had nothing in common. Tom's reporting job kept him busy all day, while Mary Andrea's stage work took care of the nights and weekends. When they managed to arrange time together, they had sex as often as possible. It was one activity in which they were synchronized in all aspects. Overdoing it spared them from having to listen to each other chatter on about their respective careers, in which neither partner honestly held much interest.

Mary Andrea had barely noticed things coming apart. The way she remembered it, one day Tom just walked in with a sad face and asked for a divorce.

Her reply: "Don't be ridiculous. In five hundred years there's never been a divorce in the Finley family."

"That," Tom had said, "explains all the psychos."

Mary Andrea related this conversation to her counselor at the Mona Pacifica Mineral Spa and Residential Treatment Center in Maui, a facility highly recommended by several of her bicoastal actor friends. When the counselor asked Mary Andrea if she and her husband had ever been wildly happy, she said yes, for about six months.

"Maybe seven," she added. "Then we reached a plateau. That's normal, isn't it, for young couples? The problem is, Tom's not a 'plateau' type of personality. He's got to be either going up, or going down. Climbing, or falling."

The counselor said, "I get the picture."

"Now he has lawyers and process servers chasing me. It's very inconsiderate." Mary Andrea was a proud person.

"Do you have reason to believe he'd change his mind about the marriage?"

"Who's trying to change his mind? I just want him to forget this absurd idea of a divorce."

The counselor looked bemused. Mary Andrea went on to offer the view that divorce as an institution was becoming obsolete. "Superfluous. Unnecessary," she added.

"It's getting late," said the counselor. "Would you like something to help you sleep?"

"Look at Shirley MacLaine. She didn't live with her husband for, what, thirty years? Most people didn't even know she was married. That's the way to handle it."

Mary Andrea's theory was that divorce left a person exposed and vulnerable, while remaining married – even if you didn't stay with your spouse – provided a cone of protection.

"Nobody else can get their meat hooks in you," she elaborated. "Legally speaking."

The counselor said, "I'd never thought of it that way."

"OK, it's just a silly piece of paper. But don't think of it as a trap, think of it as a bulletproof shield," said Mary Andrea Finley Krome. "Shirley's got the right idea. Could you ask them to bring me a cup of Earl Grey?"

"You're feeling better?"

"Much. I'll be out of your hair in a day or two."

"No hurry. You're here to rest."

"With a wedge of lemon," Mary Andrea said. "Please."

Sinclair scalded his tongue on the coffee, a gulp being his reflex to the sight of Tom Krome crossing the newsroom. Pressing a creased handkerchief to his mouth, Sinclair rose to greet his star reporter with a spurious heartiness that was transparent to all who witnessed it.

"Long time no see!" Sinclair gushed. "You're lookin' good, big guy."

Krome motioned toward the editor's private office. "We should talk," he said.

"Yes, yes, I heard."

When they were alone behind the glass, Sinclair said, "Joan and Roddy called this morning. I guess the news is all over Grange."

Krome figured as much. He said, "I'll need a week or so."

Sinclair frowned. "For what, Tom?"

"For the reporting." Krome eyed him coldly. He'd anticipated this reaction, knowing too well Sinclair's unspoken credo: *Big stories, big problems*.

The editor rocked back in a contrived pose of rumination. "I don't think we're looking at a feature takeout anymore, do you?"

Krome was amused at the collective "we." The newspaper sent its midlevel editors to a management school that taught them, among other insipid tricks, to employ the "we" during disagreements with staff. The theory was that a plural pronoun subliminally brought corporate muscle to an argument.

Sinclair went on: "I think we're looking at a ten-inch daily, max, for the city side. ROBBERS STEAL LOTTO TICKET, UNLUCKY LADY LAMENTS."

Krome leaned forward. "If that headline ever appears in *The Register*, I will personally come to your home and cut out your lungs with a trenching knife."

Sinclair wondered if it would be smart to leave the door open, in case he had to make a run for it.

"No daily story," Krome said. "The woman isn't making any public statements. She hasn't even filed a police report."

"But you've talked to her?"

"Yes, but not on the record."

Sinclair, fortifying himself with another swig of coffee: "Then I really don't see a story. Without quotes from her or the cops, I don't see it."

"You will. Give me some time."

"Know what Roddy and Joan said? The rumor is, the Lucks girl somehow lost her Lotto ticket and then made up this bit about the robbers. You know, for sympathy."

Krome said, "With all due respect to Roddy and Joan, they're positively full of shit."

Sinclair felt a foolish impulse to defend his sister and her husband, but it passed quickly. "Tom, you know how short-staffed we are. A week sounds more like an investigation than a simple feature, wouldn't you say?"

"It's a story, period. A good story, if *we* are patient."

Sinclair's policy on sarcasm was to ignore it. He said, "Until this lady wants to talk to the cops, there's not much we can do. Maybe the lottery ticket got stolen, maybe it didn't. Maybe she never had it to begin with – these big jackpots tend to bring out the kooks."

"Tell me about it."

"We've got other stories for you, Tom."

Krome rubbed his eyes. He thought about Alaska, about bears batting rainbows in the river.

And he heard Sinclair saying, "They're teaching a course on bachelorhood out at the community college. 'Bachelorhood in the Nineties.' I think it could be a winner."

Krome, numb with disdain: "I'm not a bachelor yet. And I won't be for some time, according to my lawyer."

"A minor detail. Write around it, Tom. You're living a single life, that's the point."

"Yes. A single life."

"Why don't you sit in on the classes? This week they're doing sewing – it could be very cute, Tom. First person, of course."

"Sewing for bachelors."

"Sure," said Sinclair.

Krome sighed to himself. "Cute" again. Sinclair knew how Krome felt about cute. He'd rather write obits. He'd rather cover the fucking weather. He'd rather have railroad spikes hammered into his nostrils.

With unwarranted hopefulness, Sinclair awaited Krome's answer. Which was:

"I'll call you from the road."

Sinclair sagged. "No, Tom, I'm sorry."

"You're saying I'm off the story?"

"I'm saying there *is* no story right now. Until we get a police report or a statement from this Lucks woman, there's nothing to put in the paper but gossip."

Spoken like a true newshound, Krome thought. A regular Ben Bradlee.

He said, "Give me a week."

"I can't." Sinclair was fidgeting, tidying the stack of

pink phone messages on his desk. "I wish I could do it but I can't."

Tom Krome yawned. "Then I suppose I'll have to quit."

Sinclair stiffened. "That isn't funny."

"Finally, we agree." Krome saluted informally, then strolled out the door.

When he got home, he saw that somebody had shot all the windows out of his house with a large-caliber weapon. Tacked to the door was a note from Katie:

"I'm sorry, Tom, it's all my fault."

By the time she got there, an hour later, he had most of the glass swept up. She came up the steps and handed him a check for $500. She said, "Honestly, I'm so ashamed."

"All this because I didn't call?"

"Sort of."

Krome expected to be angrier about the broken windows, but upon reflection he considered it a personal milestone of sorts: the first time that a sexual relationship had resulted in a major insurance claim. Krome wondered if he'd finally entered the netherworld of white-trash romance.

He said to Katie: "Come on in."

"No, Tommy, we can't stay here. It's not safe."

"But the breeze is nice, no?"

"Follow me." She turned and trotted toward her car – darn good speed, for a person in sandals. On the interstate she twice nearly lost him in traffic. They ended up at a Mexican restaurant near the dog track. Katie settled covertly in a corner booth. Krome ordered beers and *fajitas* for both of them.

She said, "I owe you an explanation."

"Wild guess: You told Art."

"Yes, Tom."

"May I ask why?"

"I was sad because you didn't call like you promised. And then the sadness turned to guilt – lying in bed next to this man, my husband, and me keeping this awful secret."

"But Art's been banging his secretaries for years."

Katie said, "It's not the same thing."

"Apparently not."

"Plus two wrongs don't make a right."

Krome backed off; he was a pro when it came to guilt. He asked Katie: "What kind of gun did Art use?"

"Oh, he didn't do it himself. He got his law clerk to do it."

"To shoot out my windows?"

"I'm so sorry," Katie said again.

The beers arrived. Krome drank while Katie explained that her husband, the judge, had turned out to be quite the jealous maniac.

"Much to my surprise," she added.

"I can't believe he paid his clerk to do a drive-by on my house."

"Oh, he didn't pay him. That would be a crime – Art is very, very careful when it comes to the law. The young man did it as a favor, more or less. To make points with the boss, that's my impression."

"Want to know mine?"

"Tom, I couldn't sleep Sunday night. I had to come clean with Art."

"And I'm sure he promptly came clean with you."

"He will," Katie said. "In the meantime, you might want to lay low. I believe he intends to have you killed."

The *fajitas* arrived and Tom Krome dug in. Katie remarked upon how well he was taking the news. Krome agreed; he was exceptionally calm. The act of quitting the newspaper had infused him with a strange and reckless serenity. Krome said: "What exactly did you tell Art? I'm just curious."

"Everything," Katie replied. "Every detail. That's the nature of a true confession."

"I see."

"What I did, I got up about three in the morning and made a complete list, starting with the first time. In your car."

Krome reached for a tortilla chip. "You mean . . ."

"The blow job, yes. And every time afterwards. Even when I didn't come."

"And you put that on your list? All the details?" He picked up another chip and scooped a trench in the salsa.

Katie said, "I gave it to him first thing yesterday morning, before he went to work. And, Tom, I felt better right away."

"I'm so glad." Krome, trying to recall how many times he and Katie had made love in the two weeks they'd known each other; imagining how the tally would look on paper. He envisioned it as a line score in tiny agate type, the same as on the sports page.

She said, "I almost forgot, did you take that picture for me? Of the weeping Mother Mary?"

"Not yet, but I will."

"No rush," Katie said.

"It's OK. I'm going back tonight."

"Must be some story."

"It's all relative, Katie. Not to change the subject, but you mentioned something about Art intending to kill me."

"No, to *have* you killed."

"Right. Of course. You're sure he wasn't just talking?"

"Possibly. But he's pretty mad."

"Did he hurt you?" Krome asked. "Would he?"

"Never." Katie seemed amused by the question. "If you want to know the truth, I think it turned him on."

"The confession."

"Yes. Like suddenly he realized what he was missing."

Krome said, "How about that."

He paid the check. Outside in the parking lot, Katie touched his arm and asked him to let her know, please, if the $500 wasn't enough to replace the busted windows. Krome told her not to worry about it.

Then she said, "Tommy, we can't see each other anymore."

"I agree. It's wrong."

The concept seemed to cheer her. "I'm glad to hear you say that."

Judging from the note of triumph in her voice, Katie believed that by sleeping with Tom Krome and then confessing to her low-life cheating husband, she'd helped all three of them become better human beings. Their consciences had been stirred and elevated. They'd all learned a lesson. They'd all grown spiritually.

Krome graciously chose not to deflate this preposterous notion. He kissed Katie on the cheek and told her goodbye.

*

Demencio took the stool next to Dominick Amador at the counter at Hardee's. Dominick was going through his morning ritual of spooning Crisco into a pair of gray gym socks. The socks went over Dominick's hands, to cover his phony stigmata. The Crisco served to keep the wounds moist and to prevent scabbing – Dominick's livelihood depended on the holes in his palms appearing raw and fresh, as if recently nailed to a cross. Should the wounds ever heal, he'd be ruined.

He said to Demencio: "I got a big favor to ask."

"So what else is new?"

Dominick said, "Geez, whatsa matter with you today?"

"That dippy woman lost the Lotto ticket. I guess you didn't hear."

Demencio held the gym socks open while Dominick inserted his hands. One of the socks had a fray in the toe, through which oozed a white dollop of shortening.

Dominick flexed his fingers and said, "That's much better. Thanks."

"Fourteen million dollars down the shitter," Demencio grumbled.

"I heard it was a robbery."

"Gimme a break."

"Hey, everybody in town knew she had the ticket."

"But who's got the balls," Demencio said, "to do something like that? Seriously, Dom."

"You got a point." The only robberies to occur in Grange were the holdups committed by itinerant crooks on their way to or from Miami.

Demencio said: "My guess? She lost the ticket some stupid way, then cooked up the robbery story so people wouldn't make fun of her."

"They say she's a strange one."

" 'Scattered' is the word."

"Scattered," said Dominick. He was eating a jelly doughnut, the sugar dust sticking to the socks on his hands.

Demencio told him about JoLayne's turtles. "Must be a hundred of the damn things inside her house. Tell me that's normal."

Dominick's eyebrows crinkled in concentration. He said, "Is there turtles in the Old Testament?"

"How the hell should I know." Just because Demencio owned a weeping Virgin didn't mean he'd memorized the whole Bible, or even finished it. Some of these Corinthians were rough sledding.

Dominick said, "What I'm thinking, maybe she's putting some type of exhibit together. You know, for the tourists. Except I can't remember no turtles in the Good Book. There's lambs and fishes – and a big serpent, of course."

Demencio's pancakes arrived. Drenching the plate in syrup, he said, "Just forget it."

"But didn't Noah have turtles? He had two of everything."

"Right. JoLayne, she's building a fuckin' ark. That explains it." Demencio irritably attacked his breakfast. The only reason he'd mentioned the damn turtles was to show how flaky JoLayne Lucks could be; the sort of space cadet who could misplace a $14 million lottery ticket.

Of all the people to win! Demencio fumed. It might be a thousand years before anyone in Grange hit the jackpot again.

Dominick Amador said, "Why you so pissed – it

wasn't your money." Dominick didn't know JoLayne very well, but she'd always been nice to his cat, Rex. The cat suffered from an unsavory gum disorder that required biweekly visits to the veterinarian. JoLayne was the only person besides Dominick's daughter who could manage Rex without the custom-tailored kitty strait-jacket.

"Don't you see," Demencio said. "All of us woulda cashed in big – you, me, the whole town. The story we'd put out, think about this: JoLayne won the Lotto because she lived in a holy place. Maybe she prayed at my weeping Mary, or maybe she got touched by your crucified hands. Word got around, everybody who played the numbers would come to Grange for a blessing."

Dominick hadn't thought of that: a boom for the blessing trade.

"The best part," Demencio went on, "it wouldn't be only Christians coming, it'd be anybody who does the Lotto. Jewish people, Buddhists, Hawaiians . . . it wouldn't matter. A gambler's a gambler – all they care about is luck."

"A gold mine," Dominick agreed. With a sleeve he wiped a smear of jelly from his chin.

"And now it's all turned to shit," said Demencio. In disgust he tossed his fork on the plate. How could anybody lose a $14 million lottery ticket? Lucy Fucking Ricardo couldn't lose a $14 million lottery ticket.

Dominick said, "There's more to what happened than we been told, I guarantee."

"Yeah, yeah. Maybe it was Martians. Maybe a UFO flew down in the middle of the night – "

"No, but I heard she was all beat up."

"I'm not surprised," Demencio said. "My theory?

She's so mad at herself for losing the ticket, she takes a baseball bat and clobbers herself in the goddamn head. That's what *I'd* do if I fucked up that bad."

Dominick Amador said, "I don't know," and went back to eviscerating doughnuts. After a few minutes, when it seemed Demencio had cooled off, Dominick asked another favor.

"It's regarding my feet," he said.

"The answer is no."

"I need somebody to drill 'em."

"Then talk to your wife."

"Please," said Dominick. "I got the shop all set up."

Demencio laid six dollars on the counter and slid off the stool. "Drill your own feet," he told Dominick. "I ain't in the mood."

JoLayne Lucks knew what Dr. Crawford thought:

Finally the girl gets a boyfriend, and the boyfriend beats her to a pulp.

"Please don't stare. I know I'm a sight," JoLayne said.

"You want to tell me about it?"

"Truly? No." That would clinch it with Doc Crawford, the fact that she wouldn't talk. So she added: "It's not what you think."

Dr. Crawford said: "Hold still, you little shit."

He was addressing Mickey, the Welsh corgi on the examining table. JoLayne was doing her best to control the dog but it was squirming like a worm on a griddle. The little ones always were the hardest to handle – cockers, poodles, Pomeranians – and the nastiest, too. Biters, every damn one. Give me a 125-pound Dobie any day, JoLayne thought.

To Mickey the corgi, she muttered: "Be good, baby." Whereupon Mickey sank his yellow fangs into her thumb and did not let go. As painful as it was, the attachment enabled JoLayne Lucks to control the dog's head, giving Dr. Crawford a clear shot at the vaccination site. The instant Mickey felt the needle, he released his grip on JoLayne. Dr. Crawford commended her for not losing her temper.

JoLayne said, "Why take it personally. You'd bite, too, if you had a dog's brain. I've seen men with no such excuse do worse things."

Dr. Crawford buttered her thumb with Betadine. JoLayne observed that it looked like steak sauce.

"You want some on that lip?" the doctor asked.

She shook her head, bracing for the next question. *How did that happen?* But all he said was: "A couple sutures wouldn't be a bad idea, either."

"Oh, that's not necessary."

"You don't trust me."

"Nope." With her free hand she patted the bald spot on Doc Crawford's head. "I'll be OK," she told him.

The remainder of JoLayne's workday: cat (Daisy), three kittens (unnamed), German shepherd (Kaiser), parrot (Polly), cat (Spike), beagle (Bilko), Labrador retriever (Contessa), four Labrador puppies (unnamed), and one rhinoceros iguana (Keith). JoLayne received no more bites or scratches, although the iguana relieved itself copiously on her lab coat.

Arriving home, she recognized Tom Krome's blue Honda parked in the driveway. He was sitting in the swing on the porch. JoLayne sat down next to him and pushed off. With a squeak the swing started to move.

JoLayne said, "I guess we've got a deal."

"Yep."

"What'd your boss say?"

"He said, 'Great story, Tom! Go to it!' "

"Really."

"His exact words. Hey, what happened to your coat?"

"Iguana pee. Now ask about my thumb."

"Lemme see."

JoLayne extended her hand. Krome studied the bite mark with mock seriousness.

"Grizzly!" he said.

She smiled. Boy, did it feel good, his touch. Strong and gentle and all that stuff. Which was how it always started, with a warm dumb tingle.

JoLayne hopped out of the swing and said: "We've got an hour before sunset. I want to show you something."

When they got to Simmons Wood, she pointed out the FOR SALE sign. "That's why I can't wait six months for these jerkoffs to get caught. Any day, somebody's going to come along and buy this place."

Tom Krome followed her over the fence, through the pine and palmettos. She stopped to point out bobcat scat, deer tracks and a red-shouldered hawk in the treetops.

"Forty-four acres," JoLayne said.

She was whispering, so Krome whispered back. "How much do they want for it?"

"Three million and change," she said.

Krome asked about the zoning.

"Retail," JoLayne answered, with a grimace.

They stopped on the sandy bluff overlooking the creek. JoLayne sat down and crossed her legs. "A shopping mall and a parking lot," she said, "just like in the Joni Mitchell song."

Tom Krome felt he should be writing down everything she said. His notebook nagged at him from the back pocket of his jeans. As if he still had a newspaper job.

JoLayne, pointing at the tea-colored ribbon of water: "That's where the cooters come from. They're off the logs now, but you should be here when the sun's high."

Still whispering, like she was in church. Which he supposed it was, in a way.

"What do you make of my plan?"

Krome said, "I think it's fantastic."

"You're making fun."

"Not at all – "

"Oh yes. You think I'm nuts." She propped her chin in her hands. "OK, smart guy, what would *you* do with the money?"

Krome started to answer but JoLayne motioned for him to hush. A deer was at the creek; a doe, drinking. They watched it until darkness fell, then they quietly made their way back to the highway, Krome following the whiteness of JoLayne's lab coat weaving through the trees and scrub.

Back at the house, she disappeared into the bedroom to change clothes and check her phone messages. When she came out, he was standing at the aquarium, watching the baby turtles.

"Treasure this," she said. "Chase Bank called. The assholes have already charged a truckload of stuff on my Visa."

Krome spun around. "You didn't tell me they got your credit card."

JoLayne reached for the kitchen phone. "I've got to cancel that number."

Krome grabbed her arm. "No, don't. This is wonderful news: They've got your Visa, plus they seem to be total morons."

"Yeah, I couldn't be happier."

"You wanted to find them, right? Now we've got a trail."

JoLayne was intrigued. She sat down at the kitchen table and opened a box of Goldfish crackers. The salt stung the cut on her lip, made her eyes water.

Krome said: "Here's what you do. Call the bank and find out exactly where the card's been used. Tell them you loaned it to your brother, uncle, something like that. But don't cancel it, JoLayne. Not until we know where these guys are headed."

She did what he told her. The Chase Bank people couldn't have been nicer. She took down the information and handed it to Krome, who said: "Wow."

"No kidding, wow."

"They spent twenty-three hundred dollars at a *gun show*?"

"And two hundred sixty at a Hooters," JoLayne said. "I'm not sure which is scarier."

The gun show was at the War Memorial Auditorium in Fort Lauderdale, the Hooters was in Coconut Grove. The robbers seemed to be traveling south.

"Get packed," Tom Krome said.

"Lord, I forgot about the turtles. You know how hungry they get."

"They're *not* coming with us."

"Course not," JoLayne said.

They stopped at the ATM so she could get some cash.

Back in the car, she popped a handful of Goldfish and said: "Drive like the wind, partner. My Visa maxes out at three thousand bucks."

"Then let's pay it off. Put a check in the mail first thing tomorrow – I want these boys to go hog wild."

Sportively JoLayne grabbed a handful of Krome's shirt. "Tom, I've got exactly four hundred and thirty-two dollars left in my checking."

"Relax," he told her. Then, with a sideways glance: "It's time you started thinking like a millionaire."

# SEVEN

**Chub's real name** was Onus Dean Gillespie. The youngest of seven children, he was born to Moira Gillespie when she was forty-seven, her maternal stirrings long dormant. Onus's father, Greve, was a blunt-spoken man who regularly reminded the boy that the arc of his life had begun with a faulty diaphragm, and that his appearance in Mrs. Gillespie's womb had been as welcome as "a cockroach on a wedding cake."

Nonetheless, Onus was neither beaten nor deprived as a child. Greve Gillespie made good money as a timber man in northern Georgia and was generous with his family. They lived in a large house with a basketball hoop in the driveway, a secondhand ski boat on a trailer in the garage, and a deluxe set of *World Book* encyclopedias in the basement. All of Onus's siblings made it to Georgia State University, and Onus himself could have gone there, too, had he not by age fifteen already chosen a life of sloth, inebriation and illiteracy.

He moved out of his parents' home and took up with a bad crowd. He got a job in the photo department of a drugstore, where he earned extra money sorting through customers' negatives, swiping the racy ones and peddling the prints to horny kids at the high school. (Even after entering adulthood, Onus Gillespie remained amazed there were women in the world who'd allow their boyfriends or husbands to take pictures of them topless. He dreamed of meeting such a girl, but so far it hadn't happened.)

When he was twenty-four, Onus accidentally landed a well-paying job at a home furnishings warehouse. Thanks to an aggressive union local, he managed to remain employed for six years despite a wretched attendance record, exhaustively documented incompetence and a perilous affinity for carpet glue. Stoned to the gills, Onus one day crashed a fork-lift into a Snapple machine, a low-speed mishap that he parlayed into an exorbitant claim for worker's compensation.

His extended "convalescence" involved many drunken fishing and hunting excursions. One morning Onus was observed emerging from the woods with a prostitute on one arm and a dead bear cub slung over his shoulders. The man watching him was an investigator for an insurance company, which was able to argue convincingly that Mr. Onus Gillespie was not injured in the least. Only then was he fired from the warehouse. He chose not to appeal.

Moira and Greve wrote one last check to their errant spawn, then disowned him. Onus needed no special encouragement to leave the state. In addition to the pending felony indictments for insurance fraud and game poaching, Onus had received a rather unfriendly letter from the Internal Revenue Service, inquiring why he'd never in his adult life bothered to file a tax return. To emphasize its concern, the IRS sent a flatbed and two disagreeable men to confiscate Onus's customized Ford Econoline van. It was easy to spot. An elaborate mural on the side of the vehicle depicted Kim Basinger as a nude mermaid, riding a narwhal. Onus had fallen for the beautiful Georgia actress in the movie *9½ Weeks* and conceived the mural as a love tribute.

It was the seizure of his beloved Econoline that turned Onus Gillespie bitterly against the U.S. government (although he was similarly resentful toward his parents, who not only had refused to pay his tax lien but had also tipped off the IRS agents about where to find the van). Before bolting, Onus burned his driver's license and renounced the family name. He began calling himself Chub (which is how his brothers and sisters had referred to him when he was younger and had something of a weight problem). He couldn't make up his mind on a new surname, so he decided to wait until something good popped into his head. He hitchhiked to Miami with only the clothes on his back, seventeen dollars in his wallet and, in a zippered pocket, his only tangible asset – the disabled-parking permit he'd scammed off the company doctor for the workmen's comp claim.

Pure good fortune and a round of free beers led to a friendship with an amateur forger, who entrusted Chub with his printing equipment while he went off to state prison. In no time, Chub was cranking out fake handicapped stickers and selling them for cash to local motorists. His favorite hangout was Miami's federal courthouse, infamous for its dearth of parking spaces. Among Chub's satisfied customers were stenographers, bondsmen, drug lawyers and even a U.S. magistrate or two. Soon his reputation grew, and he became known throughout the county as a reliable supplier of bootleg wheelchair emblems.

That's why he was sought out by Bodean Gazzer, who'd been having a terrible time trying to park downtown. Having recently purchased the Dodge Ram, Bode thought it was foolhardy to leave it three or four blocks away while he went to wrestle the bureaucracy of the corrections department. Those particular neighborhoods weren't such lovely places to go for a stroll; wall-to-wall Haitians and Cubans! He had nightmare visions of his gorgeous new truck stripped to its axles.

Chub felt an instant kinship with Bode, whose global theories and braided explanations struck a comforting chord. For instance, Chub had been stung when his parents scorned him as a tax cheat, but Bode Gazzer made him feel better by enumerating the many sound reasons why no full-blooded white American male should give a nickel to the Infernal Revenue. Chub brightened to learn that what he'd initially regarded as ducking a debt was, in fact, an act of legitimate civil protest.

"Like the Boston Tea Party," Bode had said, invoking his favorite historical reference. "Those boys were against taxation without representation, and that's what you're fightin', too. The white man has lost his voice in this government, so why should he foot the bill?"

It sounded good to Chub. Damn good. And Bode Gazzer was full of such nimble rationalizations.

Some of Chub's acquaintances, especially the war veterans, disapproved of his handicapped-parking racket. Not Bode. "Think about it," he'd said to Chub. "How many wheelchair people you actually see? And look how many thousands of parkin' spaces they got. It don't add up, unless . . ."

" 'Less what?"

"Unless those parkin' spots ain't really for the

handicaps," Bode had surmised darkly. "What color's them wheelchair permits?"

"Blue."

"Hmmm-mmm. And what color is the helmets worn by United Nations troops?"

"Fuck if I know. Blue?"

"Yessir!" Bode Gazzer had shaken Chub by the arm. "Don't you see, boy? There's an invasion, who you think's gonna be parked in them blue wheelchair spaces? Soldiers, that's who. UN soldiers!"

"Jesus Willy Christ."

"So in my estimation you're doin' the country a tremendous goddamn service with those imitation handicap stickers. Every one you sell means one less parkin' spot for the enemy. That's how I think of it."

And that's how Chub intended to think of it, too. He wasn't a crook, he was a patriot! Life was getting better and better.

And now here he was, on the road with his best buddy.

Soon to be multimillionaires.

Spending a long leisurely afternoon at Hooters, eating barbecue chicken wings and slugging down Coronas.

Flirting with the waitresses in them shiny orange shorts, sweet God Almighty, some of the finest young legs Chub had ever seen. And asses shaped just like Golden Delicious apples.

And outside: a pickup truck full of guns.

"A toast," said Bode Gazzer, lifting his mug. "To America."

"Amen!" Chub burped.

"This here is what it's all about."

"For sure."

Said Bode: “No such thing as too much pussy or too much firepower. That’s a fact.”

They were shitfaced by the time the check came. With a foamy grin, Bode slapped the stolen credit card on the table. Chub vaguely recalled they were supposed to ditch the nigger woman’s Visa after the gun show, where they’d used it to purchase a TEC-9, a Cobray M-11, a used AR-15, a canister of pepper spray and several boxes of ammo.

Chub preferred gun shows over gun stores because, thanks to the National Rifle Association, gun shows remained exempt from practically every state and federal firearms regulation. It had been Chub’s idea to browse at the one in Fort Lauderdale. However, he’d had strong reservations about paying for such flashy weapons with a stolen credit card, which he thought was risky to the point of stupid.

Again Bode Gazzer had put his friend’s mind at ease. He’d explained to Chub that many gun-show dealers were actually undercover ATF agents, and that the use of a phony bank card would send the bully law-men on a frantic futile search for “J. L. Lucks” and his newly purchased arsenal.

“So they’re off on a goose chase,” Bode had said, “instead of hassling law-abiding Americans all day long.”

His second reason for using a stolen Visa was more pragmatic than political: They had no cash. But Bode had agreed with Chub that they ought to throw away the credit card after the gun show, in case the Chase Bank started checking up.

Chub was about to remind his partner of that plan

when an exceptionally long-legged waitress appeared and whisked the Visa card off the table.

Bode rubbed his hands together, reverently. "*That* is what we're fightin' for, my friend. Anytime you start to doubt our cause, think a that young sweet thing and the 'Merica she deserves."

"A-fucking-men," Chub said with a bleary snort.

The waitress reminded him strikingly of his beloved Kim Basinger: fair skin, sinful lips, yellow hair. Chub was electrified. He wondered if the waitress had a boyfriend, and if she let him take topless photos. Chub considered inviting her to sit and have a beer, but then Bode Gazzer loomed into focus, reminding Chub what they both must look like: Bode, in his camo and cowboy boots, his face welted and bitch-bitten; Chub, gouged and puffy, his mangled left eyelid concealed behind a homemade patch.

The girl'd have to be blind or crazy to show an interest. When she returned to the table, Chub boldly asked her name. She said it was Amber.

"OK, Amber, if I might ast – you ever heard a the White Rebel Brotherhood?"

"Sure," the waitress said. "They opened for the Geto Boys last summer."

Bode, who was signing the Visa receipt, glanced up and said: "You are seriously mistaken, sugar."

"I don't think so, sir. I got a T-shirt at the concert."

Bode frowned. Chub twirled his ponytail and whooped. "Ain't that a kick in the nuts!"

Amber picked up the credit-card slip, which included a hundred-dollar tip, and rewarded them with a blush and her very warmest smile, at which time Chub dropped to one knee and begged permission to purchase her orange shorts as a keepsake of the afternoon. Two Hispanic bouncers materialized to escort the militiamen out of the restaurant.

Later, sitting in the truck among their new guns, Chub was chuckling. "So much for your White Rebel Brotherhood."

"Shut up," Bode Gazzer slurred, " 'fore I puke on your shoes."

"Go right ahead, brother. I'm in love."

"Like hell."

"I'm in love, and I got a mission."

"Don't you start!"

"No," Chub said, "don't *you* try and stop me."

To find out if the waitress was right about the militia's name, they stopped at a music store in a Kendall mall. Drowsily Bode pawed through the racks until he came across proof: a compact disc called *Nocturnal Omission*, recorded in Muscle Shoals, Alabama, by the White Rebel Brotherhood. Bode was aghast to see that three of the five band members were Negroes. Even Chub said: "That ain't funny."

Bode shoplifted a half dozen of the CDs, which he shot up good with the TEC-9 after they returned to Chub's trailer. They arranged it like a skeet range, Chub tossing the discs high in the air while Bode blasted away. They quit when the gun jammed. Chub unfolded a pair of frayed lawn chairs and made a fire in a rusty oil drum. Bode complained that his beer buzz was wearing off, so Chub opened a bottle of cheap vodka, which they passed back and forth while the stars came out.

Eventually Chub said, "I b'lieve our militia needs a new name."

"I'm way ahead a you." Bode cocked the bottle to his lips. "The White Clarion Aryans. It just now come to me."

"Well, I like it," said Chub, although he wasn't certain what "clarion" meant. He believed it was mentioned in a Christmas song, perhaps in connection with angels.

"Can we call us the WC . . ." and then he faltered, trying to recall if Aryan was spelled with an *E* or an *A*.

Bode Gazzer said, "WC*A*. Don't see why not."

"Because otherwise it's kind of a mouthful."

"No more 'n the first one."

"But hey, that's cool," Chub said.

*White Clarion Aryans*. He sure hoped no smart-ass rock bands or rappers or other patriot tribes had already thought of the name.

From the lawn chair Bode rose in his rumpled camos and lifted the now-empty vodka bottle to the sky. "Here's to the motherfuckin' WCA. Ready, locked and loaded."

"Damn right," said Chub. "The WCA."

At that moment the young man called Shiner, glazed by Valium, was admiring the letters *W.R.B.* that were freshly tattooed in Iron Cross-style script across his left biceps. Etched below the initials was a screaming eagle with a blazing rifle locked in its talons.

The tattoo artist worked out of a Harley joint in Vero Beach, Shiner's first stop on his way south to Florida City, where he planned to hook up with his new white brothers. He had quit the Grab N'Go, leaving on a high note – Mr. Singh, the owner, demanding to know why

Shiner's Impala was moored in the store's only handicap space. And Shiner, standing tall behind the counter: "I got me a permit."

"Yes, but I do not understand."

"Right there on the rearview. See?"

"Yes, yes, but you are not crippled. The police will come."

Shiner, coughing theatrically: "I got a bad lung."

"You are not crippled."

"Disabled is what I am. They's a difference. From the army is where I hurt my lung."

And Mr. Singh, waving his slender brown arms, hurrying outside to more closely inspect the wheelchair insignia, piping: "Where you get that? How? Tell me right now please."

Shiner beaming, the little man's reaction being a testament to Chub's skill as a forger.

Saying to Mr. Singh: "It's the real deal, boss."

"Yes, yes, but how? You are not crippled or disabled or nothing, and don't lie to me nonsense. Now move the car."

And Shiner replying: "That's how you treat a handicap? Then I quit, raghead."

Grabbing three hundred-dollar bills from the register, then elbowing his way past Mr. Singh, who was protesting: "You, boy, put the money back! Put the money back!"

Yammering about the videotape Shiner had swiped, on Bodean Gazzer's instruction, from the store's slow-speed security camera – in case (Bode explained) the cassette hadn't yet rewound and taped over the surveillance video from November 25, the date JoLayne Lucks bought her lottery numbers.

Bode Gazzer had emphasized to Shiner the importance of the tape, should the authorities question how they'd come to possess the Grange ticket. The camera could prove they didn't enter the store until the day *after* the Lotto drawing.

So, shortly after Chub and Bode had departed, Shiner obediently removed the incriminating video from Mr. Singh's recorder and replaced it with a blank. Shiner wondered, as he gunned the Impala past the Grange city limits, how Mr. Singh learned about the switch. Normally the little hump didn't check the VCR unless there'd been a robbery.

Shiner would have been more properly alarmed had he known that Mr. Singh had been visited by the same nosy man who'd accompanied JoLayne Lucks to Shiner's house. The man named Tom. He'd persuaded Mr. Singh to check the Grab N'Go's security camera, at which time they'd found that the surveillance tape from the weekend had been swapped for a new one.

Shiner's misgivings about the video theft were fleeting, for soon he was absorbed in the tattooing process. It was performed by a bearded shirtless biker whose nipples were pierced with silver skull pins. When the last indigo turn of the *B* was completed, the biker put down the needle and jerked the cord out of the wall socket. Shiner couldn't stop grinning, even when the biker roughly swabbed his arm with alcohol, which stung like a mother.

What a awesome eagle! Shiner marveled. He couldn't wait to show Bode and Chub.

Pointing at the martial lettering, Shiner asked the biker: "Know what *WRB* stands for?"

"Shit, yeah. I got all their albums."

"No," said Shiner, "not the band."

"Then what?"

"You'll find out pretty soon."

The biker didn't like wise guys. "I can't hardly wait."

Shiner said: "Here's a hint: It's in the Second Amendment."

The biker stood up and casually kicked the tattoo stool into a corner. "I got a hint for you, too, jackoff: Gimme my money and move your cherry white ass down the road."

Demencio was tinkering with the weeping Madonna when the doorbell rang. There stood JoLayne Lucks with a tall, clean-cut white man. JoLayne carried one end of the aquarium, the white man had the other.

"Evening," she said to Demencio, who could do nothing but invite them in.

"Trish is at the grocery," he said, pointlessly.

They set the aquarium on the floor, next to Demencio's golf clubs. The journey up the steps had tilted all the little turtles to one end of the tank.

JoLayne Lucks said: "Meet my friend Tom Krome. Tom, this is Demencio."

The men shook hands; Krome scrutinizing the decapitated Madonna, Demencio eyeing the agitated cooters.

"Whatcha up to?" JoLayne asked.

"No big deal. One of her eyeholes got clogged." Demencio knew lying would be a waste of energy. It was all there, spread out on the living room carpet for any fool to see – the disassembled statue, the tubes, the rubber pump.

JoLayne said, "So that's how you make her cry."

"That's how we do it."

The man named Tom was curious about the bottle of perfume.

"Korean knockoff," Demencio said, "but a good one. See, I try to make the tears smell nice. Pilgrims go for that."

"That's a fine idea," said JoLayne, though her friend Tom looked doubtful. She told Demencio she had a proposition.

"I need you and Trish to watch over the turtles until I get back. There's a bag of fresh romaine in the car, and I'll leave you money for more."

Demencio said, "Where you goin', JoLayne?"

"I've got some business in Miami."

"Lottery business, I bet."

Tom Krome spoke up: "What've you heard?"

"The ticket got lost, is what I heard," said Demencio.

JoLayne Lucks promised to reveal the whole story when she returned to Grange. "And I sincerely apologize for being so mysterious, but you'll understand when the time comes."

"How long'll you be gone?"

"Truly I don't know," JoLayne said, "but here's what I propose: one thousand dollars to take care of my darlings. Whether it's a day or a month."

Tom Krome looked shocked. Demencio whistled at the number.

JoLayne said, "I'm quite serious."

And quite nuts, thought Demencio. A grand to babysit a load of turtles?

"It's more than fair," he remarked, trying to avoid Krome's eye.

"I think so, too," JoLayne said. "Now . . . Trish mentioned you had a cat."

"Screw the cat," said Demencio. "Pardon my French."

"Has it had its shots? I don't remember seeing you folks at Doc Crawford's."

"Just some dumb stray. Trish leaves scraps on the porch."

"All right," JoLayne told him, "but the deal's off if it kills even one of my babies."

"Don't you worry."

"There's forty-five even. I counted."

"Forty-five," Demencio repeated. "I'll keep track."

JoLayne handed him a hundred dollars as an advance, plus twenty for a lettuce fund. She said he'd receive the balance when she returned from the trip.

"What about Trish?" she asked. "How does she get on with reptiles?"

"Oh, she's crazy for 'em. Turtles especially." Demencio could barely keep a straight face.

Krome took out a camera, one of those cardboard disposables. Demencio asked what it was for.

"Your Virgin Mary – can I get a picture? It's for a friend."

Demencio said, "I guess. Just give me a second to put her back together."

"That'll be terrific. Put her back together and make her cry."

"Christ, you want tears, too?"

"Please," said Tom Krome, "if it's not too much trouble."

# EIGHT

**It was past** midnight when Tom Krome and JoLayne Lucks stopped at a Comfort Inn in South Miami, near the university. Fearing her nasty cuts and bruises would draw stares, JoLayne remained in the car while Krome registered them at the motel. They got separate rooms, adjoining.

Krome fell asleep easily – a wonder, considering he had no job, thirteen hundred dollars in the bank, and an estranged wife who was pretending to be a drug addict while refusing to grant him a divorce. If that wasn't enough to cause brain fever, he'd also been marked for grievous harm by a jealous judge whose wife he'd been screwing for not even a month. All these weighty problems Krome had put aside in order to recklessly endanger himself pursuing two armed psychopaths who'd robbed and assaulted a woman Krome barely knew.

Yet he slept like a puppy. That according to JoLayne Lucks, who was sitting in the room when he awoke in bright daylight.

"Not a worry in the world," he heard her say. "That's one of the best things about my job – watching puppies and kittens sleep."

Krome rose up on both elbows. JoLayne was wearing a sports halter and bicycle shorts. Her legs and arms were slender but tautly muscled; he wondered why he hadn't noticed before.

"Babies sleep the same way," she was saying, "but watching babies makes me sad. I'm not sure why."

"Because you know what's in store for them." Krome started to roll out of bed, then remembered he was wearing only underwear.

JoLayne lobbed him a towel. "You are quite the shy one. Want me to turn around?"

"Not necessary." After the bathtub episode, there was nothing to hide.

"Go take a shower," she told him. "I promise not to peek."

When Krome came out, she was asleep on his bed. For several moments he stood there listening to the sibilant rhythms of her breathing. It was alarming how comfortable he felt, considering the lunatic risks that lay ahead. This unfamiliar sense of mission was energizing, and he resolved not to overanalyze it. A woman had been hurt, the men who did it deserved to pay – and Krome had nothing better to do than help. Anyway, chasing gun nuts through South Florida was better than writing brainless newspaper features about Bachelorhood in the Nineties.

He slipped next door to JoLayne's room, so he wouldn't wake her by talking on the telephone. Two hours later she came in, puffy-eyed, to report: "I had quite a dream."

"Bad or good?"

"You were in it."

"Say no more."

"In a hot-air balloon."

"Is that right."

"Canary yellow with an orange stripe."

Krome said, "I'd have preferred to be on a handsome steed."

"White or black?"

"Doesn't matter."

"Yeah, right." JoLayne rolled her eyes.

"As long as it runs," Krome said.

"Maybe next time." She yawned and sat down on the floor, folding her long legs under her bottom. "You've been a busy bee, no?"

He told her he'd lined up some money to finance the chase. Of course she wanted to know where he'd gotten it, but Krome fudged. The newspaper's credit union, unaware of his resignation the day before, had been pleased to make the loan. JoLayne Lucks would've raised hell if he'd told her the truth.

"I already wired three thousand toward your Visa bill," he said, "to keep the bastards going."

"Your own money!"

"Not mine, the newspaper's," he said.

"Get outta here."

"Ever heard of an expense account? I get reimbursed for hotels and gas, too."

Krome, sounding like quite the big shot. He wasn't sure if JoLayne Lucks was buying the lie. Her toes were wiggling, which could mean just about anything.

She said, "They must really want this story."

"Hey, that's the business we're in."

"The news biz, huh? Tell me more."

"The men who beat you up," Krome said, "they haven't cashed your Lotto ticket yet. I checked with Tallahassee. They haven't even left their names."

"They're waiting to make sure I don't go to the police. Just like you predicted."

"They'll hold out a week, maybe ten days, before that ticket burns a crater in their pocket."

"That isn't much time."

"I know. We'll need some breaks to find them."

"And then . . . ?"

She'd asked the same thing earlier, and Krome had no answer. Everything depended on who the creeps were, where they lived, what they'd bought at that gun show. That the men had remembered to steal the night videotape from the Grab N'Go showed they weren't as stupid as Krome had first thought.

JoLayne reminded him that her Remington was in the trunk. "The nice thing about shotguns," she said, "is the margin of error."

"Oh, so you've shot people before."

"No, Tom, but I do know the gun. Daddy made sure of that."

Krome handed her the phone. "Call the nice folks at Visa. Let's see what our party boys are up to."

Sinclair had told no one at *The Register* that Tom Krome had resigned, in the hope it was a cheap bluff. Good reporters were temperamental and impulsive; this Sinclair remembered from newspaper management school.

Then the woman who covered the police beat came to Sinclair's office with a xeroxed report he found highly disturbing. The windows of Krome's house had been shot out by persons unknown, and there was no sign of the owner. In the absence of fresh blood or corpses, the cops were treating the incident as a random act of vandalism. Sinclair thought it sounded more serious than that.

He was pondering his options when his sister Joan phoned from Grange. Excitedly she told Sinclair the latest rumor: The Lotto woman, JoLayne Lucks, left town the night before with a white man, supposedly a newspaper writer.

"Is that your guy?" Joan asked.

Sinclair felt clammy as he fumbled for a pen and paper. Having never worked as a reporter, he had no experience taking notes.

"Start again," he implored his sister, "and go slowly."

But Joan was chattering on with more gossip: The clerk at the Grab N'Go had skipped out, too – the one who'd originally said he sold the winning lottery ticket to JoLayne Lucks and then later changed his mind.

"Whoa," said Sinclair, scribbling spastically. "Run that by me again."

The shaky store clerk was a new twist to the story. Joan briefed her brother on what was known locally about Shiner. Sinclair cut her off when she got to the business about the young man's mother and the Road-Stain Jesus.

"Back up," he said to Joan. "They're traveling together – the clerk, this writer and the Lucks woman? Is that the word?"

His sister said: "Oh, there's all sorts of crazy theories. Bermuda is my personal favorite."

Sinclair solemnly jotted the word "Bermuda" on his notepad. He added a question mark, to denote his own doubts. He thanked Joan for the tip, and she gaily promised to call back if she heard anything new. After hanging up, Sinclair drew the blinds in his office – a signal (although he didn't realize it) to his entire staff that an emergency was in progress.

In solitude, Sinclair grappled with his options. Tom Krome's fate concerned him deeply, if only in a political context. An editor was expected to maintain the illusion of control over his writers, or at least have a sketchy idea of their whereabouts. The situation with Krome was complicated by the fact that he was regarded as a valuable talent by *The Register*'s managing editor, who in his lofty realm was spared the daily anxiety of working with the man. It was Sinclair's cynical theory that Krome had won the managing editor's admiration with a single feature story – a profile of a controversial performance artist who abused herself and occasionally audience members with zucchini, yams and frozen squab. With great effort Krome had managed to scavenge minor symbolism from the young woman's histrionics, and his mildly sympathetic piece had inspired the National Endowment for the Arts to reinstate her annual grant of $14,000. The artist was so grateful she came to the newspaper to thank the reporter (who was, as always, out of town) and ended up chatting instead with the managing editor himself (who, of course, asked her out). A week later, Tom Krome was puzzled to find a seventy-five-dollar bonus in his paycheck.

Was life fair? Sinclair knew it didn't matter. He was left to presume his own career would suffer if Krome turned up unexpectedly in a hospital, jail, morgue or scandal. Yet Sinclair was helpless to influence events, because of two crucial mistakes. The first was allowing Krome to quit; the second was not informing anybody else at the newspaper. So as far as Sinclair's bosses were aware, Krome still worked for him.

Which meant Sinclair would be held accountable if Krome died or otherwise got in trouble. Because Sinclair had neither the resourcefulness nor the manpower to find his lost reporter, he energetically set about the task of covering his own ass. He spent two hours crafting a memorandum that recounted his last meeting with Tom Krome, describing at length the severe personal stress with which the man obviously had been burdened. Sinclair's written account culminated with Krome's shrieking that he was quitting, upending Sinclair's desk and stomping from the newsroom. Naturally Sinclair had refused to accept his troubled friend's resignation, and discreetly put him on excused medical leave, with pay. Out of deference to Krome's privacy, Sinclair had chosen to tell no one, not even the managing editor.

Sinclair reread the memorandum half a dozen times. It was an adroit piece of management sophistry – casting doubt on an employee's mental stability while simultaneously portraying oneself as the loyal, yet deeply worried, supervisor.

Perhaps Sinclair wouldn't need the fable to bail himself out. Perhaps Tom Krome simply would forget about the nutty Lotto woman and return to work at *The Register*, as if nothing had happened.

But Sinclair doubted it. What little he could read of his own wormlike scribbles made his stomach churn.

*Bermuda*?

Chub couldn't decide where to stash the stolen lottery ticket – few hiding places were as ingenious as Bode Gazzer's condom. At first Chub tucked the prize inside one of his shoes; by nightfall it was sodden with perspiration. Bode warned him that the lottery bureau wouldn't cash the ticket if it was "defaced," a legal term Bode broadly interpreted to include wet and stinky. Dutifully Chub relocated the ticket in the box of hollowpoints that he carried with him at all times. Again Bode Gazzer objected. He pointed out that if Chub got trapped in a fire, the ammunition would explode in his trousers and the Lotto numbers would be destroyed.

The only other idea that occurred to Chub was a trick he'd seen in some foreign prison movie, where the inmate hero kept a secret diary hidden up his butthole. The guy scribbled everything in ant-sized letters on chewing gum wrappers, which he folded into tiny squares and stuck in his ass, so the prison guards wouldn't get wise. Given Bode's low regard for Chub's personal hygiene, Chub was fairly sure his partner would object to the butthole scheme. He was right.

"What if first I wrap it in foil?" Chub offered.

"I don't care if you pack it in fucking kryptonite, that lottery ticket ain't goin' up your ass."

Instead they attached it with a jumbo Band-Aid to Chub's right outer thigh, a hairless quadrant that (Bode conceded) seemed relatively untainted by Chub's potent sweat. Bode firmly counseled Chub to remove the Lotto-ticket bandage when, and if, he ever felt like bathing.

Chub didn't appreciate the insult, and said so. "You don't watch your mouth," he warned Bode Gazzer, "I'm gone do somethin' so awful to your precious truck, you'll need one a them moonsuits to go anywheres near it."

"Jesus, take it easy."

Later they went to the 7-Eleven for their customary breakfast of Orange Crush and Dolly Madisons. Bode swiped a newspaper and searched it for a mention of the Lotto robbery in Grange. He was relieved to find nothing. Chub declared himself in a mood for shooting, so they stopped by Bode's apartment to grab the AR-15 and a case of beer, and headed south down the Eighteen-Mile Stretch. They turned off on a gravel road that led to a small rock-pit lake, not far from a prison camp where Bode had once spent four months. At the rock pit they came upon a group of clean-shaven men wearing holsters and ear protectors. From the type of vehicles at the scene – late-model Cherokees, Explorers, Land Cruisers – and the orderliness with which they'd been parked, Bode concluded the shooters were suburban husbands brushing up on home-defense skills. The men stood side by side, firing pistols and semiautomatics at paper silhouettes just like the ones cops used. Bode was disquieted to observe among the group a Negro, one or two possible Cubans, and a wiry bald fellow who was almost certainly Jewish.

"We gotta go. This place ain't secure." Bode, speaking in his role as militia leader.

Chub said, "You jest watch." He peeled off his eye patch and sauntered to the firing line. There he nonchalantly raised the AR-15 and, in a few deafening seconds, reduced all the paper targets to confetti. Then, for good measure, he opened up on a stray buzzard that was flying no less than a thousand feet straight up in the sky. Without a word, the husbands put away their handguns and departed. A few drove off without removing their ear cups, a sight that gave Bodean Gazzer a good laugh.

Chub went through a half dozen clips before he got bored and offered the rifle to Bode, who declined to shoot. The blasts of gunfire had reignited the killer migraine from Bode's morning hangover, and now all he craved was silence. He and Chub sat down at the edge of the lake and worked on the beer.

After a while, Chub asked, "So when can we cash out our tickets?"

"Pretty soon. But we gotta be careful."

"That nigger girl, she ain't gonna say a word."

"Probably not," Bode said. Yet, thinking back on the beating, he recalled that the Lucks woman never seemed as scared as she should've been. Mad as a hornet, for sure, and crying like a baby when Chub shot her turtle – but there was no quivering animal panic from the woman, despite all the pain. They'd worked extra hard to make her think they'd return to murder her if she didn't keep quiet. Bode hoped she believed it. He hoped she cared.

Chub said, "Let's tomorrow me and you go straight up to Tal'hassee and git our money."

Bode laughed sourly. "You checked in the mirror lately?"

"Tell 'em we's in a car accident."

"With what – bobcats?"

"Anyways, they gotta pay us no matter how bad we look. We had leprosy, the motherfuckers still gotta pay us."

Patiently Bode Gazzer explained how suspicious it would be for two best friends to claim equal shares of the same Lotto jackpot, with tickets purchased three hundred miles apart.

"It's better," Bode said, "if we don't know each other. We ain't never met, you and me, far as the lottery bureau is concerned."

" 'K."

"Anybody asks, I bought my fourteen-million-dollar

ticket in Florida City, you got yours in Grange. And we never once laid eyes on each other before."

"No problem," Chub said.

"And listen here, we can't show up in Tallahassee together. One of us goes on a Tuesday, the other one maybe a week later. Just to play it safe."

"Then afterwards," said Chub, "we put the money all together."

"You got it."

Chub did the arithmetic aloud. "If those first checks is seven hundred grand, times two is like one million four hunnert thousand bucks."

Bodean Gazzer said, "Before taxes, don't forget." It felt like his skull was cleaving down the middle, an agony made worse by his partner's greasy persistence.

"But what I wanna ast," Chub said, "is who goes first. Cashes out, I mean."

"Difference does it make?"

"I guess none."

They got in the truck and headed down the gravel road toward the Stretch. Chub stared out the window as Bode went on: "I don't like the wait no better'n you. Sooner we get the cash, sooner we get the White Clarion Aryans together. Start serious recruitment. Build us a bomb shelter and whatnot."

Chub lit a cigaret. "So meantime what do we do for money?"

"Good question," Bode Gazzer said. "I wonder if the Negro girl's canceled out her credit card yet."

"Likely so."

"One way to find out."

Chub blew a smoke ring. "I s'pose."

"We're down to a quarter tank," Bode said. "Tell you

what. The Shell station up the highway, let's try the self-serve pump. If it spits her Visa, we'll take off."

"Yeah?"

"Yeah. No harm done."

Chub said, "And if it takes the card?"

"Then we're golden for one more day."

"Sounds good to me." Chub dragged contentedly. Already he was daydreaming about barbecued chicken wings and a certain blond-haired beauty in satiny orange shorts.

The bank's computer indicated JoLayne's Visa card hadn't been used since the previous afternoon at Hooters.

"Now what?" she asked, waving the receiver.

"Order a pizza," said Tom Krome, "and wait for them to get stupid again."

"What if they don't?"

"They will," he said. "They can't resist."

The pizza was vegetarian, delivered cold. They ate it anyway. Afterwards JoLayne stretched out on her back, locked her arms behind her neck and bent her knees.

"Sit-ups?" Tom Krome asked.

"Crunches," she said. "Wanna help?"

He knelt on the floor and held her ankles. JoLayne winked and said, "You've done this before."

He counted along in his head. After a hundred easy ones, she closed her eyes tight and did a hundred more. He gave her a minute to rest, then said: "That was a little scary."

JoLayne winced as she sat up. She pressed her

knuckles to her tummy and said, "Bastards really did a job on me. Normally I can do three-fifty or four."

"I think you should take it easy."

"Your turn," she said.

"JoLayne, please."

Then suddenly Krome was on his back, except she wasn't holding his ankles as a proper sit-up partner would do. Instead she was straddling his chest, pinning his arms.

"Know what I was thinking?" she said. "About what you said earlier, how white or black doesn't matter."

"Weren't we talking about dreams and horses?"

"Maybe *you* were."

Deliberately Tom Krome went limp. His goal was to minimize the frontal contact, which was indescribably wonderful. He was also trying to think of a distraction, something to make his blood go cold. Sinclair's face was an obvious choice, but Krome couldn't summon it.

JoLayne was saying, "It's important we should have this discussion . . ."

"Later."

"So it *does* matter. White and black."

"JoLayne?"

Now she was nose-to-nose and pressing her body down harder. "Tom, you tell me the truth."

He turned his head away. Total limpness was no longer sustainable.

"Tom?"

"What?"

"Are you mistaking this moment for some kind of clumsy seduction?"

"Call me crazy."

JoLayne pulled away. By the time he sat up, she was

perched on the bed, cutting him a look. "Back in the shower for you!"

"I thought we had a professional relationship," he said. "I'm the reporter, you're the story."

"So you're the only one who gets to ask questions? That's really fair."

"Ask away, but no more wrestling." Krome, thinking: What a handful she is.

JoLayne cuffed him. "OK, how many black friends do you have? I mean *friend* friends."

"I don't have many close friends of any color. I am not what you'd call gregarious."

"Ah."

"There's a black guy at work – Daniel, from Editorial. We play tennis every now and then. And Jim and Jeannie, they're lawyers. We get together for dinner."

"That's your answer?"

Krome caved. "OK, the answer is none. Zero black *friend* friends."

"Just like I thought."

"But I'm working on it."

"Yes, you are," said JoLayne. "Let's go for a ride."

# NINE

**JoLayne's friend was** twenty minutes late, the longest twenty minutes of Tom Krome's life. They were waiting at a bar called Shiloh's in Liberty City. JoLayne Lucks was drinking ginger ale and munching on beer nuts. She wore a big floppy hat and round peach-tinted sunglasses. It didn't matter what Tom Krome was wearing; he was the only white person there. Several patrons remarked upon the fact, and not in a welcoming tone.

JoLayne told him to put his notebook on the bar and start writing. "So you look official."

"Good idea," Krome said, "except I left it back in the room."

JoLayne clicked her tongue. "You men, you'd forget your weenies if they weren't glued on."

A gangly transvestite in a fantastic chromium wig approached Krome and offered to blow him for forty dollars.

Krome said, "No, thanks, I've got a date."

"Then I do her fo' free."

"Tempting," said JoLayne, "but I think we'll pass."

With a bony hand, the transvestite gripped one of Krome's legs. "Dolly don't take no for an answer. And Dolly gots a blade in her purse."

JoLayne leaned close to Krome and whispered: "Give him a twenty."

"Not a chance."

"Speak up now," said the Dolly person. Ridiculous fake fingernails dug into Krome's calf. "Come on, big man, let's go out to yo' cah. Bring the fancy lady if you wants."

Krome said, "I like that dress – didn't you used to be on *Shindig*?"

The transvestite gave a bronchial laugh and squeezed harder. "Dolly's gettin' the boy 'cited."

"No, just annoyed."

To unfasten the Dolly person's hand from his knee, Krome twisted the thumb clockwise until it came out of the socket. The popping sound silenced the bar. JoLayne Lucks was impressed. She'd have to find out where he'd learned such a thing.

Dropping to his knees, the transvestite prostitute shrieked and pawed at himself with his crooked digit. Lurching to avenge his honor were two babbling crackheads, each armed with gleaming cutlery. They began to argue about who should get to stab the white boy first, and how many times. It was a superb moment for JoLayne's friend to show up, and his arrival cleared the scene. The Dolly person shed a spiked pump during his scamper out the door.

The name of JoLayne's friend was Moffitt, and he made no inquiries about the crackheads or the yowling robber. Moffitt was built like a middleweight and dressed like an expensive lawyer. His gray suit was finely tailored and his checkered necktie was silk. He wore thin-rimmed eye-glasses with round conservative frames, and carried a small cellular telephone. He greeted JoLayne with a hug but scarcely nodded at Tom Krome.

The bartender brought Moffitt a Diet Coke and a bowl of pitted olives. He popped one in his mouth and asked JoLayne to remove her sunglasses.

After examining her face, he turned to Krome: "She gave me one version over the phone, but I want to hear yours – did you do this to her?"

"No."

"Because if I find out otherwise, you're going on an ambulance ride – "

"I didn't do it."

" – possibly in a bag."

JoLayne said, "Moffitt, it wasn't him."

They moved to a booth. Moffitt asked for a card, and Krome got one from his billfold. Moffitt remarked that he'd never heard of *The Register.* JoLayne told him to lighten up.

Moffitt said, "Sorry. I don't trust anyone in the media."

"Well, I'm stunned," said Krome. "We're so accustomed to being adored and admired."

Moffitt didn't crack a smile. To JoLayne he said: "What's your plan, Jo? What do you need from me?"

"Help. And don't tell me to go to the cops because if I do, I'll never get my Lotto ticket back."

Impassively Moffitt agreed. His cell phone rang. He turned it off. "I'll do what I can," he said.

JoLayne turned to Krome. "We've known each other since kindergarten. He takes a personal interest in my well-being, and I do the same for him."

"Don't lie to the man. I'm lucky to get a Christmas

card." Moffitt tapped his knuckles on the table. "Tell me about the guys who did this."

"Rednecks," JoLayne said, "red-to-the-bone rednecks. They called me, among other things, a rotten nigger slut."

"Nice." Moffitt spoke in a tight voice. When he reached for his Coke, Krome noticed the bulge under his left arm.

JoLayne said: "We're following them."

"Following." Moffitt looked skeptical. "How?"

"Her credit card," Krome explained. "They're burning a trail."

Moffitt seemed encouraged. He took out a gold Cross pen and reached for a stack of cocktail napkins. In small precise script he took down the details JoLayne gave him – the purchase of the lottery ticket, how she'd met Tom Krome, the break-in, the beating, the red pickup truck, the missing video from the Grab N'Go. By the time she finished, Moffitt had filled both sides of three napkins, which he folded neatly and tucked into an inside suit pocket.

Tom Krome said, "Now I've got a question."

JoLayne nudged him and said not to bother. Moffitt shifted impatiently.

"Who do you work for?" Krome said. "What do you do?"

"Use your imagination," Moffitt told him. Then, to JoLayne: "Call me in a day or two, but not at the office."

Then he got up and left. The bar stayed quiet; no sign of Dolly or his pals.

Fondly JoLayne said: "Poor Moffitt – I give him fits. And he's such a worrier."

"That would explain the gun," said Krome.

"Oh, that. He works for the government."

"Doing what?"

"I'll let him tell you," JoLayne said, sliding out of the booth. "I'm hungry again, how about you?"

Amber's boyfriend was named Tony. He'd been on her case to quit her job, until she made first alternate for Miss September in the Hooters Girl Calendar. After that Tony came to the restaurant three or four times a week, he was so proud. The more beers he drank, the louder he'd brag on Amber. This, she understood, was his suave way of letting the customers know she was spoken for.

Several months earlier, the Hooters people had asked Amber and three other waitresses to pose for a promotional poster, which was to be given away free to horny college guys on Fort Lauderdale beach. When Amber told Tony about the poster, he immediately joined a gym and began injecting steroids. In ten months he gained thirty-two pounds and developed such an igneous strain of acne across both shoulders that Amber forbade him to wear tank tops.

Initially she'd been flattered by Tony's surprise appearances at the restaurant, particularly since the other waitresses thought he was so handsome – quite the hunk! Amber never let on that Tony couldn't keep a job, mooched shamelessly off his parents, hadn't finished a book since tenth grade and wasn't all that great in the sack. And ever since he'd started the workout binge, he'd become moody and rough. One time he'd dragged her dripping wet from the shower to the bed, by her hair. She'd considered leaving him, but nothing better had presented itself. Tony *did* look good (at least in a sleeved shirt), and in Amber's world that counted for something.

Yet she wished he'd stop dropping in at work. His presence was not only distracting, it was a drain on her income. Amber had been keeping track: Whenever Tony was there, her tips fell off by as much as a third. Therefore the sight of her hulked-out sweetheart swaggering through the door on this particular Wednesday evening – Wednesday already being a slow night, tipwise – failed to evoke in the alternate Miss September either gladness or affection. The frisky ambience of Hooters brought out Tony's demonstrative side, and at every opportunity he intercepted his tray-laden princess with an indiscreet hug, smooch or pat on the ass. Tony's boisterous possessiveness was meant to discourage other patrons from flirting with Amber, and it did. Unfortunately, it also discouraged excessive gratuities.

Amber's only hope on this night was the icky-looking pair of rednecks at table seven, the same two who yesterday had left her a hundred-dollar tip on a credit card. The shorter man had arrived in a fresh suit of camouflage, while his ponytailed companion – the one who'd tried to buy her shorts – appeared not to have changed clothes or even shaved. Affixed across the orbit of his left eye was a new rubber bicycle patch; Amber tried not to imagine what was behind it. The faces of both men still bore the scabs of savage cuts, as if they'd gone at each other with razors. Amber could not dismiss the possibility.

But for her purposes, the rednecks could not be crude and spooky and disgusting. They were handsome and sexy and sophisticated; Mel Gibson and Tom Cruise, sharing a plate of chicken wings. That's how Amber treated them. It wasn't easy, but a hundred bucks was a hundred bucks.

"Honey," said the ponytailed one, "you's right about the White Rebel Brotherhood. They's a damn rock band."

"You should see 'em live," Amber said. She set two cold Coronas on the table.

The stumpy one in camouflage asked her if the name of the group was some kind of joke. "Considering all the Negroes they got," he added

Amber said, "I think it's meant to be funny, yeah."

The ponytailed one, lathering his palms with the condensation from the beer bottle: "Well, Bode don't think it's so funny. Can't say I do, neither."

Amber's poster-quality smile didn't flicker. "The music's killer. That's all I know."

Then she glided away with their empties and an order for more onion rings. Her path to the kitchen took her directly past Tony's table, and of course he snatched her by the elastic waistband of her shorts.

"Not now," she told him.

"Who're those dirtbags?"

"Just customers. Now let me get to work," Amber said.

Tony grunted. "They hit on you? That's what it looked like."

"You're going to get me in trouble with the boss. Let go, OK?"

"First a kiss." With one arm he pulled her close.

"Tony!"

"A kiss for Tony, that's right."

And of course he had to slip her some tongue, right there in the middle of the restaurant. Out of the corner of an eye, Amber noticed the rednecks watching. Tony must have seen them, too, because he was beaming by the time Amber pulled free.

A few minutes later, when she delivered the onion rings to the table, the ponytailed one said: "People ever tell you you look zackly like Kim Basinger."

"Really?" Amber acted flattered, though she'd always seen herself in the Daryl Hannah mold.

"Bode thinks so, too, don'tcha?"

"Dead ringer," said the camouflaged man, "and I'm the better judge. I still got both good eyes."

Amber said, "Well, you're sweet for saying so. Can I get you anything else?"

"Matter a fact, yes you can," the ponytailed man said. "How 'bout one a them red-hot kisses like you give that other guy?"

Amber blushed. With a moist leer the camouflaged man said, "Yeah, I didn't see that on no menu!"

The ponytailed one observed that Amber wasn't too keen on the kissing idea. He cocked his face upward and tapped a dirty fingertip on the bicycle patch. "Mebbe it's me. Mebbe you prejudiced against handicaps."

Amber, sensing (as all good waitresses can) that her tip was in jeopardy: "No, oh no, I can explain. That's my boyfriend."

In unison the men twisted in their chairs to reappraise Tony across the restaurant. He returned their stares with a belligerent sneer.

The ponytailed redneck said, "No shit. The hell is he, Cuban?"

Amber said no, Tony was from Los Angeles. "Sometimes he gets carried away. I'm sorry if it upset you."

Through a mouthful of onions, the one called Bode

said: "Meskin, I'll bet. They're all over California is what I heard."

On the way back to the bar station, Amber stopped at Tony's table and curtly related what had happened: "Thanks to you, they think I kiss all the customers. They think it's part of the service. You happy now?"

Tony's eyes darkened. "Those dirtbags – they wanted a kiss?"

"Do us all a favor. Go home," Amber whispered.

"No fuckin' way. Not now."

"Tony, I swear to God . . ."

He was flaring his nostrils, puffing his chest, flexing his arms. All that's missing, Amber thought, is the workout mirror.

Declared Tony: "I'll straighten those shitheads out."

"No you won't," said Amber, bitterly surveying the suddenly empty table. "They're gone."

She hurried back, hoping to find some cash. Nothing – they'd skipped on the tab. *Shit*, she thought. It would come out of her pay.

Suddenly she was enveloped by Tony's cologne, as subtle as paint thinner. She felt him looming behind her. "Goddamn you," she said, retreating to the kitchen. Predictably, Tony stormed out the door.

Two hours later, Amber's redneck customers returned, anchoring themselves at the same table.

She tried not to appear too relieved. "Where'd you fellas run off to?"

"Jest needed some fresh air," said the ponytailed one, lighting a cigaret. "You miss us? Say, where's that kissing-machine boyfriend a yours."

Amber pretended not to hear him. "What can I get for you?"

The camouflaged man ordered four more beers, two apiece, and a fresh heap of wings. "Add it on our bill," he said, flashing the Visa card with two stubby fingers.

Amber was waiting for the drink order when the barmaid handed her the phone. "For you, honey," she said. "Guess who."

Tony, of course. Screaming.

"Slow down," Amber told him. "I can't understand a word."

"My car!" he cried. "Somebody burned up my car!"

"Oh, Tony."

"Right in my fucking driveway! They torched it!"

"When?"

"During wrestling, I guess. It's still on fire, they got like five guys tryin' to put out the flames . . ."

The barmaid came with the tray of Coronas. Amber told Tony she was really sorry about the car, but she had to get back to work.

"I'll call you on my break," she promised.

"The Miata, Amber!"

"Yes, baby, I heard you."

When she brought the beers and chicken wings to the two rednecks, the one named Bode said: "Sugar, you're our rock 'n' roll expert. Is there a band called the White Clarion Aryans?"

Amber thought for a moment. "Not that I ever heard of."

"Good," Bode said.

"Not jes good," said his ponytailed friend, "fan-fucking-tastic!"

*

JoLayne Lucks demanded that Tom Krome teach her the thumb-popping trick. "That thing you did with the he-she back at Shiloh's."

When they got to a stoplight, Krome took her left hand to demonstrate.

"Not too hard!" she piped.

Gently he showed her how to disable a person by bending and twisting his thumb in a single motion. JoLayne asked where he'd learned about it.

"One time the newspaper sent me to take a class on self-defense," Krome said, "for a feature story. The instructor was a ninja guy, weighed all of a hundred and twenty pounds. But he knew all sorts of naughty little numbers."

"Yeah?"

"Fingers in the eye sockets is another good one," said Krome. "The scrotal squeeze is a crowd pleaser, too."

"These come in handy in the newspaper biz?"

"Today was the first time."

JoLayne was pleased he didn't let go of her hand until the light turned green and it was time to steer the car. They stopped at a Burger King on Northwest Seventh Avenue and ate in the parking lot with the windows down. The breeze was cool and pleasant, even with the din from the interstate. After lunch they went on a tour of JoLayne's childhood: kindergarten, elementary school, high school. The pet shop where she'd worked in the summers. The appliance store her father once owned. The auto garage where she'd met her first boyfriend.

"He took care of Daddy's Grand Prix," she said. "Good at lube jobs, bad at relationships. Rick was his name."

"Where is he now?"

"Lord, I can't imagine."

While Krome drove, JoLayne found herself spinning through the stories of the significant men in her life. "Aren't you sorry," she said, "you left your notebook at the motel?"

He smiled but didn't take his eyes off the road. "I got a helluva memory." Then, swerving around a county bus: "What about Moffitt – he's not on the List of Six?"

"Friends only." JoLayne wondered if Krome's interest was strictly professional, caught herself hoping it wasn't. "He dated both my sisters, my best friend, a cousin and also my nursing supervisor at Jackson. But not me."

"How come?"

"Mutual agreement."

"Ah," Krome said. He didn't believe it was mutual. He believed Moffitt would go to his grave asking himself why JoLayne Lucks hadn't wanted him.

"We'd been buddies so long," she was saying, "we knew too much about each other. One of those deals."

"Right," Krome said. He pulled to the curb while two police cars and an ambulance sped past. When the wail of sirens faded, JoLayne said, "Plus Moffitt's too serious for me. You saw for yourself. Why I'm telling you this stuff, Lord, I don't know."

"I'm interested."

"But it's not part of the story."

"How do you know?" Krome said.

"Because I'm telling you so. It's *not* part of the story."

He shrugged.

"What in the world was I thinking," JoLayne said, "bringing you in on this? First off, you're a man, and I've got rotten instincts when it comes to men. Second, you're a *reporter*, for heaven's sake. Only a crazy fool would believe a reporter, am I right? And last but not least – "

"I'm awfully white," Krome said.

"Bingo."

"But you trust me anyway."

"Truly it's a mystery." JoLayne removed her floppy hat and flipped it in the back seat. "Can we stop at a pay phone? I need to call Clara before it gets too late."

Clara Markham was the real estate broker who had the listing for Simmons Wood. Clara knew JoLayne wanted to buy the property, because JoLayne had phoned the night she'd won the lottery. But then, two days later, JoLayne had called back to say something had happened and it might be awhile before she could make a down payment. Clara had promised not to accept any other offers until she spoke to JoLayne again. She was a friend, after all.

Krome spotted a pay phone outside a sub shop on 125th Street. JoLayne got Clara Markham at the realty office.

JoLayne said, "Whatcha up to, working so late?"

"Busy, girl."

"How's my pal Kenny?"

Kenny was Clara's obese Persian. Because of its impeccably lush whiskers, Clara had named it after Kenny Rogers, the country singer.

"Much improved," Clara reported. "The hair-ball crisis is over, you can tell Dr. Crawford. But I'm afraid I've got some other news."

JoLayne sucked in a deep breath. "Damn. Who is it?"

"A union pension fund out of Chicago."

"And they build malls?"

"Girl, they build everything."

"What's the offer?" JoLayne asked gloomily.

"Three even. Twenty percent down."

"Damn. *Goddamn.*"

Clara said, "They want an answer in a week."

"I can do better than three million. You wait."

"Jo, I'll stall as long as I can."

"I'd sure appreciate it."

"And be sure and tell Doc Crawford thanks for the ointment. Tell him Kenny says thanks, too."

JoLayne Lucks hung up and sat on the curb. A group of teenagers spilled from the sub shop, nearly tripping over her.

Tom Krome got out of the car. "I take it there's another buyer."

JoLayne nodded disconsolately. "I've got a week, Tom. Seven lousy days to get my Lotto ticket back."

"Then let's go to it." He took her hands and pulled her to her feet.

The place known as Simmons Wood had been owned since 1959 by Lighthorse Simmons, whose father had been an early settler of Grange. Lighthorse maintained the rolling green tract as a private hunting reserve and visited regularly until he'd personally shot nearly every living creature on the property. Then he took up fishing. And although a fly rod could never provide the same hot blood rush as a rifle, Lighthorse Simmons grew to enjoy yanking feisty little bluegills and largemouth bass from the creek. Eventually, as he got older, he even stopped killing them.

Ironically, it was a hunter's bullet that led to the end of Lighthorse's long custodianship of Simmons Wood.

The mishap occurred at dusk one evening – Lighthorse was on the creek bank, bending over to cough up a wad of Red Man he'd accidentally swallowed. In the twilight, the old fellow's broad straw hat, tawny suede jacket and downward pose apparently called to mind – at least for one myopic trespasser – the image of a six-point buck, drinking.

The bullet clipped Lighthorse's right kneecap, and after three surgeries he remained unable to hike through Simmons Wood without constant, grating pain. An electric cart was given to him as part of the insurance settlement, but it proved unsuitable for the bumpy terrain. One rainy morning Lighthorse hit a pine stump and the cart overturned. He was pinned for nearly four hours, during which time he was prodigiously befouled by an excitable feral boar – a breed of pig originally introduced to Grange, for sporting purposes, by Lighthorse's own father.

After that incident, Lighthorse never again set foot in Simmons Wood. He went through the legal technicalities of rezoning it from agricultural to commercial, but ultimately he couldn't bring himself to sell. The land remained untrammeled (and the dawn unbroken by gunfire) for such a long time that wild animals finally began to reappear. But when Lighthorse passed away, at age seventy-five, the administrators of his estate put Simmons Wood on the market. The place held no sentimental attachment for the old man's son and daughter, who viewed the potentially immense proceeds from the land sale as several new oil derricks in Venezuela and a winter ski cottage in New Hampshire, respectively.

On the other end of the deal was Bernard Squires, investment manager for the Central Midwest Brotherhood of Grouters, Spacklers and Drywallers International. To Bernard Squires fell the sensitive task of dispensing the union's pension fund in such a way as to conceal the millions of dollars being skimmed annually by organized crime: specifically, the Richard Tarbone family of Chicago.

Bernard Squires' livelihood, and in all probability his very life, depended on his talent for assembling investment portfolios in which vast sums could plausibly disappear. Naturally he had a fondness for real estate developments. Not for a moment did Bernard envision for Simmons Wood a thriving, profitable retail shopping center. Grange was a perfectly ridiculous location for a major mall – one of the only municipalities in Florida to have shrunk (according to incredulous census takers) during the boom years of the eighties and nineties. And while its puny population was augmented by a modest flow of highway tourists, the demographics of the average Grange visitor could most diplomatically be typed, from a retailer's perspective, as "*low* low end." No major anchor stores or national chains would dream of locating there, as Bernard Squires well knew.

His plan, from the beginning, was to create a very expensive failure. Acting as a bank, the pension fund would finance the purchase of Simmons Wood and enter into a series of contracts with construction companies secretly controlled by Richard Tarbone and his associates. Simmons Wood would be bulldozed and cleared, a foundation would be poured, and perhaps even a wall or two would go up.

Then: a run of bad luck. Shortages of labor and materials. Weather delays. Missed payments on construction loans. Contractors unexpectedly filing for bankruptcy. And as if that weren't enough, the leasing agent would dejectedly report that hardly anyone wanted space in the soon-to-be-completed Simmons Wood Mall. The project would sputter and die, and the site would become a ruin. Florida was full of them.

Whatever true sum was lost in the Simmons Wood venture would be doubled when it appeared as red ink on the books of the Central Midwest Brotherhood of Grouters, Spacklers and Drywallers International. That is how Bernard Squires hid the Tarbone family's skimming. If other union officials suspected skulduggery, they were wise enough not to make a peep. Besides, the pension fund made a profit, overall; Squires saw to that. Even the IRS auditors didn't challenge his numbers. Investing in real estate was a crapshoot, as everybody knew. Sometimes you won, sometimes you lost.

Once the write-off had outlived its usefulness, Bernard Squires would contrive to unload Simmons Wood on an insurance conglomerate or maybe the Japanese – somebody with enough capital to finish the stupid mall, or raze it and start over. For now, though, Bernard Squires was eager to lock up the deal.

It was Richard "The Icepick" Tarbone's desire to close on the Grange property as soon as possible. "And don't call me," he had told Squires, "until you got some good fucking news. Do whatever it takes, you understand?"

Bernard understood.

The visitation got off to a rocky start. Once again, Demencio's fiberglass Madonna wasn't weeping properly – this time due to a crimp in the plastic feeder lines between the reservoir bottle and the eyes. One tear duct was barren while the other gushed like an artery. A pilgrim from Guatemala, having been spritzed in the forehead, loudly challenged the legitimacy of the miracle. Luckily the tirade was in Spanish and therefore incomprehensible to the other visitors. Trish, who was manning the Madonna, relayed the details of the plumbing problem to Demencio at the breakfast table. He told her to lay off the pump, pronto; no more crying.

"But we got a bus coming," Trish reminded him. "The mission bus from West Virginia."

"Aw, shit."

Every week Demencio changed the Madonna's weeping schedule. It was important to have "dry" days as well as "wet" days; otherwise there was no sense of heavenly mystery. Moreover, Demencio had observed that some pilgrims actually were glad when the Virgin Mary didn't cry on their first visit. It gave them a reason to come back to Grange on a future vacation, just as tourists return to Yellowstone year after year in the hopes of spotting a moose.

So Demencio hadn't been alarmed when his wife told him the Madonna was malfunctioning. Usually midweek was slow for business, a good time for an unscheduled dry day. But he'd forgotten about the damn mission bus: sixty-odd Christian pilgrims from Wheeling. The preacher's name was Mooney or Moody, something like that, and every other year he roared through Florida with new recruits. Trish would bake a lime pie and Demencio would throw in a bottle of scotch, and in return the preacher would entreat his faithful followers to donate generously at Demencio's shrine. For such a dependable throng, Demencio felt obliged to provide tears.

Thus the Madonna's hydraulic failure was potentially a crisis. Demencio didn't want to interrupt the morning visitation to haul the statue indoors for repairs – to do so would arouse suspicion, even among the most devout. Peering through the curtains, Demencio counted nine victims in the front yard, hovering attentively around the icon.

"Got any ideas?" Trish asked.

"Quiet," said her husband. "Lemme think."

But it wasn't quiet. The sounds of crunching filled the room: JoLayne's cooters, enjoying breakfast.

Demencio's somber gaze settled on the aquarium. Instead of breaking the romaine into bite-sized pieces, he'd dropped the whole head of lettuce into the tank. The sight of it had pitched the baby turtles into a frenzy, and they were now chewing their way up the leafy slopes.

It was, Demencio had to admit, weirdly impressive. Forty-five marauding turtles. He got an idea. "You still got that Bible?" he asked his wife. "The illustrated one?"

"Somewhere, yeah."

"And I'll need some paint," he said, "like they sell for model airplanes at the hobby store."

"We only got two hours before the bus."

"Don't worry, this won't take long." Demencio walked over to the aquarium. He bent down and said: "OK, who wants to be a star?"

# TEN

**On the morning** of November 28, with rain misting the mountains, Mary Andrea Finley Krome checked out of the Mona Pacifica Mineral Spa and Residential Treatment Center, on the island of Maui. She flew directly to Los Angeles, where the next day she auditioned for a network television commercial for a new home-pregnancy test. Later she flew on to Scottsdale to rejoin the road company for the *Silence of the Lambs* musical, in which she starred as Clarice, the intrepid young FBI agent. Mary Andrea's itinerary was relayed by certain sources to Tom Krome's divorce lawyer, Dick Turnquist, who arranged for a process server to be waiting backstage at the dinner theater in Arizona.

Somehow Mary Andrea got word of the ambush. Midway through the finale, with the entire cast and chorus singing,

> "Oh, Hannibal the Cannibal,
> How deliciously malicious you are!"

. . . Mary Andrea collapsed, convincingly, in a spastic heap. The process server stood back as paramedics strapped the slack-tongued actress on a stretcher and carried her to an ambulance. By the time Dick Turnquist learned the details, Mary Andrea Finley Krome had miraculously regained consciousness, checked herself out of the Scottsdale hospital, rented a Thunderbird and disappeared into the desert.

Dick Turnquist delivered the bad news to Tom Krome via fax, which Krome retrieved at a Kinko's across the highway from the University of Miami campus. He didn't read it until he and JoLayne Lucks were parked under a streetlight on what she called the Big Stakeout.

After scanning the lawyer's report, Krome ripped it into pieces. JoLayne said: "I know what that woman wants."

"Me, too. She wants to be married forever."

"You're wrong, Tom. She'll go for a divorce. It has to be her idea, that's all."

"Thank you, Dr. Brothers." Krome didn't want to think about his future ex-wife because then he would no longer sleep like a puppy. Instead he would awake with marrow-splitting headaches and bleeding gums.

He said, "You don't understand. This is a sport for Mary Andrea, dodging me and the lawyers. It's like a competition. Feeds her perverse appetite for drama."

"Can I ask how much you send her?"

Krome laughed sulfurously. "*Nada*. Not a damn penny! That's my point, I've tried everything: I cut off the monthly checks, canceled the credit cards, closed the joint accounts, forgot her birthday, forgot our anniversary, insulted her mother, slept with other women, grossly exaggerated how many – and still she won't divorce me. Won't even come to court!"

JoLayne said, "There's one thing you didn't try."

"It's against the law."

"Tell her you're dating a black girl. That usually does the trick."

"Mary Andrea couldn't care less. Hey, check this out." Tom Krome pointed across the parking lot. "Is that the pickup truck?"

"I'm not sure." JoLayne sat forward intently. "Could be."

On the morning the disposable camera arrived in the mail, Katie took it to a one-hour photo studio. Tom had done a pretty good job in Grange: only two pictures of his thumb and several of the Madonna shrine. In the close-ups, the statue's eyes glistened convincingly.

Katie slipped the photographs in her purse and drove downtown for an early lunch with her husband. In keeping with her new policy of marital sharing and complete openness, she placed the snapshots on the table between the bread basket and the pitcher of sangria.

"Tom kept his promise," she said, by way of explanation.

Judge Arthur Battenkill Jr. put down his salad fork and thumbed through the pictures. His dullness of expression and pistonlike mastication reminded Katie of a grazing sheep.

He said, "So what the hell is it?"

"The Virgin Mary. The one that cries."

"Cries."

"See there?" Katie pointed. "They say she cries real tears."

"*Who* says?"

"It's a lore, Arthur. That's all."

"A crock is more like it." He handed the photos to his wife. "And your writer boyfriend gave you these?"

Katie said, "I asked him to – and he's not a boyfriend. It's over, as I've told you a dozen times. We're through, OK?"

Her husband took a sip of wine. Then, gnawing on a chunk of Cuban bread: "Let me see if I understand. It's over, but he's still sending you personal photographs."

Katie conveyed her annoyance by pinging a spoon against the stem of her wineglass. "You don't listen very well," she said, "for a judge."

Her husband snickered. His poor attitude made Katie wonder if this whole honesty thing was a mistake; with someone as jealous as Arthur, maybe it was wiser to keep a few harmless secrets.

If only he'd make an effort, Katie thought. If only he'd open up the way she had. Out of the blue she asked, "So, how's Dana?"

Dana was one of the two secretaries whom Judge Arthur Battenkill Jr. was currently screwing.

"She's just fine," he said, cool as an astronaut.

"And Willow – she still with that ballplayer?"

Willow was the other secretary, Arthur's reserve mistress.

"They're still living together," the judge reported, "but Oscar's out of baseball. Torn rotator cuff, something like that."

"Too bad," said Katie.

"Maybe it was tendinitis. Anyway, he's gone back to get his degree. Restaurant management is what Willow said."

"Good for him," said Katie, thinking: Enough already about Oscar.

The judge looked pleased when his scrod arrived – baked in a bed of pasta, topped with crabmeat and artichokes. Katie was having the garden quiche, which she picked at listlessly. She hadn't seriously expected her husband to confess all his adulteries, but it wouldn't have killed him to admit to one. Willow would've been an encouraging start – she was no prize.

Katie said, "You were tossing and turning last night."

"You noticed."

"Your stomach again?"

"I got up," Arthur said, cheeks full, "and reread that remarkable list of yours."

Uh-oh, thought Katie.

"You and your young man," he said, swallowing emphatically, "every sordid, raunchy, sweaty detail. I can't believe you kept count."

"That's what truthful confessions are. If I went a little overboard, I'm sorry," Katie said.

"Thirteen sexual acts in fourteen days!" Her husband, twirling a pale green noodle onto his fork. "Including three blow jobs – which, by the way, is two more than you've given me in the last fourteen *months*."

Talk about keeping count, Katie thought. "Arthur, finish your fish before it gets cold."

"I don't understand you, Katherine. After everything I've done for you, I get a knife in my heart."

She said, "Stop. You're getting worked up over practically nothing."

"Three blow jobs is not 'practically nothing.' "

"You've missed the whole point. The whole darn point." She reached under the table and flicked her husband's hand off her thigh.

"Your young man," he said, "where is he now?

Lourdes? Jerusalem? Maybe Turin – getting fitted for the shroud!"

"Arthur, he's not my 'young man.' I don't know where he is. And you, you're just a hypocritical ass."

Neatly the judge buffed a napkin across his lips. "I apologize, Katherine. Tell you what, let's get a room somewhere."

"You go to hell," she said.

"Please?"

"On one condition. You quit obsessing about Tommy."

"It's a deal," said Arthur Battenkill Jr. Jovially he waved at the waiter and asked for the check.

A few hours later, Tom Krome's house blew up.

On the way to breakfast, Bodean Gazzer and Chub stopped to hassle a couple of migrant workers hitch-hiking along Highway One. Chub hovered with the .357 while Bode ran through the drill:

*Name the fourteenth President of the United States.*

*Where was the Constitution signed?*

*Recite the Second Amendment.*

*Who starred in* Red Dawn?

Personally, Chub was glad he didn't have to take the same quiz. Evidently the two Mexicans didn't do so hot, because Bode ordered them in butchered Spanish to show their green cards. Fearfully the men took out their wallets, which Bode emptied in the gravel along the side of the road.

"They legal?" Chub asked.

"They wish."

With the sharp toe of a boot, Bode kicked through the

migrants' meager belongings – driver's licenses, farm-worker IDs, passport snapshots of children, prayer tabs, postage stamps, bus passes. Chub thought he spotted an immigration card, but Bode ground it to shreds under his heel. Then he removed the cash from the men's wallets and ordered them to get a move on, *muchachos*!

Later, in the truck, Chub asked how much money they'd had.

"Eight bucks between 'em."

"Oh, man."

"Hey, it's eight bucks that rightfully belongs to white 'Mericans like us. Fucking illegals, Chub – guess who pays their doctor bills and food stamps? Me and you, that's who. Billions a dollars every year on aliens."

As usual, Chub saw no reason to doubt his friend's knowledge of such matters.

"And I mean *billions*," Bode Gazzer went on, "so don't think of it as a robbery, my friend. That was a rebate."

Chub nodded. "You put it that way, sure."

When they returned from the 7-Eleven, they found an unfamiliar car parked crookedly near Chub's trailer. It was a sanded-down Chevrolet Impala; an old one, too. One of Chub's counterfeit handicapped permits hung from the rearview.

"Easy does it," said Chub, pulling the gun from his belt.

The door of the trailer was open, the TV blaring. Bode cupped his hands to his mouth: "Get your ass out here, whoever you are! And keep your goddamn hands in the air!"

Shiner appeared, shirtless and stubbly-bald, in the

doorway. He wore the grin of a carefree idiot. "I'm here!" he proclaimed.

At first Bode and Chub didn't recognize him.

"Hey," Shiner said, "it's me – your new white brother. Where's the militia?"

Chub lowered the pistol. "The fuck you do to yourself, boy?"

"Shaved my hair off."

"May I ask why?"

"So I can be a skinhead," Shiner replied.

Bodean Gazzer whistled. "No offense, son, but it ain't your best look."

The problem was with Shiner's scalp: an angry latitudinal scar, shining like a hideous stamp on the pale dome of his head.

Chub asked Shiner if he'd gotten branded by some wild Miami niggers or Cubans.

"Nope. I fell asleep on a crankcase."

Bode crossed his arms. "And this crankcase," he said, "was it still in the car?"

"Yessir, with the engine runnin'." Shiner did his best to explain: The mishap had occurred almost two years earlier on a Saturday afternoon. He'd had a few beers, a couple joints, maybe half a roofie, when he decided to tune the Impala. He'd started the car, opened the hood and promptly passed out headfirst on the engine block.

"Fucker heated up big-time," Shiner said.

Chub couldn't stand it. He went in the trailer to take a shit, turn off the television and hunt down a cold Budweiser. When he came out he saw Bode Gazzer sitting next to Shiner on the front fender of the Chevy.

Bode waved him over. "Hey, our boy done exactly what we told him."

"How's that?"

"The Negro girl come to his house askin' about the Lotto ticket."

"She sure did," Shiner said, "and I said it wasn't her that won it. I said she must of got confused with another Saturday."

Chub said, "Good man. What'd she do next?"

"Got all pissed and run off out the door. She's beat up pretty bad, too. That was you guys, I figgered."

Bode prodded Shiner to finish the story. "Tell about how you quit your job at the store."

"Oh yeah, Mr. Singh, he said I couldn't park with the handicaps even though I got the blue wheelchair dealie on the mirror. So what I done, I grabbed my back pay from the cash register and hauled ass."

Bode added: "Took the security video, too. Just like we told him."

"Yeah, I hid it in the glove box." Shiner jerked his head toward the Impala.

"Slick move," said Chub, winking his good eye. In truth, he wasn't especially impressed by Shiner. Bode Gazzer, too, had doubts. The boy manifested the sort of submissive dimness that foretold a long sad future in minimum-security institutions.

"Look here," Shiner said, flexing his doughy left arm. "Radical new tattoo: *W.R.B.* To make it official."

Over the rim of his beer can, Chub shot Bode a look that said: *You* tell him.

"So how's it look?" Shiner asked brightly. "Seventy-five bucks, 'case you guys want one, too."

Bode slid off the fender and brushed the rust marks off the butt of his camo trousers. "Thing is, we had to change the name."

Shiner quit flexing. "It ain't the White Rebel Brotherhood no more? How come?"

"You was right about the rock band," Bode said.

"Yeah," Chub interjected, "we didn't want no confusion."

"So what's the new name?"

Bode told him. Shiner asked him to repeat it.

"White Clarion Aryans," Bode said, slowly.

Shiner's mouth drew tight. Morosely he stared at the initials burned into his biceps. "So the new ones are . . . W-C-A?"

"Right."

"Shit," said Shiner, under his breath. Looking up, he managed a smile. "Oh well."

There was an uncomfortable silence, during which Shiner rearranged his arms to cover the tattoo. Even Chub felt sorry for him. "But you know what," he said to Shiner, "that's one hell of a eagle you got there."

"Damn right," Bode Gazzer agreed. "That's one mean motherfucker of an eagle. What's he got in them claws, an M16?"

The boy perked up. "Affirmative. M16 is what I told the tattoo man."

"Well, he did you proud. How about a beer?"

Later they all went to the Sports Authority and (using the stolen Visa) purchased tents, sleeping bags, air mattresses, mosquito netting, lantern fuel and other outdoor gear. Bode said they should keep everything packed tight and ready, in case the NATO storm troopers came ashore without warning. Bode was pleased to find out that Shiner, unlike Chub, had a genuine fondness for camouflage sportswear. As a treat Bode bought him a lightweight Trebark parka – Shiner could hardly wait to get back to the trailer and try it all on.

While he ran inside to change clothes, Bode said to Chub: "He's like a kid on Christmas morning."

More like a damn retard, thought Chub. He said, "You got a spare hat? Because I don't wanna look at that skinhead's skinned head no more."

In his truck Bode found a soggy Australian-style bush hat; the mildew blended neatly into the camo pattern. Shiner wore it proudly, cinching the strap at his throat.

They spent the afternoon at the rock pit, where it quickly became evident the young recruit could not be entrusted with the serious guns. Chub had illegally converted the AR-15 to fully automatic, which proved too much, physically and emotionally, for the newest member of the White Clarion Aryans. Taking the rifle from Chub's hands, Shiner gave a Comanche-style whoop and began to shout: "Which way's the Bahamas! Which way's them cocksuckin' NATO commies!" Then he spun around and started firing wildly – bullets skipped across the water, twanged off limestone boulders, mowed down the cattails and saw grass.

Bode and Chub ducked behind the truck, Bode muttering: "This ain't no good. Christ, this ain't no good at all."

Chub cursed harshly. "I need a goddamn drink."

It took a few minutes for Shiner to relinquish the AR-15, after which he was restricted to harmless plinking with his old Marlin .22. At dusk the three of them, smelling of gunfire and stale beer, returned to Chub's trailer. When Bode Gazzer asked if anybody was hungry, Shiner said he could eat a whole cow.

Chub couldn't tolerate another hour in the

hyperactive nitwit's presence. "You gotta stay here," he instructed Shiner, "and stand guard."

"Guard of what?" the kid asked.

"The guns. Plus all the shit we bought today," Chub said. "New man always does guard duty. Ain't that right, Bode?"

"You bet." Bode, too, had grown weary of Shiner's company. He said, "The tents and so forth, that's important survivalist supplies. Can't just leave it here with nobody on watch."

"God, I'm starvin'," Shiner said.

Chub slapped him on the shoulder. "We'll bring you some chicken wings. You like the extry hot?"

According to the bank, JoLayne's credit card had been used two nights consecutively at the same Hooters – a reckless move that Krome found encouraging. The Lotto robbers clearly were not master criminals.

JoLayne figured nobody would be ballsy enough to go there three times in a row, but Krome said it was the best lead they had. Now he and JoLayne were outside the restaurant, watching a red pickup truck park in a disabled-only zone.

"Is that them?" Krome asked.

"The guys who came to my house were not crippled. Neither of them," JoLayne said gravely.

Two men – one tall, one short – got out of the truck. They entered the restaurant without the aid of a wheelchair, a crutch, or even a cane.

"Must be a miracle," said Krome.

JoLayne wasn't certain they were the same men who'd attacked her. "We're too far away."

"Then let's get closer."

He went in alone and chose a corner table. A minute later JoLayne came through the door – the floppy hat, Lolita sunglasses. She joined him, sitting with her back to the bar.

"You get the license tag?" she said.

"Yes, ma'am. And how about that bumper sticker? 'Fuhrman for President.' "

"Where are they?" she asked tensely. "Did they look at me?"

"If it's the table I think it is, they didn't notice either of us."

On the other side of the restaurant, two very distinctive customers were chatting with a pretty blond waitress. Her electric smile solved to Krome's satisfaction the mystery of why the shitkickers returned night after night with a hot credit card: They were smitten. One of the men was outfitted entirely in camouflage, including a cap. His companion wore a dirty ponytail and a vulcanized patch over one eye. Both men, Krome noted, bore deep cuts on their faces.

"You said one was dressed like a hunter."

JoLayne nodded. "That's right."

"Take a peek."

"I'm frightened."

"It's all right," Krome told her.

She turned just enough to catch a quick look. "Lord," she gasped, and turned back.

Tom Krome patted her hand. "We done good, pardner."

JoLayne's expression was unreadable behind the big sunglasses. "Give me the car keys."

"What for?" Krome asked, knowing the answer. She

didn't want to open the car; she wanted to open the trunk.

JoLayne said, "Let's wait till they leave – "

"No, not here."

"Tom, we've got the Remington. What could they do?"

"Forget it."

A waitress came, but JoLayne was unresponsive. Krome ordered hamburgers and Cokes for both of them. When they were alone again, he tried to make the case that a busy restaurant parking lot wasn't the ideal place to pull a shotgun on anybody, especially two drunk white-trash psychopaths.

JoLayne said, "I want my damn lottery ticket."

"And you'll get it. We found the bastards, that's the main thing. They can't get away from us now."

Again she peered over her shoulder, shivering at the sight of the ponytailed robber. "That face I'll never forget. But the eye patch I don't remember."

"Maybe you blinded him," Krome said.

JoLayne Lucks smiled faintly. "Lord, I hope so."

# ELEVEN

**The firebombing of** Tom Krome's house was the most serious managerial crisis of Sinclair's career. All afternoon he polished the exculpatory memorandum and awaited a summons from *The Register*'s managing editor. Like Krome's, the managing editor's training was in hard news and he viewed the world darkly. He was an angular, intense man in his mid-forties; prematurely gray, allergy prone, gruff, profane. He was famous for his laserlike glare and his lack of patience.

His last communication with Sinclair had come seven weeks earlier in a terse phone call: No frigging PMS column, you hear me! It had been one of Sinclair's rare brainstorms – a regular feature devoted to coping with PMS. The column would run once a month, of course. The managing editor despised the idea, which Sinclair promptly blamed on one of his subordinates.

Even under the mildest circumstances, direct contact with the M.E. was nerve-racking. So Sinclair whitened when, shortly after six, he was called in to discuss the Tom Krome situation. Upon entering the office, Sinclair was brusquely motioned to a covered armchair. On the other side of a mahogany desk, his boss skimmed a police report, although Sinclair (having never seen one) didn't recognize it as such. What he knew about the burning of

Krome's home had come from a gossipy city desk reporter, in a brief conversation at the urinals. Of course Sinclair had been alarmed by the news, but he was more distressed that he hadn't been notified formally, through channels. He was, after all, Krome's immediate supervisor. Didn't anybody believe in E-mail anymore?

With a contemplative snort, the managing editor turned and tossed the police report on a credenza. Sinclair seized the moment to present a crisp copy of the memorandum, which the managing editor crumpled and threw back at him. It landed in Sinclair's lap.

The managing editor said: "I already saw it."

"But . . . when?"

"In all its glorious versions, you schmuck."

"Oh."

Instantly Sinclair realized what had happened. With the touch of a button on his computer terminal, the managing editor could call up any story in the newspaper's vast bank of editing queues. Sinclair had been led to believe his boss paid no attention to what went on in the Features department, but evidently it wasn't true. The managing editor had electronically been tracking the Krome memo from the date of its perfidious inception.

Sinclair felt feverish and short of breath. He plucked the wadded paper from his lap and discreetly shoved it into a pocket.

"What I've found fascinating," the managing editor was saying, "is the creative process – how each new draft painted a blacker picture of Tom's mental state. And the details you added . . . well, I had to laugh. Maybe you missed your calling, Sinclair. Maybe you should've been a writer." The managing editor eyed him as if he were a turd on a carpet. "Would you like some water? Coffee?"

Sinclair, in an anemic murmur: "No, thank you."

"May we stipulate that your 'memo' is pure horseshit?"

"Yes."

"OK. Now I have some questions. One: Do you have any idea why Tom Krome's house was torched?"

"No, I don't."

"Do you have a clue why anyone would want to harm him?"

"Not really," Sinclair said.

"Do you know where he is?"

"The rumor is Bermuda."

The managing editor chuckled. "You're not going to Bermuda, Sinclair. You're going to the last place you sent Tom, and you're going to find him. By the way, you look like hell."

"I'm sure I do."

"Another question: Does Tom still work for us?"

"As far as I'm concerned, he does." Sinclair said it with all the conviction he could summon.

The managing editor removed his glasses and began vigorously cleaning the lenses with a tissue. "What about as far as *Tom* is concerned? Any chance he was serious about quitting?"

"I . . . I suppose it's possible."

Woozy with apnea, Sinclair thought he might be on the verge of heart failure. He'd read many articles about critically ill patients who had eerie out-of-body experiences in ambulances and emergency rooms. Sinclair felt that way now – floating above the managing editor's credenza, watching himself being emasculated. The sensation was neither as painless nor as dreamlike as other near-death survivors had described.

"The arson guys are going through the rubble tonight," said the managing editor. "They want to know if the fire could be connected to a story Tom was working on."

"I can't imagine how." Sinclair gulped air like a hippo. Slowly the feeling returned to his fingers and toes.

The managing editor said: "Suppose you tell me exactly what he was writing."

"A quickie feature. Hit and run."

"About what?"

"Just some woman who won the lottery," Sinclair said. Impulsively he added: "A black woman." Just so the boss would know Sinclair was on the lookout for feel-good stories about minorities. Maybe it would help his predicament, maybe not.

The managing editor squinted. "That's it – a lottery feature?"

"That's it," Sinclair asserted.

He didn't want it known that he'd rejected Tom Krome's request to pursue the robbery angle. Sinclair believed the decision would make him appear gutless and shortsighted, particularly if Krome turned up murdered in some ditch.

"Where is this Lotto woman?" asked the managing editor.

"Little town called Grange."

"Straight feature?"

"That's all it was."

The managing editor frowned. "Well, you're lying again, Sinclair. But it's my own damn fault for hiring you." He stood up and removed his suit jacket from the back of his chair. "You'll go to Grange and you won't come back until you've found Tom."

Sinclair nodded. He'd call his sister. She and Roddy would let him stay in the spare room. They could take him around town, hook him up with their sources.

"Next week they're announcing the Amelias," said the managing editor, slipping into his jacket. "I entered Krome."

"You did?"

Again Sinclair was caught off guard. The "Amelias" were a national writing competition named after the late Amelia J. Lloyd, widely considered the mother superior of the modern newspaper feature. No event was too prosaic or inconsequential to escape Amelia Lloyd's sappy attention. Bake sales, craft shows, charity walk-athons, spelling bees, mall openings, blood drives, Easter egg hunts – Amelia's miraculous prose breathed sweet life into them all. In her short but meteoric career, her byline had graced *The New Orleans Times-Picayune, The St. Louis Post-Dispatch, The Tampa Tribune, The Miami Herald* and *The Cleveland Plain Dealer.* It was in Cleveland that Amelia J. Lloyd had been tragically killed in the line of duty, struck down by a runaway miniature Duesenberg at a Masonic parade. She was only thirty-one.

All but an elitist handful of newspapers entered their feature sections in the annual Amelias, because it was the only contest that pretended fluff was worthwhile journalism. At *The Register*, staff entries for such awards came, as policy, from the Assistant Deputy Managing Editor of Features and Style. Sinclair had chosen not to submit Tom Krome in the Amelias because his stories invariably showed, in Sinclair's opinion, a hard or sarcastic edge that the judges might find off-putting. In addition, Sinclair feared that if by cruel fate Krome actually won the contest (or even placed), he would physically attack Sinclair in front of the staff. Krome had been heard to remark that, even with its $500 prize, an Amelia was a badge of shame.

So Sinclair was rattled to learn the managing editor had, without informing him, replaced Sinclair's hand-picked entry with Tom Krome.

"I meant to drop you a note," the managing editor said, not apologetically.

Sinclair measured his response. "Tom's turned out some super stuff this year. What category did you pick?"

"Body of work."

"Ah. Good." Sinclair, thinking: Body of work? The rules called for a minimum of eight stories, and it was generally assumed they should be upbeat and positive – just like the ones Amelia J. Lloyd used to write. Sinclair doubted whether Tom Krome had used eight upbeat *adjectives* in his whole career. And where had the boss found time to cull a year's worth of clips?

"Do you know," said the managing editor, packing his briefcase, "how long it's been since *The Register* won a national award? *Any* national award?"

Sinclair shook his head.

"Eight years," the managing editor said. "Third place, deadline reporting, American Society of Newspaper Editors. Eight fucking years."

Sinclair, sensing it was expected of him, asked: "What was the story?

"Tornado creamed an elementary school. Two dead, twenty-three injured. Guess who wrote it? Me."

"No kidding?"

"Don't look so shocked." The managing editor snapped the briefcase shut. "Here's another hot flash:

We're about to win a first-place Amelia for feature writing. As in 'grand prize.' I expect Tom to be in the newsroom next week when it moves on the wires."

Sinclair's head swum. "How do you know he won?"

"One of the judges told me. An ex-wife, if you're wondering. The only one who still speaks to me. When are you leaving for Grange?"

"First thing tomorrow."

"Try not to embarrass us, OK?"

The managing editor was three steps from the door when Sinclair said, "Do you want me to call you?"

"Every single day, *amigo*. And seriously, don't fuck this up."

Chub believed he was making progress with Amber. Each night she seemed friendlier and more talkative. Bodean Gazzer thought his friend was imagining things – the girl chatted up all her customers.

"Bull," Chub said. "See how she looks at me?"

"Spooked is how she looks. It's that damn patch."

"Fuck yourself," said Chub, though secretly he worried that Bode might be right. Amber might be one of those women who weren't aroused by scars and eye patches and such.

Bode said, "Maybe you oughta take it off."

"I tried."

"Don't tell me."

"It's the tire glue," Chub explained. "It's like goddamn see-ment."

Bode Gazzer said he was glad it was Chub's left eye that was sealed, because the right one was his lead eye for shooting. "But it'd still be better without the patch," he added. "Patch like to give you a blind spot in a firefight."

Chub bit into a chicken bone and noisily chewed it to a pulp, which he swallowed. "Don't you worry about me when it come to guns. Even my blind spots is twenty-twenty."

When Amber came to collect the empty beer bottles, Chub mischievously inquired about her boyfriend.

"He's not here," she said.

"I can see that, darling."

Chub was tempted to say something about Tony the asshole's sports car catching fire; drop a sly hint that he and Bode had done it, so Amber would know his intentions were serious. But he wasn't sure if she was sharp enough to make the connection, or even if she was the sort of woman who was favorably impressed by arson.

"Another round?" she asked.

Chub said: "Time you get off work?"

"Late."

"How late?"

"Real late."

Bode Gazzer cut in: "Bring us four more."

"Right away," Amber said, gratefully, and dashed off.

"Shit," Chub muttered. Maybe it *was* the patch. He suspected it wouldn't bother her one bit, once she found out he was soon to be a millionaire.

Bode advised him to back off. "Remember what I told you about low profiles. Plus, you're spookin' the girl."

With a thumb and forefinger, Chub deftly extracted a shard of chicken bone from the roof of his mouth. He said, "When's the last time you fucked anything besides the palm a your hand?"

Bode Gazzer said that, being a white man, he had a duty to be extra scrupulous about spreading his seed.

"Your what?" Chub sneered.

"That's what the Bible calls it. Seed."

"Man can't get enough guns and pussy. You said so yourself."

So I did, Bode thought ruefully. The truth was, he didn't want Chub distracted by a Hooters babe or any other woman until they collected the lottery money. Then there'd be plenty of time for wild poon.

Bode tried to improvise: "There's good and bad of everything, Chub. Us white men's got a responsibility – we're an endangered species. Like the unicorn."

Chub didn't fold. He recalled that he once owned a .45 semi, made in Yugoslavia or Romania or some godforsaken place, that misfired every fourth or fifth round. "Now that was a bad *gun*," he said, "but I ain't never had no bad pussy."

They debated until closing time, with Bode holding to the position that militiamen should have carnal relations only with pure white Christian women of European descent, lest the union produce a child. Chub (not wishing to limit his already sparse opportunities) insisted white men were morally obliged to spread their superior genetics near and far, and therefore should have sex with any woman who wanted it, regardless of race, creed or heritage.

"Besides, it's plain to see," he added, "Amber's white as Ivory Snow."

"Yeah, but her boyfriend's Meskin. That makes her Meskin by injection," said Bode.

"You can shut up now."

"Point is, we gotta be careful."

The manager flicked the lights twice and the restaurant began to empty. Bode asked for a box of chicken wings to go, but a Negro busboy told him the kitchen had closed. Bode paid the dinner bill with the stolen Visa, leaving another ludicrous tip. Afterwards Chub insisted on hanging around the parking lot, in the remote likelihood Amber needed a lift. After fifteen minutes she appeared, brushing her hair as she came out the door. To Chub she looked almost as beautiful in faded jeans as she did in her skimpy work shorts. He told Bode to honk the horn, so she'd see them waiting in the truck. Bode refused.

Chub was rolling down the window to call her name when none other than Tony himself drove up in a new jet-black Mustang convertible. Amber got in, and the car sped away.

"What the fuck?" said Chub, despairingly.

"Forget about it."

"Asshole must be loaded to 'ford two cars."

Bode Gazzer said, "For Christ's sake, it's probably a rental. Now forget about it."

Half drunk, Bode struggled to back the pickup out of the handicapped slot. He paid no attention to the blue Honda on the other side of the lot, and failed to notice when the same car swung into traffic behind them, southbound on Highway One.

Before the two rednecks broke into her home and attacked her, JoLayne Lucks had in her entire adult life been struck by only two men. One was black, one was white. Both were boyfriends at the time.

The black man was Robert, the police officer. He'd

slapped JoLayne across the face when, with ample evidence, she accused him of extorting sex from female motorists. The very next morning Robert found a live pygmy rattlesnake curled up in his underwear drawer, a discovery that impelled him to hop and screech about the bedroom. JoLayne Lucks gingerly collected the snake and released it in a nearby pasture. Later she teased Robert about his girlish reaction, noting that the bite of a pygmy rattler was seldom fatal to humans. That night he slept with his service revolver cocked on the bedstand, a practice he diligently maintained until he and JoLayne parted company.

The white man who hit her was, of all people, Neal the codependent chiropractor. It had happened one night when JoLayne was an hour late getting home from Jackson Memorial Hospital, a delay caused by a short-tempered cocaine importer with personnel problems. Four multiple-gunshot victims had arrived simultaneously in the emergency room, where JoLayne was on duty. Although the shooting spree was the lead story on the eleven o'clock news, Neal the chiropractor remained unconvinced. He preferred to believe JoLayne was late because she'd been dallying with a handsome thoracic surgeon, or possibly one of the new anesthesiologists. In a jealous tantrum, Neal threw a wild punch that glanced harmlessly off JoLayne's handbag. She was upon him instantly, breaking his nose with two stiff jabs. Soon Neal the chiropractor was sniveling for forgiveness. He rushed out and bought JoLayne a diamond tennis bracelet, which she returned to him in mint condition on the night they broke up.

So she was not accustomed to being struck by men of any color; did not invite it, would not tolerate it, and believed with every fiber in swift, unmitigated retribution. Which is why she couldn't get her mind off the shotgun in the trunk of Tom Krome's Honda.

"You got a plan yet?" she said. "Because I've got one if you don't."

Krome said, "I'm sure you do."

He'd dropped back to put some distance between them and the red pickup truck, which was weaving slightly and accelerating in unpredictable bursts. The driver was bombed – even a rookie patrolman could have spotted it. Krome didn't want the rednecks to crash into anybody, but he also didn't want them to get pulled over on a DUI. Who knew what they might do to a cop? And if they allowed themselves to be tossed in jail, it might be weeks before they got out, depending on how many felony warrants were outstanding. JoLayne Lucks didn't have that much time.

Krome's plan was to follow the two men to where they lived, and to case the place.

"In other words, we're stalking," JoLayne said.

Krome hoped her tone was one of impatience and not derision. "Correct me if I'm wrong, but I thought the goal was to retrieve your Lotto ticket. If you'd rather just shoot these morons and go home, let me know so I can bail out."

She raised her hands. "I'm sorry, I'm sorry."

"You're angry. I'd be angry, too."

"Furious," she said.

"Stay cool. We're close."

"You memorized the license tag?"

"I told you before. Yes," Krome said.

"Hey, they're speeding up again."

"So I noticed."

"Don't lose 'em."

"JoLayne!"

"Sorry. I'll shut up now."

They tailed the truck all the way to Homestead. On the way, it stopped three times along the side of the highway, where one or both of the rednecks nonchalantly got out to urinate. Whenever that happened, Krome kept driving. Once he got ahead, he'd quickly pull over in an unlit spot and wait for the pickup to pass by again. Eventually the rednecks turned east off Highway One, then south on a dirt road that bisected a tomato farm. Here there was no other traffic – only a rolling dust cloud kicked up by the truck. The dust smelled faintly of pesticide.

JoLayne poked her head from the car and pretended to drink the air. "Green acres! Men of the soil!" she exclaimed.

Krome slowed and turned off the headlights, so the rednecks wouldn't spot them in the rearview. After a few miles the tomato fields gave way to palmetto scrub and Dade County pines. Gradually the road turned and ran parallel to a wide drainage canal. Across the rippled water, JoLayne was able to make out the shapes of rough shacks, small house trailers and abandoned cars.

A half mile ahead on the dirt road, the pickup's brake lights flashed brightly through the whorls of dust. Krome immediately stopped the Honda and killed the engine. The silence announced that the driver of the truck had done the same.

Krome said, "Nice neighborhood."

"It's not exactly Star Island." JoLayne touched his arm. "Can we please open the trunk now?"

"In a second."

They couldn't see the red truck, but they heard the doors slam. Then came a man's voice, booming down the canal through the darkness.

JoLayne whispered: "What's that all about?"

Before Tom Krome could answer, the night was split open by gunfire.

Alone in the middle of nowhere, Shiner had wigged out. The noises were the same as those in the woods outside Grange – frogs, crickets, raccoons – but here every peep and rustle seemed louder and more ominous. Shiner couldn't stop thinking about all those NATO troops bivouacked in the Bahamas.

*Just eighty miles thataway*, Bodean Gazzer had said, pointing, *across the Gulf Stream*.

Stunted as it was, Shiner's imagination had no difficulty conjuring a specter of blue-helmeted enemy soldiers poised on an advancing flotilla. He became consumed with the idea that the United States of America might be invaded at any minute, while Bode and Chub were off drinking beer.

Acting against orders, Shiner got the AR-15 out of Chub's mobile home and climbed a trellis to the flimsy roof. There, in his moldy bush hat and new camouflage parka, he waited. And while he couldn't see as far as the Bahama Islands, he had an excellent view of the dirt road and the farm canal.

By land or by sea, Shiner thought, let the fuckers try.

The rifle felt grand in his hands; it took the edge off his nerves. He wondered what types of guns the NATO communists were carrying. Russian, Bode Gazzer had speculated, or North Korean. Shiner decided to swipe one off the first soldier he shot, for a souvenir. Maybe he'd chop off an ear, too – he'd heard of such grisly customs during his three weeks in the army, from a drill sergeant who'd been to Nam. Shiner didn't know what he would do with a severed NATO ear, but he'd surely put it someplace where his Ma wouldn't find it. Same with the guns. Ever since she'd found the Road-Stain Jesus, his mother had been down on guns.

After an hour on the roof, Shiner was overcome by a stabbing hunger. Stealthily he climbed down and foraged in Chub's refrigerator, where he located two leathery slices of pepperoni pizza and a tin of boneless sardines. These Shiner carried back to his sentry post. He forced himself to eat slowly and savor each bite – once the invasion began there'd be no more pizza for a long, long time.

On two occasions Shiner fired the AR-15 at suspicious noises. The first turned out to be a clumsy opossum (not an enemy sapper) that knocked over Chub's garbage can, just as the second turned out to be a mud hen (not a scuba-diving commando) splashing in the lily pads.

Better safe than sorry, Shiner thought.

After a while he drifted off, one cheek pressed against the cool stock of the rifle. He dreamed he was back in boot camp, trying to do push-ups while a brawny black sergeant stood over him, calling him a faggot, a pussy, a dickless wonder. In the dream, Shiner wasn't much better at push-ups than he was in real life, so the sergeant's yelling grew louder and louder. Suddenly he drew his sidearm and told Shiner he'd shoot him in the ass if his knees touched the ground once more, which of course happened on the very next push-up. In a rage, the sergeant simultaneously placed a heavy boot on Shiner's back and the gun barrel against Shiner's tremulous buttocks, and fired –

At the concussion, Shiner bolted awake, clutching the AR-15 to his chest. Then he heard it again – not a gunshot but more like a door slamming. He realized it wasn't part of the dream; it was real. Somebody was out there, in the buzzing night. Maybe it was the NATO soldiers. Maybe what Shiner had heard slamming was the turret door of a Soviet tank.

As they stepped toward the trailer, Bodean Gazzer and Chub were startled by the raw, strung-out cry that came from the roof: "Who goes! Who goes there!"

They were about to answer when the darkness exploded in orange and blue sparks. The spray of automatic rifle fire sent them diving under the pickup truck, where they cursed and cowered and covered their ears until Shiner was done.

Then Chub called out: "It's us, dickface!"

"Us who?" demanded the voice from the roof. "Who goes?"

"Us! *Us!*"

" 'Dentify you selves!"

Bode Gazzer spoke up: "The White Clarion Aryans. Your brothers."

After a significant pause, they heard: "Aw, fuck. Come on out."

Squirming from beneath the truck, Chub said: "What we got here's one brain-dead skinhead."

"Hush," Bode said. "You hear that?"

"Jesus Willy Christ."

Another car on the dirt road – driving away, fast.

Chub groped for his pistol. "What do we do?"

"We chase after the bastards," Bode said, "soon as we get John Wayne Jr. off the roof."

# TWELVE

**Tom Krome's chest** tightened when the headlights appeared in the rearview. JoLayne Lucks turned to see.

"Just like in the movies," she said.

Krome told her to hang on. Without touching the brakes, he guided the car off the farm road, over a dirt berm. They jounced and shimmied to a halt in a stand of thin Australian pines.

"Unlock your door," he said, "but don't get out till I tell you."

They ducked in the front seat, their faces inches apart. They heard the pickup truck coming, the rumble of the oversized tires on the packed dirt.

Out of nowhere, JoLayne said, "I wonder what Martha Stewart would do in a spot like this."

Krome thought: OK, she's delirious.

"Seriously," said JoLayne. "There's a woman who'd be completely useless right about now, unless you were in a hurry for a macramé or a flower box. Ever see ole Martha on TV? Planting those bulbs and bakin' them pies."

Krome said, "Get a grip." He lifted his head to peer out.

"Me, I'm all thumbs when it comes to crafts. A total klutz. However, I *can* use a gun – "

"Quiet," Krome told her.

" – which we happen to have in our possession."

"JoLayne, get ready!"

"A perfectly good shotgun."

In the darkness Krome sensed her edging closer. Her cheek touched his, and he astonished himself by kissing her. No big deal; a light brotherly kiss meant only to calm. That's what he told himself.

JoLayne turned her face but said nothing. The pick-up truck was approaching rapidly. Krome felt her arm brush his shoulder, as if she were reaching out for him.

She wasn't. She was going for his car keys, which she adroitly plucked from the ignition. In an instant she flung open her door and rolled out.

"No!" Krome shouted, but JoLayne was already at the trunk. By the time he got there, the Remington was in her hands.

Nearby, the roadbed brightened; insects swirled in the white beams of the truck's lights. Hurriedly Krome pulled JoLayne Lucks behind a pine tree. He wrapped his arms around her, pinning the shotgun awkwardly between them.

"Lemme go," she said.

"You got the safety on?"

"Don't be a jerk, Tom."

"Sshhh."

As the pickup passed, they heard the sound of men's voices raised in excitement. Tom Krome didn't relax his hold on JoLayne until the truck was gone and the night was utterly still.

He said, "That was close."

JoLayne laid the shotgun in the trunk, and not gently. "Macramé, my ass," she said.

Demencio was still basking in the praise of the Reverend Joshua Moody, who before departing had turned to his curious flock and proclaimed:

"In thirty-three years of touring miracles, this is one of the most astounding things I've ever seen!"

He was speaking of the apostolic cooters.

Later, after the Christian pilgrims from West Virginia had keened and swooned and ultimately placed in Trish's wicker collection basket the sum of $211 (not including what was spent on soft drinks, T-shirts, angel food snacks and sunblock), Reverend Moody had pulled Demencio aside: "You gotta tell me exactly where this came from."

"It's like I said."

"Hey, I been doin' this since before you were born." The preacher, arching one of his snowy-white eyebrows. "Come on, son, I won't give it away."

Demencio had coolly stuck to his spiel. "One day the turtles are normal. The next day I look in the aquarium and there's the apostles. All twelve of 'em."

"Sure, sure." With an impatient sigh, Reverend Moody had turned Demencio loose. "Of all the places for a holy apparition – on a cooter's shell, I swear to God, boy."

"Not an apparition," Demencio had said coyly, "just a likeness."

The concept of using turtles is what had intrigued Reverend Moody – how had a mere layman such as Demencio dreamed up something so original? The man simply wouldn't say. So, out of professional courtesy, the preacher had backed off. Amiably he'd pumped Demencio's hand and told him: "You are one brilliant bastard." Then he'd shepherded the pilgrims back onto the bus.

Demencio had stood waving on the sidewalk until they were out of sight. With a self-congratulatory smirk he'd turned toward his wife, who was sorting the tear-dampened clumps of cash.

"We did it!" she said elatedly.

"Un-fucking-believable."

"You were right, honey. They'll go for anything."

As a kid, Demencio had seen painted turtles for sale at an outdoor flea market in Hialeah. Some of them had roses or sunflowers lacquered on their shells; others had flags or hearts or Disney characters. Demencio had figured it would be no less absurd to decorate JoLayne's cooters with the faces of religious figures. It had seemed Demencio's only hope for salvaging a profit from Reverend Moody's visitation, since the weeping Madonna was temporarily out of service.

After Trish had brought home the art supplies, Demencio had selected a dozen of the liveliest specimens from JoLayne's big aquarium. The delicate process of painting had been preceded by a brief discussion about how the apostles could be most respectfully portrayed on the carapace of a mud-dwelling reptile. Neither Demencio nor his wife could name even half of the original disciples, so they'd consulted a Bible (which, unfortunately, had not provided a complete set of portraits). Trish then had fished through a box of her late father's belongings and found a *Time-Life* volume about the world's greatest masterpieces. In it was a photograph of Leonardo's *The Last Supper*, which Trish had torn out and placed on the workbench in front of her husband.

"This is peachy," he'd said, "but who's who?"

Trish, pointing: "I believe that's Judas. Or maybe Andrew."

"Christ."

"Right there," Trish had said helpfully, "in the middle."

Whereupon Demencio had expelled her and settled down with the cooters to paint. There was no sense getting fancy, because the animals' corrugated shells were difficult to work with – as small as silver dollars. Beards was the way to go, he'd told himself. All the big shots in the Bible wore beards.

Soon Demencio had found a rhythm – restraining each baby turtle with his left hand, wielding the brush with his right. He'd been steady and precise, finishing the job in less than three hours. Although every apostle was given lush facial hair, Demencio had tried to make each one distinct.

Beholding the miniature visages, Trish had asked: "Which is which?"

"Beats the hell outta me."

And, as Demencio had expected, it hadn't mattered. One pilgrim's Matthew was another pilgrim's John.

Avidly Reverend Moody's followers had clustered around the cooter corral that Trish had fashioned out of plastic gardening fence. Demencio had called out the names of each apostle as he pointed with deliberate ambiguity among the scrabbling swarm. The pilgrims hadn't merely been persuaded, they'd been overwhelmed. In the center of the small enclosure Demencio had stationed the fiberglass Virgin Mary, who (he'd announced) would not be crying on this special day. The pilgrims had understood completely – the Holy Mother obviously was cheered by the unexpected arrival of her Son's inner circle.

The apostolic turtles proved such a smash that Demencio decided to use them again the next morning. By noon the yard was jammed. Demencio was fixing a sandwich in the kitchen when Trish urgently reported that the cooters were dehydrating in the sun and that the paint on their shells was beginning to flake. Demencio solved the problem by digging a small moat around the fiberglass Madonna and filling it with a garden hose. Later a divinely inspired tourist from South Carolina asked if that was holy water in which the turtles were swimming. When Demencio assured him it was, the man asked to buy a cupful for four dollars. The other visitors rushed to queue up, and before long Demencio had to refill the moat.

He was aglow at his windfall. Turtle worship! Reverend Moody had been right – it was pure genius.

The visitation proceeded smoothly until midafternoon, when Dominick Amador showed up to hustle Demencio's overflow, exhibiting his seeping stigmata in a most vulgar way. Trish chased him away with a rake. The altercation took place in full view of Mayor Jerry Wicks, who made no attempt to intervene on the shameless Dominick's behalf.

Mayor Wicks had arrived at the shrine in the company of three persons who definitely weren't pilgrims. Two of them Demencio recognized from around town; the third was a stranger. Demencio acknowledged the group with the air of a busy man on his way to the bank, which he was.

"Please," the mayor said. "We won't be long."

"You caught me at a bad time." Demencio, stuffing the last of three fat envelopes.

Jerry Wicks said, "It's about JoLayne Lucks."

"Yeah?" Demencio, thinking: Shit, I knew it was too good to be true. The damn turtles are probably stolen.

Trish popped her head in the front door: "More lettuce!"

Demencio locked the bank deposits in a drawer and headed for the refrigerator. "Have a seat," he said indifferently to his visitors. "Be with you in a minute."

Roddy and Joan were thrilled to assist Joan's brother on such an important journalistic assignment; in fact, they'd have been ecstatic to help with the weekly crop report. Roddy worked for the state, inspecting gasoline pumps, while Joan taught third grade at the county elementary school. They didn't get much company in Grange so they were delighted when Sinclair asked if he could come over for a few days, to work on the lottery story. Because it had been their tip to the newspaper that had gotten the ball rolling, Roddy and Joan felt duty-bound to help Sinclair locate his star reporter, missing with JoLayne Lucks. The Lotto mystery was the most commotion to sweep Grange in ages, and Roddy and Joan were pleased to be in the thick of it. Sinclair hadn't been in town twenty minutes before they introduced him to the mayor, who listened to Sinclair's account of Tom Krome's disappearance with puzzlement and a trace of dismay.

"Whatever's happened," Jerry Wicks said, "rest assured it wasn't Grangians who are responsible. We are the most hospitable folks in Florida!"

Sinclair balanced the notebook on his knees while writing down every word. Sinclair assumed that's how real reporters worked; like a supercharged stenographer, preserving each article and preposition. He didn't know any better, and was too proud to ask around the newsroom for guidance before he'd left on his trip.

One drawback to Sinclair's exact note-taking technique was the extended silence between the moment a sentence was spoken and the moment Sinclair finished transcribing it. He was an uncommonly slow writer; years at the computer keyboard had left him unaccustomed to the feel of a pen in his hand. To make matters worse, he was a neat freak. Copying every trivial comment wasn't enough; Sinclair painstakingly put in the punctuation, too.

Roddy and Joan loyally remained alert while Joan's brother hunched for what seemed like an eternity over the notebook. The mayor, however, was growing antsy.

"I won't mind," he finally said, "if you want to use a tape recorder."

Sinclair's only response was a fresh burst of scribbling.

Jerry Wicks turned to Roddy: "Why's he writing *that* down?"

"I'm not sure."

"Who cares what I said about the tape recorder – "

"I don't know, Mr. Mayor. He must have a reason."

Sinclair reined himself, midsentence. Sheepishly he glanced up and capped the pen. Jerry Wicks seemed relieved. He suggested they all go visit the last person to see JoLayne Lucks before she left town. The man's name was Demencio, the mayor said, and he had a popular religious shrine. Sinclair agreed that he should speak with the man as soon as possible. He tucked the notebook in his back pants pocket, like he'd often seen the male reporters at *The Register* do.

Sliding into the back seat of the mayor's car, Joan murmured to her brother that she kept a portable Sony at the house.

"Thanks anyway," Sinclair said stiffly, "but I'm fine."

And upon meeting Demencio, he whipped out the notebook once again. "Could you spell your name for me?" he asked, pen poised.

"You a cop?" Demencio turned to the mayor. "Is he some kinda cop?"

Jerry Wicks explained who Sinclair was and why he'd come all the way to Grange. They were seated in Demencio's living room – the mayor, Roddy, Joan and Sinclair. Demencio was in his favorite TV chair, nervously tossing a head of romaine lettuce from one hand to the other, like a softball. He was leery of the stranger but he didn't want to blow a shot at free press coverage for the shrine.

Sinclair asked, "When's the last time you saw JoLayne Lucks?"

"Other night," Demencio said, "when she dropped off the cooters."

Roddy and Joan were very curious about the tank of baby turtles, as well as the painted ones in the moat outside, but for some reason Sinclair didn't follow up. Meticulously he wrote down Demencio's answer, then asked:

"Was there a man with Miss Lucks?"

"A white man?"

"Yes. Mid-thirties," Sinclair said. "About six feet tall."

"That's the guy. He took pictures of my Virgin Mary statue. She cries real tears."

Roddy, trying to be helpful: "People come from everywhere to pray at his weeping Madonna."

"There's a visitation every morning," Demencio added. "You oughta stop over."

Sinclair made no response. He was still working frenetically on the first part of Demencio's answer. He'd gotten as far as the word "Virgin" when Roddy's interruption had thrown him off track, causing him to lose the rest of Demencio's quote. Now Sinclair was forced to reconstruct.

"Did you say 'It cries' or 'She cries'?"

"*She* cries," said Demencio, "like a drunken priest."

Neither Roddy nor Joan could imagine seeing such a coarse remark printed in a family newspaper, but Sinclair transcribed it anyway.

"And twelve of my turtles," Demencio said, "got the apostles on their backs. It's the damnedest thing you ever saw – check out the moat!"

"Slow down," said the frazzled Sinclair. His fingers had begun to cramp. "The man who was with Miss Lucks – they left together?"

"Yeah. In his car."

While Sinclair scribbled, Roddy, Joan and the mayor maintained silence. Any distraction would only slow him down more. Demencio, though, had grown restive. He began to shuck the head of lettuce, arranging the leaves in piles, according to size, on the ottoman. He was worried the newspaperman would ask about his financial arrangement with JoLayne Lucks regarding the turtle-sitting. Demencio had no illusion that one thousand dollars was a customary or reasonable fee, or that the newspaperman would believe it was JoLayne's idea.

But when Sinclair finally looked up from his notes,

all he said was: "Did they mention where they were headed?"

"Miami," Demencio answered, in relief.

Joan, her track record as a tipster at stake, piped in: "We heard Bermuda. They say anything about Bermuda?"

"Miami's what they told me. JoLayne said she had some business down that way."

"Slower," Sinclair protested, bent over the pad like a rheumatic jeweler. "Please."

Demencio had run out of hospitality. "It's M-i-a – "

"I *know* how to spell it," Sinclair snapped.

The mayor wedged a knuckle in his mouth, to keep from laughing.

They rode for miles on the farm roads without finding the other car. Bodean Gazzer was too drunk and tired to continue. Chub offered to take the wheel but Bode wouldn't hear of it; nobody else was allowed to drive his new Dodge Ram. He parked on the edge of a tomato field and passed out to the strains of Chub and Shiner bickering about the shooting fiasco at the trailer. At first Bode thought Chub was being too rough on the kid, but his opinion changed at daybreak when he noticed the two ragged bullet holes in the truck's quarter panel.

Bode said to Chub: "Shoot his damn nuts off."

"I didn't know it was you guys!" Shiner protested.

Bode angrily grabbed for the gun in Chub's belt. "Here, gimme that thing."

Chub knocked his hand away. "Somebody'll hear."

"But I thought you was NATO!" Shiner cried. "I said I was sorry, dint I?"

"Look what you done to my truck."

"I'll pay for it, I swear."

"Fucking A you will," snarled Bodean Gazzer.

Shiner was a jittery wreck. "Gimme another chance," he begged.

"Another chance? Shit," Chub said. He'd already concluded the boy was a hopeless fuckup – they had to cut him loose. He and Bode could toss a coin to see who'd break the news.

Chub got out to take a leak, and immediately came upon a rusty aerosol can of spray paint – in the middle of a tomato field! It seemed too wonderful to be true. Because Bode disapproved of sniffing, Chub kept his back to the truck. He knelt in the loamy sand and excitedly shook the can. The rattle soothed him, the beat of an old familiar song. He cupped his hands around the nozzle and pressed down with his chin, but no paint shot out. He held the nozzle beneath his nostrils and sniffed fruitlessly for a trace of fumes; not a whiff. He swore, stood up and hurled the empty can as far as possible.

When he unzipped his pants to pee, a horsefly landed on the tip of his pecker. Chub couldn't imagine feeling less like a millionaire. Despondently he shooed the fly away and finished his business. Then he removed the Colt Python from his belt and tucked it in his left armpit. He groped carefully down his right pants leg until he found the bandage: At least the lottery ticket was safe. He wondered what his parents would say if they knew he had 14 million bucks taped to his thigh!

When he returned to the pickup truck, he saw that Bodean Gazzer had settled down. Shiner was earnestly inquiring about the pending NATO attack on the United States, wondering if there was something particular he should be watching for; a clear signal it was all right to go for the guns.

"Like helicopters. I heard about them secret black helicopters," he was saying, "from the Internet."

Bode said, "I wouldn't go by the helicopters no more. Hell, they might switch to blimps. All depends."

"Damn," said Shiner.

"Tell you what, I wouldn't be surprised if it happened the dead of night, real quiet. You wake up one morning and the fuckin' mailman's wearing a blue helmet."

Shiner recoiled. "Then what – they kill all us white people, right?"

Chub said, "Not the women. Them they rape. The men is who they'll kill."

"No," Bode Gazzer said. "First thing they do is make us all so dirt poor we can't afford food or medicine or clothes on our back."

"How in the world?" Shiner asked.

"Easy. Suppose they decided all our money's illegal. Everything you saved up, worthless as toilet paper. Meanwhile they print up all new dollars, which they give out by the millions to Negroes and Cubans and such."

Chub sat on the bumper of the truck and tried to massage the hangover from his forehead. He'd already heard Bode's conspiracy theory about U.S. currency replacement. The subject had come up the night before, at Hooters, when Chub again recommended that they get rid of the nigger woman's credit card before it could be traced. Bode had said they ought to hang on to it, in case the New World Tribunal took over all the banks and issued new money. Then everybody's hard-earned American cash would be no good.

*What* cash? Chub had wondered. They were dead fucking broke.

"And the new money," Bode was telling Shiner, "instead of George Washington and U. S. Grant, it'll have pitchers of Jesse Jackson and Fy-del Castro."

"No shit! Then what do we do?"

"Plastic," Bode replied. "We use plastic. Ain't that right, Chub?"

"For sure." Chub got up, scratching at his crotch. It had been so long since he'd seen a fifty-dollar bill, he couldn't remember whose face was on it. Might as well be James Brown, for all it mattered to Chub.

"Let's get some goddamn food," he said.

On the drive to Florida City, Shiner fell asleep with his teeth bared, like a mutt. Bode and Chub used the quiet time to discuss the events of the night before. Were they really followed, or was the car they'd heard simply lost in the farmlands?

Bode Gazzer voted for lost. He insisted he would have noticed somebody tailing them from the restaurant.

"Maybe if you was sober," Chub said.

"It was nobody after us, I guarantee. We was just jumpy from all the boy's shootin'."

Chub said, "I ain't so sure."

He had a strong feeling that their luck was going rotten. He became certain after breakfast, at the diner, when the waitress failed to return promptly with the credit card. Chub spotted her consulting with the restaurant manager at the cash register. In one hand the manager was holding the stolen Visa. In his other hand was the telephone.

Chub whispered across the table, "Jig's up."

Bodean Gazzer went rigid. Working his toes back into

his cowboy boots, he accidentally kicked Chub in the knee. Irritably Chub glanced under the table and said, "Watch it."

Shiner, bug-eyed, twisting his paper napkin into a knot: "What the hell do we do now!"

"Run, boy. What else?" Chub playfully rapped his knuckles on Shiner's bare marbled scalp. "Run like the fuckin' wind."

# THIRTEEN

**Bode Gazzer's fondness** for stolen credit cards was evident from the double-digit entry on his rap sheet, which also included nine convictions for check kiting, five for welfare fraud, four for stealing electricity, three for looting lobster traps and two for willful destruction of private property (a parking meter and an ATM machine).

All this was revealed to Moffitt soon after JoLayne Lucks called to report the license tag of the red pickup truck carrying the men who'd attacked her. The tag number was fed into one computer, which produced the name and birth date of Bodean James Gazzer, and that was fed into another computer, which produced Mr. Gazzer's arrest record. Moffitt was surprised by nothing he found, least of all the fact that, despite his many crimes, Bode Gazzer had cumulatively spent less than twenty-three months of his whole worthless life behind bars.

Although the information wasn't available from the computers, it wouldn't have shocked Moffitt to know that Bode Gazzer was an avowed white supremacist and founder of a fledgling right-wing militia. By contrast, Bode Gazzer would have been stunned and appalled to find out that he'd attracted the attention of an agent from the despised Bureau of Alcohol, Tobacco and Firearms, and that the agent was a damn Negro.

For Moffitt, seeing JoLayne Lucks was simultaneously excruciating and heavenly. She never flirted or strung him along even slightly. It wasn't necessary. All she had to do was laugh, or turn her face, or walk across a room. One of *those* deals.

Moffitt's condition was bad but not pathetic. Sometimes for months he wouldn't think about her. When he did, there was no moon-eyed pining – just a stoic wistfulness he had fine-tuned over the years. He was a realist; he felt what he felt. Whenever she called, he called back. Whenever she needed something, he came through. It made him feel good in a way that nothing else could.

They met at a rib joint on Highway One in South Miami. JoLayne didn't wait half a minute to ask about the man who owned the pickup truck.

"Who is he? Where does he live – out by the tomato farms?"

"No," Moffitt said.

"What's his address?"

"Forget about it."

"Why? What're you going to do?"

"Toss the place," Moffitt said.

JoLayne wasn't sure what he meant.

"Search it," Tom Krome explained, "with extreme prejudice."

Moffitt nodded. "Meantime, cancel your Visa. We got a name now, and that's all we need."

All three of them ordered combo platters and iced tea.

JoLayne didn't eat much. She was feeling left out of the hunt.

"When you 'toss' this guy's house – "

"Apartment." Moffitt dabbed a napkin at his mouth.

"OK, but when you do it," said JoLayne, "I'd like to be there."

Moffitt shook his head firmly. "*I* won't even be there. Officially, that is." He took out his ID and set it open on the table, in front of Tom Krome. "Explain to her," Moffitt said, pointing with a sparerib.

When Krome saw the ATF badge, he understood. The agency had been pilloried after the Waco raid. Gun nuts clamored for its abolition and compared its agents to jackbooted Nazis. Congress investigated. Heads rolled at the top; the field staff was put on ultra-low profile.

"A real shitstorm," Krome said to JoLayne.

"I get the papers, Tom. I can read." She gave Moffitt a scalding look. "Don't you be talkin' to me like I'm a child."

The agent said, "No more headlines, that's our orders from Washington. And that's why I'll be doing this burglary alone."

JoLayne Lucks picked at her coleslaw with a plastic fork. She was aching to know who these redneck bastards were, how they lived, and what had possessed them to come after her, of all the lucky people who'd ever won the lottery. Why drive up to Grange to steal a ticket instead of waiting until somebody in Miami or Lauderdale hit the jackpot, which happened all the time?

It made no sense. JoLayne wanted to go with Moffitt and break into the man's home. Dig through his closets, peek under his bed, steam open his mail. JoLayne wanted some answers.

"All I can promise," said Moffitt, "is the ticket. If it's there, I'll find it."

"At least tell me his name."

"Why, Jo – so you can look it up in the phone book and beat me there? No way."

They finished the meal in silence. Krome followed Moffitt to the parking lot while JoLayne stayed to work on a slice of apple pie.

The agent said, "She won't stop with the lottery ticket. You realize that, don't you?"

"She might."

Moffitt smiled. "That girl gets an idea, she'll leave you in the dust. Believe me." He got in his car, a standard government-issue behemoth, and plugged the cell phone into the lighter jack. "Why you doin' this?" he asked Krome. "I hope your reason is better than mine."

"Probably not." Here Krome expected a warning that he'd better take excellent care of JoLayne Lucks, or else.

But instead Moffitt said: "Here's as far as it got between us: two dates. A movie and a Dolphins game. She hates football."

"What was the movie?"

"Something with Nicholson. We're going back ten, eleven years. The Dolphins got their asses kicked, that much I remember. Anyway, after that it was back to being friends. Her choice, not mine."

Krome said, "I'm not after anything."

Moffitt chuckled. "Man, you're not listening. It's *her* choice. Always." He started the car.

Krome said, "Be careful at the apartment."

"You're the one who needs to be careful." Moffitt winked.

When Krome returned to the restaurant, JoLayne

reported that the pie was excellent. Then she asked what Moffitt had told him in the parking lot.

"We were talking about football."

"Yeah, I'll bet."

"You realize," Krome said, "he's taking one helluva risk."

"And I appreciate it. I do."

"You've got a funny way of showing it."

JoLayne shifted uneasily. "Look, I've got to be careful what I say with Moffitt. If I sound ungrateful, it's probably because I don't want to sound *too* grateful. I don't want . . . Lord, you know. The man's still got some strong feelings for me."

"The hots is what we call it."

JoLayne lowered her eyes. "Stop." She felt bad about dragging Moffitt into the search. "I know he's supposed to get a warrant, I know he could lose his job if he's caught – "

"Try jail."

"Tom, he wants to help."

"In the worst way. He'd do anything to make you happy. That's the curse of the hopelessly smitten. Here's my question: Do you want your Lotto money, or do you want revenge?"

"Both."

"If you had to choose."

"The money, then." JoLayne was thinking of Simmons Wood. "I'd want the money."

"Good. Then leave it at that. You'll be doing Agent Moffitt a big favor."

And me, too, Krome thought.

*

Champ Powell was the best law clerk Judge Arthur Battenkill Jr. had ever hired; the most resourceful, the most hardworking, the most ambitious. Arthur Battenkill liked him very much. Champ Powell didn't need to be taught the importance of loyalty, because he'd been a policeman for five years before entering law school: a Gadsden County sheriff's deputy. Champ understood the rules of the street. The good guys stuck together, helped each other, covered for one another in a jam. That's how you got by, and got ahead.

So Champ Powell was flattered when Judge Battenkill sought his advice about a delicate personal problem – a fellow named Tom Krome, who'd come between the distinguished judge and his lovely wife, Katie. Champ Powell was working late in the law library, researching an obtuse appellate decision on condominium foreclosures, when he felt Arthur Battenkill's hand on his shoulder. The judge sat down and gravely explained the situation with Krome. He asked Champ Powell what *he* would do if it was his wife fooling around with another man. Champ (who'd been on both ends of that nasty equation) said first he'd scare the living shit out of the guy, try to run him out of town. Judge Battenkill said that would be excellent, if only he knew how to do such a thing without getting himself in hot water. Champ Powell said don't worry, I'll handle it personally. The judge was so profusely grateful that Champ Powell could see his future in the law profession turning golden. With one phone call, Arthur Battenkill could get him a job with any firm in the Panhandle.

That very night, the law clerk drove to Tom Krome's house and shot out the windows with a deer rifle. The judge rewarded him the next morning in chambers with a collegial wink and a thumbs-up. Two days later, though, Arthur Battenkill phoned Champ Powell to irately report that Krome was still communicating with Katie, sending her photographs of an occult nature: weeping statuary. Champ was outraged. With the judge's blessing, he left work early so he could get to the hardware store before it closed. There he purchased twelve gallons of turpentine and a mop. Any experienced arsonist could have told Champ Powell that twelve gallons was excessive and that the fumes alone would knock an elephant on its ass.

But the law clerk had no time for expert consultations. With resolve in his heart and a bandanna over his nostrils, Champ Powell vigorously swabbed the turpentine throughout Tom Krome's house, slicking the floors and walls of each room. He was in the kitchen when he finally passed out, collapsing against the gas stove, groping wildly as he keeled. Naturally his hands latched onto a burner knob and unconsciously twisted it to the "on" position. When the explosion came, it was heard half a mile away. The house burned to the foundation in ninety minutes.

Champ Powell's remains were not discovered until many hours after the blaze had died, when firefighters overturned a half-melted refrigerator and found what appeared to be a charred human jaw. Larger bone fragments and clots of jellied tissue were collected from the debris and placed in a Hefty bag for the medical examiner, who determined that the victim was a white male about six feet tall, in his early thirties. Beyond that, positive identification would be nearly impossible without dental records.

Based on the victim's race, height and approximate

age, fire investigators conjectured that the dead body was probably Tom Krome and that he'd been murdered or knocked unconscious when he surprised the arsonist inside his house.

The grisly details of the discovery, and the suspicions surrounding it, were given the following morning to *The Register*'s police reporter, who promptly notified the managing editor. Somberly he assembled the newsroom staff and told them what the arson guys had found. The managing editor asked if anybody knew the name of Tom Krome's dentist, but no one did (though a few staff members remarked upon Krome's outstanding smile, cattily speculating that it had to be the handiwork of a specialist). An intern was assigned the task of phoning every dental clinic in town in search of Krome's X-rays. In the meantime, a feature writer was assigned to work on Krome's obituary, just in case. The managing editor said the newspaper should wait as long as possible before running a story but should prepare for the worst. After the meeting, he hurried back to his office and tried to reach Sinclair in Grange. A woman identifying herself as Sinclair's sister reported he was "at the turtle shrine" but offered to take him a message. The managing editor gave her one: "Tell him to call the goddamn office by noon, or start looking for a new job."

As it happened, Champ Powell and Tom Krome had, in addition to their race and physique, one other characteristic in common: a badly chipped occlusal cusp on the number 27 tooth, the right lower canine. Champ Powell had damaged his while drunkenly gnawing the cap off a bottle of Busch at the 1993 Gator Bowl. Tom Krome's chip had been caused by a flying brick during a street riot he was covering in the Bronx.

One of Krome's second cousins, trying to be helpful, mentioned the broken tooth (and its semiheroic origin) to a *Register* reporter, who mentioned it to the medical examiner, who dutifully inspected the charred jawbone retrieved from Krome's house. The number 27 canine looked as if it had been busted with a chisel. With confidence, the medical examiner dictated a report that tentatively identified the corpse in the ruins as Tom Krome.

*The Register* would run the news story and sidebar obituary on the front page, beneath a four-column color photograph of Tom Krome. It would be the picture from his press badge – an underexposed head shot, with Tom's hair windblown and his eyes half closed – but Katie would still fall apart when she saw it, dashing to the bedroom in tears. Judge Arthur Battenkill Jr. would remain at the breakfast table and reread the articles several times. Try as he might, he would not be able to recall the condition of Champ Powell's dentition.

Arriving at the courthouse, he would find that for the second consecutive day his eager law clerk hadn't shown up for work. The secretaries would offer to go to Champ's apartment and check on him, but the judge would say it wasn't necessary. He would pretend to recall that Champ had mentioned driving to Cedar Key, to visit his parents. Later Arthur Battenkill Jr. would go alone into his chambers and shut the door. He would put on his black robe, untie his shoes and sit down to figure out what would be worse for him, from the standpoint of culpability – if the burned body belonged to Champ Powell or to Tom Krome.

Either way meant trouble, the judge would reason, but a live Krome was bound to be more trouble than a dead Champ. Arthur Battenkill Jr. would find himself hoping the newspaper was right, hoping it was Krome's barbecued bones that were found in the house, hoping Champ Powell was lying low somewhere – like the savvy ex-cop he was – waiting for things to cool off. He'd probably contact the judge in a day or two, and together they'd invent a plausible alibi. That's how it would go. In the meantime there was Katie, who (between heaving sobs) would accuse Arthur Battenkill Jr. of arranging the cold-blooded murder of her former lover. The judge wouldn't know what to do about *that*, but he'd find himself wondering whether a new diamond pendant might soothe his wife's anguish.

On his lunch hour he would go out and buy her one.

When they returned to the motel, JoLayne changed to her workout clothes and went for a walk. Tom Krome made some phone calls – to his voice mail at *The Register*, where his insurance agent had left an oddly urgent message regarding Krome's homeowner policy; to his answering machine at home, which apparently was out of order; to Dick Turnquist, who reported a possible sighting (in, of all places, Jackson Hole, Wyoming) of Krome's future ex-wife.

Krome fell asleep watching a European golf tournament on ESPN. He woke up gasping for air, JoLayne Lucks astride him, jabbing his sides with her supernatural-blue fingernails.

"Hey!" she said. "Hey, you, listen up!"

"Get off – "

"Not until you tell me," she said, "what the hell's going on."

"JoLayne, I can't breathe – "

" 'Helluva risk,' that's what you said. But then it dawned on me: Why in the world would a federal lawman tell *you* – a newspaper guy, for Lord's sake! – that he's about to commit a break-in? Talk about risk. Talk about stupid."

"JoLayne!"

She shifted some of her weight to her knees, so that Krome could inhale.

"Thank you," he said.

"Welcome."

She leaned forward until they were nose to nose. "He's a smart man, Moffitt is. He wouldn't blab anything so foolish in front of the press unless he knew there wasn't going to be any story. And there's *not*, is there? That's why you haven't taken out your damn notebook the whole time we've been on the road."

Krome prepared to shield his ribs from a fresh attack. "I told you, I don't write down every little thing."

"Tom Krome, you are full of shit." She planted her butt forcefully on his chest. "Guess what I did? I called Moffitt on his cellular, and guess what he told me. You're not working for the paper now, you're on medical leave. He checked it out."

Krome tried to raise himself up. Medical leave? he thought. That idiot Sinclair – he's managed to muck up a perfectly splendid resignation.

"Why didn't you tell me?" JoLayne demanded. "What's going on with you?"

"OK." He slipped his arms under her knees and gently rolled her off. She stayed on the bed, stretched out, propped on her elbows.

"I'm waiting, Tom."

He kept his eyes on the ceiling. "Here's what really happened. My editor killed the lottery story, so I resigned. The 'medical leave' stuff is news to me – Sinclair probably made it up to tell the boss."

JoLayne Lucks was incredulous. "You quit your job because of me?"

"Not because of you. Because my editor's a useless, dickless incompetent."

"Really. That's the only reason?"

"And also because I promised to help you."

JoLayne scooted closer. "Listen: You can't quit the newspaper. You absolutely cannot, is that understood?"

"It'll all work out. Don't worry."

"You damn men, I can't believe it! I found another crazy one."

"What's so crazy about keeping a promise?"

"Lord," said JoLayne. He was perfectly serious. A cornball, this guy. She said, "Don't move, OK? I'm gonna do something irresponsible."

Krome started to turn toward her, but she stopped him, lightly closing his eyes with one hand.

"You deaf? I told you not to move."

"What is this?" he asked.

"I owe you a kiss," she said, "from last night. Now please be still or I'll bite your lips off."

# FOURTEEN

**Tom Krome was** caught by surprise.

"Well, say something," JoLayne said.

"Something original."

"You taste like Certs."

She kissed him again. "Spearmint flavored. I think I'm hooked on the darn things."

Krome rolled on his side. He could see she was highly amused by his nervousness. "I'm lousy at this part," he said.

"In other words, you'd rather skip the chitchat and get right to the fucking."

Krome felt his cheeks get hot. "That's not what – "

"I'm teasing."

He sat up quickly. She was too much.

"Tom, you were sweet to quit your job. Misguided, but sweet. I figured you deserved a smooch."

"It was . . . very nice."

"Try to control yourself," JoLayne said. "Here's what you do now: Get in the car and go home. Back to work. Back to your life. You've done more than enough for me."

"No way."

"Look, I'll be fine. Once Moffitt gets my lottery ticket, I'm outta here."

"Yeah, right."

"I swear, Tom. Back to Grange to be a land baroness."

Krome said, "I don't quit on stories."

"Gimme a break."

"What if Moffitt can't find the ticket?"

JoLayne shrugged. "Then it wasn't meant to be. Now start packing."

"Not a chance. Not until you get your money." He fell back on the pillow. "Suppose you wound up on the wet T-shirt circuit again. I couldn't live with myself."

She laid her head on his chest. "What is it you want?"

"One of those mints would be good."

"From all this, I mean. All this wicked craziness."

"A tolerable ending. That's it," Krome said.

"Makes for a better story, right?"

"Just a better night's sleep."

JoLayne groaned. "You're not real. You can't be."

Krome made a cursory stab at sorting his motives. Maybe he didn't want Moffitt to find the stolen Lotto ticket, because then the adventure would be over and he'd have to go home. Or maybe he wanted to recover the ticket himself, in some dramatic flourish, to impress JoLayne Lucks. It probably wasn't anything noble at all; just dumb pride and hormones.

He said, "You want me to go, I'll go."

"Your tummy's growling. You hungry again?"

"JoLayne, you're not listening."

She lifted her head. "Let's stay like this awhile, right here in bed. See what happens."

"OK," Tom Krome said. She was too much.

*

Chub was gloating about the getaway. He said they wouldn't have made it if Bode's pickup hadn't been parked in the blue zone, steps from the diner's front door. He said the guy at the counter never saw three handicaps move so goddamn fast.

As the truck cruised toward Homestead, Shiner kept looking to see if they were being chased. Bode Gazzer was taut behind the wheel – he'd been expecting the Negro woman to cancel her credit card, but it jarred him anyway. The manager of the diner would be calling the law, no doubt about that.

"We gotta have a meeting," Bode said. "Soon as possible."

"With who?" Shiner asked.

"Us. The White Clarion Aryans." It was time to start acting like a well-regulated militia. Bode said, "Maybe this afternoon we'll hold a meeting."

Chub leaned forward. "What's wrong with right now?"

"Not in the truck. I can't preside and drive at the same time."

"Hell, you can't piss and whistle at the same time." Chub ran a mossy-looking tongue across his front teeth. "We don't need a damn meeting. We need our Lotto money."

Bode said, "No, man, it's too soon."

Chub took out the .357 and placed it on the floorboard at his feet. "Before somethin' else goes wrong," he said.

Wedged between the squabbling criminals in the front seat, Shiner felt inexplicably safe. Chub was the toughest, and not only because of the guns. Bode could be a hardass, too, but he was more of a thinker; the idea man. Shiner liked his suggestion for a real militia meeting, liked his attention to orderliness and strategy. But before the White Clarion Aryans held a meeting, Shiner wanted to get his tattoo fixed. It couldn't be that difficult, changing the *W.R.B.* to *W.C.A.* The screaming eagle was perfect the way it was.

When he inquired about stopping at a tattoo parlor, Chub laughed and said, "Just what you need."

"I'm dead serious."

Bode, stiffening in the driver's seat: "We ain't stoppin' for no such nonsense."

"Please, I got to!"

Chub said, "Aw, look at your damn arm. It's still bruised up from last time, like a rotten banana."

"You don't unnerstand." Shiner's chin dropped as he slid into a sulk.

Not this again, Chub thought. He snatched up the Colt and twisted the barrel into the kid's groin. "Son, you 'bout the whiniest little fuck I ever met."

Shiner's head came up with a jerk. "I'm s-sorry."

"Sorry don't begin to cover it."

Bode told his partner to take it easy. "We're all three of us still jacked up from last night. Tell you what, let's stop over to the trailer and fetch the automatics. Go out by the rock pit and let off some steam."

"Way cool," Shiner said, expectantly.

"Then, after, we'll have a meeting."

Chub said, "Whoop-dee-doo." He put the pistol in his belt. "Fuck the rock pit. I wanna shoot at somethin' that moves. Somethin' bigger 'n' faster than a goddamn turtle."

"Such as?"

"Wait and see," said Chub. "Shoot a Jew, cap a Jap – "

"Pop a wop," Shiner chimed.

"Yeah!"

Bode Gazzer hoped his partner's sinister mood would pass before they broke out the serious toys.

Moffitt wasn't supposed to get mad. He was a pro. He dealt with low-rent shitheads all the time.

But sneaking through the cramped apartment of Bodean James Gazzer, the agent felt his anger rise.

The wall poster of David Koresh, the Waco wacko himself. Moffitt had lost a friend in that fiasco of a raid.

Then there were the bullet holes in the plaster. Empty ammo clips. Stacks of gun magazines and *Soldier of Fortune*. Porno videos. A paperback book called *The Poacher's Bible*. A pepper mill trimmed with a Nazi armband. A how-to pamphlet on fertilizer bombs. A clipped-out cartoon proposing a humorous aspect to the Holocaust. An assortment of NRA patches and bumper stickers. A closetful of camouflage clothes. Tacked to the peeling wallpaper behind the toilet: a Confederate flag. In the bedroom, a calico cross-stitched portrait of David Duke.

Moffitt thought: These guys must've had a blast, working on JoLayne.

He locked the front door behind him, bracing it with a chair. He opened a back window and punched out the screen, as an escape in case Bodean James Gazzer returned. The fresh air didn't hurt, either – the place smelled of soiled laundry, cigaret ash and stale beer. Methodically, Moffitt began to search. He knew from experience that even the dimmest of thugs occasionally could be brilliant at concealing contraband – and a lottery ticket was easier to hide than an AK-47 or a kilo of hash.

The kitchen was first. One glance at the crusty silverware made Moffitt glad he wore surgical gloves. With a heavy forearm he cleared the cluttered dinette. There he dumped every box and tin from Bodean James Gazzer's cabinets – sugar, flour, instant coffee, Cocoa Krispies, croutons, Quaker Oats.

No Lotto stub.

He took a deep breath before opening the refrigerator, but it wasn't as rancid as he'd feared. The food section was practically empty except for Budweisers, marshmallow-filled cookies, ketchup and a fuzzy chunk of Gouda. Finding nothing hidden there, Moffitt hacked his way into the freezer compartment, a favorite stash of novice dopers and smugglers. A half-gallon container of ancient fudge-ripple ice cream went into a mixing bowl, which went into the stove. When the slop was melted, Moffitt strained it through a colander. Then he emptied the ice trays on the counter and examined each cube.

No ticket.

He grabbed a steak knife and headed for the bedroom, where he eviscerated the pillows, gutted the mattress and box spring, pried up the musty corners of the carpet. Inside Bodean James Gazzer's dresser, Moffitt came across something he'd never before seen: camo-style underwear. There was also a World War II bayonet, a gummy-looking *Penthouse* and a pile of dunning notices from the National Rifle Association for unpaid dues. Moffitt was certain he had hit pay dirt in the bottom drawer, beneath a tangle of frayed socks, where he uncovered five crisp tickets from the Florida Lotto.

But none of the sequences matched JoLayne's winning numbers, and the date of the drawing was wrong: December 2.

That's tomorrow, thought Moffitt. Unbelievable – the $14 million they stole from her wasn't enough. The fuckers want more.

He pocketed the tickets and, with some dread, moved to the bathroom. A colony of plump carpenter ants had taken over the sink, demonstrating a special fondness for Bodean James Gazzer's toothbrush. Moffitt dove into the medicine chest and emptied the pill bottles. Several had been prescribed to persons other than Mr. Gazzer, who'd undoubtedly stolen them or forged the scrips. Moffitt took his time with a dispenser of Crest and a tube of hemorrhoid cream, which he flattened under a shoe and then opened with a wire cutter.

Nothing.

The vanity held an empty box of Trojan nonlubricated condoms, which intrigued Moffitt. Bodean James Gazzer's apartment showed no signs of a woman's presence – certainly no woman who was worried about catching a disease. Maybe Gazzer was gay, the agent thought, although it seemed unlikely, given the homophobic tendencies of gun nuts. Also, the pornographic videos stacked near the TV set bore heterosexually oriented titles.

Maybe the loon wore rubbers when he jacked off. Or maybe he used them with hookers. In any event, he'd been a busy boy.

The answer to the riddle of the Trojans turned up in a plastic trash can: five foil condom wrappers and a razor blade. Moffitt aligned them on the toilet seat. The condoms were inside the packages, and Moffitt cautiously removed them with a tweezers. Each of them bore visible nicks or slices, which presumably was why they'd been discarded.

Moffitt concentrated on the bright wrappers. Clearly they hadn't been torn open in the ordinary haste of lust. Instead they'd painstakingly been cut along one edge, undoubtedly with the razor blade. Even with such care, Bodean James Gazzer had damaged all five rubbers.

The sixth must have been the winner. Moffitt was pretty sure he knew where it was and what was hidden inside it.

"Fucker," he said aloud.

Mr. Gazzer must be quite the optimist, the agent reflected. Why else would he care whether the condom in which he'd concealed the lottery ticket was usable?

On his way out of the apartment, Moffitt encountered a stout rat gorging itself in the mounds of sugar and cereal on the dinette. His first impulse was to shoot it, but then he thought: Why do Gazzer any favors? With luck, the critter was rabid.

By nature Moffitt was not a mischievous person, but he was inspired by the shabby trappings of hate. He had a nagging image of Bodean Gazzer and his sadistic partner – one would be stretched out in his underwear on the futon, the other might be slouched at the dinette. They'd be slugging down Budweisers, laughing about what they'd done to JoLayne Lucks, trying to remember who'd punched her where. The look in her eyes. The sounds she made.

Moffitt simply could not slip away and allow such shitheads to go on with their warped lives, exactly as before. After all, how often did one get the opportunity to make a lasting impression upon paranoid sociopaths?

Not often enough. Moffitt felt morally obligated to fuck with Bodean James Gazzer's head. It took only a few extra minutes, and afterwards even the rat seemed amused.

Sinclair was overcome the instant he touched the cooters: a warm tingle that started preternaturally in his palms and raced up both arms to his spine.

He was sitting cross-legged in Demencio's yard, on the lip of the moat. The daily visitation was over, the pilgrims were gone. Sinclair had never handled a turtle before. Demencio said go ahead, help yourself. They don't bite or nothin'.

Sinclair picked up one of the painted cooters and set it delicately in his lap. The bearded face gazing up from the grooved carapace was purely beatific. And the turtle itself was no less exquisite – bright gemlike eyes, a velvety neck striped in greens, golds and yellows. Sinclair reached into the water and picked up another one, and then another. Before long, he was acrawl with baby turtles – rubbery legs pumping, tiny claws scratching harmlessly on the fabric of his pants. The sensation was hypnotic, almost spiritual. The cooters seemed to emanate a soft, soothing current.

Demencio, who was refilling the moat with "holy" water, asked Sinclair if he felt all right. Sinclair spontaneously began to tremble and hum. Demencio couldn't make out the tune, but it was nothing he was dying to hear on the radio. Turning to Joan and Roddy: "I'd say it's time to take the boy home."

Sinclair didn't want to go. He looked up at Roddy.

"Isn't this amazing?" Thrusting both hands high, full of dripping turtles: "Did you see!"

Demencio, sharply: "Be careful with them things. They ain't mine." That's all he'd need, some city dork accidentally smushing one of JoLayne's precious babies. Say *adiós* to a thousand bucks.

Demencio was tempted to turn the hose on the guy – it had worked like a charm on Trish's tomcat. Sinclair's face pinched into a mask of concentration. His head began to flop back and forth, as if his neck had gone to rubber.

"*Nyyah nurrha nimmy doo-dey,*" he said.

Roddy glanced at his wife. "What is that – Spanish or somethin'?"

"I don't believe so."

Again Sinclair cried: "*Nyyah nyyah doo-dey!*" It was a mangled regurgitation of a newspaper headline he'd once written, a personal all-time favorite: NERVOUS NUREYEV NIMBLE IN DISNEY DEBUT.

The translation, had Demencio known it, would have failed to put him at ease. "That's it," he said curtly. "Closing time."

At Roddy's urging, Sinclair returned the twelve painted turtles to the water. Roddy led him to the car, and Joan drove home. Roddy began stacking charcoal briquettes in the outdoor grill, but Sinclair said he wasn't hungry and went to bed. He was gone when Joan awoke the next morning. Under the sugar bowl was his journalist's notebook, opened to a fresh page:

*I've returned to the shrine.*

That's where she found him, rapt and round-eyed.

Demencio took her aside and whispered, "No offense, but I got a business here."

"I understand," said Joan. She walked to the moat and crouched next to her brother. "How we doing?"

"See that?" Sinclair pointed. "She's crying."

Demencio had repaired the Madonna's plumbing; teardrops sparkled on her fiberglass cheeks. Joan felt embarrassed that Sinclair was so affected.

"Your boss called," she told him.

"That's nice."

"It sounded real important."

Sinclair sighed. Cupped in each hand was a cooter. "This is Bartholomew, and I think this one's Simon."

"Yes, they're very cute."

"Joan, please. You're talking about the apostles."

"Honey, you'd better call the newspaper."

Demencio offered to let him use the telephone in the house. Anything to get the goofball away from the shrine before the first Christian tourists arrived.

The managing editor's secretary put Sinclair through immediately. In a monotone he apologized for not calling the day before, as promised.

"Forget about it," said the managing editor. "I've got shitty news: Tom Krome's dead."

"No."

"Looks that way. The arson guys found a body in the house."

"No!" Sinclair insisted. "It's not possible."

"Burned beyond recognition."

"But Tom went to Miami with the lottery woman!"

"Who told you that?"

"The man with the turtles."

"I see," said the managing editor. "What about the

man with the giraffes – what did he say? And the bearded lady with penguins – did you ask her?"

Sinclair wobbled and spun, tangling himself in the telephone cord. Joan shoved a chair under his butt. Breathlessly he said: "Tom can't be dead."

"They're working on the DNA," the managing editor said, "but they're ninety-nine percent sure it's him. We're getting a front-page package ready for tomorrow."

"My God," said Sinclair. Was it possible he'd actually lost a reporter?

He heard his boss say: "Don't come home."

"What?"

"Not just yet. Not till we figure out what to say."

"To who?" Sinclair asked.

"The wires. The networks. Reporters don't get murdered much these days," the managing editor explained, "especially feature writers. It's a pretty big deal."

"I suppose, but – "

"There'll be lots of sticky questions: Where'd you send him? What was he working on? Was it dangerous? It's best if I handle it. That's why they pay me the big bucks, right?"

Sinclair was gripped by a cold fog. "I can't believe this."

"Maybe it had nothing to do with the job. Maybe it was a robbery, or a jealous boyfriend," said the managing editor. "Maybe a fucking casserole exploded – who knows? The point is, Tom's going to end up a hero, regardless. That's what happens when journalists get killed – look at Amelia Lloyd, for Christ's sake. She couldn't write a fucking grocery list, but they went ahead and named a big award after her."

Sinclair said, "I feel sick."

"We all do, believe me. We all do," the managing editor said. "You sit tight for a few days. Take it easy. Have a good visit with your sister. I'll be in touch."

For a time Sinclair remained motionless. Joan took the receiver from his hand and carefully unwrapped the cord from his shoulders and neck. With a tissue she dabbed the perspiration from his forehead. Then she dampened another and wiped a spot of turtle poop from his arm.

"What did he say?" she asked. "What's happened?"

"It's Tom – he's not in Miami, he's dead."

"Oh no. I'm so sorry."

Sinclair stood up. "Now I understand," he said.

Nervously his sister eyed him.

"Finally I understand why I'm here. What brought me to this place," he said. "Before, I wasn't sure. Something fantastic took hold of me when I touched the turtles, but I didn't know what or why. Now I do. Now I know."

Joan said, "Hey, how about a soda?"

Sinclair slapped a hand across his breast. "I was sent here," he said, "to be reborn."

"Reborn."

"There's no other explanation," Sinclair said, and trotted out the door toward the shrine. There he stripped off his clothes and lay down in the silty water among the cooters.

*"Nimmy doo-dey, nimmy nyyah!"*

Trish, who was setting up the T-shirt display, dropped to one knee. "I believe he's speaking in tongues!"

"Like hell," said Demencio. "Coo-ca-loo-ca-choo."

Balefully he stomped to the garage in search of the tuna gaff.

*

Krome looked preoccupied. Happy, JoLayne thought, but preoccupied.

She said, "You passed the test."

"The white-guy test?"

"Yep. With flying colors."

Krome broke out laughing. It was nice to hear. JoLayne wished he'd laugh like that more often, and not only when she made a joke.

He said, "When did you decide this would happen?"

They were under the bedcovers, holding each other. As if it were freezing outdoors, JoLayne thought, instead of seventy-two degrees.

"Pre-kiss or post-kiss?" Krome asked.

"Post," she answered.

"You're kidding."

"Nope. Strictly a spur-of-the-moment deal."

"The sex?"

"Sure," JoLayne said.

Which wasn't exactly true, but why tell him everything? He didn't need to know the precise moment when she'd made up her mind, or why. It amused JoLayne that men were forever trying to figure out how they'd managed to get laid – what devastatingly clever line they'd come up with, what timely expression of sincerity or sensitivity they'd affected. As if the power of seduction were theirs whenever they wanted, if only they knew how to unlock it.

For JoLayne Lucks, there was no deep mystery to what had happened. Krome was a decent guy. He cared about her. He was strong, reliable and not too knuckleheaded. These things counted. He had no earthly clue how much they counted.

Not to mention that she was scared. No denying it.

Chasing two vicious robbers through the state – insane is what it was. No wonder they were stressed out, she and Tom. That certainly had something to do with it, too; one reason they were hugging each other like teenagers.

JoLayne retreated to standard pillow talk.

"What are you thinking about?"

"Moffitt," he said.

"Oh, very romantic."

"I was hoping he takes his time searching that guy's place. A week or so would be OK. In the meantime we could stay just like this, the two of us."

"Nice comeback," JoLayne said, pinching his leg. "You think he'll find the ticket?"

"If it's there, yeah. He gives the impression of total competence."

"And what if it's not there?"

"Then I suppose we'll need a plan, and some luck," Krome said.

"Moffitt thinks I'll do something crazy."

"Imagine that."

"Seriously, Tom. He won't even tell me the guy's name."

"I've *got* the name," Krome said, "and an address."

JoLayne sat upright, bursting out of the covers. "What did you say?"

"With all due respect to your friend, it doesn't take Sherlock Holmes to run a license-tag check. All you need is a friend at the highway patrol." Krome shrugged in mock innocence. "The creep with the pickup truck, his name is Bodean James Gazzer. And we can find him with or without intrepid Agent Moffitt."

"Damn," said JoLayne. The boy was slicker than she'd thought.

"I'd have told you sooner," he said, "but we were preoccupied."

"Don't give me that."

They both jumped when the phone rang. Krome reached for it. JoLayne scooted closer and silently mouthed: "Moffitt?"

Krome shook his head. JoLayne hopped out of bed and headed for the shower. When she came out, he was standing at the window, taking in a grand view of the Metrorail tracks. He didn't seem to notice that she'd repainted her nails a neon green or that she was wearing only the towel on her head.

"So who was it?" she asked.

"My lawyer again."

Uh-oh, she thought, reaching for her robe. "Bad news?"

"Sort of," Tom Krome said. "Apparently I'm dead." When he turned around, he appeared more bemused than upset. "It's going to be on the front page of *The Register* tomorrow."

"Dead." JoLayne pursed her lips. "You sure fooled me."

"Fried to a cinder in my own home. Must be true, if it's in the newspaper."

JoLayne felt entitled to wonder if she really knew enough about this Tom fellow, nice and steady as he might seem. A burning house was something to consider.

She said, "Lord, what are you going to do?"

"Stay dead for a while," Krome replied. "That's what my lawyer says."

# FIFTEEN

**Bodean Gazzer instructed** Chub to cease shooting from the truck.

"But it's *him*."

"It ain't," Bode said. "Now quit."

"Not jest yet."

Shiner cried, "My eardrums!"

"Pussy." Chub continued to fire until the black Mustang skidded off the highway on bare rims. Fuming, Bode braked the pickup and coasted to the shoulder. He was losing his grip on Chub and Shiner; semiautomatics seemed to bring out the worst in them.

Chub hopped from the truck and loped with homicidal intent through the darkness, toward the disabled car. Bode marked his partner's progress by the bobbing orange glow of the cigaret. The man was setting a damn poor example for Shiner – there was nothing well-regulated about sniping at motorists on the Florida Turnpike.

Shiner said, "Hell we do now?"

"Get out, son." Bode Gazzer grabbed a flashlight from the glove box and hurried after Chub. They found him holding at gunpoint a young Latin man whose misfortune was to vaguely resemble the obnoxious boyfriend of a Hooters waitress, who even more vaguely resembled the actress Kim Basinger.

Bode said: "Nice work, ace."

Chub spat his cigaret butt. It wasn't Tony in the Mustang.

Shiner asked, "Is it the same guy or not?"

"Hell, no, it ain't him. What's your name?" Bode demanded.

"Bob." The young man clutched the meaty part of his right shoulder, where a rifle slug had grazed it.

Chub jabbed at him with the muzzle of the Cobray. "Bob, huh? You don't look like no Bob."

The driver willingly surrendered his license. The name on it made Chub grin: Roberto Lopez.

"Jest like I thought. Goddamn lyin' sumbitch Cuban!" Chub crowed.

The young man was terrified. "No, I am from Colombia."

"Nice try."

"Bob and Roberto, it is the same thing!"

Chub said, "Yeah? On what planet?"

Bodean Gazzer switched off the flashlight. The heavy traffic on the highway made him jumpy; even in Dade County a bullet-riddled automobile could attract notice.

"Gimme some light here." Chub was pawing through the young man's wallet. "I mean, long as we gone to all the trouble and ammo."

Jauntily he held up four one-hundred-dollar bills for Bode to see. Shiner gave a war whoop.

"And lookie here – 'Merican Express," Chub said, waggling a gold-colored credit card. "Fuck is the likes a you doin' with *anything* 'Merican?"

Roberto Lopez said, “Take whatever you want. Please don’t kill me.”

Chub commanded Shiner to search the trunk. Bode Gazzer was a basket case; any second he expected the blue flash of police lights. He knew there would be little chance of satisfactorily explaining a shot Colombian to the Florida Highway Patrol.

“Hurry it up! Goddamn you guys,” he growled.

They found a briefcase, a holstered Model 84 Beretta .380 and a new pair of two-tone golf shoes. Shiner said, “Size tens. Same as me.”

“Keep ’em!” Roberto Lopez, calling from the front seat.

Bode aimed the flashlight inside the briefcase: bar charts, computer printouts and financial statements. A business card identified Roberto Lopez as a stockbroker with Smith Barney.

Here Chub saw a chance to salvage merit from the crime. Even though the guy had turned out not to be Amber’s asshole boyfriend, he was still a damn foreigner with fancy clothes and too much money. Surely Bode would agree that the rifle attack wasn’t a total waste of time.

In a tone of solemn indignation, Chub accosted the fearful young Colombian: “You fuckers sneak into this country, steal our jobs and then take over our golf courses. If I might ast, Mister Roberto Stockbroker, what’s next? You gone run for President?”

Shiner was so stirred that he patriotically kicked the car, the golf cleats leaving a flawless perforation. Bode Gazzer, however, showed no sign of indignation.

Chub set aside the rifle and seized Roberto Lopez by the collar. “OK, smart-ass,” Chub said, recalling Bode’s piercing roadside interrogation of the migrant workers, "gimme the fourteenth President of the U.S.A."

Tightly the young Colombian answered, "Franklin Pierce."

"Ha! Frankie who?"

"*Pierce.*" Bode's voice dripped bitterness. "President Franklin Pierce is right. The man got it right."

Deflated, Chub stepped back. "Jesus Willy Christ."

"I'm outta here," Bodean Gazzer said, and headed toward the pickup truck. Chub vented his disappointment by punching the luckless stockbroker in the nose, while Shiner concentrated his energies on the exterior of the Mustang.

To elude the process servers hired by her estranged husband, Mary Andrea Finley Krome began calling herself "Julie Channing," a weakly veiled homage to her two all-time-favorite Broadway performers. So determined was Mary Andrea to resist divorce court that she went a step further: At a highway rest stop outside Jackson Hole, Wyoming, she cut her bounteous red hair and penciled in new full eyebrows. That same afternoon she drove into town and unsuccessfully auditioned for a ragged but rousing production of *Oliver Twist*.

Back in Brooklyn, the resourceful Dick Turnquist had compiled from the World Wide Web a list of theater promoters in the rural western states. He faxed to each one a recent publicity shot of Mary Andrea Finley Krome, accompanied by a brief inquiry hinting at a family emergency back East – had anyone seen her? The director in Jackson Hole was concerned enough to reply, by telephone. He said the woman in the photograph bore a keen resemblance to an actress who had, only yesterday, read for the parts of both Fagin and the Artful Dodger. And while Miss Julia Channing's singing voice was perfectly adequate, the director said, her Cockney accent needed work. "She could've handled Richard the Second," the director explained, "but what I needed was a pickpocket."

By the time Dick Turnquist retained and dispatched a local private investigator, Mary Andrea Finley Krome was already gone from the mountain town.

What impressed Turnquist was her perseverance for the stage life. Knowing she was being pursued, Mary Andrea continued to make herself visible. And although changing one's professional name might tax the ego, as subterfuge it was pretty feeble. Mary Andrea could have melted into any city and taken any anonymous job – waitress, receptionist, bartender – with only a negligible decline of income. Yet she chose to keep acting despite the risk of discovery and subpoena. Perhaps she was indomitably committed to her craft, but Turnquist believed there was another explanation: Mary Andrea needed the attention. She craved the limelight, no matter how remote or fleeting.

Well, Turnquist reflected, who didn't?

She could call herself whatever she wanted – Julie Channing, Liza Bacall, it didn't matter. The lawyer knew he would eventually catch up to the future ex-Mrs. Krome and compel her presence in the halls of justice.

He therefore was not at all distressed when *The Register* called to inform him that Tom Krome had died in a suspicious house fire. Having only an hour earlier chatted with his client, alive and uncharred in a Coral Gables motel, Turnquist realized the newspaper was about to make a humongous mistake. It was about to devote its entire front page to a dead man who wasn't.

Yet the lawyer chose not to edify the young reporter on the end of the line. Turnquist was careful not to lie outright; it wasn't required. Conveniently the young reporter failed to ask Turnquist if he'd spoken to Tom Krome that day, or if he had any reason to believe Tom Krome was not deceased.

Instead the reporter said: "How long had you known each other? What are your fondest memories? How do you think he'd like to be remembered?"

All questions that Dick Turnquist found it easy to answer. He didn't say so, but he was grateful to *The Register* for saving him further aggravation in tracking Mary Andrea Finley Krome. Once she heard the news, she'd naturally assume she could stop running. Tom's dying would get her off the hook, litigation-wise, and she'd have no reason to continue the dodge. Mary Andrea had always been less concerned with saving the marriage than with avoiding the stigma of divorce. The last true Catholic, in her estranged husband's words.

She was also a ham. Dick Turnquist expected Mary Andrea would get the first plane for Florida, to play the irresistible role of grief-stricken widow – sitting for poignant TV interviews, attending weepy candlelight memorials, stoically announcing journalism scholarships in her martyred spouse's name.

And we'll be waiting for her, thought Dick Turnquist.

On the phone, the reporter from *The Register* was winding up the interview. "Thanks for talking with me at such a difficult time. Just one more question: As Tom's close friend, how do you feel about what's happened?"

The lawyer answered, quite truthfully: "Well, it doesn't seem real."

On the morning of December 2, Bernard Squires telephoned Clara Markham in Grange to inquire if his generous purchase offer had been conveyed to the sellers of Simmons Wood.

"But it's only been three days," the broker said.

"You haven't even spoken to them?"

"I've put in a call," Clara fudged. "They said Mr. Simmons is in Las Vegas. His sister is on holiday down in the islands."

Bernard Squires said, "They have telephones in Las Vegas, I know for a fact."

Normally Bernard was not so impatient, but Richard "The Icepick" Tarbone urgently needed to make a covert withdrawal from the union pension accounts. The nature of the family emergency was not confided to Bernard Squires, and he pointedly exhibited a lack of curiosity on the matter. But since the Florida real estate purchase was crucial to the money laundering, The Icepick had taken a personal interest in expediting the deal. None of this could be frankly communicated by Bernard Squires to Clara Markham, who was saying:

"I'll try to reach them again this morning. I promise."

"And there are no other offers?" Bernard asked.

"Nothing on the table," said Clara, which was strictly the truth.

As soon as the man from Chicago hung up, she dialed the number in Coral Gables that JoLayne had given her. A desk clerk at the motel said Miss Lucks and her friend had checked out.

With heavy reluctance Clara Markham then phoned the attorney handling the estate of the late Lighthorse Simmons. She described the pension fund's offer for the forty-four acres on the outskirts of Grange. The attorney said three million sounded like a fair price. He seemed sure the heirs would leap at it.

Clara was sure, too. She felt bad for her friend, but business was business. Unless JoLayne Lucks found a miracle, Simmons Wood was lost.

An hour later, when Bernard Squires' telephone rang, he thought it must be Clara Markham calling with the good news. It wasn't. It was Richard Tarbone.

"I'm sicka this shit," he told Squires. "You get your ass down to Florida."

And Squires went.

They'd checked out of the Comfort Inn shortly after Moffitt's visit. The agent had come straight from the redneck's apartment. His tight-lipped expression told the story: no Lotto ticket.

"Damn," JoLayne had said.

"I think I know where it is."

"Where?"

"He hid it in a rubber. The camo guy."

"A rubber." JoLayne, pressing her knuckles to her forehead, trying not to get grossed out.

"A Trojan," Moffit had added.

"Thanks. I've got the picture."

"He's carrying it on him somewhere, I'm willing to bet."

"His wallet," Tom Krome had suggested.

"Yeah, probably." Moffitt matter-of-factly told them

about the search of Bodean James Gazzer's place – the anti-government posters and bumper stickers, the gun magazines, the vermin, the condoms in the wastebasket.

"What now? How do we find the ticket?" Krome had asked.

"Gimme a week."

"No." JoLayne, shaking her head. "I can't. Time's running out."

Moffitt had promised he'd take care of it as soon as he returned from San Juan. He had to go testify in a seizure case – illegal Chinese machine guns, routed through Haiti.

"When I get back, I'll deal with these guys. Do a traffic stop, pat 'em down real hard. Search the pickup, too."

"But what if – "

"If it's not there, then . . . hell, I don't know." Moffitt, working his jaw, stared out the window.

"How long will you be gone?"

"Three days. Four at the most."

Moffitt had handed JoLayne Lucks the lottery tickets from Bodean Gazzer's sock drawer. "For Saturday night," he'd said. "Just in case."

"Very funny."

"Hey, weirder things've happened."

JoLayne had tucked the tickets in her handbag. "By the way, Tom's dead. It'll be in the papers tomorrow."

Moffitt had glanced quizzically at Krome, who'd shrugged and said, "Long story."

"Murdered?"

"Supposedly. I'd prefer to keep it that way for now. You mind?"

"I've never laid eyes on you," Moffitt had said, "and you've never laid eyes on me."

At the door, JoLayne had given the ATF agent a warm hug. "Thanks for everything. I know you stuck your neck out."

"Forget it."

"Nothing happened? You sure?"

"Easy as pie. But the place is trashed – Gazzer'll know it wasn't some chickenshit burglar."

As soon as Moffitt was gone, they'd started to pack. Krome insisted. The robber's address was in Krome's notebook, the one JoLayne said he never used.

The first formal meeting of the White Clarion Aryans was held by lantern light at an empty cockfighting ring. It began with a dispute over titles; Bode Gazzer said military discipline was impossible without strict designations of rank. He declared that henceforth he should be called "Colonel."

Chub objected. "We's equal partners," he said, " 'cept for him." Meaning the kid, Shiner.

Bode offered Chub the rank of major, which he assured him was on a par with colonel. Chub pondered it between swigs of Jack Daniel's, purchased (along with beer, gas, cigarets, T-bone steaks, onion rings and frozen cheesecake) with the cash stolen from the young Colombian stockbroker.

*Major Chub* didn't sound particularly distinguished, Chub thought. *Major Gillespie* wasn't half bad, but Chub wasn't psychologically prepared to revert to the family name.

"Fuck this whole dumb idea," he mumbled.

Shiner raised a hand. "Can I be a sergeant?"

Bode nodded. "Son, you're reading my mind."

Chub raised the liquor bottle. "Can I be a Klingon? Please, Colonel Gazzer, sir. Purty please?"

Bode ignored him. He handed each of the men a booklet distributed by the First Patriot Covenant, an infamously disagreeable cell of supremacists headquartered in western Montana. The First Patriot Covenant lived in concrete pillboxes and believed blacks and Jews were the children of Satan; the Pope was either a first or a second cousin. Simply titled "Starting Up," the group's booklet contained helpful sections about organizing militia wings: fund-raising, tax evasion, rules of order, rules of recruitment, dress codes, press relations and arsenals. Shiner could hardly wait to read it.

"Page eight," Bode said. " 'Be Discreet.' Everybody understand what that means? It means you don't go blastin' away with rifles on the goddamn turnpike."

From Chub came a scornful grunt. "Blow me."

Shiner was startled. This was nothing like the army. He felt a sticky arm settle around his shoulders. Turning, he got a faceful of whiskey breath.

"Funny thing," Chub said, fingering his ponytail, "how it's fine and dandy for him to roust a couple beaners for eight lousy bucks, but I swipe four C-notes off poor 'Bob' Lopez and all of a sudden I'm a shitty soldier. You tell the colonel he can blow me, OK?"

An angry cry arose, and the next thing Shiner knew, they were locked together – Bodean Gazzer and Chub – thrashing in the dry dirt of the rooster pit. Shiner wasn't convinced it was a serious fight, since no hard punches were being struck, but he was nevertheless disturbed by the unseemly clawing and hair pulling. The two men on the ground didn't look like battle-ready officers, they looked like barroom drunks. Shiner found himself wondering, with a twinge of shame, whether the White Clarion Aryans had a snowball's chance against crack NATO troops.

Pure fatigue ended the scuffle. Bode got a torn shirt and a bloody nose, Chub lost his eye patch. The colonel announced they were all going to his apartment and cook up the steaks. Shiner was surprised the drive was so peaceful; no one mentioned the fight. Bode talked expansively about the many militias in Montana and Idaho, and said he wouldn't mind moving out there if it weren't for the winters; cold weather aggravated the gout in his elbows. Meanwhile Chub had twisted the rearview mirror to inspect his split eyelid, observing that the whole orb socket had taken on a rank and swampy appearance beneath the airtight bicycle patch. Shiner recommended antibiotics, and Bode said he had a tube of something orange and powerful in the medicine cabinet at home.

Upon arriving at the apartment building, Bode Gazzer neatly gunned the Dodge Ram into the first handicapped slot. A scolding stare from an insomniac neighbor made no impression. Bode asked his white brothers to mind the guns, while he toted the food inside.

Chub and Shiner were perched on the tailgate, finishing their beers, when they heard it – more a moan than a scream. Yet it was riven with such horror as to raise the fuzz on their necks. They scrambled toward Bode's apartment, Chub drawing the .357 as he ran.

Inside, unaware that the colonel had dropped the groceries, Shiner slipped on an onion ring and went down headfirst. Chub, stepping in cheesecake, skated hard into the television set, which toppled sideways with a crash.

Bodean Gazzer never turned to look. He remained stock-still in the living room. His pale face shone with perspiration. With both hands he clutched his camouflage cap to his belly.

The place had been taken apart from the kitchen to the john; a maliciously thorough job.

Dumbstruck, Chub stuck the Colt in his belt. "Jesus Willy," he gasped. Now he saw what Bode saw. So did Shiner, one cheek smeared with rat shit, peering up from the kitchen tiles.

The intruders had ripped down the posters of David Koresh and the other patriots. On the bare wall was a message scrawled in red, in letters three feet high. The first line said:

WE KNOW EVERYTHING

The second line said:

FEAR THE BLACK TIDE

It took only fifteen minutes for the White Clarion Aryans to load the pickup – guns, gear, bedding, water, plenty of camo clothes. Wordlessly the men piled into the front, Shiner in the middle as usual. Chub's head lolled against the side window; he was too shaken to ask Bode Gazzer for a theory.

To Shiner it seemed the colonel knew exactly where he was going. He looked determined behind the wheel, taking the truck on a beeline to Highway One, then making a sharp left.

South, by Shiner's reckoning. The Everglades, maybe. Or Key Largo.

Bode flicked on the dome light and said, "There's a map under the seat."

Shiner spread it across his lap.

"Flip it over," Bode told him.

Instead he should've been paying attention to his mirrors. Then he might have noticed the headlights of the compact car that had been following them from the apartment.

Inside the Honda, JoLayne Lucks turned down the radio and asked: "How did you know they'd run?"

Tom Krome said, "Because these are not brave guys. These are guys who beat up women. Running away is second nature."

"Especially with the 'Black Tide' on their tails." JoLayne chuckled to herself. She and Tom had arrived an hour earlier and peeked in the apartment window, to make sure it was the right place. That's when they'd seen Moffitt's menacing valentine on the wall.

Now, pointing at the truck in front of them, JoLayne said: "Think they've got my ticket on 'em?"

"Yep."

"Still no game plan?"

"Nope."

"I like an honest man," JoLayne said.

"Good. Here's more: I'm not feeling so brave myself."

"OK. When we get to Oz, we'll ask the wizard to give you some courage."

Krome said, "Toto, too?"

"Yes, dear. Toto, too."

JoLayne leaned over and put a lemon drop in his mouth. When he started to say something, she deftly popped in another one. Krome was hopelessly puckered. He didn't know where the pickup truck was leading them, but he knew he wasn't turning back. Bachelorhood in the Nineties, he thought. What a headline Sinclair could write:

DEAD MAN DOGS DANGEROUS DESPERADOS

# SIXTEEN

**The farther they** got from Coconut Grove, the stronger grew Chub's conviction that he would never see his treasured Amber again. He was seized by a mournful panic, a talon-like snatch of his heart.

Neither of his companions noticed. Shiner was preoccupied with the mysterious "Black Tide," and Bodean Gazzer was brimming with theories. Both men were shaken by the scene inside the ransacked apartment, and chatting about niggers and communists seemed to steady their nerves. An even flow of conversation also preserved the illusion of a calm orderly flight, when in fact Bode had no plan beyond running like hell. They were being pursued; chased by an unknown evil. Bode's instinct was to hide someplace remote and out of reach, and to get there as fast as possible. Shiner's naive and breathless queries, which otherwise would have provoked the harshest sarcasm, now worked as a tonic by affirming for Bode his role as the militia's undisputed leader. Although he hadn't the foggiest clue who the Black Tide was, Bode gave the full weight of his authority to wild speculation. This kept his mind busy and his spirits up, and Shiner hung on every word. Chub's lack of participation was of small concern, for Bode was accustomed to his partner's nodding off.

He was therefore flabbergasted to feel the gun barrel at the base of his neck. Shiner (who'd detected Chub's arm slipping behind the seat and figured he was just stretching) jerked at a sharp noise near his left ear – the click of the hammer being cocked. He turned only enough to see the Colt Python pointed at the colonel.

"Pull over," Chub said.

"What for?" Bode asked.

"Yer own good."

As soon as his partner stopped the truck, Chub eased down the hammer of the gun. "Son," he said to Shiner, "I got another mission for you. Provided you wanna stay in the brotherhood."

Shiner flinched like a spanked puppy; he'd thought his place in the White Clarion Aryans was solid.

"It's no sweat," Chub was saying. "You'll dig it." He stepped out of the pickup and motioned with the gun for Shiner to do the same.

Being half drunk and exhausted did not affect Bodean Gazzer's low threshold of annoyance. Chain of command obviously meant nothing to Chub; the goon operated on blood impulse and reckless emotion. If it continued, they'd all end up in maximum security at Raiford – not the ideal venue for a white-supremacy crusade.

When Chub reentered the truck, Bode said, "This shit's gotta stop. Where's the boy?"

"I sent him back up the road."

"For what?"

"To finish some bidness. Let's go." Chub, laying the revolver on the front seat between them; Shiner's spot.

"Well, goddamn." Bode could hear the kid's golf spikes clacking on the pavement.

"Jest drive," Chub said.

"Anywheres in particular?"

"Wherever you was goin' is fine. Long as it ain't too fur from Jewfish Creek." Chub launched a brown stream of spit out the window. "Go 'head and ast."

Bode Gazzer said, "OK. How come Jewfish Creek?"

"On account of I like the name."

"Ah." On account of you're a certified moron, Bode thought.

By daybreak they were at a marina in Key Largo, picking out a boat to steal.

Tom Krome's death was announced with an end-of-the-world headline in *The Register*, but the news failed to shake American journalism to its foundations. *The New York Times* didn't carry the story, while the Associated Press condensed *The Register*'s melodramatic front-page spread to eleven sober inches. The AP's rewrite desk circumspectly noted that, while the medical examiner was confident of his preliminary findings, the body found in Tom Krome's burned house had yet to be positively identified. *The Register*'s managing editor seemed certain of the worst – he was quoted as saying Krome was "quite possibly" murdered as the result of a sensitive newspaper assignment. Pressed for details, the managing editor replied he was not at liberty to discuss the investigation.

Many papers across the United States picked up the Associated Press story and reduced it to four or five paragraphs. A slightly longer version appeared in *The Missoulian*, the daily that serves Missoula and other communities in the greater Bitterroot valley of Montana. Fortuitously, it was here Mary Andrea Finley Krome had hooked up with a little-theater production of *The Glass Menagerie*. Although she was not a great fan of Tennessee Williams (and, in any case, preferred musicals over dramas), she needed the work. The prospect of performing in small-town obscurity depressed Mary Andrea, but her mood brightened after she made friends with another actress, a dance major at the state university. Her name was Lorie, or possibly Loretta – Mary Andrea reminded herself to check in the playbill. On Mary Andrea's second morning in town, Lorie or Loretta introduced her to a cozy coffee shop where students and local artists gathered, not far from the new city carousel. The coffee shop featured old stuffed sofas upon which Mary Andrea and her new pal contentedly settled with their cappuccinos and croissants. They spread the newspaper between them.

It was Mary Andrea's habit to begin each morning with an update of entertainment and celebrity happenings, of which several were capsulized in *The Missoulian*. Tom Cruise was being paid $22 million to star in a movie about a narcoleptic heart surgeon who must attempt a six-hour transplant operation on his girlfriend (Mary Andrea wondered which of Hollywood's anorexic blowjob artists had won the part). Also, it was reported that one of Mary Andrea's least-favorite television programs, *Sag Harbor Saga*, was being canceled after a three-year run. (Mary Andrea feared it wasn't the last America would see of Siobhan Davies, the insufferable Irish witch who'd beaten her out for the role of Darien, the predatory textile heiress.) And, finally, a drug-loving actor with whom Mary Andrea once had done Shakespeare in the Park was under arrest in New York after disrobing in the lobby of Trump Tower and, during his flight to escape, head-butting the beefeater at the Fifth Avenue entrance. (Mary Andrea took no joy from the actor's plight, for he had shown her nothing but kindness during *The Merchant of Venice*, when a disoriented June bug had flown into Mary Andrea's right ear and interrupted for several awkward moments Portia's famous peroration on the quality of mercy.)

Having digested, and sagely commented upon, each item in the "People" column, Mary Andrea Finley Krome then turned to the weightier pages of *The Missoulian*. The headline that caught her attention appeared on page three of the front section: NEWS REPORTER BELIEVED DEAD IN MYSTERY BLAZE. It wasn't the slain-journalist angle that grabbed Mary Andrea so much as the phrase "mystery blaze," because Mary Andrea adored a good mystery. The sight of her estranged husband's name in the second paragraph was a complete shock. The newspaper drifted from Mary Andrea's fingertips, and she emitted an oscillating groan that was mistaken by fellow coffee drinkers for a New Age meditative technique.

"Julie, you OK?" asked Lorie, or Loretta.

"Not really," Mary Andrea rasped.

"What is it?"

Mary Andrea pressed her knuckles to her eyes and felt genuine tears.

"You need a doctor?" asked her new friend.

"No," said Mary Andrea. "A travel agent."

Joan and Roddy got a copy of *The Register* at the Grab N'Go and brought it to Sinclair at the shrine. He refused to read it.

"You're mentioned by name," Joan beseeched,

holding up the newspaper for him to see, "as Tom Krome's boss."

Roddy added: "It explains how you're out of town and not available for comment."

"*Nyyah nimmy doo-dey!*" was Sinclair's response.

The yammering sent a sinusoidal murmur through the Christian tourists gathering along the narrow moat. Some knelt, some stood beneath umbrellas, some perched on folding chairs and Igloo coolers. Sinclair himself lay prone at the feet of the fiberglass Madonna.

Joan was so concerned about her brother's behavior that she considered notifying their parents. She'd read about religious fanatics who fondled snakes, but a turtle fixation seemed borderline deviant. Roddy said he hadn't heard of it either. "But personally," he added, "I'm damn glad it's cooters and not diamondbacks. Otherwise we'd be coffin-shopping."

Sinclair had cloaked himself toga-style in a pale bed-sheet, upon which a confetti of fresh lettuce was sprinkled. With surprising swiftness the apostolic turtles scrambled from their sunning stones to ascend the gleaming buffet. Zestfully they traversed Sinclair from head to toe, while he cooed and blinked placidly at the passing clouds. Cameras clicked and video cameras whirred.

Trish and Demencio monitored the visitation from the living room window. She said, "He's really something. You gotta admit."

"Yeah. A fruit basket."

"But aren't you glad we let him stay?"

Demencio said, "A buck's a buck."

"He must've snapped. Stripped a gear."

"Maybe so." Demencio was distracted by a sighting

of Dominick Amador, clumping unscrupulously among the pilgrims.

"Sonofabitch. He got him some crutches!"

Trish said, "You know why?"

"I can sure guess."

"Yeah, he finally got his feet drilled. I heard he paid the boy at the muffler shop, like, thirty bucks."

"Psycho," said Demencio.

Then Dominick Amador spotted him in the window and timorously waved a Crisco-filled mitten. Demencio did not return the greeting.

Trish said, "You want me to chase him off?"

Demencio folded his arms. "Now what – who the hell's that?" He pointed at a slender person in a hooded white robe. The person carried a clipboard and moved with clerical efficiency from one tourist to the next.

"The lady from Sebring Street," Trish explained, "the one with the Road-Stain Jesus. She's working on a petition to the highway department."

"Like hell. She's workin' on my customers!"

"No, honey, the state wants to pave over her shrine – "

"Is that my problem? I got a business going here."

"All right," Trish said, and went outside to have a word with the woman. Demencio had always been leery of his competition – he liked to stay ahead of the pack. It bothered him when Dominick or the others came snooping. Trish understood. The miracle racket was no picnic.

And the queer histrionics of the visiting newspaperman had made Demencio edgier than usual. He could cope with hydraulic malfunctions in a weeping statue; a flesh-and-blood lunatic was something else. For the time being, the recumbent and incoherent Sinclair was drawing plenty of customers. But what if he freaked out? What if his marble-mouthed gibberish turned to violent rant?

Demencio fretted that he might lose control of his shrine. He sat down heavily and contemplated the aquarium, where the unpainted baby turtles eagerly awaited breakfast. JoLayne Lucks had phoned to check on the smelly little buggers, and Demencio reported that all forty-five were healthy and fit. He hadn't told her about the apostle scam. JoLayne had promised she'd be home in a few days to collect her "precious babies."

They're precious to me, too, thought Demencio. I've got to milk 'em for all they're worth.

When Trish returned he said: "Let's do the rest."

"What?"

*"Them."* He nodded at the tank.

"How come?"

"More painted cooters, more money. Think of how happy Mister Born Again'll be." Demencio cut a glance toward the front window. "Crazy dork can bury himself under the damn things."

Trish said, "But, honey, there's only twelve apostles."

"Who says it's gotta be just apostles? Go find that Bible. All we need is thirty-three more saint types. Most anybody'll do – New Testament, Old Testament."

How could Trish say no? Her husband's instincts on such matters were invariably sound. As she gathered the brushes and paint bottles, she showed Demencio the front page of *The Register*, which had been given to her by Joan and Roddy. "Isn't that the fella went to Miami with JoLayne?"

"Yeah, only he ain't dead." With a forefinger, Demencio derisively flicked the newspaper. "When she called up this morning, this Tom guy was with her. Some phone booth down in the Keys."

"The Keys!"

"Yeah, but don't go tellin' the turtle boy. Not yet."

"I suppose you're right," Trish said.

"He finds out his man's still alive, he might quit prayin'. We don't want that."

"No."

"Or he might stop with them angel voices."

"Tongues. Speaking in tongues," Trish corrected.

"Whatever. I won't lie," Demencio said. "That crazy dork is good for business."

"I won't say a thing. Look here, he's mentioned in the same article."

Demencio skimmed the first few paragraphs while he struggled to uncap a bottle of thinner. "You see this? 'Assistant Deputy Managing Editor of Features and Style.' Hell kinda job is *that*? Ha, no wonder he's rolling in the mud."

Trish handed him a bouquet of paintbrushes. "What do you think about Holy Cooter T-shirts? And maybe key chains."

Her husband looked up. "Yeah," he said, with the first smile of the day.

When Tom Krome got his turn on the pay phone, he called his parents on Long Island to tell them not to believe what they saw in the papers.

"I'm alive."

"As opposed to what?" his father asked.

*Newsday* had run the story somewhere other than the sports section, so Krome's old man had missed it.

Tom gave a sketchy explanation of the arson, instructed his folks on fielding future media inquiries, then called Katie. He was genuinely touched to hear she'd been crying.

"You should see the front page, Tommy!"

"Well, it's wrong. I'm fine."

"Thank God," Katie sniffled. "Arthur also insists you're dead. He even bought me a diamond solitaire."

"For the funeral?"

"He thinks I think he had something to do with killing you – which I *did* think, until now."

Krome said, "I'm assuming he's the one who burned down my house."

"Not personally."

"You know what I mean. The dead body in the kitchen must have been his law clerk, faithful but careless."

"Champ Powell. I guess so," Katie said. "Tom, what'm I going to do? I can't stand the sight of Arthur but I honestly don't believe he meant for anyone to get hurt . . ."

"Pack a bag and go to your mother's."

"And the diamond *is* beautiful. God knows what it cost. So, see, there's a part of him that wants to be true – "

"Katie, I gotta go. Please don't tell anyone you spoke with me, OK? Keep it a secret for now, it's important."

"I'm so glad you're all right. I prayed so hard."

"Don't stop now," Tom Krome said.

It was a bright and breezy fall morning. The sky was cloudless and full of gulls and terns. The marina stirred but didn't bustle, typical of the dead season between Thanksgiving and New Year's, when the tourists were still up North. For the locals it was a glorious and special time, despite the wane of revenues. Many charter captains didn't even bother to go down to the docks, the chance of walk-ons was so remote.

JoLayne Lucks had dozed off in the car. Krome touched her arm and she opened her eyes. Her mouth was sour, her throat scratchy.

"Yekkk," she said, yawning.

Krome handed her a cup of coffee. "Long night."

"Where are our boys?"

"Still in the truck."

JoLayne said, "What d'you think – they meeting somebody?"

"I don't know. They've been up and down, scoping out the boats."

Squinting at the windshield's glare, JoLayne groped for her sunglasses. She saw the red Dodge pickup at the opposite end of the marina, parked by the front door of the tackle shop.

"Again with the wheelchair zone?"

"Yep."

"Assholes."

They'd decided that the man driving the truck must be Bodean Gazzer, because that was the name on the registration, according to Tom's source at the highway patrol. Bullet holes notwithstanding, the pristine condition of the vehicle suggested an owner who would not casually loan it to fleeing felons. Tom and JoLayne still had no name for Gazzer's partner, the one with the ponytail and the bad eye.

And now a new mystery: a third man, who'd been abruptly put out along the road in the pitch dark of the night – JoLayne and Tom watching from the parking lot of a video store, where they'd pulled over to wait.

Something in the bearing of the third man had looked familiar to JoLayne, but in the blue-gray darkness his facial features were indiscernible. The headlights of a passing car had revealed a chubby figure with a disconsolate trudge. Also: an Australian bush hat.

There was no sign of him in the morning, at the marina. Krome didn't know what to make of it.

JoLayne asked if he'd phoned his folks.

"They didn't even know I was dead. Now they're really confused," Krome said. "Whose turn on the radio?"

"Mine." She reached for the dial.

During the long hours in the car, the two of them had encountered a potentially serious divergence of musical tastes. Tom believed that driving in South Florida required constant hard-rock accompaniment, while JoLayne favored songs that were breezy and soothing to the nerves. In the interest of fairness, they'd agreed to alternate control of the radio. If she lucked into a Sade, he got a Tom Petty. If he got the Kinks, she got an Annie Lennox. And so on. Occasionally they found common ground. Van Morrison. Dire Straits. "The Girl with the Faraway Eyes," which they sang together as they rode through Florida City. There were even a few mutual abominations (a Paul McCartney-Michael Jackson duet, for instance) that propelled them to lunge simultaneously for the tuning button.

"Here's what I noticed," said JoLayne, adjusting the volume.

"Who's that?" Krome demanded.

"Céline Dion."

"Geez, it's Saturday morning. Have some mercy."

"You'll get your turn." JoLayne wore a shrewd,

schoolteacher smile. "Now, Tom, here's what I noticed: You don't like many black musical artists."

"Oh, bullshit." He was truly stung.

"Name one."

"Marvin Gaye, Jimi Hendrix – "

"A *live* one."

"B.B. King, Al Green, Billy Preston. The Hootie guy, what's his name – "

"You're pushing it," JoLayne said.

"Prince!"

"Oh, come on."

Krome said, "Damn right. 'Little Red Corvette.' "

"I guess it's possible."

"Christ, what if I said something like that to you?"

"You're right," said JoLayne. "I take it all back."

" 'A live one.' Gimme a break."

She eyed him over the rims of her peach-tinted shades. "You're pretty touchy about this stuff, aren't you? I suppose that's the white man's burden. At least the liberal white man."

"Who said I was liberal?"

"You're cute when you're on the defensive. Want the rest of my coffee? I gotta pee."

"Not now," Tom Krome said. "Take off your hat and duck."

The red pickup was rolling toward them, in reverse. The driver backed up to a slip where a twenty-foot boat was tied. It had twin outboards, a flecked blue-and-gray finish and a folding Bimini top. From the tackle shop you couldn't have seen it, moored between a towering Hatteras and a boxy houseboat.

Peering over the dashboard, Krome watched a tall, unshaven passenger get out of the truck: the ponytailed man. He carried a bottle of beer and some tools – a screwdriver, a wire cutter, a socket wrench. The man climbed somewhat unsteadily into the boat and disappeared behind the steering console.

"What's going on?" JoLayne, inching up in the seat.

Krome told her to stay down. He saw a puff of blue smoke, then heard the outboards start. The ponytailed man stood up and signaled laconically at the driver of the pickup truck. Then the ponytailed man untied the lines and with both hands pushed the boat away from the pilings.

"They're stealing it," Krome reported.

JoLayne said: "My neck hurts. May I sit up?"

"In a second."

Barely fifty yards from the dock, the ponytailed man shoved forward the throttle of the stolen boat. Momentarily the bow rose upward like a gaily striped missile, then leveled off under a collar of foam as the boat took out across the shallows of Florida Bay. At the same instant, and with a sudden yelp of rubber, the red pickup truck shot toward the marina exit.

"Now?" asked JoLayne.

"All clear," Krome told her.

She rose, glancing first at the departing truck and then at the receding gray speck on the water. "All right, smart guy. Which one's got my ticket?"

"Beats me," Krome said.

# SEVENTEEN

**It was Shiner's** first kidnapping, and despite a shaky start it came off pretty well.

He had hitchhiked to the Grove, where he'd fallen asleep in Peacock Park. In midafternoon he'd awakened and wandered down Grand Avenue to buy a handgun. His street-corner inquiries had been so poorly received that he'd been chased from the neighborhood by a group of black and Hispanic teenagers. Naturally he'd lost his bush hat and the golf spikes, which were ill-suited for a footrace.

Armed only with a stubby Phillips-head screwdriver he'd found beneath a banyan tree, Shiner arrived at Hooters shortly before five o'clock. Remembering Chub's instructions, he struck up a conversation with the bartender, who was glad to point out Amber among the servers. Shiner scoped her out – hot-looking, like Chub had said, but as a rule most waitresses were hot-looking to Shiner. And while Chub had made a great point of detailing Amber's uncanny resemblance to Kim Basinger, the information was useless to Shiner. He didn't know who Kim Basinger was. While preparing for the crime, Shiner became apprehensive over the possibility of snatching the wrong girl. What if Hooters had more than one Amber? Chub would shoot him dead, that's what.

Hours later, Shiner was crouched behind a hedgerow when the waitress identified by the bartender left work. She slipped behind the wheel of a giant Ford sedan, which momentarily rattled Shiner (who'd been expecting a sports car – in his mind, all hot-looking babes belonged in sports cars). He recovered his composure, flung himself in the passenger side and placed the tip of the screwdriver against Amber's soft and flawless neck.

"Whoa," she said.

Not a scream, but a *whoa*.

"You Amber?"

She nodded carefully.

"The one looks like the actor – Kim something?"

Amber said, "You're the second guy this week who's told me that."

Shiner was flooded with relief. "All right. Now drive."

"That a knife?"

Shiner pulled the screwdriver away from Amber's neck. The grooved tip left a small, stellate impression in her skin; Shiner could see it in the green glow of the dashboard.

Hastily he slipped the tool into his pocket. "Yeah, it's a knife. I got a damn gun, too."

"I believe you," Amber said.

After a few wrong turns, he got her pointed south. She didn't ask where they were going, but Shiner was ready if she did. *Base camp*, would be his answer. Base camp of the White Clarion Aryans! That'd give her something to think about.

"This your car?" he asked.

"My dad gave it to me. Runs great," Amber said.

Not the least bit shy. That's cool, Shiner thought.

"My boyfriend has a Miata," she added. "Well, *had* a Miata. Anyhow, I like this better. More legroom – I've got super-long legs."

Shiner felt his cheeks flush. Up close, Amber was very beautiful. Whenever headlights passed in the other direction, he could see glimmers of gold in her long eyelashes. Plus she smelled absolutely fantastic for someone who worked with chicken wings and burgers, not to mention the onions. Shiner believed Amber smelled about a thousand times sweeter than the baskets of orange blossoms his mother would take to the Road-Stain Jesus. True, they were week-old orange blossoms (purchased in bulk from a turnpike gift shop) but still they held a fragrance.

Amber said, "What happened to your head?" She was talking about the crankcase scar.

"I got hurt."

"Car accident?"

"Sort of." Shiner was surprised she noticed it, since she'd barely taken her eyes off the road since he'd hopped in.

"How about buckling your seat belt," she said.

"No way." Shiner remembered what Bodean Gazzer had said about seat belts being part of the government's secret plot to "neutralize the citizenry." If you're wearing seat belts, Bode had explained, it'll be harder to jump out of the car and escape, once the NATO helicopters start landing on the highways. That's the whole reason they made the seat-belt law, Bode had said, to make sure millions of Americans would be strapped down and helpless when the global attack was launched. As intriguing as Bode's explanation was, Shiner decided the information was too sensitive to share with Amber.

"What's that on your arm?" she asked. She turned on the domelight for a better look at Shiner's tattoo.

"It's a eagle," he said, self-consciously.

"I meant the *W.R.B.* Is that for the White Rebel Brotherhood?"

Shiner said, "Man, it's a long story."

"I saw 'em in concert. They were killer."

"Yeah?"

"The best is 'Nut-Cutting Bitch.' Ever heard it? You like hip-hop?"

"Metal." Shiner gave his decorated biceps a subtle flex; it wasn't often he had a pretty girl's undivided attention.

She said, "Then what's the deal with your *W.R.B.*? They are so *not* heavy metal."

Shiner told Amber there'd been a mix-up on his tattoo. He was pleased to hear her say she could fix it.

"But only if you let me go," she added.

"No way."

"My best friend worked in a tattoo parlor for two summers. I hung out there, God, for hours. It's not as hard as it looks."

Shiner's lips drew tight. Ruefully he said: "I can't let you free. Not right away."

"Oh." Amber turned off the dome light. For a long time she didn't speak to him. When two tank-topped frat boys in a Beemer convertible nearly sideswiped them, she said: "Fuckheads." But it was practically a whisper, not intended as conversation. Soon Shiner grew nervous again. He'd been doing fine while Amber was chatty, but now his feet were tapping with the jitters. Plus he felt like a dolt. He felt like he'd blown something.

Finally she said, "You're going to rape me, aren't you?"

"No way."

"Don't lie. It's better if I know."

"I ain't lyin'!"

"Then what is all this?" Both hands were fixed on the wheel. Her thin arms were straight and stiff. "What's going on?"

Shiner said, "It's a favor for a friend."

"I get it. Then *he's* going to rape me."

"Over my dead body!" Shiner was startled by his own vehemence.

It drew a hopeful glance from Amber. "You mean it?"

"Damn straight I do."

"Thanks," she said, turning her attention back to the traffic. "You don't really have a gun, do you?"

"Naw."

"So, what's your name?" Amber asked.

Both of Arthur Battenkill's secretaries knew something was wrong, because he'd stopped pestering them for sex. The women didn't complain; they much preferred typing and filing. The judge's deportment in bed was no different from that in the office – arrogant and abrupt.

Dana and Willow often discussed their respective intimacies with Arthur Battenkill, and this was done with no trace of possessiveness or jealousy. Rather, the conversations served as a source of mutual support – the man was a burden they shared.

Willow reported: "He didn't ask me to stay after work."

"Me, neither," said Dana. "That's two days in a row!"

"What do you think?" Willow said.

"He's upset about Champ quitting."

"Could be."

"If that's what really happened," Dana added, lifting an eyebrow.

Both secretaries were puzzled by the sudden departure of the law clerk, Champ Powell. At first Arthur Battenkill had said he'd gone home for a family emergency. Then the judge had said no, that was merely a cover story. Actually, Champ had been called back to the Gadsden County sheriff's department for a special undercover operation. The project was so secret and dangerous that even his family wasn't told.

Which explained, the judge had said, why Champ's mother kept calling the office, looking for him.

Dana and Willow remained unconvinced. "He didn't seem like the undercover type," Dana remarked. "B'sides, he really loved his job here."

"Plus he idolized the judge," Willow said.

"That he did."

Champ Powell's devotion was almost an unnatural thing, both women agreed. The clerk was so enamored of Arthur Battenkill that initially the secretaries suspected he was gay. In fact they'd privately discussed the possibility of Champ's seducing the judge, which wouldn't have bothered them one bit. Anything to distract the man.

But it hadn't yet happened, at least to their knowledge.

Said Dana: "Whatever's got into Art, let's just leave it be."

"Amen," Willow said.

"Sit back and enjoy the peace."

"Right."

"Hey. Maybe he's found God."

Willow laughed so hard that Diet Pepsi jetted out of her nostrils. Naturally that's when the judge walked in. As Willow grabbled for a box of Kleenex, Arthur Battenkill said, "How elegant."

"Sorry."

"It's like having Princess Grace answering the phones."

With that, the judge disappeared into his chambers, closing the door. Willow was somewhat battered by his first-thing-in-the-morning sarcasm, so Dana took him coffee.

She told the judge he didn't look well.

"It's Saturday," he grumbled. The chief judge had been on Arthur Battenkill's ass about clearing the case backlog, so he'd been putting in hours on weekends.

"You haven't slept." Dana, affecting a motherly tone.

"Pollens. Mold spores." Arthur Battenkill took a sip of coffee. "I sleep fine."

It was the scene at breakfast that had disturbed him – Katie gobbling down four huge buttermilk flapjacks and a bagel, a clear signal she was no longer grieving. Clearing the dishes, she'd exhibited a perkiness that could have at its root only one explanation: She'd come to believe her precious Tommy wasn't dead.

Reluctantly the judge had already reached the same conclusion. The strongest evidence was the uncharacteristic lack of communication from Champ Powell, who by now should have called to seek Arthur Battenkill's praise and gratitude for the arson. Nearly as ominous: Champ's Harley-Davidson motorcycle had been found and towed from a Blockbuster parking lot three blocks from Tom Krome's house. The judge was certain Champ never would have abandoned the bike were he still alive.

The unexpected upswing of Katie's mood had clinched it for Arthur Battenkill. Picking indifferently at his pancakes, he'd recalled hearing the telephone ring while he was in the shower – probably Krome, calling to tell Katie not to worry. The mannerly motherfucker.

Now Dana, arms folded: "You've got that emergency hearing in ten minutes. Would you like me to press your robe?"

"No. Who is it?"

"Mrs. Bensinger."

"God. Let me guess."

Dana dropped her voice. "Another alimony problem."

Arthur Battenkill said, "I hate those horrible people. Thank heaven they never had children."

"Not so loud. She's out in the hall."

"Yeah?" The judge cupped his hands to his mouth: "Greedy freeloading twat!"

Dana looked at him blankly.

The judge said, "Her husband's a thieving shit, too."

"Yes, he is."

"By the way, I've decided to take some time off. I suppose you and Willow will survive without me. I get that impression."

Dana fixed her gaze safely on the coffeepot. "How long will you be gone?"

"I can't say. Mrs. Battenkill and I are going away together." The judge thumbed his appointment book. "See if Judge Beckman will cover for me starting late next week. Can you do that?"

"Certainly."

"And, Dana, this is supposed to be a surprise for my wife, so don't blow it."

Willow buzzed on the speakerphone to report that Mr. Bensinger had arrived and that the atmosphere in the hallway was growing tense.

"Fuck 'em." Arthur Battenkill snorted. "I hope they slaughter each other with blunt objects. Save the taxpayers a few bucks. Dana, isn't it Judge Tigert over in Probate who's got the bungalow in Exuma?"

"The Abacos."

"Whatever. See if it's available."

The notion of the judge taking his wife on a romantic trip to the Bahamas was stupefying. Obviously the man was suffering a breakdown. Dana could hardly wait to share the gossip with Willow.

As she was leaving his chambers, Arthur Battenkill called out: "Dana, darling, you're doing a superb job of concealing your amusement."

"What on earth are you talking about?"

"Don't pretend to know everything about me. Don't pretend to have me figured out. I *do* have feelings for Mrs. Battenkill."

"Oh, I believe you," Dana said. "By the way, Art, how'd she like the new necklace?"

The judge's smug expression dissolved. "Send in the goddamn Bensingers," he said.

JoLayne Lucks hadn't been to the Keys since she was a small girl. She was amazed at how much had changed, the homey and congenial tackiness supplanted by franchise fast-food joints, strip malls and high-rise resorts. To take her mind off the riffraff, JoLayne recited for Tom

Krome a roster of local birds, resident and migratory: ospreys, snowy egrets, white herons, blue herons, kingfishers, flycatchers, cardinals, grackles, robins, red-tailed hawks, white-crowned pigeons, flickers, roseate spoonbills . . .

"Once there were even flamingos," she informed him. "Guess what happened to them."

Krome didn't respond. He was watching Bodean James Gazzer strip and clean a large semiautomatic rifle. Even from a distance of a hundred yards, the barrel glinted ominously in the noon sun.

"Tom, you don't even care."

"I like flamingos," he said, "but what we have here is a rare green-breasted shithead. Broad daylight, he's playing with guns."

"Yes, I can see."

Tom had rejected her latest plan, which involved ambushing Bodean Gazzer alone, jamming her twelve-gauge into his groin and demanding under threat of emasculation that he return the stolen lottery ticket.

Not here, Krome had told her. Not yet.

They were parked on a bleached strip of limestone fill, along a rim of lush mangroves. Not far away was a gravel boat ramp, blocked at the moment by Bodean Gazzer's red pickup. The driver's door was open and he stood in full view; neck-to-knees camouflage, cowboy boots, mirrored sunglasses. He had a chamois cloth spread on the hood, the assault rifle in pieces before him.

"Steel balls. I give him that," Krome said.

"No, he's just a fool. A damn fool."

JoLayne feared a cop would drive by and see what Bodean Gazzer was doing. Once the idiot got himself arrested, the chase would be over. The thing would boil down to JoLayne's word against the redneck's, and he'd never produce the ticket.

A small black bird landed in the trees and began to sing. Krome said, "OK, what's that one?"

"Redwing," JoLayne answered stiffly.

"They endangered?"

"Not yet. Don't you find it obscene – their presence in a place like this? They're like . . . *litter.*" She was talking about the two robbers. "They don't deserve this – to feel the sun on their necks and breathe this fine air. It's completely wasted on men like that."

Krome rolled down the car window and took in the cool salt breeze. In a sleepy voice he said, "I could get used to this. Maybe after Alaska."

JoLayne, thinking: How can he act so relaxed? She could no longer distract herself with the island wildlife, so unnerving was the spectacle of Bodean Gazzer toiling ritually at his gun. She couldn't shake the memory of that awful scene in her house – not just the man's punches and kicking, but his voice:

*Hey, genius, she can't talk with a gun in her mouth.*

Talking to his filthy, ponytailed friend:

*You wanna make a impression? Look – here.*

Snatching one of the baby turtles from the glass tank, putting it on the wooden floor, coaxing his ponytailed friend to shoot it. That's what Bodean Gazzer had done.

Yet here he was, fit and free in the Florida sunshine. With a $14 million Lotto ticket hidden somewhere, possibly inside a rubber.

JoLayne said to Tom: "I can't just sit here doing nothing."

"You're absolutely right. You should drive to the grocery." Krome took out his wallet. "Then you should stop at one of those motels and rent a boat. I'll give you some money."

JoLayne said she had a better idea. "I'll stay here and keep an eye on the archpatriot. *You* go get the boat."

"Too risky."

"I can handle myself," she insisted.

"JoLayne, there's no doubt in my mind. I was talking about *me*. Dead persons should always keep a low profile – my face has been in *The Herald*, probably even on TV."

She said, "It was a shitty picture, Tom. Nobody'll recognize you."

"I can't take that chance."

"You looked like Pat Sajak on NyQuil."

"The answer is no."

Tom didn't trust her, of course. Didn't trust her not to mess with the redneck. "This is ridiculous," she complained. "I've never driven a boat."

"And I've never fired a shotgun," Krome said, "so we have something new to learn from each other. Just what every romance needs."

"Please."

"Speaking of which." He got out, popped the trunk and removed the Remington. "Just in case."

JoLayne said, "Bad news, Rambo. The shells are in my purse."

"Just as well," he said. "I figure we've got another forty-five minutes, maybe an hour. Ice is priority one. Get as much ice and fresh water as you can carry."

"Forty-five minutes until what?"

"Until our sailor with the ponytail gets here," Krome said.

"Is that so? When were you planning to clue me in?"

"When I was sure."

JoLayne Lucks was determined to appear skeptical. "You think they're going by sea."

"Yup."

"Where?"

"No idea. That's why we need a boat of our own. And a chart would be good, too."

Listen to him, thought JoLayne. Mr. Take-Charge.

She considered holding her ground, telling him off. Then she changed her mind. It did look like a grand day to be out on the bay, especially if the alternative was six more hours in a cramped Honda.

"How big a boat?" JoLayne asked.

Chub was almost at ease on the water. One of the few bearable memories of his childhood was the family ski boat, which the Gillespies had used on weekend outings to Lake Rabun. The young Onus's pudginess had prevented him from developing into a first-rate water-skier, but he'd loved steering the boat.

The thrill returned to him now, at the helm of the *Reel Luv*, which he had hot-wired in the name of the White Clarion Aryans. With its twin Merc 90s, the stolen twenty-footer was much peppier than the boat Chub had captained as a boy. That was fine; he could handle the extra speed. What he couldn't cope with was the irregular layout of Florida Bay, with its shifting hues, snaking channels and treacherous flats. It was nothing like Lake Rabun, which was deep and well-defined and relatively free of immovable obstacles such as mangrove islands. Chub's somewhat rusty navigational skills were further tested by the impaired vision of his wounded left eye (covered by a new rubber patch, purchased for two dollars at an Amoco station) and by his relatively high blood alcohol.

It was only a matter of minutes before he beached the boat. The broad tidal bank was highly visible because of its brown color, which contrasted boldly with the azure and indigo of the deep channels. Also in evidence was a phalanx of wading birds, whose long-legged presence should have signaled the dramatic change of water depth. Chub didn't notice.

The grounding was drawn-out and panoramic, the big outboards roaring and throwing great geysers of cocoa-colored silt. Chub was hurled hard against the console, knocking the wind out of him. The egrets and herons took flight in unison, wheeling once over the noisy scene before stringing out westbound in the porcelain morning sky. When the spewing engines finally died, the *Reel Luv* was at rest in approximately seven inches of water. The hull drew exactly eight.

As soon as Chub regained his breath, he got up and saw there was but one way off the shallows: Get out and push. Swearing bitterly, he pulled off his shoes and slipped overboard. Immediately he sank to his nuts in the clammy marl. With great thrashing he managed to position himself at the stern and lean his weight against the transom.

The boat actually moved. Not much, but Chub felt somewhat encouraged.

Every sloppy inch of progress was muscle-sapping, like trying to march in wet cement. The mud sucked at Chub's legs, and his bare skin stung from the sea lice. Fastening to his arms and belly were tiny purple leeches, no larger than rice kernels, which he swatted away savagely. Additional concern was generated by an unfamiliar tingle in his crotch, and it occurred to Chub that some exotic parasite might have entered his body by swimming into the hole of his pecker. No other millionaire in the entire world, he thought rancorously, had these kinds of problems. He was thankful Amber wasn't there to witness the degrading scene.

Finally the stolen boat came free of the grassy bank. Chub boosted himself aboard and manically stripped off his pants to attend to the stinging.

That's when he remembered it.

*The ticket.*

"Jesus!" he cried hoarsely. "Jesus Willy Christ!"

His right thigh was bare and dripping wet. The jumbo Band-Aid had fallen off. The Lotto ticket was gone.

Chub uttered an inhuman croak and sorrowfully toppled back into the water.

# EIGHTEEN

**Bodean Gazzer was** obsessed with the specter of the Black Tide. He could recall no mention of the group in the stacks of white-supremacist pamphlets he'd collected.

Black Panthers, MOVE, Nation of Islam, NAACP – Bode had read extensively about them. But nothing called the Black Tide.

Whoever they were, they'd been through his apartment. Negroes, almost certainly! Bode thought he knew why he'd been singled out: They'd learned about the White Clarion Aryans.

But how? he asked himself. The WCA had been together scarcely one week – he hadn't even composed a manifesto yet. His pulse fluttered as he mulled the only two possible explanations: Either the Negro force possessed a sophisticated intelligence-gathering apparatus, or there was a serious leak within the WCA. Bode Gazzer regarded the latter as almost inconceivable.

Instead he would proceed on the assumption that the Black Tide was exceptionally cunning and resourceful, probably connected to a government agency. He would also presume that no matter where the White Clarion Aryans took up hiding, the devious Negroes would eventually track them down.

That's all right, Bode thought. He'd have his militia ready when the time came.

Meanwhile, where was that fucking Chub with the boat?

Panic nibbled at Bode Gazzer's gut. The idea of deserting his trigger-happy partner began to make some sense. Bode had, after all, fourteen million bucks tucked in a condom. Once he cashed the lottery ticket, he could go anywhere, do anything – build himself a fortress in Idaho, with the mother of all hot tubs!

Lately Bode had been thinking a lot about Idaho, lousy winters and all. From what he'd heard, the mountains and forests were full of straight-thinking white Christians. Recruiting for the WCA would be so much easier in a place like that. Bode was thoroughly fed up with Miami – everywhere you turned were goddamn foreigners. And when you finally came across a real English-speaking white person, there was a better than even chance he'd turn out to be a Jew or some ultraliberal screamer. Bode was sick and tired of walking on egg-shells, whispering his true righteous beliefs instead of declaring them loud and proud in public. In Miami you always had to be so damn careful – God forbid you accidentally insulted somebody, because they'd get right in your face. And not just the Cubans, either.

Bodean Gazzer felt sure the minorities out West were more docile and easily intimidated. He decided it might be a good move, providing he could adjust to the cold weather. Even in summer camos, Bode Gazzer thought he could fit right in.

As for Chub, he probably wouldn't go over big in Idaho. He'd probably spook even decent white people away from the Aryan cause. No, Bode thought, Chub belonged in the South.

And it wasn't as if Bode would be leaving the man high and dry. Chub still held the other Lotto ticket, the one they'd taken off the Negro woman in Grange. Hell, he'd be rich enough to start his own militia if he wanted. Be his own colonel.

Bode checked his wristwatch. If he left now, he could make Tallahassee before midnight. This time tomorrow, he'd have his first Lotto check.

Unless they got to him first – the vicious bastards who'd ransacked his apartment.

Ironically, that's when a crazy stoner like Chub was most useful – in the face of violence. He didn't spook easily, and he'd do just about anything you told him. He'd be damn handy to have around if shooting started. It was something to consider, something to mark on the positive side of the Chub ledger. An argument could be made for keeping the man nearby.

Pacing the boat ramp, Bode sweated through his Timber Ghost jumpsuit. The weekend road traffic zipped past, Bode feeling the curious eyes of the travelers on his neck – not all were tourists and fishermen, he felt certain. Undoubtedly the Black Tide enlisted many watchers, and they'd be scouting for a red Dodge Ram pickup with a FUHRMAN FOR PRESIDENT sticker (which Bode Gazzer had tried unsuccessfully to scrape off the bumper with a penknife).

That's when he'd decided to haul out the AR-15. Let the fuckers see what they're up against.

He laid a chamois across the hood of the truck and disassembled the semiautomatic exactly as Chub had taught him. He hoped the Black Tide was catching all this. He hoped they'd come to the conclusion he was mentally deranged, displaying an assault rifle in broad daylight along a U.S. government highway.

When it was time to put the AR-15 back together, Bodean Gazzer ran into difficulty. Some parts fit together, some didn't. He wondered if he'd accidentally misplaced a screw or two. The pieces of the gun were slick and oily, and Bode's fingers were moist with perspiration. He began dropping little things in the gravel.

In exasperation, he thought: *How hard can this be? Chub can do it when he's drunk!*

After half an hour, Bode angrily gave up. He folded the chamois cloth around the loose components of the rifle and set the bundle in the bed of the pickup truck. He tried to act nonchalant, for the benefit of the spying Negroes.

He got behind the wheel and cranked the AC up full blast. He scanned the bottle-green water in all directions. A low-riding fishing skiff crossed his view. So did a pretty girl, cutting angles on a sailboard. Then came two hairy fat guys on jet skis, jumping each other's wakes.

But there was no sign of Chub in the stolen boat. Sourly Bode thought: Maybe the dickhead's not coming. Maybe he's ditching *me*.

Five more minutes, he told himself. Then I'm gone.

On the highway, cars streamed southbound as if loaded on a conveyor belt. Staring at them made Bode drowsy. He'd been up for almost two days and in truth was physically incapable of driving to Cutler Ridge, much less Tallahassee. He would've loved to take a nap, but that would be suicide. That's when they'd make their move – the Black Tide, whatever and whoever it was.

When Bode closed his eyes, a question popped belatedly into his brain: What the hell do they want?

He was not too exhausted to figure it out. They seemed to know everything, didn't they? Who he was, where he lived. They knew about the White Clarion Aryans, too.

So surely they also knew about one, if not both, of the lottery tickets. That's what the greedy bastards had been searching for inside his apartment!

Bodean Gazzer was snapped alert by the icy realization that the only stroke of good fortune he'd ever experienced was in danger of being ripped from his grasp. Alone on the road, with the AR-15 in pieces, he was a sitting duck.

Impulsively Bode dug into his pants for his wallet, took out the Trojan packet, peeked inside. The Lotto coupon was safe. He put it away. He didn't need to look at his watch to know five minutes was up. Maybe Chub had bailed. Or got busted by the marine patrol. Or found some fiberglass resin to sniff, fell off the boat and drowned.

*Adiós, muchacho.*

Bode's heart was hammering like a rabbit's. Recklessly he gunned the truck across Highway One and fishtailed into the northbound lane. With trembling fingers he adjusted the rearview mirror, something he should've done the night before. With only a Molson truck on his bumper, Bode was breathing easier by the time he reached Whale Harbor. Crossing the bridge, he glanced along a broad tree-lined channel to the west. As if seized by a cramp, his foot sprang off the accelerator.

A blue-and-gray speedboat was snaking down the

waterway. The driver's ponytail flapped like a gray rag in the breeze.

"Aw, hell," Bodean Gazzer said. He made a noisy U-turn at the Holiday Isle charter docks and hauled ass back to the ramp.

The grocery store was a treat; everyone friendly, helpful. Not so at the motel marina. The man in charge of the boats – old fart, pinched gray face with a yellow three-day stubble – was clumsy with edginess and indecision. Clearly he'd never done business with a solitary black woman, and the prospect had afflicted him with the yips.

"Is there a problem?" JoLayne Lucks inquired, knowing full well there was. She drummed her daunting fingernails on the cracked countertop.

The dock guy coughed. "I'll need your driver's license."

"Fine."

"And a cash deposit." More coughing.

"Certainly."

The dock guy gnawed his lower lip. "You done this before? Mebbe you wanna try a water bike 'stead."

"Lord, no." JoLayne laughed. She spotted a calico cat curled beside the soda cooler. She scooped it off the floor and began stroking its chin. "Poor lil princess got ear mites, don't ya?" Then, addressing the dock guy: "Chlorhexidine drops. Any veterinarian carries them."

The old man fumbled his pen. "Ma'am, is the boat fer fishin' or divin' or what azackly? How fur you gone take it?"

JoLayne said, "I was thinking Borneo."

"Now, don't you get huffy. It's jest the boss owner makes me do all this shit paperwork."

"I understand." Tacked to a wall of the shack was a marine chart of Florida Bay. JoLayne surreptitiously scanned it and said: "Cotton Key. That's as far as I'm going."

The dock guy looked disappointed as he wrote it down on the rental form. "They's a grouper hole out there. I guess the whole damn world knows."

JoLayne said, "Well, they won't hear it from me." The cat jumped from her arms. She opened her purse. "How about a tide table," she asked, "and one of those maps?"

The dock guy seemed pleasantly surprised by the request, as if most yahoo tourists never thought to ask. JoLayne could see his estimation of her rise meteorically. In his scarlet-rimmed eyes appeared a glimmer of hope that the motel's precious sixteen-foot skiff might actually be returned in one piece.

"Here go, young lady." He handed her the chart and the tide card.

"Hey, thanks. Could you warm up the boat for me? I'll be there in a jiff – I've got ice and food out in the car."

The dock guy said OK, which was a good thing because JoLayne didn't know how to start a cold outboard. The old man had it purring by the time she stepped aboard with the grocery bags. He even held the lid of the cooler while she stocked it. Then he said, " 'Member. Back by sunset."

"Gotcha." JoLayne examined the controls, trying to recall what Tom had told her about working the throttle. The old guy hobbled out of the boat and, with a creaky grunt, pushed it away from the pilings. JoLayne levered the stick forward.

The man stood on the dock, eyeing her like a bony old stork. "Sunset!" he called out.

JoLayne gave him the thumbs-up as she motored slowly away, aiming the bow down a marked channel. She heard the dock guy call to her once more. A funereal droop had come to his shoulders.

"Hey!" he cried.

JoLayne waved; the robotic sort of wave you got from the girl on the homecoming float.

"Hey, what about some b-bait!"

JoLayne waved some more.

"The hell you gone catch fish without no bait?" he shouted at her. "Or even a damn rod and reel?"

She smiled and tapped a forefinger to her temple. The old guy sucked in his liver-colored cheeks and stomped into the shack. JoLayne accelerated as much as she dared in the bumpy chop and then concentrated on not crashing. The chief hazards were other recreational vessels, a large percentage of which seemed to be piloted by lobotomized young men holding beer cans. They regarded JoLayne as if she were an exotic squid, causing her to conclude that not many African-American women were seen alone on the waters of the Florida Keys. One witty lad even sang out: "Are you lost? Nassau's *thata* way!" JoLayne congratulated herself for not flipping him the finger.

To avoid being noticed by Bodean Gazzer, Tom had arranged to meet a safe distance from the gravel ramp where the pickup truck was parked. He'd pointed out a break in the mangroves, a bare gash of rocky shoreline on the ocean side of the highway. A deepwater cut strung with red-and-blue lobster buoys would help JoLayne locate the place.

She navigated with excessive precision, cleaving two of the bright Styrofoam balls on her way in. Krome was waiting by the water's edge, to catch the bow. After patiently untangling the trap ropes from the skeg, he climbed in the boat and said, "OK, Ahab, scoot over. They've got a ten-minute head start."

"Aren't you forgetting something?"

"JoLayne, come on."

She said, "The shotgun." Expecting another argument.

But Tom said, "Oh yeah." He jumped out and dashed across the road. In a minute he'd returned with her Remington, concealed in a plastic garbage bag. "I really *did* forget," he said.

JoLayne believed him. She had one arm around his shoulders as they headed across the water.

According to Chub's orders, Shiner wasn't supposed to talk to Amber except to give directions. He found this to be impossible. The longest and closest he'd ever been with such a beautiful girl was a thirty-second elevator ride with an oblivious stenographer at the Osceola County Courthouse. Shiner burned to hear everything Amber had to say – what stories she must have! Also, he felt crummy about poking her with the screwdriver. He longed to reassure her that he wasn't some bloodthirsty criminal.

"I'm in junior college," she volunteered, sending his heart airborne.

"Really?"

"Prelaw, but leaning toward cosmetology. Any advice?"

Now, what was he supposed to do? For all his crude faults, Shiner was essentially a polite young fellow. This was because his mother had flogged the rudeness out of him at an early age.

And it was rude, his mother always said, not to speak when one was spoken to.

So Shiner said to Amber: "Cosmetology – is that where they teach you to be a astronaut?"

She laughed so hard she nearly upended her bowl of minestrone. Shiner perceived that he'd said something monumentally stupid, but he wasn't embarrassed. Amber had a glorious laugh. He'd have gladly continued to say dumb things all night long, just to listen to that laughter.

They'd stopped at a twenty-four-hour sub shop on the mainland, Shiner being in no hurry to get down to Jewfish Creek. It was possible his white brethren were already waiting there, but he wasn't concerned. He wanted nothing to spoil these magical moments with Amber. In her skimpy Hooters uniform she was drawing avid stares from the dining public. Shiner despaired at the thought of turning her over to Chub.

She said, "What about you, Shiner? What do you do?"

"I'm in a militia," he replied without hesitation.

"Oh wow."

"Saving America from certain doom. They's NATO troops gonna attack any day from the Bahamas. It's what they call a international conspiracy."

Amber asked who was behind it. Shiner said communists and Jews for sure, and possibly blacks and homos.

"Where'd you come up with this?" she said.

"You'll find out."

"So how big is this militia?"

"I ain't allowed to say. But I'm a sergeant!"

"That's cool. You guys have a name?"

Shiner said, "Yes, ma'am. The White Clarion Aryans."

Amber repeated it out loud. "There's, like, a little rhyme."

"I think it's on purpose. Hey, remember what you said about fixin' my tattoo? What I need is somebody knows how to make the *W.R.B.* into a *W.C.A.*"

She said, "I'd like to help. Really I would, but first you've got to promise to let me go."

Not this again, Shiner thought. Nervously he rolled the screwdriver between his palms. "How 'bout if I pay ya instead?"

"Pay me what?" Amber said, skeptically.

Shiner saw her cast a glance at his dirty bare feet. Quickly he said: "The militia's got a shitload a money. Not right now, but any day."

Amber leisurely finished her soup before she got around to asking how much they had coming. Fourteen million, Shiner answered. Yes, dollars.

What a laugh *that* brought! This time he felt compelled to interject: "It's no lie. I know for a fact."

"Oh yeah?"

Decisively he lit a cigaret. Then, in a tough voice: "I helped 'em steal it m'self."

Amber was quiet for a while, watching a long white yacht glide under the drawbridge. Shiner worried that he'd said too much and now she didn't believe any of it. Desperately he blurted, "It's the God's truth!"

"OK," said Amber. "But where do I fit in?"

Shiner thought: I wish I knew. Then he got an idea. "You believe in the white man?"

"Honey, I'll believe in Kermit the Frog if he leaves twenty percent on the table." She reached over and took hold of Shiner's left arm, causing him to tremble with enchantment. "Let's have a look at that tattoo," she said.

Chub was in no mood to hear whining about the pickup truck.

"Leave it," he snapped at Bode Gazzer.

"Here? Right by the water?"

"Won't nobody fuck with it, you got the handicap deal on there."

"Yeah, like *they* care."

"They who?"

"The Black Tide."

"Look here," Chub said, "the boat thing was your idea, so don't go chickenshit on me now. Not after the motherfucker of a day I've had."

"But – "

"Leave the goddamn truck! Jesus Willy, we got twenty-eight million bucks. Buy a whole Dodge dealership, you want."

Sullenly Bode Gazzer joined Chub in loading the stolen boat. The last thing to come out of the pickup was the rolled-up chamois.

"The hell's in there?" Chub said. "Or shouldn't I ast. Sounds like a bag a Budweiser cans."

Bode said, "The AR-15. I took it apart to clean."

"God help us. Let's go."

Bode knew better than to ask for the wheel; he could see there'd been problems on the boat. Chub's clothing was soaked, and his ponytail was garnished with a strand of cinnamon-colored seaweed. The deck and vinyl bucket seats were littered with small broken pieces of what appeared to be bluish ceramic, as if Chub had smashed a plate.

As they idled away from the ramp, Bode turned for one last look at his red Ram truck, which he fully expected to be stripped or stolen outright by dusk. He noticed a man standing a short distance up the shore, at the fringe of some mangroves. It was a white man, so Bode Gazzer wasn't alarmed; probably just a fisherman.

As the boat labored to gain speed, Bode shouted: "How's she run?"

"Like a one-legged whore."

"What's all the mud and shit in here?"

"I can't hear you," Chub yelled back.

Given the slop on deck and the halting performance of the outboards, it was pointless for Chub to deny that he'd run the thing aground. He saw no reason, however, to tell Bodean Gazzer how close he'd come to losing half the lottery jackpot.

Bravely kicking back to the shallows.

Flailing and groping in the marl and grasses until he'd found it in eighteen inches of water: the Lotto ticket, waving in the current like a small miracle.

Naturally it was in the claws of a blue crab. The nasty fucker had staked a claim to the moldy Band-Aid on which the ticket was stuck. The delirious Chub hadn't hesitated to leap upon the feisty scavenger, which gouged him mercilessly with one claw while clinging with the other to its sodden prize. With the crab fastened intractably to his right hand, Chub had clambered over the transom and thrashed the little bastard to pieces against the gunwale. In this manner he had reclaimed the Lotto ticket, but victory came with a price. The only intact segment of the defunct crab was the cream-blue pincers that hung from the web of skin between his thumb and forefinger; a macabre broach.

Bodean Gazzer noticed it immediately, but decided not to say a word. Thinking: *I shoulda kept drivin' straight to Tall'hassee. I shoulda never turnt around.*

"I got a map," he shouted over the hack of the mud-choked Mercurys.

No audible response from Chub.

"I picked out a island, too."

Chub seemed to nod.

"Pearl Key!" Bode shouted. "We'll be safe there."

Chub launched a gooey hawker over the windshield. "First we gotta make a stop."

"I know, I know." Bode Gazzer let the engines drown his words. "Jewfish goddamn Creek."

# NINETEEN

**Demencio spent all** day painting the rest of JoLayne's cooters. Without a reliable biblical archive, it was difficult to find thirty-three separate portraits for duplication on turtle shells. In the interest of time Demencio chose a generic saintly countenance, varying the details only slightly from cooter to cooter.

While the reptiles were drying, Trish burst into the house and exclaimed: "Four hundred and twenty bucks!"

Demencio's eyebrows danced – it was a gangbuster of a visitation.

"They flat-out love this guy," said his wife.

"Sinclair? My theory, it's more the apostles."

"Honey, it's the whole package. Him, the weeping Mary, the cooters . . . There's a little something for everybody."

It was true; Demencio had never seen a group of pilgrims so enthralled.

Trish said, "Just think what we could clear, Christmas week. When did JoLayne say she'll be back?"

"Any day." Demencio began capping the paint bottles.

"I bet she'd loan us the cooters over the holidays!"

One thing about Trish, she had a ton of faith in human

nature. "Loan or *rent*?" said Demencio. "And even if she did, what about him?"

"Sinclair?"

"He ain't wrapped for the long haul. By tomorrow he's liable to be flashin' his weenie at old ladies."

Trish said, "You should go have a talk."

Demencio reminded her that he couldn't understand very much Sinclair said. "It's like his tongue come off the hinges."

"Well, Mister Dominick Amador doesn't seem to have any trouble communicating." Trish stood at the front window, parting the drapes to get a view of the shrine.

Demencio jumped up. "Sonofabitch!"

He hurried outside and chased Dominick from the property. In retreat the stigmata man hastily discarded his new crutches, slick with Crisco, which Demencio snatched up and beat to pieces against a concrete utility pole. Demencio meant the outburst to serve as a warning. He scanned the distant ficus hedge into which Dominick Amador had disappeared, and hoped the pesky con artist was watching.

To Sinclair he admonished: "That guy's bad news."

Sinclair sat Buddha-style among the apostolic turtles. The white sheet he wore was bunched and soiled, criss-crossed with diminutive muddy tracks.

Demencio said, "What'd that asshole want? Did he ask you to work with him?"

Sinclair's expression was quizzical and remote, an accurate reflection of his state of mind.

"Did he show you his hands?" Demencio demanded.

"Yes. His feet, too," Sinclair said.

"Ha! Now here's a bulletin: He did that to *himself*.

Bloody holes and all. That Dominick, he's one twisted sonofabitch."

Demencio felt he could speak freely, since the tourists were gone. "He bothers you again, let me know," he said.

"Oh, I'm fine," said Sinclair, which was the truth. Never had he felt such spiritual peace. Watching the clouds was as good as floating: cool and weightless, free from earthly burdens. Except for lemonade breaks, he'd scarcely moved a muscle all day. Meanwhile the turtles had explored him – up one arm, down one leg, back and forth across his chest. The march of miniature toenails tickled and soothed Sinclair. One of the cooters – was it Simon? – had made it up the steep slope of Sinclair's skull and settled on his vast unlined forehead, where it sunned itself contentedly for hours. The sensation had put Sinclair into a Zen-like trance; he lolled among the tiny creatures like a Gulliver, without the ropes. The crushing guilt of sending Tom Krome to his death evaporated like a gray mist. *The Register*'s frenetic newsroom and the job that Sinclair had once taken so seriously receded into the vaguest of recollections, appearing to him in cacophonous and incoherent flashes. Every so often, all the headlines he'd ever composed would scroll through his consciousness one after another, like a demonic Dow Jones ticker, causing Sinclair to yodel alliteratively. He understood these eruptions to mean he was forever finished with daily journalism, a revelation that contributed in no small way to his serenity.

Demencio dropped to a crouch, to secure better eye contact with the dreamy turtle boy. "Can I get you anything – soda? Half a sandwich?"

"Nuh-uh," Sinclair said.

"You wanna stay for supper? Trish is doing one of her angel foods for dessert."

"Sure," said Sinclair. He was too drowsy for the walk to Roddy and Joan's house.

"Sleep over, if you like. There's a daybed in the spare room," Demencio offered, "and plenty of clean sheets to wear, in case you wanna hang around tomorrow."

Sinclair had given no thought whatsoever to the future, but for the moment he couldn't imagine parting with the holy cooters.

Demencio said, "Plus I got a surprise for you."

"Ah."

"But you gotta promise not to faint or nothin', OK?"

Demencio ran into the house and came out lugging the aquarium, which he placed at Sinclair's feet. In breathless reverence Sinclair gazed at the freshly painted turtles; he reached out, tenuously fingering the air, like a child trying to touch a hologram.

Demencio said, "Here you go. Enjoy!"

When he tipped the tank on one side, thirty-three newly sanctified cooters swarmed forth to join the others in the moat. Sinclair joyfully scooped up several and held them aloft. He tossed back his chin and began to croon, "*Muugghhh meeechy makk-a-mamma*," a subconscious rendition of the classic MUGGER MEETS MATCH AGAINST MARTIAL-ARTS MOM.

Demencio edged away from the ranting turtle boy and returned to the house. Trish was in the kitchen with the cake mix. "Did you ask about the T-shirts? Will he give us permission?"

Her husband said, "The guy's so far gone, he'd let us yank out his kidneys if we wanted."

"So I should fix up the guest room?"

"Yeah. Where are the car keys?" Demencio patted his pockets. "I gotta make a lettuce run."

Also disengaging from the newspaper business was Tom Krome, though in the opposite manner of his editor and without the mystic balm of reptiles. While Sinclair escaped transcendentally from the headlines, Krome had become one of them. He'd hurled himself into a tricky cascade of events in which he was a central participant, not a mere chronicler.

He'd become a news story. Off the sidelines and into the big game!

Joining JoLayne Lucks meant Krome couldn't write about her mission; not if he still cared about the tenets of journalism, which he did. Honest reporters could always make a good-faith stab at objectivity, or at least professional detachment. That was now impossible regarding the robbery and beating of a black woman in Grange, Florida. Too much was happening in which Tom Krome had sway, and there was more to come. Absolved of his writerly duties, he felt liberated and galvanized. It was an especially good buzz for someone who'd been declared dead on the front page.

Yet Krome still caught himself reaching for the spiral notebook he no longer carried. Sometimes he could still feel its stiff, rectangular shape in his back pocket; a phantom limb.

Like now, for instance. Watching the bad guys.

Ordinarily Krome would've had the notebook opened on his lap. Hastily jotting in what Mary Andrea once described as his "serial killer's scrawl."

*3:35 pm Jewfish Crk.*
*Camo, Ponytail fueling boat.*
*Arguing – about what?*
*Buying beer, food, etc.*
*Joined by 2 people, unidentif. m and f. He bald and barefoot. She blond w/orange shorts.*
*Who?*

These observations compiled automatically in Tom Krome's brain as he sat with JoLayne in the scuffed old Boston Whaler she'd rented. Both of them were stiff and tired from a long night aboard the cramped skiff. They'd closed the gap on the rednecks, only to watch the stolen ski boat plow sensationally into a shallow grass bank. It was the first of several detours, as the robbers would spend hours pinballing from one nautical obstruction to another. Tom and JoLayne, astounded at their quarry's incompetence, followed at a prudent distance.

Now their skiff was tied to a PVC stake at the mouth of a shallow inlet. The makeshift mooring afforded a partially obstructed view of the busy docks at Jewfish Creek, where the rednecks finally had managed an uneventful landing.

Krome grumbling, for the second time: "I should've got some binoculars."

JoLayne Lucks saying she didn't need any. "It's the kid. I'm sure of it."

"What kid?"

"Shiner. From the Grab N'Go."

"Hey . . . you might be right." Krome, cupping both hands at his eyes to cut the glare.

JoLayne said, "The rotten little shit. That explains

why he lied about my Lotto ticket. They gave him a piece of the action."

All things considered, Krome thought, she's taking it well.

"Guess what else," she said. "The girl in the shorts and T-shirt? – it looks like the Hooters babe."

Krome broke into a grin. "The one they were hitting on the other night. Yes!" He could see them boarding the stolen boat: Bodean Gazzer first, followed by the skinhead Shiner, then the ponytailed man, tugging the blond woman behind him.

Pensively JoLayne said, "That's four of them and two of us."

"No, it's fantastic!" Krome kissed her on the forehead. "It's the very best thing that could happen."

"Are you nuts?"

"I'm talking about the babe. Her being there changes everything."

"The babe."

"*Yes*. Whatever grand plan these guys had, it's in tatters as of this moment!"

JoLayne had never seen him so excited. "In one small boat," he said, "we've got three smitten morons and one beautiful woman. Honey, there's an incredible shitstorm on the horizon."

She said, "I'm inclined to be insulted by what you just said. On behalf of all womanhood."

"Not at all." He untied the Whaler from the trees. "It's men I'm talking about. The way we are. Look at those googans and tell me they know how to cope with a girl like that."

JoLayne realized he was right: The stolen boat had become a time bomb. Any kind of a dispute would set the men off – over cigarets, the last cold beer . . . or a stolen lottery ticket.

Krome said, "We needed these boys to be distracted. I would say our prayers have been answered."

"Then God bless Hooters." JoLayne jerked her chin toward the docks. "Tom, they're heading back this way."

"So they are."

"Shouldn't we duck?"

"Naw," Krome said. "Just stay cool until they go past. Turn toward me, OK?"

"Hold on a second. Is this another kiss?"

"A long romantic one. To make sure they don't see our faces."

"Aye, aye, captain."

Judge Arthur Battenkill Jr. was an intelligent man. He knew Champ Powell's remains would eventually be identified. A medium-rare lump of tissue was already on its way to the FBI for DNA screening, or so the judge had heard.

A dead law clerk in the torched house of your wife's lover was not easy to explain, especially if the lover was to return and make an issue of the arson. Which that bastard Tom Krome likely would.

Arthur Battenkill knew his judicial career would soon end in scandal if he didn't take the bull by the horns. So, being as practical as he was smart, he began making plans to quit the bench and leave the country.

Starting over would be expensive. As a matter of convenience, the judge decided that the insurance carrier for Save King Supermarkets should pay for his new life in the Bahamas, or wherever he and Katie chose to relocate. This meant placing a call to Emil LaGort's lawyer.

Emil LaGort was a plaintiff in a civil lawsuit filed in Arthur Battenkill's court. In fact, Emil LaGort was a plaintiff in numerous lawsuits from Apalachicola to Key West – a habitual fraud, a renowned slip-and-fall artist. He was also seventy-four years old, which meant that one of these days he would *really* slip and fall.

Why not now? mused Arthur Battenkill. Why not in the aisle of a Save King Supermarket?

Emil LaGort was suing the store for $5 million, but he gladly would've settled out of court for fifty grand and costs. He did it all the time. Therefore his attorney was greatly surprised to receive a phone call, at home, from Judge Arthur Battenkill Jr.

As a rule, Emil LaGort shied from judges – if a deal couldn't be cut, he'd quietly drop the case. Going to trial was a time-consuming inconvenience that Emil LaGort simply could not afford, what with so many irons in the fire. He had a good thing going with the quickie settlements. Most insurance companies were pushovers when it came to frail senior citizens who claimed to have fallen on their policyholders' premises. Most insurance companies wished to spare jurors the sight of Emil LaGort, enfeebled in a neck brace and a wheelchair. So he got paid to go away.

The complaint scheduled to be heard in Arthur Battenkill's court was fairly typical. It alleged that, while shopping one morning at the Save King, Emil LaGort had slipped and fallen, causing irreparable harm to his neck, spine and extremities; furthermore, that the accident was due to the gross negligence of the store, whereas an extra-large tube of discount hemorrhoid ointment was left lying on the floor of the health-care-and-hygiene aisle, where it subsequently was run over by one or possibly more steel-framed shopping carts, thus distributing the slippery contents of the broken tube in a reckless and hazardous manner; and furthermore, that no timely efforts were made by Save King or its employees to remove said hazardous ointment, or to warn customers of the imminent danger, such negligence resulting directly in the grave and permanent injury to Emil LaGort.

Emil LaGort's attorney figured that Judge Arthur Battenkill Jr., like everyone else familiar with the case, knew that Emil had purposely knocked the tube of goop off the shelf, stomped it with both feet and then laid himself very gingerly on the floor of the health-care-and-hygiene aisle. The attorney certainly was not expecting the judge to call him at home on a Sunday morning and say:

"Lenny, it would be in your client's interest to hang tough."

"But, Your Honor, we were preparing to settle."

"That would be precipitous."

"A hundred even was the offer."

"You can do better, Lenny. Trust me."

The attorney tried to stay cool. "But I'm not ready for a trial!"

"Put on a little show," Arthur Battenkill said, needling. "That snotty bone guy you always use as an expert witness, the one with the ratty toupee. Or that lying dipshit of a so-called neurologist from Lauderdale. Surely you can manage."

"Yeah, I suppose." The attorney was beginning to get the picture.

The judge said, "Let me ask you something. Do you

think Mr. LaGort would be satisfied with, say, $250,000?"

"Your Honor, Mr. LaGort would be fucking jubilant." And I would, too, the attorney thought. Me and my thirty-five percent.

"All right, Lenny, then I'll tell you what. Let's see if we can save the taxpayers some dough. First thing tomorrow we'll all meet in chambers, after which I anticipate the defendants will be motivated to settle."

"For two fifty."

"No, for half a million. Are you following me?" said Arthur Battenkill.

There was an uncomfortable pause on the other end. The attorney said, "Maybe we should have this conversation in person."

"The phones are clean, Lenny."

"If you say so."

"Five hundred is a smart number," the judge continued, "because Save King's insurance company can live with it. A trial is too risky, especially if you get a couple old geezers on the jury. Then you're looking at seven figures, automatic."

The attorney said, "Amen."

"Next question: Can Mr. LaGort be persuaded that the court's costs are unusually high in this case?"

"For the kind of money he's getting, Your Honor, Mr. LaGort can be persuaded that cows shit gumdrops."

"Good," said Arthur Battenkill. "Then you know what to do with the other two fifty."

"Do I?"

"Escrow, Lenny. You do have an escrow account?"

"Of course."

"That's the first place it goes. Then it's wired overseas. I'll give you the account number when I get one."

"Oh."

"What's the matter now?"

The attorney said, "It's just . . . I've never done it this way before."

"Lenny, do I strike you as a brown-bag-in-the-alley sort of fellow? Do you see me as some kind of low-class bumpkin?"

"No, Your Honor."

"I hope not," Arthur Battenkill said. "By the way, next week there will be an announcement of my pending retirement, for unspecified health reasons. Tell Mr. LaGort not to be alarmed."

The attorney endeavored to sound genuinely concerned. "I'm sorry to hear that. I didn't know you'd been ill."

The judge laughed acidulously. "Lenny, you're not too swift, are you?"

"I guess not, Your Honor."

Not for a moment did it occur to Mary Andrea Finley Krome that the newspapers might be wrong and that her husband was still alive. She departed Missoula on an upswelling of sympathy from Loretta (or was it Lorie?) and her other new acquaintances among the *Menagerie* cast, and with the director's personal assurance that the role of Laura Wingfield would be waiting when she returned.

Which, of course, Mary Andrea had no intention of doing. She believed that being a famous widow would open new doors, careerwise.

The long flight to Florida gave Mary Andrea time to prepare for the bustle of attention that awaited. Knowing she'd be asked by interviewers, she tried to reconstruct the last time she'd seen Tom. Incredibly, she could not. Probably it was at the apartment in Brooklyn, probably in the kitchen over breakfast. That was usually when he'd tried to initiate the so-called serious discussions about their marriage. And probably she'd gotten up from the table and moseyed into the bathroom to pluck her eyebrows, her customary response to the subject of divorce.

All Mary Andrea could remember with certainty was that one morning, four years ago, he hadn't been there. Poof.

The previous night, she'd come home from rehearsals very late and fallen asleep on the sofa. She expected to be awakened, as she had so many days, by the sound of Tom munching on his cereal. He was partial to Grape-Nuts, which had the consistency of blasted granite.

What Mary Andrea recalled most distinctly from that morning was the silence in the apartment. And of course the brief note, which (because it had been Scotch-taped to the cereal box) had been impossible to take seriously:

*If you won't leave me, I'll find somebody who will.*

Only later did Mary Andrea discover that Tom had lifted the line from a Warren Zevon song, an irritating detail that merely fortified her resolve to stay married.

As for the last time she'd actually laid eyes on her husband, what he'd said to her, his mood, the clothes he'd been wearing – none of this could Mary Andrea remember.

She did recall what she'd been doing on the afternoon the lawyer phoned, that asshole Turnquist. She'd been reading *Daily Variety* and running through her vocal exercises; octaves and whatnot. She remembered Turnquist saying Tom wanted to give her one more chance to sit down and work out the details, before he filed the papers. She remembered manufacturing a giggle and telling the lawyer he'd been the victim of an elaborate practical joke her husband arranged every year, on their anniversary. And she remembered hanging up the telephone and breaking into tears and wolfing three Dove bars.

Compared to other newsworthy breakups it seemed mundane, and Mary Andrea saw no benefit in launching her public widowhood by boring the media. So, gazing from the window of the plane at the scooped-out cliffs of the Rocky Mountains, she invented a suitable parting scene that she could share with the press. It had happened, say, six months ago. Tom had surprised her in, say, Lansing, where she'd landed a small part in a road tour of *Sunset Boulevard*. He'd slipped in late and sat in the rear of the theater, and surprised her with pink roses backstage after the show. He'd said he missed her and was having second thoughts about the separation. They'd even made plans to get together for dinner, say, next month, when she was scheduled to come back east with the production of *Lambs*.

Sounds pretty good, Mary Andrea thought. And who's to say it didn't happen? Or wouldn't have happened, if Tom hadn't died.

As the flight attendant freshened her Diet Coke, Mary Andrea thought: Crying won't be a problem. When the cameras show up, I'll have gallons of tears. Heck, I could cry right now.

Because it *was* terribly sad, the senseless death of a young and moderately talented and basically goodhearted man.

So what if she didn't lie awake at nights, missing him. She'd really never known him well enough to miss him. That was sort of sad, too. Imagining the intimacy and caring that might have been; the kind of closeness only years of separation could bring.

Mary Andrea Finley Krome dug through her handbag until she located the rosary beads she'd found at a Catholic thrift shop in Missoula. She would clutch them in her left hand as she got off the plane in Orlando, and mention in a choked voice that they'd been a gift from Tom.

Which they might have been, someday, if the poor guy hadn't been murdered.

# TWENTY

**JoLayne Lucks sat** up so abruptly she made the boat rock.

"Lord, what an awful dream."

Krome put a finger to his lips. He'd killed the engine, and they were drifting in the dark toward the island.

"Get this," she said. "We're in the hot-air balloon, the yellow one from before, and all of a sudden you ask for half the lottery money."

"Only half?"

"This is after we get the stolen ticket back. Out of nowhere you're demanding a fifty-fifty split!"

Krome said: "Thank you, Agent Moffitt, wherever you are."

"What?"

"He put that idea in your head."

"No, Tom. As a matter of fact, he said you didn't strike him as a typical moneygrubbing scumbag."

"Stop. I'm blushing."

It was a windy night, wispy clouds skating overhead. A cold front was moving in from the north. The starlight came and went in patches. They'd approached the island on a wide arc. The tree-lined shore looked black and lifeless – the robbers were nowhere in sight, having disappeared up a creek on the lee side. Krome surmised it was too soon for the group to send a lookout; the men would be busy unloading their gear.

JoLayne said, "You're sure they didn't see us following them?"

"I'm not sure of anything."

She thought: That makes two of us.

Evidently Tom was sticking with her, shotgun and all. She couldn't help but wonder why, a riddle she'd been avoiding since the first day. Why was he doing this? What was in it for him? Krome had said nothing in particular to trigger these doubts in JoLayne; it was only the backwash from a lifetime of being let down by men she trusted.

As the skiff floated closer to the mangroves, she heard Tom say: "Hang on." Then they were tilting, and she saw he was over the side and wading for shore. He held the bow rope in one fist, pulling the Whaler quietly across the flat toward the tree line.

JoLayne sat forward. "You be careful," she whispered.

"Water's nice."

"Skeeters?"

Krome, keeping his voice low: "Not too bad."

It's the breeze, JoLayne thought. Mosquitoes like hot still nights. If this were August, they'd be devouring us.

"See any place to tie off?" she asked. "What about over there?"

"That's where I'm headed."

The opening wasn't much wider than the skiff itself. Krome advised JoLayne to lie flat and cover her face as he led them through a latticework of mangroves. The branches raked at her bare arms, and a gossamer fragment of a spider's web caught in her hair. She was more alarmed by the sound of the roots screaking along the hull, but Tom seemed unconcerned. He hauled the skiff to the bank and helped her step out.

In fifteen minutes they had the gear unpacked and sorted. By flashlight they wiped down the Remington and loaded two shells. It was the first time since sunset that JoLayne had been able to see Tom's face, and it made her feel better.

She said, "How about a fire?"

"Not just yet." He stood the gun against a tree and clicked off the light. "Let's just sit and listen."

The vibrant quiet was a comfort; nothing but the hum of insects and the whisk of wavelets against the shore. The peacefulness reminded JoLayne of the evening at Simmons Wood when she and Tom had stopped to watch the deer.

Except this time he was squeezing her hand. He was tense.

She told him: "This is a good place you found. We'll be safe here."

"I keep hearing noises."

"It's just the wind in the trees."

"I don't know."

"It's the wind, Tom." She could tell he hadn't spent much time in the outdoors. "Let's have a fire."

"They'll smell the smoke."

"Not if they've got one burning, too," she said, "and I'll bet you five bucks they do. I'll bet that cute little waitress is freezing her buns in those shorts."

Tom broke up some driftwood while JoLayne dug out a small pit in the sand. For tinder they used handfuls of the crispy, dried-out seaweed that ringed the shore. It didn't take long for a spark to catch. JoLayne stood close, enjoying the heat on her bare arms. Tom unsnapped the faded blue canvas from the skiff's Bimini top and spread it on the ground. JoLayne tactfully suggested he should move it to the upwind side of the fire, so the smoke wouldn't blow in their eyes.

"Good thinking," he said tightly.

They sat close to the flames – Tom with a Coke and a granola bar; JoLayne with a Canada Dry, a box of Goldfish crackers and the Remington.

She said, "All the comforts of home."

"Yeah."

"Except a radio. Wouldn't Whitney hit the spot right now?" JoLayne, trying to loosen him up, singing in a tinny voice: "Aaahheeeayyyyy will all-ways love you-aaaooooo . . ."

A small laugh; not much. "Something wrong?" she asked.

"I guess I'm just tired."

"Well, it's about time."

"We should do some scouting at dawn, while they're still asleep."

"They might be up early."

"I doubt it. They bought a shitload of beer," Tom said.

"Dawn it is. Then what?"

"We get as close as possible to their camp – close enough to see and hear what's going on. That way we'll know when things go sour."

JoLayne said, "I sure hope you're right about that. OK, then what happens?"

"We get them one by one."

"You serious?"

"Not with the shotgun, JoLayne. Not unless they leave us no choice."

"I see."

Tom opened a can of tuna fish and forked it onto a paper plate. JoLayne waved it off before he could offer.

"I was thinking about your dream," he said.

"Uh-oh."

"I don't blame you for being suspicious of me. Only a fool wouldn't be – "

"That's not the right word – "

"Look," he said, "if I were reporting this story instead of participating, that's the first thing I'd ask: 'How do you know that guy isn't after your Lotto money, too?' And all I can say is, I'm not. The idea never crossed my mind, that's the truth. Which raises the obvious question: What in the hell's wrong with me? Why risk my neck for a woman I've only known a week?"

"Because I'm extra-special?" JoLayne, through a mouthful of Goldfish crackers.

"Hey. I'm trying to be serious."

"Wild," she said. "You really can't explain why you're here. You, who are in the profession of putting words together. An intelligent, successful guy who doesn't hesitate to drop everything, to walk away from a whole other life."

"Unbelievable, I know. I *do* know." He stared beyond the flames. "It just seemed . . . necessary."

JoLayne took a slug of ginger ale. "All right, Mister Krome. Since neither of us can figure out your motives, let's look at the possibilities."

"The fire's dying."

"Sit your ass down," JoLayne said. "Let's start with sex."

"Sex."

"Yes. That thing we were doing last night in the motel.

Remember? We take off all our clothes and one of us climbs on top – "

"You're suggesting that I'd risk being massacred by vicious psychopaths just to charm you into the sack?"

"Some men'll do anything."

"No offense," Tom said, "but I'm not quite that starved for affection."

"Oh really? Before last night, when was the last time you made love to a woman."

"A week ago."

"Yipes," said JoLayne, with a blink.

"The wife of a judge." Krome got up to toss more driftwood on the embers. "Apparently she kept a scorecard. I could probably get a copy, if you want."

JoLayne recovered admirably. "So we've ruled out money and nooky. What about valor?"

Tom chuckled mirthlessly. "Oh, how I wish."

"White man's guilt?"

"That's possible."

"Or how about this: You're just trying to prove something to yourself."

"Now we're getting somewhere." He lay back, entwining his hands behind his head. In the firelight JoLayne could see he was exhausted.

He said, "Hey, we missed the lottery."

"Lord, that's right – it was last night, wasn't it? I believe we were distracted." In her handbag she found the Lotto coupons Moffitt had confiscated from Bodean Gazzer's apartment. She fanned them, like a royal flush, for Tom to see.

"You feeling lucky?"

"Very," he said.

"Me, too." She leaned forward and dropped the tickets, one by one, into the flames.

By the time they reached Pearl Key, Bodean Gazzer and Chub were hardly speaking. At issue was the newly purchased marine chart of Florida Bay, which neither of them was able to decipher. Chub blamed Bode, and Bode blamed the mapmakers from the National Oceanic and Atmospheric Administration, who (he insisted) had purposely mislabeled the backcountry channels to thwart the flight of survivalists such as the White Clarion Aryans. This time Chub wasn't buying it.

The inability of either man to make sense of the navigational markers resulted in a succession of high-speed groundings that seriously eroded the aluminum propellers. The ski boat was shaking like a blender long before the militiamen got to the island.

Chub seethed – he had so hoped to impress Amber with his nautical skills. Yet, during their third mishap after departing Jewfish Creek, he'd heard her say: "This is a joke, right?"

At the time he was waist-deep in water, fighting the tide, pushing against the transom with all his strength. Bode Gazzer sloshed next to him in the shallows, working on the starboard side. Amber was in the boat with Shiner.

*This is a joke, right*?

And Chub had heard Shiner say, "If only."

The snotty fuck.

Panting in the marl, Chub found his worries turning to the lottery tickets. Both were hidden in the steering console – the stolen one still damp from the previous near disaster; the one in Bode's wallet relocated when Chub made him go overboard to push.

The console had cheap plastic doors that didn't lock. Chub resolved to shoot Shiner in the kneecaps if he went anywhere near it.

Night had fallen before they beached at Pearl Key. Bode Gazzer used liquid charcoal lighter to get a fire going. Chub stripped down and hung his sopping clothes in the mangroves. Shiner was ordered to unload the boat. He couldn't believe Chub was sauntering around camp in his underwear, right in front of Amber.

"Want some bug spray?" Chub asked her.

"I'm cold," she said.

In an instant Shiner was there with an army blanket. Chub snatched it and wrapped Amber's shoulders. He handed her an aerosol can of insect repellent and said: "Squirt a lil on my legs, wouldya?"

She did as she was told, her expression concealed by Chub's lanky shadow. Bode Gazzer glanced up from the campfire – it was foolishness; such a girl had no place in a paramilitary unit. Shiner was equally dismayed, but for different reasons.

He piped, "They's some dry camos in the duffel."

Chub ignored him. He seemed entirely relaxed in mud-splattered Jockey shorts.

"So, Amber," he said, "where'd y'all sleep last night?"

"The car."

Chub cut a hard look at Shiner, who said: "By the side of the road."

"Is that right?"

"Whatsa big damn deal?" Shiner didn't appreciate how Chub was putting him on the spot: giving him the eye, acting like Shiner was holding something back.

Amber came to his defense. "It's a Crown Victoria. You can fit a football team in there," she said. "I slept in the back seat, Shiner slept in front. Anything else you want to know?"

Chub got red and flustered. The last thing he'd wanted to do was piss her off – hell, some girls were flattered when you got jealous. He offered Amber a Budweiser.

"No, thanks."

"Some jerky?"

"I think I'll pass."

Bodean Gazzer said, "We got to have a meeting. Sugar, can you leave us men alone for 'bout thirty minutes."

Amber looked out toward the gray woods, then turned back to Bode. "Where exactly am I supposed to go?"

Shiner cut in, saying it was all right for her to stay. "She knows who we are, and she's a hundred percent with the program."

Now it was the colonel's turn to shoot him the evil eye. Shiner didn't cave. "She's even gonna fix my tattoo!"

"Too bad she can't fix your fuckin' brain." Chub, picking at his eye patch as if it were a scab.

Bodean Gazzer sensed that his hold on the newborn militia was slipping. Amber would have to shut up and behave, that's all. Her presence was disrupting the group; the scent of her in particular. While Bode was grateful for any fragrance potent enough to neutralize the stink of Chub's perspiration, he felt throttled by Amber's perfume. It fogged his brain with impure thoughts, some of them jarringly explicit. Bode was angry at himself for entertaining base fantasies when he should be concentrating totally on survival.

He spread an oilskin tarpaulin and called the meeting

to order. Amber sat cross-legged in the center of the tarp, with Shiner and Chub on each side.

"As you know," Bode began, "we're here on this island because something – somebody – calls themselves the Black Tide is out to destroy us. I got no doubt it's a Negro operation, a pretty slick one, and I expect they'll find us eventually. We come all the way out here to regroup, get our weapons in tiptop shape and make a stand.

"Now, I believe with all my Christian heart we're gonna prevail. But to whip these black bastards we gotta be prepared, and we gotta be a team: armed, disciplined and well-regulated. Pretty soon 'Merica's gonna come under attack – I don't need to tell you about that. The New World Tribunal, the communists, NATO and so forth. But this here's our first big test, this Black Tide . . . now what?"

The Hooters girl had raised her hand.

"You got a question?" Bode Gazzer said, perturbed.

"Yeah. Where do you guys see this going?"

"Pardon?"

"The plan," Amber said. "What's the long-range plan?"

"We are the White Clarion Aryans. We believe in the purity and supremacy of the Euro-Caucasian people. We believe our Christian values been betrayed and forsaken by the United States government . . ."

As he spoke, Bodean Gazzer glowered at Chub. How were they going to win a race war with a damn waitress hanging around?

Chub wasn't annoyed by Amber's interruption; he was too busy trying to cop a peek up her shorts. Shiner, by contrast, was painfully attentive. Taking Amber's lead, he raised his right arm and waved at Bode.

"What!"

"Colonel, you said Euro something . . ."

"Euro-Caucasian."

"Could you 'xplain what that is?" Shiner asked.

"White people," Bode Gazzer snapped. "White people whose folks come from, like, England or Germany. Places such as that."

"Ireland?" asked Amber.

"Yeah, sure. Denmark, Canada . . . you get the goddamn idea." He couldn't believe these nimrods – the concept of ethnic purity wasn't that complicated.

Then Shiner said: "They got white people in Mexico."

"Bullshit."

"Guy used to work days at the Grab N'Go. Billy was his name. He looked awful white, Colonel."

Bode was steaming. He walked over to Shiner and kicked him in the side of the head. Shiner cried out and toppled across Amber's lap. Chub looked on, abject with envy.

Leaning over, Bode took Shiner by the chin. "Listen, you pimple-faced little shitweasel. Ain't no such thing on God's earth as a white Meskin named Billy or Hay-zoos or any other damn thing. They's no white Cubans or Spaniards, neither."

"But Spain *is* in Europe." Amber, calm as you please, stroking Shiner's bestubbled scalp.

Chub, who was tired of being left out, declared: "She got a point there." Then, turning with a smirk toward the girl: "And here's a man won't even say the word 'nigger.' "

Bodean Gazzer took a deep breath and walked a slow

circle around the campfire. He had to cool off; he had to be the calm, clear-thinking one.

"When I talk about Euro-Caucasians," he said, "I'm referrin' to *white* white people, all right? That's the easiest way to explain it. I'm talkin' about Aryan ancestry, which is something all four of us share."

Impatiently Chub said, "Get on with it." To his immense relief, Shiner sat up, uncluttering Amber's thighs. The glow of the flames gave a delicious sheen to her nylon stockings; it was all Chub could do to restrain himself from stroking them. It was, in fact, only a matter of moments before he tried.

When he did, Amber whacked him in the face. "Look what you did!" she exclaimed.

The aborted grope had snagged Chub's hand in her hose. It was the crab claw, he was disheartened to see.

"What's the matter with you!" Amber said, and took another swipe. She wanted the kidnappers to know she was a fighter and that every touch would cost them dearly. It was a cardinal rule of waitressing: Defend your dignity.

Chub knocked over his beer as he fumbled to disentangle himself. "*I'll* do it," Amber snapped.

In disgust Bode Gazzer spit a chunk of jerky into the campfire. Shiner was stunned by the scene. Amber's fear of a rape no longer seemed far-fetched; the same could not be said of Shiner's gallant vow to protect her. Chub was so much stronger and meaner; short of killing him in his sleep, Shiner's options were limited.

The crab pincers left a ragged hole in Amber's nylons.

"Damn," she muttered. Then to Chub: "Hope you're happy, Romeo." It was the sort of asshole stunt that boyfriend Tony might pull, pawing at her crotch in public.

Chub told her to chill. He dug in the cooler for another beer. Then he opened the chamois and tackled (with a scathing cackle) the reassembly of the AR-15. Bode pretended not to pay attention.

Amber picked up a flashlight and went into the woods to change clothes. She came out wearing one of Bode Gazzer's camouflage jumpsuits; Mossy Oak.

Instantly a gloom settled over Chub. He pined for the cutoff T-shirt and the silky shorts. He tried to imagine Kim Basinger as a bear hunter and could not. Bodean Gazzer, however, found himself helplessly intoxicated by the flickering vision in mottled camos. *His* camos. The dainty white Keds added a devastating element.

"Meeting's over," he said, and sat down heavily.

Amber, who was soundly apprehensive, resolved not to let it show. She walked forthrightly up to Chub and said: "We need to talk."

"Gimme a minute with this rifle."

"No. Right now."

She took his hand – the claw-hobbled hand! – and led him into the shadows of the mangroves. Shiner was dumbfounded. Was the girl crazy?

Bode Gazzer didn't like it, either. He caught himself grinding his molars; the only thing that could make him do that was a woman. Don't get stupid, he warned himself. It's no time to grow horns. Yet he couldn't stop thinking about her; about what the Mossy Oak jumpsuit would smell like after she removed it. Or after Chub tore it off, in which case Bode might have to blow the man's brains out. Purely for the sake of maintaining discipline.

Twenty yards into the woods, Amber turned and put

the flashlight on Chub's face. She said, "I know what you want."

"It don't take a genius."

"Well, this can go two ways," she told him. "You can be a pig and rape me, and I'll hate your guts forever. Or we can get to know each other and see what happens."

With his good eye Chub squinted against the spear of light, trying to read Amber's expression. He said, "I thought you already liked me jest fine. Seemed that way at the resty-rant."

"Let me explain something: Just because I smile at a customer doesn't mean I want to fuck him."

The word rocked Chub on his heels.

"And if you rape me," Amber said, "it will be the worst time you ever had with a woman. The *worst*."

"Wh-why?"

"Because I'm not moving a muscle, I'm not making a sound. I'm going to lie there like a cold sack of mud, bored out of my mind. I might even *time* you." She held up her wrist, so he could get a glimpse of her watch.

Chub said, "Jesus Willy." Feeling himself wither, he now wished he'd put on some pants.

"Or we can try to be friends," Amber said. "Think you can handle that?"

"Sure." His ears were buzzing. He slapped at them.

"Bugs," Amber said. She shooed them away.

"Thanks."

"We got a deal?" She held out her hand. Chub took it. Briefly he considered throwing her down and sticking it to her right there, but he decided against it. Fucking a cold sack of mud didn't sound like much fun, even if the sack looked like a movie star. He thought: Hell, at least hookers *acted* like they were having a good time.

"What kinda guys you go for?" he asked. "Your boyfriend don't seem all too polite, neither."

Amber said, "Sometimes he's not."

"Then how come you stay with him? He rich?"

"He does all right." A big fat lie.

"I bet I'm richer," Chub said.

"Oh, sure."

"How does fourteen million damn dollars sound?"

The flashlight clicked off. In the shadows he heard Amber say, "You're kidding." The smell of perfume was stronger than before, as if she'd moved closer.

"No, I ain't kidding. Fourteen million."

Amber said, "I want to hear all about it."

There was a break in the rolling clouds, and for a few moments Chub could see her eyes by the light of the stars. He felt himself twitching back to life; inadvertently his claw hand went to his groin.

She said, "Maybe tomorrow we can go for a walk. Just the two of us."

"Fine by me." The excitement made him light-headed.

The next time Amber spoke, it was a whisper: "Oh, I've got something for you." She took his unwounded hand – the one clenched at his side – opened it gently and pressed something soft into the palm.

Even in the blackness Chub knew what it was.

Her orange Hooters shorts.

"A little token of our friendship," she said.

# TWENTY-ONE

**Cold rain fell** after midnight, slapping at the leaves. Bodean Gazzer was curled up beside the hissing embers, where he'd passed out from exhaustion. Chub was splayed in the cockpit of the *Reel Luv.* To his chest he clutched Amber's waitress shorts, a beer bottle and a tube of polyurethane marine adhesive he'd come across while rifling a hatch. He had gnawed off the plastic nipple and placed the glue inside a paper grocery bag, leaving space for his head. Amber doubted if the storm would rouse him; his snoring sounded like a locomotive.

Shiner was pulling guard duty, sopping and forlorn. Amber shook out the oilskin tarpaulin and draped it across the mangroves, for a lean-to. She tugged Shiner out of the rain and said: "You're going to catch your death."

"No, I can't sit down."

"Don't be ridiculous."

"But the colonel put me on perimeter."

"The colonel's out like a light. Relax," Amber said. "What kind of gun is that? It's ugly."

"TEC-9," said Shiner.

"I'd be scared to even hold it."

"Piece a crap."

"Sure beats the screwdriver."

Shiner said, "I like the AR-15 better." The wind snapped the corners of the tarp. "God, this weather sucks. You hear that?"

"It's just the waves."

"I hope." Through the trees he could make out the shape of the boat at the waterline. Chub had anchored it in a skinny channel that ran along the shore of the island.

"It's, like, zero visibility," Shiner remarked.

Amber blinked the flashlight in his face. "Just in case," she said.

"Don't tell me you gonna make a run for it."

She laughed emptily. "Where?"

"I'd have to stop you. That's my orders."

Amber said, "I'm not going anywhere. Tell me about the money."

Shiner fell silent for a short while. Then he thought he heard a helicopter. "The NATO troops got Blackhawks. They's lined up on the beach at Andros Island, is what Colonel Bode says."

Water streamed off the tarp in sheets. Amber said, "There are no helicopters coming tonight, all right? Not in this shitty storm. Maybe submarines, but no helicopters."

"You think this is funny?"

"Oh yeah. Getting kidnapped, that really cracks me up."

Shiner asked, "What'd Chub want? Before, when you guys went in the woods."

"What do you think?"

"He dint try nothin', did he?"

"Yeah, he tried something. He tried to tell me he was a millionaire."

"The brotherhood, he means."

"No. Him personally," said Amber.

"I don't think so." Shiner looked troubled.

"Fourteen million dollars is what he said. That's the same money you helped to steal, right?" Amber poked his arm. "Well?"

Again Shiner turned away, toward the boat. "Did he take your pants? He said he took your pants."

She could scarcely hear him above the wind and the shake of the trees.

Shiner said, "He showed 'em to us. Them orange ones."

"He didn't *take* anything. I gave him the damn shorts." Amber put the light on his face. "Don't worry, it's all right."

"You say so."

"I'm a big girl."

"Yeah, but he's crazy," Shiner said.

A string of cold drops landed on Amber's forehead. Glancing up, she noticed a shiny bulge in the skin of the tarpaulin, where the water had puddled on the other side.

She told Shiner: "Watch out, it's dripping on your Tex." Turning the flashlight on the gun.

"It's T-e-c, not T-e-x." He dried the stubby barrel on one of his sleeves.

"You still worried about helicopters?"

"Naw," Shiner said.

"The money?"

"Right." He sniffed sarcastically.

"Where'd you guys get so much?" Amber asked. "Rob Fort Knox or something?"

"Try a lottery ticket."

"You're kidding."

"It was easy."

"Well, tell me about it," Amber said.

And Shiner did.

Tom Krome couldn't get to sleep in the slashing storm. The shadows swayed in the wind, and it got chilly without a fire. He and JoLayne bundled beneath the boat canvas, raindrops popping on the stiff fabric.

"I'm freezing," she said.

"This is nothing."

JoLayne briskly rubbed her hands on the knees of her jeans.

Tom said, "Incredible. It was sunny all day."

"Florida," she said.

"You like it down here?"

"I like what's left."

"Ever been to Alaska?"

"Nope," she said. "They got black folks up there?"

"I'm not sure. Let me get back to you on that."

They took out the marine chart and tried to figure out where they were. Tom guessed it was one of three keys in the middle of Florida Bay – Calusa, Spy or Pearl. They wouldn't know for sure until they got enough daylight to see the horizon.

"Not that it really matters. They're all uninhabited," Tom said.

JoLayne nudged him. A tall, long-necked bird was perched regally on the stern of the Whaler. It cocked its head and studied them with blazing yellow eyes. Rain dripped off the tip of its lancelike beak.

"Great blue," JoLayne whispered.

The bird was really something. Tom said, "Hey, big guy. What's up?"

The heron took off, croaking and bellowing across the treetops.

JoLayne said, "He's pissed. We must be in his spot."

"That, or something spooked him."

They listened for movement in the mangrove. The shotgun was positioned under the canvas at JoLayne's feet.

She said, "I don't hear a thing."

"Me, neither."

"They're not exactly Green Berets, these guys. They won't be sneaking around in this weather."

"You're right," said Tom.

To pass the time until the skies cleared, they compared futures. He told her his plan to move to Alaska and write a novel about a man whose wife wouldn't divorce him, no matter what he did. JoLayne said she liked the premise.

"It could be very funny."

"Funny wasn't the direction I was going," Tom said.

"Oh."

"I had a darker tone in mind."

"I see. More Cheever than Roth."

"Neither," he said, "I was thinking along the lines of Stephen King."

"A horror story?"

"Sure. *The Estrangement*. What do you think?"

JoLayne said, "Scary."

She told him her idea to make a nature preserve of Simmons Wood. She intended to speak to a lawyer about inserting a conservation easement in her deed, so the property could never be developed.

"Even after I'm dead," she said. "That'll fix the greedy bastards."

"Will you stay in Grange?"

"Depends."

"On what?"

"On whether there's any other black folks in Alaska," she said. "Doesn't have to be many – one would be fine, as long as it's Luther Vandross."

"Might as well aim high," Tom said.

"Hey, I'm inviting myself, in case you hadn't noticed."

He wondered if she was serious. It sounded like it.

"Try to control yourself, Tom."

"I was just thinking it's too good to be true." He slipped an arm around her.

"You mean it?"

"I was about to ask you the same thing."

"Let's say I do. Say we both mean it," JoLayne said. "What happens if we don't find the lottery ticket? If we're broke and bummed out."

"We'll go anyway. Don't you want to see a grizzly before they're all gone?"

JoLayne loved the thought of a northern wilderness, but she wondered about the redneck quotient. Alaska was almost as famous for its shitkickers as for its wildlife.

Tom said, "And the place is loaded with eagles, according to what I've read."

"That would be something."

She fell asleep with her head against his shoulder. He remained awake, listening for intruders. With his free arm he moved the Remington closer. A cool gust made him shiver. Sixty-three degrees, he thought, and already my bones are cold. Perhaps the Kodiak scenario needed more thought. Also, he'd gotten the impression JoLayne wasn't bowled over by his idea for the divorce novel. He had a feeling she was humoring him.

He was tinkering with the plot when he was startled by flapping behind him – the stately heron, returning. This time it stood on the bow of the boat. Tom Krome saluted. The bird paid no attention; a small silvery fish wriggled in its beak.

Nice work, Krome thought, especially in a deluge.

Then the heron did something unexpected. It let go of the fish, which bounced off the slick deck and landed on the grass-covered beach. The bird made no move to retrieve its meal. Instead it froze like an iron weather vane, its head erect and its snakelike neck extended.

Uh-oh, Krome said to himself. What does it hear?

He didn't have to wait long. Between the stutter of the gunshots and the woman's scream, the great blue flared its wings and took off. This time it flew away from the island, into the teeth of the squall, and this time it made no sound.

Amber had never witnessed gunfire.

She'd heard it before, of course; everyone who lived in Dade County knew the sound of a semiautomatic. Yet she'd never actually seen a flame-blue muzzle flash until Shiner cut loose with the TEC-9. Her shriek was involuntary but hair-raising, cutting like a sickle through the respective stupors of Bodean Gazzer and Chub. Spewing curses, they lumbered bleary-eyed into the clearing – first Bodean Gazzer, brandishing the .380 stolen off the Colombian motorist; then Chub, in his droopy underwear, stoned and waving the Colt.

Shiner met them at the edge of the clearing. "I seen somebody! I did!" He radiated uncertainty and shame.

Bode snatched the TEC-9 and turned to Amber. "Tell the damn truth," he said.

"There *was* something out there. I heard it."

"A man? A critter?"

"I couldn't say – it's too dark."

Chub said, "Un-fucking-believable." He coughed up something that landed near Shiner's feet.

The kid knew he was in trouble. After the earlier fiasco at the trailer, the colonel had given him a stern lecture about wasting ammo. "It was a human bean," Shiner insisted in a mumble. "A nigger is what it looked like, a small un."

Impatiently Bode Gazzer motioned for the flashlight. Amber handed it to him. He ordered everyone to stay put and stalked into the trees. Ten minutes later he returned to report finding no signs of a human prowler, Negro or otherwise.

"Figgers." It was Chub growling. With a difficulty born of distaste and insobriety, he was attempting to insert his legs and arms into a set of Bode's camos. His own clothes were soaked by the rain, and he was freezing his ass off in the Jockey shorts.

Amber saw Shiner's stock sliding and tried to help. "It was making all kinds of noise. Right over there." Pointing where Shiner had fired.

"Yeah, I bet it did," said Bode Gazzer. From the pocket of his parka he produced a bloodied tuft of brown fur. "Got this off a leaf."

Amber declined an offer to inspect the evidence. Shiner shrunk away in embarrassment.

"You shot a mean ole bunny rabbit." Chub, with a sneer. "Or maybe a killer mouse."

Amber rose. Chub asked where she was going.

"To get some sleep. You mind?" She walked to the lean-to and lay down beneath the tarp.

Chub said, "We got us a Girl Scout. She made her own tent."

Bode told Shiner to go back out in the boat. "I need to talk to Major Chub alone."

"Don't call me that," Chub grumped. The camos looked absurd; the cuffs were six inches short, and the seat was about to rip out of the trousers. Yet he couldn't work up much indignation, he was still so high from the marine glue. He announced he was beat and headed for the lean-to to join his dream girl.

Bode intercepted him. "Not right now." Then, under his breath: "You got the tickets, right?"

"Yeah. Somewheres." Chub gingerly probed at his nose, which felt scalded on the inside. "I think they's still in the boat."

"You *think*." Bode wheeled and called to Shiner: "Hey, sergeant, change of plans!" Motioning toward the tarp. "You go ahead and sleep there. Chub and me'll take the perimeter."

Wordlessly Shiner did what he was told. He stretched out next to Amber, whose lovely eyes were closed. The wind had dropped off noticeably, and the rain had waned to an irregular drizzle that made whispers on the oilskin. Shiner was half dozing when he heard Amber's voice:

"It's going to be OK."

"I don't think so."

"Don't underestimate yourself," she told him.

Nothing could have puzzled Shiner more.

They waited until the kid and the waitress were asleep before checking the *Reel Luv.* The lottery tickets were safe in the console. Bodean Gazzer returned the precious condom to his wallet. Chub rolled up the other ticket, the stolen one, and slipped it into an empty bullet chamber in the .357. He laughed dopily at his own cleverness.

"Bang bang," he said.

Bode was buoyed by the sight of Chub in camouflage, even if it wasn't a tailored fit. At least they were finally dressed like an honest-to-God militia; Bode, Chub, Amber and Shiner.

Shiner, God Almighty . . .

They'd lucked out again. Thanks to the heavy weather, nobody seemed to have heard the kid's reckless shooting or the girl's scream. No planes or boats had come out to the island to investigate. The group's secret position seemed safe, for now.

Bode said to Chub: "The dumb fuckup, he's gonna get us killed."

"No shit."

"I say we cut him loose."

"You got my vote."

They agreed Shiner had outlived his usefulness to the White Clarion Aryans. While he'd faithfully backed up their story for the Lotto scam and delivered Amber to Jewfish Creek as ordered, he had become a security risk. It was only a matter of time before he'd blow away one of them by mistake.

"Maybe even the girl," Chub said, though in truth he

was more worried about Shiner putting the moves on Amber than shooting her. Not that she'd ever sleep with a zit-faced skinhead, but she did seem awful protective of the kid. Chub didn't go for that one bit.

He said, "We kick him out, he's like to rat on us. How 'bout we kill him?"

Bode flatly said no. "I'll never shoot no Christian white man, I can help it."

"Then let's pay the fucker off."

"How much?"

"I dunno. A grand?" Glue fumes always made Chub generous.

Bode Gazzer said, "You gotta be jokin'."

A thousand dollars wouldn't put a ding in the $28 million, but it was still too much money for a half-wit. Especially since Bode still suspected Shiner as a possible leak in the organization. What if the kid was working undercover for the Black Tide? What if the nutball shooting sprees were an act and he was actually using the guns to signal the Negroes? Bode had no proof, but the doubts nagged at him like an itch.

He said, "How about this: a thousand bucks, less what it costs for a new quarter panel on my pickup. On account a the bullet holes he made."

"Fair by me. Tell him he gets his money soon as we get ours," Chub said, "long as he keeps his trap shut."

The decision was made to inform Shiner of his expulsion first thing in the morning. Chub would transport him by boat to the Overseas Highway, where he could hitch a ride up to Homestead and retrieve his car.

"Meanwhiles I can pick up s'more beer," Chub said. "Cigarets, too. And ice."

"And A.1 sauce for my scrambly eggs."

Bode Gazzer said, "I better make a list."

"You do that now."

Chub took out the grocery bag containing the tube of marine adhesive. He squeezed out a moist curlicue and offered a hit to Bode, who declined. Chub buried his face in the bag and luxuriantly sucked in the vapors.

Bode said, "Easy."

Chub whooped. He had a rubber patch stuck on one eye and a rotting crab claw poking through one hand, and still he felt fucking wonderful. He wasn't the least tiny bit worried about the Black Tide or NATO or the Tri-fucking-Lateral Commission, no siree. Nobody was gonna find 'em out here on this faraway island, not even the trickiest niggers. It was OK to get wasted tonight because him and Bode was white and free and well-armed, and best of all they was goddamn m-millionaires.

"You imagine?" Chub wheezed with glee.

Bode refrained from reminding him that the lottery proceeds were to be used strictly for militia building. There would be a better time for that conversation.

"Little Amber," Chub was saying. "You shoulda seed her face when I tole her about the money. All of a sudden she wants to go for a walk in the woods tomorrow, just her and me."

"Aw, shit," Bode said. He should've seen it coming. "What all did you tell her?"

"Only that I's worth fourteen million dollars. You might say it changed her opinion a me."

So would a bath, Bode thought.

"That look she give me," Chub went on dreamily, "like she could suck a golf ball through a garden hose."

"Careful what you say to her. Understand?"

With a hiccup Chub thrust the paper bag to his face.

"Knock that shit off!" Bode said. "Now listen: Pussy's fine, but there's a time and a place. Right now we're in a battle for the heart and soul of America!"

Chub made a noise like a tire going flat. "Hilton Head," he rasped euphorically.

"What?"

"I wanna buy Amber and me a condo up at Hilton Head. That's a island, too, and it beats the hell outta *this* one."

"You serious?"

But later, after Chub had nodded off, Bode Gazzer caught himself warming to his partner's fantasy. Strolling a sunny Carolina beach with a half-naked Hooters girl on your arm sounded much more appealing than sharing a frigid concrete pillbox with a bunch of hairy white guys in Idaho.

Bode couldn't help wondering what Amber's attitude toward him might be if she knew that he, too, was about to become a tycoon.

When JoLayne Lucks woke up, Tom Krome was sighting the shotgun across his kneecaps. That's when she realized the screaming wasn't part of a dream.

"What do you see?" she asked in a low voice. "Honey, don't forget the safety."

"It's off." He squinted down the barrel, waiting. "Did you hear the shots?"

"How many?"

"Five or six. Like a machine gun."

JoLayne wondered if the rednecks shot the waitress. Or possibly they shot each other while fighting *over* the waitress.

As long as the waitress didn't shoot *them*. Not until I get my Lotto ticket back, JoLayne thought.

Tom said, "Listen!"

His shoulders tightened; he moved his finger on the trigger.

JoLayne heard it, too – in the woods, something running.

"Wait, it's small." She touched Tom's elbow. "Don't fire."

The rustling got closer, changed direction. Krome followed the noise with the barrel of the Remington. The movement came to a halt behind an ancient buttonwood trunk.

JoLayne grabbed the flashlight and crawled out of the makeshift blanket. She said, "Don't you go shooting me by accident. I blend in pretty good with the night."

There was no stopping her. Tom lowered the gun and watched her sneak up to the tree. She was met by an unearthly, high-pitched chittering that descended to a low snarl. Tom got goose bumps.

He heard JoLayne saying: "Now hush and behave." As if talking to a child.

She came back holding a runty-looking raccoon. There was a smear of blood on the breast of her sweatshirt; one of the animal's front paws had been grazed by a bullet.

"Assholes," said JoLayne. With the flashlight she showed Tom what had happened. When she touched the coon, it growled and bared its teeth. Krome believed the animal was well-equipped to rip open his throat.

He said, "JoLayne – "

"Could you get me the first-aid kit?"

She'd bought a ten-dollar cheapo at the grocery store before renting the boat.

"You're going to get bit," Tom said. "We're *both* going to get bit."

"She's just frightened, that's all. She'll settle down."

"She?"

"Could you find the bandages, please?"

They worked on the raccoon's leg until nearly daybreak. They both got bit.

JoLayne beamed when the animal scurried away, feisty and muttering. As Tom dressed a punctured thumb, he said, "What if she gave us rabies?"

"Then we find ourselves somebody to chew on," JoLayne replied. "I know just the guys."

They tried to light another fire but the rain swept in, harder than before, though not as chilly. Huddling beneath the boat canvas, they worked to keep the food and the shotgun shells dry. Soon after the downfall stopped, the damp blue-gray darkness faded to light. JoLayne lay down and did two hundred crunches, Tom holding her ankles. The eastern rim of sky went pink and gold, ahead of the sun. They snacked on corn chips and granola bars – everything tasted salty. In the dawn they moved the Whaler out of the mangroves to a spit of open shore, for an easier get-away. From camp they gathered what they needed and began making their way to the other end of the island.

# TWENTY-TWO

**When Mary Andrea** Finley Krome stepped off the plane, she thought she was at the wrong airport. There were no news photographers, no TV lights, no reporters. She was greeted only by a brisk, sharp-featured man with prematurely graying hair. He introduced himself as the managing editor of *The Register.*

Mary Andrea said, "Where's everybody else?"

"Who?"

"The reporters. I was expecting a throng."

The managing editor said, "Consider me a throng of one."

He picked up Mary Andrea's bag. She followed him outside to the car.

"We're going to the newspaper office?"

"That's right."

"Will the media be there?" Mary Andrea, peevishly twirling her rosary beads.

"Mrs. Krome, we *are* the media."

"You know what I mean. Television."

The managing editor informed Mary Andrea that the interest in her husband's tragic death was somewhat less avid than anticipated.

She said, "I don't understand. A journalist gets burned to smithereens – "

"Tell me about it."

The managing editor drove at excessive speed with one hand on the wheel. With the other he poked irritably at the radio buttons, switching between classical music stations. Mary Andrea wished he'd settle on something.

"I know it's made the papers," she persisted, "all the way out to Montana."

"Oh yes. Even television," said the managing editor, "briefly."

"What happened?"

"I would describe the public reaction," he said, "as a mild but fleeting curiosity."

Mary Andrea was floored. A despondency settled upon her; it might have been mistaken for authentic grief, although not by those aware of Mary Andrea's background as an actress.

The managing editor said: "Don't take it personally. It's been a humbling experience for all of us."

"But they should make Tom a hero," she protested.

The managing editor explained that the job of newspaper reporter no longer carried the stature it had in the days of Watergate. The nineties had brought a boom in celebrity journalism, a decline in serious investigative reporting and a deliberate "softening of the product" by publishers. The result, he said, was that daily papers seldom caused a ripple in their communities, and people paid less and less attention to them.

"So your husband's death," said the managing editor, "didn't exactly generate an uproar."

Gloomily Mary Andrea stared out the car window. If only Tom had made it to *The New York Times* or *The Washington Post*, then you'd have seen a damn uproar.

"Was he working on something big?" she asked hopefully.

"Not at all. That's part of the problem – it was just a routine feature story."

"About what?"

"Some woman who won the lottery."

"And for that he got blown up?"

"The police are skeptical. And as I said, that's part of our problem. It's far from certain Tom was killed in the line of duty. It could have been a robbery, it could have been . . . something more personal."

Mary Andrea gave him a sour look. "Don't tell me he was doing somebody's wife."

"Just a rumor, Mrs. Krome. But I'm afraid it was enough to spook Ted Koppel."

"Shit," Mary Andrea said. She would've gargled battery acid to get on *Nightline*.

The managing editor went on: "We gave it our best shot, but they wanted it to be a mob hit or some cocaine kingpin's revenge for a front page exposé. They were disappointed to find out Tom was just a feature writer. And after the adultery rumor, well, they quit returning our calls."

Mary Andrea slumped against the door. It was like skidding into a bad dream. That the media had already lost interest in Tom Krome's murder meant vastly reduced exposure for his bereft wife – and a wasted plane fare, Mary Andrea thought bitterly. Worse, she'd put herself in position to be humiliated if the fatal "mystery blaze" was traced to a jealous husband instead of a vengeful drug lord.

Damn you, Tom, she thought. This is my career on the line.

"How's the hotel?" she asked glumly.

"We got you a non-smoking room, like you requested." Now the managing editor was chewing on a toothpick.

"And there's a gym with a StairMaster?"

He said: "No gym. No StairMaster. Sorry."

"Oh, that's great."

"It's a HoJo's, Mrs. Krome. We put up everybody at the HoJo's."

After a ten-minute sulk, Mary Andrea announced she'd changed her mind; she wished to return to the airport immediately. She said she was too grief-stricken to appear at the newspaper to accept the writing award Tom had won.

"What's it called again – the 'Emilio'?"

"Amelia," said the managing editor, "and it's quite a big deal. Tom's the first journalist to win it posthumously. It would mean a lot if you could be there in his place."

Mary Andrea sniffed. "Mean a lot to who?"

"Me. The staff. His colleagues." The managing editor rolled the toothpick with his tongue. "And possibly your future."

"Come on, you just told me – "

"We've got a press conference scheduled."

Mary Andrea Finley Krome drilled him with a stare. "A *real* press conference?"

"The TV folks will be there, if that's what you mean."

"How do you know for sure?"

"Because it's a safe story."

"Safe?"

"Fluff. Human interest," the managing editor explained. "They don't want to get into the murky details of the murder, but they're thrilled to do twenty seconds on a pretty young widow receiving a plaque for her slain husband."

"I see."

"And I'd be less than frank," the managing editor added, "if I didn't admit my paper could use the publicity, too. This is a big award, and we don't win all that many."

"When you say TV, are we talking network?"

"Affiliates, sure. CBS, ABC and Fox."

"Oh. Fox, too?" Mary Andrea, thinking: I'll definitely need a new dress, something shorter.

"Will you do it?" the managing editor asked.

"I suppose I could pull myself together," she said.

Thinking: Twenty seconds of airtime, my ass.

Katie Battenkill made a list of things for which she had forgiven Arthur, or overlooked, because he was a judge and being married to a judge was important. The inventory included his annoying table manners, his curtness to her friends and relatives, his disrespect for her religion, his violent jealousy, his cheap and repeated adulteries, his habit of premature ejaculation and of course his rancid choice of cologne.

These Katie weighed against the benefits of being Mrs. Arthur Battenkill Jr., which included a fine late-model car, a large house, invitations to all society events, an annual trip to Bermuda with the local bar association, and the occasional extravagant gift, such as the diamond pendant Katie was now admiring in the vanity mirror.

She hadn't thought of herself as a shallow or materialistic woman, but the possibility dawned upon her. Art was quite the unrepentant sinner, yet for eight years Katie had put up with it. She'd spent little time trying to change him, but allowed herself to be intimidated by his caustic tongue and mollified by presents. Ignoring what he did became easier than arguing about it. Katie told herself it wasn't a completely loveless marriage, inasmuch as she honestly loved being the wife of a circuit court judge; it was Arthur himself for whom she had no deep feelings.

Many Sundays she'd gone to church and asked God what to do, and at no time had He specifically counseled her to start an illicit affair with an itinerant newspaperman. But that's what had happened. It had caught Katie Battenkill totally by surprise and left her powerless to resist – like one of her uncontrollable cravings for Godiva chocolate, only a hundred times stronger. The moment she'd laid eyes on Tom Krome, she knew what would happen . . .

She was in a walkathon for attention-deficit children when all of a sudden this good-looking guy came jogging down James Street in the opposite direction, weaving through the phalanx of T-shirted marchers. As he approached Katie, he slowed his pace just enough to smile and press a five-dollar bill in her palm. For the kids, he'd said, and kept running. And Katie, to her astonishment, immediately turned and ran after him.

Tom Krome was the first man she'd ever seduced, if that's what you call a hummer in the front seat.

Now, looking back on those wild and guilt-ridden weeks, Katie understood the purpose. Everything happens for a reason – a divine force had brought Tommy jogging into her life. God was trying to tell her something: that there were good men out there, decent and caring men whom Katie could trust. And while He probably didn't intend for her to have torrid reckless sex with the first one she met, Katie hoped He would understand.

The important thing was that Tom Krome made her realize she could get by without Arthur, the lying snake. All she needed was some self-confidence, a reordering of priorities and the courage to be honest about the empty relationship with her husband. There hadn't been enough time to fall in love with Tommy, but she certainly *liked* him better than she liked Arthur. The way Tom had apologized for forgetting to call that night from Grange – Katie couldn't remember hearing Arthur say he was sorry for anything. Tom Krome wasn't special or outstanding; he was just a kind, affectionate guy. That's all it took. The fact that Katie Battenkill was so easily drawn astray portended a dim future for the marriage. She decided she had to get out.

Katie recalled a line from an Easter sermon: "To tolerate sin is to abet it, and to share in the sinning." She thought of Arthur's many sins, including Dana, Willow and others whose names she never knew. That was bad enough, the adultery, but now the judge had commissioned an arson and a man was dead.

Not an innocent man, to be sure; an evil little shit. Yet still precious in the eyes of a benevolent God.

That was a sin Katie could not tolerate, if she hoped to save herself. What to do now?

In the mirror the diamond necklace glinted like a tiny star among her many freckles. Of course it was nothing but a bribe to ensure her silence, but dear God, was it gorgeous.

The bathroom door opened and out came her husband with *The Register* folded under one arm.

"Art, we need to talk."

"Yes, we do. Let's go to the kitchen."

Katie was relieved. The bedroom was no place to drop the bomb.

She noticed her hands fluttering as she filled the coffeemaker. Over her shoulder she heard Arthur say, "Katherine, I've decided to retire from the bench. How would you like to live in the islands?"

Slowly she turned. "What?"

"I've had enough. The job is killing me," he said. "I'm up for reelection next year but I don't have the stomach for another campaign. I'm burned out, Katie."

All she could think to say was: "We can't afford to retire, Art."

"Thank you, Ms. Dean Witter, but I beg to differ."

In that acid tone of voice that Katie had come to despise.

"Shocking as it may seem," the judge went on, "I made a few modest investments without consulting you. One of them's paid off very handsomely, to the tune of a quarter-million dollars."

Katie gave no outward sign of being impressed, but it was a struggle to remain composed. "What kind of investment?"

"A unit trust. It's a bit complicated to explain."

"I bet."

"Real estate, Katherine."

She made the coffee and poured a cup for Arthur.

"You're forty-three years old and ready to retire."

"The American dream," said the judge, smacking his lips.

"Why the islands? And which islands?" Katie, thinking: I can't even get him to take me to the beach.

Arthur Battenkill said, "Roy Tigert has offered to loan us his bungalow in the Bahamas. At Marsh Harbour, just to see if we like it. If we don't, we'll try someplace else – the Caymans or Saint Thomas."

Katie was speechless. Bungalow in the Bahamas – it sounded like a vaudeville song.

Awkwardly her husband reached across the table and stroked her cheek. "I know things haven't been perfect around here – we need to make a change, Katherine, to save what we've got. We'll go away and start over, you and me, with nobody else to worry about."

Meaning Tom Krome – or Art's secretaries?

Katie asked, "When?"

"Right away."

"Oh."

"Remember how much you liked Nassau?"

"I've never been there, Arthur. That must've been Willow."

The judge sucked desperately at his coffee.

Katie said, "This isn't about saving our marriage, it's about Tommy's house burning down with a dead body inside. You're scared shitless because it's your fault."

Arthur Battenkill Jr. stared blankly into his cup. "You've developed quite an imagination, Katherine."

"You're running away. Admit it, Arthur. You stole some getaway money, and now you want to leave the country. Do you think I'm stupid?"

"No," said the judge, "I think you're practical."

*

On that same Monday morning, the fourth of December, the real estate office of Clara Markham received an unexpected visitor: Bernard Squires, investment manager for the Central Midwest Brotherhood of Grouters, Spacklers and Drywallers International. He'd flown to Florida on a private Gulfstream jet, chartered for him by Richard "The Icepick" Tarbone. The mission of Bernard Squires was to place a large deposit on the Simmons Wood property, thereby locking it up for the union pension fund from which the Tarbone crime family regularly stole. After driving through Grange, Bernard Squires felt more confident than ever that the shopping mall planned for Simmons Wood could be devised to fail both plausibly and exorbitantly.

"We spoke on the phone," he said to Clara Markham.

"Yes, of course" she said, "but I'm afraid I've got nothing new to report."

"That's why I'm here."

Clara Markham asked if Squires could come back later, as she had an important closing to attend.

Squires was courteous but insistent. "I doubt it's as important as this," he said, and positioned a black eelskin briefcase on her desk.

The real estate agent had never seen so much cash; neat, tight bundles of fifties and hundreds. Somewhere among the sweet-smelling stacks, Clara knew, was her commission; probably the largest she'd ever see.

"This is to show how serious we are about acquiring the property," Squires explained, "and to expedite the negotiations. The people I represent are eager to get started immediately."

Clara Markham was in a bind. She'd heard nothing over the weekend from JoLayne Lucks. Their friendship was close – and JoLayne was an absolute saint with Kenny, Clara's beloved Persian – but the real estate agent couldn't permit her personal feelings to jeopardize such a huge deal.

She waved a hand above the cash and said, "This is very impressive, Mr. Squires, but I must tell you I'm expecting a counteroffer."

"Really?"

"There's nothing in writing yet, but I've been assured it's on the way."

Squires seemed amused. "All right." With a well-practiced motion he quietly closed the briefcase. "We're prepared to match any reasonable counteroffer. In the meantime, I'd ask that you contact your clients and let them know how committed we are to this project."

Clara Markham said, "Absolutely. First thing after lunch."

"What's wrong with right now?"

"I . . . I'm not sure I can reach them."

"Let's try," said Bernard Squires.

Clara Markham saw that stalling was fruitless; the man wouldn't return to Chicago without an answer. Bernard Squires settled crisply into a chair while she telephoned the attorney for the estate of Lighthorse Simmons. Five minutes later the attorney called back, having patched together a conference call with Lighthorse's two profligate heirs – his son, Leander Simmons, and his daughter, Janine Simmons Robinson. Leander dabbled in fossil fuels and thoroughbreds; Janine spent her money on exotic surgeries and renovating vacation houses.

Leaning close to the speakerphone, Clara Markham

carefully summarized the union's offer for Simmons Wood, the key detail being the figure of $3 million.

"In addition," she concluded, "Mr. Squires has delivered to my office a substantial cash deposit."

On the other end, Leander Simmons piped, "How much?" He whistled when the real estate agent told him.

An old pro at conference calls, Bernard Squires raised his voice just enough to be heard: "We wanted everyone to know how serious we are."

"Well, you got *my* attention," said Janine Simmons Robinson.

"Me, too," her brother said.

On behalf of JoLayne Lucks and the doomed wildlife of Simmons Wood, Clara Markham felt compelled to say: "Mr. Squires and his group want to build a shopping mall on your father's land."

"With a playground in the atrium," Squires added coolly.

"And a Mediterranean fountain in front," the attorney chimed, "with real ducks and geese. It'll be a terrific attraction for your little town."

From the speakerphone came the instant reaction of Leander Simmons: "Personally, I don't give a shit if you guys want to dig a coal mine. How about you, Sis?"

Said Janine: "Hey, three million bucks is three million bucks."

"Exactly. So what the hell are we waiting for?" Leander demanded. "Just do it."

Bernard Squires said, "We're ready to go. However, Ms. Markham informs me there may be another offer."

"From who?" asked Janine Simmons Robinson.

"How much?" asked her brother.

Clara Markham said, "It's a local investor. I intended

to call you as soon as I received the papers, but they haven't arrived."

"Then screw it," said the attorney. "Let's go with Squires."

"Whatever you wish."

"Now just hold on a second." It was Leander Simmons. "What's the big rush?"

He smelled more money. Bernard Squires' expression blackened at the prospect of a bidding duel. Clara Markham noticed some fresh veins pulsing in his neck.

As it happened, Janine Simmons Robinson was on the same opportunistic wavelength as her brother. "What's the harm in waiting a couple three days?" she said. "See what these other folks have in mind."

"It's your call," said their attorney. Then: "Ms. Markham, will you get back to us as soon as you hear something – say, no later than Wednesday?"

"How about tomorrow?" said Bernard Squires.

"Wednesday," said Leander Simmons and his sister in unison.

There was a series of clicks, then the speaker box went silent. Clara Markham looked apologetically first at Bernard Squires, then at the eelskin briefcase on her desk. "I'll deposit this in our escrow account," she said, "right away."

Gravely Squires rose from the chair.

"You don't strike me as a deceitful person," he said, "the sort who'd try to jack up her commission by cooking up phony counteroffers."

"I'm not a sneak," said Clara Markham, "nor am I an imbecile. Simmons Wood will be my biggest deal of the year, Mr. Squires. I wouldn't risk blowing the whole enchilada for a few extra bucks."

He believed her. He'd seen the town; it was a miracle she hadn't starved to death.

"A local investor, you said."

"That's right."

"I don't suppose you'd be kind enough to tell me the name."

"I'm afraid I can't, Mister Squires."

"But you're confident they've got some resources."

"They do," said Clara Markham, thinking: Last I heard.

Shiner's mother overslept. The road machines woke her.

Hurriedly she squeezed into the bridal gown, snatched her parasol and sailed out the door. By the time she reached the intersection of Sebring Street and the highway, it was too late. The Department of Transportation was ready to pave the Road-Stain Jesus.

Shiner's mother shrieked and hopped about like a costumed circus monkey. She spat in the face of the crew foreman and used her parasol to stab ineffectively at the driver of the steamroller. Ultimately she flung herself facedown upon the holy splotch and refused to budge for the machines.

"Pave me, too, you godless bastards!" she cried. "Let me be one with my Savior!"

The crew foreman wiped off his cheek and signaled for his men to halt work. He telephoned the sheriff's office and said: "There's a crazy witch in a wedding dress out here humping the road. What do I do?"

Two deputies arrived, followed later by a television truck.

Shiner's mother was kissing the pavement, on the

place she imagined to be Jesus' forehead. "Don't you worry, Son of God," she kept saying. "I'm right here. I'm not goin' nowheres!" Her devotion to the stain was remarkable, considering its downwind proximity to a flattened opossum.

A vanload of worried-looking pilgrims arrived, but the deputies ordered them to stay out of the right-of-way. Shiner's mother raised her head and said: "That's the collection box on top of the cooler. Help yourselves to a Sprite!"

By now traffic was blocked in both directions. The crew foreman, who was from Tampa and unfamiliar with the local lore, asked the deputies if there was a mental institution in town.

"Naw, but we're overdue," said one of them.

They each grabbed an arm and hoisted Shiner's mother off the highway. "He's watching! He sees you!" she screamed.

The deputies deposited her in the cage of a patrol car and chased the curious tourists away. Before continuing with the paving job, the crew foreman and his men assembled in a loose semicircle at the center line. They were trying to figure out what the lunatic biddy was ranting about.

Bending over the stain, the foreman said, "If that's Jesus Christ, I'm Long Dong Silver."

"Hell, it's fuckin' brake fluid," declared one of his men, a mechanic.

"Oil," asserted another.

Then the driver of the steamroller said: "From here it kinda looks like a woman. If you close one eye, a naked woman on a camel."

That was it for the foreman. "Back to work," he snapped.

The TV crew stayed for the paving. They got an excellent close-up of the Road-Stain Jesus disappearing beneath a rolling black crust of hot asphalt. The scene was deftly crosscut with a shot of a young pilgrim sniffling into a Kleenex as if grieving. In reality she was merely trying to stave off dead-opossum fumes.

The story ran on the noon news out of Orlando. It opened with videotape of Shiner's mother, tenderly smooching the sacred smudge. Joan anxiously phoned Roddy at work. "There's TV people in town. What if they hear about the turtle shrine?"

"Pretend we don't know him," Roddy said.

"But he's my brother."

"Fine. Then you do the interviews."

Shiner's mother was booked for disturbing the peace and after three hours was released without bail. Immediately she took a cab to the intersection of Sebring and the highway. The asphalt had hardened, dry to the touch; Shiner's mother wasn't even positive where the stain had been. She observed that somebody had stolen her collection box and most of the cold sodas. She was officially out of business.

She made her way to Demencio's house and set her empty cooler in the shade of an oak tree, away from Sinclair's crowd. Trish noticed her sitting there and brought a lemonade.

"I heard what happened. I'm so sorry."

"Pigs tore my gown," Shiner's mother said.

"We can mend that in no time," said Trish.

"What about my shrine. Who's gonna fix *that*?"

"Just you wait. There'll be new stains on the highway."

Shiner's mother said, "Ha."

Trish glanced at the front window of the house, in case Demencio was watching; he'd be miffed if he spotted the old lady on the premises. Her ice-blue parasol stood out like a pup tent.

"You should go home and get some rest," Trish said.

"Not after I've lost the two things in the world I care about most – the Road-Stain Jesus, and my only son."

"Oh, Shiner will be back." Trish, thinking: As soon as he needs money.

"But he won't never be the same. I got a feeling he is bein' corrupted by the forces of Satan." Shiner's mother drained the glass of lemonade. "How about some of that angel food?"

"I'm afraid it's all gone. Need a lift home?"

"Maybe later," Shiner's mother said. "First I got to talk to the turtle boy. My heart's been steamrolled, I need some spiritual healing."

"Poor thing." Trish excused herself and hurried inside to warn Demencio. Shiner's mother lit a cigaret and waited for the line around the moat to dwindle.

# TWENTY-THREE

**The Everglades empties** off the Florida peninsula into a shimmering panorama of tidal flats, serpentine channels and bright-green mangrove islets. The balance of life there depends upon a seasonal infusion of freshwater from the mainland. Once it was a certainty of nature, but no more. The drones who in the 1940s carved levees and gouged canals throughout the upper Everglades gave absolutely no thought to what would happen downstream to the fish and birds, not to mention the Indians. For the engineers, the holy mission was to ensure the comfort and prosperity of non-native humans. In the dry season the state drained water off the Everglades for immediate delivery to cities and farms. In the wet season it pumped millions of gallons seaward to prevent flooding of subdivisions, pastures and crops.

Over time, less and less freshwater reached Florida Bay, and what ultimately got there wasn't so pure. When the inevitable drought came, the parched bay changed drastically. Sea grasses began to die off by the acre. The bottom turned to mud. Pea-green algae blooms erupted to blanket hundreds of square miles, a stain so large as to be visible from NASA satellites. Starved for sunlight, sponges died and floated to the surface in rotting clumps.

The collapse of the famous estuary produced the

predictable dull-eyed bafflement among bureaucrats. Faced with a public-relations disaster and a cataclysmic threat to the tourism industry, the same people who by their ignorance had managed to starve Florida Bay now began scrambling for a way to revive it. This would be difficult without antagonizing the same farmers and developers for whom the marshlands had been so expensively replumbed. Politicians were caught in a bind. Those who'd never lost a moment's sleep over the fate of the white heron now waxed lyrical about its delicate grace. Privately, meanwhile, they reassured campaign donors that – screw the birds – Big Agriculture would still get first crack at the precious water.

For anyone seeking election to office in South Florida, restoring the Everglades became not only a pledge but a mantra. Speeches were given, grandiose promises made, blue-ribbon task forces assembled, research grants awarded, scientific symposiums convened . . . and not much changed. The state continued to siphon gluttonously what should have been allowed to flow naturally toward Florida Bay. In the driest years the bay struggled; turned to a briny soup. In the rainiest years it rebounded with life.

The condition of the place could be assessed best at remote islands such as Pearl Key. When the mangroves were spangled with pelicans and egrets, when the sky held ospreys and frigate birds, when the shallows boiled with mullet and snook – that meant plenty of good water was spilling from the 'Glades; enough for a reprieve from the larceny perpetrated upstream.

It was Chub's misfortune to have arrived at Pearl Key after an exceptionally generous rainy season, when the island was lush and teeming. Scarcely two months later the flats would be as murky as chocolate milk, the game fish and wading birds would have fled, and in the water would swim few creatures of serious concern to a glue-sniffing kidnapper, passed out with one hand dangling.

His wounded hand, as it happened; swollen and gray, still adorned with a severed crab claw.

As fishermen know, the scent of bait is diffused swiftly and efficiently in saltwater, attracting scavengers of all sizes. Chub knew this, too, although the information currently was stored beyond his grasp. Not even a doctorate in marine biology would've mitigated the stupefying volume of polyurethane fumes he'd inhaled from the tube of boat glue. He was completely unaware that his wounded mitt hung so tantalizingly in the water, just as he was unaware of the cannibalistic proclivities of *Callinectes sapidus*, the common blue crab.

In fact, Chub was so blitzed that the sensation of extreme pain – which ordinarily would have reached his brain stem in a nanosecond – instead meandered from one befogged synapse to another. By the time his subconscious registered the feeling, something horrible was well under way.

His screams ruined an otherwise golden morning.

The other three had been awake for hours. Bodean Gazzer was patrolling the woods not far from the campsite. Amber was attempting to revise Shiner's tattoo, using a honed fishhook and a dollop of violet mascara. Before starting she'd numbed his upper arm with ice, but the pricking still stung like hell. Shiner hoped the procedure would be brief, since only two of the three initials required altering. Amber warned him it wasn't an easy job, changing the letters from *W.R.B.* to *W.C.A.*

"The *B* won't be bad. I'll just add legs to make it look like a capital *A*. But the *R* is tricky," she said, frowning. "I can't promise it'll ever pass for a *C*."

Shiner, through clenched teeth: "Do your best, 'K?"

He turned away, so he wouldn't see the punctures. Occasionally he'd let out a grunt, which was Amber's cue to apply more ice. Despite the discomfort, Shiner found himself enjoying being the focus of her concentration. He liked the way she'd rolled up the sleeves of the camouflage jumpsuit and pinned her hair in a ponytail; all business. And her touch – clinical as it was – sent a pleasurable tickle all the way to his groin.

"I had a friend," she was saying, "he was paranoid about dying in a plane crash. So he got his initials tattooed on his arms and his legs, his shoulders, the soles of his feet, both cheeks of his butt. See, because he'd read where that's one way they can identify the body parts, if there's tattoos."

Shiner said, "That's pretty smart."

"Yeah, but it didn't help. He was, like, a smuggler."

"Oh."

"His plane went down off the Bahamas. Sharks got him."

"There wasn't nothin' left?"

"One of his Reeboks is all they found," Amber said. "Inside was something that looked like a toe. Of course, it wasn't tattooed."

"Damn."

To Shiner's surprise, Amber began to sing as she went at him with the fishhook:

*"Smile like a princess but bite like a snake –*
*Got ice in her veins and a heart that don't ache.*
*She a nut-cutting bitch and that's no lie,*
*Hack 'em both off with a gleam in her eye . . ."*

Shiner said, "You got a nice voice."

"White Rebel Brotherhood," said Amber, "the song I told you about. It's killer." As she worked on the tattoo, her face was so close he could feel the soft breath on his skin.

He said, "Maybe I'll check out the CD."

"They do it more hip-hop."

"Yeah, I figgered."

"Am I hurting you?"

"Naw," Shiner lied. "Matter a fact, I was wonderin' if mebbe you could add somethin' extry. Under the eagle."

"Such as?"

"A swatch ticker," said Shiner.

"A what?"

"You know – a swatch ticker. Like the Nazis had."

Amber glanced up sharply. "Swastika, you mean."

"Yeah!" He practiced the proper pronunciation. "That'd be cool, don'tcha think?"

"I don't know how to draw one. Sorry."

Shiner mulled it over, wincing every so often at the stabs of the fishhook. "I seen some good ones at the colonel's place," he said eventually, "if I can only 'member how they went. Look here . . ."

He cleared a place in the sand and, using a forefinger, drew his version of the infamous German cross.

Amber shook her head. "That's not right."

"You sure?"

"You made it look like . . . like something from the Chinese alphabet."

"Now hold on," said Shiner, but he was stumped. Just then Bodean Gazzer came stomping out of the mangroves. He sat near the fire and began wiping dew from his rifle. Shiner called him over.

"Colonel, can you do a swatch ticker?"

"No problem." Bode saw an opportunity to impress Amber at the kid's expense. He put down the gun and joined them under the tarp. With a sweep of a hand he erased Shiner's chicken-scratch swastika. In broad, sure strokes he sketched his own.

Amber briefly scrutinized the design before declaring it had "too many thingies." She was referring to the tiny stems that Bode had drawn on the ends of the secondary legs.

"You're wrong, sweetheart," he told her. "That's exactly how the Nasties done it."

Amber didn't argue, but she thought: Any serious white supremacist and Jew-hater would know how to make a swastika. Bode and Shiner's confusion on the topic reaffirmed her suspicions that the White Clarion Aryans were a pretty lame operation.

"OK, you're the expert," she said to Bode, and began reheating the point of the fishhook with a cigaret lighter.

Shiner felt his stomach jump. He had a hunch Amber was right – the colonel's swastika was odd-looking; too many angles, and the lines seemed to point in the wrong directions. The damn thing was either upside down or inside out, Shiner couldn't tell which.

"Where you gone put it?" Bode asked.

"Under the bird." Amber tapped the designated location on Shiner's left biceps.

Bode said, "Perfect."

Shiner didn't know what to do. He didn't want to offend his commanding officer but he sure as hell didn't want another defective tattoo. And a fucked-up swastika would be difficult to fix, Shiner knew; difficult and painful.

Amber pressed a fresh batch of ice cubes against his arm. "Let me know when you can't feel the cold."

Bode Gazzer edged closer. "I wanna watch."

Shiner fixed his gaze on the blackened barb of the fishhook and instantly became dizzy.

"Ready?" asked Amber.

Shiner sucked in a deep breath – he'd made up his mind. He'd do it for the brotherhood.

"Anytime," he said thickly, and locked his eyes shut.

At first he believed the screams he heard were his own. Then, as the animal howling tapered to a stream of profanity, Shiner recognized the timbre of Chub's voice.

Then Amber saying: "Oh my God."

And Bodean Gazzer: "What the hell!"

Shiner looked up to see Chub, nude except for Amber's orange shorts, which he wore upon his head. The shorts were pulled down as snugly as a skullcap, fitted at an angle to hide Chub's eye patch.

But that's not what made the others stare.

It was fastened to the end of Chub's right arm, which hung limp and heavy at his side. Where once there was only a pair of dead crab pincers there was now a complete live crab; one of the largest crabs Amber had ever seen, outside the Seaquarium.

"What do I do?" Chub pleaded. "Jesus Willy, what the fuck do I do?" Gummy-eyed from either sleep or glue, he displayed his other hand – his functional hand – for them to see. The knuckles were bloody knobs, from beating on the crustacean.

Amber cast her eyes at Shiner, who had not much experience with marine life and, thus, no counter-strategy. Despite his white brother's awful predicament, he couldn't help feeling a sense of reprieve. While the others stood transfixed by the sight of Chub, Shiner discreetly scuffed his feet across the dirt until he'd obscured Bode Gazzer's dubious swastika sketch.

"The crab!" Chub was bellowing. "The crab, it's after that g-g-god-damn claw!"

Gravely Bode surmised: "It's either trying to eat it or fuck it."

In its bloated and discolored state, Chub's hand could have been mistaken by a farsighted crab for another member of its species; that was Bode's hypothesis. Amber had nothing more plausible to offer.

Shiner asked, "How come he got your pants on his head?"

"God only knows," she said with a sigh.

Chub bolted toward the water. When the others caught up, they found him madly slinging his lifeless crab arm against the stump of an ancient buttonwood.

Shiner stepped forward. "I'll take care a that goddamn thing."

Bode was alarmed to see the Beretta glinting in the kid's paw. "Oh, no you don't," he said, snatching it away. "I'll do the honors, son."

"Do what?" Amber asked.

She felt Shiner's hand on her shoulder. "Better stand back," he advised.

*

Although he was unaware of it, Bodean Gazzer almost hadn't made it back to camp. Tom Krome and JoLayne Lucks almost caught him alone.

They'd spotted him from about a hundred yards, moving across a salt flat on the crown of the island. The flat was wide and oval-shaped, ringed by mangroves and hurricane deadfall. Normally it filled up as a lagoon during the big autumn tides, but two days of heavy winds had blown out much of the water. Assault rifle in hand, Bode had scattered groups of stilt-legged birds as he clomped through the custardlike marl.

JoLayne and Tom had emerged from the tree line no more than two minutes behind him. They couldn't risk following the same path across the flat because there was no cover. So they kept low to the ground and skirted the fringe, picking their way through the stubborn mangroves. It was slow going; Tom leading the way, holding the springy branches until JoLayne could squeeze past with the Remington. When they reached the place where the stumpy redneck had reentered the woods, they could make out his heavy-footed crackles and crunches ahead of them. They moved forward carefully, baby-stepping, so he wouldn't hear.

Then the twig-snapping stopped. JoLayne tugged Tom's sleeve and motioned him to be still. She came up beside him and whispered: "I smell wood smoke."

The sound of conversation confirmed it. They were very near the robbers' camp; possibly too near. Quietly JoLayne and Tom backed off, concealing themselves in a tangled canopy. All around them, the tree limbs were necklaced with freshly spun spiderwebs. Tom leaned back, dazzled.

"Golden-orbed weaver," JoLayne said.

"It's gorgeous."

"Sure is." She found it interesting that he was so calm, almost relaxed, as long as they were on the chase. It was doing nothing that seemed to unsettle him, the sitting and waiting.

When JoLayne mentioned it, Tom said, "That's because I'd rather be the hunter than the hunted. Wouldn't you?"

"Well, we got pretty close to the bastard."

"Yeah. You're good at this."

"For a black girl, you mean?"

"JoLayne, don't start with that."

"Not all of us hang out on street corners. Some of us actually know our way around the woods . . . or maybe were you referring to women in general."

"Actually, I was." Tom decided it was better to be thought a chauvinist than a racist – assuming JoLayne was half serious.

She said, "Are you saying your wife never took you stalking?"

"Not that I can recall."

"And none of your girlfriends?" Now JoLayne was smiling. Obviously she enjoyed giving him a start now and then.

Kissing his neck sweetly: "I'm sorry to be jerking your chain, but it's more fun than I can stand. You don't know how long it's been since I've had a guilt-ridden white boy all to myself."

"That's me."

"We should've made love again," she said, suddenly pensive. "Last night – to hell with the rain and cold, we should've done it."

Tom thought it an odd moment to raise the subject,

what with a gang of heavily armed lunatics three hundred feet away.

"I decided a long time ago," she said, "that if I knew exactly when I was going to die, I'd make a point of screwing my brains out the night before."

"Good plan."

"And we *could* die out here on this island. I mean, these are very bad guys we're chasing."

Tom said he preferred to think positive thoughts.

"But you do agree," JoLayne said, "there's a chance they'll kill us."

"Hell, yes, there's a chance."

"That's all I'm saying. That's why I wish we'd made love."

"Oh, I think we'll get another shot." Tom, trying to stay upbeat.

JoLayne Lucks closed her eyes and rolled her head back. "Mortal fear makes for great sex – I read that someplace."

"Mortal fear."

"It wasn't *Cosmo*, either. I'm sorry for babbling, Tom, I'm just really – "

"Nervous. Me, too," he said. "Let's concentrate on what to do about these assholes who stole your lottery ticket."

The dreamy expression passed from JoLayne's face. "That wasn't all they did."

"I know."

"But still I'm not sure if I can make myself pull the trigger."

"Maybe it won't come to that," he said.

JoLayne pointed up in the mangrove branches. A tiny barrel-shaped beetle had become trapped in one of the gossamer webs. Slowly, almost casually, the spider was crossing the intricate net toward the struggling insect.

"That's what we need. A web," JoLayne said.

They watched the stalking until a drawn-out cry broke the stillness; not a woman's cry, this time, but a man's. It was no less harrowing.

JoLayne shuddered and rose to her knees. "Damn. What now?"

Tom Krome got up quickly. "Well, I'd rather have them screaming than singing campfire songs." He held out his hand. "Come on. Let's go see."

Chub didn't trust either Bode or Shiner to shoot the crab safely off his hand. He didn't even trust himself.

"I feel like dogshit," he admitted.

They persuaded him to lie down, and the panic passed after a few minutes. The piercing pain subsided into a dead throbbing weight. Bode brought a lukewarm Budweiser and Shiner offered a stick of beef jerky. From Amber, nothing; not a peep of sympathy.

"I'm cold," Chub complained. "I got the shakes."

Bode told him the wound was badly infected. "What I can see of it," he added. The crab had quite a mouthful.

"Is the fucker dead or alive?" Chub, squinting fretfully.

Shiner said, "Dead."

Bode said, "Alive."

Chub looked to Amber for the tiebreaker. "I can't honestly tell," she said.

"God, I'm freezin'. My skin's on fire but the rest a me is freezin' cold."

Amber pulled the tarpaulin off the tree and blanketed

Chub, up to his neck. He was thrilled by what he perceived, incorrectly, as an act of comfort and affection. Amber's true intent was selfish: to conceal from plain view Chub's stringy nakedness, as well as the ghastly crab.

He said, "Thank you, darling. Later we'll go on that walk you promised."

"You're in no shape to walk anywhere."

Shiner said, "Amen, that's a fact." Dreading the thought of the two of them alone.

Bodean Gazzer warmed a pot of coffee on the fire. Chub began to doze. Amber furtively tried to retrieve her waitress shorts but they caught on Chub's ponytail, which snapped him awake. "No, don't you dare! They're mine, goddammit, you gave 'em to me!" Twisting and shaking his head.

"OK, OK." Amber backed off.

From beneath the tarp emerged Chub's good hand. It readjusted the shiny pants across his nose and mouth, leaving his unpatched eye exposed through one of the leg holes.

Shiner, his back turned to Chub, mouthed the words: "He's crazy."

"Thanks for the news flash," said Amber.

They drank the coffee while Bodean Gazzer read aloud from the writings of the First Patriot Covenant. When he got to the part about Negroes and Jews being descended from the devil, Amber waved a hand. "Where does it say *that* in the Scriptures?"

"Oh, it's in there. 'Those who lay down with Satan will bring forth from his demon seed only children of darkness and deceit.' " Bode was winging it. He hadn't cracked a Bible since junior high.

Amber remained skeptical, but Shiner chirped: "If the colonel says it's in there, it's in there." Though Shiner couldn't recall his fanatically reborn mother invoking such a potent verse. It seemed like something she would've mentioned, too; demon seeds!

Chub lifted his head and requested his sack of marine glue. Angrily Bode said, "You're done with that shit."

"I ain't, either." Whenever Chub spoke, the satiny fabric of Amber's shorts puckered around his mouth. Amber expected she would carry the freaky vision to her grave.

Bodean Gazzer was saying, "Christ, you already got a fucked-up eye, a fucked-up hand – last thing you need is a fucked-up brain. You're a soldier, remember? A major."

"My ass." Chub, glowering through the pants.

Bode resumed reading, but only Shiner remained attentive. His questions mostly concerned the living accommodations provided in Montana by the First Patriot Covenant. Did the pillboxes have central heating? Was there cable TV, or a dish?

Chub, who'd nodded off again, suddenly sprung to a sitting position. "My gun! Where's it at?"

"Probably in the boat," Bode said disapprovingly, "with your camos."

"Go find it!"

"I'm busy."

"Now! I ast for my goddamn gun!" Chub had remembered the lottery ticket, hidden in one of the chambers.

Shiner said, "I'll go."

"Like hell," Chub snarled. His eye fell upon Amber. She was on the other side of the campfire, sitting beside the kid; real close, too. *Touching* him – touching his pudgy arm!

Chub didn't realize she was icing the tattoo, but it likely wouldn't have mattered. To Bode Gazzer he said: "Time for a meetin'."

"What?"

"Of the WCA. We got 'portant bidness, remember?"

"Oh yeah," said Bode. He'd have preferred to wait until the crab crisis was resolved. Encumbered as he was, Chub had lost some of the menacing presence that was so useful in tight confrontations.

Bode called the meeting to order with such a lack of enthusiasm that it put Amber on alert. She gave Shiner a quick jab with an elbow, to let him know it was coming; what they'd debated privately in the hours before dawn. Shiner looked crushed, like a kid who just found there was no such thing as Santa Claus.

"Son," Bode Gazzer began, "first I want you to know how much we 'preciate all you done for the militia. We ain't gonna forget it, neither. Down the road we intend to settle up fair and square. But the thing is, it's not workin' out so good. Particularly with the weapons, son – you're just too damn excitable."

Chub cut in: "You like to get ever' one of us kilt, shootin' at birds and bunny rabbits. Jesus!"

"I said I'm sorry," Shiner reminded them. "And, Colonel, didn't I promise to pay for them holes in your truck?"

"You did, you will, and I respect that. Truly I do. But we're in a high-risk scenario here. We got the Black Tide on our asses, not to mention the NATO problem over in the Bahamas. That's wall-to-wall Negroes, son. We can't afford no mistakes."

Chub said: "Life or death. This ain't a game."

"And that's how come we got to let you go," said Bode

Gazzer. "Go on home and watch over your momma. Ain't no shame in that."

Shiner surprised them both. He stood up and said, "No way." He glanced at Amber, who gave a nod of support. "You can't kick me out. You can't." He pointed at the bruised and scabby tattoo. "See there? *W.C.A.* I'm in for life."

"Son, I'm sorry, but it's no good." Bode understood it was up to him to reason with the boy, because Chub had no tolerance for argument. "All we can say is thanks for everything, and so long. Also, we're gonna give you a thousand bucks for all your loyalty."

Amber chuckled sarcastically. These guys were unbelievable.

Emboldened, Shiner said, "A thousand dollars is a goddamn joke."

Bode asked him what he wanted.

"To stay in the militia," Shiner answered briskly, "plus I want one-third of the lottery money. I earned it."

Chub hurled the tarpaulin aside and lurched to his feet. "Shoot the motherfucker," he said to Bode.

"Just hold on."

"If you don't, I will."

Bode Gazzer scowled at Shiner. "Goddammit, son." He took the stolen .380 out of his belt. "Why'd you put me in this posture?"

Amber saw that Shiner was scared out of his mind. She said: "Colonel, there's something you ought to know. Tell him, Shiner. Tell them what you did at Jewfish Creek."

Here was the big bluff. Shiner struggled to remember what Amber had coached him to say, exactly the way she'd said it last night. But he couldn't quite piece it all together – the sight of the Beretta had unnerved him.

"About the videotape," Amber prodded.

"Oh . . . yeah."

"The phone call you made," she said.

Bode asked, "What phone call?"

"That's right," Shiner said. "The store video, 'member? You guys had me swipe it from the Grab N'Go. On account of it proves you didn't win the Lotto – "

"Shut the fuck up," Chub barked.

" – because you didn't even show up in Grange till the day after. It's all on the tape."

Bode, tapping the .380 against his thigh. "*What* phone call?"

"Tell him," Amber said to Shiner.

"To my ma," Shiner lied. "The tape's hid in my car and the car's at Major Chub's trailer. I called my ma and told her come down get it, she don't hear from me by Thursday – "

"Tuesday," Amber interjected.

"Right, Tuesday. I told her come get the car."

"Then what?" Bodean Gazzer's throat was like chalk.

Shiner said, "I told her to give the video to the black girl. JoLayne. She'll know what to do."

"You're full a shit," Bode said, without conviction.

"I ain't."

"I heard him make the phone call," said Amber.

"Then goddamn the both a you."

Amber announced she was going for a swim, alone. Shiner was relieved, because he'd been waiting to take a world-record leak.

Chub and Bode withdrew to the *Reel Luv* for an

urgent conference. Even in his dazed and febrile condition, Chub comprehended what the kid had done; gotten hisself some insurance. "Does this mean we can't kill the fucker?"

"I don't see how," Bode said.

"And what's all this about the money?"

"He wants a cut, we gotta give it to him," Bode said. "Thank God he only knows about one a them lottery tickets. So, like . . . what's a third of fourteen million?"

Chub strained to do the division in his head. "Four something. Four point five, four point six."

"So that'll be his share. Long as he don't find out about the other goddamn ticket."

Chub felt like puking. Four and a half million bucks for that dumb dork! It wasn't right. Sinful was what it was.

"Blackmail," Bode said morosely. There was no denying the gravity of their predicament. Saving white America would have to wait; first they had to save themselves.

"Tell you what else," he said to Chub. "Your pretty blond sweetheart's in on the deal."

"Not Amber. Ain't no way."

"You think Shiner's smart enough to dream this shit up? Kid can't find his own dick with a pair of salad tongs."

"But still." Chub didn't want to believe Amber had hooked up with Shiner. Why would she be with him, he wondered, when she could have me?

Bode Gazzer told him to put on some clothes. "Before your pecker gets fried."

"But I'm burnin' up. Feel how hot." He flopped his tumescent crab arm on the deck of the boat.

"No, thanks," Bode said, stepping away. A notion had come to him. "Today's Monday, right?"

"Don't ask me."

Bode drummed his fingers on the gunwale. "That gives us a whole day until Shiner's momma hits the launchpad. Say we leave right now – run this puppy back to the highway, hop in the truck and haul ass. We could make Tall'hassee by lunchtime tomorrow."

Chub peeped ferretlike from inside Amber's orange shorts. "What about the video?"

"We stop at the trailer on the way north. Find the damn tape and burn it. Burn the whole car if we got to, just like we done to that asshole's Miata."

"Fan-fucking-tastic." Chub's laugh came out as a dry rattle. He couldn't wait to get off that miserable island. "Leave the sneaky bastard out here to rot. I love it, man."

"Her, too."

"Aw, no!"

Bode Gazzer said, "We better."

"But I haven't got to fuck her yet. Not even a b.j."

"Come on. Let's load the boat."

Chub said, "We got time, man, if we hurry. Time for both of us to get a piece."

Bode should've short-circuited the idea, but instead he allowed it to float around his imagination. He was beset by a vision of Amber nude, on her knees.

"We tie up the skinhead," Chub proposed, "we each take a turn with the girl and then we split."

"Will she go for it?" Bode didn't feel right about raping a white woman. More important, it was a big-time felony.

Chub said, "S'pose it was her only way off the island. Then she'd go for it, you bet she would."

"Good point," Bode said.

It was a historic moment, Chub with an actual brainstorm. He climbed into the *Reel Luv* to search for his bag of glue.

Bode heard footsteps and wheeled around. He should've been ready with the Beretta, but he wasn't.

Amber stood there in the camo jumpsuit, the top half open, her hair slick and shining from her swim. "I can't find Shiner," she said.

"Ain't that a shame." Chub, leering through the crotch of her waitress shorts.

Bode Gazzer matter-of-factly told Amber the plan, told her the price of the boat ride back to the Keys. She didn't sob, didn't run, didn't get mad. Her expression was totally neutral, giving both men a misplaced sense of expectation. Chub had a bounce in his step as he got out of the boat.

Amber said, "Take those ridiculous pants off your face."

Bode was momentarily distracted by the crab attached to Chub's hand; he thought he detected movement.

Amber repeated her demand. "Take 'em off. You look like a pervert."

"Listen to you," Chub said, and made a step toward her. That's when he saw the Colt Python .357. *His* Colt. His Lotto ticket, his life's fortune, his entire mortal future – all in the hands of a pissed-off Hooters babe.

"Jesus Willy," he said.

Bodean Gazzer was amazed at how fast it was unraveling, all because of rotten luck, blind lust and stupidity.

"Have some more glue," he told his partner. "See what else you can fuck up."

Amber fired the pistol at Chub's feet. The bullet kicked sand on his shins and ankles. He yanked the orange pants off his head and tossed them.

"Thank you," Amber said. "Now, what did you guys do with Shiner?"

"Nothin'," they answered, Bode first and then Chub.

None of them could know that Shiner was exactly one hundred and twenty-seven paces away, wetting himself in stark terror.

# TWENTY-FOUR

**As he pointed** the shotgun, Tom Krome wrote the lead of the story in his head:

*An unidentified convenience store clerk was shot to death Monday in a bizarre attack on a remote island off the Florida Keys.*

*Police said the victim apparently was stalked and ambushed while relieving himself in a mangrove thicket. Arrested for first-degree murder was Thomas Paine Krome, 35, a newspaper reporter who had been missing and believed dead.*

*Coworkers described Krome as a moody and volatile "loner." One of his former editors said he wasn't "the least bit surprised" by the homicide charge.*

Krome made Shiner put up his hands. JoLayne Lucks instructed him not to move a muscle.

"But I peed on myself," the kid said.

"I expect it'll be the high point of your day."

Shiner blinked wildly.

Krome said, "OK, Goober, where's the Lotto ticket?"

"I d-don't got it." Shiner's eyes jumped from the Remington to the dark crescent radiating across his trousers. "Can I least tuck myself in?"

"No, you cannot," JoLayne said sternly. "I want your little white wacker right where it is, hangin' in the fresh air so we can shoot it off if necessary."

The clerk looked as if he would weep.

"But, JoLayne, I don't got your ticket. I don't know what they done with it, I swear up to God."

JoLayne turned to Tom Krome. "Give me my gun."

"Stay cool."

"Tom, don't be difficult."

With a mix of dread and relief, Krome passed her the shotgun. Immediately Shiner began mewling. He saw that he'd shrunk entirely into his pants. JoLayne Lucks poked the barrel inside his zipper.

"Anybody home?" Her voice was so cheery that it gave Shiner an arctic chill.

"Please don't," he squeaked.

"Then tell me where the ticket is."

Krome tapped the face of his watch. "Hurry up, son." He didn't think JoLayne would shoot the kid point-blank; the two shitkickers, maybe, but not Shiner.

Unless he tried something stupid.

*An unidentified convenience store clerk was shot to death Monday in a bizarre attack on a remote island off the Florida Keys.*

*Police said the victim apparently was ambushed by a disgruntled customer who believed she had been cheated out of a $14 million lottery ticket. Arrested for first-degree murder was JoLayne Lucks, 35, who works at a veterinary clinic in Grange.*

*Neighbors described her as a quiet, gentle person, and expressed shock and disbelief at the homicide charge.*

Krome said to Shiner: "If you're the least bit fond of those testicles, I'd tell the lady what she wants to know."

"But I ain't even seen the damn thing, and that's the God's truth!" Shiner, hissing through his teeth.

JoLayne looked at Tom. "You believe him?"

"I hate to say so, but yeah."

"Well, I'm still not sure."

She took a step back. True to form, Shiner chose the moment to lunge for the Remington. He was surprised that JoLayne released it without a struggle. He was further surprised to find himself unable to hold on to it, as both his thumbs were abruptly dislocated and rendered useless.

While Shiner flopped on the ground like a mullet, JoLayne thanked Tom for teaching her the trick. He calmly grabbed Shiner around the neck and urged him in the strongest terms to suffer in silence, so as not to alert his travel companions.

"Now, where's the videotape?"

"It's hid in my car," Shiner whispered hoarsely, "back at Chub's trailer."

"Chub is the man with the ponytail?"

"And a tire patch on his eye, yessir. Plus a big ole crab on his hand."

Krome let go of Shiner's neck and yanked him upright. "What's his real name?"

"Chub? I never heard him tell." The kid was moist-eyed and panting. When he snuck a peek at his crooked thumbs, he almost passed out.

"What would your momma say about all this? Lord, I can just imagine." JoLayne's tone was scorching. She picked up the shotgun and sat on the sand beside Shiner. He recoiled as if she were a tarantula.

"Why'd you do this?" she asked. "Why'd you help those bastards?"

"I dunno." Shiner turned away and clammed up. It was the same strategy he tried whenever his mother hassled him about skipping his hymns or sneaking beer to his room.

Tom Krome said, "He's hopeless, Jo. Let's go."

"Not yet." Gently she put a fingernail under the young man's chin and turned his head, so their eyes met.

Shiner said, "It's just a club, OK? They asked did I wanna join up and I said sure. A brotherhood is what they tole me. That's all."

"Sure," said Tom. "Like Kiwanis, only for Nazis."

"It ain't what you think. Least it dint start out that way." Shiner, mumbling in a childish tone.

JoLayne's eyes glistened. "You know what your 'brothers' did to me? Want me to show you?"

Wordlessly the skinhead pitched forward and threw up. JoLayne Lucks took this as an unqualified no.

Unlike some women her age, Amber held a realistic view of life, love, men and her prospects. She knew where her good looks could carry her and how far to let things go. She would not fall for the blond modeling routine (drawing the line at calendar tryouts), and she would not dance tables (despite the staggering sums involved). She would remain a waitress at Hooters and finish junior college and get a respectable job as a cosmetologist or perhaps a paralegal. She would stay with jealous Tony until someone better came along, or until she could no longer tolerate his foolishness. She would not become the mistress of any man old enough to be her father, no matter how much money he had or how great a bayfront apartment he offered to rent for her. She would borrow from her parents only in emergencies, and she would pay back every dime as soon as she could. She would keep only one credit card. She would not fake an orgasm two nights in a row. She would stay off cigarets, which had killed her uncle, and avoid Absolut vodka, which caused her to misbehave in public. She would not be automatically impressed by men with black convertibles or foreign-language skills.

Yet even the most centered and well-grounded young woman would have been rightfully terrified to be kidnapped by an armed militia. However, waitressing in ludicrously skimpy shorts had given Amber an unshakable confidence in her ability to handle jerks of all kinds. Of the three rednecks, Shiner was the weak link and consequently the chief target of her attentions. Amber of course had never actually worked in a tattoo parlor and knew nothing about the art, but she'd correctly surmised that young Shiner was so hungry for her touch that he would allow her to poke holes in his flesh with a rusty fishhook.

Early on, she'd sensed that Shiner's heart wasn't in hate crimes and that he'd joined up with Chub and Bodean Gazzer mainly out of small-town boredom and curiosity. After Shiner confided about the stolen Lotto ticket and the $14 million prize, Amber realized his two buddies intended to ditch him at their earliest convenience. Which meant she'd be left alone with the camouflaged colonel and the one-eyed panty-sniffing stoner, both of whom she perceived as more brutish and less malleable than the novice skinhead. Almost certainly they were not averse to the notion of forcible sexual intercourse.

Amber believed that keeping Shiner in the equation would improve her chances of avoiding a rape, and also of escape.

To that end, she'd devised for the young man a strategy of rudimentary blackmail. She was astounded he hadn't thought to demand a cut of the lottery prize – he was like a half-witted busboy, too thick or too shy to ask for his tip-out at the end of the night. The hammer (as Amber patiently explained to Shiner) was the security video from the Grab N'Go.

She had only one misgiving about helping the kid get a piece of the Lotto jackpot: It was somebody else's money. Some black chick, according to Shiner. A girl from his hometown. Amber felt crummy about that, but decided it was premature to get the guilts.

For now the priority was emplacing the blackmail plan. It wasn't a bad one, either, concocted on short notice under adverse conditions, with an accomplice of limited cognitive range. The made-up business about the phone call to Shiner's mother, about her readiness to retrieve the videotape in the event of a double cross – those were nifty touches. The plan's chief flaw, as Amber now realized, was the time line. It gave Bode and Chub almost a whole day's grace, enough of a window to leave the island, destroy the incriminating tape and bolt to Tallahassee to claim the lottery.

Which is what they were preparing to do when she confronted them at the boat after her morning swim.

"Take those ridiculous pants off your face." One hand zipping up the top of the jumpsuit, the other clenching Chub's pistol, which earlier Amber had removed from the *Reel Luv* and concealed in some bushes near the campfire.

"Take 'em off. You look like a pervert." Then shooting once at Chub's feet, just to find out what it felt like; a huge heavy gun going off. And also to make the rednecks understand she was serious and would not negotiate with any grown man wearing shorts over his face.

"Now, what did you guys do with Shiner?"

Nothing, they replied.

"He went off to have a piss," Bodean Gazzer said.

"Well, he's gone."

"Bull," said Chub.

"Let's go find him. Get some clothes on," Amber said.

"Not jest yet." Chub, grinning lopsidedly. "Sure you don't see somethin' you like? Somethin' hot 'n' tasty?"

He waggled his sunburned peter, inspiring Amber to fire once again. This time the Colt nearly jumped out of her hand. The slug passed between Bode and Chub, snapping through the mangroves and splooshing in the water.

As leaves and twigs fluttered into the boat, the demon crab unaccountably dropped off Chub's ripening hand. The animal was long dead, it turned out. Chub jabbed the rancid blue husk with a bare toe and muttered, "Motherfucker."

Bode Gazzer raised his arms for Amber. "OK, sweet thing, quit with the damn gun. You made yer point."

"Tell your friend."

"Don't worry. He's on board."

Chub said, "Like hell. Not till we play some lollipop, her and me."

Bode scowled disgustedly. The man was unbelievable; no sense of priorities. No sense at all.

Amber said, "He's pushing it, Colonel."

"What can I say? Sometimes he's a complete fuckhead."

"Think I should shoot him?"

"I'd rather you didn't."

Chub was studying his infected hand like it was a busted carburetor. "I still got the damn claw, though."

"One thing at a time," Bode Gazzer told him. "Put on your clothes and let's go find the skinhead."

"Not until my darling Amber blows me."

"She's gonna blow you, awright. She's gonna blow your sorry ass to kingdom come."

Chub said, "No, I don't believe so. I believe I'm due for some good luck."

"Hell's *that* mean?"

"It means Amber ain't gone shoot nobody. That's azackly what it means."

He stepped toward her; an exaggerated Hitler-style goose step. Then another. By now she was gripping the pistol with both fists.

"He's asking for it," she warned Bode.

"So I see. My opinion, it's the damn glue."

Chub clucked. "It ain't the glue, Colonel. It's true fucking love."

With a giddy warble he attacked. Amber pulled the trigger but all she heard was a flat harmless click. The gun didn't fire – the cylinder turned, the hammer fell, but no slug came out.

Because there was no bullet in that particular chamber; instead, a small piece of sand-gritted paper, bleached by sweat and saltwater, and folded tightly to fit the small round hole. If she'd been able to remove the paper and examine it, Amber would have seen that it bore six numerals and the likeness of a pink flamingo, official mascot of the Florida lottery.

"I tole you!" Chub crowed.

He was naked on the ground, and waving with his undamaged arm the recaptured Colt Python. Pinned in the sand and seaweed beneath him was Amber, struggling in silence.

"I tole you, yes I did." Chub, broke into coarse, vicious laughter. "I tole you fuckers I was due for some decent luck!"

Bodean Gazzer hadn't had sex in eleven months, his excuse for celibacy being that it was against the Bible to consort with nonwhite women, and all the white women he met demanded too much money. Still, his feverish pent-up desires regarding the fragrant and available Amber were clouded by misgivings.

Her unwillingness to service the White Clarion Aryans was evident from her vigorous resistance to Chub as he ungently disrobed her. And although Bode was intoxicated by the vision of Amber's breasts spilling out of the Mossy Oak camo, he nonetheless was disturbed to be participing in the rape – and that's where this was headed – of a white Christian woman of European descent. In fact, Bode would've been reluctant even if she were a Negro or a Cuban, not so much for the immorality of the crime but for the legal risks. Unlike Chub, Bode Gazzer had spent enough months behind bars to know it wasn't worth knocking off a Burger King or boosting a Cadillac, or even two minutes of humping natural-blond pussy. Rape was felony time, and in

Florida the rape of a white woman – even by a white man – could mean a long stretch in not-so-scenic Starke.

Bode also knew that Chub, in his current frame of mind, was immune to such logic. All Bode could do was hold the Colt revolver and stand there, hoping it wouldn't take long, hoping they wouldn't make much noise. The shiver of arousal sparked by Amber's nudity had already died of distraction at the heaving, pink-butted spectacle of Chub; grimy and grunting and drool-flecked. The arresting sights and smells graphically reminded Bode Gazzer of his partner's many hygienic lapses and killed any spark of temptation to join in the fun.

"Hol' still! Hol' still!" Chub kept huffing.

But the agile Amber would not.

"Hurry up," Bode said, checking over his shoulder. The skinhead Shiner would go ballistic if he saw what was happening.

"I can't get it in! Goddamn, make her hol' still!" Chub used his weight to constrain her. Ribbons of brown turtle grass clung to his thighs.

"Use the damn gun!" he hollered at his partner.

"Shit." Bode knelt and placed the barrel to Amber's head. She stopped squirming. Behind a tangle of yellow-blond hair, her eyes narrowed with acceptance; not coldness and wild anger, like that crazy Negro woman up in Grange.

This is the way it's supposed to be, Bode mused. You see the gun, you quit trying to fight. "Be still now," he said. "It'll be over soon."

"Listen to the man." Chub seized Amber's wrists, pulling them away from her chest. "And do your lips . . .

all pushed out and pouty . . . you know, like how Kim Basinger does."

Amber said, "OK, on one condition. Tell me your name."

"What for!"

"I can't make love to a man," she said, "unless I know his name. I just can't do it, I'd rather die."

Bode Gazzer told Chub: "Don't be a idiot."

Chub, pinning Amber's arms over her head, catching his breath. "Gillespie," he said. "Onus Gillespie."

Bode was relieved – it was such a strange name, he thought his partner had made it up.

Coolly Amber said, "Pleased to meet you, Otis."

"Naw, it's *Onus*. O-n-u-s."

"Oh. Mine's Amber." She blinked innocently. "Amber Bernstein. That's B-e-r-n-s-t-e-i-n."

It was as if Bodean Gazzer had been mule-kicked in the gut.

"Get off!" he shrieked at Chub.

"No sir!"

"But didn't you hear? She's . . . she's a Jew!"

"I don't care if she's Vietcong, I'm gone stick my weenie in."

"No! NO! Get off, and that's an order!"

Chub closed his eyes and tried to block out Bode's carping. *Hilton Head*, he told himself. *You and Blondie are at Hilton Head, doin' it on the beach. Naw, even better – you're doin' it on the balcony of your brand-new condo*!

But Amber's obstinate wriggling was giving him fits; it was like trying to screw an eel. Plus, in his glue-dazed condition, Chub found himself wielding something less than a world-class, diamond-cutter erection.

"No white Christian man" – Bode, somber as a coroner, leaned over them – "no white Christian man shall give his seed to an infidel child of Satan!"

Amber interrupted her evasions to mention that her father was a rabbi. Bode Gazzer emitted a mournful groan. Chub glared up at him. "You worry about your own damn seed. Now back off so's I kin plant mine."

"Negative! As commanding officer of the White Clarion – "

Chub rose to his knees and, with his clawless hand, snatched the pistol from the colonel. He jammed it to Amber's throat and told her to spread her legs.

Bode remembered the Colombian's Beretta in his belt. He considered drawing the gun, not so much for Amber's sake but to reinforce his superior rank. Without a steep improvement in discipline, Bode felt, the fledgling militia would soon go to pieces.

His consternation was heightened by the unexpected arrival of Shiner, the young blackmailer himself, stumbling through the trees. His cheeks were puffy and his pants were soiled and his twisted-looking fists were extended oddly at his sides, like a scarecrow's. Upon seeing Major Chub naked atop Amber, Shiner roared into a headlong assault.

Bodean Gazzer was poised to tackle the hapless skinhead when something exploded from the shoreline behind him. Chub was lifted off Amber as if there were springs in his ass. Then Bode heard a frightfully heavy thump, which he later learned was the butt of a Remington shotgun impacting his own skull.

When he regained consciousness, Bode was aware of being constricted. A white man he didn't know was tying him with a length of anchor rope to a buttonwood stump. Still flat on the ground was Chub, gurgling curses and drenched in his own blood. Shiner sat downcast in the bow of the stolen boat; his melancholy gaze was fixed on the bruised scabby mess of a tattoo. Amber stood back, wrapped in the oilskin tarpaulin. Irritably she plucked leaves and turtle grass from her hair.

All the militia's weapons had been piled on the ground. The captured arsenal was being inspected by a muscular young Negro woman with neon-green nails and a Remington shotgun. Bode Gazzer recognized her immediately.

"Not you!" was all he could say.

"That's right, bubba. Say hi to the Black Tide."

The sky and earth and universe began to spin madly for Bode Gazzer, as his fate appeared to him with sickening lucidity. The white man finished with the knots and stepped away from the tree. The Negro woman came forward, carrying the gun so casually as to cause a spasm in Bode's fragile sphincter.

"What do you want?" he asked.

JoLayne Lucks slipped the shotgun between his lips.

"Let's start with your wallet," she said.

# TWENTY-FIVE

**The case of** *LaGort* v. *Save King Enterprises, Allied-Cagle Casualty, et al.* was settled in a courthouse hallway after a pretrial conference lasting less than two hours. The attorneys for the supermarket's insurance carrier, having detected in Judge Arthur Battenkill Jr. a frosty and inexplicable bias, chose to pay Emil LaGort the annoying but not unpalatable sum of $500,000. The purpose was to avoid a trial in which the defense clearly would get no help from the judge, who'd already vowed to prohibit any testimony attacking the past honesty of the plaintiff, including but not limited to his very long list of other negligence suits. Emil LaGort attended the conference in a noisy motorized wheelchair with maroon mica-fleck armrests, and wore around his neck a two-tone foam cervical brace. The brace was one of nine models available in Emil LaGort's walk-in closet, where he saved all medical aids acquired during the phony recoveries from his many staged accidents.

After the settlement papers were signed and the sourpuss insurance lawyers filed into the elevator and Emil LaGort rolled himself across James Street to a topless luncheonette, his lawyer discreetly obtained from Judge Arthur Battenkill Jr. the number of a newly opened

Nassau bank account, into which $250,000 would be wired secretly within four weeks.

Not exactly a king's ransom, Arthur Battenkill knew, but enough for a fast start on a new life.

The judge's wife, however, wasn't packing for the tropics. While Arthur Battenkill was tidying up the details of the Save King payoff, Katie was on her knees in church. She was praying for divine guidance, or at least improved clarity of thought. That morning she'd read in *The Register* that Tom Krome's estranged wife had come to town to receive a journalism award on her "late" husband's behalf. Regardless of Tommy's ill feelings toward the elusive Mary Andrea Finley, it seemed possible to Katie Battenkill that the woman might be mourning an imagined loss; that she still might love Tom Krome in some significant way.

Shouldn't somebody tell her he's not really dead? If it were me, Katie thought, I'd sure want to know.

But Katie had assured Tommy she wouldn't say a word. Breaking her promise would be a lie, and lying was a sin, and Katie was trying to give up sinning. On the other hand, she couldn't bear the thought of Mrs. Krome (whatever her faults) needlessly suffering even a sliver of widow's pain.

Knowing Tom was alive became a leaden weight upon Katie's overtaxed conscience. There was a second secret, too; equally troubling. She was reminded of it by another item in *The Register*, which reported that the human remains believed to be those of Tom Krome were being shipped to an FBI laboratory "for more sophisticated analysis." This meant DNA tests, which meant it wouldn't be long before the dead man was correctly identified as Champ Powell, law clerk to Circuit Judge Arthur Battenkill Jr.

The devious shitheel with whom Katie was about to flee the country forever.

"What do I do?" she whispered urgently. Head bowed, she knelt alone in the first pew. She prayed and waited, then prayed some more.

God's answer, when it eventually came, was typically strong on instruction but weak on details. Katie Battenkill didn't push it; she was grateful for anything.

As she walked out of church, she removed her diamond solitaire and deposited it in the slot of the oak collection box, where it landed with no more fanfare than a nickel. Lightning didn't flash, thunder didn't clap. No angels sang from the rafters.

Maybe that'll come later, Katie thought.

After the last of the pilgrims were gone, Shiner's mother approached the besheeted Sinclair, who was sloshing playfully with the cooters in the moat. She said, "Help me, turtle boy. I need a spiritual rudder."

Sinclair's unshaven chin tilted toward the heavens: "*Kiiikkkeeeaay ka-kooo kattttkin.*"

His visitor failed to decipher the outcry (KICKING BACK WITH ULTRA-COOL KATHLEEN – from a feature profile of the actress Kathleen Turner).

"How 'bout giving that a shot in English?" Shiner's mother grumped.

Sinclair beckoned her into the moat. She kicked off her scuffed bridal heels and stepped in. Sinclair motioned her to sit. With cupped hands he gathered several baby turtles and placed them on the billowing white folds of her gown.

Shiner's mother picked one up to examine it. "You paint these suckers yourself?"

Sinclair laughed patiently. "They're not painted. That's the Lord's imprint."

"No joke? Is this little guy 'posed to be Luke or Matthew or who?"

"Lay back with me."

"They paved my Jesus this morning, did you hear? The road department did."

"Lay back," Sinclair told her.

He sloshed closer, taking her shoulders and lowering her baptismally. Shiner's mother closed her eyes and felt the coolness of the funky water on her neck, the tickle of tiny cooter claws across her skin.

"They won't bite?"

"Nope," said Sinclair, supporting her.

Soon Shiner's mother was enfolded by a preternatural sense of inner peace and trust, and possibly something more. The last man who'd touched her so sensitively was her periodontist, for whom she'd fallen head over heels.

"Oh, turtle boy, I lost my son and my shrine. I don't know what to do."

"*Kiiikkkeeeaay ka-kooo*," Sinclair murmured.

"OK," said Shiner's mother. "*Kiki-kakeee-kooo*. Is that the Bible in, like, Japanese?"

Unseen by the meditators in the moat was Demencio, who stood with knuckles on hips at a window. To Trish he said: "You believe this shit – she's in with the turtles!"

"Honey, she's had a rough day. The D.O.T. paved her road stain."

"I want her off my property."

"Oh, what's the harm? It's almost dark."

Trish was in the kitchen, roasting a chicken for supper. Demencio had been mixing a batch of perfumed water, refilling the tear well in the weeping Madonna.

"If that crazy broad's not gone after dinner," he said, "you go chase her off. And be sure and count them cooters, make sure she don't swipe any."

Trish said, "Have a heart."

"I don't trust that woman."

"You don't trust anybody."

"I can't help it. It's the nature of the business," said Demencio. "We got any red food coloring?"

"For what?"

"I was thinking . . . what if she started crying blood? The Virgin Mary."

"Perfumed blood?" said his wife.

"Don't gimme that face. It's just an idea is all," Demencio said, "just an idea I'm playing with. For when we don't have the turtles no more."

"Let me check." Trish, bustling toward the spice cabinet.

Under less stressful circumstances Bernard Squires might have enjoyed the farmhouse quaintness of Mrs. Hendricks' bed-and-breakfast, but even the caress of a handmade quilt could not dissolve his anxiety. So he took an evening walk – alone, in his sleek pin-striped suit – through the little town of Grange.

Bernard Squires had spent a tense chunk of the afternoon on the telephone with associates of Richard "The Icepick" Tarbone and, briefly, with Mr. Tarbone himself. Squires considered himself a clear-spoken person, but he'd had great difficulty making The Icepick understand why Simmons Wood couldn't be purchased until the competing offer was submitted and rejected.

"And it *will* be rejected," Bernard Squires had said, "because we're going to outbid the bastards."

But Mr. Tarbone had become angrier than Squires had ever heard him, and made it plain that closing the deal was requisite not only for Squires' future employment but for his continued good health. Squires had assured the old man that the delay was temporary and that by week's end Simmons Wood would be secured for the Central Midwest Brotherhood of Grouters, Spacklers and Drywallers International. Squires was instructed not to return to Chicago without a signed contract.

As he strolled in the cool breezy dusk, Bernard Squires tried to guess why the Tarbones were so hot to get the land. The likeliest explanation was a dire shortfall of untraceable cash, necessitating another elaborately disguised raid on the union pension fund. Perhaps the family intended to use the Simmons Wood property as collateral on a construction loan and wanted to lock in before interest rates shot up.

Or perhaps they really *did* mean to build a Mediterranean-style shopping mall in Grange, Florida. As laughable as that was, Bernard Squires couldn't eliminate the possibility. Maybe The Icepick had tired of the mob life. Maybe he was trying to go legit.

In any case, it truly didn't matter why Richard Tarbone was in such a hurry. What mattered was that Bernard Squires acquire the forty-four acres as soon as possible. In tight negotiations Squires was unaccustomed to losing and had at his disposal numerous extralegal methods of persuasion. If there were (as Clara Markham asserted) rival buyers for Simmons Wood, Squires felt certain he could outspend them, outflank them, or simply intimidate them into withdrawing.

Squires was so confident that he probably would've drifted contentedly into a long afternoon nap, had old man Tarbone not uttered what sounded over the phone like a serious threat:

"You get this done, goddammit! You don't wanna end up like Millstep, you'll fucking get this done."

At the mention of Jimmy Millstep, Bernard Squires had felt his silk undershirt dampen. Millstep had been a lawyer for the Tarbone family until the Friday he showed up twenty minutes late at a bond hearing for Richard Tarbone's homophobic nephew Gene, who consequently had to spend an entire weekend in a ten-by-ten cell with a well-behaved but flamboyant he-she. Attorney Millstep blamed a needful mistress and an inept cabbie for his tardiness to court, but he got no sympathy from Richard Tarbone, who not only fired him but ordered him murdered. A week later, Jimmy Millstep's bullet-riddled body was dumped at the office of the Illinois Bar Association. A note pinned to his lapel said: "Is this one of yours?"

So it was no wonder Bernard Squires was jumpy, a condition exacerbated by the abrupt appearance of a rumpled stranger with bloody punctures in the palms of his hands.

"Halt, sinner!" said the man, advancing with a limp. Bernard Squires warily sidestepped him.

"Halt, pilgrim," the man implored, waving a sheaf of rose-colored advertising flyers.

Squires snatched one and backed out of reach. The stranger muttered a blessing as he shuffled off into the twilight. Squires stopped beneath a streetlamp to look at the paper:

ASTOUNDING STIGMATA OF CHRIST!!!!
Come see amazing Dominick Amador,
the humbel carpenter who woke up one day
with the exactly identical crucifiction wounds of
Jesus Christ himself, Son of God!
Bleeding 9 a.m. to 4 p.m. daily.
Saturdays Noon to 3 p.m. (Palms only).
Visitations open to the publix. Offerings welcomed!
4834 Haydon Burns Lane
(Look for The Cross in the front yard!)

And in small print at the bottom of the paper:

As feachered on Rev. Pat Robertson's
"Heavenly Signs" TV show!!!

Bernard Squires crumpled the flyer and tossed it. Sickos, he thought, no matter where you go on this planet. Sickos who never learned to spell. Squires stopped at the Grab N'Go, where his request for a *New York Times* drew the blankest of stares. He settled for a *USA Today* and a cup of decaf, and headed back toward the b-and-b. Somewhere he made a wrong turn and found himself on a street he didn't recognize – the chanting tipped him off.

Squires heard it from a block away: a man and a woman, vocalizing disharmoniously in some exotic tongue. The tremulous sounds drew Squires to a floodlit house. It was a plain, one-story concrete-and-stucco, typical of Florida tract developments in the 1960s and

'70s. Squires stood out of sight, behind an old oak, watching.

Three figures were visible – four, counting a statue of the Virgin Mary, which a dark-haired man in coveralls was positioning and repositioning on a small illuminated platform. Two other persons – the chanters, it turned out – sat with legs outstretched in a curved trench that had been dug in the lawn and filled with water. The man in the trench was cloaked in dingy bed linens, while the woman wore a formal white gown with lacy pointed shoulders. The pair was of indeterminate age, though both had pale skin and wet hair. Bernard Squires noticed V-shaped wakes pushing here and there in the water; animals of some kind, swimming . . .

Turtles?

Squires edged closer. Soon he realized he was witness to an eccentric religious rite. The couple in the trench continued to join arms and spout gibberish while scores of grape-sized reptile heads bobbed around them. (Squires recalled a cable-television documentary about a snake-handling cult in Kentucky – perhaps this was a breakaway sect of turtle worshipers!) Interestingly, the dark-haired man in coveralls took no part in the moat-wallowing ceremony. Rather, he intermittently turned from the Madonna statue to gaze upon the two chanters with what appeared to Bernard Squires as unmasked disapproval.

"*Kiiikkeeeaay ka-kooo katttkin!*" the couple bayed, sending such an icy jet down Squires' spine that he crossed the street and hurried away. He was not a devout man and certainly didn't believe in omens, but he was profoundly unsettled by the turtle handlers and the stranger with blood on his palms. Grange, which initially had impressed Squires as a prototypical tourist-grubbing southern truck stop, now seemed murky and mysterious. Weird vapors tainted the parochial climate of sturdy marriages, conservatively traditional faiths and blind veneration of progress – *any* progress – that allowed slick characters such as Bernard Squires to swoop in and have their way. He returned straightaway to the bed-and-breakfast, bid an early good night to Mrs. Hendricks (taking a pass on her pork roast, squash, snap beans and pecan pie), bolted the door to his room (quietly, so as not to offend his hostess), and slipped beneath the quilt to nurse a hollow, helpless, irrational feeling that Simmons Wood was lost.

The *Reel Luv* smelled of urine, salt and crab parts. How could it not?

Shiner slouched over the wheel. They were cruising at half-speed to conserve gas. Bode Gazzer's marine chart was unrolled across Amber's lap. The route to Jewfish Creek had been marked for them in ballpoint pen by the helpful Black Tide lady.

Florida Bay had a brisk chop; no rollers to make the travelers queasy. Still, Shiner's cheeks took on a greenish tinge, and there were dark circles under his eyes.

"You all right?" Amber asked.

He nodded unconvincingly. The pudge on his arms and belly jiggled with each bump. He steered gingerly; the Black Tide lady had popped his dislocated thumbs back into the sockets, but they remained painfully swollen.

"Stop the boat," Amber told him.

"I'm OK."

"Stop it. Right now." She reached across the console and levered back the throttle. Shiner didn't argue because she had the gun; Chub's Colt Python. The tip of the barrel peeked from beneath the chart.

As soon as the boat stopped moving, Shiner leaned over the side and puked up six of the eight Vienna sausages he'd wolfed down for breakfast on Pearl Key.

"I'm sorry." He wiped his mouth. "Usually I don't get seasick. Honest."

Amber said, "Maybe you're not seasick. Maybe you're just scared."

"I ain't scared!"

"Then you're a damn fool."

"Scared a what?"

"Of getting busted in a stolen boat," she said. "Or getting the shit beat out of you by my crazy jealous boyfriend back in Miami. Or maybe you're just scared of the cops."

Shiner said, "What cops?"

"The cops I ought to call the second we see a phone. To say I was kidnapped by you and nearly raped by your redneck pals."

"Oh God." Noisily Shiner launched the remainder of breakfast.

Afterwards he restarted the engines and off they went, the hull of the *Reel Luv* pounding like a tom-tom. Amber was still trying to sort out what had happened on the island. Shiner hadn't been much help; the more earnestly he'd tried to explain it, the nuttier it sounded.

This much she knew: The woman with the shotgun was the one the rednecks had robbed of the lottery ticket.

"How'd she find you guys all the way out here?" Amber had wondered, to which Shiner had proposed a fantastically muddled scenario involving liberals, Cubans, Democrats, commies, armed black militants, helicopters with infrared night scopes, and battalions of foreign-speaking soldiers hiding in the Bahamas. Wisely Shiner had refrained from tossing in the Jews, although he couldn't stop himself from asking Amber (in a whisper) if her last name was actually Bernstein, as Chub had raged.

"Or d'you make that up?"

"What's the difference?" she'd said.

"I don't know. None, I guess."

"You'd still marry me, wouldn't you? In about ten seconds flat." Amber winking at her joke, which had caused Shiner to redden and turn away.

That was after Chub had been shot and the colonel had been knocked out and Amber had fixed herself up and put on some clean clothes. Then the black woman and the white guy had collected the militia's guns – the AR-15, the TEC-9, the Cobray, the Beretta, even Shiner's puny Marlin .22 – and heaved them one after another into the bay. The only thing that didn't get tossed was a can of pepper spray, which the black woman placed in her handbag.

Afterwards she'd told Shiner and Amber to take the stolen boat back to the mainland. The black woman (JoLayne was her name) had marked the way on the chart and had even given them bottled water and cold drinks for the journey. Then the white guy had pulled Shiner aside, into the woods, and when they'd returned Shiner was ashen. The white guy had handed Chub's Colt Python to Amber with instructions to "shoot the little creep if he tries anything funny."

Amber didn't have much faith in the big revolver since

it had misfired once already, but she didn't mention that to Shiner. Besides, he looked too sick and dejected for mischief.

Which he was. The white guy, JoLayne's friend, hadn't laid a hand on him in the mangroves. Instead he'd looked the kid square in the eyes and said, "Son, if Amber doesn't get home safe and sound, I'm going straight to your momma in Grange and tell her everything you've done. And then I'm going to put your name and ugly skinheaded picture on the front page of the newspaper, and you're going to be famous in the worst possible way."

And then he'd calmly escorted Shiner back to the shore and helped him into the boat. JoLayne Lucks had been waiting with the shotgun, watching over Bodean Gazzer and Chub. The white guy had waded in, shoving the stern into deeper water so Shiner and Amber could lower the outboards without snagging bottom.

"Have a safe trip," the black woman had sung out. "Watch out for manatees!"

An hour later Shiner finally heard what he'd been dreading – a helicopter. But it was blaze orange, not black. And it wasn't NATO but the U.S. Coast Guard, thwock-thwocking back and forth in search of a woman overdue in a small rental boat; a woman who'd said she was going no farther than Cotton Key.

Shiner had no way of knowing this. He was convinced the chopper had been sent to strafe him. He dove to the deck, yanking Amber with him.

"Look out! Look out!" he hollered.

"Would you please get a grip."

"But it's them!"

The helicopter dipped low over the boat. The crew

spotted the couple entwined on the deck and, accustomed to such amorous sightings, flew on. Clearly it wasn't the vessel they'd been sent to find.

Once the chopper disappeared, Shiner sheepishly collected himself. Amber shoved the chart under his chin and told him to quit behaving like a wimp. An hour later, the Jewfish Creek drawbridge came into view. They nosed the *Reel Luv* into the slip farthest from the dockmaster (its owner would be puzzled but pleased to find it there, and the theft would be ascribed to joyriding teenagers). Mindful of his throbbing thumbs, Shiner struggled to tie off the bow rope. Amber scouted for the marine patrol, just in case. She was relieved to spot her car, undisturbed in the parking lot.

Shiner gave a glum wave and said, "See ya."

"Where you going?"

"To the highway. Try and hitch a ride."

Amber said, "I'll drop you in Homestead."

"Naw, that's OK." He was worried about her boyfriend, jealous Tony. Maybe she was setting him up for an ass-whupping.

"Suit yourself," she said.

Shiner thought: God, she's so pretty. To hell with it. He said, "Maybe I will bum along."

"That's a good way to describe it. You drive."

They were halfway up Highway One to Florida City when Amber took Chub's pistol out again, leading Shiner to believe he'd misjudged her intentions.

"You're gone kill me, ain't you?"

"Oh right," Amber said. "I'm going to shoot you in broad daylight in all this traffic, when I had all morning to blow your head off in the middle of nowhere and dump your body in the drink. That's what a dumb bimbo I am. Just drive, OK?"

The way Shiner was feeling, a hot slug in the belly couldn't have hurt much worse than her sarcasm. He clamped his eyes on the road and tried to cook up a story for his ma when he got back to Grange. The next time he glanced over at Amber, she'd gotten the Colt open. She was spinning the cylinder and peering, with one eye, into the chambers.

"Hey," she said.

"What's that?"

"Stop the car."

"OK, sure," said Shiner. Carefully he guided the gargantuan Ford to the grassy shoulder, scattering a flock of egrets.

The gun lay open on Amber's lap. She was unfolding a small piece of paper that had fallen from one of the bullet chambers.

Shiner said, "Lemme see."

"Just listen: Twenty-four . . . nineteen . . . twenty-seven . . . twenty-two . . . thirty . . . seventeen."

Shiner said, "God, don't tell me it's the damn Lotto!"

"Yup. Your dumb shitkicker buddies hid it inside the gun."

"Oh man. Oh man. But – d-damn, what do we do now?"

Amber snapped the revolver shut and slipped the lottery coupon in a zippered pocket of her jumpsuit.

"You want me to keep drivin'?" Shiner asked.

"I think so, yes."

They didn't speak again until Florida City, where they stopped at a McDonald's drive-thru. They were fifth in the line of cars.

Amber said, "We've got a decision to make, don't we?"

"I always get the Quarter Pounder."

"I'm talking about the Lotto ticket."

"Oh," said Shiner.

"Fourteen million dollars."

"God, I know."

"Sometimes there's a difference," Amber said, "between what's right and what's common sense."

"Good."

"All I'm saying is, we need to think this out from all angles. It's a big decision. Order me a salad, would you? And a Diet Coke."

Shiner said, "You wanna split some fries?"

"Sure."

Later, sitting at the traffic light near the turnpike ramp, Shiner heard Amber say: "What do you think they did to your buddies? Back on the island, I mean. What do you think happened after we left?"

Shiner said, "I don't know, but I can guess." Sadly he examined the mutilated militia tattoo on his arms.

"Light's green," Amber said. "We can go."

# TWENTY-SIX

**Bodean Gazzer watched** the Negro woman pick through his wallet until she found the condom packet. How could she have possibly known?

Another mystery, Bode thought despondently. Another mystery that won't matter in the end.

As nonchalant as a nurse, the woman unrolled the rubber and plucked out the lottery ticket, which she placed in a pocket of her jeans.

"That ain't yours," Bode Gazzer blurted.

"Pardon?" The Negro woman wore a half smile. "What'd you say, bubba?"

"That one ain't yours."

"Really? Whose might it be?"

"Never mind." Bode didn't like the way her eyes kept cutting to the shotgun, which she'd handed to the white guy while she searched the wallet.

"Funny," she said. "I checked the numbers on that ticket. And they were *my* numbers."

"I said never mind."

Chub began to moan and writhe. The white guy said, "He's losing lots of blood."

"Yes, he is," said the Negro woman.

Bode asked, "Is he gone die?"

"He most certainly could."

The white guy said to the woman: "It's your call."

"I suppose so."

She walked briefly out of Bode's view. She reappeared carrying a flat white box with a small red cross painted on the lid. She knelt beside Chub and opened it.

Bode heard her saying: "I wish I could stand here and let you die, but I can't. My whole life, I've never been able to watch a living thing die. Not even a cockroach. Not even a despicable damn sonofabitch like you . . ."

The words lifted Bode's hopes for reprieve. Covertly he began rubbing his wrists back and forth, to loosen the rope that held him to the tree.

The shotgun blast had excavated from Chub's left shoulder a baseball-sized chunk of flesh, muscle and bone. He was not fortunate enough to pass out immediately from pain. The woman's touch ignited splutter and profanity.

Firmly she told him to be still.

"Get away from me, nigger! Get the hell away!" Chub, wild-eyed and hoarse.

"You heard the man." It was the white guy, holding the Remington. "He wants to bleed out. You heard him, JoLayne."

Another agitated voice. Sounded like Bode Gazzer. "For God's sake, Chub, shut up! She's only trying to save your life, you stupid fuck!"

Yep. Definitely the colonel.

Chub shook himself like a dog, spitting blood and sandy grit. The bicycle patch had peeled, so now he had two open eyes with which to keep a bead on the nigger girl; more like one and a half, since the unhealed lid drooped like a ripped curtain.

"What're you gone do to me, if I might ast?"

"Try to clean this messy gunshot and stop your bleeding."

"How come?"

"Good question," the woman said.

Craning his head, Chub saw it was attached to a striped, sand-caked body that could not possibly be his. The cock, for example, was puckered to the size of a raspberry; definitely not a millionaire's cock.

Had to be a nightmare is all, a freak-out from the boat glue. That must be how come the nigger girl looks 'zackly like the one they'd robbed upstate, the one clawed the shit outta us with those hellacious electric-looking fingernails.

"You ain't no doctor," Chub said to her.

"No, but I work in a doctor's office. An animal doctor – "

"Jesus Willy Christ!"

" – and you're about the dumbest, smelliest critter I ever saw," the woman said matter-of-factly.

Chub was too weak to hit her. He wasn't even a hundred percent sure he'd heard it right. Delirium slurred his senses.

"Whatcha gone do with all that lottery money, nigger?"

"Well, I thought I'd buy me a Cadillac or two," JoLayne said, "and a giant-screen color TV."

"Don't you talk down to me."

"And maybe a watermelon patch!"

"You gone kill me, girl?" Chub asked.

"Well, it's tempting."

"Why can't you jes answer me straight?"

The white guy's face appeared over the woman's shoulder. He whistled and said, "Hey, sport, what happened to your eye?"

Chub exerted himself to make a sneer. "You muss be some kind a nigger-lover."

"Just a beginner," the white man said.

The last thing Chub heard before blacking out was Bodean Gazzer bellowing: "Hey, I changed my mind! You kin let him die! Go 'head and let the asshole die!"

JoLayne Lucks couldn't do it.

Couldn't, although the stench of the robber had brought everything rushing back, the bile to her throat and the stinging to her eyes. All that had happened that night inside her own house – the horrible words they'd used, the casual way they'd punched her, the places on her body where they'd put their hands.

She still could taste the barrel of the man's revolver, oily and cool on her tongue, yet she couldn't let him die.

Even though he deserved it.

JoLayne willed herself to think of Chub as an animal – a sick confused animal, not unlike the raccoon she'd patched up the night before. It was the only way she could suppress her rage and concentrate on the seeping crater in the man's shoulder; cleaning the wound as best she could, squeezing out the whole tube of antibiotic and dressing the pulp with wads of thin gauze.

The bastard finally passed out, which made it easier. Not having to listen to him call her nigger: that sure helped.

At one point, maneuvering to get the tape on, JoLayne

wound up with his head in her lap. Instead of feeling repulsed, she was overwhelmed by an anthropological curiosity. Studying Chub's slack unconscious face, she searched for clues to the toxic wellspring. Was the hatred discernible in his deep-set eyes? The angry-looking creases in his sunburned brow? The dull unhappy set of his stubbled jaw? If there was a telltale mark, a unique congenital feature identifying the man as a cruel sociopath, JoLayne Lucks couldn't find it. His face was no different from that of a thousand other white guys she'd seen, playing out hard fumbling lives. Not all of them were impossible racists.

"Are you all right?" Tom Krome, stooping beside her.

"Fine. Brings back memories of my trauma-unit days."

"How's Gomer?"

"Bleeding's stopped for now. That's about all I can do."

"You want to talk with the other one?"

"Most definitely," JoLayne said.

As Krome approached the buttonwood stump, he sensed something was different. He should've stopped right away to figure it out, but he didn't. Instead he picked up the pace, hurrying toward Bodean Gazzer.

By the time Krome saw the limp rope and noticed the prisoner's legs were tucked under his butt – boot heels braced against the tree trunk – it was too late. With a martial cry the stubby thief vaulted from the ground, spearing Krome in the chest. He toppled backward, sucking air yet clinging madly with both fists to the shotgun. From a bed of damp sand he raised his head to see Bode Gazzer running away, into the mangroves.

Running toward the other end of Pearl Key, where Tom and JoLayne had hidden the other boat.

Which was, now, the only transportation off the island.

Krome hadn't slugged anybody for years. The last time it happened was in the Meadowlands stadium, where he and Mary Andrea were watching the Giants play the Cowboys. The temperature was thirty-eight degrees and the New Jersey sky looked like churned mud. Sitting directly behind Tom Krome and his wife were two enormous noisy men from somewhere in Queens. Longshoremen, Mary Andrea speculated with a scowl, although they would later be revealed as commodities brokers. The men were alternating vodka screwdrivers and beer, and had celebrated a Giants field goal by shedding their coats and jerseys and pinching each other's bare nipples until their eyes watered. By the second quarter Krome was scouting the stands for other seats, while Mary Andrea was packing to go home. One of the New Yorkers produced a pneumatic boat horn, which he deployed in sustained bursts six to ten inches from the base of Krome's skull. Irately Mary Andrea wheeled and snapped at the two men, impelling one of them – he sported a beer-flecked walrus mustache, Krome recalled – to comment loudly upon the modest dimensions of Mary Andrea's breasts, a subject about which she was known to be sensitive.

The colloquy quickly degenerated (despite the distraction of a blocked Dallas punt) until one of the men aimed the boat horn at Mary Andrea's flawless nose and let 'er rip. Krome saw no other option but to punch the fat fuck until he fell down. His bosom buddy of course took a wide sloppy swing at Krome's noggin, but Tom had plenty of time to duck (Mary Andrea was way ahead of him) and unleash a solid uppercut to the scrotal region. The decking of the rude men drew flurries of cheers, the other football fans mistaking Krome's outburst for an act of husbandly chivalry. In truth it was pure selfish anger, as Krome demonstrated by grabbing the boat horn, placing it flush against the right ear of fallen Walrus Face, and blasting away until the canister emptied, its plangent blare ebbing with a sequence of comical burps.

Cops arrived, jotted names, arrested no one. Krome himself fractured two knuckles in the fight but had no regrets. Mary Andrea scolded him for flying off the handle, but phoned every one of her friends to brag on him. A month later the Kromes heard from an attorney representing one of the commodities brokers, who claimed to be suffering from chronic headaches, deafness and myriad psychological problems resulting from the beating. A companion lawsuit was being hatched by the other fan, who was said to be in need of delicate surgery for cosmetic repair of a displaced left testicle. Tom Krome's own lawyer strongly advised him to avoid a trial, which he did by agreeing to purchase Giants season tickets for each of the aggrieved brokers and also providing (thanks to the connections of a sportswriter pal) official-looking NFL footballs personally autographed by Lawrence Taylor.

Krome anticipated no such nuisance suits from Bodean Gazzer and would take all steps necessary to prevent the robber from escaping Pearl Key and stranding Tom and JoLayne without a boat. To prevent shooting off his own toes, Krome prudently set down the shotgun before he started running. The redneck had a fifty-yard head start but he wasn't hard to track, crashing through branches like a crazed rhinoceros. Any concealment provided by Gazzer's camouflage outfit was offset by his unstealthiness. The longer-legged Krome was able to gain ground and at no time mistook the fleeing felon for a mangrove tree.

He overtook Gazzer in a clearing and tackled him. The redneck extracted one chunky leg and slammed his boot smartly into Tom Krome's cheekbone. Quickly Gazzer was up and running again. He got to the Boston Whaler, which he was laboring to drag into the water when Krome again overtook him. They went down in a splash, the camouflaged man windmilling his arms.

Krome felt a lifetime of emotional detachment dissolve in a stream of bubbles and galvanizing, uncontrollable fury. It was the first purely murderous impulse of his life, and for a split second it gave a perverse clarity to all the murderous acts he'd written about for newspapers. Krome understood that he ought to be terrified, but he felt only a primitive rage. He wrapped Bodean Gazzer in a brutal headlock and held him underwater with the gravest intention. When a wildly flung elbow struck Krome in the throat, he realized that he was (at age thirty-five) engaged in his first life-or-death struggle.

He would have preferred it more neatly choreographed, like the altercation at Giants Stadium, but that was unusual. In his work Krome had attended enough crime scenes to know that violence was seldom cinematic. Usually it was clumsy, careless, chaotic: a damn mess.

Exactly like this, he thought. If I can't get my head up even for half a second, I'm probably going to drown.

In four lousy feet of water, I'm going to drown.

They'd stirred up so much marl that Krome couldn't see anything but a greenish haze in suspension. He released his hold on Gazzer's neck but they remained tangled – he and the crook, no longer fighting each other but flailing for air.

As the mortal darkening began, words came unspooled in Tom Krome's brain.

REPORTER FOUND DEAD . . .

REPORTER BELIEVED DEAD FOUND DEAD . . .

REPORTER BELIEVED DEAD FOUND DEAD ON MYSTERY ISLAND . . .

Krome thinking: Headlines!

He pictured them vividly as they would appear in the paper, below the fold of the front page. He beheld a vision of scissors flashing, the article about his drowning meticulously being clipped by a faceless someone – his father, Katie, JoLayne or even Mary Andrea (strictly for insurance purposes).

Tom Krome envisioned the span of his life condensed to one shitty, potentially ungrammatical newspaper caption. The prospect was more depressing than death itself.

With a last measure of strength, he pulled away from Bodean Gazzer and thrashed to the surface. Wheezing and half choked, Krome now saw that the darkness was spreading not in his mind but in the water; a deep reddish cloud, lustrous and undulant around his legs.

Blood.

Krome thinking: God, don't let it be mine.

*

One moment Bode Gazzer had the boat, the next he was being heaved in the drink. He'd been outrun, naturally; the curse of short legs and tar-gummed lungs. Thank you, Mom and Dad. Thank you, Philip Morris.

Who else could he blame?

Chub, for being stoned, blind-horny and incompetent.

The government, for allowing Negro terrorists to purchase Lotto tickets.

And his own bad fortune, for unknowingly robbing and assaulting a card-carrying member of the feared Black Tide, whatever the hell that was; a woman who obviously used her NATO cohorts to track the White Clarion Aryans to the remotest of islands so she could pick off his troops one by one, like baby harp seals.

Not me, Bode vowed, submerging in the grasp of the Negro woman's white accomplice. Nosir, you ain't leavin' me out here to starve with that sorry-ass Chub.

Major, my ass. Major fuckup is more like it.

Bode battled with no style but loads of determination. The heavy shitkicker boots were an encumbrance, filling rapidly with saltwater – he might as well have strapped cinder blocks to his feet. Nor was the sodden camo suit an ideal choice for swimwear, but Bode coped as well as he could. Having been choked two or three times before, in prison fights, he recognized the onset of oxygen deprivation.

The white guy was stronger than Bode Gazzer expected, so Bode undertook a strategy of mad pawing and thrashing. The effect was to muddy the bay bottom so thoroughly that Bode initially failed to see the stingray lying there, as flat as a cocktail tray.

Like most criminals who relocate to South Florida,

Bodean Gazzer had spent little time familiarizing himself with the native fauna. He was keenly aware that lobsters had a weakness for lobster traps, but otherwise his knowledge of marine wildlife was sketchy. A minimal amount of scholarship – say, a visit to the Seaquarium – would have provided two lifesaving facts about the common southern stingray.

One: It doesn't actually sting. The detachable barb on the end of its tail, although coated with an infectious mucus, is used defensively as a lance.

Two: Should one encounter a ray dozing in the shallows, the worst possible thing to do is kick it.

Which is what Bodean Gazzer (mistaking it for an extremely large flounder) did. The agony he experienced was the result of the stingray barb penetrating deep flesh. The blood he saw in the water jetted from his own femoral artery.

Once Bode poked up for air, he saw the white guy wading doggedly in pursuit of the boat, which was drifting away. Bode aimed himself toward dry land but discovered he couldn't stand upright, much less walk. A chill shook him to the marrow, and suddenly he felt woozy.

What now? he thought. Then he keeled sideways.

"Wake up," JoLayne said to the moaning redneck.

"It might be too late," Tom Krome told her.

"No, it's not."

Bodean Gazzer cracked his eyelids. "Get the fuck away."

"Told you," JoLayne said.

"Get away!"

"No, I've got a question. And I'd like an honest answer, Mr. Gazzer, before you die: Why'd you pick me? Of all people, why me? Because I'm black, or because I'm a woman – "

Tom said, "He's out of it."

"Hell I am," the redneck murmured.

"Then please answer me," JoLayne said.

"It wasn't none a them reasons. We picked you on account a you won the damn Lotto. It just worked out you was a Negro – hell, we didn't know." Bode Gazzer chuckled weakly. "It just worked out that way."

"But it made it easier, didn't it? That I was black."

"We believe in the s-s-supremacy of the white race. If that's what you mean. We believe the Bible preaches genetic p-p-purity."

They'd hauled him up on shore and peeled off his hunting camos. Once they saw the gushing leg wound, they knew it was over.

The redneck said, "You tell me I'm dyin' – I look dumb enough to fall for that?" His eyelids closed. JoLayne cupped his cheeks and urged him to stay awake.

"Please," she said, "I'm trying to understand the nature of your hatefulness. Let's sort this out."

"Oh, I got it. You ain't gonna shoot me, you're gonna talk me to death."

"What did I ever do to you?" she demanded. "What did any black person ever do to you?"

Bodean Gazzer grunted. "Prison once, there was a Negro stole the magazines out from under my whatchacallit. My bunk. Plus some NRA decals."

Tom said, "He's going into shock."

JoLayne nodded disappointedly. "I wish I understood

– there was no cause for all this. Man doesn't even know me, comes to my house and does what he did – "

" 'Nother time they got my car stereo." Bode's voice trailed. "Happened in Tampa, either them or Cubans for sure . . ."

Tom said, "It won't be long, Jo. Let's go."

She stood up. "Lord have mercy," she said to the dying man. "There's nothing I can do for you."

"No shit." The redneck tittered. "Nothin' anybody can do. I'm on God's shit list, that's the story my whole damn life. Numero uno on God's shit list."

"Goodbye, Mr. Gazzer."

"You ain't gonna shoot me? After all this?"

"Nope," said JoLayne.

"Then I sure don't understand."

Tom Krome said, "Maybe it's just your lucky day."

The helicopter pilot decided to make one more pass and call it quits. The ride-along said he understood; the Coasties were on a bare-bones budget like everybody else.

Search conditions were ideal: a cloudless sky, miles of visibility and a light clean chop on the water. If the lost boat was anywhere on Florida Bay, they probably would've found her by now. The pilot was certain of one thing: There was no sixteen-foot Boston Whaler near Cotton Key. Either the woman who'd rented it had gotten lost in the foul weekend weather or she'd lied to the man at the motel marina.

Flying at five hundred feet, the pilot took the chopper on a sinuous course from the Cowpens along Cross Bank toward Captain Key, Calusa, the Buttonwoods and

Roscoe. Then he arced back across Whipray Basin toward Corinne Key, Spy and Panhandle. He was coming up fast on the Gophers when he heard his spotter say: "Hey, we've got something."

It was an open skiff, zipping through a stake channel on Twin Key Bank. The Coast Guard pilot throttled down and put the bird in a hover.

"Whaler sixteen?"

"Roger," said the spotter. "Two aboard."

"Two? Are you sure?"

"That's a roger."

The ride-along said nothing.

"They OK?" the pilot asked the spotter.

"Seem to be. Heading for Islamorada, it looks like."

The pilot leaned toward the jump seat. "What do you think, sir?"

The ride-along had brought his own binoculars, weatherproof Tascos. "A little closer if you can," he said, peering.

Perched in the chopper door, the spotter reported it was a man and a woman. "She's waving. He's giving us a thumbs-up."

The Coast Guard pilot said, "Well, Mr. Moffitt?"

"That's her. Definitely."

"Good deal. You want us to hang by?"

"Not necessary," the agent said. "She's as good as home."

# TWENTY-SEVEN

**Shiner never contemplated** stealing the Lotto ticket from Amber and cashing it for himself. He was too infatuated; they'd spent so much time together, he felt they were practically a couple. Moreover, he was by nature an accomplice; a follower. Without someone to boss him around, Shiner was adrift. As his mother often said, this was a young man who needed firm direction. Certainly he hadn't the nerve to travel alone to Tallahassee and attempt to claim the lottery jackpot. The idea was petrifying. Shiner knew he made a poor first impression, knew he was an unskilled and transparent liar. The vile tattoo could be concealed, but how would he explain his corkscrew thumbs and the skinhead haircut? Or the crankcase scar? Shiner couldn't conceive a circumstance in which the State of Florida willingly would hand him $14 million.

Amber, on the other hand, could pull off anything. She was smooth and self-confident, and her dynamite looks sure couldn't hurt. Who could say no to a face and a body like that! Shiner figured the best thing to do was concentrate on the driving (which he was good at) and let Amber handle the details of collecting the Lotto winnings. Certainly she'd cut him in for *something* – probably not fifty percent (on account of the kidnapping and then what happened on the island with Chub), but maybe four or five million. Amber did need him, after all. It would be foolish to turn in the lottery ticket without first destroying the videotape from the Grab N'Go, and only Shiner could take her where it was hidden. He resolved to be the best damn chauffeur she ever saw.

"Where's this trailer?" she asked.

"We're almost there."

"What's all that, corn or something?"

"The colonel said corn, tomatoes and I think green beans. You grow up on a farm?"

"Not even close," Amber said.

Shiner thought she seemed a little cranky. To loosen her up, he sang a few lines from "Nut-Cutting Bitch," tapping a beat on the dashboard and hoping she'd join in. He gave up when he ran out of lyrics.

Amber blinked impassively at the passing crop fields. "Tell me about the black girl," she said. "JoLayne."

"What's to tell?"

"What does she do?"

Shiner shrugged one shoulder. "Works at the vet. You know, with the animals."

"She got any kids?"

"I don't think so."

"Boyfriend? Husband?" Amber, biting her lower lip.

"Not that I heard of. She's just another girl around town, I don't know much about it."

"Do people like her?"

"My Ma says so."

"Shiner, are there many black people where you live?"

"In Grange? Some. What's 'many'? I mean, we got a few." Then it occurred to him that she might be considering a move, so he added: "But not many. And they stick pretty much to theyselves."

Showing good sense, Amber thought.

"You all right?"

"How much farther?"

"Just up the road," Shiner said. "We're almost there."

He was relieved to see his Impala next to the trailer, where he'd parked it, although he'd apparently left the trunk ajar. Dumb-ass!

Amber said, "Nice paint job."

"I done the sanding myself. When I'm through, it'll be candy-apple red."

"Look out, world."

She stood and stretched her legs. She noticed an opossum curled on the trailer slab; the mangiest thing she'd ever seen. It blinked shoe-button eyes and poked a whiskered pink snout in the air. When Shiner clapped his hands, it ambled into the scrub. Amber wished it had run.

She said, "I can't believe anybody lives like this."

"Chub's tough. He's about the toughest I ever met."

"Yeah. Look where it got him – a dump." Amber meant to shatter any notions Shiner might have about inviting her inside. "So where's the tape?" she asked impatiently.

He stepped to the Impala and opened the passenger-side door. The glove compartment was open, and empty.

"Oh shit."

"Now what?" Amber leaned in to see.

"I can't fucking believe this." Shiner wrapped his arms around his head. Someone had been inside his car!

The videotape was gone. So was the bogus handicapped parking emblem, which Shiner had hung from the rearview. Also missing was the Impala's steering wheel, without which the car was scrap.

"It's them again. The goddamn Black Tide!" Shiner gasped out the words.

Amber looked inappropriately amused. He asked her what was so damn funny.

"Nothing's funny. But it *is* sort of perfect."

"Glad you think so. Jesus, what about the Lotto!" he said. "And what about my car? I hope you got Plan B."

Amber said, "Let's get going." When he balked, she lowered her voice: "Hurry. Before 'they' come back."

She made Shiner drive, an enforced distraction. Soon he blabbered himself into a calm. In Homestead she instructed him to pull over by a drainage canal. She waited for a dump truck to pass, then tossed Chub's Colt Python into the water. Afterward, Shiner stayed quiet for many miles. Amber knew he was thinking about all that money. She was, too.

"It wasn't meant to be. It wasn't right," she said, "not from any angle."

"Yeah, but for fourteen million bucks – "

"Know why I'm not upset? Because we're off the hook. Now we don't have to make a decision about what to do. Somebody made it for us."

"But you still got the ticket."

Amber shook her head. "Not for long. Whoever came for that video knows who really won the lottery. They *know*, OK?"

"Yeah." Shiner went into a sulk.

She said, "I've never been arrested before. How about you?"

He said nothing.

"You mentioned your mom? Well, I was thinking

about my dad," Amber said. "About what my dad would do if he turned on the TV one night and there's his little blond princess in handcuffs, busted for trying to cash a stolen Lotto ticket. It'd probably kill him, my dad."

"The rabbi?"

She laughed softly. "Right."

Shiner wasn't sure how to get back to Coconut Grove, so Amber (who needed to pack an overnight bag, check in with Tony and arrange for her friend Gloria to cover her shift at Hooters) told him to stick with U.S. 1, even though there were a jillion stoplights. Shiner didn't complain. They were stopped in traffic at the Bird Road intersection when the car was approached by an elderly Cuban man selling long-stemmed roses. Impulsively Shiner dug a five-dollar bill from his camos. The old man grinned warmly. Shiner bought three roses and handed them to Amber, who responded with a cool dart of a kiss. It was the first time he ever got flowers for a woman, and also his first experience with a genuine Miami Cuban.

What a day, he thought. And it still ain't over.

The videotape gave Moffitt a headache. Typical convenience-store setup: cheapo black-and-white with stuttered speed, so the fuzzy images jerked along like Claymation. A digitalized day/date/time flickered in the bottom margin. Impatiently Moffitt fast-forwarded through a blurry conga line of truckers, traveling salesmen, stiff-legged tourists and bingeing teenagers whose unwholesome diets and nicotine addictions made the Grab N'Go a gold mine for the Dutch holding company that owned it.

Finally Moffitt came to JoLayne Lucks, walking

through the swinging glass doors. She wore jeans, a baggy sweatshirt and big round sunglasses, probably the peach-tinted ones. The camera's clock flashed 5:15 p.m. One minute later she was standing at the counter. Moffitt chuckled when he saw the roll of Certs; spearmint, undoubtedly. JoLayne dug into her purse and gave some money to the pudgy teenage clerk. He handed her the change in coins, plus one ticket from the Lotto machine. She said something to the clerk, smiled, and went out the door into the afternoon glare.

Moffitt backed up the tape, to review the smile. It was good enough to make him ache.

He'd left Puerto Rico a day early, after the de la Hoya cousins wisely discarded their original explanation of the three hundred Chinese machine guns found in their beach house at Rincón (to wit: they'd unknowingly rented the place to a band of leftist guerrillas posing as American surfers). Attorneys for the de la Hoyas realized they were in trouble when they noticed jurors smirking (and, in one case, suppressing a giggle) as the surfer alibi was presented during opening statements. After a hasty conference, the de la Hoyas decided to jump on the government's offer of a plea bargain, thus sparing Moffitt and a half dozen other ATF agents the drudgery of testifying. Once the case was settled, Moffitt's pals headed straight to San Juan in search of tropical pussy, while Moffitt flew home to help JoLayne.

Who was, naturally, nowhere to be found.

Moffitt had known she wouldn't take his advice, wouldn't back off and wait. There was nothing to be done; she was as stubborn as a mule. Always had been.

Finding her, if she was still alive, meant finding the Lotto robbers whom she undoubtedly was tracking. For clues Moffitt returned to the apartment of Bodean James Gazzer, which appeared to have been abandoned in a panic. The food in the kitchen was beginning to rot, and the ketchup message on the walls had dried to a gummy brown crust. Moffitt made another hard pass through the rooms and came up with a crumpled eviction notice for a rented trailer lot in the boonies of Homestead. Scratched in pencil on the back of the paper were six numbers that matched the ones on JoLayne's stolen lottery ticket.

Moffitt was on his way out the apartment door when the phone rang. He couldn't resist. The caller was a deputy for the Monroe County sheriff's office, inquiring about a 1996 Dodge Ram pickup truck that had been found stripped near the Indian Key fill, on the Overseas Highway. The deputy said the truck was registered to one Bodean J. Gazzer.

"That you?" the deputy asked on the phone.

"My roommate," Moffitt said.

"Well, when you see him," said the deputy, "could you ask him to give us a holler?"

"Sure thing." Moffitt thinking: So the assholes ran to the Keys.

Immediately he began calling marinas, working south from Key Largo and asking (in his most persuasive agent-speak) about unusual rentals or thefts. That's how he learned about the Whaler overdue in Islamorada, rented to a "nigrah girl with a sassy tongue," according to the old cracker at the motel dock. The Coast Guard already had a bird up, so Moffitt made another call and got cleared to tag along. He was waiting at Opa-Locka when the chopper came in for refueling.

Ninety minutes later they'd spotted her – JoLayne

with her new friend, Krome. Tooling along in the missing skiff.

Watching through the binoculars, Moffitt had felt sheepish for worrying so much about her. But who in his right mind wouldn't?

After the helicopter dropped him off, Moffitt drove to Homestead to locate the house trailer from which a man known to his landlord as "Chub Smith" was being evicted. It was a dented single-wide on a dirt road way out in farm country. Inside, Moffitt came across piles of old gun magazines, empty ammo boxes, a WHITE POWER T-shirt, a FRY O.J. sweatshirt, a GOD BLESS MARGE SCHOTT pennant, and (in the bedroom) a makeshift forgery operation for handicapped-parking permits – the quality of which, Moffitt noted, was pretty darn good.

The mail was sparse and unrevealing, bills and gun-shop flyers addressed to "C. Smith" or "C. Jones" or simply "Mr. Chub." Not a scrap of paper offered a hint to the tenant's true identity, but Moffitt felt certain it was the ponytailed partner of Bodean James Gazzer. A clot of grimy long strands in the shower drain seemed to confirm the theory.

Parked outside the trailer was an old Chevrolet Impala. Moffitt made a note of the license tag before popping the trunk (where he found a canvas rifle case and a five-pound carton of beef jerky), checking under the seats (two roach clips and a mangled *Oui* magazine) and unlatching the glove box (the video cassette now playing in his VCR).

Moffitt turned off the tape player and opened a beer. He wondered what had happened while he was out of the States, wondered where the white-trash robbers were. Wondered what JoLayne Lucks and her new friend Tom had been up to.

He dialed her number in Grange and left a message on the machine: "I'm back. Call me as soon as you can."

Then he went to sleep wondering how much he ought to ask, and how much he really needed to know.

Mary Andrea Finley Krome sparkled like a movie star.

That's what everyone at *The Register* was saying. Even the managing editor admitted she was a knockout.

She'd gotten her short hair highlighted and her nails done, put on tiny gold hoop earrings, pale-rose lipstick, sheer stockings and a stunningly short black skirt. The coup de grâce was the rosary beads, dangling sensually from Mary Andrea's fingertips.

When she entered the newsroom, the police reporter turned to the managing editor: "Tom must've been nuts to walk out on *that*."

Maybe, thought the managing editor. Maybe not.

The elegant widow walked up to him and said, "So, where are they?"

"In the lobby."

"I just came through the lobby. I didn't see any cameras."

"We've got ten minutes," the managing editor said. "They'll be here, don't worry."

Mary Andrea asked, "Is there a place where I can be alone?"

The managing editor glanced helplessly around the newsroom, which offered all the privacy of a bus depot.

"My office," he suggested, unenthusiastically, and

headed downstairs for a Danish. When he returned, he was intercepted by an assistant city editor.

"Guess what Mrs. Krome is doing in there."

"Weeping uncontrollably?"

"No, she's – "

"Doubled over with grief?"

"Get serious."

"Rifling through the desk. That's my bet."

"No, she's rehearsing," the assistant city editor reported. "Rehearsing her lines."

"Perfect," said the managing editor.

When they got to the lobby, crews from three local television stations were waiting, including the promised Fox affiliate. A still photographer from *The Register* arrived (properly sullen about the assignment), boosting the media contingent to four.

"Not exactly a throng," Mary Andrea griped.

The managing editor smiled coldly. "It is, by our modest standards."

Soon the room filled with other editors, reporters and clerks, most of whom didn't know Tom Krome very well but had been forced to attend by their supervisors. There were even clusters from Circulation and Advertising – easy to spot, because they dressed so much more neatly than the newsroom gang. Also among the audience were curious civilians who had come to *The Register* to take out classified ads, drop off pithy letters to the editor or cancel their subscriptions because of the paper's shameless left- or right-wing bias.

One person missing from the award ceremony was the publisher himself, who hadn't been especially shattered by the news of Tom Krome's probable incineration. Krome once had written a snarky article about a restricted country club to which the publisher and his four golfing sons belonged. After the story appeared, the membership of the country club had voted to spare the sons but expel the publisher for not firing Tom Krome and publicly apologizing for exposing all of them to scorn and ridicule (Krome had described the club as "blindingly white and Protestant, except for the caddies").

The managing editor would have loved to use that line (and a dozen other zingers) in his tribute to Krome, but he knew better. He had a pension and stock options to consider. So instead, when the TV lights came on, he limited himself to a few innocuous remarks, gamely attempting to invest the first-place Amelia with significance and possibly even prestige. The managing editor of course invoked the namesake memory of the late Ms. Lloyd, noting with inflated irony that she, too, had been cut down midcareer in the line of journalistic duty. Here several reporters exchanged doubtful glances, for the prevailing gossip held that Tom Krome's death was in no way connected to his job and was in fact the result of imprudent dating habits. Fueling the skepticism was the conspicuous absence of Krome's own editor, Sinclair, who normally wouldn't pass up an opportunity to snake credit for a writer's good work. Obviously something was screwy, or Sinclair would have been in the lobby, buoyantly awaiting his turn at the lectern.

The managing editor was aware of the rumors about Tom's death, yet he'd made up his mind to venture out on this limb. One reason was his strong belief that local authorities were too incompetent to sort out the true facts (whatever they were) about the fatal blaze at Krome's house. And in the absence of competing explanations, the managing editor was willing to promote his newspaper's first Amelia as a posthumous homage to a fallen star. If, come spring, Krome's tenuous martyrdom still hadn't been shot down in a hail of embarrassing personal revelations, the managing editor might just try to float it past a Pulitzer committee. And why the hell not?

"My regret – *our* regret," he said in conclusion, "is that Tom couldn't be here to celebrate this moment. But all of us here at *The Register* will remember him today and always with pride and admiration. His dedication, his spirit, his commitment to journalism, lives on in this newsroom . . ."

Inwardly the managing editor cringed as he spoke, for the words came out corny and canned. It was a tough audience, and he expected to hear a muffled wisecrack or a groan. Quickly he pushed on to the main event.

"Now I'd like to introduce someone very special – Tom's wife, Mary Andrea, who came a very long way to be with us and share some memories."

The applause was respectful and possibly heartfelt, the most vigorous burst erupting (out of gung-ho reflex) from the crisp-shirted advertising reps. Slightly more reserved was the newsroom crew, although the managing editor snapped his head around upon hearing a crude wolf whistle; one of the sportswriters, it turned out. (Later, when confronted, the kid would claim to have been unaware of the occasion's solemnity. Bearing late-breaking news of a major hockey trade, he'd been hurrying through *The Register*'s lobby toward the elevator when he had spotted Mary Andrea Finley Krome at the podium and was overcome by her rocking good looks.)

As she stepped to the microphone, the managing editor presented her with the standard slab of lacquered pine, adorned by a cheap gold-plated plaque. An appalling etching of the late Amelia J. Lloyd, full-cheeked and chipper, was featured on the award, which Mary Andrea enfolded as if it were a Renoir.

"My husband . . ." she said, followed by a perfect pause.

"My husband would be so proud."

A second burst of applause swept the lobby. Mary Andrea acknowledged it by hugging the Amelia to her breasts.

"My Tom," she began, "was not an easy man to know. During the last few years, he threw himself into his work so single-mindedly that, I'm sad to say, it pushed us apart . . ."

By the time Mary Andrea got to their imaginary backstage reunion in Grand Rapids (which, she'd decided at the last moment, sounded more romantic than Lansing), the place was in sniffles. The TV cameras kept rolling; two of the crews even reloaded with fresh batteries. Mary Andrea felt triumphant.

Twenty seconds, my ass, she thought, dabbing her cheeks with a handkerchief provided by the managing editor.

Most surprising: Mary Andrea's tears, which had begun as well-practiced stage weeping, had bloomed into the real deal. Talking about Tom in front of so many people made her truly grief-stricken for the first time since she'd learned about the fire. Even though she was largely fictionalizing their relationship – inventing anecdotes, intimacies and confidences never shared – the act nonetheless thawed Mary Andrea's heart. Tom was, after all, a pretty good guy. Confused (like all men) but decent at the core. It was a pity he hadn't been more adaptable. A damn pity, she thought, blinking away the teardrops.

One person who remained unmoved during the ceremony was the managing editor of *The Register.* The other was Tom Krome's lawyer, Dick Turnquist, who politely waited until Mary Andrea was finished speaking before he edged through the well-wishers and served her with the court summons.

"We finally meet," he said.

And Mary Andrea, being somewhat caught up in her own performance, assumed he was a fan from the theater who wanted an autograph.

"You're so kind," she said, "but I don't have a pen."

"You don't need a pen. You need a lawyer."

"What?" Mary Andrea, staring in bafflement and dismay at the documents in her hand. "Is this some kind of sick joke? My husband's dead!"

"No, he's not. Not in the slightest. But I'll pass along all the nice things you said about him today. He'll appreciate it." Turnquist spun and walked away.

The managing editor stood frozen by what he'd overheard. Among the onlookers there was a stir, then a bang caused by lacquered pine hitting terrazzo. The managing editor whirled to see his prized Amelia on the lobby floor, where the nonwidow Krome had hurled it. Only inches away: a discarded rosary, coiled like a baby rattler.

The last conscious act of Bodean Gazzer's life was brushing his teeth with WD-40.

In a survivalist tract he'd once read about the unsung versatility of the popular spray lubricant, and now (while exsanguinating) he felt an irrational urge to brighten his smile. Chub pawed through the gear and found the familiar blue-and-yellow can, which he brought to Bode's side, along with a small brush designed for cleaning pistols. Chub knelt in the blood-crusted sand and tucked a camouflage bedroll under his partner's neck.

"Do my molars, wouldya?" Groggily Bode Gazzer opened his mouth and pointed.

"Jesus Willy," Chub said, but he aimed the nozzle at Bode's brown-stained chompers and sprayed. What the hell, he thought. The fucker's dying.

Bode brushed in a listless mechanical way. He spoke from the uncluttered side of his mouth: "You believe this shit? We just lost twenty-eight million bucks to a Negro terrorist and a damn waitress! They got us, brother. NATO and the Tri-Lateral Negroes and the damn com'nists . . . You believe it?"

Chub was in a blinding misery, his bandaged shoulder afire. "You know . . . you know what I *don't* believe?" he said. "I don't believe you still won't say 'nigger' after all she done to us. Goddamn, Bode, I wonder 'bout you!"

"Aw, well." Bodean Gazzer's eyelids drooped to half-staff. One hand flopped apologetically, splatting in a puddle of blood. His face was as pallid as a slab of fish.

"She shot you. She *shot* you, man." Chub hunched over him. "I wanna hear you say it. 'Nigger.' Before you go and croak, I want you to act like a upright God-fearin' member of the white master race and say that lil word just once. Kin you do that for me? For the late, great White Clarion Aryans?" Chub laughed berserkly against the pain.

"Come on, you stubborn little prick. Say it: N-i-g-e-r."

But Bodean James Gazzer was done talking. He died with the gun brush in his cheeks. His final breath was a soft necrotic whistle of WD-40 fumes.

Chub caught a slight buzz from it, or so he imagined. He snatched up the aerosol can, struggled to his feet and staggered into the mangroves to mourn.

# TWENTY-EIGHT

**The pilgrims were** restless. They wanted Turtle Boy.

Sinclair wouldn't come out until he had a deal. Shiner's mother sat beside him on the sofa; the two of them holding hands tautly, as if they were on an airplane in turbulence.

The mayor, Jerry Wicks, had rushed to Demencio's house after hearing about the trouble. Trish prepared coffee and fresh-squeezed orange juice. Shiner's mother declined the pancakes in favor of an omelette.

Demencio was in no mood to negotiate, but the crazy fools had him pinned. Something had gone awry with the food-dye formula and his fiberglass Madonna had begun to weep oily brown tears. Hastily he'd hauled the statue indoors and shut down the visitation. Now there were forty-odd Christian tourists milling in the yard, halfheartedly snapping photos of baby turtles in the moat. Sales of the "holy water" had gone flat-line.

"Lemme get this straight." Demencio paced the living room. "You want thirty percent of the daily collection *and* thirty percent of the concessions? That ain't gonna happen. Forget about it."

Sinclair, still numb and loopy from his revelations, had been taking his cues from Shiner's mother. She pressed a smudged cheek against his shoulder.

"We told you," she said to Demencio, "we'd settle for twenty percent of the concessions."

"What's this 'we' shit?"

"But only if you find a place for Marva," Sinclair interjected. Marva was the name of Shiner's mother. "A new shrine," Sinclair went on, brushing a clod of lettuce from his forelock, "to replace the one that was paved."

He hardly recognized his own voice, a trillion light-years beyond his prior life. The newsroom and all its petty travails might as well have been on Pluto.

Demencio sagged into his favorite TV chair. "You people got some goddamn nerve. This is *my* business here. We built it up by ourselves, all these years, me and Trish. And now you just waltz in and try to take over . . ."

Shiner's mother pointed out that Demencio's pilgrim traffic had tripled, thanks to Sinclair's mystical turtle handling. "Plus I got my own loyal clientele," she said. "They'll be here sure as the sun shines, buying up your T-shirts and sodey pops and angel food snacks. You two'll make out like bandits if only you got the brains to go along."

Trish started to say something, but Demencio cut her off. "I don't need you people, that's the point. You need *me*."

"Really?" Shiner's mother, with a smirk. "You got a Virgin Mary leakin' Quaker State out her eyeballs. Who needs who? is my question."

Demencio said, "Go to hell." But the loony witch had a point.

Even in his blissfully detached state, Sinclair wouldn't budge off the numbers. He knew a little something about business – his father ran a gourmet cheese shop in

Boston, and there were plenty of times he'd had to play hardball with those blockhead wholesalers back in Wisconsin.

"May I suggest something?" Mayor Jerry Wicks, playing mediator. The manager of the Holiday Inn, fearing a dip in the bus-tour trade, had implored him to intervene. "I've got an idea," said the mayor. "What if . . . Marva, let me ask: What would you need in the way of facilities?"

"For what?"

"Another manifestation."

Shiner's mother crinkled her brow. "Geez, I don't know. You mean another Jesus?"

"I think that's the ticket," the mayor said. "Demencio's already got dibs on the Mother Mary. The turtle boy – may I call you Turtle Boy? – he's got the apostles. That leaves a slot wide open for the Christ child."

Shiner's mother wagged a bony finger. "No, not the baby Jesus. The growed-up one is what I favor."

"Fine," said the mayor. "My point is, this place would make a helluva shrine, would it not? Talk about having all your bases covered!" He cocked his chin toward Demencio. "Come on. You gotta admit."

Demencio felt Trish's hand on his shoulder. He knew what she was thinking: *This could be big*. If they did it right, they'd be the number one stop on the whole Grange bus tour.

Nonetheless, Demencio felt impelled to say: "I don't want no stains on my driveway. Or the sidewalks, neither."

"Fair enough."

"And I won't give up no more than fifteen percent on the collections."

Sinclair looked at Shiner's mother, who smiled in approval. "That we can live with," she said.

They gathered at the dining table to brainstorm a new Christ shrine. "Wherever He appears, that's where it is," Shiner's mother explained, raising her palms. "And maybe He won't appear at all, not after what happened out on the highway – them heathens from the road department."

Ever the optimist, Mayor Jerry Wicks said: "I bet if you went outside and started praying real hard . . . Well, I just have a feeling."

Shiner's mother squeezed Sinclair's arm. "Maybe that's what I'll do. Get down on my knees and pray."

"Not in my driveway," Demencio said curtly.

"I heard you the first time, OK? Geez."

Trish said: "Who needs more coffee?"

From where he sat, Demencio had a clear view of the scene out front. The crowd was thinning, the pilgrims bored to tears. This was bad. The mayor noticed, too. He and Demencio exchanged apprehensive glances. Unspoken was the fact that Grange's meager economy had come to rely on the seasonal Christian tourist trade. The town couldn't afford a downturn, couldn't afford to lose any of its prime attractions. Around Florida there was growing competition for the pilgrim dollar, some of it Disney-slick and high-tech. Not a week went by when the TV didn't report a new religious sighting or miracle healing. Most recently, a purported three-story likeness of the Virgin Mary had appeared on the wall of a mortgage company in Clearwater – nothing but sprinkler rust, yet three hundred thousand people came to see. They sang and wept and left cash offerings, wrapped in handkerchiefs and diapers.

Offerings, at a mortgage company!

Demencio didn't need Jerry Wicks to tell him it was no time to slack off. Demencio knew what was out there, knew it was vital to keep pace with the market.

"Wait'll you see," he told the mayor, "when I got my Mary cryin' blood. You just wait."

The telephone rang. Demencio went to take it in the bedroom, where it was quiet. When he came out, his expression was dour. Shiner's mother asked what was wrong.

"You said you were gonna pray? Well, go to it." Demencio waved an arm. "Pray like crazy, Marva, because we'll need a new miracle, ASAP. Any new Jesus'll do just fine."

Jerry Wicks sat forward, planting his elbows on the table. "What happened?"

"That was JoLayne on the phone. She's coming home," Demencio reported cheerlessly. "She's on her way home to pick up her cooters."

Sinclair went pale. Shiner's mother stroked his forehead and told him not to worry, everything was going to be all right.

They bought some new clothes and went to the best restaurant in Tallahassee. Tom Krome ordered steaks and a bottle of champagne and a plate of Apalachicola oysters. He told JoLayne Lucks she looked fantastic, which she did. She'd picked out a long dress, slinky and forest green, with spaghetti straps. He went for simple slate-gray slacks, a plain blue blazer and a white Oxford shirt, no necktie.

The lottery check was in JoLayne's handbag: five

hundred and sixty thousand dollars, after Uncle Sam's cut. It was the first of twenty annual payments on JoLayne's share of the big jackpot.

Tom leaned across the table and kissed her. Out of the corner of an eye he saw a starchy old white couple staring from another table, so he kissed JoLayne again; longer this time. Then he lifted his glass: "To Simmons Wood."

"To Simmons Wood," said JoLayne, too quietly.

"What's wrong?"

"Tom, it's not enough. I did the math."

"How do you figure?"

"The other offer is three million even, with twenty percent down. I promised Clara Markham I could do better, but I don't think I can. Twenty percent of three million is six hundred grand – I'm still short, Tom."

He told her not to sweat it. "Worse comes to worse, get a loan for the difference. There isn't a bank in Florida that wouldn't be thrilled to get your business."

"Easy for you to say."

"JoLayne, you just won fourteen million bucks."

"I'm still black, Mr. Krome. That *do* make a difference."

But after thinking about it, she realized he was probably right about the loan. Black, white or polka-dotted, she was still a tycoon, and bankers adored tycoons. A financing package with a fat down payment could be put together, a very tasty counteroffer. The Simmons family would be drooling all over their foie gras, and the union boys from Chicago would have to look elsewhere for a spot to erect their ticky-tacky shopping mall.

JoLayne attacked her Caesar salad and said to Tom Krome: "You're right. I've decided to be positive."

"Good, because we're on a roll."

"I can't argue with that."

They'd returned the overdue Boston Whaler with a minimum of uproar, blunting the old dock rat's ire by pleasantly agreeing to forfeit the deposit. After grabbing a cab down to the boat ramp, they'd retrieved Tom's Honda and sped directly to Miami International Airport, where they lucked into a nonstop to Tallahassee. By the time they arrived, the state lottery office had closed for the day. They'd gotten a room at the Sheraton, hopped in the shower and collapsed in exhaustion across the king-sized bed. Dinner was cocktail crackers and Hershey's kisses from the minibar. They'd both been too tired to make love and had fallen asleep laughing about it, and trying not to think of Pearl Key.

When the Lotto bureau opened the next morning, JoLayne and Tom were waiting at the door with the ticket. A clerk thought she was joking when she matter-of-factly remarked it had been hidden inside a nonlubricated condom. The paperwork took about an hour, then a photographer from the publicity office made some pictures of JoLayne holding a blown-up facsimile of the flamingo-adorned check. Tom was pleased they'd avoided TV and newspaper coverage by showing up unannounced. By the time a press release was issued, they'd be back in Grange.

"This is all going to work out," he assured JoLayne, pouring more champagne. "I promise."

"What about you and me?"

"Absolutely."

JoLayne studied him. "Absolutely, Tom?"

"Oh brother. Here it comes." Krome set down his glass.

She said, "I think you deserve some of the money."

"Why?"

"For everything. Quitting your job to stay with me. Risking your neck. Stopping me from doing something crazy out there."

"Anything else?"

"I'd feel so much better," she said, "giving you something."

Tom tapped a fork on the tablecloth. "Boy, that guilt – it's a killer. I sympathize."

"You're wrong."

"No, I'm right. If I won't take the money, it'll make it harder for you to dump me later. You'll feel so awful you'll keep putting it off, stringing me along, probably for months and months – "

"Eat your salad," JoLayne said.

"But if I *do* take a cut, then you won't feel so lousy saying goodbye. You can tell yourself you didn't use me, didn't take advantage of a hopelessly smitten sap and then cut him loose. You can tell yourself you were fair about it, even decent."

"Are you finished?" JoLayne inwardly ached at the truth of what he said. She definitely was looking for an escape clause, in case the romance didn't work. She was looking for a way to live with herself if someday she had to break up with him, after all he'd done for her.

Tom said, "I don't want the damn money. You understand? *Nada*. Not a penny."

"I believe you."

"Finally."

"But just for the record, I've got no plans to 'dump' you." JoLayne kicked off a shoe and slipped her bare foot in Tom's lap, under the table.

Tom's eyes widened. "Oh, *that's* fighting fair."

"I've had a bad run with men. I guess I'm conditioned to expect the worst."

"Understood," he said. "And just for the record, you should feel free to string me along. Drag it out as long as you can stand to, because I'll take every minute with you that I can get."

"You're pretty polished at this guilt business."

"Oh, I'm a pro," Tom said, "one of the best. So here's the deal: Give us six months together. If you're not happy, I'll go quietly. No wailing, no racking sobs. The only thing it'll cost you is a plane ticket to Alaska."

JoLayne steepled her hands. "Hmmm. I suppose you'll insist on first class."

"You bet your ass. Up front with the hot towelettes and sorbets, that's me. Deal?"

"OK. Deal."

They shook. The waiter came with the steaks, big T-bones done rare. Tom waited for JoLayne to take the first bite.

"Delicious," she reported.

"Whew."

"Hey, I just thought of something. What if you dump *me*?"

Tom Krome grinned. "You just thought of that?"

"Smart-ass!" she said, and poked him with her big toe in quite a sensitive area. They wolfed their steaks, skipped dessert and hurried back to the room to make love.

Judge Arthur Battenkill Jr. came home to an empty house. Katie was probably at the supermarket or the hairdresser. The judge put on the television and sat down to savor a martini, in celebration of his retirement. The early news came on but he didn't pay much attention. Instead he absorbed himself with the challenge of selecting a Caribbean wardrobe. Nassau would be the logical place to shop; Bay Street, where he'd once bought Willow a hand-dyed linen blouse and a neon thong bikini, which he'd brutishly gnawed off in the cabana.

Arthur Battenkill tried to imagine himself in vivid teal walking shorts and woven beach sandals; him with his hairy feet and chalky, birdlike legs. He resolved to do whatever was needed to be a respectable exile, to blend in. He looked forward to learning the island life.

The name Tom Krome jarred him from the reverie. It came from the television.

The judge grabbed for the remote and turned up the volume. As he watched the footage, he stirred the gin with a manicured pinkie. Some sort of press conference at *The Register.* A good-looking woman in a short black dress; Krome's wife, according to the TV anchor. Picking up a journalism plaque on behalf of her dead husband. Then: chaos.

Arthur Battenkill rocked forward, clutching his martini with both hands. God, it was official – Krome was indeed alive!

There was the man's lawyer on television, saying so. He'd just served the astonished and now flustered Mrs. Krome with divorce papers.

Ordinarily the judge would've smiled in admiration at the attorney's cold-blooded ambush, but Arthur Battenkill wasn't enjoying the moment even slightly. He was climbing the stairs, taking three at time, anticipating what he'd find when he reached the bedroom; preparing himself for the catastrophic fact that Katie wasn't at the grocery or the salon. She was gone.

Her drawers in the bureau were empty; her side of the bathroom vanity was cleaned out. A suitcase was also missing, the big brown one with foldaway casters. A lavender note in Katie's frilly handwriting was Scotch-taped to the headboard of their bed, and for several moments it paralyzed the judge:

*Honesty, Arthur. Remember?*

Which meant, of course, that his wife, Katherine Battenkill, had been to the police.

The judge began packing like the frantic fugitive he was about to become. Tomorrow's front-page newspaper headline would exhume Tom Krome but, more important, rekindle the mystery of the corpse found in the burned house. Detectives who might otherwise have dismissed Katie's yarn as spousal bile (and done so without a nudge, being longtime court-house acquaintances of Arthur Battenkill) would be impelled in the scorching glare of the media to take her seriously.

Which meant a full-blown search would begin for Champ Powell, the absent law clerk.

I could be fucked, thought Arthur Battenkill. Seriously fucked.

He filled their second-string suitcase, a gunmetal Samsonite, with underwear, toiletries, every short-sleeved shirt he owned, jeans and khakis, a windbreaker, PABA-free sunscreen, swim trunks, a stack of traveler's checks (which he'd purchased that morning at the bank) and a few items of sentimental value (engraved cuff links, an ivory gavel and two boxes of personalized Titleists). He concealed five thousand in cash (withdrawn during the same sortie to the bank) inside random pairs of nylon socks. He packed a single blue suit (though not the vest) and one of his judge's robes, in case he needed to make an impression on some recalcitrant Bahamian immigration man.

One thing Arthur Battenkill found missing from the marital bureau was his passport, which Katie undoubtedly had swiped to thwart his escape.

Clever girl, the judge said to himself.

What his wife did not know (and Arthur Battenkill did, from his illicit travels with Willow and Dana) was that U.S. citizens didn't need a passport for entry into the Commonwealth of the Bahamas. A birth certificate sufficed, and the judge had one in his billfold.

He latched the suitcase and dragged it to the living room, where he got on the phone to a small air-charter service in Satellite Beach. The owners owed him a favor, as he'd once saved them a bundle by overruling a catastrophic jury verdict. The case involved a 323-pound passenger who'd been injured by a sliding crate of roosters on a flight to Andros. Jurors blamed the air-charter service for the mishap and awarded the passenger $100,000 for each of her fractured toes, which numbered exactly four. However, it was Arthur Battenkill's view, based on the expert testimony, that the woman herself shared much of the blame since it was her jumbo presence in the rear of the aircraft that had caused the cargo to shift so precipitously upon takeoff. The judge sliced the jury award by seventy-five percent, a decision upheld on appeal and received buoyantly by the air-charter firm.

Whose owners now assured Arthur Battenkill Jr. that

it would be no trouble flying him to Marsh Harbour, none whatsoever.

As the judge showered and shaved for the last time as an American resident, he imagined how it would be, his new life in the islands. It would have been better with Katie, for a single middle-aged man surely would attract more notice and even suspicion. Still, he could easily picture himself as the newly arrived gentleman divorcé – no, a widower. Polite, educated, respectful of native ways. He'd have a small place on the water and live modestly off investments. Discreetly he would let it drop that he'd held a position of prominence in the States. Perhaps eventually he would take on some piecework, advising local attorneys who had business with the Florida courts. He also would learn how to snorkel, and would order some books to help him identify the reef fish. He would go barefoot and get a nut-brown tan. There would be time for painting, too (which he hadn't done since his undergraduate days) – watercolors of passing sailboats and swaying palms, bright tropical scenes that would sell big with the tourists in Nassau or Freeport.

Leaning his forehead against the tiles in the steamy shower, the Honorable Arthur Battenkill Jr. could see it all. What he couldn't see was the plain blue sedan pulling into his driveway. Inside were three men: an FBI agent and two county detectives. They'd come to ask the judge about his law clerk, whose name had been helpfully provided by the judge's wife and secretaries, and whose toasted remains had been (less than one hour ago) positively identified by a series of DNA tests. If, as Mrs. Battenkill stated, the judge had assigned the late Champ

Powell to the arson in which he'd perished, then the judge himself would stand trial for felony murder.

It was a topic that would arise soon enough, after Arthur Battenkill toweled off, got dressed, picked up his suitcase and – gaily humming the tune of "Yellow Bird" – walked out his front door, where the men stood in wait.

"What'll happen to your husband?"

Katie Battenkill said, "Prison, I guess."

"God." Mary Andrea Finley Krome, thinking: This one's tougher than she looks.

"There's a Denny's off the next exit. Are you hungry?"

Mary Andrea said, "Tell me again where we're going. The name of the place."

"Grange."

"And you're sure Tom's there?"

"I think so. I'm pretty sure," Katie replied.

"And how exactly do you know him? Or did you already say?"

Mary Andrea wasn't in the habit of road-tripping with total strangers, but the woman had seemed trustworthy and Mary Andrea had been frantic – spooked by Tom's divorce lawyer and rudely shouted at by the reporters. She would never forget the heat of the TV lights on her neck as she fled, nor the dread as she fought for a path through the crowd in the newspaper lobby. She'd even considered feigning another medical collapse but decided against it; the choreography would've been dicey amid the tumult.

All of a sudden a hand had gripped her elbow, and she'd spun to see this woman – a pretty strawberry blonde, who'd led her out the door and said: "Let's get you away from all this nonsense."

And Mary Andrea, stunned with defeat and weakened from humiliation, had accompanied the consoling stranger because it was the next best thing to running, which was what Mary Andrea felt most like doing. The woman introduced herself as Katie something-or-other and briskly took Mary Andrea to a car.

"I tried to get there sooner," she'd said. "I wanted to tell you your husband was still alive – you deserved to know. But then I got tied up at the sheriff's office."

Initially Mary Andrea had let pass the last part of the woman's remark, but she brought it up later, as an icebreaker, when they were on the highway. Katie candidly stated that her husband was a local judge who'd committed a terrible crime, and that her conscience and religious beliefs required her to rat him out to the police. The story piqued Mary Andrea's curiosity but she was eager to steer the conversation back to the topic of her scheming bastard husband. How else to describe a man so merciless that he'd burn down his own house to set up his own wife – even an estranged one – for publicly televised ridicule!

"You're mistaken. It wasn't like that," said Katie Battenkill.

"You don't know Tom."

"Actually, I do. See, I was his lover." Katie was adhering to her new-found doctrine of total honesty. "For about two weeks. Look in my purse, there's a list of all the times we made love. It's on lavender notepaper, folded in half."

Mary Andrea said, "You're serious, aren't you?"

"Go ahead and look."

"No, thanks."

"Truth matters more than anything in the world. I'll tell you whatever you want to know."

"And then some," Mary Andrea said, under her breath. She considered putting on a show of being jealous, to discourage the woman from further elaboration.

But Katie caught her off guard by asking: "Aren't you glad he's alive? You don't look all that thrilled."

"I'm . . . I guess I'm still in shock."

Katie seemed doubtful.

Mary Andrea said, "If I weren't so damn mad at him, yes, I'd be glad." Which possibly was true. Mary Andrea knew her peevishness didn't fit the circumstances, but young Katie couldn't know what the Krome marriage was, or had become. And as good a performer as Mary Andrea was, she wasn't sure how an ex-widow ought to act. She'd never met one.

Katie said, "Don't be mad. Tom didn't set you up. What happened was my husband's fault – and mine, too, for sleeping with Tom. See, that's why Arthur had the house torched – "

"Whoa. Who's Arthur?"

"My husband. I told you about him. It's a mess, I know," said Katie, "but you've got to understand that Tommy didn't arrange this. He had no clue. When it happened he was out of town, working on an article for the paper. That's when Art sent a man to the house – "

"OK, time out!" Mary Andrea, making a T with her hands. "Is this why your husband's going to jail?"

"That's right."

"My God."

"I'm so glad you believe me."

"Oh, I'm not sure I do," said Mary Andrea. "But it's quite a story, Katie. And if you *did* cook it up all by yourself, then you should think about a career in show business. Seriously."

They were thirty minutes outside Grange before Katherine Battenkill spoke again.

"I've come to believe that everything happens for a reason, Mrs. Krome. There's no coincidence or chance or luck. Everything that happens is meant to guide us. For example: Tom. If I hadn't made love thirteen times with Tom, I would never have seen Arthur for what he truly is. And likewise he'd never have burned down that house, and you wouldn't be here with me right now, riding to Grange to see your husband."

For once Mary Andrea was unable to modulate her reaction. "Thirteen times in two weeks?"

Thinking: That breaks *our* old record.

"But that's counting oral relations, too." Katie, attempting to soften the impact. She rolled down the window. Cool air streamed through the car. "I don't know about you, but I'm dying for a cheeseburger."

"Well, I'm dying to speak to Mr. Tom Krome."

"It won't be long now," Katie said lightly. "But we do need to make a couple of stops. One for gas."

"And what else?"

"Something special. You'll see."

# TWENTY-NINE

**On the morning** of December 6, Clara Markham drove to her real estate office to nail down a buyer for the property known as Simmons Wood. Waiting in the parking lot was Bernard Squires, investment manager for the Central Midwest Brotherhood of Grouters, Spacklers and Drywallers International. As Clara Markham unlocked the front door, JoLayne Lucks strolled up – jeans, sweatshirt, peach-tinted sunglasses and a base-ball cap. She'd done her nails in glossy tangerine.

The dapper Squires looked uneasy; he shifted his eelskin briefcase from one fist to the other. Clara Markham made the introductions and started a pot of coffee.

She said, "So how was your trip, Jo? Where'd you go?"

"Camping."

"In all that weather!"

"Listen, hon, it kept the bugs away." JoLayne moved quickly to change the subject. "How's my pal Kenny? How's the diet coming?"

"We've lost two pounds! I switched him to dry food, like you suggested." Clara Markham reported this proudly. She handed a cup of coffee to Bernard Squires, who thanked her in a reserved tone.

The real estate broker explained: "Kenny's my Persian blue. Jo works at the vet."

"Oh. My sister has a Siamese," said Squires, exclusively out of politeness.

JoLayne Lucks whipped off her sunglasses and zapped him with a smile. He could scarcely mask his annoyance. *This* was his competition for a $3 million piece of commercial property – a black woman with orange fingernails who works at an animal hospital!

Clara Markham settled behind her desk, uncluttered and immaculate. JoLayne Lucks and Bernard Squires positioned themselves in straight-backed chairs, almost side by side. They set their coffee cups on cork-lined coasters.

"Shall we begin?" said Clara.

Without preamble Squires opened the briefcase across his lap, and handed to the real estate broker a sheaf of legal-sized papers. Clara skimmed the cover sheet.

For JoLayne's benefit she said, "The union's offer is three million even with twenty-five percent down. Mr. Squires already delivered a good-faith cash deposit, which we put in escrow."

They jacked up the stakes, JoLayne brooded. Bastards.

"Jo?"

"I'll offer three point one," she said, "and thirty percent up front." She'd been to the bank early. Tom Krome was right – a young vice president in designer suspenders had airily offered an open line of credit to cover any shortfall on the Simmons Wood down payment.

Squires said, "Ms. Markham, I'm not accustomed to

this . . . informality. Purchase proposals on a tract this size are usually put into writing."

"We're a small town, Bernard. And you're the one who's in the big hurry." Clara, with a saccharine smile.

"It's my clients, you see."

"Certainly."

JoLayne Lucks was determined not to be intimidated. "Clara knows my word is good, Mr. Squires. Don't you think things will move quicker this way, all three of us together?"

Disdain flicked across the investment manager's face. "All right, quicker it is. We'll jump to 3.25 million."

Clara Markham shifted slightly. "Don't you need to call your people in Chicago?"

"That's not necessary," Squires replied with an icy pleasantness.

"Three three," JoLayne said.

Squires closed the briefcase soundlessly. "This can go on for as long as you wish, Miss Lucks. The pension fund has given me tremendous latitude."

"Three point four." JoLayne slipped from worried to scared. The man was a shark; this was his job.

"Three five," Bernard Squires shot back. Now it was his turn to smile. The girl was caving fast. What was I so worried about? he wondered. It's this creepy little hole of a town – I let it get to me.

He said, "You see, the union has come to rely upon my judgment in these matters. Real estate development, and so forth. They leave the negotiations to me. And the value of a parcel like this is defined by the market on any given day. Today the market happens to be, quite frankly, pretty good."

JoLayne glanced at her friend Clara, who appeared

commendably unexcited by the bidding or the rising trajectory of her commission. What *was* evident in Clara's soft hazel eyes was sympathy.

Gloomily JoLayne thought: If only the lottery paid the jackpots in one lump sum, I could afford to buy Simmons Wood outright. I could match Squires dollar for dollar until the sweat trickled down his pink midwestern cheeks.

"Excuse me, Clara, may I – "

"Three point seven!" Bernard Squires piped, from reflex.

" – borrow your phone?"

Clara Markham pretended not to have heard Squires. As she slid the telephone toward JoLayne, it rang. Clara simultaneously lifted the receiver and twirled her chair, so she could not be seen. Her voice dropped to a murmur.

JoLayne snuck a glance at Bernard Squires, who was flicking invisible dust off his briefcase. They both looked up inquisitively when they heard Clara Markham say: "No problem. Send him in."

She hung up and swiveled to face them. "I'm afraid this is rather important," she said.

Bernard Squires frowned. "Not another bidder?"

"Oh my, no." The real estate agent chuckled.

When the door opened, she waved the visitor inside – a strong-looking black man wearing round glasses and a business suit tailored even more exquisitely than Squires' own.

"Oh Lord," said JoLayne Lucks. "I should've known."

Moffitt pecked her on the crown of her cap. "Nice to see you, Jo." Then, affably, to Squires: "Don't get up."

"Who're you?"

Moffitt flipped out his badge. Bernard's reaction, Clara Markham would tell her colleagues later, was so priceless that it was almost worth losing the extra commission.

When he hadn't heard from JoLayne, Moffitt had driven to Grange, jimmied the back door of her house and (during a neat but thorough search) listened to the voice messages on her answering machine. That's how he'd come across Clara Markham, a woman who (unlike some Florida real estate salespersons) wholeheartedly believed in cooperating with law enforcement authorities. Clara had informed Moffitt of JoLayne's interest in Simmons Wood and brought him up to speed on the negotiations. Something ticked in the agent's memory when he learned the competing buyer was the Central Midwest Brotherhood of Grouters, Spacklers and Drywallers International. Moffitt had spent the early part of the morning talking to the people in his business who talked to the computers. They were exceptionally helpful.

Clara Markham invited him to sit. Moffitt declined. His hovering made Bernard Squires anxious, which was for Moffitt's purpose a desirable thing.

Squires examined the agent's identification. He said: "Alcohol, Tobacco and Firearms? I don't understand." Then, for added smoothness: "I hope you didn't come all this way on government business, Mr. Moffitt, because I don't drink, smoke or carry a gun."

The agent laughed. "In Florida," he said, "that puts you in a definite minority."

Bernard Squires was compelled to laugh, too – brittle

and unpersuasive. Already he could feel his undershirt clinging to the small of his back.

Moffitt said, "Do you know a man named Richard Tarbone?"

"I know who he is," Squires said – the same answer he'd given to three separate grand juries.

"Do you know him as Richard or 'Icepick'?"

"I know *of* him," Squires replied carefully, "as Richard Tarbone. He is a legitimate businessman in the Chicago area."

"Sure he is," Moffitt said, "and I'm Little Richard's love child."

JoLayne Lucks covered her mouth to keep from exploding. Clara Markham pretended to be reading the fine print of the union's purchase offer. When Moffitt asked to speak to Mr. Squires privately, the two women did not object. JoLayne vowed to hunt down some doughnuts.

Once he and Squires were alone in the office, Moffitt said: "You don't really want to buy this property. Trust me."

"The pension fund is very interested."

"The pension fund, as we both know, is a front for the Tarbone family. So cut the crap, Bernie."

Squires moved his jaws as if he was working on a wad of taffy. He heard the door being locked. The agent was standing behind him now.

"That's slander, Mr. Moffitt, unless you can prove it – which you cannot."

He waited for a response: Nothing.

"What's your interest in this?" Squires pressed. He couldn't understand why the ATF was snooping around a commercial land deal that had no connection to illegal guns or booze. Gangsters bought and sold real estate in Florida every day. On the infrequent occasions when the government took notice, it was the FBI and Internal Revenue who came calling.

"My interest," Moffitt said, "is purely personal."

The agent sat down and scooted even closer to Bernard Squires. "However," he said, "you should be aware that on May 10, 1993, one Stephen Eugene Tarbone, alias Stevie 'Boy' Wonder, was arrested near Gainesville for interstate transportation of illegal silencers, machine-gun parts and unlicensed firearms. These were found in the trunk of a rented Lincoln Mark IV during a routine traffic stop. Stephen Tarbone was the driver. He was accompanied by a convicted prostitute and another outstanding public citizen named Charles 'The Gerbil' Hindeman. The fact Stephen's conviction was overturned on appeal in no way diminishes my interest in the current firearms trafficking activities of the young man, or of his father, Richard. So officially *that* is my jurisdiction, in case I need one. You with me?"

A metallic taste bubbled to Squires' throat from places visceral and ripe. Somehow he mustered a stony-eyed demeanor for the ATF man.

"Nothing you've said interests me in the least or has any relevant bearing on this transaction."

Moffitt jovially cupped his hands and clapped them once, loudly. Squires jumped.

"Transaction? Man, here's the transaction," the agent said with a grin. "If you don't pack up your lizard valise and your cash deposit and go home to Chicago, your friend Richard the Icepick is going to be a front-page headline in the newspaper: ALLEGED MOB FIGURE TIED TO LOCAL MALL DEAL. I'm not a writer, Mr. Squires, but you get the gist. The article will be real thorough regarding Mr. Tarbone and his family enterprises, and also his connection to your union. In fact, I'll bet Mr. Tarbone will be amazed at the accuracy of the information in the story. That's because I intend to leak it myself."

Bernard Squires struggled to remain cool and disdainful. "Bluffing is a waste of time," he said.

"I couldn't agree more." From a breast pocket Moffitt took a business card, which he gave to Squires. "That's the reporter who'll be doing the story. He'll probably be calling you in a few days."

Squires' hand was trembling, so he slapped the card flat on the table. It read:

> *Thomas P. Krome*
> *Staff Writer*
> *The Register*

"A real prick," Moffitt added. "You'll like him."

Bernard Squires picked up the reporter's card and tore it in half. The gesture was meant to be contemptuous, but the ATF agent seemed vastly entertained.

"So Mr. Tarbone doesn't mind reading about himself in the press? That's good. Guy like him needs a thick hide." Moffitt rose. "But you might want to warn him, Bernie, about Grange."

"What about it?"

"Very conservative little place. Folks here seem pretty serious about their religion. Everywhere you go there's a shrine to one holy thing or another – haven't you noticed?"

Dismally Squires thought of the gimp with the bloody

holes in his hands and the weird couple chanting among the turtles.

"People around here," Moffitt went on, "they do not like sin. Not one damn bit. Which means they won't be too wild about gangsters, Bernie. Gangsters from Chicago or anyplace else. When this story breaks in the paper, don't expect a big ticker-tape parade for your man Richard the Icepick. Just like you shouldn't expect the Grange town fathers to do backflips for your building permits and sewer rights and so forth. You follow what I'm saying?"

Bernard Squires held himself erect by pinching the chairback with both elbows. He sensed the agent shifting here and there behind him, then he heard the doorknob turn.

"Any questions?" came Moffitt's voice.

"No questions."

"Excellent. I'll go find the ladies. It's been nice chatting with you, Bernie."

"Drop dead," said Squires.

He heard the door open, and Moffitt's laughter trailing down the hall.

Without rising, Demencio said: "You're early. Where's the lucky lady?"

"She's got an appointment," said Tom Krome.

"You bring the money?"

"Sure did."

Trish invited him inside. It was a peculiar scene at the kitchen counter: she and her husband in yellow latex gloves, scrubbing the shells of JoLayne's baby turtles.

Krome picked up one of the cooters, upon which a bearded face had been painted.

"Don't ask," Demencio said.

"Who's it supposed to be?"

"One of the apostles, maybe a saint. Don't really matter." Demencio was despondently buffing a tiny carapace to perfection.

Trish added: "The paint comes right off with Windex and water. It won't hurt 'em."

Tom Krome carefully placed the cooter in the tank with the others. "Need some help?"

Trish said no, thanks, they were almost done. She remarked upon how attached they'd become to the little buggers. "They'll eat right out of your fingers."

"Is that right?"

"Lettuce and even raw hamburger."

"What my wife's trying to say," Demencio cut in, "is we'd like to make JoLayne an offer. We'd appreciate the opportunity."

"To do what?"

"Buy 'em. All forty-five," he said. "How's two grand for the bunch?"

The man wasn't joking. He wanted to own the turtles.

Trish chirped: "They'll have a good home here, Mr. Krome."

"I'm sure they would. But I can't sell them, I'm sorry. JoLayne has her heart set."

The couple plainly were disappointed. Krome took out his billfold. "It wouldn't be hard to catch your own. The lakes are full of 'em."

Demencio said, "Yeah, yeah." He finished cleaning the last turtle and stepped to the sink to wash up. "I told you," he muttered to his wife.

Tom Krome paid the baby-sitting fee with hundred-dollar bills. Demencio took the money without counting it; Trish's job.

"How about some coffee cake?" she offered.

Krome said sure. He figured JoLayne would be tied up at the real estate office for a while. Also, he felt the need to act friendly after squelching the couple's cooter enterprise.

To give Demencio a boost, he said: "I like what you did with the Madonna. Those red tears."

"Yeah? You think it looks real?"

"One-hundred-proof jugular."

"Food coloring," Trish confided. She set two slices of walnut cinnamon coffee cake in front of Krome. "It took a day or so for us to get the mixture just right," she added, "but we did it. Nobody else in Florida's got one that cries blood. *Perfumed* blood! You want butter or margarine?"

"Butter's fine."

Demencio said the morning's first busload of Christian pilgrims was due soon. "From South Carolina – we're talkin' hellfire and brimstone, a damn tough crowd," he mused. "If *they* go for it, we'll know it's good."

"Oh, it's good," Trish said, loyally.

As Krome buttered the coffee cake, Demencio asked: "You see the papers? They said you was dead. Burned up in a house."

"So I heard. It was news to me."

"What was that all about? How does somethin' screwy like that happen?" He sounded suspicious.

Tom Krome said, "It was another man who died. A case of mistaken identity."

Trish was intrigued. "Just like in the movies!"

"Yep." Krome ate quickly.

Demencio made a skeptical remark about the bruise on Krome's cheek – Bodean Gazzer's last earthly footprint. Trish said it must hurt like the dickens.

"Fell off a boat. No big deal," Krome said, rising. "Thanks for the breakfast. I'd better run – JoLayne's waiting on her cooters."

"Don't you wanna count 'em?"

Of course, Krome already had. "Naw, I trust you," he said to Demencio.

He grabbed the corners of the big aquarium and hoisted it. Trish held the front door open. Krome didn't make it to the first step before he heard the cry, quavering and subhuman; the sound of distilled suffering, something from a torture pit.

Krome froze in the doorway.

Trish, staring past him: "Uh-oh. I thought he was asleep."

A slender figure in white moved across the living room toward them. Demencio swiftly intervened, prodding it backward with a long-handled tuna gaff.

"*Nyyahh froohhmmmm! Hoodey nyyahh!*" the frail figure yodeled.

Demencio said, sternly: "That'll be enough from you."

Incredulous, Tom Krome edged back into the house. "Sinclair?"

The prospect of losing the cooters had put him into a tailspin. Trish had prepared hot tea and led him to the spare bedroom, so he wouldn't see them swabbing the holy faces off the turtle shells. That (she'd warned Demencio) might send the poor guy off the deep end.

To make sure Sinclair slept, she'd spiked his chamomile with a buffalo-sized dose of NyQuil. It wasn't enough. He shuffled groggily into the living room at the worst possible moment, just as the baby cooters were being carried away. Sinclair's initial advance was repelled by Demencio and the rounded side of the gaff. A second lunge aborted when the crusty bedsheet in which Sinclair had cloaked himself became snagged on Demencio's golf bag. The turtle fondler was slammed hard to the floor, where he thrashed about until the others subdued him. They lifted him to Demencio's La-Z-Boy and adjusted it to the fully reclined position.

When Sinclair's eyes fluttered open, he blurted at the face he saw: "But you're dead!"

"Not really," Tom Krome said.

"It's a blessed miracle!"

"Actually, the newspaper just screwed up."

"Praise God!"

"They should've waited on the DNA," said Krome, unaware of his editor's recent spiritual conversion.

"Thank you, Jesus! Thank you, Lord!" Sinclair, crooning and swaying.

Krome said: "Excuse me, but have you gone insane?"

Demencio and his wife pulled him aside and explained what had happened; how Sinclair had come to Grange searching for Tom and had become enraptured by the apostolic cooters.

"He's a whole different person," Trish whispered.

"Good," Krome said. "He needed to be."

"You should see: He lies in the water with them. He speaks in tongues. He . . . what's that word, honey?"

Demencio said, " 'Exudes.' "

His wife nodded excitedly. "Yes! He exudes serenity."

"Plus he brings in a shitload of money," Demencio added. "The pilgrims, they love it – Turtle Boy is what they call him. We even had some T-shirts in the works."

"T-shirts?" said Krome, as if this were an everyday conversation.

"You bet. Guy who does silk screen over on Cocoa Beach – surfer stuff mostly, so he was hot for a crack at something new." Demencio sighed. "It's all down the crapper now, since your girlfriend won't sell us them turtles. What the hell use are T-shirts?"

Trish, in the true Christian spirit: "Honey, it's not JoLayne's fault."

"Yeah, yeah," said her husband.

Krome eyed the linen-draped lump in the recliner. Sinclair had covered his head and retracted into a fetal curl.

Turtle Boy? It was poignant, in a way. Sinclair peeked out and, with a pallid finger, motioned him closer. When Krome approached he said, "Tom, I'm begging you."

"But they don't belong to me."

"You don't understand – they're miraculous, those little fellas. You were dead and now you're alive. All because I prayed."

Krome said, "I wasn't dead, I – "

"All because of those turtles. Tom, please. You owe me. You owe *them*." Sinclair's hand darted out and snatched Krome by the wrist. "The inner calm I feel, floating in that moat, surrounded by those delicate perfect creatures, God's creatures . . . My whole life, Tom, I've never felt such a peace. It's like . . . an epiphany!"

Demencio gave Trish a sly wink that said: Write that one down. Epiphany.

Krome said to Sinclair: "So you're here to stay?"

"Oh my, yes. Roddy and Joan rented me a room."

"And you're never coming back to the newspaper?"

"No way." Sinclair gave a bemused snort.

"You promise?"

"On a stack of Bibles, my brother."

"OK, then. Here's what I'll do." Krome pulled free and went to the aquarium. He returned with a single baby turtle, a yellow-bellied slider, which he placed in his editor's upturned palm.

"This one's yours," Krome told him. "You want more, catch your own."

"God bless you, Tom!" Sinclair, cupping the gaily striped cooter as if it were a gem. "Look, it's Bartholomew!"

Of course there was no face to be seen on the turtle's shell; no painted face, at least. Demencio had sponged it clean.

Tom Krome slipped away from Sinclair and lifted the aquarium tank off the floor. As he left the house, Trish said, "Mr. Krome, that was a really kind thing to do. Wasn't it, honey?"

"Yeah, it was," Demencio said. One cooter was better than none. "JoLayne won't be pissed?"

"No, I think she'll understand perfectly."

Tom Krome told them goodbye and carried the heavy tank down the front steps.

The two women arrived in Grange on Tuesday night, too late for Katie Battenkill's sightseeing. They rented a room at a darling bed-and-breakfast, where they were served a hearty pot-roast supper with a peppy Caesar salad. Over dessert (pecan pie with a scoop of vanilla) they tried to make conversation with the only other guest, a well-dressed businessman from Chicago. He was taciturn and so preoccupied that he didn't make a pass at either of them; the women were surprised but not disappointed.

In the morning Katie asked Mrs. Hendricks for directions to the shrine. Mary Andrea Finley Krome pretended to be annoyed at the detour, but truthfully she was grateful. She needed more time to rehearse what to say to her estranged husband, if they found him. Katie was confident they would.

"In the meantime, you won't be sorry."

"Should we bring something?" Mary Andrea asked.

"Just an open mind."

The visitation was only a few blocks away. Katie parked behind a long silver bus that was disgorging the eager faithful. They carried prayer books and crucifixes and umbrellas (for the sun) and, of course, cameras of all types. Some of the men wore loose-fitting walking shorts and some of the women had wide-brimmed hats. Their faces were open and friendly and uncluttered by worry. Mary Andrea thought they were the happiest group she'd ever seen; happier even than *Cats* audiences.

Katie said, "Let's get in line."

The Virgin Mary shrine was in the lawn of an average-looking suburban house. The four-foot icon stood on a homemade platform beyond a water-filled trench. A cordial woman in a flower-print pants suit moved among the waiting pilgrims and offered soft drinks, snacks and sunscreen. Mary Andrea purchased a Snapple and a tube of Hawaiian Tropic #30. Katie went for a Diet Coke.

Word came down the line that the weeping Madonna was between jags. The tourist ahead of Katie leaned back and said, "Cripes, I hope it's not another dry day."

"What do you mean?"

"That's what happened last time I was here, in the spring – she never cried once, not one darn teardrop. Then the morning after we leave, look out. Some friends mailed us pictures – it looked like Old Faithful!"

Mary Andrea was diverted by a weather-beaten woman in a bridal gown. Perched on a stool beneath a tree, the woman was expounding in low tones and gesticulating theatrically. A half dozen of the bus tourists stood around her, though not too close. As an actress Mary Andrea had always been drawn to such colorful real-life characters. She asked Katie Battenkill to hold her place in line.

Shiner's mother was alerted by the click of high heels, for the typical pilgrim didn't dress so glamorously. The brevity of the newcomer's skirt also raised doubts about her piety, yet Shiner's mother wasn't ready to pass judgment. Couldn't redheaded rich girls be born again? And couldn't they, even as sinners, be generous with offerings?

"Hello. My name's Mary Andrea."

"Welcome to Grange. I'm Marva," said Shiner's mother, from the stool.

"I love your gown. Did you make it yourself?"

"I'm married to the Word of the Lord."

"What've you got there," Mary Andrea inquired, "in the dish?"

Other tourists began moving in the direction of the

Madonna statue, where there seemed to be a flurry of activity. With both arms Shiner's mother raised the object of her own reverence. It was a Tupperware pie holder; sea green and opaque.

"Behold the Son of God!" she proclaimed.

"No kidding? May I peek?"

"The face of Jesus Christ!"

"Yes, yes," Mary Andrea said. She opened her handbag and removed three dollar bills, which she folded into the slot of the woman's collection box.

"We thank you, child." Shiner's mother centered the Tupperware on her lap and, with a grunt, prized off the lid.

"Behold!"

"Isn't that an omelette?" Mary Andrea cocked her head.

"Do you not see Him?"

"No, Marva, I do not."

"Here . . . now look." Shiner's mother rotated the Tupperware half a turn. Instructively she began pointing out the features: "That's His hair . . . and them's His eyebrows . . ."

"The bell peppers?"

"No, no, the ham . . . Look here, that's His crown of thorns."

"The diced tomatoes."

"Exactly! Praise God!"

"Marva," said Mary Andrea, "I've never witnessed anything like it. Never!" Not since the last time I ate at Denny's, she thought.

The omelette looked like absolutely nothing but an omelette. The woman was either a loon or a thief, but who cared?

"Bless you, child." Shiner's mother, slapping the lid on the Tupperware and burping it tight. In this manner she announced that the high-heeled pilgrim had gotten her three bucks' worth of revelation.

Mary Andrea said, "I'd love for my friend to see. Would you mind?" Waving gaily at Katie, she thought: At least it beats sitting alone at the HoJo's.

"Katie, come over here!"

But Katie Battenkill was otherwise engrossed. The queue at the weeping Madonna had dissolved into a loose and excited swarm, buzzing toward the moat.

Shiner's mother shrugged. "Crying time. You better get a move on."

Mary Andrea found herself feeling sorry for the wacko in the wedding dress. It couldn't be easy, competing with a weeping Virgin. Not when all you had was a plate of cold eggs in Tabasco. Mary Andrea slipped the woman another five bucks.

"You wanna see Him again?" Shiner's mother was aglow.

"Maybe some other time."

Mary Andrea began working her way to the house. She walked on tip-toes, trying to spot Katie among the surging pilgrims. Even in their fervor they remained orderly and courteous; Mary Andrea was impressed. In New York it would've been a rabid stampede for the shrine; like a Springsteen concert.

Suddenly Mary Andrea found the sidewalk blocked – a tall man lugging, of all things, an aquarium filled with turtles.

Boy, she thought, is this town a magnet for crackpots!

Mary Andrea stepped aside to let the stranger pass. He was lifting the tank high, at eye level, to protect it from the jostle of the tourists; apologizing to them as he went along.

Through the algae-smudged plate of aquarium glass Mary Andrea recognized the man's face.

"Thomas!"

Curiously he peered over the lip of the tank. Her husband.

"I'll be damned," he said.

Cried Mary Andrea Finley Krome: "Yes, you will! I believe you will be damned!"

Angrily she snapped open her pocketbook and groped inside. For an instant, Thomas Paine Krome wondered if irony could be so sublime, wondered if he was about to be murdered for real, with an unexplained armful of baby cooters.

# THIRTY

**Leander Simmons and** Janine Simmons Robinson were miffed to learn Bernard Squires had withdrawn his offer for their late father's property. In a conference call with Clara Markham, the siblings said they didn't appreciate getting jerked around by some fast-talking Charlie from up North. They'd gotten their hopes sky-high for a bidding war, and now they were stuck with one buyer and one offer.

"Which," Clara reminded them, "is more than you had two weeks ago."

She didn't let on that JoLayne Lucks was sitting in the office, listening over the speakerphone.

Leander Simmons argued for rejecting the $3 million offer, as the old man's land obviously would fetch more. All they needed was patience. His sister argued strenuously against waiting, since she'd already pledged her share of the proceeds for a clay tennis court and new guest cottages at her winter place in Bermuda.

They went back and forth for thirty minutes, the bickering interrupted only by an occasional terse query to Clara Markham on the other end. Meanwhile JoLayne was having a ball eavesdropping. Poor Lighthorse, she thought. With kids like that, it was no wonder he spent so much time skulking in the woods.

Eventually Janine and Leander compromised on a holdout figure of $3.175 million, to which JoLayne silently assented (flashing an "OK" sign to Clara). The real estate agent told the siblings she'd bounce the new number off the buyer and get back to them. By lunchtime the deal was iced at an even three one. The new owner of Simmons Wood got on the line and introduced herself to Leander and Janine, who suddenly became the two sweetest people on earth.

"What've you got in mind for the place?" the sister inquired cordially. "Condos? An office park?"

"Oh, I'll leave the land the way it is," JoLayne Lucks said.

"Smart cookie. Raw timber is one helluva long-term investment." The brother, endeavoring to sound shrewd.

"Actually," JoLayne said, "I'm going to leave it exactly the way it is . . . *forever.*"

Baffled silence from the siblings.

Clara Markham, brightly into the speakerphone: "It's been a joy doing business with all of you. We'll be talking soon."

Moffitt was waiting outside. He offered JoLayne a lift, and on the way apologized for searching her house.

"I was worried, that's all. I tried not to leave a mess."

"You're forgiven, you sneaky little shit. Now tell me," she said, "what happened between you and Bernie boy – how'd you scare him off?"

Moffitt told her. With a grin, JoLayne said, "You're so bad. Wait'll I tell Tom."

"Yeah. The power of the press." Moffitt wheeled the big Chevy into her driveway.

"How about some lunch?" she asked.

"Thanks, but I gotta run."

She gave him a kiss and told him he was still her hero; it was a running gag between them.

Moffitt said, “Yeah, but I’d rather be Tom.”

Which gave JoLayne a melancholy pause. Sometimes she wished she’d fallen for Moffitt the way he’d fallen for her. He was one of the best men she’d ever known.

“Hang in,” she said. “Someday you’ll meet the right one.”

He threw his head back, laughing. “Do you hear yourself? God, you sound like my aunt.”

“Geez, you’re right. I don’t know what got into me.” She slid from the car. “Moffitt, you were sensational, as usual. Thanks for everything.”

He gave a mock salute. “Call anytime. Especially if Mister Thomas Krome turns out to be another sonofabitch.”

“I don’t think he will.”

“Be careful, Jo. You’re a rich girl now.”

Her brow furrowed. “Damn. I guess I am.”

She waved until Moffitt’s car disappeared around the corner. Then she jogged up the sidewalk to the porch, where the mail lay stacked by the front door. JoLayne scooped it up and unlocked the house.

The refrigerator was a disaster – ten days’ worth of congealment and spoilage. One croissant, in particular, had bloomed like a Chia plant. The only item that appeared safe for consumption was a can of ginger ale, which JoLayne cracked open while thumbing through letters and bills. One envelope stood out from the others because it was dusty blue and bore no address, only her name.

*Ms. Jo Lane Lucks* was how it had been spelled, in ballpoint.

Inside the blue envelope was a card that featured a florid Georgia O'Keeffe watercolor, and tucked inside the card was a piece of paper that caused JoLayne to exclaim, "Oh Lord!"

And truly, devoutly, mean it.

Amber kept the engine running.

"You feel OK about it? Tell the truth."

Shiner said, "Yeah, I feel pretty good."

"Didn't I tell ya?"

"You wanna come in? It don't look like she's home." All the lights were off, including upstairs.

Amber said, "I can't, hon. Gotta get back to Miami and see if I've still got a job. Plus I've already missed way too much school."

Shiner didn't want to say goodbye; he believed he'd found his true love. They'd spent two more nights together – one at a turnpike rest stop near Fort Drum, and the other parked deep in the woods outside of Grange. Nothing sexual had occurred (Amber sleeping in the back seat of the Crown Victoria, Shiner in the front) but he didn't mind. It was rapture, being so near to such a woman for so long. He'd become intimate with the scent of her hair and the rhythm of her breathing and a thousand other things, all exotically feminine.

She said, "We did the right thing."

"Yep."

"But I still wonder who that was in the other car."

I don't know, Shiner thought, but I guess I owe him. He bought me a few more hours with my darling.

The first time they'd cruised past JoLayne Lucks' place, the other car was idling at the curb: a squat gray

Chevrolet sedan. The buggy-whip antenna said cop. Shiner had cussed and stomped the accelerator.

They'd tried again later, with Amber at the wheel. This time the watcher had been parked around the corner, by a newspaper rack. Shiner had gotten a pretty good look at him – a clean-cut black guy with glasses.

"Don't stop! Keep driving!" Shiner had urged Amber.

He'd been too freaked to go directly home. He feared that the Black Tide (and who else could it be, lurking around JoLayne's?) would ransack his house and kidnap his mother to the Bahamas. Amber had been anxious, too. To her, the guy in the gray sedan looked like heavy-duty law enforcement – and he could be looking for only one thing.

So she'd kept driving, all the way past the Grange city limits to a stretch of light woods off the main highway. She'd spotted a break in the barbed-wire fence, and that's where she'd turned. They'd spent a clear chilly night among the pines and palmettos; no big deal, after Pearl Key. Through the wispy fog at dawn they'd seen a herd of white-tailed deer and a red fox.

It was still early when they'd arrived back at JoLayne's place. The gray cop car was gone; they'd circled the block three times to make certain. Amber had backed the Ford up to the house, getaway style, and said: "Want me to do it?"

Shiner had said no, he wanted to be the one.

The way she'd looked at him, damn, he felt like an honest-to-God champ. When all he really was trying to do was make something right again.

She'd passed him the blue envelope and he'd trotted to JoLayne's porch – Amber watching in the rearview, to make sure he didn't get any cute ideas. Afterwards they'd gone to breakfast, and now home. Shiner wished it wouldn't end.

She motioned him closer in the front seat. "Roll up your sleeve. Lemme see."

His muscle was a marquee of contusions, the tattoo lettering crusty and unreadable.

"Not my best work," Amber remarked, with a slight frown.

"It's OK. Least I got my eagle."

"For sure. It's a beauty, too." With a fingertip she lightly traced the wings of the bird. Shiner felt strangled with desire. He squeezed his eyes closed and heard the pulse pounding in his ears.

"Whoa," Amber said.

A stranger was peering through the windshield – an odd fellow with fuzzy socks on his hands.

"Hey, it's Dominick," said Shiner, pulling himself together. He rolled down the window. "How's it goin', Dom?"

"You're back!"

"Yeah, I am."

"Who's your friend? Geez, what happened to your thumbs?"

"That's Amber. Amber, this here's Dominick Amador."

The stigmata man reached into the car for a handshake. Amber obliged politely, although her face registered stark alarm at the creamy glop that oozed from the stranger's sock-mitten.

Shiner told her not to worry. "It's only Crisco."

"That would've been my second guess," she said, wiping it brusquely on his sleeve.

Dominick Amador was unoffended. "You lookin' for

your ma, Shiner?" he asked. "She's over at Demencio's. They hooked up on some kinda co-op deal."

"What for?"

"The state come in and paved her stain. Didn't you hear?"

"Naw!"

"Yeah, so she's over with the Turtle Boy."

"Who?"

"Y'know, it was me that first give Demencio the idea for the cooters – a Noah-type deal. Now you should see what they done with JoLayne's bunch! It's a damn jackpot."

Amber had heard enough. She whispered emphatically to Shiner that she had to leave. He acknowledged with a lugubrious nod.

"That's where I'll end up, too," Dominick rambled, "workin' for Demencio, I 'xpect. He's got a good setup, plus on-street parking for them pilgrim buses. Him and me got a 'pointment tomorrow. We're pretty close on the numbers."

Amber was about to interrupt even more forcefully when the man flung himself on the grass and thrust both legs in the air. Proudly he displayed his bare soles. "Look, I finally got 'em done!"

"Nice work." Shiner forced a smile.

Amber averted her eyes from the stranger's punctured feet. Surely this could be explained – a radiation leak in the maternity ward; a toxin in the town's water supply.

Dominick hopped up and gave each of them a pink flyer advertising his visitations. Then he limped away.

Shiner felt himself being nudged out of the car. Slump-shouldered, he circled to the driver's side and rested his forearms on the door.

He said to Amber, "I guess this is it."

"I hope things are OK between you and your mom."

"Me, too." He brightened at the sight of the three roses in the back seat. They were gray and dead, but Amber hadn't discarded them. To this slender fact Shiner attached unwarranted significance.

Amber said, "If it doesn't work out, remember what I told you."

"But I never bused tables before."

"Oh, I think you can handle it," she said.

Certainly it was something to consider. Miami scared the living piss out of Shiner, but a gig at Hooters could be the answer to most, if not all, of his problems.

"Are they like you?" he asked. "The other waitresses, I mean. It'd be cool if they all was as nice as you."

Amber reached up and lightly touched his cheek. "They're all just like me. Every one of them," she said.

Then, leaving him wobbly, she drove off.

Later Shiner's mother would remark that her son seemed to have matured during his mysterious absence from Grange, that he now carried himself with purposefulness and responsibility and a firm sense of direction. She would tell him how pleased she was that he'd turned his heathen life around, and she'd encourage him to chase his dreams wherever they might lead, even to Dade County.

And not wishing to cloud his mother's newfound esteem for him, Shiner would elect not to tell her the story of the $14 million Lotto ticket and how he came to give it back.

Because she would've kicked his ass.

*

It wasn't a loaded firearm in Mary Andrea's purse. It was a court summons.

"Your attorney," she said, waving it accusingly, "is a vicious, vicious man."

Tom Krome said, "You look good." Which was very true.

"Don't change the subject."

"OK. Where did Slick Dick finally catch up with you?"

"At your damn newspaper," Mary Andrea said. "Right in the lobby, Tom."

"What an odd place for you to be."

She told him why she'd gone there. "Since everybody thought you were dead – including yours truly! – they asked me to fly down and pick up your stupid award. And this is what I get: ambushed by a divorce lawyer!"

"What award?" Tom asked.

"Don't you dare pretend not to know."

"I'm not pretending, Mary Andrea. What award?"

"The Emilio," she said sourly. "Something like that."

"Amelia?"

"Yeah, that's it."

He shot a wrathful glare toward the house, where Sinclair was holed up. That asshole! Krome thought. The Amelias were the lamest of journalism prizes. He was appalled that Sinclair had entered him in the contest and infuriated that he hadn't been forewarned. Krome fought the impulse to dash back and snatch the yellow-bellied slider from the editor's grasp, just to see him whimper and twitch.

"Come on." Tom led his wife away from the bustle of the shrine, around to the backyard. He set the bulky aquarium in the sun, to warm the baby cooters.

Mary Andrea said, "I suppose you saw it on television, Turnquist's big coup. You probably got a good laugh."

"It made the TV?"

"Tom, did you set me up? Tell the truth."

He said, "I wish I were that clever. Honestly."

Mary Andrea puffed her cheeks, which Tom recognized as a sign of exasperation. "I don't think I'm going to ask about those turtles," she said.

"It's a very long story. I like your hair, by the way. Looks good short."

"Stop with that. You hear me?" She very nearly admitted she'd started coloring it because it had become shot full of gray, no thanks to him.

Tom pointed at the summons, with which Mary Andrea briskly fanned herself. He had to grin. Fifty-nine degrees and she's acting like it's the Sahara.

"So when's our big day in court?"

"Two weeks," she said curtly. "Congratulations."

"Oh yeah. I've already ordered the party hats."

"What happened to your face?"

"A man stomped it. He's dead now."

"Go on!" But she saw he wasn't kidding. "My God, Tom, did you kill him?"

"Let's just say I was a contributing factor." That would be as much as he'd tell; let her make up her own yarn. "Well," he said, "what's it going to be? Are you going to keep fighting me on this?"

"Oh, relax."

"Gonna take off again? Change your name and all that nonsense?"

"If you want the truth," Mary Andrea said, "I'm tired of running. But I'm even more tired of road tours and working for scale. I need to get back East and jump-start this acting career of mine."

"Maybe look for something off Broadway."

"Exactly. I mean, God, I ended up in the middle of *Montana*."

"Yeah?" Krome thinking: Not a megamall for a thousand miles.

"Me in cowboy country! Can you imagine?"

"All because you didn't want a divorce."

"I'll be the first Finley woman in five centuries to go through with it."

"And the sanest," Tom said.

Mary Andrea gave a phony scowl. "I saved your goodbye note. The lyric you ripped off from Zevon."

"Hey, if I could write worth a lick," he said, "I wouldn't be working for schmucks like Sinclair."

"What about your novel?" she asked.

Stopping him cold.

"Your girlfriend told me about it. *The Estrangement*. Catchy title."

Mary Andrea's tone was deadly coy. Tom angled his face to the sky, shielding his eyes; pretending to watch a flight of ducks. Buying time. Wondering when, why and under what unthinkable circumstances JoLayne Lucks and Mary Andrea Finley Krome had met.

"So how far along are you?"

"Uh?" Tom, with a vague, sidelong look.

"On your book," prodded Mary Andrea.

"Oh. Bits and pieces are all I've got."

"Ah."

A knowing smile was one of her specialties, and now she wore a killer. Just as Tom was about to surrender and ask about JoLayne, Katie Battenkill came around the corner, humming contentedly. Then he understood.

"*Ex*-girlfriend," he whispered to Mary Andrea.

"Whatever."

Katie rushed up and unabashedly hurled her arms around his neck. "We rode over together," she said. "Your wife and I."

"So I gather."

The information had a paralytic, though not entirely disagreeable, effect. Tom had never before been bracketed by two women with whom he'd slept. Though awkward, the moment enabled him to understand perfectly why he'd been attracted to each of them and why he couldn't live with either one.

"Tell her she looks great," Mary Andrea said archly to her husband. "We *all* look great."

"Well, you do."

Katie said, "I think you guys need to be alone."

Tom snagged her around the waist before she could slip away. "It's all right. Mary Andrea and I have finished our serious chat."

His wife asked: "What's that on your hand, Katie? Did you cut yourself?"

"Oh no. That's an actual teardrop from the world-famous weeping Madonna." Katie gaily displayed a red-flecked ring finger. "My guess is tap water, food coloring and perfume. Charlie, it smells like."

After a discreet sniff, Mary Andrea concurred.

Krome said to Katie: "I hope you're not too disappointed."

"That it's not real? Geez, Tommy, you must think I'm a total sucker. It's a beautiful shrine, that's what matters. The tears are just for hype."

Mary Andrea was on the verge of enjoying herself. "His book," she reported confidentially to Katie, "is still in the very early stages."

"Eeeeek." Katie covered her face in embarrassment. She knew she shouldn't have mentioned to Tom's wife his idea for a divorce novel.

"What else did you tell her," he said, "or am I foolish to ask?"

Katie's green eyes widened. Mary Andrea responded with a quick shake of the head.

Krome caught it and muttered: "Oh, terrific." Katie and her carnal scorecard. "You should get a job on the sports desk," he told her.

She smiled wanly. "I might need it."

Mary Andrea gave her new friend's arm a maternal pat and suggested it was time to leave. "We've got a long drive, and you need to get home."

"It's Art," Katie volunteered to Tom. "He's been arrested – it was all over the radio."

Krome couldn't fake so much as a murmur of sympathy. His house burned down because of Arthur Battenkill; burned down with a man inside. The judge deserved twenty to life.

"The police want to talk to me some more," Katie explained.

"It's good you're cooperating."

"Of course, Tommy. It's the only honest thing. Oh, look at all the little cooters – they're adorable!"

Lugging the turtle tank, Tom Krome escorted the two women through the ebullient pilgrims, past the blood-weeping Virgin and the runny Jesus Omelette, and out to the street.

Katie Battenkill was delighted to learn what was

planned for the baby reptiles. "That's so lovely!" she said, kissing Tom on the nose. She primly scissored her long legs into the car and told him she'd see him at Arthur's trial. Tom waved goodbye.

Mary Andrea stood there looking tickled; savoring the sight of her long-lost spouse trying to balance his swirling emotions and an exotic cargo. The only possible explanation for the turtle project was a new woman, but Mary Andrea didn't pry. She didn't want to know anything that might weaken the story in the retelling.

"Well," Tom said, "I guess we'll be seeing each other at a different trial, won't we?"

"Not me. I don't have time."

She sounded sincere but Krome remained wary; Mary Andrea could be so smooth. "You mean it?" he said. "We can finally settle this thing?"

"Yes, *Tommy*. But only if I get a first edition of *The Estrangement*. Autographed personally by the author."

"Christ, Mary Andrea, there's no book. I was just ranting."

"Good," she said to her future ex-husband. "Then we've got a deal. Now put down that damn aquarium so I can give you a proper hug."

Bernard Squires was a light drinker, but after supper he accepted one glass of sherry from Mrs. Hendricks at the bed-and-breakfast; then another, and one more after that. He wouldn't have drunk so much liquor in front of other guests, particularly the two attractive women who'd arrived the previous night. But they'd already checked out, so Squires felt that seemly comportment was no longer a priority.

The poor fellow was suffering, Mrs. Hendricks could see that. He told her the deal had fallen through, the whole reason he'd come all the way to Grange from Chicago, Illinois.

Kaput! Finished!

Mrs. Hendricks sympathized – "Oh dear, these things happen" – and tried to nudge the conversation toward cheerier topics such as the Dow Jones, but Mr. Squires clammed up. Slouched on the antique deacon's bench, he stared dolefully at his shoe tops. After a while Mrs. Hendricks went upstairs, leaving him with the sherry bottle.

When it was empty, he snatched up his briefcase and went wandering. Crumpled in a pocket of his coat were three telephone messages in Mrs. Hendricks' flawless penmanship. The messages had come from Mr. Richard Tarbone and were progressively more insistent. Bernard Squires could not summon the courage to call the hot-tempered gangster and tell him what had happened.

Squires himself wasn't sure. He didn't know who the black girl was, or where she'd gotten so much dough. He didn't know how the hard-ass ATF agent got involved, or why. All Bernard Squires knew for certain was that neither the pension fund nor the Tarbone crime family could afford another front-page headline, and that meant the Simmons Wood deal was queered.

And it wasn't his fault. None of it.

But that wouldn't matter, because Richard the Icepick didn't believe in explanations. He believed in slaying the messenger.

Each passing minute reduced the odds of Bernard Squires' surviving the week. He knew this; drunk or sober, he knew.

In his career as a mob money launderer, Squires had faced few predicaments that a quarter million dollars cash could not resolve. That was the amount he'd brought to Grange, to secure the Simmons Wood parcel. Afterwards, when the deal officially turned to dogshit, Clara Markham had made a special trip to the bank to retrieve the money and had even helped Squires count the bundles as he repacked the briefcase.

Which he now carried nonchalantly through the sleeping streets of Grange. It was a lovely, still autumn evening; so different from how he'd always pictured Florida. The air was cool, and it smelled earthy and sweet. He stepped around an orange tomcat, snoozing beneath a street lamp, which barely favored him with a glance. Occasionally a dog barked in a backyard. Through the windows of the homes he could see the calming violet flicker of televisions.

Squires hoped the stroll might clear his muddled brain. Eventually he would figure out what to do – he always did. So he kept walking. Before long he found himself on the same street where he'd been two nights before, under the same oak in front of the same bland one-story house. From behind the drawn curtains he heard lively conversation. Several cars were parked in the driveway.

But Bernard Squires was alone at the glazed shrine of the Virgin Mary. No one attended the spotlit statue, its fiberglass hands frozen in benediction. From his distance it was impossible for Squires to see if there were teardrops in the statue's eyes.

Edging forward, he spotted a lone figure in the moat; the linen-clad man, his knees pulled up to his chest.

Hearing no chanting, Squires ventured closer.

"Hello, pilgrim," the man said, as if he'd been watching the entire time. His face remained obscured by a shadow.

Squires said, "Oh. Am I interrupting?"

"No, you're fine."

"Are you all right in there?"

"Couldn't be better." The man lowered his knees and reclined slowly into the water. As he spread his arms, the white bedsheet billowed around him, an angelic effect.

"Isn't it cold?" Squires said.

"*Sah-kamam-slamasoon-noo-slah*!" came the reply, though it was more a melody than a chant.

SOCCER MOMS SLAM SUNUNA FOR SLUR – another of Sinclair's legendary headlines. He couldn't help it; they kept repeating themselves, like baked beans.

Bernard Squires asked, "What language is that?"

"Into the water, brother."

Sinclair welcomed any company. A noisy meeting was being held in the house – Demencio and his wife, Joan and Roddy, dear lusty Marva, the mayor and the plucky stigmata man. They were talking money; commissions and finder's fees and profit points, secular matters for which Sinclair no longer cared.

"Come on in," he coaxed the visitor, and the man obediently waded into the shallow moat. He did not remove his expensive suit jacket or roll up his pants or set aside his briefcase.

"Yes! Fantastic!" Sinclair exhorted.

As Bernard Squires drew closer, he noticed in the wash of the floodlights a small object poised on the floating man's forehead. At first Squires believed it to be a stone or a seashell, but then he saw it scoot an inch or so.

The object was alive.

"What is it?" he asked, voice hushed.

"A sacred cooter, brother."

From the shell a thimble-sized head emerged, as smooth as satin and striped exquisitely. Bernard Squires was awestruck.

"Can I touch it?"

"Careful. He's all that's left."

"Can I?"

The next day, during the long flight to Rio de Janeiro, Bernard Squires would fervidly describe the turtle handling to a willowy Reebok account executive sitting beside him in business class. He would recount how he'd experienced a soul soothing, a revelatory unburdening, an expurgation; how he'd known instantly what he was supposed to do with the rest of his life.

Like a cosmic window shade snapping up, letting the sunlight streak in – "blazing lucidity" is how Bernard Squires would (while sampling the in-flight sherry) describe it. He would tell the pretty saleswoman about the surrealistic little town – the weeping Madonna, the dreamy Turtle Boy, the entrepreneurial carpenter with the raw holes in his hands, the eccentric black millionaire who worked at the animal clinic.

And afterwards he would tell the woman a few personal things: where he was born, where he was educated, his hobbies, his tastes in music and even (sketchily) his line of work. He would under no circumstances, however, tell her the contents of the eelskin briefcase in the overhead compartment.

# EPIPHANY

**Tom Krome carried** the turtle tank up the porch and backed it slowly through the front door. The house was warm and fragrant with cooking; spaghetti and meatballs.

JoLayne was sampling the sauce when he came in. She was barefoot and blue-jeaned, in a baggy checked shirt with the tails knotted at her midriff.

"Where've you been?" she sang out. "I'm in my Martha Stewart mode! Hurry or you'll miss it." She breezed over to check on the cooters.

"We're one shy," Tom said. He told her about Demencio's "apostles" and the weirdness with Sinclair. "I felt so sorry for the guy," he said, "I gave him a slider. He thinks it's Bartholomew."

JoLayne, with consternation: "What exactly does he do with them? Please tell me he doesn't . . ."

"He just sort of touches them. And chants like a banshee, of course."

She said, "You've gotta love this town."

The remaining forty-four seemed perky and fit, although the aquarium needed a hosing. To the turtles JoLayne crooned, "Don't worry, troops. It won't be long now."

She felt Tom's arms around her waist. He said, "Let's hear the big news – are you a baroness, or still a wench?"

JoLayne knighted him grandly with the sauce spoon. He snatched her up and twirled with her around the floor. "Watch the babies! Watch out!" she said, giggling.

"It's fantastic, Jo! You beat the bastards. You got Simmons Wood."

They sat down, breathless. She pressed closer. "Mostly it was Moffitt," she said.

Tom raised an eyebrow.

"He told the guy you were writing a big exposé on the shopping-mall deal," JoLayne said. "Told him it was bound to make the front pages – Mafia invades Grange!"

"Priceless."

"Well, it worked. Squires bolted. But, Tom, what if they believe it? What if they come after you? Moffitt said they won't dare, but – "

"He's right. The mob doesn't kill reporters anymore. Waste of ammo, and very bad for business." Krome had to admire the agent's guile. "It was a great bluff. Too bad . . ."

"What?"

"Too bad I didn't think of it myself."

JoLayne gave him a marinara kiss and headed for the kitchen. "Come along, Woodward, help me get the food on the table."

Over dinner she went through the terms of the land sale. Tom worked the math and said: "You realize that even after taxes and interest payments, you'll still have quite a comfortable income. Not that you care."

"How comfortable?"

"About three hundred grand a year."

"Well. That'll be something new."

OK, JoLayne thought, here's the test. Here's when we find out if Mr. Krome is truly different from Rick the mechanic or Lawrence the lawyer, or any of the other winners I've picked in this life.

Tom said, "You could actually afford a car."

"Yeah? What else?" JoLayne, spearing a meatball.

"You could get that old piano fixed. And tuned."

"Good. Go on."

"Decent speakers for your stereo," he said. "That should be a priority. And maybe a CD player, too, if you're really feeling wild and reckless."

"OK."

"And don't forget a new shotgun, to replace the one we tossed overboard."

"OK, what else?"

"That's about it. I'm out of ideas," Tom said.

"You sure?"

JoLayne, hoping with all her heart he wouldn't get a cagey glint in his eye and say something one of the others might've said. Colavito the stockbroker, for instance, would've offered to invest her windfall in red-hot biotechs, then watched the market dive. Likewise, Officer Robert would've advised her to deposit it all in the police credit union, so he could withdraw large sums secretly to spend on his girlfriends.

But Tom Krome had no schemes to troll, no gold mines to tout, no partnerships to propose. "Really, I'm the wrong person to give advice," he said. "People who work for newspaper wages don't get much experience at saving money."

That was it. He didn't ask for a penny.

And JoLayne knew better than to offer, because then he'd suspect she was setting him up to be dumped. Which was, now, the farthest thing from her mind.

Bottom line: From day one, the man had been true to

his word. The first I've ever picked who was, she thought. Maybe my luck *has* changed.

Tom said, "Come on – you must have your own wish list."

"Doc Crawford needs a new X-ray machine for the animals."

"Aw, go nuts, Jo. Get him an MRI." He tugged on the knot of her shirttail. "You're only going to win the lottery once."

She hoped her smile didn't give away the secret.

"Tom, who knows you're staying here with me?"

"Am I?"

"Don't be a smart-ass. Who else knows?"

"Nobody. Why?"

"Look on top of the piano," she said. "There's a white envelope. It was in the mail when I got home."

He examined it closely. His name was hand-printed in nondescript block letters. Had to be one of the locals – Demencio, maybe. Or the daffy Sinclair's sister, pleading for an intervention.

"Aren't you going to open it?" JoLayne tried not to appear overeager.

"Sure." Tom brought the envelope to the table and meticulously cut the flap with the tines of a salad fork. The Lotto ticket fell out, landing in a mound of parmesan.

"What the hell?" He picked it up by a corner, as if it were forensic evidence.

JoLayne, watching innocently.

"Your numbers. What were they?" Tom was embarrassed because his hand was shaking. "I can't remember, Jo – the six numbers you won with."

"I do," she said, and began reciting. "Seventeen . . ."

Krome, thinking: This isn't possible.

"Nineteen, twenty-two . . ."

It's a gag, he told himself. Must be.

"Twenty-four, twenty-seven . . ."

Moffitt, the sonofabitch! He's one who could pull it off. Print up a fake ticket, as a joke.

"Thirty," JoLayne said. "Those were my numbers."

It looked too real to be a phony; water-stained and frayed, folded then unfolded. It looked as if someone had carried it a long way for a long time.

Then Krome remembered: There had been two winners that night.

"Tom?"

"I can't . . . This is crazy." He showed it to her. "Jo, I think it's the real thing."

"Tom!"

"And this was in your mail?"

She said, "Unbelievable. *Unbelievable*."

"That would be the word for it."

"You and me, two of the most cynical people on God's green earth . . . It's almost like a revelation, isn't it?"

"I don't know what the hell it is."

He tried to throttle down and think like a reporter, beginning with a list of questions: Who in their right mind would give up a $14 million Lotto ticket? Why would they send it to him, of all people? And how'd they know where he was?

"It makes no damn sense."

"None," JoLayne agreed. That's what was so wondrous. She'd been over it again and again – there were no sensible answers, because it was impossible. What had happened was absolutely impossible. She didn't believe in miracles, but she was reconsidering the concept of divine mystery.

"The lottery agency said the other ticket was bought in Florida City. That's three hundred miles away."

"I know, Tom."

"How in the world . . ."

"Honey, put it away now. Someplace safe."

"What should we do?" he asked.

" 'We'? It's your name on that envelope, buster. Come on, let's get moving. Before it's too dark."

It was a few hours later, after they'd returned from their mission and JoLayne had drifted to sleep, when Tom Krome found the answer to one of the many, many questions.

The only answer he'd ever get.

He slipped out of bed to catch the late TV news, in case the men on Pearl Key had been found. He knew he shouldn't have been concerned – dead or alive, the two robbers wouldn't say much. They couldn't, if they wished to stay out of prison.

Nonetheless, Krome was glued to the tube. As though he needed independent proof, a confirmation that the events of the past ten days were real and not a dream.

But the news had nothing. So he decided to surprise JoLayne (and demonstrate his domestic suitability) by washing the dinner dishes. He was scraping a tangle of noodles into the garbage when he spotted it in the bottom of the can:

A blue envelope made out to "Ms. Jo Lane Lucks."

He retrieved it and placed it on the counter.

The envelope had been opened cleanly, possibly with a very long fingernail. Inside the envelope was a card, a bright Georgia O'Keeffe print.

And inside the card . . . nothing. Not a word.

And Tom Krome knew: That's how the second lottery ticket had been delivered. It was sent to JoLayne, not him.

He could've cried, he was so happy. Or laughed, he was so mad.

Again she'd been one step ahead of him. It would always be that way. He'd have to get used to it.

She was too much.

Vultures starred in his nightmares, and Chub blamed the nigger woman.

Before boarding the skiff, she'd warned him in harrowing detail about black vultures. The sky over Pearl Key was full of them. "They're gonna come for your friend," she'd said, kneeling beside him on the shore, "and there's nothing you can do."

People think all buzzards hunt by smell, she'd said, but that's not so. Turkey vultures use their noses; black vultures hunt purely by sight. Their eyeballs are twenty or thirty times more powerful than a human's, she'd said. When they're circling like that – the nigger woman pointing upward and, sure enough, there they were – it means they're searching for carrion.

"What's that?" Chub, fumbling to open his ragged eyelid, so he might see the birds better. Every part of him burned with fever; he felt infected from head to toe.

"Carrion," the woman had replied, "is another word for dead meat."

"Jesus Willy."

"The trick is to keep moving, OK? Whatever you do, don't lie down and doze off," she'd said, "because they might think you're dead. That's when they'll come for you. And once they get started, Lord . . . Just remember to do like I said. *Don't stop moving*. Arms, legs, whatever. As long as they see movement, buzzards'll usually keep away."

"But I gotta sleep."

"Only when it's dark. They feed mainly in the daytime. At night you should be safe."

That's when she'd pressed the can of pepper spray into his crab-swollen fist and said, "Just in case."

"Will it stop 'em?" Chub peered dubiously at the container. Bode Gazzer had purchased it at the Lauderdale gun show.

"It's made to knock grizzly bears on their asses," the woman had told him. "Ten percent concentration of oleoresin capsicum. That's two million Scoville Heat Units."

"What the fuck's that mean?"

"It means big medicine, Gomer. Good luck."

Moments later: the sound of an outboard engine revving. Sure as shit, they'd left him out here. She and the white guy – deserted him on this goddamn island with his dead friend, and the sky darkening with vultures.

They'd come down for Bode in the midafternoon, just as the woman predicted. At the time, Chub was squatting in the mangroves, huffing the last of the WD-40. It didn't give a fraction of the jolt that boat glue did, but it was better than nothing.

Teetering from the woods, he'd spotted the buzzards picking eagerly at his partner's corpse – six, seven, maybe more. Some had held strings of flesh in their beaks, others nibbled shreds of camouflage fabric. On the ground the birds had seemed so large, especially with their bare, scalded-looking heads and vast white-tipped wings – Chub had been surprised. When he ran at them they'd hissed and spooked, although not far; into the treetops.

On the bright sand around him he'd noticed the ominous shrinking shadows of others dropping closer, flying tighter circles. That's when Chub decided to run far away from Bode's dead body, to a safer part of the island. He grabbed the pepper spray and half lurched, half galloped through the mangroves. Finally he came to a secluded clearing and keeled in exhaustion, landing on his wounded shoulder.

Almost immediately the first nightmare began: invisible beaks, pecking and gouging at his face. He bolted upright, sopped in sweat. In his next dream, which followed quickly, the rancid scavengers encircled him and, by aligning wing to wing, formed a picket from which he couldn't escape. Again he awakened with a shiver.

It was all her fault, the nigger girl from the Black Tide – she'd put the crazy buzzard talk in his head. They were only birds, for chrissake. Stupid, smelly birds.

Still, Chub kept his good eye trained on their glide pattern, the high thermals.

At dusk he made his way back to the abandoned campsite, in hopes of finding a dry tarp and some beer. When he spotted the paper grocery bag in the bushes, he got an idea about how to pass the long nerve-racking night. He dumped out the crinkled tube of marine adhesive and gave one last squeeze, to make sure he hadn't missed any. Then he shook the can of pepper spray and shot a stream inside the empty bag.

Thinking: Stuff's gotta be heavy-duty to take out a fuckin' grizzly.

Chub had never heard of "Scoville heat" but he assumed from its potent-sounding name that a whiff of two million units would produce a deliriously illicit high – exactly what he needed to take his mind off the buzzards and Bodean Gazzer. Chub further assumed (also mistakenly) that the pepper spray was designed to impair only an attacker's vision and that the fumes could be ingested as easily as those of common spray paint, and that he'd be safe from the caustic effects if he merely covered his eyes while inhaling.

Which is what he did, sucking the bag to his face.

The screams lasted twenty-five minutes; the vomiting, twice as long.

Chub had never known such volcanic misery – skin, throat, eyes, lungs, scalp, lips; all aflame. He slapped himself senseless trying to wipe off the poison, but it seemed to have entered chemically through his pores. Daft from pain, he clawed at himself until his fingertrips bled.

When his strength was gone, Chub lay motionless, mulling options. An obvious one was suicide, a sure release from agony, but he wasn't ready to go that far. Possibly, if he'd had his .357 . . . but he surely couldn't work up the nerve to hang himself from a tree or slice his own wrists.

A sounder choice, Chub felt, was to club himself unconscious and remain that way until the acid symptoms wore off. But he couldn't stop thinking about the vultures and what the nigger woman had told him: Keep moving! Once the sun came up, blacking out would be dangerous. The deader you looked, the faster the hungry bastards would come for you.

So Chub made himself stay awake. In the end, what he most wanted was to be saved, plucked off the island. And he wasn't picky about whether the rescue helicopter was black or red or canary yellow; or whether it was being flown by niggers or Jews or even card-carrying communist infiltrators. Nor did he give two shits whether they carried him back to Miami or straight to Raiford prison, or even to a secret NATO fortress in the Bahamas.

The main thing was to get away from this horrible place, as soon as possible. *Away.*

And if, at dawn the next morning, there actually had been a rescue chopper searching Florida Bay, and if it had flown low over Pearl Key, the crew would have noticed something that would have brought them banking around sharply for a second pass:

A lone naked man waving for help.

The spotter in the helicopter would've seen through his high-powered binoculars that the stranded man had a lank gray ponytail; that his body was dappled with dried blood; that one shoulder was heavily bandaged and one hand was swollen to the size of a catcher's mitt; that his sunburned face was raw and striated, and that one eye appeared scabbed and black.

And the crew would have been impressed that, despite the stranded man's severe injuries and evident pain, he'd managed to construct a device for signaling aircraft. The crew would've admired how he had lashed together mangrove branches to make a long pole, and on the end of it he had fastened a swatch of shiny fabric.

But in the end, there was nobody to see the stranded

man. No helicopters were in the sky over Pearl Key at dawn the next day, or the day after, or for many days that followed.

No one was searching for Onus Gillespie, the person known as Chub, because no one knew he was missing.

Every morning he stood in the sunniest spot on the island and feverishly waved his makeshift flag at glistening specks in the blue – 727s from Miami International, F-16s from Boca Chica, Lears from North Palm Beach, all of which were flying far too high over Florida Bay to see him.

Finally the beer was gone, then the beef jerky and then the last of the fresh water. Not long afterwards, Chub lay down in the coarse bleached sand and did not move. Then the vultures came, just like the bitch had said they would.

Nine months later a poacher would find a skull, two femurs, a rusty can of pepper spray and an oilskin tarpaulin. He would be appropriately intrigued by the doomed man's handmade pole and the unusual streamer tied to it:

A pair of skimpy orange shorts, just like babes at Hooters wore.

On the drive to Simmons Wood, they went back and forth with the radio. Tom got a Clapton, while JoLayne took a Bonnie Raitt and a Natalie Cole (on the argument that "Layla" was long enough to count as two songs). They wound up in a discussion of guitarists, a topic as yet unexplored in the relationship. JoLayne was delighted to hear Tom include Robert Cray in his personal pantheon, and as a reward yielded the next two selections. "Fortunate Son" was playing, full blast, when they arrived.

JoLayne bolted from the car and ran to the FOR SALE sign, which she yanked triumphantly from the ground. Tom took the baby cooters out of the tank one at a time and placed them in a linen pillowcase, which he knotted loosely at the neck.

"Careful," JoLayne told him.

A chapel-like stillness embraced them as soon as they entered the woods, and they didn't speak again until they got to the creek. JoLayne sat on the bluff. She patted the ground and said, "Places, Mr. Krome."

The sun was almost down, and the pale dome of sky above them was tinged softly with magenta. The air was crisp and northern. JoLayne pointed out a pair of wild mergansers in the water and, on the bank, a raccoon prowling.

Tom leaned forward to see more. His face was bright. He looked like a kid at a great museum.

"What are you thinking?" she asked.

"I'm thinking anything is possible. Anything. That's how I feel when I'm out here."

"That's the way it's supposed to feel."

"Anyway, what's a miracle? It's all relative," he said. "It's all in somebody's head."

"Or in their heart. Hey, how're my babies?"

Tom peeked in the pillowcase. "Excited," he reported. "They must know what's up."

"Well, let's wait till Mister Raccoon is gone."

JoLayne smiled to herself and wrapped her arms around her knees. A flight of swallows came top-gunning out of the tree line, gulping gnats. Later Tom was certain he heard the whinny of a horse, but she said no, it was just an owl.

"I'll learn," he promised.

"There's another piece of land, not far from here. Once I found a bear track there."

In the twilight Tom could barely make out her expression.

"A black bear," she said, "not a grizzly. You'll still need to go to Alaska for one of those."

"Any old bear would be fine."

She said, "It's also for sale, that land where I saw the track. I'm not sure how many acres."

"Clara would know."

"Yes. She would. Come on, it's time."

She led him down to the creek. They walked along the bank, stopping here and there to place baby turtles in the water.

JoLayne was saying, "Did you know they can live twenty, twenty-five years? I read a paper in *BioScience* . . ."

Whispering all this – Tom wasn't sure why, but it seemed natural and right.

"Just think," she said. "Twenty years from now we can sit up there and watch these guys sunning on the logs. By then they'll be as big as army helmets, Tom, and covered with green moss. I can't wait."

He reached into the sack and took out the last one.

"That's a red-belly," she said. "You do the honors, Mr. Krome."

He placed the tiny cooter on a flat rock. Momentarily its head emerged from the shell. Then out came the stubby curved legs.

"Watch him go," JoLayne said. The turtle scrambled

comically, like a wind-up toy, landing with a quiet plop in the stream.

"So long, sport. Have a great life." With both hands she reached for Tom. "I need to ask you something."

"Fire away."

"Are you going to write a story about all this?"

"Never," he said.

"But I was right, wasn't I? Didn't I tell you it would be a good one?"

"You did. It was. But you'll never read about it in the paper."

"Thank you."

"In a novel, maybe," he said, playfully pulling free. "But not in a newspaper."

"Tom, I'll kill you." She was laughing as she chased him up the hill, into the tall pines.